A DARK BILLIONAIRE ROMANCE

SERIES COLLECTION

DEVIL'S KISS

USA TODAY BESTSELLING AUTHOR

GEMMA JAMES

DEVIL'S KISS
SERIES COLLECTION

Devil's Kiss Series Collection: A Dark Billionaire Romance

Cover design by Gemma James

ISBN: 9798873749287

BOOK ONE
THE DEVIL'S KISS

Note To Readers

This book is intended for readers 18+ who enjoy dark and explicit themes. Reader discretion is advised.
For detailed content warning information, please visit authorgemmajames.com/trigger-warnings

CHAPTER ONE

"You wanted to see me?" My unsteady voice betrayed the deceptive nonchalance in the question.

"Yes, shut the door, Kayla." His tone issued a warning that echoed in my ears, and I almost jumped as the door clicked shut. As usual, his presence caused an unsettling tickle in my stomach.

Gage Channing left no room for mistakes or excuses—every single one of his employees displayed their best behavior, or else. I shuddered to think of the woman he'd fired last week; she'd scurried from the building as mascara tracked down her cheeks.

"Sit down." He gestured to the leather chair in front of his desk.

I sat, crossed my legs, and forced myself to meet his gaze. He had a way of piercing people with his eyes. They were startling—the kind of blue that dolphins played in. I got the feeling he saw right through me, as if he'd known what I'd been doing and had bided his time until the perfect moment presented itself to pounce. Was that moment now?

He slapped a folder on the desk. "Do you know what's in here?"

"N-no, Mr. Channing."

"I'm disappointed, Ms. Sutton."

My heartbeat tumbled twice, then sped up. He rarely addressed me so formally, a fact which caused a fair amount of gossip in the office. Some speculated the boss had a thing for me, and others went so far as to claim we were screwing like rabbits after hours. "I'm sorry, I'm not sure what you're getting at." *Liar!* He'd found me out; I was sure of it.

"I'm referring to the ten grand you stole from Channing Enterprises." He opened the folder and pushed the evidence in front of me. Account statements. Ledgers.

Oh God...

"I trusted you, Kayla. I even promoted you to personal assistant, and this is how you repay me?"

"I was desperate." I swallowed hard as the reality of my situation threatened to choke me. He'd have me thrown in jail, and Eve...Eve would die without me by her side. "My daughter is sick. I needed money...please, I'll pay you back. Every penny." I lifted my head and faced his granite expression. "Just don't turn me in."

If he was affected by my plea, he didn't show it. "I don't plan to alert the authorities." He snapped the incriminating file shut. "But you're correct when you say you'll pay me back." He steepled his fingers and rested his chin on them. "There is something I want. I've had a contract drawn up outlining my terms, and if you want my silence—and the evidence destroyed—you'll sign it."

"What do you want from me?" My voice quivered, and when he flashed a devilish grin, I gripped the chair to keep from bolting.

Gage got up and rounded the desk. His body overshadowed mine as he knelt beside me. A line of stubble darkened his jaw, giving him an undeniable hint of danger. "I want you as my slave."

"Your slave?" My jaw dropped. Did I even want to know what that meant?

"Hmm, yes. My slave." He lowered his gaze to my mouth, then lingered on my breasts, and his inspection burned a hole through my blouse. In response, my nipples tightened underneath the silk. "Surely you've heard of BDSM," he added.

I screwed my mouth shut. I didn't like where this conversation was going at all.

"Bondage, discipline," he said, inching closer, "punishment." The last word he savored, as if fine wine dampened his lips. "I'd say you've earned quite a bit. Wouldn't you agree?"

"I can pay you back," I said. "It'll take time, but I'll get the money."

"I don't want your money." Warm and minty breath breezed across my lips, inviting my mouth to mate with his. I edged away and clung to the side of the chair.

"I want your submission," he continued, "absolute ownership of you and your body. That's what I want."

I worked my jaw, searching for the words to express my disbelief, but only ended up staring at him in stunned silence. The man could have any woman he wanted, and all it would take was a crook of his executive finger. "Why are you doing this?"

His face darkened. "I have my reasons."

"You're crazy if you think I'll agree to this."

"You're too gorgeous to waste away in prison." He placed a hand on my leg, right above my knee. I tensed, afraid to move, afraid he'd push his possession further if I resisted. "You know"—he gently slid his palm upwards—"the penalty for embezzlement in Oregon is up to five years."

My breath hitched as he grazed the skin underneath the hem of my skirt. "Don't."

He raised an eyebrow. "No?" Gage reached for the phone. "Are you sure?"

The futility of my situation spilled from my eyes. Upset with myself for displaying weakness, I wiped the tears from my cheeks. "Don't call."

As if I'd given him permission, he uncrossed my legs and wedged them apart. "I love natural redheads." He slipped his fingers under the edge of my panties and smoothed them over my crotch. "Are you just as red here?" he asked, grabbing a pinch of hair.

With a nod, I closed my eyes. My entire body tingled, and not in a good way. I couldn't believe my boss was doing this to me...in his office in the middle of a workday.

"I'm tempted to leave you natural, at least for a while. I want to see you first."

My face burned with humiliation, and it took everything I had to keep my legs apart. I balled my hands until my fingernails bit into skin. "This is sexual harassment, you bastard. It's illegal, and so is blackmail."

He withdrew his hand, and by the time I looked up, Gage had reclaimed his seat. "Don't think of it as blackmail. Think of it as an alternative to prison. I'd much rather punish you myself." He opened another folder and slid the contents across the desk. "You either submit to me or go to jail. Either way, the decision is yours."

With unsteady fingers, I fiddled with the paperwork but couldn't bring myself to read his demands. "What exactly do you have in mind?"

"Let's start with the basics." He gestured toward the contract. "You'll be my submissive for the next six weeks, beginning immediately upon your signature. I prefer a live-in arrangement on the weekends. During the week I expect you to follow my rules." He leaned back in his chair and kept a steady gaze on me. "You'll come to work as usual, but under no circumstances will you flirt or date other men, or entertain or go out with friends—"

"What about Eve? I spend most of my time at the hospital."

"I'm aware of that, and I don't have an issue with you seeing her, but the weekends belong to me, understand?"

If I could shoot daggers with a single glance, he'd feel my pain. "What else?" I tossed the contract down and crossed my arms.

"I expect absolute obedience." The corner of his mouth curled. "I won't hesitate to punish you when necessary. Of course, you'll choose a safe word." He frowned, as if the idea didn't please him. "However, should you decide to use it, our contract will become null and void, and I'll turn you over to the police. If you speak with anyone about this, the same stipulation applies."

Tears of desolation dripped down my cheeks, and I no longer cared about hiding them. His ultimatum terrified me. I wasn't a stranger to abuse, but being someone's slave—in every sense of the word—was a terrifying concept. "Eve will wonder where I am on the weekends."

"She'll benefit from our agreement. I'm allowing you to keep the money, which in turn ensures she gets the treatment she needs. I understand it's experimental and that you don't have the luxury of time."

I narrowed my eyes. "How did you know about that?" I hadn't talked to anyone about Eve's treatment. It was too painful a subject, and the last thing I wanted were platitudes thrown in my face. The insurance had refused to cover it, and Eve was out of options.

"I have my sources." He leaned forward with a smirk. "I have vested interest in you, Kayla—ten thousand dollars worth. You're desperate, and I know you'll give me what I want because even though I'm giving you a choice, your love for your daughter won't."

"There's a hole in your logic. Even with the ten grand, I'm still short."

"You underestimate me. I'll pay for her medical bills in full. She'll be taken care of."

The bastard had me, and he knew it. "What will you do to me?"

"It's all there in the contract...but to put it succinctly"—he leaned forward with a glimmer of excitement in the depths of his eyes —"whatever I damn please."

I forced my attention onto the papers. Certain words and phrases popped out: Flogging. Bondage. Nipple torture. Anal play. I stared at him, slack-jawed. "You'd hurt me like this?"

"Yes," he lowered his voice, and something about his deep timbre shot through me, "but there's a flimsy line between pain and pleasure."

"I think I'm gonna be sick."

"Decide now. I'm growing impatient."

"Please, Gage. Don't make me do this. Please, I'll—"

"You'll save your begging for later, preferably while on your knees." He held out a pen. "But either way, decide."

I glared at him. "Do I have a choice?"

"Of course, just as you have the option of backing out of our agreement whenever you wish." He tapped the pen against the desktop. "That's the beauty of this. The choice is yours."

"But if I don't agree, you'll turn me in and Eve won't get her treatment."

"Correct."

"That doesn't sound like much of a choice. That sounds like coercion."

"I want you, and I'm willing to cross a line to get what I want. Just as you did to save your daughter's life."

I snatched the pen from his hand and stabbed the paper with my signature, essentially signing over my soul to the devil incarnate. I'd only experienced this kind of claustrophobic captivity one other time in my life, and it was a time capsule of hell I'd buried deep in my memory. Would Gage unearth it?

"Excellent." He grabbed the contract and enclosed it in a safe. "And since today is Friday"—he scribbled something on a piece of paper—"here's my address. Go to BodyScape Spa first and ask for Glenda. I'll call ahead and make arrangements."

I moved toward the door, my steps heavy, as if he'd already shackled my ankles.

"Oh, and Kayla?"

I stiffened at the sound of his voice. "Yes?"

"I want you on my doorstep wearing nothing but a trench coat in two hours."

He was insane if he thought I was going to do that.

CHAPTER TWO

I gagged for what seemed like the tenth time and heaved more of my lunch into the toilet. I'd probably never eat chow mein again. Getting to my feet, I braced against the stall and closed my eyes. Gage was all I thought about. Nothing else penetrated past the haze in my mind. I tried to imagine him touching me...doing more than touching me, but my stomach rolled again at the thought.

I stumbled out of the stall, still shaking, but at least I'd stopped vomiting. Katherine, the receptionist, quirked an eyebrow as she reapplied her lipstick. "Let me guess, knocked up?"

"Bad food at lunch today." Refusing to rise to her bait, I joined her at the sink and calmly washed my hands. Katherine was one of those preppy girls, the kind who never had a hair out of place and wouldn't be caught in a morgue wearing anything other than a designer label. She also didn't hesitate to bare her claws if she thought someone was poaching on her turf. In her ice-blue eyes, Gage Channing was off-limits to everyone but herself.

Why couldn't he have chosen her to torment and terrorize?

I left the restroom, praying she wouldn't feed the office grapevine with stories of a pregnancy, and got stuck in rush-hour traffic on my way to BodyScape Spa, which proved to be a more humiliating experience than I imagined. Maybe it was because of Glenda's familiarity with "Mr. Channing's preferences," but I couldn't help but speculate on the number of women he'd sent there. Had there been others like me? Women he'd coerced and blackmailed? Or had they gone willingly? Gage was exceptionally attractive, and he was wealthy and successful to boot. A formidable package for sure, rolled into six feet of toned body, a head full of black hair, and a striking gaze that had the ability to pin you to the wall. I wasn't immune to how easy on the eyes my boss was.

For the past three years, I'd been immune to men period, and I'd certainly never entertained the idea of going to bed with my employer. It weirded me out to realize he'd been waiting for the perfect moment to ensnare me—to subject me to his twisted brand of sexual games.

"This'll hurt," Glenda warned. She ripped the wax off my leg like a Band-Aid, and I bit my lip to keep from groaning. I should be grateful it wasn't my bikini area; Gage had given Glenda instructions to leave me natural but trimmed down there.

The rest of the appointment went by much like the past hour had—in a daze. By the time I unlocked my car, night had fallen, and my nerves had multiplied. I wasn't ready for this. I didn't think twice about driving to the Hospital. I'd be late due to the detour, but I wasn't about to disappear on Eve without saying goodbye. Two days was a long time to a three-year-old.

Downtown Portland reflected a glittering skyline on the

Willamette River, and Christmas lights lit up Pill Hill—which was home to the hospital. The temperature had dropped, and I was still rubbing my hands together when I arrived on Eve's floor.

"Good evening, Kayla," the nightshift nurse said. "Eve's been asking for you."

Guilt clawed at my gut. How could I expect my baby to understand? "Thanks, Mel." I headed to Eve's room, and her tiny face lit up the instant she saw me. Every day she grew paler, smaller—the hospital bed nearly swallowed her whole—but her eyes still sparkled with innocence.

"Hi, baby."

"Mama! Look what I color?" She proudly displayed her scribbled doodle.

"You drew this? You're so talented." I pulled her into a tight hug and held on a little longer than I normally would. The thought of being away for two days broke my heart. God, I was going to miss her. I blinked back tears and tucked her into bed. She jabbered on for a few minutes, words only a mother could detect without asking her to repeat them a dozen times.

"Eve," I began gently, "I've gotta go away—"

"Hello, Kayla."

My breath stalled at the sound of his voice. Time had done nothing to erase it from my mind. I slowly turned. He stood in the doorway, a stethoscope dangling from his neck. God, he was a doctor now. Last I'd seen him, he'd been on the verge of entering medical school.

Last I'd seen him, I'd broken both of our hearts.

"Ian...it's been a long time." What kind of idiotic response was that? Seven years and that was all I could come up with?

His hazel gaze darted to Eve, and I didn't have to guess at the confusion on his face. Seven years ago I'd been pregnant;

Eve was only three. "And apparently a lot has happened since." He brought a hand up and fiddled with the pen in his shirt pocket, and his eyes drifted to my left hand. Sometimes I still felt the phantom weight of my wedding band.

"You work here now?" I asked before he could voice the questions I saw in his eyes—the ones I didn't want to answer.

"Just transferred from Salem." He stepped inside and closed the door. "I heard your daughter was here. I wanted to come by and see you. See if I could do anything to help." He opened his mouth, then snapped it shut. "I'm sorry. I shouldn't have intruded like this."

"It's okay, you're not."

He moved to Eve's bedside. She'd settled into a light doze. "Leukemia?"

I wrapped my arms around myself and nodded.

"What phase is she?"

"Acute. She stopped responding to chemo."

"Jesus, Kayla." He ran a hand through his short hair; it was lighter than I remembered. "I'm sorry."

"We're not giving up." I lost count of how many times I recited the phrase daily.

Ian was about to say more when my cell vibrated in my pocket. I pulled it out, and upon recognizing Gage's number, willed my face into a neutral mask. "I'm sorry, I have to go. I...I have a business trip this weekend. I tried getting out of it." I nibbled on my lip and looked at Eve. "I hate leaving her."

Ian pulled out a prescription tablet and wrote down his number. "Call me if you need anything. Or even if you don't...well, you know how to reach me now." His fingers brushed mine, lingering a few seconds as he passed me the slip of paper, and that familiar spark that had been dormant for so long sprung to life. My heart thundered in my ears as our eyes met. He started to move away, but I grabbed his arm.

"Ian, wait...there is something you can do for me." I let go of his sleeve. "Can you keep an eye on Eve for me? You know, if you're gonna be here?"

"That's not a problem. I can do that."

A lock of hair fell over his brow, and I clenched my fists to keep from brushing it back. "Thank you."

"No problem. I'll see you when you get back." He hesitated a few seconds, and then he noiselessly disappeared into the hall.

CHAPTER THREE

I barely remembered the drive to Gage's place in Portland Heights. My GPS directed me there, but if I needed to repeat the trip without assistance I'd more than likely get lost. A wall of trees cradled his massive house, affording a sense of seclusion even though the city sparkled below. Willing my skittish feet to stay put, I rapped on the door.

He yanked it open. "You're late." He took one look at my business suit and frowned. "Training you is going to be a challenge, I see." The corner of his mouth turned up, as if he relished the idea. Gage gestured for me to enter the foyer. He grabbed my purse before I could protest and rifled through it. "Hand over your phone, too."

"I need it in case the hospital calls."

"I've arranged for them to call me in case of an emergency."

Wondering how he'd managed that, I reluctantly handed him my cell. He also took my coat, and then he locked all of my belongings in a closet by the door. We stepped down into the living room. His home had been designed with a modern edge; vaulted ceilings, light oak flooring, and taupe walls that had surely never been victim to small, sticky fingerprints. His personality was stamped all over the sharp angles, the glass and steel.

I didn't get the grand tour. He ushered me to a door, which opened into a black hole of a basement.

"Where are you taking me?"

"You'll address me as Master when we're alone." He grabbed my chin and forced me to look at him. "Is that clear?"

"You're kidding, right?"

"No, I assure you, I am definitely not kidding, and the sooner you accept your place here, the easier it'll be on you. You've just arrived and already you've got two strikes against you, Kayla."

"For what?"

"Disobeying me. I told you to come naked, and you arrived late." He gestured for me to precede him down the stairs.

"I had to say goodbye to Eve. I couldn't disappear on her for the weekend without seeing her first." I grasped his arm to keep from stumbling. He flipped a switch, and the basement flooded with soft light.

The room was rectangular, dark and windowless, with deep crimson walls that matched the comforter on the king-sized bed; Gage had already laid several items on the end. A rack of cuffs, chains, whips, paddles, and God only knew what else hung on the far wall. An odd-looking bench sat in front of the display. Not certain what the X on the wall, the hooks in the floor and ceiling, or the plethora of items on the shelves were used for, I tore my gaze from the terrifying sight. A group of comfy chairs and a couch were arranged on a throw rug at the opposite end. Across from the bed a swanky bathroom, outfitted with a whirlpool tub and separate shower, could be seen through an archway.

Gage fisted my hair and yanked me against him. "These are my rules. Remember them." He trailed a hand down my throat, and his fingers settled on the buttons of my blouse. "Number one, don't fight me. If you do you'll be punished." He slowly unfastened each one, taking the time to brush his fingers against my skin. "Two, unless I've given you permission to speak freely, always call me Master when we're alone." He slid his hand inside and palmed my breast. "And three, obey without hesitation. Do you understand these rules?"

"I-I understand." I forced the words past my quivering lips.

He let out a low chuckle. "I don't think you do. I think it's time for your first punishment." He gripped my hair even tighter. "Before we go any further, you need to choose a safe word."

"And if I say this word...you'll stop?"

"Yes. And then I'll turn you over to the authorities. Neither of us wants that."

"Then what's the point in choosing a safe word? You know I won't use it."

"Because what happens here will be on my terms, but ultimately your choice. I won't move forward without it, so choose wisely, something you won't forget or accidentally say." He withdrew his hand from my breast and put a few inches between us. "It's the only word that will save you from your punishment. Screaming, crying, begging me to stop... none of those tactics will work."

"You sick bastard."

"You might consider showing me some respect—I'm the only person standing between you and a jail cell."

"Rick."

"Rick what?"

"Rick is my safe word."

"Who is Rick?"

I wrapped my arms around myself. "Someone I don't like to talk about."

"Answer the question. You'll withhold nothing from me."

"He's my ex-husband."

"An interesting choice for a safe word. Why'd you choose it?"

"Because I don't like to think about him, much less speak his name."

He whirled me around and curled his fingers around my wrists, then forced them to my sides. "Don't ever close yourself off to me again. I want your legs open and your arms at your sides. Always." He parted my blouse, and the material slid down my arms and floated to the floor.

Gage grabbed a thin strip of leather from the bed. "A collar to mark you as mine. It's discreet enough to wear in public. Don't take it off." He encircled my neck before reaching for a set of leather cuffs. "Give me your hands."

Instinctively, I shook my head. "Gage, what are you gonna do?"

His startling eyes pinned me. "I've been lenient. Until you agree to address me as Master, you'll not be allowed to speak." He grasped an odd ball contraption and mashed it against my lips. "Open your mouth."

Trepidation set in. "You don't need to do this. I'll call you Master."

"Yes you will. Now open your mouth." I feared the command in his tone, the underlying threat that if I didn't do as told, being gagged would be the least of my worries. I parted my lips, and the taste of rubber assaulted my tongue. He fastened the straps tight enough to make my jaw ache.

"Whenever your mouth is otherwise engaged"—his lips curved into a wicked grin, and I could only imagine what he was thinking—"you can snap your fingers in lieu of saying your safe word." He grabbed my hands and yanked them up, hooking them above my head. "Spread your legs."

My skirt bunched around my thighs as I obeyed, revealing a scrap of white panties. My pulse drummed in my ears, drowning out everything else as he kneeled down and fastened two more cuffs around my ankles. He placed a bar between them, ensuring I remained spread for him.

Gage stood and slowly pulled on a tether. "On your toes."

My eyes grew wide as he hoisted me up, and an unintelligible sound escaped me. The position made my breasts jut out and caused my legs to wobble until I was able to gain balance. I shifted my wrists, but they wouldn't budge. My arms and shoulders burned. How long was he going to make me stand like this? Better yet, what was he going to do?

I had my answer a moment later. He grabbed a pair of scissors and moved toward me. I panicked and let out a muffled cry as he came closer.

"Relax. I'm not going to hurt you. I want you naked." He slid the cool metal along my skin and cut away my bra, and tears overflowed as my breasts spilled free, right into the warmth of his waiting palms.

Gage fondled them, weighed them in his hands, and his gaze zeroed in on my hardened peaks. "Perfect, just the right size." He flicked his thumbs back and forth. I gasped for breath, vacillating between shame and arousal as every touch zinged to my core. Unable to take anymore, I tried to jerk away. He pinched each nipple and twisted, and I squeezed my eyes shut against the pain.

"Look at me, Kayla." He increased the pinch. I lifted my lashes and silently begged him to stop.

"You've got spirit, and you're stubborn. The more you resist, the more it turns me on." He released me and bent to his knees again. I couldn't stop trembling as he cut the skirt and panties from my body.

"You're so gorgeous strung up like that, helpless and open. Naked." His gaze journeyed over me, finally arriving at the juncture between my thighs. "Red indeed." He delved a finger inside, and I shot to the very tips of my toes.

"God, baby, you're so tight. How is that possible after giving birth?" His warm hand smoothed across my abdomen, and he traced the wounds left behind from my four years of marital hell. "What happened here?" The question was a rhetorical one, since I couldn't answer him verbally. "They look like knife wounds." He thrust another finger inside, gliding in and out, never breaking eye contact. I was helpless to do anything but accept his invasion. My eyes drifted shut.

"Don't." Another hard pinch of my nipple reminded me of his power. "I want you to watch me." With a twitch of a smile, Gage circled my clit with precision. My belly clenched, and I throbbed deep within as liquid heat ignited between my legs. "You're not allowed to hide your shame from me." He closed his mouth over a nipple and teased with his tongue, lightly nipped.

I squirmed as the fire in my body spread and intensified. God, it'd been so long. Too long. It was the only explanation for my reaction.

"You don't want to want me, but you do." He stroked me languidly, caressing in a sensual rhythm that drove me out of my mind. "I've been watching you, Kayla, noticing those shy glances you aim my way when you think no one's looking. If I didn't think this would work between us, I would've had you thrown in jail."

My muscles tightened, and I shamefully moved against his hand. I hadn't expected this, for him to make me want to come. A low moan escaped, and I almost did.

He pulled away abruptly. "You're not allowed to orgasm without my explicit permission. Like clothing, sexual gratification is a gift you must earn." He grabbed my chin and brought his face close to mine. "Take this time to think about your behavior."

Gage stepped away and smiled, as if we were conversing about something as mundane as the weather. His eyes wandered to my breasts, and my nipples begged for his touch, his mouth. "The room is under surveillance, so trust I'll keep an eye on you for safety reasons. I'm not a careless Master, but you must know where you stand with me. Disobedience will always earn you punishment. You'll stand like that for an hour."

An hour? I let out a pitiful cry.

He crossed his arms. "If you can't handle it, snap your fingers now."

Using my only way out wasn't an option, and we both knew it. Eve's pale face swam in my vision. I'd do anything for her. Anything. I shook my head, and by doing so gave him the okay. His heavy steps pounded the stairs, growing fainter the further he climbed. He was leaving! Oh God...an hour.

Fear enveloped me like a stifling blanket; an hour loomed ahead like eternity.

CHAPTER FOUR

Time had no measure. Seconds, minutes...they all bled into each other until the only thing that mattered was the rampant ache in my muscles, the dimming of the room, the goose bumps forming on my skin as the chill set in. After a while I became numb. Listless. Found a place outside myself where I could tolerate existing. It was a familiar place, one I hadn't visited in a long time. I sagged toward the floor a little more with each minute, heels refusing to touch ground, wrists taking the burden of my weight.

And then I felt the warmth of his hands, grazing my ankles as he removed the bar from between my legs, circling my wrists and lifting...until they dropped like noodles at my sides. In a dizzying whirl, I slumped toward the floor. He engulfed me in his arms.

"Open your eyes, Kayla." His breath whisked across my face, tinted with brandy.

I stared into his sapphire gaze...and felt nothing.

He held me up with one hand and removed the gag with the other. "Have you learned your lesson?"

I worked my aching jaw, and only then did I realize I had drool trailing down my chin.

"Answer me. Have you learned your lesson?"

"Yes."

"I'm giving you one chance, because I know your punishment wasn't easy. Show me the respect I'm owed."

My apathetic state diminished; swift anger welled and overflowed. I hated him. Truly despised him. "Go to hell, Gage."

He swept me up, threw me over his shoulder, and stalked to the bench.

"What are you doing?" I cried.

Ignoring my question, he dropped me to my feet. I grabbed onto the bench to keep from falling, which was a bad idea because my actions only helped him position me. Gage pressed onto my back and wedged my knees apart. He strapped my hands, knees, and ankles in place, and then he adjusted the bench until my butt tilted up for easy access.

The snap of leather sent ice through my blood. "What is that?" I cranked my neck around to see.

"A whip."

"Don't you dare hit me with that!" I couldn't breathe. Everything flooded back; the beatings, the bruises and cuts. The fractured bones.

"I told you what I expect from you, yet you continue to disobey me. If you can't take your punishment, say your word and end it." He punctuated his words with a swift strike to my ass.

I jerked and cried out, and the whip whistled through the air again, a split second warning before he struck me a second time.

Crack!

He hit me again and again, never giving me a moment to catch my breath, never allowing the sting to alleviate before he escalated the pain with another strike. I sobbed and pleaded with every blow, and eventually I found that place again—the place I'd lived in for the duration of my marriage.

Stop, stop, stop, stop...

Finally he did.

Tears drenched my face, and I couldn't see him, though the sound of his breath, coming fast and hard, told me he wasn't far. I ticked off the seconds in my mind and stopped counting when his legs came into view.

"Who am I, Kayla?"

I lifted my head. He still had a death grip on the whip; his knuckles had gone white around the handle. "You're my Master."

"That's right. Don't you forget it."

He put the whip away and then freed me from the restraints. "Don't move yet." He disappeared, only to reappear a few seconds later with a bottle of massage oil. He dripped some onto my back and went to work in rubbing the tension from my body. His fingers glided over my back and down my legs. I felt myself sinking, losing myself to the allure of my cloudy mind. Confusion niggled on the outskirts, and I vaguely wondered why he'd beat me only to massage away some of the pain afterward.

"Who am I?" His voice drifted above, rich and warm like hot chocolate. His hands chased the chills away from my skin.

"My Master," I mumbled.

He gripped my hand. "You can get up." Gage helped me to my feet and steadied me when I stumbled. "If you behave, I won't restrain you." He pointed to the bed. "Stand at the end and bend over the mattress." He reached for the button of his slacks.

The fog cleared, unveiling fear in its wake. "Please... Master..." I faltered. Would he be rough? Would it be quick?

"Do it now, Kayla."

My legs shook as I moved clumsily across the room. He pressed a hand against my back, and my breasts and stomach slid along the satiny comforter.

"Spread your legs."

On the verge of tears, I obeyed and opened for him. Chills traveled the length of my body; I couldn't stop shaking. I jumped when he grabbed my hips.

"Arms straight out in front of you." He massaged my sore ass. "Good, just like that. I want you to remain in this position, do you understand?"

I rested my cheek on the mattress as a tear escaped. "Yes, Master," my voice cracked, and I heard the distinctive slide of a zipper, the tear of a foil packet. For several seconds I waited, barely breathing, muscles tense in preparation for his intrusion.

He glided his fingers between my thighs. Keeping perfectly still, I bit down on my lower lip. Unwelcome warmth flared again, and I prayed he'd stop caressing and just get it over with already.

"Please, Master, just do it."

"Oh, no, I'm not about to make this easy for you." He probed me with his fingers. "Do you know how many times I had to get myself off in my office after watching you prance around in your skirts?" He groaned. "You're getting wet, baby."

I arched my spine and bit back a moan.

"God, you're so responsive. I've wanted you for such a long time, wet and on the brink, begging for release." He plunged in, filling me with his pulsating heat, slowly stretching until I felt nothing but him.

I dug my fingernails into the bedding and closed my eyes in shame.

"If you come, I'll punish you." His breath fanned across my back. "Don't disobey me."

Yet the bastard took his time. I locked my jaw to keep quiet and trembled from the effort of holding back as he pumped in and out. I hated my body for betraying me.

It's only biology.

I held on to that thought as he pushed deeper. "You feel so good," he groaned. He increased his thrusts, exploiting a rhythm designed to send me spiraling out of control.

I fisted the comforter and unwittingly let out a long moan. "Master..."

"Don't come, Kayla."

I gritted my teeth and did the only thing I could think of to cool the fire. I thought of Rick; replayed the day I escaped with Eve. I'd been two weeks postpartum when he'd beaten me in a drunken rage. Hours later, when I thought he'd finally passed out for the night, I'd grabbed Eve and hobbled toward the door. He'd come out of nowhere with the knife. Eve had been thrown into the corner, and I thanked God every day she hadn't been seriously hurt, though a broken arm had been serious enough.

After a while Gage tensed and shuddered, and I knew it was over. For now.

He withdrew and disposed of the condom "You've got impressive restraint. Not many women can hold back so well, not that they come here under your circumstances. I suspect that might have more to do with it. You feel forced."

My emotions were too close to the surface. On the heels of remembering in vivid detail how I'd escaped with my life —how Eve's future had depended on it—my rage exploded. I whirled around and pushed him. "That's because you did force me! Master," I bit out the last word as if it were poison.

"You might be able to elicit a reaction from my body, but you'll never get the one you're truly after. You'll never have my eager participation." I took a step forward, emboldened by the stunned expression on his face. "It was easy to control myself. All I had to do was think of my ex-husband and how he nearly stabbed me to death."

Gage pressed his hand over my mouth. "I'd watch your tone. Don't villainize me—you're the one who stole ten grand. You signed the contract."

I pushed his hand away. "What you're doing is wrong, Gage. Punish me if you wish. Do your worst. You couldn't possibly hurt me more than he did." I turned my back on him, mostly because I figured it would piss him off.

I wasn't prepared for his laughter. "I do love a challenge. Sleep well, Kayla."

I hugged myself, and as his feet thumped up the stairs, I wanted to curl into a ball and cry myself to sleep. He shut the door, and the sound echoed through the basement, through the empty chamber of my heart.

CHAPTER FIVE

The following morning Gage ordered me into the bathtub. He sat on the edge, instructing me on how he expected me to bathe daily. The regimen he wanted me to follow would take a nice chunk out of my mornings, but I wasn't about to negotiate with him, not so long as the hard glint remained in his eyes. The new day had dawned with clarity; I'd gone too far the previous night. Now I had nothing to do but wait until he decided to dish out my punishment. My ass still stung from the one he'd given the night before—a constant reminder to call him "Master."

"I'm going to prepare breakfast. After you finish here, I expect you to wait on your knees until I return."

I gulped. "Why, Master?" I stood on the bathmat, tightly clutching the towel around my body. It didn't matter that he'd already seen me, had touched my most private places. I'd never be comfortable parading around naked in front of him.

"Because I ordered you to."

He left, and I waited until the echo of the door rang

through the basement before I dried off. I took my time blow-drying my hair and applying makeup, but eventually I couldn't stall any longer. He still hadn't returned. With nothing else to do, I moved to the middle of the room and sank to my knees.

My thoughts drifted to Eve. I wondered what she was doing. Was she eating breakfast? I hoped they were able to get her to eat something. I also thought of Ian. Had he checked on her already? Suddenly, excitement fluttered in my stomach. If I behaved the way Gage wanted me to, took my punishment without complaint and sucked up to the bastard, maybe he'd let me call to check on her. I wondered if I'd get lucky enough to catch Ian at the hospital. Gage didn't have to know that "Dr. Kaplan" was more to me than a doctor.

I jumped as the door opened. He leisurely strolled down the stairs and stopped inches in front of me. He had no qualms about displaying the bulge behind his zipper. I looked up at him as dread squeezed my insides.

"I expect you to greet me on your knees from here on out. Understand?"

"Yes, Master," I answered automatically, though in reality I didn't understand any of it. How could anyone treat another human being this way? Maybe I was the damaged one and abusive men naturally flocked to me.

"Hungry?" he asked.

How did I answer that? My stomach growled, yet I feared he wasn't talking about food. "Yes, Master."

His mouth curved into a grin. "Seeing you on your knees, calling me Master..." He rubbed himself. "Do you know what that does to me?"

"No, Master," I said, as if denying the evidence of his arousal would make it go away.

"You please me, Kayla. You've caught on quickly, faster than I thought you would."

I lowered my eyes.

"Look at me when I'm talking to you."

There was no mistaking the authority in his tone. I raised my eyes and didn't dare look away. Not with my ass still sore from the whipping he'd given me last night. Twenty-four hours hadn't passed and already I'd been reduced to a pathetic woman on my knees, my sole purpose to service and obey a man. Deep within, I silently screamed in rebellion and indignation. I hadn't hated myself this much since before my divorce.

He held out his hand, oblivious to my inner turmoil. "Come on, breakfast awaits."

I couldn't begin to describe my relief as I rose to my feet. Confronted with his arousal while on my knees made me ill. He led me upstairs, and I fought the urge to cover my breasts. I'd never walked around my own apartment naked, so the idea of walking around his home in the nude made me vulnerable on a whole new level. I suspected that was his intention.

We entered the dining room, and he dumped a bag of uncooked rice onto the hardwood floor next to the table. "Your punishment for getting mouthy with me last night." He pointed to the rice. "On your knees again."

I sank down, gritting my teeth as the grains dug into my skin.

Gage sat in a chair and began feeding me fruit. He fed me breakfast bite-by-bite, and by the time he spooned up some yogurt, I wanted to slather my burning knees with it.

"I want to talk about your previous sexual experience." He fed me another spoonful of yogurt. "I'm going to ask you some questions," he continued, "and I want your complete honesty. Do you understand?"

"Yes, Master."

"Have you ever had anal sex?"

I lowered my head without thinking. What the question implied terrified me. I couldn't breathe.

"Kayla? I won't remind you again to look at me when I'm talking to you. Next time it happens, you'll be punished."

My gaze immediately shot to his.

He smiled. "That's better. Now answer the question."

"Once, Master," I said, my voice so low that he asked me to repeat myself.

"Did you like it?"

I shook my head, my throat constricting as the memories I'd worked so hard to bury burst through and flooded my mind.

"Why not?" He sounded genuinely curious.

"I-I...he forced me."

His face darkened. "And now you think I'm doing the same." It was a statement rather than a question.

I narrowed my eyes. "Because you are. You blackmailed me." I tempered my tone and added, "I had no choice, Master."

He rubbed the bridge of his nose and sighed. "I know I crossed a line with you, Kayla. I've had many women, and to be perfectly honest, they bored me. I want a woman who values self-respect, who is classy enough to refrain from bedding every man she meets. I wanted you."

I wanted to ask how I'd gotten so unlucky to be wanted by him, but remembering my hope to call the hospital, I bit my tongue.

He held out a hand. "You can get up now." I grabbed his hand and stood, and then I wiped the rice from my knees. Gage gestured toward the chair closest to him. "You can sit."

I sat down and didn't think twice about crossing my legs and arms. One look at his heated expression reminded me of his rules. I let my arms fall like noodles at my sides and uncrossed my legs, opening them several inches so he could see all of me.

He gave an imperceptible nod of approval and pushed my plate in front of me. "Finish eating. I have a few more questions."

I remained silent and bit into a piece of toast.

"How many men have you slept with?"

"Two, Master," I said, then immediately shook my head. "I mean three...since you..."

A smile teased his lips. "That's what I thought. I respect you for abstaining from the slutty behavior of most women. "Who were your lovers?

"My ex-husband and..."

Gage tapped his fingers on the table. "And?"

"A guy I knew in college, Master."

He frowned. "Sounds like there's more about this guy from college than you're letting on. Did you love him?"

"That's none of your business!"

His mouth flattened into a line, and I immediately regretted the outburst. "That's where you're wrong. If I say it's my business, then it is." He pushed his chair back and stood, and his hands bunched at his sides. "Were you in love with him?" There was no bend to his expression, no room for sympathy. Certainly no room for compromise. I was his, and he'd do with me as he pleased. Even if it meant making me answer what should have been a simple question.

"Yes, Master. I loved him." My rebellious nature rose, but I squashed it.

"Are you still in love with him?"

Oh shit. Would he believe me if I lied? Probably not. "It's been years, Master."

"That isn't what I asked. Answer the question, Kayla."

"Why does it matter to you?" *Smooth move, idiot. Keep pissing him off and he'll never give you access to a phone.*

He jerked a chair out from the table and sat. "Come here now."

I inched toward him. With swift agility, he reached out and pulled me over his knee.

My body tensed as his hand came down. "Are you in love with him?"

"Yes!" This punishment was more humiliating than painful.

"I want you to say 'I will not back talk my Master' after every swat of your ass."

Smack!

"I will not back talk my Master."

Smack!

I was wrong. Every strike of his hand grew more painful, and he didn't stop after just a few. He counted the spankings, his voice cool and mechanical. I was openly crying, struggling to recite the words with a semblance of coherency by the time he passed forty. He released me at fifty. "Sit down, Kayla."

I staggered back and eased into my chair with a wince.

"Don't test me again. You won't like the outcome." He picked up his coffee mug and took a sip. "Now, let's see if we can have a civilized conversation free of outbursts."

I was seething inside as I swiped the tears from my face. I scooped up a bite of yogurt before I lost my temper again.

"What is it about this man that has captured you so?"

I didn't know how to answer. It'd been so long since Ian had been a part of my life, and we'd barely had a chance before a surprise pregnancy had tipped my world upside down and I'd made the mistake of going back to my ex. That mistake had cost me my first baby. "I can't answer, Master. Not because I'm being difficult, but it's been seven years. A lot has happened. I don't know why there's still a part of me holding on."

"Did he satisfy you in bed?"

I felt my face grow warm. "Yes, Master."

Gage went silent for a few moments, and I took the opportunity to broach the subject of a phone call. "Can I ask you something, Master?"

He considered me carefully. "Go ahead."

"I'm worried about Eve. Would you...allow me the privilege of calling the hospital to check on her?"

"No."

I jumped out of my chair. "How can you be such a cold-hearted bastard?"

Displaying an irritating air of calm that nicked at my anger, Gage rose from his chair and crossed the dining room without a word. He halted in front of the tall hutch in the corner and withdrew something from a drawer. My stomach sank when I recognized the ball gag in his hands, similar to the one he'd used the previous night. He closed the distance between us and held it to my mouth. I clinched my jaw, displaying one last hint of fiery anger, and then parted my lips. Fighting him would only make things worse—I was beginning to understand this game he played.

Gage grabbed my hand and led me back to the basement. He took a seat in an overstuffed chair and pointed to the floor. I gave him a questioning look, as I wasn't sure what he wanted.

"I shouldn't have to spell it out for you, Kayla." He raised a brow. "You know your place by now, so stop being stubborn. Obey me."

I dropped to my knees.

"We'll discuss phone privileges another time, perhaps when you've found a way to rein in that mouth."

He didn't speak to me for the next hour. Drool trailed

down my chin, dripped onto my breasts, and my knees ached and burned. He sat, a perfect picture of calm, reading a book while I suffered in silence. The stubborn part of me refused to give an inch. I wouldn't move, wouldn't shift and squirm or make a sound. I'd match him calm and raise him in strength any day.

CHAPTER SIX

Dinner went much more smoothly than breakfast. I managed to make it through the entire meal without a cross look from Gage or a punishment. Upon returning to the basement, he led me straight to the bench. My composure shattered.

"What are you doing, Master?" I resisted, which only caused him to firm his hold on me. "Why? What did I do?" I made him drag me across the room, thrashing the whole way.

"Knock this off right now!" He bent me over and spanked my ass. "Now crawl onto the bench before I issue a repeat of this morning."

I climbed up and got into position, and like the night before, he strapped me in. My body shook, from the chill in the room, from my absolute vulnerability. I jerked when his hands kneaded my ass.

"Don't hurt me, Master."

His hands smoothed up my back. "You need to learn to trust me. I won't punish you unless you deserve it. Have you done anything to deserve it tonight?"

I hadn't thought so.

"Answer me."

"No, Master."

"This isn't about punishment." He swept my hair to the side and trailed his fingers down my spine. "We're going to explore anal play," he said. "I don't want this to be traumatic for you, so we'll ease into it by using a butt plug, but eventually I want to fuck your ass."

"Don't do this." My voice broke.

"If you want me to stop, you have the power in one little word, Kayla."

I whimpered as he spread my cheeks. Oh God, it was going to hurt. He was bigger than my ex, and when Rick had forced himself into that tight space, I hadn't been able to sit down for days. I'd been a week postpartum, and he hadn't wanted to wait for me to heal after giving birth.

He moved away and opened a cupboard. When he returned, his cool hands slid over my butt again. I felt trapped, absolutely helpless. I could do nothing to stop him, short of saying the word that would void our contract. We both knew that wasn't going to happen. A squirting sound broke the utter quiet in the basement, and Gage applied a cold, jelly-like substance.

I automatically tensed as he dipped a finger inside.

"How does that feel?" he asked.

I gritted my teeth. "It burns, Master."

"Relax your ass."

I willed my mind past the pain and concentrated on releasing the tension in my body.

"Better?" he asked.

Surprisingly, it was. "Yes."

He used his fingers for a while before introducing the butt plug. "You need to stay relaxed. If you don't it'll only hurt more."

"Please, Master, don't. I'm not ready for this."

"Yes, you are. You're only fighting it because you're scared. I won't hurt you, but you've gotta loosen up." He slowly inched in the plug, and I let out a screeching cry.

"Stop," I sobbed. "Please...stop." I fought against the restraints until the leather cuffs bit into my tender skin.

"Relax your muscles," he said again. The pressure in my rectum increased as he shoved it all the way in. He reached between my legs and circled my clit. "Let your body adjust to it." Something about the husky quality of his voice caused tingles to spread through me; I was stunned to find myself aroused.

What the hell was this man doing to me?

"How does it feel now?"

I wet my lips and tasted the salt of my tears. "Weird, Master."

"Does it still hurt?"

"A little." Not like it had when my ex had forced his way in there. Maybe the difference lie in the preparation.

He crawled onto the bench and straddled me from behind, and I heard him unzip his pants. Gage pressed against my back and whispered directly into my ear, "Are you turned on?"

"Yes, Master." Humiliation washed over me.

"Do you want me to fuck you?"

I gave him the answer he wanted to hear. "Yes, Master."

Before I could take my next breath, he thrust into me. I was already wet and ready for him. The pressure from the butt plug heightened the pleasure, making each plunge a sensation that drove me closer to losing control. I moved with him as he pumped in and out, no longer caring if I was acting like a desperate hussy. The need inside me clawed to the surface; I could deny it no longer. I was on the verge of release, breaths coming in gasping pants, when he painfully fisted my hair.

"Not yet, baby. Not until I give you permission."

"Gage!" I cried out again, barely managing to rein in my orgasm. "I can't, Master!"

He groaned. "Yes you can."

I dug my fingernails into the leather of the bench, groaning as the pressure built to the erupting point. "Please, Master...please..."

He shot upright onto his knees and smacked my ass. "Not yet."

I let out a scream as the violent orgasm tore through my body. "Oh God!" I arched my back, curled my feet, and wondered if the wave would ever end.

Gage came then, releasing a hoarse cry that caused my insides to clench all over again.

"I couldn't stop it, Master."

"You know I'll have to punish you for that, right?"

Gasping for breath, I let my head fall to the bench and nodded. At the moment I didn't care. I'd never experienced such an intense orgasm. Ever. I closed my eyes, my heart still pounding a fast beat, and allowed the overwhelming surge of emotion to spill over.

CHAPTER SEVEN

As part of my slave duties, Gage assigned me a list of chores Sunday morning. After I'd done the dishes, folded his laundry, and vacuumed, he reinserted the butt plug and ordered me to scrub both of his bathrooms on my hands and knees.

Only his idea of clean surpassed mine by a hundred miles. He'd made me redo my first attempt, instructing me to use a toothbrush. I'd since moved on to the bathroom in the basement and was now scrubbing the grout between the tiles with a vengeance, all the while silently cursing him.

"R" is for rotten scoundrel.

"S" is for Satan.

"T" is for—

I gasped as the pressure in my ass shifted—it had been there for so long, I'd begun to get used to it. I stilled as he teased me by sliding the plug out a couple of inches, only to push it back in. I couldn't decide if I liked the sensation or not. He did it again, and I unconsciously raised my ass.

"You like that, huh?" He dipped his fingers between my legs, and the toothbrush fell from my hand and clattered to the floor.

I moaned with each thrust, with every motion of his fingers. I didn't recognize the woman I'd become; on hands and knees on a bathroom floor, coming undone as my boss fucked me in the ass with a butt plug.

Gage pulled away. "Get up."

I obeyed and slowly turned to look at him. He was completely naked. Warmth flushed my cheeks. Ashamed of what he'd reduced me to, I had a difficult time meeting his gaze.

He pulled me against him. "You need a shower, and I need you to take care of this." He grabbed my hand and closed my fingers around his erection. I stroked him as he backed me toward the stall. Gage guided me inside and switched on the shower. Hot water cascaded over us, coming from all directions from the multiple shower heads.

He pushed my back against the wall. "Hold on to these," he said, lifting my arms and folding my fingers around the two handles built into the shower stall. "Close your eyes. I want you to feel every touch, every sensation."

My eyes drifted shut, and his soapy hands glided over my skin, fingers teasing breasts, smoothing down my stomach, caressing between my thighs. He left no area untouched. My pulse fluttered at my throat, and when he laved his tongue there, I arched my neck and let out a sigh.

"You're so beautiful," he whispered against my skin. "So responsive to my touch."

The warmth of his mouth closed around a nipple. I whimpered, overcome with need, and tightened my grip on the handles. The way he set me off reminded me of the night I'd spent with Ian all those years ago. I hadn't experienced such intense desire in years; my ex had surely never made my body hum.

Gage grabbed my ass and hoisted me against him. "Wrap your legs around me," he said. "Keep your eyes closed."

I obeyed his command. He ran his hands up my back and burrowed them in my hair. I parted my lips and tasted water as it streamed down my face. His mouth came down on mine, and my mind fogged over as his tongue swept inside. His kiss was sensual, urgent, possessive, and erotic, all rolled into one. He kissed like he smiled—with a devilish edge that was too tempting to ignore. He delved deeper, and I lost my mind as he thoroughly possessed my mouth. For a few blissful minutes, I forgot how he'd forced me there, forgot about the beating, the humiliation. For the first time in years, I felt alive.

He broke away, and without thinking, I opened my eyes; I'd never seen his so bright. In that moment I saw him for the first time. Really saw him, his face softened in vulnerability.

"Turn around," he said hoarsely.

Limbs shaking, I did as I was told.

"Grab the handles and climb up."

I looked down and noticed the built-in seat, made specifically to accommodate a woman's knees. I got into position, and Gage ran his fingers down my spine. He palmed my ass and then dipped the plug in and out.

"Master..." I moaned and arched my back.

"Yes, baby, just like that. You're gorgeous in this position." He lightly spanked me. I jumped, not because it hurt, but because the slap was so unexpected. He slapped my ass again, and then he spread my cheeks.

My heart thundered in my ears as he removed the plug and applied lubricant. Apprehension twisted my insides.

"Hold on to those handles," he said.

Gage's thick cock slowly pressed in. His intrusion stretched me further, and I gasped for breath at the intensity of the burn, clamped my fingers around the handles, and focused on breathing. I now knew how pleasurable it could feel if I let my mind and body accept it.

"How does it feel?"

"It burns, Master."

"Try to relax." He pushed in another inch.

"I can't!" My knuckles turned white. "Stop—"

"Relax your muscles, Kayla. I'm not trying to hurt you." He groaned softly against my ear. "I'm being as gentle as I can, but if you can't loosen up you'll have to endure the pain. This won't be the last time I fuck you like this." He took his time, easing in a little more with each thrust. My knees trembled, and Gage wound his arms around me and palmed my breasts, supporting me with his strength. He sipped at the water sluicing down my neck and dove deeper. "You feel so good."

I squeezed my eyes shut, and after a while my body grew accustomed to his. With a final jerk, he came and collapsed onto my back. We stayed frozen like that for a while, me relieved it was over, and him coming down from the high he'd achieved.

He got up and shut off the water. "Come on," he said, gently tugging on my arm. I got to my feet. We dried off with fluffy towels, and he ushered me into the basement. I eyed the bench, remembering my forbidden orgasm from the day before, and wondered if he planned to strap me onto it and beat me again.

But he bypassed the bench and headed for the bed. "Have you been wondering how I'm going to punish you?"

I bit my lip and nodded.

He crawled onto the mattress and sat with his back to the headboard. He patted his lap. "Come here."

I blinked. "Do-do you want me to straddle you, Master?"

"No, I want you to sit facing away."

I hesitated a second before climbing onto the bed. The friction of my skin sliding along his excited me.

"Lie against me."

I reclined against his chest. Gage wedged his legs between mine and spread my thighs.

"I want you to touch yourself until you reach the point where you're about to orgasm, then I want you to stop. If you come, there will be consequences."

I swallowed hard. I'd never gotten myself off before in front of another person, and I'd certainly never had to hold back. With tentative fingers, I reached down and stroked myself, slowly rubbing in a way that was familiar and sensual. Yet the usual build-up was absent. I squirmed and tried to force myself into the right mindset, but after several minutes my breathing was still too even, the tingles in my body too weak.

He kissed the hollow of my shoulder. "Close your eyes," he whispered, "do whatever you have to, but get yourself to the edge. You're not stopping until you do."

I inhaled a deep breath, closed my eyes, and turned my mind off to anything but the feel of his warm skin underneath me, the zinging sensation deep in my stomach as his hands brushed across my breasts. My center liquefied as my fingers circled with increasing speed. A blissful ache rushed through my limbs, and my heartbeat reached a thundering roar. I jerked my hand away. My chest heaved in his hands, and I panted and squirmed, hating how the ache lingered between my legs.

Gage's own breathing had grown heavy. Just as the pressure started to subside, he pushed my hand back to my crotch. "Do it again, and stop before you come."

I tunneled my fingers through my slick folds, and my body immediately responded. He made me rub myself to the edge several times, until I was openly moaning and grinding my butt against his erection. Blood rushed through me, molten lava coalescing at the epicenter between my legs. On the brink of exploding, I trembled so violently that my legs cramped. He whisked his thumbs across my nipples and I almost burst into flames.

"Please," I groaned. "I can't..."

He trapped my hands in his. "Control it. Hold it in. You don't have my permission to come."

I arched and dug my fingernails into his skin. Several minutes passed in silence, and when he pushed my hand back to the center of all that throbbing heat, I thought I'd die. He forced me to the edge one last time, and then he slid from the bed and fastened my hands to the headboard. "Wouldn't want you to give in to temptation," he said with a crooked grin. "I'll be back in an hour. Hopefully you'll have calmed down by then."

CHAPTER EIGHT

As a reward for my iron-like control over my body, Gage took me out to dinner that night. After existing in a naked state for two days, I found the sensation of clothing against my skin wonderful. Now I almost felt normal, seated like a lady, surrounded by fashionable people at a fancy restaurant with an attractive man smiling back at me from across the table.

Almost.

Beyond the surface, nothing about the situation was normal, especially since the man in question had inserted a butt plug in my ass before we'd left the house. I recrossed my legs for the fifth time and tried not to squirm.

"You're gorgeous. I'm a lucky man to be accompanied by the most beautiful woman in the restaurant."

Luck had nothing to do with it, but I kept my thoughts to myself. I'd managed to get through the rest of the day without further punishment or pain, if you didn't count the pulsing ache between my thighs that refused to subside. He'd given me more chores to complete and had come to me for sex twice already. I hadn't been allowed to orgasm; as a result I was tense with sexual frustration.

He lowered his gaze to my breasts and smiled in amusement. "Still feeling a little uncomfortable?"

I clenched my jaw. My nipples had been hard pebbles of need for most of the evening. I felt them poking out now.

"Answer me, Kayla." Even in public, he didn't hesitate to wield his authority over me.

"Yes, Mast—" I broke off, remembering that I wasn't supposed to call him Master in public. "I'm sorry. Yes, I'm "uncomfortable."" That was one way of putting it.

The waiter arrived at our table. He was young, maybe a couple years younger than my twenty-eight years. He flashed a boyish grin at me, and Gage's expression darkened.

"Good evening," he said, "we have several specials on the menu tonight. Can I interest you in a bottle of wine?" He directed the question at Gage and then took a small step back at the dangerous look in his eyes.

"A bottle of Pinot Grigio, please."

The waiter scurried away, and Gage blasted me with his granite expression. "Don't look at him when he returns. I'll order for you."

I lowered my gaze. *Just bite your tongue. The weekend's almost over, just get through it.*

The waiter returned a few minutes later, and in my peripheral vision I saw him present a bottle. Gage went through the whole swirl and taste routine and gave a nod. Wine swished into my glass an instant later, and the waiter left after taking our orders.

"Are you going to visit Eve tonight?" Gage asked.

"Yes. I'm sure she's missing me."

An uncomfortable silence settled over us. How odd that he had nothing more to say to me, considering he knew my body inside and out by now. When the food arrived, I kept my eyes on my hands. The meal went by painfully slow, filled with long silences and small talk that was unnatural and awkward. It was as if the two of us didn't know how to operate together outside of the office or the bedroom.

Gage had shaken up my world with a new dynamic: I didn't know how to act around him anymore. Would things be this tense at the office?

I let out a sigh of relief when we returned to his house. At least there I knew where I stood. He'd trained me well over the weekend, had made it clear where my place was; on my knees at his feet. He shut the door, and as soon as I shed my coat, he picked me up and pressed me against the wall. His fingers tore through nylon, shoved aside panties, and his cock slammed into me before I could catch my breath. He pulled the butt plug out, and I heard it drop to the floor.

It was, perhaps, our shortest session yet. After climaxing, he zipped up and walked into the living room without a word.

"Did I do something wrong, Master?"

"No." He grabbed a notebook from the coffee table and turned to me. "I want you to remember who you belong to. I don't take kindly to other men undressing you with their eyes."

He was blowing it out of proportion—the guy had only smiled at me—but I wasn't about to argue with him.

"Before you go, we need to discuss a few things." He handed me the notebook. "It's a journal, and on the first page you'll find a list of rules. Also included are my expectations outlining what you should eat and wear during the week. I want you to write in the journal every night. List what you did during the day, who you saw, what you ate and wore, and I especially want you to list any rules you broke."

I took the notebook from him. Despite his demands, a sense of freedom awaited me through that door, even if the next five days would go by too fast. God, how I was going to hate the end of each day, bringing me that much closer to next weekend.

"Can I go now, Master?"

"Yes. I'll see you tomorrow morning at the office."

I shrugged into my coat, concealing the torn state of my nylons, and opened the door. Gage's hand shot out and blocked my exit.

"Kayla—" He grabbed the back of my head and brought my mouth to his. The kiss went on for what seemed like forever. By the time he broke away, my pulse pounded in my ears. "If you disobey me, I *will* find out. Don't forget you're mine."

I averted my eyes, and he jerked my face back to his. "Do you understand?"

"Yes, Master." I stepped outside and shivered; I wasn't entirely certain the chill was from the weather. The next five days promised blessed freedom. Time spent with Eve, maybe even a few forbidden moments at the hospital with Ian. I planned to make every one of them count.

CHAPTER NINE

Whoever said crying was a form of cleansing hadn't cried over the shit I had in my lifetime, the most recent of which took the cake—namely that my daughter was fighting for her life. I'd stolen from the devil himself in order to save her, and now I was paying the ultimate price: six weeks of forced slavery of the most vile variety.

The fact that a part of me enjoyed it only compounded the problem.

I unlocked my door and finally allowed the floodgates to break. I'd barely kept my tears at bay while at the hospital, where I'd pulled Eve into my arms and rocked her long after she'd fallen asleep. I wasn't sure if I'd held on so long to comfort her or me, but the weight of her in my arms and the smell of her soft skin had righted my world, if only for a while. I'd needed someone in that moment, and sadly I had no one but my three-year-old daughter.

I shed my clothes and collapsed into bed, and the sense of safety I usually felt within these walls was absent. Gage Channing's lingering intrusion permeated every corner of my sanctuary. I curled into a ball and hugged my naked body, letting it all out in gulping sobs. The rest of the night blurred—hours blending together as the clock on my nightstand moved time...moved time closer to when I'd have to see him again.

Confusion and grief were powerful emotions; they haunted me now as heavily as my guilt did—the most disturbing case imaginable. I tortured myself with the vivid memory of his sculpted body moving against mine, demanding my submission, and his whip lancing my bare skin in unforgiving blows. Worse was how he'd forced me to pleasure...how even now I craved it.

I still ached from being denied so long. Despite his damn rules, I slid my hand between my thighs and closed my eyes, burrowing my fingers into slick, throbbing heat. My frenzied touch brought me to an exquisite build-up. Gage's blue-eyed gaze flashed in my head, and as I recalled the experience of grinding against him—again and again without release—I plunged into inevitable rapture, coming long and hard. A deep moan poured from my throat, and I spread my legs wider as my body cramped and shuddered. Heart pounding a deafening rhythm, I gave over to my release as it pulsed around my fingers. A blessed haze engulfed me, and I drifted to sleep a couple hours before the sun peeked through the blinds.

The blaring alarm interrupted an alternate replay of Gage and me in my dreams. There had been no cruelty, no hunger for power and dominance—he'd touched me with the gentlest patience and whispered the sweetest words, unlike the language he'd used over the weekend.

I want to fuck your ass.

Yes, dream-Gage had been ten times better than foul-mouthed, sadistic Gage with his demands and a whip to ensure I bowed to him. I got to my feet and began his mandatory hygiene regimen.

Bath oil in the water—check.

Wash and condition hair—check.

Shave underarms, bikini area, and legs from thigh to ankle—check.

Rub jasmine scented lotion over every inch of skin—check.

I'd have to stop by the department store on my way to work to pick up a pair of four-inch heels—another requirement. He even demanded I wear them to the hospital and while running errands. With a sigh, I ransacked my closet in search of a short skirt. A deep forage into my lingerie drawer produced a lacy bra and thong set I'd forgotten about long ago. I hadn't worn such things in...

Shit, I couldn't remember the last time I'd worn something so sexy. If Gage hadn't promised to set up an account for me at Victoria's Secret, I'd be in real trouble. As I moved toward the kitchen to turn on the coffee maker, a drift of cool air hit my ass. I hated thongs.

I hated Gage Channing even more.

I picked up the journal he'd given me and re-read his "rules..."

No masturbating.

Oops, already broke that one.

No dating, flirting, or touching/having sex with other men. No talking to men, unless work, errands, or hospital personnel require it.

Not likely to happen, since my social life was non-existent. A niggling thought bothered me. Ian might fall into this category. I couldn't help my feelings for him, years ago buried but never forgotten, and I couldn't help if I ran into him at the hospital. What was I supposed to tell him? That I wasn't allowed to speak to him? Yeah, as if that wouldn't raise a few questions, not to mention an eyebrow or two.

Must maintain hygiene regimen daily.

I already despised this rule.

Must always wear the collar.

The damn thing choked me, if not literally then figuratively. The thin strip of leather was a constant reminder that no matter how close freedom seemed within my grasp, it truly wasn't.

Must follow the specified menu plan.

This one could be a problem, since most days I didn't have an appetite at all.

Must wear four-inch heels, short skirts, and thong underwear at all times (work, hospital, errands).

Perverted bastard.

Must sleep naked.

Ditto.

CHAPTER TEN

I was shaking by the time I exited the elevator, anxious and terrified of facing Gage again after what had happened between us over the weekend. The office bustled with the normal Monday morning activity I'd become accustomed to during my employment at Channing Enterprises. Katherine gave me her patented sugary smile as I stumbled toward Gage's office in my new heels. I cursed the squished nature of my toes, and then cursed again when some of his coffee splashed onto my hand. Already on the verge of being late, I licked up the bitter liquid and hoped no one noticed. The caffeine went straight to the butterflies in my stomach; they fluttered with the energy of a crack addict. I knocked on his door and pushed it open upon his order to enter.

He sat behind his desk, a phone wedged between his ear and shoulder as he entered data into his laptop. He didn't acknowledge me as I set down the coffee cup with a trembling hand. I pulled my iPad from my briefcase and shuffled my feet as he finished the call.

"Good morning, Kayla." He grabbed the cardboard cup and took a sip before going about his normal morning routine, which involved dictating what he needed me to do for him. My fingers flew over the screen, adding meetings, notes, and anything else he specified. He said nothing remotely related to our weekend together—not even a hint. He resumed typing, and I kept my mouth shut, though I had to admit to being completely flustered. He acted as if nothing out of the ordinary had happened. I couldn't help but stand there like an idiot, waiting for some sort of response—something to indicate how I should behave around him. Was I supposed to call him Master while in his office when no one else was around? Did he want me on my knees as long as the door was closed?

I cleared my throat. "Mr. Channing?" Uttering that name left an odd taste in my mouth after the weekend I'd endured. Not only had he effectively programmed me to call him "Master," but addressing him so formally after he'd had his cock buried in me seemed ridiculous. I licked my lips, thinking of the one place he had yet to penetrate. I'd be naive to assume it wasn't going to happen eventually.

He glanced up. "Yes?"

"Is there anything else?"

"No, that's all. I'll need that report by lunch." He returned to his work, and I didn't know what confused me more—his casual dismissal, or the fact that it stung.

I put Gage's behavior out of my mind and got to work. Shortly before lunchtime, as I was gathering a printout, Tom from the marketing department approached me.

"How was your weekend?" he asked.

I blinked. "It was...nothing unusual. How was yours?"

"Could've been better. Cindy and I broke up."

"I'm sorry."

"Don't be. It was a long time coming. Actually, I wanted to ask you out for coffee. You busy this week?" He took a step closer and brushed a stray hair out of my eyes. "Or we could do something more private. Whatever you're up for."

I gave him an uneasy smile. "I'm sorry, I can't. My daughter's in the hospital." I stumbled back until a couple of feet separated us.

Apparently he didn't pick up on my subtle hint. "How's she doing?" he asked, closing the distance.

"Her doctor's hopeful. We're waiting on some test results." I looked toward Gage's office and found his thunderous expression aimed in our direction. He crossed the space with a purposeful stride.

Oh, shit.

"You're fired," he snapped at Tom. "Security will escort you from the premises." Gage gave a slight nod toward a man who materialized from the periphery. He grabbed Tom by the arm.

"What the hell?" Tom's eyes widened as he took in our employer's furious expression. "Why? What'd I do?"

"I won't tolerate sexual advances between my employees. You obviously made Ms. Sutton very uncomfortable."

"Let's go," the security guard ordered.

Tom protested, his voice ringing through the fifth floor as the guard escorted him to the elevator. "I'll have you sued for this!" As soon as they disappeared behind the sliding doors and all the prying eyes pretended to go back to work, I set my hands on my hips and glared at Gage.

"Was that really necessary? He has a kid to take care of!" I wasn't sure who was more surprised by my outburst—him or me.

"In my office *now*."

I closed my eyes on an exhale. Once again I'd let my mouth run rampant. Every gaze in the room weighed on me as I trailed behind Gage. He shut and locked the door, and I swallowed hard, preparing to grovel.

"I'm sorry. I was way out of line."

He grabbed my arm and yanked me over to his desk. There wasn't much on it—a few papers, a stapler, and the coffee cup from this morning. He swept everything to the floor, and black coffee splashed the wall.

"How dare you disrespect me in front of my employees. It's bad enough I had to watch that idiot manhandle you."

"You're right. I was wrong to question you in front of everyone."

"Has one night of freedom erased your training already? You will address me as Master, and so we're clear, you were wrong to question me at all." He unbuckled his belt and gestured to the desk. "Bend over."

I didn't dare hesitate. If I did as told, maybe he would go easy on me.

"Lift up your skirt. If you drop it, I'll make your hands bleed."

With shaking fingers, I lifted the back of my skirt and exposed my bare bottom.

"You've brought this on yourself, Kayla." The slide of his belt shattered the quiet as he removed it. "If you ever let another man touch you again, I'll do far worse." The strap of leather came down hard enough to steal my breath.

I blinked back tears, knowing that leaving his office with blotchy eyes and streaking mascara was more humiliation than I could stand. I pressed into the desk to brace myself and gripped my skirt tighter in preparation for the next blow.

"How many strikes do you think you deserve?"

Was he fucking serious? How could I answer without getting ensnared in his trap?

"As many as you see fit, Master."

"Very diplomatic answer. That's one thing I like about you—you're a smart woman."

Crack! I jumped at the stinging bite. Holy hell it hurt.

"Do you think I enjoy this, Kayla?"

"Yes, Master," I choked out.

"You'd be wrong." He struck me again, and I couldn't hold back a sob. I squeezed my eyes shut, but it did little to shut out the pain. "I won't deny that the sound of your cries, the display of your submission and vulnerability, gets me hard, but I'd much rather get past the need to punish you at all." The belt whooshed through the air again, and I bit into my lip as it connected with my tender skin.

He stopped at ten. "Come here."

I turned around in time to see him drop the belt. Upon my hesitation, he flexed his hands. Slowly, I crossed the three feet that separated us, my skirt swishing against my burning ass as I moved. He reached out and gripped my shoulders, pushing down until I was kneeling before him. The hard ridge behind his zipper stared me in the face.

Gage unbuttoned his slacks, and the slight tremble in his hands didn't go unnoticed; he was worked up, though from anger or desire, I couldn't be sure. "Unzip me."

I raised my head, though I knew my silent pleading wouldn't do any good.

"Don't look at me like that. You're only going to piss me off more."

"Please, Master—"

"I want my cock in your mouth *now*."

Holding back another sob, I pulled down his zipper, and his shaft popped out, hard and ready for my lips and tongue.

He fisted my hair with both hands and held me in place.

"Don't make me do this, Master. Please, not here."

His cock twitched. "Beg some more. It turns me on."

I clenched my jaw. I wondered what he'd do if I refused? Did I want to find out?

No, I didn't.

Several seconds went by, during which neither of us moved. He was waiting for me to take the initiative, and I was waiting for him to force me. It would be easier if he did. Every inch I gave him felt like a betrayal to myself. He tickled my mouth with the tip, bathing my lips with his desire. He'd win this standoff; I'd lost the game before I even knew how to play.

I darted my tongue out to taste him. More moisture collected at the head, and his salty taste lingered on my tongue. It'd been years since I'd given a blow job, but I was pretty sure I still remembered how. I reached out and fisted the base, and then teased him with my lips, swirling a wet path around the soft tip a few times before fastening my mouth around him.

Gage expelled a deep moan, and his grip on my hair tightened to an unbearable pull. The fact that his response tingled between my legs shouldn't have shocked me by now, but it did. And it shamed me. A part of me got off on the power I had in this moment. He might have forced me to my knees, but I could bring him to his with the heat of my mouth, the kiss of my tongue. I took him in as far as I could stand and worked him for all I was worth.

His choppy breathing infused the air, and he began to thrust, forcing my head back with each forward motion. Pumping in and out, deeper, faster, keeping time to the friction of my mouth and hands. His gaze intensified, and unsettled with how he watched me, I closed my eyes.

"Look at me," he ordered on a groan. I met his glazed-over eyes as he jerked to the back of my throat. His taste flooded my mouth, and when I tried to pull away, he immobilized me in his grasp. I couldn't keep from gagging as his cum shot down my throat. The way he tightened his fingers, pulling against my tender scalp, told me he enjoyed making me gag as much as he enjoyed spilling into my mouth.

He withdrew, zipped up with casual patience, and then indicated the spilt coffee on the floor—the evidence of his rage and jealousy. "Clean this up before you go to lunch. I have a meeting I'm late for." He picked up his belt and looped it through his pants, and just like that the bastard left me kneeling in the middle of his office, wet between my thighs as his cum dribbled down my chin.

I got up on jittery legs and stumbled to his private bathroom. A few splashes of cold water to my face, followed by the mindless task of cleaning up after his fit, helped me find composure. When I left his office, grabbing a file folder on the way to make it look like I'd had legitimate business in there, I did my best to appear unfrazzled. I cringed to think of the office grapevine catching wind of what Gage had forced me to do.

My lunch hour passed much too quickly, and upon my return I managed to avoid my coworkers and Gage for the duration of the day by hiding away with a laptop in a vacant windowless office. Privacy was a must, since I couldn't sit without grimacing. I was unprepared for the whispers and incredulous looks as I gathered my briefcase and purse at the end of the day.

One glance into Gage's office revealed it was empty. He was either away at a late meeting, or he'd already left. I stiffened when someone whispered the word "slut" as I made the long journey toward the elevator. From the corner of my eye I recognized Katherine. She laughed, her blond head bent close to someone else's. They both snickered, and I felt their eyes bore holes into my back. I was content to ignore them until I heard the term "blow job" drift through the office.

Rage and mortification collided in my chest, and I hardly breathed as I sought refuge behind the elevator doors. I blinked, silently repeating *I will not cry* over and over again as the elevator descended. If everyone knew what had happened today in Gage's office, then he must have told someone. Barreling out into the pounding rain, I was thankful for Oregon's weather as the raindrops disguised my tears. I slid into the privacy of my car and pulled out my cell.

Gage answered on the third ring. "This better be important."

"You're damn right it's important!" I dashed the tears from my face and lowered my voice. "Everyone knows." God, how was I going to keep this job now? It was difficult enough to envision working for the devil himself after entering into a contract with him, but to withstand the ridicule of his employees...and not be able to defend myself with the truth...I couldn't do it. Yet I had no choice. The pay was too good, and even with Gage covering Eve's medical bills, I was still entrenched in debt. I couldn't afford to change jobs.

I heard him speak to someone else, and then the distinctive sound of a door closing filtered to my ear. "What are you talking about, Kayla?"

"They called me a slut, and someone mentioned 'blow job.' How could you tell anyone? Haven't you tortured me enough?"

"First off, watch your tone. Don't forget who you're speaking to. Secondly, I don't flaunt my business, so I have no idea what you're talking about."

"Someone found out. They know what happened today in your office."

He let out a heavy sigh. "I need to finish up here. Are you on the way to the hospital?"

"Yeah."

"Are you alone right now?"

"I'm in my car."

"Then why aren't you addressing me as Master? This

changes nothing. You'll be punished for your lack of protocol tonight. Come to my house at nine."

A violent shudder tore through me. Freedom didn't exist within Gage's contract—I wouldn't be free for another five and half weeks. Like a trained dog, I replied, "Yes, Master."

A small part of me wondered if I'd ever be free of him.

CHAPTER ELEVEN

The hair on the back of my neck stood on end as I rushed through the rain toward the hospital. The uneasy sensation of being watched settled over me, though in the back of my mind I knew the feeling was likely a result of what had happened in the office earlier. I felt exposed and on display, as if every person I crossed paths with thought the word "slut" after a single glance.

The instant I entered Eve's room, my paranoid worry about gossip and rumors vanished. Dr. Leah Gordon's weary expression threatened to strangle me. My heart plummeted, and I instinctively sensed something was wrong.

"Kayla, maybe you should have a seat."

I shook my head. "No, just tell me."

Her shoulders slumped slightly. "Eve's blood work came in. It's not encouraging."

"But...but..." I suddenly couldn't form a coherent sentence. The walls in the room closed in as the doctor's words percolated in my head. "You said her chances were good..."

Dr. Gordon laid a comforting hand on my shoulder. "I

was optimistic, yes, but we're not seeing the results I'd hoped for."

I brought a trembling hand to my mouth. Eve was fast asleep in bed, her skin so pale it nearly matched the pasty color of the bed sheets. My eyes zeroed in on the dried blood caking the skin underneath her nostrils. "She had another nose bleed?"

"Yes, and she became quite agitated. The nurse got her to calm down by rocking her. She's been resting for the past hour."

I grabbed a washcloth and ran it under warm water, then gently wiped her face. She stirred but didn't wake. She looked peaceful. Sick, but peaceful.

I faced Dr. Gordon again. "What can we do?"

"I don't want to get your hopes up, but there is a clinical trial we can try...if we can get her enrolled in time, that is. It's a long shot." Her face softened in sympathy.

"Do it." I blinked away tears. "Do whatever you have to."

The doctor hesitated. "Getting her into the trial isn't the only issue. Like the last treatment, your insurance won't cover it. You've indicated your finances aren't—"

"I'll get the money. How soon can she get in?"

"I'll do my best, but you might want to prepare...making her comfortable is about all we can do at this point unless something changes."

I blinked several times until the sting in my eyes abated. A knock sounded, and the door creaked open behind me. Dr. Gordon gave me one last sympathetic look. "I'll let the two of you visit."

I turned around in time to see her nod at Ian on her way out.

"Hi." His eyes traveled the length of my body, from the red locks of my hair to the spiky heels encasing my feet. "How was the business trip?"

"Exhausting." That much was true; Gage Channing had put me through the wringer. Nothing compared to this, though. My eyes burned with more unshed tears.

You are not breaking down in front of him.

I turned back to Eve and planted a kiss on her forehead. "Can you give me a minute?" I closed my eyes and breathed in her scent, and my throat tightened. "Please."

"What's wrong?" The rustling of his clothing reached my ears.

"The treatment isn't-isn't..."

"Kayla...I don't know what to say. " His breath whispered across the back of my neck. "I'm so sorry. I don't have any kids...I can't even begin to imagine what you're going through right now."

I couldn't stop despair from overflowing, and when I sensed him reaching for me, I jerked out of his grasp. "Please...don't." Speaking to him about my daughter was one thing, but allowing myself to fall apart in his embrace was another. I wouldn't be able to stop crying if he wrapped those strong arms around me; I remembered much too vividly the comfort and shelter they offered. I finally turned and faced him.

"Don't shut me out," he pleaded. "You need me...I'm here."

"Why now?" I was playing with fire, but I couldn't stop the question from escaping. "It's been seven years, Ian."

"Seven years too long." He shook his head. "You pushed me out of your life, moved away, wouldn't take my calls... why'd you disappear like that?"

"Can we not get into this right now?"

"We used to mean everything to each other." He drew in a breath. "I came back for you, Kayla."

I wanted to lean on him so badly. He'd been my rock, the one person I could trust no matter what. But leaning on him was off-limits. Gage would go ballistic if he found out I was talking to him. "Eve and I will be okay," I whispered, needing to believe it was true more than anything. "Dr. Gordon mentioned a clinical trial."

"She's a fighter," he said. "Just like her mom."

No three-year-old should have to fight so hard to live. Another piece of my heart broke off and shattered. If I lost Eve...I couldn't fathom living.

"Is there anything I can do?" he asked, looking about as helpless as I felt.

I shook my head. Ian couldn't step back into the role of protector and comforter...lover. Things change, and as much as I hated to admit it, the only person who could help me now was my sadistic boss. I'd do whatever Gage wanted, so long as he made sure my daughter had a fighting chance. With his money and resources...

"I just need some time. Please, Ian."

He ran his hand over his mouth and reluctantly nodded. "You know where to find me."

"I know."

He went to the door, and I sensed him wavering. "I've missed you," he said as he slipped from the room.

I stretched out next to Eve and pulled her into my arms. "I've missed you too."

CHAPTER TWELVE

It was fifteen past nine when I pounded on Gage's door. He jerked it open, and I immediately recognized the hardened glint in his eyes. He halted and did a double take.

I could only imagine what I must look like; tear-streaked face, drenched hair and clothes. I was broken on the inside and tattered on the outside. I imagined my eyes were depths of vacancy.

"I—" My voice hitched on a sob. Until that moment, I hadn't allowed myself to acknowledge how scared I was. I'd had so much hope that the treatment would work. Now it felt as if someone was gripping my heart and squeezing a little more as each second passed.

"What's wrong?"

"It's Eve..."

"Come here." He grabbed my arm and pulled me inside, and then he enfolded my shivering body into his arms. "What happened?"

I clung to him. "The treatment isn't working." A hiccup escaped as he rubbed some warmth back into my body. "I need more money. There's one last trial her doctor wants to try..." I untangled from his embrace and fell to my knees. "Please, Master. I'll do anything you want."

His hands sifted through my hair. "I'm a bastard for being so turned on right now. What I want is to hurt you. Will you let me?"

Nothing could hurt worse than the terror eating away at my insides. "Yes, Master. Do as you wish. Just save my daughter."

He pulled my hair until I tilted my head back. "Your lack of faith in me is insulting. I told you I'd take care of her."

"This is an additional cost, Master. A really expensive one."

"You have my assurance. I'll drop off another check at the hospital first thing in the morning." He paused, and his steady gaze froze me to the spot. "So long as you fully submit to me."

"Master...I have." I forced the words out. "I do."

He shook his head slowly, as if taking the time to weigh his words. "No, you haven't. Not completely. There's a strong, stubborn...*independent*...part of you that still resists."

I parted my lips, but nothing came out; what he said was true.

"Tonight won't be easy." His gaze lowered to my mouth. "I'm going to push you to your limits. I'm tired of playing games. I shouldn't have to punish you so often." He let go of my hair, and his face hardened with determination. "You want my help? I want your total submission. Are we clear?"

I searched his eyes for a spark of empathy and found the slightest hint of an ember. "Yes, Master."

"Did you break any of my rules?"

I chewed on my lip. "I made myself..." I really didn't want to say the words. My cheeks warmed at the memory because I'd been thinking of him as I came.

"Go on," he prompted.

"I made myself orgasm."

"How many times?"

"Once."

"Anything else?"

"I haven't eaten much today."

"I see." He frowned. "What is your least favorite food?"

I squinted up at him, wondering where he was going with this. "Master?"

"Answer the question."

"I guess...fish."

"Then you will eat fish every night this week for dinner. I'm sure this menu will make you grateful for the one I expect you to follow."

I became nauseated at the thought but wisely remained quiet. He'd proven time and again that arguing or questioning him wouldn't change the outcome of what he decided, and I couldn't afford to piss him off. I needed to be on my best behavior...

Do it for Eve.

"As for your forbidden orgasm, you'll be denied again tonight. Get up."

My stomach dropped as I stood. Wordlessly, he led me down to the basement. Rather than turn on the lights, Gage took the time to set several candles ablaze. "Strip."

I obeyed his command without hesitation. Our eyes never wavered as I shed my clothing piece by piece. My nipples ached, forming two hard pebbles that drew his hungry gaze, and the magic spot between my legs began to throb. I swallowed the self-loathing that rose in my throat.

"Leave the heels on. I like them." He held out a hand. "Come."

I slid my hand into his, and in that moment—a moment I instinctively recognized as a pivotal one—I knew I'd succumbed. I was at his mercy, and there was no going back.

The fear still lingered, as did hatred, but renewed purpose filled me. The confusing part was how I hated and craved him so much at the same time.

Gage led me over to the big X on the wall. I couldn't stop shivering as he encircled my wrists and ankles with chains.

"I'm so cold, Master."

"You won't be for long." He pushed me against the wall, and his dexterous fingers locked me in place. I stood spread-eagled, naked except for my heels.

"I want to void your safe word, but I'll leave the choice up to you."

Why did this feel like a trick? "Why, Master?"

"It'll be a sign that you've given yourself to me completely. You said you'd do anything, and I believe you. Will you relinquish your safe word?"

I swallowed hard. "For tonight?"

"No, until our contract ends."

A shiver drifted across my breasts. He wanted to shatter my last thread of resistance. There would be nothing to stop him from doing as he wished—not that there was much now that would cease his torture. But knowing I'd had the option to end it at any time...somehow that small, inconsequential thing made his demands bearable. Now, if I couldn't handle what he dished out, my only option would be to flee and turn myself in.

"I-I can't use it, Master. I can't go to jail."

"It's a yes or no question, Kayla."

I wanted to say no. Something deep inside—self-preservation, perhaps—set the word on the tip of my tongue. Yet... if I eliminated the option, there would be no way out. I'd never have to face the temptation of wagering Eve's life against my pain and torture. She'd be safer this way.

"Yes."

"Are you sure?"

"Yes, Master."

He moved quickly, taking my sight with a blindfold, the ability to beg and plead with a ball gag. Nausea rose with panic, and my heartbeat thundered in my ears as he silenced everything with earplugs. I could hear nothing past the roar in my head, see nothing beyond the suffocating darkness pressing on me. Gage had effectively isolated me within my own mind. I made protesting, terrified pleas—garbled muffles to my plugged ears—and pulled against the restraints. Legs trembling violently, I barely had the strength to keep myself upright. Had I not been chained to the wall, I would have crumbled to the floor.

What have I done?

At the first graze of his teeth to my nipple, every muscle in my body stiffened. I held my breath, not knowing if he planned to serve pain or pleasure, and not knowing was excruciating. He sucked my nipple into the scorching cavity of his mouth. I wasn't sure if I whimpered or moaned—maybe it was a little of both. His fingers teased my other breast, and he trailed a hand down my stomach, making my muscles quiver beneath his touch. He dipped a finger into my wetness, teasing a moment before he pulled away.

Nothing could have prepared me for the first strike between my thighs. I would have screamed if he'd left me with the choice. Good God, he was whipping my most intimate place. He wasn't kidding when he said he wanted to hurt me. My legs cramped with each strike, and I sobbed for mercy as tears escaped the blindfold.

Several long minutes passed. I was beginning to grow numb when the heat of his mouth replaced the whip. I jerked to my toes as his tongue swirled the pain away with expert strokes, delving deeper as he simultaneously released my ankles from the restraints. He lifted me, urged my legs around his shoulders, and probed my ass with a finger as he kissed me intimately. The closer his tongue brought me to oblivion, the more I gave myself over to him.

I wanted to come so badly—was certain I begged for it in muffled pleas—but knew it was off-limits. Gage Channing knew how to take a woman to the edge, and he was even better at pulling back at the last second. He did it relentlessly. Tears dripped from my chin onto my heaving breasts, and I could think of nothing but how I wish he'd let me come...let me fall into oblivion where nothing had the power to touch me.

He abruptly pulled away, leaving me suspended in a combination of anticipation and apprehension. I had no way to measure time, and the longer he left me there—bound, gagged, unable to see, hear, or speak—the closer I reached hysteria. Where was he? Surely he wouldn't leave me alone like this? In the midst of my thundering heartbeat, I suddenly remembered his words over the weekend.

"You need to learn to trust me."

Was this a test? Gage wasn't careless—he'd said as much himself. He was probably standing in front of me, enjoying my internal struggle not to let blinding panic take over. I couldn't help but wonder what made a man like him tick. He'd certainly pushed me to my limits and beyond, and I was positive he was sporting a raging erection at witnessing my helplessness.

I jerked when something cold pressed against my nipples, and when he clamped them to an unbearable pinch, I screeched around the gag, my throat on fire from the strain. Only his tongue on my clit had the power to distract me. He took me to the edge again, almost pushed me over, but like the cruel sadist he was, he pulled away at the last second. Gage removed the gag, blindfold, earplugs...released my hands. I slumped into his arms, and his mouth plundered mine as he carried me to bed. We dipped into the mattress as one.

"Do you belong to me?" Bracing above me, he looked into my eyes.

"Yes, Master," I mumbled, studying him through the haze. "Why do you like to hurt me?"

He brushed a lock of hair out of my eyes. Several moments went by, in which he ran his hands through my hair, trailed his fingers down my collarbone, and teased the valley between my breasts. He pulled on the clamps and yanked painfully.

"Knowing that I can do anything to you, that I can bring you intense pain or pleasure...there's no better feeling than that."

His mouth was on mine before I was able to respond. He removed the clamps and fondled my breasts, then squeezed and pinched, refusing to let go until I begged him to stop. Sitting back long enough to unbutton his slacks, he kicked them off before carelessly flinging them across the room. He attacked my mouth again, burying his hands in my hair as he wedged apart my legs. I moaned deep in my throat as he slid into me.

This was not the Gage I'd come to know over the weekend. This man was different, his brutality in direct contrast with his gentleness; he confused the heck out of me. So did my eager response to him. He laced our fingers together and held my hands to the bed. Every thrust was sensual yet demanding, each plunge a testament of his possession and power.

"Look at me, Kayla."

I found his eyes and couldn't have looked away if I tried.

"Who am I?"

"My Master..." I curled my fingers around his until my nails bit into his skin. He didn't even flinch. I arched up to meet his thrusts. "I want you," I gasped. "Let me come, Master."

"No." He let go of my hands and gripped my hair, yanking my head back hard. "Control it, you don't have my permission. I'll deny you all weekend if you disobey me."

"Oh God! Please…I can't…please…"

He pulled out and pumped his cock in the palm of his hand until he spilled onto my stomach.

I stared at him in shock. I'd been so out of my mind, I'd failed to notice that he hadn't used a condom. The mixture of our heavy breathing filled the basement for several long moments. Gage broke it with a voice left husky from his orgasm.

"I want nothing more than to make you come. When I do, you'll never want to leave me." He collapsed beside me and rolled onto his back.

I shuddered at the implication of his words. For the first time since entering into this madness, I doubted his intentions. What if he wanted more from me than six weeks? What the hell was I supposed to do then?

"Your daughter is going to be okay." The change of subject intruded upon my thoughts, and a different fear arose.

"I don't know what I'll do if she…"

"I'll do everything in my power to make sure she has the best doctors, the best treatments."

I rolled to my side and looked at him. "Thank you."

He grabbed my chin. "Who am I?" His eyes hypnotized me as they searched my face.

"You're my Master."

"I'll hold up my end of the bargain, so long as you hold up yours." He gave me a wry smile. "I'm not heartless, Kayla, despite what you might think when I'm whipping you or shoving my cock into this tempting mouth of yours." He cradled my head and kissed me; a deep, tender exchange of tongues that made me throb between my legs all over again. He broke away and brushed his thumb across my lips. "I can't wait to fuck you here again."

My heart thudded at the reminder. "What about the gossip at work, Master? Someone found out."

"I'll take care of it. I have an idea of who's behind the rumors. She's only guessing because she's been in my office on her knees a time or two."

I wanted to ask if it was Katherine but refrained from giving voice to the question. "How do you know, Master?"

"Nothing goes on in my office without my knowing."

Gage sat up and pulled on his slacks. "I'll have a new contract drawn up to eliminate your safe word." He paused for a moment. "This changes things, Kayla. It's more responsibility for both of us. I'm giving you a homework assignment to help you prepare for what's to come. I want you to write a thousand word research paper on what it means to be a slave. I expect you to learn how to please and obey me."

Dread sat heavy in my gut, and I wondered what I'd gotten myself into.

"And I have one more stipulation, non-negotiable." He got to his feet and turned to me. "I demand absolute honesty from you. No lies, and no withholding anything from me. If I find out you've lied or kept something from me, you won't be punished—you'll go straight to jail. Do you understand?"

A lump formed in my throat, and I swallowed. "There's something you need to know, Master."

"What is it?"

"The man from college...the one you asked about? He's back. He works at the hospital."

"Why is this something you think I need to know?"

"Because he's stopped by Eve's room a couple of times, Master."

Gage's mouth flattened into a hard line. "Then you'll tell him you don't want to see him again." He zipped up his pants and gave me a hard look. "And you won't. I'll see you tomorrow at the office. Don't forget to write in your journal tonight, and for God's sakes, go eat something. You're already so damn thin."

He climbed the stairs without a backward glance.

CHAPTER THIRTEEN

I didn't know what to expect the following morning when I arrived at work, but I had to admit to being shocked that not a single person looked my way as I exited the elevator. Most noticeable was Katherine's absence. An older woman sat in her place; she answered the phone as I passed by on my way to Gage's office. Holding his coffee in one hand, I knocked on his door with the other...and froze as a loud moan filtered through. I was debating on what to do when the door jerked open a few moments later. Katherine aimed her iciest glare in my direction as she brushed by me.

"Come in, Kayla." Gage casually zipped his pants and took a seat behind his desk. "Shut the door."

I went to do as told, only I didn't merely shut the damn thing—I slammed my fingers in the process. "Ow!" The coffee dropped to my feet, coating my heels in brown liquid. Gage shot up and crossed the office before I could take a breath.

"Let me see." He grabbed my hand and inspected my fingers. "They're a little purple, but they don't appear broken."

I couldn't see beyond the front of his pants; he hadn't tucked in his shirt fully. "Did I do something wrong, Master?"

His eyes zeroed in on my face, eyebrows slightly raised. "Why would you think that?"

"Well...I'm assuming Katherine was in here doing what I...did yesterday?"

His mouth twitched. "Does that bother you?"

Not for the reason he apparently assumed it did. I couldn't afford to displease him, and if he felt the need to go to other women... "No, I just don't want to displease you, Master." I'd started my research the previous night and had been overwhelmed with information. Being a "proper" or "good" slave wouldn't be the easiest thing I ever did. I was beginning to understand what Gage wanted from me; he wanted me meek and pliable, willing to drop to my knees on demand and obey his every command. He expected me to anticipate his needs, as his pleasure was to be my first priority, as was serving him.

The center of my being revolted at the notion, but I'd do it for Eve.

"You do please me."

"Do you want me on my knees, Master?"

"No. We'll keep our office relationship as normal as possible, notwithstanding special circumstances." He tilted my chin up so I met his gaze head on. "Katherine was in here because I fired her. Considering what she pulled yesterday, sucking my cock was a fitting punishment." He smirked. "Or rather, my reaction afterward was. She thought she could manipulate me with her mouth."

Hadn't I had a similar thought yesterday? What the hell was happening to me? He was drawing me in, and I was helpless to stop it. Just remembering how he had the power to cast me into a void so intense in pleasure was enough to stall my breath. I was addicted to that void...that blissful escape from reality. I'd stumbled onto the term "subspace," and now I wondered if Gage was sending me there with every strike of his whip, every scorching touch of his mouth and hands. I couldn't deny he was one of the sexiest men I'd set eyes on, and on some level I was very much attracted to him, whether I liked it or not.

But I wasn't in love with him. I'd move on when our six weeks ended.

"What are you thinking?" he asked.

"Am I that obvious?"

"You wear everything on your face, Kayla. You always have."

My first instinct was to lie, but then I remembered his non-negotiable terms—terms I assumed he'd have me sign today. "I was thinking how I'd move on from you when this is all over."

His eyes darkened. "Can't wait to get away from me, huh?"

I wrung my hands. "You won't like the truth, Master."

"Maybe not, but I demand it."

"I can't be who you want me to be. I'll pretend for Eve's sake, and I'll do whatever I have to in the meantime, but it'll be a lie. As soon as our six weeks are up, I'll walk."

Gage slid his hand along my cheek. "We'll see." He returned to his desk. "The company Christmas party is this Friday night. We'll attend together." He'd switched gears so fast, my head spun.

"Won't that fuel the gossip?"

He waved away my concern. "No one will dare treat you badly after today. You have nothing to worry about." He leaned back in his chair. "As far as anyone needs to know, you and I are dating. I'm not about to squander the opportunity to have you on my arm for the next five weeks." He focused his attention on his computer. "Let's get to work."

I hastily pulled out my iPad as he began dictating to me. After he'd armed me with the day's instructions, he slid a piece of paper across the desk. "Your new contract. No safe word, and no lies." A pen accompanied the paper.

My hand shook as I scrawled my name at the bottom. "Master...will you let me visit Eve on Friday? I won't be long —I just can't stand the thought of going a whole two days without seeing her, especially now that her condition is so rocky."

"I'll give you an hour. And if you behave well, you can call the hospital on Saturday too."

"Thank you." I let out a breath. Deep down, I hadn't expected him to say yes.

"Speaking of the hospital, do you expect to get a visit from Dr. Kaplan this evening?"

I froze at his words. "I don't know, Master."

"Don't forget what you have to do. I want him out of your life, is that clear?"

"Yes, Master."

"Good, then I'll see you at lunchtime." Gage casually dismissed me as he went back to work.

I left his office, and only after I'd closed the door did it occur to me that I'd never mentioned Ian's name.

CHAPTER FOURTEEN

The week passed amidst a torrential downpour before I saw Ian again. Caught up in the daily grind of work and spending every free moment at the hospital, I wasn't prepared to face him yet. If I was being honest, I wouldn't ever be ready to cast him aside again. I watched Eve slumber peacefully, grateful for the hour Gage had given me, and thought back to the day seven years ago when I told Ian goodbye. We'd stood in my driveway, too consumed with despair to care about the rainstorm soaking us. After being inseparable friends for three years, we'd finally given in to the feelings neither of us could deny any longer. If I had to list my favorite moments in life, that night with Ian would be at the top. No one had ever made me feel the way he had... cherished, worshipped, loved.

But then everything fell apart when I realized I was pregnant with Rick's baby. Rick and I had been together for a year—a rocky on-again, off-again year filled with screaming arguments and too many tears to count. He'd revealed a hint of his dark nature as the months went by: jealous, possessive, mean-spirited. I'd eventually hit a crossroads—either continue down a destructive path with him, or risk my friendship with Ian by turning it into something more. I'd chosen the latter, experienced a small taste of happiness, and had thrown it all away before something truly amazing could bloom. Going back to my ex had been a misguided attempt at doing the right thing by my baby.

How naive I'd been. I closed my eyes to the memory of that first beating, the one that began them all...the one that ended my first pregnancy just shy of twelve weeks. Even now I asked myself why I'd stayed so long...even knowing how I would never regret the decision; Eve wouldn't be here if I'd left sooner. I didn't allow myself to think of the past often, but I didn't have a choice now. The memories seeped through the cracks of the metaphorical room in which I'd locked them. They flooded me, especially the night I'd told Ian I didn't love him. Raindrops had disguised his tears, but not the devastation in the depths of those hazel eyes I still dreamed about seven years later.

"Hey, if you're gonna cry every time I come near you, maybe I should bring chocolate." I raised my head and found the object of my thoughts standing in the doorway. He frowned, despite the light tone of his words, and closed the door behind him. "How's Eve?"

I took a deep breath. "You should go."

"You have a habit of telling me that." He folded his arms and leaned against the door.

"I can't handle seeing you right now. Eve started a new treatment yesterday, and I'm under a lot of pressure at work right now..." *Under Gage Channing's watchful eye.* "I'm glad you're back, but I think we need a few weeks to let things settle first."

"Meaning you're gonna barricade yourself from people and deal with her illness alone." He shook his head and pulled up a chair, legs scraping the linoleum, and settled across from me on the other side of the bed. "You look like hell. Have you gotten any sleep at all?"

"Not much," I admitted quietly. Unable to tear myself away as the weekend approached, I'd slept at Eve's bedside for the past two nights. "You really need to go."

He leaned forward, and his eyes—greener today than usual—froze me to the spot. "Don't shut me out. I won't walk away this time. I've regretted it every day for seven years."

"I need you to stay away from me and Eve for the next few weeks. Please...I'm begging you."

"Why?"

"I can't tell you—" I broke off, cringing at the slip-up. "Please, just go."

"You're worrying me, Kayla." He rubbed a hand down his face and sighed. "What's going on with you?"

"Nothing." Firming my resolve, I met his unyielding stare. "I need for you to leave me alone. I don't want to see you, or hear from you—"

He sprung to his feet, and every muscle in his body tensed. "So we're doing this again? Is it someone else? If you're involved with someone, just say so. I won't like it, but I can deal with it." He shoved his hands into his pockets, and his shoulders relaxed a fraction as he waited for a reply.

Waited for me to deny it.

I stared at my shoes—spiky heels that made my feet ache and reminded me of the man who'd trapped me. Saying I was seeing someone would be the easiest solution to this dilemma. "There's no one else." I looked up and met Ian's gaze. "There's no one else," I repeated. "I just need time."

"Take all the time you need." He flung the door open. "I hope you don't take another seven years to figure it out."

CHAPTER FIFTEEN

I stood on Gage's doorstep, allowing myself one last minute of reflection before I entered his domain of pain. Ian's stormy exit from my life—once again—still clung to my emotions, making me susceptible to acts of unpredictability. I couldn't afford feeling this way when Gage opened that door. The foundation of my acquiescence had shifted since I'd first stood in this spot a week ago...funny, how it seemed much longer. I no longer had a safe word, but more importantly, I owed Gage. Whatever he'd done, whatever strings he'd pulled, had gotten Eve into the trial faster than her doctor thought possible. I couldn't mess this up. Forcing my turbulent thoughts to the back of my mind, I knocked on his door.

He treated me to a real smile from the other side. "Right on time. I take it you've learned your lesson this week?" He raised an eyebrow.

"Yes, Master," I said as he ushered me into the foyer.

He held out his hand. "Your journal?"

I removed it from my oversized purse. "The research paper is tucked in the back."

"Go ahead and put your things in the closet," he instructed as he flipped through the pages. "Did you break anymore rules?"

"No, Master."

He smiled in a way that made my stomach drop. The smile of the devil. "For your sake, I hope you're telling the truth. Lie detectors aren't easy to fool."

"What are you talking about, Master?"

"You'll undergo a polygraph." Setting the journal aside, he grabbed my arm and led me into a home office. A wall of windows opened to a view of the swimming pool in the backyard. If not for the nervous flutters in my stomach, I would have laughed; only Gage Channing would have an outdoor pool in the Pacific Northwest. Rain beat against the glass, and watching all that water made me shiver.

We weren't alone. Someone sat behind the desk where an odd machine was displayed on the surface. "Have a seat," he invited with a reassuring smile.

"This is Mr. Hughes," Gage said as I slid into a chair. "He's aware of the nature of our relationship, so there's no need to feel uncomfortable at the intimacy of the questions. He's heard it all, trust me."

I quirked an eyebrow but didn't voice my incredulity.

"I'll be back when you've finished." Gage pinned me to the chair with his deep blue eyes. "I'll advise you not to lie here, Kayla."

I hadn't planned to, but that still didn't calm my apprehension. Lie detectors weren't fail-proof, were they?

"Don't be nervous," Mr. Hughes said after Gage had disappeared through the doorway. "Just be honest and everything will go smoothly."

Sure, says the guy administering the test. I folded my hands in my lap and remained silent as he hooked me up to the machine. He pressed a few buttons, made some adjustments, and pulled out a sheet of paper.

"Do you take any medications?"

"No."

He asked several more questions—all of them related to my personal and medical background. "All right, I'm going to ask you two questions that you'll answer yes to. This is to calibrate the machine." He cleared his throat. "Is your name Kayla Sutton?"

"Yes."

"Do you live in Europe?"

"Yes."

He cleared his throat again and peered at the paper in his hands. "Let's begin. Did you have any inappropriate contact with a man other than your Master?"

I swallowed hard and thought about Ian. Considering he hadn't even touched me, and I'd only spoken to him briefly to push him out of my life—probably for good—I was fairly certain in my answer. "No."

"Did you break any of your Master's rules?"

"N-no."

Mr. Hughes marked something on the printout. "Did you eat fish for dinner every night this week?"

"Yes."

"Did you take off your Master's collar?"

"No."

"Did you masturbate?"

My face burned at such an intimate question. "No." But God, how I'd wanted to.

He asked a few more questions, and when it was over I experienced the sweetest sense of relief. Gage reentered the room after I'd been unhooked from the machine.

"Did she pass?"

"Yes."

"Go on down to the basement and prepare. I'll be down shortly."

"Yes, Master." I hurried from the room and entered the basement with flaming cheeks. That had been more mortifying than going to the gynecologist. A few moments snuck by as I leaned against the door, breathing heavy as uncertainty took hold of me. He wanted me to "prepare." I suddenly felt lost; without Gage to dictate my every move, I wasn't sure what to do. Descending the stairs, I entered his "dungeon" and remembered how the cold leather of the bench chilled my skin, how the sharp sting of his whip struck with the speed of a snake; and more recently how that strip of leather had the power to set my crotch on fire...how his tongue ignited a different kind of burn.

I stepped into the room, brought my fingers to my blouse, and began unhooking the buttons. Instinctively, I knew what he wanted. My nipples pebbled in the chilly air, and as I laid my clothing neatly on the couch, tingles shivered to my toes. I moved to the center of the floor and fell to my knees.

And closed my eyes and waited.

A drift of air was the only indication he'd entered. His clothes whispered as he came near, and I hated myself for craving the warmth he radiated.

Dampness flooded the spot between my thighs. I craved much more than body heat. Gage had done something to me —flipped a switch—and despite the harsh punishments he issued, I yearned for another taste of explosive liberation. I'd taken it once without permission; somehow, I knew he'd send me into another realm when he coaxed an orgasm from me of his own free will. It was that foggy-headed reality I hungered for most—a time when thought wasn't possible, when pain and difficult decisions didn't exist. Gage had enslaved me, and by doing so he also freed me on some level.

"Are you ready to fully submit, Kayla?"

"Yes, Master."

He ran a hand over my hair. "Why are you on your knees?"

"To please you, Master."

He groaned. "You are, baby, and I can't wait to return the favor." My heart began to race. The haze was taking over already, and he had barely touched me. "Though your pleasure will come with pain." He tilted my chin up. "Did you send the doctor away?"

"Yes, Master."

"How did he take it?"

Ian's angry, hurt expression flashed in my mind. "Not well."

"And he won't come back?"

I blinked. "I don't think so."

"How does that make you feel?"

"Upset, Master." The truth spilled from my lips without thought or effort. The way he commanded my compliance, his strong voice floating above me as I kneeled on the hard floor, reinforced the dynamics of our relationship.

"Yet you obeyed me, and you're being truthful about it."

"Yes, Master. I told you I was yours, and I meant it." Five more weeks. I could give him that.

"I needed to know you'd be honest with me no matter what. Your absolute honesty is important to me. I'll accept nothing less."

"I know, Master." It was one of two rules I would never break, the other being confidentiality.

He slipped a blindfold over my eyes before guiding me to my feet. "Undress me," he said, bringing my hands to his shirt.

I fumbled with the buttons, blindly undoing them. His shirt whispered to the floor, and my hands drifted to his belt. Sliding it from the loops reminded me of the beating I'd taken in his office earlier that week. I shuddered at the thought and reached for what I thought was the button of his slacks. Instead I found his erection straining against the zipper. He jerked my hands up a few inches and helped me remove the last barrier to his body.

"Good girl." He pressed down on my shoulders until I sank to my knees again. Unlike in his office, where he'd given me most of the control, he swatted my hands away, grabbed my head, and forced his cock between my lips. I gagged the deeper he dove, but that didn't deter him. I couldn't see his expression, but I imagined the tightness of his features, the tension in his shoulders as he neared climax. I didn't fight him as he slipped in and out, his balls flapping against my chin. The loud groan he released as he spilled into my mouth sent fire between my legs. I ached in a way that was exhilarating and humiliating all at once—the two emotions fought for space in my heart. No matter how many times he forced me to my knees, demanded I bend to his will, my body still responded in a primal way even I didn't understand.

Gage expelled a heavy breath. "You know how to love a man's cock."

I raised my head and waited for his instruction.

He removed the blindfold. "We have a Christmas party to get to." Gage helped me to my feet, and I gasped when he spun me around and pushed me to the bed. "Bend over." I hadn't noticed the cocktail dress he'd set out on the mattress...or the butt plug and nipples clamps. I cringed to think of the pain those things would inflict.

"You'll wear them to the party," he said, as if he'd heard my thoughts. He grabbed the plug, and I tensed in preparation, hissing a breath through my teeth as he pushed it in. He grabbed my arm and twirled me until I faced him again. I shrank away when he reached for the clamps.

"I-I'm sorr—"

"Don't be sorry, Kayla. Just obey. I can restrain you, if you won't behave yourself."

I shook my head and stepped toward him.

His eyes lingered on my nipples, and the edges of his mouth turned up. "Stand up straight and clasp your hands behind your back. You'll learn to present your breasts properly."

I lengthened my spine and laced my fingers together at the small of my back, and the position put my chest on display. He bent down and slid his tongue across each nipple. A delicious chill raced through me, only to be obliterated when he clamped the first sensitive peak. I whimpered, and Gage responded by tightening the clamp further. I screwed my eyes shut as he did the same to the other side. I could only imagine how excruciating they'd feel if I hadn't breastfed.

He brought his mouth to my ear. "I want you uncomfortable. I want your tits aching, your ass full. By the time we return tonight, you'll beg me to fill every part of you."

A shiver of excitement tore through me.

"Get dressed. Come upstairs when you're ready." His lips drifted down my chest, and he bit down on the chain connecting my breasts and pulled. "Don't take too long—we're almost late."

I dressed quickly, gritting my teeth as the material scraped across my aching nipples, and then climbed the stairs. Gage's voice rang through the house as I edged the door open, though judging by his low tone, I figured he didn't want to be overheard. Whoever was on the other end of the call had sure pushed a button.

"I'm tired of your threats!" he hissed.

I should have announced my presence, but in the end my curious nature won. I pressed against the door and listened.

"You have no idea who you're dealing with, do you?" Silence followed, until he muttered something indistinguishable. The sound of his feet hitting the floor reverberated in my ears. I scrambled to open the door behind me, and when Gage rounded the corner, it appeared as if I'd just exited. He smoothed the anger from his features and ended the call. "Ready to go?"

"Yeah..." My mouth parted, and I couldn't help but stare at the sight of Gage Channing in a tux.

CHAPTER SIXTEEN

The Sheraton Hotel hosted the company Christmas party. Gage opened the door for me and then tucked my arm in his as we approached the room where the event was being held. Everyone in the room took notice upon our arrival, but Gage was correct in people's reactions. Apparently, Katherine's absence served as a reminder for people to mind their own business.

Gage nuzzled my neck and spoke into my ear. "Would you like some champagne?"

I nodded, unable to speak.

He leaned into me. "Enjoy yourself tonight. You'll have plenty of time to surrender to me later." My breath went thready at his words. Gage planted a kiss on my cheek before heading in the direction of the bar.

The instant I was alone, Jody waltzed up to me. I'd known her for years, and it was on her referral that I'd gotten the job. I frowned when I realized we'd barely spoken, let alone spent time together, since she'd moved on from Channing Enterprises. She'd left months ago, around the time I'd been promoted to Gage's personal assistant, to take a job as managing accountant at a smaller firm.

"Are you really dating Gage?"

My cheeks warmed. "Is that what everyone's saying?"

She nodded. "Holy smokes, Kayla, the man is hot." She raised her eyebrows and shot me a playful grin. "I should know—like most of the female employees at Channing Enterprises, I've had a turn at him."

"Are you serious?" I leaned closer and lowered my voice. "When?"

"A few years ago. Around the time you and Rick split."

"I hadn't realized you'd worked for him that long."

"Yep. I still miss it sometimes." She gazed across the room at her date, who I vaguely recognized from the mail room. "That's why I finagled a plus one from Rob. I couldn't pass up this party." She winked at me. "Good to see you again. We should do lunch sometime."

"I'd like that."

"Great," she said as Rob gestured at her. "Oops, gotta go. Rob's a hot one too, though he's not into kink like Gage was. Is he still into that shit?" she threw the question over her shoulder.

The butt plug vibrated to life for a moment, and I gulped. Is that what they were calling it? Kink?

Gage returned a few moments later, champagne in hand. Sporting a knowing smirk, he handed me a crystal flute. "Dinner's about to start." He ushered me to a table. The room was decorated in whites, blacks, and silvers, with splashes of red and gold. The tables were adorned with black table cloths and silver candles. White linens accompanied the red and gold patterned china. A huge Christmas tree took up one corner of the room. Gage pulled out a chair and gestured for me to take a seat. He settled next to me and immediately placed his hand on my knee.

Two other couples joined us, and conversation revolved around work for the short period before dinner was served. As the meal wore on, Gage inched his hand up my thigh. Certain my cheeks were turning the color of tomato paste, I leaned away from him, but all that got me was a hard look and more determination on his part. He carried on his conversation easily as he forced my thighs apart.

My only defense was to focus on cutting my chicken into small bites and chewing until the meat practically slid down my throat. I bit my tongue when his fingers slipped inside my panties. His touch scorched me from the inside out, and suddenly, the heavy ache in my nipples only added fuel to his public seduction. God...armed with sexual frustration and champagne, I became dizzy with it and prayed no one would guess what was going on underneath the table. He tilted his head and gave me a knowing smile as he stroked me, spreading my wetness to my clit. His other hand disappeared under the table, and the plug vibrated to life in my ass again. I gripped my chair and took a deep breath through my nose.

"So, Kayla, how is Eve?"

What a way to douse the fire. I cast my attention on the woman across from me, and though I couldn't remember her name, I was more than grateful for the distraction. "It's been up and down, but her doctor is confident this new trial will help."

Gage slid a finger inside, and a groan escaped.

The woman furrowed her brows. "Are you all right? You don't look well, dear."

I sprang up from the table. "I think it was something I ate. Please, excuse me." I nearly crashed into the women's restroom in my haste to escape Gage. A quick check of the stalls assured me I was alone. Grabbing hold of the counter, I focused on breathing and closed my eyes, but the plug still vibrated incessantly, making me moan as my insides clenched.

The door creaked open, and Gage entered. "Are you alone in here?"

I nodded.

He locked the door, and I watched his reflection wearily, wondering if I'd earned myself another punishment for bolting from the table. He stood behind me and rested his hands next to mine, caging me in between the counter and his impressive body. Pure desire reflected from his eyes in the mirror—a maniacal glint that both frightened and excited me. We said nothing as we stared at each other, and when Gage removed his hands, I didn't dare move. He gripped my skirt and inched it up before sliding his hand beneath my panties again.

"Your eyes darken to the deepest brown when you're turned on, did you realize that?"

"No," I said on a moan. My head fell back against his shoulder, and his lips devoured my throat as he stroked me.

"You're so wet, baby."

I groaned and arched into his hand. "What are you doing to me?"

"Making you mine." He took my mouth, and I kissed him back with abandon, chasing his tongue again and again.

"I'm losing myself to you," I gasped, tearing my mouth from his.

"Not yet, you're not." He stepped away. "Come back to the table."

Five minutes later I obeyed, only stumbling twice on my journey back to my seat. Dessert had already been served. Gage wasted no time in reclaiming the hot, damp place between my legs. He stroked me relentlessly, and not even the decadent cake had the power to distract me. By the time he pulled me into his arms on the dance floor, I'd downed four more glasses of champagne and was more than a little tipsy. Bodies flush, our champagne breaths mingling, I melted against him and let him pull me into the sway. Something shifted within me during that dance. For the first time, I returned his touch. Sliding my hands into his hair, I curled my fingers into the dark strands as he swept me across the room. I didn't care if everyone was watching, if what I was doing and feeling was wrong.

And it was so wrong. Nothing about this situation should feel romanticized, but I was lost and never wanted to be found.

He tightened his arms around me, pulling me close enough that his hard-on strained against my stomach. "Wanna get out of here?"

Our faces were inches apart, and for a moment I thought he was going to kiss me in front of everyone. "Yeah."

We left in a flurry of goodbyes, and the only thing more dizzying than my champagne-induced state was the commotion of grabbing our coats. The drive back to Gage's place was but a fuzzy memory. We stumbled through the front door, his mouth hot and wet on my throat as my thighs locked around his waist. My hands gripped his hair as he carried me through the house. Maybe later I'd question why he took me to his bedroom instead of the basement, or why he seemed so un-Gage like as he ripped the bodice of my dress in an impatient fit of desire. The material tore to my waist, exposing my clamped breasts. He yanked on the chain, propelling me toward him and the bed, and his mouth closed over an aching nipple. We shed our clothing and tumbled onto the mattress, where he wrapped my fingers around the bars of the headboard.

"Don't let go." His breath fanned across my face an instant before he blinded me with a silk tie. "I'm going to remove the clamps." My heart jackhammered under his touch, and I squeezed the bars as blood rushed to my nipples, flooding them with pain.

His mouth moved over my breasts. "Tell me what you want," he whispered.

"I want you."

"Be specific, Kayla."

I bent my knees and spread wide for him. "I want you inside of me."

He pulled away, and though I couldn't see him, I imagined him gazing down at me, eyes the color of sapphires as he savored my surrender. He splayed his hands on my inner thighs, spreading me further and torturing me with the tickle of his thumbs. "Tell me more."

"I-I want...you sliding in and out slowly, your mouth on my breasts...everywhere." I sucked in a breath when he reached around and lifted me. "I want to feel you everywhere, Master."

He scooted down and smothered his face against my mound. I bucked against his mouth as his kiss spread through my body—in the tingle along my spine, in the ache of my curling feet. My fingers tightened a death grip around the bars, and I dug my feet into the mattress, meeting each thrust of his tongue and fingers.

He slid up my stomach and plunged into me without warning, filling me so fully, I almost climaxed.

"You feel so fucking good." He buried his face in my hair and folded his hands around mine, and we began to move, building a tempo that was both tender and explosive—a contradiction comparable to Gage. "Don't come until I give you permission."

I gritted my teeth as he moved inside me. It wasn't going to take much to send me over the edge, but knowing Gage, he'd probably do this all night before he let me come. Our bodies slicked together like two lovers on the beach oiled down with coconut lotion. Muscles tensing, moans escalating, we chased release. I wrenched my hands from underneath his and gripped his shoulders.

"I can't hold back much longer. Master...please..."

He removed the blindfold and froze, going perfectly still. The light from the hall illuminated the apprehension in his features. "Do you hate me?"

I blinked. "What?"

"You heard me. Do you hate me for what I've done to you?"

I parted my lips, denial on the tip of my tongue, but denying it would be dishonest. "Part of me does, Master." I closed my eyes on a sigh and raised my hips. "The other part can't get enough."

He groaned and sunk his hands into my hair. I was about to burst when he reared up onto his knees and carried me with him.

Clinging to him, I panted. "Please..."

"Say you'll never leave me."

"I'll never leave you." The lie escaped before I could stop it. I'd sunk so far into the abyss, I didn't know which way was up anymore.

"Come for me now, baby," he commanded, burrowing even deeper.

"Gage!" I screamed as the orgasm tore through me. I wrapped my body around his and rode the waves, digging my fingernails into his shoulders so hard, I was sure I drew blood.

CHAPTER SEVENTEEN

Gage awoke me the next morning with breakfast in bed. As soon as I sat up, I gripped my throbbing head.

"Hungover?" he asked, setting the tray on the nightstand. He held out two white tablets and a glass of orange juice.

I nodded, and then swished down the pills.

"I'm afraid we hit the champagne a little too heavily last night. Now we'll both have to suffer the consequences." He sat down next to me, and only then did I notice the belt in his hand. My eyes shot to his. He immediately adverted his gaze. "Last night was...incredible...but that doesn't give you free rein to call me anything other than Master."

"I-I'm sorry, Master. It just slipped out." His name had more than slipped out; I'd screamed it to high heaven as I came undone in his arms.

He rose to his feet. "I am too, Kayla. Let's get this over with." He gestured to the space in front of him. "On your feet. Bend over and grab your ankles."

I slid from bed, and as I held onto my ankles, preparing for the strike of his belt, I went back to despising myself.

He'd gotten to me last night, had snuck into a small corner of my heart. Now that little piece shattered to dust.

Bastard.

I mentally chanted the epithet with every strike, though I had to admit the punishment hurt more on an emotional level than a physical one; perhaps I'd gotten under his skin as well because he was now going easy on me, though recognizing that didn't make me feel any better.

Gage calmly put his belt away once he was satisfied I'd been thoroughly punished. "I promised you a phone call. Check on your daughter." He handed me his cell phone.

I studied him, trying to find a hint of the man I'd seen last night hiding under his cool exterior, but all I found was impenetrable steel. "Why do you do this?"

He tilted his head. "Do what?"

"Shut yourself off from emotion."

His body stiffened. "Are you *trying* to earn another punishment?"

I stepped closer and placed my hand on his chest; he flinched under my touch. "I'm trying to understand you." I peeked up and met his eyes. "You're tender one minute, and a brute the next. I can't keep up with your mood swings."

"You know nothing about me, except that disobeying will earn you another punishment." He gestured toward the bed. "Bend over the bed this time."

I turned and placed my hands on the mattress. "I know you care enough to let me contact Eve." The snap of his belt made me jump. I couldn't hold back a yelp as it landed on my bottom.

"Stop analyzing me!" He put more strength into the lashes, releasing his anger on the back of my thighs as well as my ass.

"I'm sorry!" I cried. God, would he ever stop hitting me?

"I'm a bastard, Kayla—don't fool yourself otherwise." I heard the belt buckle hit the floor, and neither of us moved.

"I know what you are, Master." A walking contradiction. So were my feelings for him.

"Good. Now call your daughter before I change my mind." He stomped from the room and slammed the door upon his exit.

Exhaling a long breath, I dialed the hospital from memory. Guilt lanced through me at the sound of Eve's voice. She cried, wanting to know where I was. I held my breath and sought composure. I'd give anything to be with her, and as I recalled how effortlessly Gage had made me forget everything, if only for a while, my self-loathing intensified. I hung up after her doctor assured me she was doing okay—the only thing bothering her at the moment was how much she missed her mother. All things considered, I had to find the silver lining; the new treatment seemed to be helping.

I paced Gage's bedroom, taking in the furnishings for the first time. The bed and dresser overpowered the room with mahogany-toned masculinity. Unlike the crimson of his basement, this room had been decorated in shades of brown, complemented with touches of royal blue. I eyed the breakfast tray. I didn't have an appetite, but I forced down what I could. A half hour had passed, and he still hadn't returned. I was completely naked, my dress lying in tatters on his floor. Wringing my hands, I went over my options for my next move. Did he want me to leave the room and find him? Or was I supposed to wait here? Not knowing what else to do, I sank to my knees and waited.

Eventually, he pushed open the door. I let out a breath of relief at the sight of him. My knees ached to a point that was unbearable.

"How long have you been waiting on your knees?"

"A while, Master."

The corner of his mouth turned up. "You know how to behave when you want to."

"Can I get up now, Master?"

He held out a hand. "Yes. You have chores to get to." He pulled the nipple clamps from his pocket. "Present your breasts."

I almost begged for mercy, but in the end I stood up straight, clasped my hands behind my back, and suffered in silence as he clamped my nipples. The passionate, lustful, *out-of-control* Gage from the night before was long gone, overpowered by a man who apparently guarded his emotions above all else.

He kept me busy with chores for hours. After dinner, he returned me to the basement, where he abused my bottom some more for his perverse pleasure. Like the previous weekend, he took me anally. Wrists and ankles locked into place on the spanking bench—a term I'd learned through my research—I was powerless to stop him as he probed my tight hole.

"Stop," I sobbed. Every last shred of composure I'd held on to vanished as he slowly inched his way in.

"It'll get easier each time we do it. Relax your muscles." It burned like hell for the first few minutes, but then Gage buried his fingers in the place he'd staked as his, and a different kind of fire erupted. "Relax," he repeated, "eventually you'll learn to enjoy it." He pushed all the way in with a hoarse groan. My body opened for him, and as he rubbed me to pleasure, my cries took on the sound of ecstasy. His body owned me, demanded my surrender, and with a smack to my crimson bottom, he commanded my orgasm. Completion crashed over me, like a tsunami that couldn't be stopped. He held his own orgasm at bay for a long time, forcing me to release twice more before he withdrew from my ass.

"Sweet dreams, Kayla," he whispered after he'd unfastened the restraints. The door to the basement clicked shut. I remained on the bench for a while, replaying what had just happened in my head. Not only had he made me enjoy it, but he'd brought me to orgasm three times. The realization stunned me, yet on some level I realized it shouldn't have. Gage had slowly knocked down my defenses, gaining compliance, and if my heart didn't yield to his intrusion, my body sure as hell did.

Again and again, whether I liked it or not.

I fell into bed and questioned my very being. What was wrong with me? What kind of person enjoyed being forced like this? How could I enjoy anything in life—least of all something so sinfully twisted—while my daughter fought for her life in the hospital? Tears trickled onto my pillow as sleep pulled at the edge of consciousness. My last thought before I fell asleep was how I'd need to find a good therapist after Gage was finished making me his plaything.

CHAPTER EIGHTEEN

The biggest surprise on Sunday was how quickly the day flew by. Gage kept me busy with additional chores, three more rounds of sex, and even the absurdity of a board game. You haven't played Scrabble until you've done it naked with a sadist who makes up his own rules. The only words allowed in Gage's rulebook were those of a sexual nature, and his prize for winning was a blow job.

Now I stood in the foyer, but unlike last Sunday, I didn't hold fast to any grand illusions of freedom. Gage's dominance would follow me out the door. He molded his body to mine from behind, one hand palming my breast as the other fell on my thigh. The hem of my dress inched up with his fingers. We'd just returned from dinner, and now the time for us to part had arrived.

Until the following morning when I'd see him at work again.

He slid his hand into my panties. "You're so sexy." His mouth left a wet trail down my neck, and every flick of his tongue coiled between my thighs. Excitement ignited at the idea of him taking me in the foyer, against the wall like he had the previous weekend. I spread my legs to give him better access.

"Do you want me, Kayla?"

I nodded, my breath coming in short spurts.

"Who am I?"

"My Master."

"You want your Master's cock inside here?" He stroked my opening, then dipped a finger into that pleasurable place.

My head fell back against his shoulder. "Yes, Master."

"I'm not going to give you what you want right now." He rubbed a circle around my clit. "And you know the rules—no masturbation. If you want it badly enough, come to me on your lunch hour tomorrow and beg for it." He gripped my hair, holding my head in place. "Is that clear?"

"Yes, Master," I breathed.

He helped me into my coat, and then he relinquished my purse and cell phone. "I was impressed by your research paper, by the way. You've learned a lot, and your behavior has showcased it." He whirled me around and pulled me against him. His mouth descended, and we said goodbye with a long slide of tongues.

"See you tomorrow at work." He opened the door for me, and I stepped into the late evening winter chill. As I hurried to my car, I felt the weight of his stare and almost looked back twice. Only after I'd slid into the driver's seat did I allow my gaze to linger on him. His eyes never strayed as I backed down the driveway. The notion was naive, but I couldn't help but smile as a sense of freedom settled over me. Freedom to see Eve. I couldn't wait to hold her. Visiting the hospital didn't take long, as it was late and Eve was tired, but I did get my cuddle time in and was relieved to find some color in her cheeks for the first time in weeks. Apparently Ian had taken my request to be left alone seriously—there'd been no sight of him, not even a quick passing in the halls as I left.

So I was stunned to find him waiting for me in my driveway, especially since I hadn't told him where I lived.

"You shouldn't be here!" I shouted the instant I exited my car. Swift anger rose until it burst free—anger at Gage for making my life so damn complicated, and anger toward Ian for making me want something I'd made myself give up years ago. I remembered in vivid clarity all the times we'd sat thigh-to-thigh on the couch watching movies during college, or how he'd wrapped his body around mine, holding on as I cried. His mere presence had been enough to set my head spinning back then; now was no different, despite the passing years.

Despite my crazy circumstances of which he knew nothing—and could know nothing—about.

I halted a few feet in front of him and crossed my arms. My angry display didn't deter him. He narrowed the short distance, standing close enough to make me high off the spicy scent of his cologne.

"I shouldn't be here? Or you don't want me here? There's a big difference."

I studied his white sneakers, jarred by how easily he sliced through my defenses with calm patience.

He tilted my chin up. "Tell me to leave...tell me you feel nothing for me, and I'll never bother you again, I promise."

I blinked several times, hating how Gage had turned me into a blubbering, crying female. I hadn't cried this often in years. Not since Rick had pushed and beat until the tears flowed, until he'd known he had the power to pound on me just as easily with hurtful words as he did his fists. "I can't tell you that." My voice cracked, as did my self-control. He opened his arms, and I fell into them.

"What's going on, Kayla? I've been trying to get a hold of

you all weekend. I wanted to apologize, but you wouldn't answer your phone, and you haven't been at the hospital..." He inched back and looked at me. "You've had me really worried."

"I'm fine."

"No, you're not. Is it Rick? I saw him at the hospital Saturday."

His words turned my blood to ice. "What?" I gripped his shoulders as panic took hold of me. "Rick was there?" Impossible. He'd been arrested twice already for violating the restraining order. I hadn't seen or heard from him in over a year—I'd figured he'd finally gotten the message.

Ian opened his mouth, appearing to struggle for words. "I...I always got the impression he didn't treat you good, but you wouldn't talk to me, and then you moved and changed your number, and when I did manage to track you down, he made it clear you wanted nothing to do—"

"Wait—you came to see me? When?"

"About three years ago."

I shuddered. Rick's rage made more sense now. The final and last beating had been the most brutal, and he'd almost killed me in the end. "Let's go inside. It's freezing out here."

"I wasn't sure you'd let me in."

"I wasn't planning to, but I've already broken the rules —" And now I'd said too much; going down that path would lead straight to the subject of Gage's contract.

Ian shut the door. "What rules?"

"My rules," I said quickly. "I don't want complications in my life right now. Eve is the only one who matters."

"Of course she is," he whispered, and I suddenly found myself between him and the door. He encased me in his arms, and his breath drifted across my face as he leaned in. "She's your daughter. But you're a horrible liar, Kayla. You about shatter every time I see you. You're nervous all the time, constantly looking over your shoulder."

I was? I thought I'd hidden my inner turmoil better than that.

"Is Rick harassing you? How bad was it?"

I focused on his mouth, because looking into his eyes hurt too much. "Bad. Really bad."

He dropped his forehead against mine. "I should've done something. I suspected he was controlling, and you'd mentioned how possessive—"

"Going back to him was the worst mistake of my life."

"Letting you go was the worst mistake of mine." He dipped his head, and I stilled, barely breathing.

"Don't."

"Why?"

"Because I'm not free to be with you right now." I was terrified. Ian and I were about to cross a line. He was a part of my past, a place where he should stay. And me? I was enslaved—literally—to a man who liked to play with my head.

"Kayla, talk to me."

I gripped his waist, wanting to keep him close even though I needed to send him packing. "I can't. You need to go."

"Like hell I do." His mouth claimed mine, and he assaulted me with the kind of hair-tingling kiss that meant something. His hands were everywhere, pulling me close at the small of my back, tangling in my hair, palming my breasts. His erection strained against my stomach, and I tore my mouth from his with a small cry.

"Stop." This was impossible. I couldn't do this.

But then I was kissing him again. He groaned and hoisted me against him. I wrapped my legs around him, and our clothing provided the only barrier between us.

"Shit, Kayla..." He buried his face in the hollow of my shoulder and moved against me.

"Ian...stop."

"Don't ask me to stop...please don't." He fastened his mouth over mine again, silencing my protests.

I was in a daze until the feel of his hands on my thighs evaporated the fog. I pushed him away, hard enough to make him stumble. "I said stop!"

His expression crumbled, and he slid to the floor, holding his head in his hands. "I'm sorry."

Shame, swift and intense, clung to me like Ian's scent did. How could I go from wanting Gage to wanting Ian in the space of two hours? What kind of person had I become? Gage would know. There was no way I could hide this from him.

"I'd never force you...this isn't like me."

I wanted to say it wasn't like me either, but I guess there wasn't much I hadn't done now, thanks to the man who'd placed metaphorical shackles around my ankles.

He looked up, and his eyes were brighter than usual. "Please, say something. God, I hate that I made you cry."

And that did me in. I fell to my knees and let him pull me against him. I let it all go—the confusion, guilt, and fear. It'd been a long time since someone cared. Of course, that only made me cry harder, but I did it in the shelter of his embrace, and a small part of me pieced itself back together again.

CHAPTER NINETEEN

Going to work made me a nervous wreck, and it didn't help my mental state when I couldn't find my journal. That was just what I needed—punishment to compound punishment. I went through the normal morning ritual of placing his coffee on the desk, and then I pulled out my iPad. I couldn't meet Gage's eyes as he delegated the morning tasks. I avoided him as much as possible until lunchtime, when he called me into his office.

"Lock the door."

I obeyed and stood before him, eyes downcast, feeling as if my disobedience was a flashing sign on my forehead; withholding this from him all morning was eating me alive.

I have to tell him...

"Is something wrong?" he asked.

I nodded. "I need to tell you something, Master, but I'd rather not tell you here. Can I come to your place tonight?"

He tapped his fingers on the desk, and when I found the courage to face him, his eyes had darkened to indigo. "Why don't we just get this over with now? Your punishment can wait until tonight, but you need to be upfront with me."

I bit my lip. "You're going to be angry."

"Angry doesn't describe it, Kayla." His mouth flattened into an unforgiving line. "You forgot your journal at my house last night. I drove to your place to drop it off."

My body went cold, and I folded myself into my arms, as if I could simply disappear into them. "You saw?"

"I expect you on my doorstep at nine. In the meantime, you need to get out of here before I explode."

I scampered from his office and made myself scarce for the rest of the day. That evening I spent as much time as possible at the hospital, playing a memory card game with Eve. The only bright point in my day was how much healthier she looked. I kissed her goodnight and left shortly after eight-thirty. I wasn't about to arrive at Gage's a second late.

The instant he opened the door, I threw myself at his feet. "Please, Master, forgive me." I planted my sweaty palms on the floor and studied the varying colors in the hardwood. Several seconds ticked by—seconds that seemed more like minutes. I held my breath and counted every beat of my heart.

"Look at me."

I raised my head. Tears spilled over, and no amount of willpower would stop them. Dread roiled in my stomach, and I knew with absolute certainty I wouldn't get a smidgeon of mercy from him.

"Did you have sex with him?"

"No, Master."

He narrowed his eyes. "But you wanted to."

I paused at his tone; he sounded much too confident. "Yes, Master."

"Get up."

I scrambled to my feet, limbs shaking, and bowed my head. "I'm sorry, Master. Please forgive me."

He grabbed my hand. "Come."

"Are you going to punish me, Master?" Stupid question. Punishment was inevitable; it was the way in which he planned to carry it out that worried me.

"Yes." He was too calm. He'd shown more reaction at innocent things, like when Tom had asked me out at work, or even when the waiter had smiled at me. Gage's cool demeanor was more terrifying than his rage. I wanted to turn and bolt for the door, but entertaining the notion of escape was an impossible temptation I couldn't succumb to. Like the dutiful slave he'd turned me into, I didn't fight him as he ushered me down to the basement.

And my world came to a grinding halt. Oh my God...I blinked several times, but Ian was still standing in front of me. He wouldn't look me in the eyes.

I fell to my knees and grabbed onto Gage's slacks. "Please, Master, *please*, I'm begging you. Don't involve him in this."

"I didn't involve him, Kayla. You did."

I gasped for air, as if he'd punched me in the stomach. From the corner of my eye, I noticed Ian take a step toward me. He faltered when Gage raised a hand.

"Tell him who you belong to," Gage demanded, and when I didn't answer, he yanked me back by the hair.

"I belong to you, Master."

Ian sprung into motion. "You're not a fucking possession!" He closed the distance in three long strides. "Get up, Kayla. I'm taking you home."

Gage glared at him. "You said you'd cooperate, or do I need to carry out my threat?"

Ian bunched his hands. "I'll beat the shit out of you if you hurt her."

"I haven't done anything she hasn't agreed to." Gage let go of my hair.

"Is this true?" Ian asked, his eyes wandering to mine.

My face flamed under his perusal. "Permission to speak to him, Master?"

"Go ahead."

"I did it for Eve. He was going to send me to jail if I didn't."

"Jesus...that's not consent, that's blackmail."

"Technicalities," Gage said with a wave of his hand. "She'll agree to whatever I want, and what I want is to fuck her hard while you watch. If you care about her, you'll cooperate."

"Give us a minute alone," Ian demanded.

"Absolutely not."

"This is bullshit! I'm going to the police."

"No!" I cried. "You can't."

"You've got five minutes," Gage snapped, "but keep your damn hands off her, got it?" He drew my attention back to him. "Don't you dare move from your knees."

Ian waited until we were alone before he spoke. "Why didn't you tell me you were being blackmailed?"

"I couldn't." I shifted, uncomfortable with being on my knees in front of him. "I don't know how much he told you—"

"He said you embezzled money for Eve's medical bills, and in return for his...discretion...you agreed to..." He shook his head, and I said the words for him, since there was no point watering down anything in this situation.

"I agreed to be his sex slave."

"Jesus, Kayla, this is insane. We can go to the police—I'm sure they'll be able to do something—"

"No. If I do that, he won't pay for Eve's treatment. She's getting better—" I broke off, overcome with emotion. "If they stop now, she'll die."

Ian took a deep breath and closed his eyes. "I can't watch him rape you. Don't ask me to do this."

"It's not rape." My voice shook as I said the words. I'd become an expert at convincing myself of half-truths, of justifying the thin line on which I'd found myself. Now I had to do the same with Ian. "I wouldn't ask otherwise, but it's Eve...please, Ian, I know she's not yours, but—"

"Don't." He fisted his hands. "You know how I feel about you. I'd do anything for you, but this?" He shook his head, and my heart dropped. Would he ever look at me the same way again after tonight? "I can't watch him hurt you."

"You won't have to," Gage announced as he came down the stairs. "She enjoys my cock." He stood, feet shoulder-width apart, and crossed his arms. "However, I doubt she'll enjoy watching you fuck another woman." He smiled toward the top of the stairs, and the axis of my world all but shattered when Katherine sauntered into the basement. She halted at Gage's side and looked down her nose, giving me a haughty once-over.

This wasn't happening...the thought of Ian with that... that complete bitch was too much. "Please, Master, don't ask him to do this."

"I'm not, you are, and if he doesn't agree, he'll live knowing that you suffered the consequences."

Ian took a step forward. "You sick—"

"Ask him, Kayla," Gage interrupted.

"No."

He narrowed his eyes. "Seems my slave has backpedaled in her training. Yes or no, Dr. Kaplan?"

My pulse pounded through my body as Ian appeared to battle with himself. Half of me—the young girl who still loved him—wanted to scream for him to say no, but the more dominant half remained silent; maternal instinct would always win in the end.

Ian folded his arms and gave a small nod.

"Katherine, treat our guest to your services. The couch will suffice."

"My pleasure." She glided across the room and curled her hand around his bicep. "C'mon, lover, I'll show you a good time."

Ian didn't budge. He trapped me in his questioning gaze —a silent plea in the depths of intense hazel.

I mouthed, "I'm sorry," and then blinked back tears as he let Katherine haul him over to the couch. He collapsed and dragged a hand down his face.

"Strip," Gage commanded me.

I rose to my feet and brought my hands to my blouse, going on autopilot as I unhooked the buttons. Much too conscious of Ian sitting a few feet away, I kept my eyes on Gage the whole time, hoping to catch a glimpse of the man I'd seen lurking underneath during the weekend. His face displayed only calculated focus, driven by jealousy. Out of all the mistakes I could have made, this was surely the worst, for I belonged to him and he'd accept nothing less. The blouse fell from my shoulders. I reached for the front hook of my bra and sensed Ian's gaze on my breasts, so tangibly it could have been his touch.

Gage kneeled, yanking my skirt and panties down, and I stepped outside the puddle of clothing. Tears streamed down my cheeks—a testament of lost dignity. Not that he'd left me with much to begin with.

"How does it make you feel to know he'll see who you really are?"

I almost vomited at the thought.

He pulled me against him. "Does the idea excite you?"

"No, Master."

"Do you love him?"

"You know I do, Master."

Gage turned me around and bent me over the bed. Grabbing my hair, he forced my face in Ian's direction. "Do you think he'll still love you after I've fucked you and made you scream my name in front of him?"

Through my tears, I saw Katherine kiss her way down Ian's chest, and my heart shattered when he twisted his head away. "No," I choked.

Ian clenched his hands when Gage took me from behind, his thrusts rough and unforgiving. He whispered into my ear, "You're going to come for me, or I'll take your disobedience out on him." He buried his fingers between my legs and did what he did best.

I closed my eyes and shut off my mind to Ian's tortured expression, Katherine's smugness, and Gage's cruelty. And I did what Gage had trained me to do—I obeyed, only I imagined it was Ian pounding into me, that it was his body slick against mine as I neared climax. When I opened my eyes, the sight on the couch stole my breath in agony. Katherine's head was buried in Ian's lap, and his knuckles had gone white as he gripped the cushions. He flung his head back and groaned. Hatred rushed through my blood, every last ounce of it compelling me to rebel. I made an even bigger mistake, though I didn't delude myself into believing I did it accidentally. As Gage wrenched my head back and commanded my orgasm, I screamed Ian's name at the top of my lungs.

CHAPTER TWENTY

I found Ian's car parked in my driveway when I returned home early the next morning. Maybe I should have been more alarmed, considering how our forbidden embrace had started this madness to begin with, but after suffering through an intense beating from Gage, I was numb as I struggled to make it to the doorway. Gage had obliterated any positive feelings I'd harbored for him when he'd forced Ian and me into such a sick situation. The last root of that connection withered away as he'd strung me up on my toes, whipping me for hours and showing no mercy until I'd uttered the name I'd vowed to never say. The only thing saving me from jail was the fact that "Rick" was no longer my safe word, since according to our contract, I didn't have one anymore. But Gage had honored it anyway; he'd dropped the bloodied whip before unhooking me, and then he'd fallen to his knees as I collapsed to mine.

He hadn't protested as I dressed and headed toward the stairs, and I'd left without a word.

"What'd he do to you?" Ian choked out. Redness rimmed his eyes. "I didn't want to leave you—"

"You didn't have a choice." I moved past him to my door. "You shouldn't be here. This is how it all started."

"I know...Kayla, I had to see you." His presence overpowered the small space of my front porch. "Did he hurt you?"

"Nothing he hasn't done before." Another half-truth. Gage had never been so brutal. I probably wouldn't sit for days. My arms were like deadweight, and I couldn't hide a wince as I lifted my key toward the lock. Thank God my coat sleeves hid the red marks circling my wrists. "I'm sorry I got you caught up in this." I pushed the door open and held it between us. "Please go. You're better off forgetting about me."

How could he not want to after what had happened?

"Not a chance." He shoved his way inside, kicking the door shut behind him as he pulled me into his arms. I cried out in pain, and he immediately let go, though his hands never left my shoulders as he studied me. "What did he do to you?" His voice rose with every word.

"He whipped me."

"I'll kill him." He reached for my jacket. "How bad is it?"

"Don't." I shrank away from him.

"This is my fault—" he broke off, swallowing hard. "You told me to stay away and I didn't listen."

"No, it's mine. I screamed your name..." My gaze fell to the floor, and the image of him with Katherine speared through me more painfully than the impact of Gage's whip.

Ian grimaced. "I can't stop thinking of you bent over the bed..." Avoiding my eyes, he sucked in a breath. "I'd give anything to get that out of my head."

"I have a few memories I'd like to forget as well." Namely Katherine's loud, obnoxious moans as she rode him. Only the fact that he did it for me, for Eve, kept the hurt and anger from consuming me. Though guilt was an emotion I'd live with forever. How could I be angry with him when I was the reason he'd ended up with Katherine in the first place?

"He's going to pay, Kayla. I'll make sure of it."

"You can't go there right now. If not for him, Eve wouldn't have gotten into the trial. He's paid for everything..."

"And he's about as saintly as Lucifer himself. Kayla, I hired a PI to follow Rick."

I blinked. "Why'd you do that?"

"You unsettled me on Friday, and seeing your ex the next day was too coincidental. I know you, Kayla...you wouldn't disappear on your daughter two weekends in a row without good reason."

"What are you saying? What does Rick have to do with anything?"

"I'm saying he's been in contact with your boss a lot during the past few weeks."

My jaw dropped. "What? Why didn't you tell me this last night?"

He sighed. "I didn't know last night. The PI just called me an hour ago."

Goosebumps broke out on my arms. Gage had never given me any indication he'd known my ex. "But how...why do they know each other?" I paced my living room as my mind tried to catch up. "This doesn't make any sense."

"The only connection the PI found was a woman named Jody Palmer."

"She's a friend of mine from work—" I halted. Jody, who'd gotten me the job...who'd also known Rick.

Who had also admitted to sleeping with Gage.

"The guy I hired is still digging, but he's pretty sure Rick's been blackmailing your boss."

"Why does he think this?"

"He found records. Apparently there's been several large deposits in Rick's account that match Channing's financial statements." Ian sank onto my couch and rubbed his hands down his face. "He thinks your boss has been embezzling from his clients for years. Hopefully by the end of the day, we'll have enough evidence to take to the police. You should be able to make a deal with them."

I shook my head. "No. If I turn him in, he'll stop paying for Eve's treatment."

"We'll come up with the money for it on our own."

"He did more than pay for it. He got her in that trial in less than twelve hours." I hugged myself as the force of Gage's rage washed over me. "He's furious...he won't hesitate to undo whatever it was he did to get her in."

"Don't tell me you're gonna go back to him!" Ian sprung up from the couch. "I can't stand the thought of you anywhere near that monster."

"I'm not going back to him." I met his eyes and an idea formed—a way out that wouldn't hurt my daughter's progress. "But he no longer holds all the cards. I think it's time Gage Channing got a taste of his own medicine."

CHAPTER TWENTY-ONE

Power was an interesting thing. It rose in me now, spurring me forward and stomping down the timid, scared woman Gage had molded with his thirst for domination. I clutched the manila folder—the source of my salvation—in one hand and knocked on his door.

No answer.

I pounded harder, using enough force to bruise my knuckles. The bastard was going to face me. After everything he'd put me through, he owed me that much.

"Open the door, Gage! I know you're in there!" Another few seconds of blatant knuckle abuse passed, and I finally yanked on the handle, surprised when it turned. The evening shadows darkened his foyer, but not so much as to hide the destruction of his home. I halted, stunned as the scene in front of me gave an alarming visual. Overturned furniture littered the space, picture frames had been knocked from the walls, and glass was strewn across the hardwood floor. My sneakers crunched on a piece of light-bulb as I took a cautious step into the living room. The area opened into the kitchen, which didn't look much better.

Several dishes lay in pieces, and one of the cabinets had a gaping hole in the dark wood.

"Gage?" Silence greeted me—an unsettling void that raised the hair at my nape. The urge to flee was strong. I was stupid for coming, especially after what he'd done the night before, but I wanted to shove what Ian had found down his throat and see him cower for a change.

A quick scan of the dining room revealed empty space. After finding the same in his bedroom, I moved on from the sight of his bed—from the memory of the night we'd spent there—and stopped at the basement's entrance. The door stood wide open, like a cavernous mouth inviting me into the bowls of hell. I flicked on the light to chase the darkness away, and then questioned my sanity as I descended the stairs. The basement didn't fair much better than the rest of his house. His collection of whips and paddles were scattered across the floor, and the St. Andrew's cross had been torn from the wall.

"Go home, Kayla."

I clenched my jaw and closed the distance between us. Looking down, I realized two things: he was still wearing the same clothes from the previous evening, and this was the first time Gage Channing had ever sat at my feet. He kept his head bowed toward the bottle of rum clutched between his hands.

"I'm not going anywhere until I've said this." I threw the folder at his feet. "You'll find enough evidence in there to send you to jail for a long time."

"What evidence?"

"Proof of your embezzlement. How ironic that you blackmailed me for doing what you're guilty of yourself." I let out a bitter laugh. "Isn't this a tidy little circle we've got here? You steal from your clients, I steal from you. He blackmails you, you blackmail me." I gritted my teeth. "If I didn't have Eve to think about, I might find some humor in it all."

"Why are you here, Kayla?"

"The rules have changed." I paced a few steps before stopping in front of him again. "I'm here to call a truce. End our contract, pay for Eve's care, and I'll consider us even."

"Fine. You can go now." He tipped the bottle back and took a swig.

"That's all you have to say?" A tremor laced my voice. Dammit, I'd wanted so much to remain calm, just as cold and detached as him. He was more of a master at cold and calculating than he was a "Master" in anything else. "Look at me, Gage."

He raised his eyes, and I reached up and unhooked the buttons of my jacket. I stood before him without makeup, wearing sweatpants and a T-shirt because anything else hurt too much. My fingers disappeared under the hem, and I inched it up, removing my clothes and watching his reaction as I revealed the welts and bruises he'd left behind.

He took another swig, and something in his expression shifted from indifferent to pained as his gaze wandered over my body. My breasts and bottom had taken the brunt of his rage, but every inch of me showed evidence of his cruelty.

"Is this why you're hiding in that bottle? Did your conscience finally claw its way out of the grave?" I wouldn't look away or back down. I wanted...no, I needed him to acknowledge the line he'd crossed. I tapped my foot and waited. "Dammit, say something!"

"What do you want me to say? That I'm sorry?"

"Are you?"

He sprung to his feet, so unexpectedly that I jerked back. "I'll *never* be sorry for fucking you in front of him." He hurtled the bottle against the wall, and the sound of shattering glass competed with the warning going off in my head. I shrank away as he advanced, but he grabbed me anyway. His hands dug into the bruises and welts. "I'd do it again and again until he gouged his fucking eyes out."

"Let go, you're hurting me!"

"Then stop me." He caught me in his vise-like embrace, and his mouth crashed onto mine, his tongue infusing my taste buds with the bitterness of rum. I struggled until every ounce of strength seeped from my bones. Finally giving in, I sagged against him and submitted my mouth.

He tangled his hands in my hair and tilted my head back, and I was helpless against the lure of him, split down the middle between logic and need.

With a groan, he pushed me away and staggered back a few feet. "Go home, before I fuck you again, and no amount of crying or begging will stop me."

"Why are you holding back now?" My voice cracked. "What's so different?"

He collapsed to the floor and buried his head in his hands, and he said nothing. I told myself I hadn't glimpsed a seed of remorse in his expression, that he was an ice cube underneath all that anger, incapable of feeling anything real. Problem was...I didn't believe it. I'd been ready to let his actions shatter whatever I might have felt for him, but then I'd walked into his disaster zone and seen the image of a broken man.

"If there's a speck of humanity in you, Gage"—I reached up and removed the collar—"you'll do the right thing."

The thin strip of leather drifted to the floor, and still, he said nothing. I dressed, and his silence followed me up the stairs and out the door.

CHAPTER TWENTY-TWO

I couldn't remember the last time I'd gotten drunk, but that's exactly what I was, and the culprit was a continuous supply of some fruity drink I found too easy to consume. It was like drinking Kool-Aid, only better. Kool-Aid didn't give me this amazing floaty sensation; weightless and free. I didn't have to think or feel.

Who was Gage Channing? Who was Ian? Who the fuck was I?

A persistent hand landed on my thigh, and I had to stop and think about who it belonged to. Oh, right...the guy who'd bought me the last round of drinks. What was his name?

Kyle?

Kevin?

I settled for calling him "Guy." Did it matter if I remembered his name? Likely not. Nothing mattered, which was how I wanted it. Guy's hand inched upward, and I was thankful for the ugly sweatpants I wore. He leaned in, and his beer breath overwhelmed my senses.

"Wanna get outta here, baby?"

I shook my head and stumbled to my feet, experiencing a sudden and urgent need to use the restroom.

"Hey, darlin', where're you goin'?" he protested.

I broke into laughter and had no clue why. "The lil girls' room. You can't come."

"Aw, that's not fair..."

His voice faded as I hobbled toward the bathroom. I pushed the door open and stalled at the sight of my reflection in the mirror. I looked like a zombie from a horror flick with bloodshot eyes and traces of mascara on my cheeks... right...I'd given in to a crying jag earlier. I should've stuck with bawling; drinking only made me look like hell, and in the end it was a temporary fix anyway. Tomorrow morning I'd feel just as miserable, if not more so. But I didn't indulge in alcohol often, and if Gage Channing could drown his demons in a bottle, why couldn't I?

Why do I let him get to me?

I squatted over the toilet and considered the question. I'd been prepared for all kinds of scenarios upon walking into his house. Rage, disbelief after seeing the evidence, and even his usual smugness followed by his demands, because even though I held power in my hands, surely something like the threat of jail wouldn't cause him to back down.

I'd expected a fight, only I'd gotten my first real glimpse of remorse, and it reminded me that underneath all his complexity, Gage was still a man. I finished taking care of business and crashed through the door of the restroom. I'd hit cab status long ago, but I couldn't bring myself to regret this foolish indulgence.

"There you are." Guy pulled my body flush with his, and we fell against the wall outside the restrooms. His mouth and hands were everywhere, and my first instinct was to push him away...until I realized that I needed to know. I needed to know if someone else could spark the same all-consuming feelings in me as Gage. I pulled him closer and gripped his hair, wrapped my leg around his calf, and rubbed against the bulge in his pants. His mouth plundered mine, slick and wet and all wrong, and his body moved against me, too rough and too fast.

I shoved him away. "I can't do this."

"Sure you can."

I jerked my face away as he descended again, and he slobbered on my cheek. Lifting my knee, I blindly aimed for where I knew it'd hurt most. I must have found my target, because he struggled for air. I slipped from his grasp, and his voice sounded odd as he called after me. I ignored him. In fact, I ignored everyone. Keeping my head bowed, I headed for the exit. He didn't follow. Maybe he figured I wasn't worth the trouble. And I wasn't. I wasn't worth anything. Not after what Gage had turned me into.

His whore.

Icy air hit me as I stumbled from the bar, though it was exquisite relief to my flushed cheeks. The sidewalk spun, and the brick wall of the bar blurred in my peripheral vision, as if I'd entered a funhouse...except the word "fun" didn't exist in this carnival. I fell into the wall and pounded my fists against the rough texture of the brick. Who was Gage, that he could propel me to hit bottom like this? The pain in my knuckles failed to register, and that was my problem; I was attracted to things that hurt me, even now in the way I chose to unleash my anger. Finally spent, I slumped to the ass-numbing concrete and pulled out my cell. He was the last person I wanted to face...and the one I needed to.

He'd come; I knew he would.

Ian pulled up twenty minutes later and hurried to where I sat on the deserted sidewalk. "Are you okay?" He helped me to my feet, and his gaze fell to my hands. "What happened?"

"I'm drunk."

"I can see that."

"The wall pissed me off."

"You really did a number on your hands." He put his arm around me. "Come on, I'll take you home."

I tripped over my feet and grasped his jacket. "I don't wanna go home." My empty apartment was the last place I wanted to go. "Take me home with you."

"Kayla..." His voice dropped in warning. "You need to sleep it off." He opened the passenger door of his SUV and helped me inside.

"I need you." He moved to shut the door, but I grabbed his hand and laced our fingers together. "Make me feel something."

"Not while you're drunk." He extracted his fingers from mine, and the door slammed with an echo of finality. I settled into the seat with a sigh as he rounded the vehicle.

"I went to see him," I said as he slid in beside me.

"I thought we agreed you wouldn't go alone."

"No, you *told* me not to go alone."

"How did he take it?"

"He was drunk."

"That seems to be a theme tonight." He ran a hand through his short, brown hair. "Are you all right? He didn't hurt you, did he?"

"He kissed me." Why was I telling him this?

His fingers tightened around the steering wheel. He turned onto the road and stomped on the gas. "What did he tell you?"

I laughed. "Absolutely nothing."

We fell silent, and I stewed the whole way to my apartment. He deposited me on the doorstep and straightened my jacket collar, as if I was a wayward ribbon on a present that needed fixing. Too drunk to unlock my own door, he did it for me. Nothing but loneliness and despair awaited me on the other side.

"I'll come back in the morning and take you to get your car."

"Don't leave." I gripped the front of his jacket, willing him to come inside, though I hadn't thought much on what we'd do once we got past the door. "Please, don't go." I collapsed into his arms and sobbed, body shaking violently as I let it all pour out of me. "I'm such a mess. He fucked me up, Ian." Gage was still in my system, a parasitic itch I still wanted to scratch. He'd wanted to own me, and now he did. Underneath the fear, the hatred and rage, lurked a sense of gratitude. He'd saved my daughter's life...how could I hate anyone who'd done that?

I gulped in mouthfuls of air, but it wasn't enough to calm me. Hesitantly, he tightened his arms around me, and I sensed him battling with himself. He closed and locked the door, decision made. My heart skipped as he picked me up, but then he set me on my feet next to the couch.

"No, take me to bed."

"Kayla—"

"Just hold me," I interrupted. "Please. I want to wake up with you tomorrow morning." I wanted the warmth of his body next to mine, then maybe Gage wouldn't haunt my dreams while I slept.

He cursed under his breath and lifted me again, and the last thing I recalled as my head sank into the pillow was the safety of his arms surrounding me.

CHAPTER TWENTY-THREE

The gentle way he touched me bespoke of reassurance. His fingers glided along my skin, igniting want and need in their wake. He pushed a little deeper, past the resistance of my innocence and into the center of my heat, and I knew I was dreaming...dreaming of the night Ian made love to me for the first time. The one and only time.

I cried out, overcome by him filling me, pressing into me, devouring me. Never before had I dreamed so vividly in life-like detail. His skin slid against mine, hot and damp, and something beyond the physical touched me. Maybe it was the way he trembled as he grasped my hands and held them to the mattress, as if he needed to hold on to something to keep from coming apart. We hadn't needed words. The brush of our lips, the tender union of tongues, the claiming sensation of his thrusts—the way we came together said more than words ever could.

The dream evaporated, and as the light of day seeped behind my lids, I recalled how the morning after—so many years ago—I'd ended up puking. I'd puked every morning after that for a few weeks. My eyelids fluttered open, the dream still a tickle at my conscious mind, and he was looking straight at me. The previous evening came flooding back. Oh my God...had I really begged him to take me to his place? Or even worse...had I let some random stranger stick his tongue down my throat?

"I'm sorry about last night. I shouldn't have called you." I should have called a cab and fallen into bed alone, but now here we were, seven years later.

"Don't apologize for calling me. I'm glad I was there. You weren't exactly in the best part of town."

I avoided his eyes and inspected the nasty scrapes covering my knuckles. "I was in a bad place, and I'm not talking about the area of town."

"You don't deserve what he's done." He rolled to his back and sighed. "I wish I knew what to say or do, but I don't. I don't know how to handle this..."

The memory of what Gage had put us through hit me square in the chest, and I wondered if the impact would ever lessen with time. If I could withstand the humiliation of that, then last night shouldn't bother me. "We should talk about it."

"I know."

I didn't know what to say either. He'd basically been raped—if not by force, then by threat—and I couldn't help but obsess over the fact that he'd managed to reach orgasm with Katherine. That alone was messed up on so many levels, as I'd learned firsthand how someone could coax pleasure from an unwilling participant if they put some effort into it. I closed my eyes, but the memory of them together still burned like a scorching brand on my mind and heart. His torment had shone from his gaze, but then he'd shuttered his expression and had moaned right along with her, if only for a moment.

"I don't want you to feel ashamed about it, Kayla."

Had he pretended it was me? Maybe that was the one question I wanted answered, only I didn't know how to ask, so I remained silent.

"I hate that you paid the price for saying my name, but I don't think I would've been able to…do what he demanded if you hadn't." He rolled over and faced me, close enough to breathe the same air. "I thought of you and that was enough to send me over the edge. I want you to know I wasn't with her—every part of me was with you."

I couldn't resist kissing him. To hell with the consequences, to what was right and wrong. Getting involved with him was cruel and irresponsible, but I couldn't fight the draw of him. He was my safety net, and I was falling headfirst toward concrete.

I hoped he was strong enough to catch me, because in that moment I was fresh out of strength.

For a few stolen moments, we lost ourselves in each other, our mutual moans the only sounds louder than my thumping heartbeat. Trapped underneath his body, I found freedom. We finally came up for air, and he dropped his forehead against mine.

"Kayla…" His breath caressed my lips, and I parted them, wanting more of him. "I want you so badly right now."

"I want you too. That hasn't changed from last night."

He closed his eyes. "But sobriety has brought back reason."

Sobriety had brought back a lot of things. "Yeah." If we gave into our desire now, I might never know for certain, and I couldn't move on with him until I knew it was for the right reasons.

My phone buzzed on the nightstand, and one glance told me it was Gage. I questioned why I didn't just ignore the call —I had called in sick for a few days, after all. But the reasons were complicated, a mess of convoluted truth I didn't want to deal with. Power still tipped in his favor; in the way I submitted to him, in the way I was compelled to answer simply because he called. And with four terse words that formed a demand, he had me sliding out of bed.

"Come into the office."

CHAPTER TWENTY-FOUR

Ian wanted me to quit my job. He had driven me to get my car, but then he'd had to go to work. I still recalled the apprehension on his face, even now as I approached the fifth floor of Channing Enterprises. He had pleaded with me not to go.

Gage Channing is a monster.

He'll only hurt you again.

At least let me go with you.

I'd agreed with the first two statements, but I wouldn't let him take time off from his job to deal with my problems. He'd been dragged into my life enough already.

A ding announced the fifth floor, and as the doors slid open, I wondered what Gage wanted. After his non-reaction to the evidence I'd presented him with, I was more than curious. Maybe he was going to fire me. A part of me hoped he would so I wouldn't have to face the decision of whether or not to put in my resignation. The idea of searching for a new job was a daunting one, though staying on as his personal assistant didn't sit well either.

I exited the elevator, not at all recovered from Gage's

beating or my bar excursion, but at least no one would tell by looking at me. I wore my usual heels and skirt ensemble, only the inches on my shoes were shorter and the hem of my skirt longer than his more recent requirements. I looked like the put-together woman I wanted the world to see. No one would know that every inch of my body still ached from the impact of his whip.

"Good morning, Kayla." Katherine's sing-song greeting iced my blood. I avoided her smug face and rushed into Gage's office without knocking. The door slammed shut behind me, making him jump.

"I'll have to call you back," he said into his cell. He ended the call and leaned back in his chair, staring at me, though instead of his usual cocky air, his face was bathed in uncertainty.

I hadn't expected uncertainty. "I was debating whether or not to put in my resignation, but I can't work here with Katherine." How interesting that his presence didn't bother me half as much as hers did.

Pinching the bridge of his nose, he closed his eyes, and I assumed he was suffering from the effects of his drinking binge. "I'll have her transferred. I can't fire her—she and I have an agreement."

I bet. "Let me guess, her job back in exchange for destroying me?"

He ignored my scathing question and gestured to the seat in front of his desk. "Sit down. We have a few things to discuss."

"I'll stand, thank you. And you're the one who needs to do the talking. Why is my ex blackmailing you? Is he doing it for money, or does it have something to do with me?"

"He thinks he can keep me away from you," he said with a smirk. "Your ex is an ass."

"A bit hypocritical, don't you think?"

His face darkened, and he rose and rounded the desk.

I took a step back, remembering how he'd kissed me last night. "Don't come any closer."

"What do you think I'm gonna do, Kayla? Bend you over my desk and put a belt to your ass?" He had me against the door before I was able to blink. "You made it clear the rules have changed, remember?" His eyes lowered to my trembling mouth. "Only I'm a little unclear on what they are now. Am I still allowed to touch you?" He feathered his fingers across my nipples, as if testing how far he could push me. "Kiss you?" His words whispered across my lips, breath laced with the richness of coffee. "You didn't seem to mind last night."

"No, you don't get to touch me." I shoved him back a few inches, hating how he still had the power to make my pulse race. The bastard still turned me on; that out of everything pissed me off the most.

"I called you in here to negotiate my own terms."

I raised a brow. "I didn't realize you had anything left to negotiate with."

He laughed. "You didn't quite achieve checkmate yet—my king is still in the game, believe me."

I flattened myself against the door, but it didn't give me the distance I wanted. His chest felt like steel under my hands as I pushed against him. "I'll scream."

"Do it, then the cops can come and arrest you." His grin was too triumphant, and I wondered how he'd so easily turned the tables on me.

"And you think the police will ignore your embezzlement? You're not above the law, even though it's clear you think otherwise."

"You won't turn me in."

"Really? What makes you so certain?"

"Because upon further investigation, the Feds will

discover that your friend Jody Palmer is also guilty. If I go down, she does too."

My jaw went slack. "You're lying."

"Am I? Do you want to test me?" He quirked an eyebrow. "Why do you think she resigned?"

A chill traveled through my body. He was basically telling me I had no leverage. Oh my God...this wasn't over yet. "Gage, don't do this to me. I can't take anymore."

Something flickered in the depths of his eyes, something that gave me hope, but he dashed it with the words he whispered against my ear. "Doing the right thing isn't in my nature. I want you." He grabbed my ass and lifted, and his erection pushed against my opening.

Where I instantly throbbed for him.

"No!" I shoved him away. "Turn me in, if you want, but I can't do this anymore."

"You'd risk your daughter's life?"

"No," I choked out. "God, you're despicable. The fact that you'd use her like this tells me everything I need to know about you."

He frowned. "Maybe you don't know me as well as you think." He returned to his chair, which shocked the heck out of me. Deep down, I'd expected him to take me right there in his office.

"Then do the right thing. Let me go."

"So you want me to let you out of our contract, but I'm supposed to keep paying for Eve's medical bills?"

"Haven't I paid enough? You've put me through hell and you know it."

"I'll do it under one condition."

His words stunned me, but then suspicion set in. "What do you want?"

The edge of his mouth turned up. "I already told you what I want."

He wanted me. "Why, Gage? I don't understand. You could have any woman you wanted."

"Not any woman," he said wryly.

And that was it. I was the forbidden fruit on the tree, though why he'd placed me into that category was unclear. If he'd approached me like a decent human being, I might have liked him. Now all he had going for him was my chemical reaction to him. It was just sex—really fantastic sex mixed with really horrific pain. "I'll ask again, *what do you want from me*?"

"I want your trust."

"Are you kidding me?"

He shook his head and stared at the scattered papers on his desk. "I'm a jealous man, Kayla. I don't like sharing. But I admit that I went too far with you."

"Is this the part where I tell you it's okay?" I'd locked my anger away too long, and now it exploded in a rare display of fury. I stalked across the room and swiped the papers from his desk. Even his computer crashed to the floor, but I couldn't bring myself to care. "I don't like being raped, but that didn't matter to you."

He tensed, and for a moment I was sure he was going to explode. He stared at me for several long moments before speaking. "A part of you does like it, or you'd walk away right now."

I opened my mouth but nothing came out.

"Eve is getting better," he said. "I could stop paying for her care and she'd still recover." He leaned forward. "So why are you still here, Kayla?"

My mouth hung open, a dozen replies forming on my tongue, but the truth gagged me.

I didn't know why I was still there.

"Give me one more weekend. We'll leave the contract behind."

"And if I say no?"

He shrugged. "Well, if you'd rather carry out the rest of your six weeks, I guess I can punish you now for your blatant disobedience."

I clenched my teeth. "One weekend, then I'm free?"

He nodded. "One weekend, and then you're free."

CHAPTER TWENTY-FIVE

Rain pelted my windows as I sat in my car, debating on whether or not to knock on Jody's door, but I was here so I might as well get it over with. I reached for the door handle but snapped my hand back when two people emerged from her house. The sight of Rick speared through me, and I gripped the steering wheel as the fight or flight instinct kicked in. He grabbed her in a way that was too familiar; hands gripping her hair so she couldn't move while he kissed her, his body trapping her between him and her front door. A passerby would see two people locked in a passionate embrace, but I saw it for what it was. Possession—the same kind Gage had wielded over me. He and Rick were made of the same cloth.

They finally broke apart, and the heat boiling in my stomach wasn't born of jealousy. I pitied the poor woman who fell for Rick's charm, for his crooked, boyish smile that was bright enough to disguise the viciousness lurking within him. No, it was hatred that set my blood afire; hatred for the man who'd taken my innocence and trust and had used them to shatter me. Flesh wounds heal—even the evidence of the beating Gage had issued would disappear—but the damage inflicted on the soul would last a lifetime.

Never taking my eyes off them, I dialed Ian's number.

"Hi…" I said once he'd answered. "It's me."

His sigh came over the line. "I was so worried. Why'd you ignore my calls?"

I shrugged. "I don't know." Only I did. My confrontation with Gage still lingered, as did the questions he'd asked that I had no answers to. Rick finally broke away from Jody, and I sank down in my seat as he crossed the street to where a shiny BMW was parked. If that wasn't evidence of Gage Channing's money, I wasn't sure what was.

"Are you okay?" Ian asked.

I hesitated, searching for an answer that wasn't total BS. "Okay" was difficult to define. "Yeah…I'm at Jody's. Gage said she's also responsible for the embezzlement."

"Jesus, Kayla. You can't trust anything he says."

"I know, but Rick just left her house, so something is definitely up. I'm gonna talk to her." I waited until the BMW disappeared around the corner before opening my door.

"I called the PI. He didn't find anything else." His frustration was obvious.

"Thanks for trying. I'll call you after I talk to her." I ended the call as I darted across the street, keeping my head ducked low against the rain. And then I found myself facing her much too soon. I opened my mouth, but no words came out.

"Kayla? What are you doing here?"

"I need to talk to you."

She stepped back and opened the door wide. "Come in."

"Thanks." I stepped inside, and I didn't miss the worried glance she sent down the street as she closed the door. I'd met her shortly after my wedding, and at one time we'd been close. Now there was a huge divide between us, only I hadn't realized how far apart we'd drifted until now. I hadn't realized the divide was Rick himself. There was no point in beating around the bush. "I saw you with Rick."

She swallowed hard, and her attention landed on anything other than me; the plush burgundy runner on the floor, the large poinsettia plant on the hutch in the foyer, even her own reflection in the oversized mirror. "I don't know what to say..."

"Why don't you start with the truth? Why is Rick blackmailing Gage?"

Her gaze jerked to mine. "What are you talking about?"

"Don't play dumb. I know about the embezzlement. Gage told me you were involved." I still wasn't sure if I believed him, but I had nothing else to go on.

She crossed her arms. "Gage Channing is crazy. You can't trust anything he tells you."

"How about his financial records? Should I trust those? The evidence doesn't lie, Jody. Money went into Rick's account, and it coincides with Gage's statements." I wondered how long her affair with Rick had been going on. Had she been sleeping with him while he'd been married to me? "Since I just saw Rick leave here, I'm going to assume Gage was telling the truth."

"I have no idea what you're talking about. Look, I know this must be a shock to find out about Rick and me this way, but—"

"It's more than a shock—it's crazy! Jody, do you have any idea what he's capable of?"

She pursed her lips. "It's been three years. I thought you'd be over him by now."

I was sure my eyes bulged. "You think I'm still hung up on the man who beat the shit out of me?" I took a step toward her. "How long has this been going on? Has he hit you yet?"

Jody shuffled back and wrapped her arms around herself. "He's changed. He never meant to hurt you."

I arched my brows. "Really?"

"He told me what happened. You don't have to be ashamed—a lot of women suffer from postpartum depression and do things they regret."

I stared at her, incredulous. "This should be good. Please, enlighten me—what bullshit did he feed you?"

"It's in the past." She shook her head. "I know you'd never try to hurt yourself or your daughter under normal circumstances, and obviously you got the help you needed—"

"Obviously," I snapped, folding my arms. "I can't believe you're buying into his lies."

"He wouldn't lie to me. He loves me."

I almost snorted. "Rick doesn't love anyone."

"He loves me, and he loves Eve. You can't keep him from her forever. He already lost a year and half in prison."

I blinked, struggling to form a reply to such a crazy statement. "He should have been locked away a lot longer for what he did to me." His expensive attorney had gotten him a lenient plea bargain, otherwise he'd still be in jail, and I'd still be safe from the threat of him. "How long has it been going on?" I asked.

She studied the purple nail polish on her toes. "Since before you guys split. I'm sorry. I never meant to hurt you, Kayla."

"You're going to be the sorry one. Rick is rotten underneath his appeal." I headed toward the door and opened it. "Tell him if he comes anywhere near Eve, I'll have him thrown in jail again."

Her expression iced over. "It's not fair to keep him from her. He just wants to be part of her life—we both do."

"Over my dead body." I slammed the door behind me,

and Ian called before I reached my car. He started talking the instant I answered.

"I'm going on my lunch break now. Can I come over? I need to see you."

"I need time, Ian." I slid in behind the wheel and slumped in my seat. Letting him past my defenses that morning had been a mistake.

"Why do you keep shutting me out?"

"I don't want to shut you out, but..."

"But what?"

I'm ashamed.

"I've got some stuff to sort out. I'm sorry." I hung up, shut off my phone, and headed to the hospital to spend the rest of my day with Eve. And I prayed to God Ian would stick to the wing he worked in.

CHAPTER TWENTY-SIX

Eve's doctor gave me the best Christmas present I could've hoped for. My baby was coming home in two weeks.

I must have cried happy tears for an hour straight, and thankfully Eve was too preoccupied with opening her gifts and visiting with Santa to notice that her mother was a basket case. Only this time I was a basket case in the best sense of the word; I hadn't been this happy in months.

So of course Gage would have to ruin my Christmas with his mere presence.

"Merry Christmas," he said, nodding toward Santa as the big guy in red and white exited Eve's room. Gage shut the door and took the empty seat on the opposite side of her bed.

I gawked at him as he began removing presents—all of them wrapped in shiny paper splashed with Santa's reindeer and adorned with fancy bows. I wondered if he'd wrapped them himself or if he'd paid the department store to do it for him. He smiled at Eve, a grin so huge and unguarded that I did a double take. When she sat up and grinned back, something within me unleashed. I bolted from my chair and pulled him away from her.

"What the hell do you think you're doing here?"

He had the nerve to look offended. "It's Christmas. What do you think I'm doing here?"

"Mommy! Can I open them?"

"Of course you can," he answered before I was able to. "I brought them especially for you."

I glared at him. "I won't let you use her to get to me. I don't want you anywhere near her." I lowered my voice amidst Eve's enthusiastic package-opening. "Do you understand? She's off-limits to your sick games. You can play them with me all you want, but you'd better leave her out of it." If I hadn't been so worked up myself, I would have been alarmed by the fury that crossed his face.

His gaze darted behind me, and I turned around and noticed Eve's curious expression. He grabbed my hand and pulled me toward the door. "I need to talk to your mom. Merry Christmas, Eve." He practically dragged me from her room, and I saw him strain under the effort it took to keep from slamming the door. He moved against me, both arms trapping me between him and the wall.

"Let me go. This is *not* the place."

"Don't you think I realize that?" He ground his teeth. "Let's get something straight *right now*." He leaned even closer and spoke to me nose-to-nose. "I would never...*never*... hurt Eve."

"You expect me to believe that after the last beating you gave me?"

He buried his face in the hollow of my shoulder, and I felt him inhale deeply. "If I could take it back, I would."

I went still. I'd guessed he was dealing with some amount of guilt, but I never thought he'd admit it. "Why'd you do it?" I squeezed the question past my constricted throat.

"Get your hands off her."

Gage pushed away from the wall and glanced at Ian, who looked ready to greet him with his fists. "Dr. Kaplan," he said, his tone unworried. He returned his attention to me, as if Ian's presence didn't matter. "Next weekend, Kayla. I'll pick you up at seven." He brushed his lips across my cheek. "Wear something sexy." My face flamed, both from anger and embarrassment as he took off down the hall.

"What is he talking about?"

I studied the worn carpet. "He said he'd let me out of the contract if I gave him one more weekend."

"And you believe him?"

I was tired of trying to figure everyone out, of trying to understand my own reactions to a man whose presence should send me running in the opposite direction. "I don't know what to believe."

"He's gotten under your skin."

I wanted to deny it, but it'd be a lie. Gage *had* gotten under my skin, only I hadn't realized to what extent until now. Until Ian had thrown the truth in my face. Gage hadn't just cast the line; I'd opened my mouth and let him hook me.

Ian let out a curse. "After everything he's done, how can you have feelings for him?"

"I don't." I stepped back against the wall and folded my arms.

"Then why are you agreeing to this?"

"It seems like the best way out."

"You could go to the police. It's not too late."

"Not if Jody's involved." It didn't matter if she'd betrayed me as a friend. I wouldn't drag her through this situation. "It's only one more weekend, and then it'll be over."

He dropped his head. "I can't talk you out of this, can I?"

I silently pleaded for him to talk me out of it, to pull me back, because I feared Gage had me in his sights and there was nowhere to hide. Nowhere for me to go but downhill from here, and what really sucked was how familiar this path was.

So was the same sense of helplessness I felt.

His composure fell apart, and he leaned against the wall, his arm hiding his face. "This is my fault. I did this." Before I could refute or question his claim, he pushed away from the wall. "I've gotta go."

He bolted down the hall, and I felt more confused than ever.

CHAPTER TWENTY-SEVEN

The week sped by too fast. Ian was obviously avoiding me, something I had to admit was a relief. Gage and I barely spoke, another source of relief. He'd kept me busy at work with tasks that kept me out of the office for the majority of the workday, and I spent my nights at the hospital with Eve.

I'd been a nervous wreck all week. I couldn't help but wonder what Gage had planned for me at the week's end, and considering how he'd chosen New Year's Eve to begin our last weekend together, I couldn't deny I was edgy...and curious.

Now as I slipped into a red halter dress, I recognized something was different about this weekend. Gage had told me on Wednesday that he was taking me out of town—not far in case Eve needed me—which only heightened the nervous flutters in my gut. I prepared my hair and put on my makeup. He hadn't even arrived yet, but I sensed it; this weekend was significant, only I didn't know why. It felt more like a date. I floundered at the thought, but I didn't have time to dwell on it. A knock sounded on the door.

The reality of his arrival trembled through me. The idea

that he wanted my trust was absurd. It didn't matter how much I warred with myself—I would always remember the brutality of his hands. I took a deep breath and opened the door. He wore a dark suit, black on smoke gray, and he'd left the tie at home. He'd unfastened the top two buttons of his collar. I stumbled back a little. He looked good enough to eat, though taking a bite of that would likely poison me.

His wandering gaze heated, and I was certain he'd already undressed me in his head. "Are you ready to go?"

With a nod, I picked up the overnight bag I'd left by the door. "Where are we going?"

"You'll see." He grabbed my bag, and I shut and locked the door. Moments later we were in his car speeding down the highway, and it became apparent that we were headed to the airport.

"You said we weren't going far."

"We're not. It's only a two-hour flight on my jet. I can have you home in no time if need be."

I wasn't happy about this development, but I let it go. One more weekend, and it would be over. I was prepared to take whatever the next two days gave me. He parked next to a sleek jet where a man materialized next to the car and pulled our bags from the trunk. Gage placed his hand on the small of my back as we climbed the steps. His touch had a possessive connotation, and when he clamped his fingers around my side, I resisted the urge to squirm out of reach.

The inside of the plane was bigger than it appeared from the outside. I'd expected a few seats and little more. I should've known better. The inside was just as luxurious as everything else he owned. Every detail testified of money and power; the large flat screen television on the wall, the abstract pieces of art, the plush rug under our feet. He ushered me to the cream leather couch that spanned one side.

"Straddle me," he demanded, pulling me onto his lap and denying me the chance to object. He slid his hands under my dress and grabbed my ass, bringing me against his erection. My reaction was instantaneous. A flood of warmth crashed at my center, and I struggled to catch my breath through lips that parted of their own volition. His hands kneaded my bottom. "You feel that?" Awareness zinged between us as he watched me. "We connect here, Kayla."

"It's just sex." My voice sounded weak, and I despised myself for it, especially since my body rocked against his.

"No, you're not the type of woman who engages in 'just sex' arrangements." He brought his hands up and spanned my ribcage. "The fact that you're sitting here hot for my cock after everything I've done"—he circled my nipples with his thumbs—"turning to liquid at my touch, gives you away. You can have 'just sex' with anyone. There's more here between us."

I couldn't look at him anymore. I closed my eyes, but I still felt his hands on me, still felt him hard and hot underneath me.

"I could fuck you right now, and you'd still beg for more." He grabbed the back of my neck and pulled me in. "You're just as addicted to me as I am you." Pressing his mouth to mine, his tongue swept inside, and I wondered what he was waiting for.

"Do it, Gage." I moaned against his lips. Later I'd beat myself up for this. Later I'd walk away.

"No. Just because you're not my slave anymore, that doesn't mean you call the shots." He palmed my ass and squeezed hard. "And I'm still Master to you in the bedroom." His tone left no room for argument. Before I could argue with him anyway, he was kissing me again. He freed my hair from my up-do, and the heavy locks fell in waves around his face.

I curled my fingers in the silk of his hair, but he grabbed my hands and held them behind my back, clenched together in his strong fist. His other hand held me to him so I couldn't pull out of the kiss until he allowed it. And I didn't want to escape his mouth. We kissed long after the jet left the ground, and only a patch of turbulence severed our lips, though he didn't release me.

"Let's talk," he rasped against my cleavage.

I could hardly breathe or think, and he wanted to talk? I inched away and studied his expression, looking for a clue as to what he was thinking. "You want to talk? Now?" My head spun—from his kiss, from his rapid mood-shift.

"Yes. Talk. We haven't done much of that."

No, we hadn't. He'd always distanced himself. He gently pushed me from his lap and patted the seat beside him. I sat, expecting him to dominate the conversation, to drill me with questions he demanded answers to, much like he had over breakfast during my first weekend with him. "What do you want to talk about?"

"You." He ran his hand along the back of the couch and played with my hair. "Why did you marry him?"

The question hit me in the gut. "Do we really have to talk about this?"

"Yes."

"Okay, but as long as you promise to be open with me. Conversation is a two way street."

"Fine."

"I got pregnant. I was young, and I thought marrying him was the right thing to do."

"Did you know he was abusive beforehand?"

"No. I mean, he was possessive, and I knew he angered easily. But he'd never hurt me before."

"Did you love him?"

I rubbed the silky hem of my dress between two fingers.

"At one time, maybe I did." Raising my eyes to his, I asked, "Have you ever been in love?"

"No." His reply was too quick.

I raised a brow. "Not even a little? Most people fall in love at least once in their lifetime."

"Maybe I was waiting for the right woman." His gaze, hot and suggestive, pinned me to the seat.

I refused to back down. "So there was no one...?"

"Once, a long time ago." He said it like it was ancient history—as if this part of his past didn't mean anything, but I was certain it did mean something. I sensed that whatever happened was a factor in what had made him so deranged. Normal people didn't enjoy inflicting pain on others in the manner he did. Even the normally kinky people knew where to draw the line. Gage didn't.

"So what happened?"

"This isn't open for discussion, Kayla."

"We had an agreement. You promised to be open with me."

"I'm modifying that agreement now. Drop it."

I crossed my arms. "No."

"Are you purposely trying to make me angry? Maybe you like punishment more than you've let on."

"I like a lot of things, Gage, but pain isn't one of them. I'm asking because I want to know you. Don't you think I deserve that much, after everything you've done to me?"

He ran a hand through his hair. "You deserve everything." He turned his face toward the blackness outside the small window, contemplation shadowing his features. "She was my high school sweetheart." Several moments of thick silence passed, as if he thought those six words explained everything.

"Was she...was she your slave?"

His mouth twitched. "I never had a slave before you. She

was the opposite of you. I'd whip her and she'd beg me to do it harder. She loved it."

Sounded like they were made for each other. "So what happened?"

"She was fucking someone else."

Okay...so he'd had his heart broken. Not exactly the precipice I'd been looking for to clue me in on why he was such a sadistic bastard. "And there's been no one since?" I found that hard to believe. I knew he'd had an immeasurable amount of women, but surely he'd had at least a couple of relationships.

"No."

"So she cheated on you, broke your heart, and you what? Decided to go the rest of your life hating women?"

"She died." He glared at me, and I felt every facet of that hostile gaze. "I told you to drop it."

The fear came back then, creeping up my spine, tingling along my skin and reminding me that Gage wasn't a romantic lover, this wasn't a date, and he wasn't going to whisper endearments in my ear as we made love. He'd whittled away my guard, making me forget how he could turn on me in an instant. Like a rabid dog.

"I'm sorry," I said, adverting my gaze.

He forced my chin up, though his touch was more gentle than usual. "There are things about my past you don't need to know about. I don't want you to think you can't talk to me, or ask whatever is on your mind, but when I tell you to drop something, I mean it. Understand?"

I nodded. Obviously, I'd pushed too far. If he wanted to dish out punishment now, I deserved it. In the back of my mind, I realized how skewed that notion was, but there it was.

The next hour passed in uncomfortable silence, and I couldn't help but wonder about his past, about the woman who'd stolen his heart. What had happened to her? Did he hold himself responsible for her death? I shrugged off the tense silence and the questions as we began to descend. Peering out the window, I spied a neon expanse below, and the closer we got, the bigger the buildings appeared. He'd taken me to Las Vegas. I'd never been, but I recognized the infamous strip, and I'd heard how spectacular Vegas was on New Years Eve.

What the hell was he up to?

After the jet came to a stop, he rose and held out his hand. The next half-hour sped by in a blur. People opened doors as if we were royalty, and during the limo ride down the strip, the bustling atmosphere called to me, called to the flutters of excitement in my stomach.

Him bringing me here...it was beginning to make sense. He wanted to show me how good it could be at his side, but what he hadn't stopped to think about was how he'd already shown me the worst of him. No amount of seduction, sexual or otherwise, would erase that, though I had to admit I was being lured in for a weekend of the best of Gage Channing...at least I hoped he'd left the sadist at home.

After arriving at the hotel, we bypassed the registration desk and went straight to the bank of elevators off the lobby. I watched the numbers light up as we climbed upward. Of course, we didn't exit until we reached the top floor. He placed his hand on the small of my back, a touch so light that outsiders would think nothing of it. I knew better. His every touch signified ownership.

"I want to blindfold you," he said once we'd stopped in front of the door to our room.

My heart galloped ahead of me for a moment. "Why?"

"Trust me."

"You think you've earned my trust?"

"No, but I think you're going to give it to me anyway." He produced a blindfold from his pocket and reached for me.

I opened my mouth to protest, but he was already slipping it over my eyes. I felt silly standing in the hall, blindfolded while he opened the door. No one else was around to witness my compliance, but that didn't stop me from wondering about surveillance cameras. After a few moments I heard a beep, and he guided me inside.

"Watch your step," he murmured. The floor dipped, and he walked me further into the room, his hands on my hips guiding me the whole way. "Stop here."

I halted and waited, holding my breath, wondering what he'd do. I'd agreed to the blindfold but nothing else...and he hadn't mentioned anything else. I reminded myself that I wasn't under his control any longer. He'd promised no contract.

So why did I feel like this whole trip was a sham? Like I had even less freedom than I'd had before? I drew in a quick breath, and something deep inside me called to him, something craving the unknown—that tingle of anticipation mixed with fear. The part of me that fell back into the dynamic of submissive too easily. The word "Master" was on my tongue, begging to be spoken.

"Will you whip me if I call you by your name?"

"Yes."

"Will you stop if I tell you to?"

A few seconds went by, and I heard him inhale. "Yes, but I don't think you want to."

He was only partly right. I wanted to tell him to stop, but I felt as if I couldn't.

"Lift your arms," he instructed, and clearly, that line of questioning was over. Whatever he had in mind, he was ready to begin.

"Gage—" I broke off, cringing as I lifted my arms above

my head. Had I slipped up on purpose? Did I want to test the new perimeters of our agreement?

He chuckled...the bastard actually chuckled. He dragged the zipper of my dress down, his fingers lighting a fire down my back. My breath hitched when he bent and placed his hands on my thighs. His fingers were close to the wetness between my legs, tantalizingly close, and I bit back a moan as the ache spread. I couldn't hold it in when his hands glided upward, palms caressing my stomach and breasts as he pushed the dress up my body and over my head. Goose-flesh broke out on my arms and traveled down my legs, and as he walked me forward a few more feet, I couldn't stop shaking.

"Cold?"

"A little."

"Brace yourself," he said, and I was clueless about what he meant until he pushed me against the cold, hard surface of what I assumed was a window. I gasped at the contact, and my nipples pebbled against the glass. I was probably visible to God knew who, naked except for a thong and heels, but I didn't care. All that mattered was the next moment...and whether he planned to unleash his sadistic or sensual side.

He grabbed my hands and placed them flat against the glass, and something soft and silky encircled my wrists. "I'm going to whip you," he said, voice gentle as the bindings tightened.

His words elicited a deep freeze in my bones, much colder than the chill on my skin, and I replayed the agony of being struck for hours in my head. I tried to jerk away from the glass, but he'd tethered my hands to something. "Master..." The name tumbled out, a plea for mercy I knew didn't exist within him. "Please, I can't take another beating like that."

"Shhh..." He swept my hair aside and placed the heat of his mouth on my neck. "I'm not going to hurt you...much." He left a wet trail down my back, and by the time he cupped my mound and slipped his fingers inside, I was dripping wet. He owned me there, with the simplicity of his touch, with the way he made my insides pulse around his fingers. Forgetting that I should be scared, I opened up for him and moaned.

"I won't lose control like I did last time." He increased his strokes. In and out...in again, slowly caressing, dipping deeper until I started humming. Sweet tension spread from my belly to my limbs, and my breasts heated against the glass, no longer cold.

I was on fire.

Holy hell...

I held my breath, knowing I was about to come, but he stopped.

"Master—"

Without warning, he shoved a gag into my mouth. "Quiet." That single word, spoken calmly but with enough warning to let me know he meant business, silenced me more effectively than the gag. I wanted to beg and plead, but I didn't dare, even though one important question screamed in my head; how could I say no if he wouldn't allow it?

"I want you to trust me," he said, as if he heard the turmoil of my thoughts. "I know I've given you no reason to, but I'm going to change that. I won't hurt you like I did last time, but I am going to punish you, and if you make a sound I'll extend the punishment." He ran his hands over my bottom. "Can you behave yourself?"

I nodded.

"Can you remain quiet?"

I nodded again but doubted my ability to obey.

"I'm giving you the chance to say no now, but once this

moment passes, you're mine." He squeezed my ass, and I bit back another moan. "Shake your head if you want to say no."

Part of me pleaded with me to do it—the more logical, level-headed, self-respecting part. Just a simple shake of my head would stop this. I had power now. But what if I did... and he stopped...everything? God, I was pathetic. I wanted him so badly, I ached.

My moment of escape passed, and he stepped away. The sound of him removing his belt made me cringe, and the whoosh of that familiar strip of leather reached my ears an instant before it hit my ass. I bit down on the gag to keep silent, though the pain wasn't bad. Yet. It'd get worse; it always did. I jerked each time he struck my tender bottom and counted the lashes in my head. Fourteen...fifteen... sixteen...seventeen...

My eyes flooded with unshed tears at twenty, and by twenty-five the first drop fell. I felt dirty and worthless—much worse then ever before, because I'd allowed this to happen this time. He'd given me a choice, and I was still restrained, trapped by my body's need for him, helpless and at the mercy of his belt.

Why hadn't I stopped this? This was insane.

A whimper escaped my throat, and he stopped. "Naughty girl."

I jumped when he pulled the thong aside and inserted a small vibrator between my damp folds.

"Close your legs to hold it there. If you drop it, you won't be allowed to orgasm tonight. And you won't have my permission until I'm deep inside your ass." He swatted my bottom to make his point. "Not a sound, Kayla."

He was the devil.

I scratched at the window as he continued the lashes. In the back of my mind I realized he wasn't putting all his strength behind them. I knew how unbearable a real whipping was at his hands, and this wasn't it. But it stung like hell, and I held onto the sensation to keep from climaxing.

I wanted him. Inside me, in my mouth. I didn't care—I just wanted him, and fooling myself otherwise was a waste of time.

"Your ass is such a sexy shade of red."

Smack!

Unforgiving leather delivered punishment for several more minutes, and just when he was about to stop, I'd moan or whimper and it'd start all over again. The pain was harder to handle, more intense, as were the vibrations going through my body. Tears and sweat drenched my face, and I stood straight as a pillar, clenching my thighs to keep the vibrator in place. Orgasm teased from the outskirts, there... but just out of reach.

The pain overshadowed the pleasure.

I bit hard on the gag as the last few minutes drove me to my limits. Finally, he dropped the belt. "Keep that vibrator where it belongs." He bent me over and pushed into my ass, inch by inch, and I didn't even consider protesting.

A loud boom sounded outside, followed by another, and another...he slid in further, removed the blindfold and gag, and a guttural scream tore from my throat. I arched my spine as an orgasm washed over me—swift in the onslaught, but deliciously long in duration. The Las Vegas strip exploded in a dizzying whirl of color, and I knew the fireworks outside couldn't begin to compete with the ones between Gage and me.

CHAPTER TWENTY-EIGHT

The man liked to gamble. A lot. He'd been at it for most of the day, and if I'd harbored any guilt about the amount of money he'd spent on Eve's care, I didn't now. I was disgusted at how easily he threw away his money, but I couldn't help but watch in morbid fascination.

So *this* was how the other half lived. I still couldn't wrap my mind around it.

The guy next to us arranged the dice the way he wanted them. His blond hair brushed his collar, and every time he leaned forward to roll, his shirt sleeve grazed my arm. He shot a grin at me before tossing the dice toward the opposite end of the craps table. The large crowd pressed in on all sides, and everyone erupted in cheers.

"Easy six!" One of the gaming attendants said.

Gage just won some of this money back. He leaned against my back and reached in to collect. We'd been standing in this position for the past hour; him behind me, his arms caging me in and his cock nudging my ass. He'd been rock-hard the whole time, and not even the man next to us, with his bold and inviting smile, distracted Gage from his desire. I tensed every time the guy aimed his flirtations in my direction, but so far Gage hadn't unhinged.

But he was about to.

His rum-scented breath drifted across my bare shoulder, and he brought his lips to my ear. "If he looks at you like that one more time, neither of you are going to like the outcome." He pushed his erection into my left butt cheek a little harder and tightened his arm around my waist. "Quit being so damn sexy."

Of course, in Gage Channing's twisted mind, this would be *my* fault.

Poker chips were dropped and picked up, clacking together in the triumph of a win, and excited chatter charged the air as everyone prepared for the next come-out roll. Mr. Big Flirt did something stupid; he touched me.

"It was all you, baby! You're my lucky charm!" His fingers circled my wrist, and he wrenched my arm up in the air, as if we were champions celebrating a win.

Oh no. No, no, no...

Gage clamped his fingers around the guy's wrist and squeezed until my hand fell free. "Touch her again, and I'll break off your fucking fingers."

The guy shrank back, his eyes going wide. I couldn't blame him. If Gage hadn't so effectively trapped me between him and the table, I would have done the same thing. I didn't have to see his face to know his features were twisted in rage.

"Dude, you need to chill out. I didn't mean anything by it."

One of the table attendants interrupted their argument. "Is there a problem here, Mr. Channing?"

"Yes. This asshole thinks it's okay to harass and paw at my date."

And that was the last I saw of Mr. Big Flirt, though his indignation at being escorted away like a criminal lingered. Just like Tom's had at work. Hating how everyone's focus was drawn to me, I pushed away from the table. "Let me out." I cranked my neck and glared at him. "*Right* now, Gage. I'm not kidding."

He backed away, and I bolted. Tears threatened to spill over as I weaved through the multitude of gamblers. Heavy smoke drifted in the air, which only made my eyes burn more. Gage caught up to me at the elevators. We both entered, and I kept my attention fastened on the doors, unwilling to look or speak to him.

And he didn't speak to me.

I wasn't sure what was going to happen when we got back to our room, but it couldn't be good. Would he be able to see through his haze of red to hear me say no? Or was I in for another horrendous beating? Hysteria rushed up and lodged under my breastbone, and I could hardly breathe as the doors slid open at our floor. He dug his fingers into my arm and dragged me to our suite. My face was already wet with tears.

"Please, Gage—"

"Shut up."

He swiped his card, the light flickered green, and the beep signaled the beginning of what I knew was going to be a hellish night.

"I'm saying no," I said as soon as he shoved me through the door. "Wha...whatever"—I swallowed the vomit rising in my throat—"whatever you're gonna do, stop."

The door slammed, and he pushed me against it. "I said shut up." His hands shook, which only intensified the terror fisting my heart. "What I'm going to do," he said, his gaze dropping to my mouth, "is kiss the fuck out of you." He tangled his hands in my hair, leaned in, and sighed against my lips. "Do you have a problem with that?"

No, but I should have.

It was my only thought as he took control of my mouth. Hot tongues swirling together, the taste of rum on his lips, the way he moaned my name before sucking my lower lip between his teeth, and his fingers tightening in my hair, pulling against my scalp—every sensation zipped through me like a firefly. I should definitely have a problem with this.

I couldn't recall the space of time between the door and the bed, but the mattress welcomed the weight of my body, and Gage blanketed me, his mouth never leaving mine, never failing to suck the free will from my soul with the poison of his kiss. He grabbed at my dress, ripping and tearing, and his frantic fingers clutched handfuls of me; my hips, my thighs, shoving my legs wide open, pushing my knees up an instant before he slammed into me. He was like a beast, desire his claws, and I came apart under his lethal need.

"Gage!" I urged him deeper, spreading my thighs further and arching to meet him. He pressed high into me, so high all I could feel was him.

He grunted, his forearms shaking on either side as he pumped. "Who am I, Kayla?" He plunged one more time, violently, and then went still.

I met his gaze—maniacal eyes possessing me—and shuddered. My heart feared him, but the gate of my sexual need was manned by him, owned by him.

And he knew it.

"Say it, or I'll stop right now and cuff your hands to the headboard. I'll make you edge all night until you're begging me to fuck you."

"Master." I tilted my hips upward. "You're my Master. Don't stop."

With a growl, his body engulfed mine, smothering and

consuming, and the only thing more painful than being devoured so thoroughly was the sound of my unrestrained moans, a traitorous testimony of his control over me. My need for him ripped from my throat and poured from my being with every thrust.

And then I was chanting his name. "Master...Master... Master..." Moaning and moaning and moaning. "Master... Master...Master." More moaning, more thrusting...and he was getting off on every sexual plea.

I was getting off on *him*.

I dug my nails into his shoulders and scratched my unbridled desperation down his back, on the cusp of splintering. It was right there for the taking—and with stunned frustration, I realized why my body wasn't shattering.

I was waiting for his permission.

"Let me come, Master."

He groaned. "Say it again. Tell me how bad you want it."

I grabbed fistfuls of bedding, and a pitiful, keening cry broke loose. I rose to meet him, again and again, and gasped my plea. "Please! Give me permission, Master!"

He groaned again, an unrestrained sound that vibrated to my core. "Fuck, woman, I'm never letting you go." He gripped my head and forced my gaze to his. "Come for me."

I fell into oblivion.

His sapphire eyes drank me in as I came undone, holding me prisoner in their depths until the last wave carried me to a place only he could send me. I was gasping, struggling just to breathe, when his control began to slip. I watched him in wonder, in awe by the raw pleasure twisting his features. We'd never been so close as we were in this moment; he'd never allowed himself to go like this, had never allowed me to see it. He buried himself to the hilt, and his forehead fell against mine.

"Kayla..." He squeezed his eyes shut and moaned. "Baby..."

I buried my hands in his hair, fingers brushing the sweat at his nape. The sound of his vulnerability was the sexiest thing I'd ever heard. He cried out, hoarse and powerful, sensual and conquering, a sound of unstoppable release that poured out of him as he spilled into me.

CHAPTER TWENTY-NINE

Gage gave me the ultimate Vegas experience on our last night in Sin City. Cirque du Soleil, a ridiculously expensive dinner at Guy Savoy—even a helicopter tour at nightfall. He was the epitome of charm, from the way he opened doors for me to the way he guided me with a hand to the small of my back. All the women we came in contact with flirted with him, and he fooled them all into believing the facade.

He'd even fooled me, for a while. But then we'd boarded his jet, and he'd reverted back to the same old Gage by pushing to me to my knees. And I hadn't protested. I'd grown wet between my legs as I swallowed every last drop of him. That was how he'd left me on my doorstep—hot and wanting him, despite the chilly late night air. With one final kiss, a quick brush of his lips to mine, he'd disappeared from my life. Just like that.

That had been two weeks ago.

He'd transferred me to another department the week following our trip, and there'd been no phone calls or demands. He hadn't sought me out once, other than to send a copy of our voided contract. Now I was a bewildered mess because his actions disappointed me. I couldn't explain it—this hollow in my chest he'd left behind. I wanted my freedom, and I still despised him for the way he'd hurt me, but...

I missed him. I missed the way he consumed me, missed the way he sent me crashing into deep space. I thought about scheduling an appointment with a shrink, but the thought of divulging the cause of my stress humiliated me too much. He'd used and abused me, and now that he'd let me go, I couldn't stop thinking about him.

And all the while, Ian stood by, kind, understanding, and displaying the patience of a saint. He'd stopped by every day to see me—at the hospital, at home, even after work. But we didn't talk about it. Gage sat between us, an unspoken entity. My horror at what I'd done—at how easily I'd succumbed to my desire for Gage—made me keep Ian at arm's length.

I wiped the unsettling thoughts from my mind as the elevator approached the fifth floor. The doors slid open, and as a tall brunette entered, I let the tension slowly seep from my body. The doors narrowed toward the center, but a black dress shoe stopped them from completing their slide. Gage's eyes met mine. I sought the farthest corner and tried to fold myself into it—obviously my body understood the threat he represented, even if my heart didn't, and my heart was beating like a caffeinated little drummer boy.

The elevator stopped at the third floor where the woman got off and left Gage and me alone. The air was instantly stifling, heavy with fear and the undeniable spark of sexual tension. I jumped when he moved and studied my shoes upon the funny look he gave me.

"How's Eve?"

"She's good. They're letting her come home tomorrow."

A smile broke out on his face—one so rare I wanted to snap a picture just to have proof that Gage Channing was capable of such a grin. "I'm glad." The doors opened into the parking garage, and without another word, he exited.

I puzzled over the strange encounter as I approached my car, heels tapping an echo through the deserted garage. Gage backed out of his spot and disappeared through the exit, and as I opened my car door, a voice from behind stopped me cold. I jumped and whirled.

Jody stood there, sporting two black eyes and a busted lip.

"Rick's been drinking again." Her mouth trembled, and like a scared child, she folded her arms around herself. "He really had changed, Kayla. He was doing so good." She dropped her arms to her sides and formed two tight fists. "But you kept him away from Eve, and now he's going crazy. Why'd you have to be such a bitch?"

I slammed my door. "Don't you dare put this on me. He's dangerous." I shook my head. "I thought we were friends, Jody. Let me help you."

Her bitter laughter bounced off the walls of the garage. "Friends? We haven't been friends in a long time. Why, Kayla?"

"I-I don't know. Eve got sick..." And I'd checked out on life for a while. I'd lost touch with everyone. "I'm worried about you."

"Well don't. Just quit provoking him already." She took off toward a bright red Honda parked nearby. The tires screeched as she slammed on the gas and raced through the exit.

Her words percolated in my head all evening, an unwanted distraction that intruded on my time with Eve. I tossed and turned next to her for hours after she fell asleep, unable to stop thinking about my encounters with both Gage and Jody.

It was past midnight when I found myself in his driveway. I needed to figure out why he drew me to him like a magnet, regardless of how much he hurt me…would always hurt me. People didn't change, and I wasn't about to kid myself otherwise. He'd always be the same sadistic bastard with a taste for my pain. I shut off the ignition, and the utter quiet of the night surrounded me. Haunted me. Ghosts weren't so easily laid to rest in the still of the night.

Why am I here?

I had no answer—none that made any sense. He'd let me go. I was free…yet here I was walking into the lion's den. My limbs quaked as I approached his door, and I almost turned back. I told myself to turn back, even chanted the words in my mind over and over again as if doing so would be enough to convince me. My traitorous fist wasn't listening; it rose and announced my presence.

Oh God. Oh my freaking God…what the hell am I doing?

I whirled, intending to sprint to my car, but the door opened.

"Kayla?"

Damn. I wished for invisibility as I turned to face him, though I would have settled for the earth fissuring under my feet. The image of him standing there wearing nothing but flannel pajama pants was enough to render me speechless. I'd never seen him in something so casual. I wondered if the fabric was as soft as I imagined. Soft flannel against hard man.

I shouldn't have come. I should have stayed far, far away.

"What are you doing here?"

"Honestly? I don't know."

He quirked a brow. "You don't know?" I shook my head, and the edge of his mouth turned up. "What do you want, Kayla?"

You.

Only I had no idea why. He was like a disease, and the

bad cells had multiplied and taken over. He'd infiltrated my system, and now I couldn't get him out. Even now, standing in the freezing cold, my body flushed with warmth as I liquefied between my legs. Some crazy, destructive instinct rose within me, and I catapulted the last step and launched myself at him. Our mouths crashed together, open and hot and ravenous. We kissed like we were possessed, and maybe we were.

At least I was. I heard the door slam behind us an instant before he released me.

"Get on your knees."

I fell to them without a second thought and reached for the waistband of all that soft flannel. Trembling with impatient desire—and maybe a little fear—I freed his cock and closed my mouth around him. A groan rumbled from his throat, evidence of his tightly held control. He grabbed my head, his hands shaking, and trapped me between them. No way would he allow me control—he was too close to losing it himself.

"Hands behind your back," he ground out between tight lips. I obeyed, and his eyes, so ridiculously blue, never left mine as he fucked my mouth. "Kayla..." His composure fell apart, and his hips took on the rhythm of madness.

I'd never felt so powerful.

He screwed his eyes shut and pushed to the back of my throat, roaring his release as his essence gushed into my mouth. Despite the fact that my panties were drenched, I gagged. Which only meant he shoved his cock deeper. His pleasure wouldn't be complete without my pain.

Still breathing irregularly, he pulled his pants up, and without a word, grabbed my hand. I followed him down to the basement. His fingers tightened around mine, as if he thought I might change my mind and bolt. I was considering it as we reached the last step. He'd had the damage repaired.

The room looked as it always had; painful and cold. A dungeon indeed, though in this case I'd given away the key to my own freedom. I took one look at the St. Andrew's cross and remembered how he'd buried his face between my thighs, and all thoughts of cold evaporated.

He hoisted me against him, and we fell to the bed where he trapped me between his braced arms. "What's your safe word?"

I blinked. I hadn't expected him to give me one. "I-I don't know."

"You don't know much tonight, do you?"

"I know I want you."

His eyes widened, but then his face settled into the Gage I knew and loved to hate.

"I don't want to give you the option of telling me no, but I will. Last chance before I gag you and make you mine."

"I'm already yours." Anyone who could admit such a thing without breaking down must be insane. Which I was.

"Are you seriously arguing with me about a safe word?"

"Master—that's my safe word."

He laughed. "I might have to push you to your hard limits just to hear you say it."

"You could ask nicely."

He grabbed my left wrist and stretched it over my head. "I'm not nice."

"I'm not blind to how cruel you are, Gage." His name rolled off my tongue, forbidden. He clicked the locks in place and bent down to secure my ankles. I was still fully clothed.

"Don't gag me."

"I'll give you one request. Are you sure that's it?"

I scrambled to think of all the bad things. The whips, the nipple clamps, the butt plugs...actually, those weren't too horrible. I nodded. "I'm giving myself to you. Give me the right to cry or scream if I need to." I remembered Vegas and cringed.

Don't make me hold it all in again.

"Okay, no gags, but everything else is fair game."

With those words, he wielded a pocketknife and cut the clothes from my body. I'd been naked in front of him too many times to count, had lost all dignity in front of Ian and Katherine, but something about this time, this night, made me feel more vulnerable in my nudity. I was there of my own free will. He hadn't blackmailed or coaxed me; it was a truth I couldn't hide from, and being spread out before him brought it to the forefront of my mind.

He slid the flannel down his legs and stood tall, naked and unashamed. Gage was a lot of things, but ashamed wasn't one of them. His gaze traveled the length of my body, and his mouth turned up in a smile of conquer. He had me right where he wanted me, and suddenly I wondered if he'd been working toward this all along.

"If I asked you to let me go, would you?"

"If you say your safe word. You're not my slave anymore."

But I was, in all the ways that counted.

He crawled onto the bed and settled between my legs. "If you say it, I'll send you home."

I'd figured as much. It was all or nothing with him. "Sounds to me like establishing a safe word is pointless. If I don't do what you want, you'll just punish me for it by denying me." I yanked at my restraints, but he'd tightened them to the point where my limbs burned from the stretch.

He dropped his face to my stomach, his hair brushing my skin, lips and tongue teasing my belly button. "I don't want to deny you anything." His words vibrated against my belly. He lifted his head. "I want to make you come until you're screaming."

I had no doubt he'd succeed.

"But I like being in control." He dipped his fingers inside me. "If you can't live with that, then you need to leave now."

"I don't want to leave."

"Good, because I don't want you to either."

I couldn't think or breathe after that. He buried his head between my thighs and flicked his tongue across my clit, teasing for what seemed like forever until my fingers and toes were in a constant curl. He must have kept me in that state for an hour, lapping and swirling me to the edge while his fingers caressed my breasts. Unable to stand it any longer, I begged him with every moan.

He finally pulled away.

"Don't stop."

He ignored me and crossed to the other side of the basement, and when he approached the bed again, I knew the games were about to begin. He held three items in his hand; a butt plug, a nasty-looking set of nipple clamps, and a whip...*the* whip...the one he'd used the night he'd fucked me in front of Ian. It was long and thin, and I'd learned from experience how excruciating the strike of that thing was.

I started sobbing at the sight of it. "Don't."

He set the items on the bed, much too calmly, and watched as I pulled at my restraints. He didn't say anything, just waited until my body went limp and I gave up.

"Why?" I tasted the salt of my tears.

"Because I want you to trust me. I screwed up, Kayla." He picked up the whip. "Let me show you that you don't have to be scared of me. You have a safe word. Use it if you need to, and I'll stop."

"You don't need to do this."

"Yes, I do."

Something in the intensity of his expression terrified me, and I suddenly sensed that this was about more than earning my trust. This was the ultimate tipping point.

Either I walked...or I stayed and gave him my pain. Pleasure for pain—it was the way he'd always operated, only now he was giving me a choice, and if I stayed, he really would own me.

He released my ankles and wrists. "Stand up."

I got up and stood before him, trembling and not knowing what to do or say.

Stupid! Say the word and go!

Pressing my lips together, I prepared to form the two syllables that would set me free, but the word lodged in my throat.

"Present your breasts."

"I-I'm not your slave anymore."

"I never said you were." The clamps dangled from his fist, big and clunky and painful-looking.

I folded my arms across my chest. "Why are you doing this?"

"This is who I am." His face hardened. "Hands behind your back now, or I'll make the whipping a punishment."

"There's a difference?"

"Yes, and you're going to learn what it is."

Go, go, go!

I couldn't budge, couldn't make my voice work. Slowly, I brought my hands behind me and clasped them together. He bent down and sucked at each nipple until they peaked. He took his time clamping them.

I gritted my teeth, squeezed my eyes shut and held my breath, but the pain didn't subside.

"Bend over the bed."

My mind shut down. It seemed like a bad dream, like someone else was obeying his every command. He slipped the plug in, and intense vibrations drowned out the agony of the clamps. And then he was whipping me, blazing caresses against my bottom. It hurt—I couldn't deny it—but he was holding back, and some of the strikes were so light, they were a tease.

"Stand up," he ordered.

I obeyed, but lost my balance and almost tipped over.

"Hold onto the footboard for support." He left a trail of fire down my right butt cheek, and I reached out and gripped the wood, breasts heavy and aching as the chain swung between them.

"Spread your legs."

His commands continued to come in clipped words, and I followed every one. I didn't allow myself to think beyond the sting of his whip. If I allowed awareness in, I knew I wouldn't like what I'd find. The strap snaked around my hip and kissed my crotch, eliciting a moan from my throat. He put more strength into it, and the caress became pain. I cried out—a plea for him to stop…a plea for him to continue.

"Master."

The whip thumped to the floor. "Is that your safe word?"

"I don't know." I shook my head. "No. Don't make me leave."

He pressed against me, chest to back, groin to buttocks, one hand pulling at the clamps as the other dipped inside wet need. "You're not going anywhere." His lips and tongue devoured my neck, and I moaned again, my center clenching as an orgasm built.

"I'm so close," I whispered.

"Not yet." He turned me around to face him. "Are you scared of me?"

"Yes." I said it without hesitation. I was scared of him all right—terrified of what he made me feel.

"You don't need to be." He grabbed the chain linking my breasts and tugged. "I want you in my bed." He picked me up and stomped up the steps, and as we entered his bedroom, I wondered how many other women he'd brought into this room. I couldn't stop from voicing the question.

He went rigid. "Why?"

"I'm curious." I sank into his mattress and stared up at him, waiting to see if he'd answer.

Our eyes connected and held. Long seconds passed, but he didn't answer until after he'd removed the clamps. "No one else has been in here but you." He plunged into me, and I was lost.

Warm fingers feathered down my spine. I was sprawled on my stomach, sinking into the softness of the mattress and the allure of sleep. I hadn't slept late in a long time, but judging from the brightness behind my eyelids, I guessed it was at least nine. I snuggled closer to the warm body pressed against my side, glad that it was Saturday and I didn't have to get out of bed at the crack of dawn. He draped a leg over mine and splayed his fingers across my ass.

"Why did you cry last night?"

My eyes popped open, and I met Gage's questioning stare. "I don't know."

He swept my hair aside and kissed my shoulder. "Yes you do. I won't allow you to keep secrets from me. That hasn't changed."

I shrugged him off and scooted to the edge of the bed. "Last night was a mistake."

"You came to me, remember?"

I did remember, which made the light of day more difficult to face. Every time I was near him, I lost another piece of myself. "I shouldn't have come."

"But you did, and you screamed while doing it."

"That's not what I meant, and you know it."

The bed dipped, and his fingers curled around my side. "Then why did you come back?"

"Because you live inside of me!" I jumped up and whirled around to face him. "I can't eat, I can't sleep, I can't get you out of my head. And this is so wrong. You're a fucking monster, Gage, and you keep pulling me in. Are you happy now?"

"I'm happy you're in my bed. I'm not happy that you're still fighting it."

"Fighting what?"

"You and me."

"There is no you and me!" I searched the floor for my clothes until I remembered that he'd cut them from my body. "I need something to wear. I have to be at the hospital soon." Eve was coming home today, and I didn't have the time or energy to argue with him. Her discharge changed everything. This had to end.

He slid out of bed and opened the door to a walk-in closet bigger than my bathroom. "Not the most fashionable, but they should fit." He handed me a pair of sweatpants with a drawstring waist and a large T-shirt. "You look sexy in anything you wear."

I clutched them to my bare chest and inhaled a whiff of the detergent he used. Damn him. That scent would always remind me of him. Avoiding his gaze, I dressed quickly and left his bedroom. Taking a detour to the basement, I wedged my feet into my shoes and headed toward the front door. He followed, completely naked, his towering form on my heels the whole way. I reached for the handle, but he pulled me against him.

"Stop fighting it, Kayla."

"It's just sex."

"Didn't we already have this conversation?"

I glared at him. "Apparently you need to hear it again. I'm not in love with you."

"I never said you were. This isn't about love. It's about connecting, and you damn well know we connect."

"Again...*just* sex." I pushed against him, but he refused to let go. "You're the last person I want around my daughter. She deserves better." *I* deserved better. "I'm done here." I untangled myself from his arms.

He smirked and leaned in until our noses almost touched. "You'll be back."

"I won't." I left the house, slid into the driver's seat of my car, and met his steady gaze from across the driveway. God, the man stood buck-naked in his doorway. He truly had no shame. A knowing glint lingered in the depths of his sapphire eyes. Smug bastard. He was one hundred percent certain I'd be back, begging him to take me.

At that precise moment, I knew he was right. I'd come back again and again, a glutton for his sadism. I'd lie down and let him do whatever he wanted—I was that addicted to him. I could think of no other way out, other than going cold turkey. I'd have to leave town—that seemed the best way to wash him from my life. Leaving wasn't going to be easy. I'd need to make preparations, get clearance from Eve's doctor, and find a place with an excellent children's cancer treatment center.

It was going to take some time and a lot of creative penny pinching, but I could do this...I only hoped he didn't ruin me in the meantime.

I backed down his driveway, and on my way to the hospital, I stopped by my apartment to shower and change. Eve was already picking at her lunch tray when I entered her room. Ian sat next to her, his bagged lunch open in his lap. They were watching Dora, and something about seeing a grown man watch a cartoon with a three-year-old floored me. This wasn't the first time I'd found him in her room, sharing lunch or playing a game with her.

Spotting me in the doorway, she broke into a huge smile. She jumped from bed and crashed into my arms with the power of a locomotive. The urge to cry overwhelmed me. Happy tears because Eve was healthy again, and desperate tears because I was so mixed up on the inside. I pushed it down and focused on her, on this day—the day she was coming home. She'd come so far. Just four weeks ago, I'd thought she wasn't going to make it.

I had Gage to thank for the reality of her in my arms.

"Hi, baby. Sorry I'm late." I deposited her in bed and took the seat next to her. "What're you having for lunch?"

"Yucky peas." She made a face, and I laughed.

Ian grinned at me from the other side of her bed. "No amount of bribing works. She won't touch them. She did eat the macaroni and cheese though." He rose to his feet and gestured toward the door. "Can I talk to you for a minute?"

"Sure." I swallowed my nervousness as he ushered me into the hall. He guided me down the corridor to where the elevators where. "Where are we going?" I asked.

"My office. We need some privacy for this conversation."

I already dreaded what was coming. He'd given me plenty of space during the past two weeks, never voicing the questions he tried to hide. Apparently, that was about to change. We descended two floors, and he led me down a maze of hallways.

"How do you keep from getting lost?"

His mouth turned up as he unlocked the door to what I guessed was his office. "Trust me, I still get lost sometimes." We entered a small, tidy space, and he pulled out a chair. "Have a seat."

I sat twiddling my thumbs as he settled next to me.

"What's this about, Ian?" Something about the uncertain set of his mouth made my heart jump.

"I know the timing is shitty. You're about to bring Eve home, and this definitely isn't how I'd envisioned doing this..." He let out a breath and stood, and my heart started pounding when he bent to one knee. "But I love you, Kayla. I've spent the past seven years trying to right wrongs, trying to be good enough." He withdrew a white box from the pocket of his slacks and opened it to reveal a tasteful solitaire. "Marry me." His fingers curled around mine and squeezed. "I want to be here for you and Eve."

I blinked, but the room wouldn't stop spinning. His face swam in my vision. "I...I can't."

"If this is about Gage..." He trailed off and lowered his head. "If it's about that last weekend you spent with him, I don't need to know about it. It's in the past. You did what you had to do. I understand that."

"You don't understand." My voice cracked, and when he looked up, my tears spilled over.

"You're in love with him? Kayla...what he did to you...

"I'm not in love with him." I blinked and prepared to spill my guts. I hadn't wanted him to know what I'd done, but he deserved the truth; at the very least, he deserved an explanation. "I went back to him last night. He didn't blackmail me, didn't force me. It was all me."

He glanced up, his pain evident in the firm set of his jaw. "I don't believe you."

I swiped rivulets of moisture from my cheeks. "I slept with him. I even let him whip me." Burying my face in my hands, I mumbled, "I don't deserve you."

He pulled my hands away. "Look at me."

"I'm going to leave town as soon as I can."

"No." He shook his head. "Don't leave. You mean everything to me. You think you don't deserve me? It's the other way around, Kayla." He swallowed, and his hands trembled as he dragged them through his hair. "I'm not innocent in all this. Whatever you feel for him...he brainwashed you, but I put you in that position."

I shook my head. "You didn't know he was blackmailing me. It was a simple hug. Gage went off the deep end all on his own and for no reason at all."

"I'm not talking about that. I'm talking about the reason he's doing this to you." He sucked in a deep breath. "I haven't been honest with you. There are things in my past I never told you about."

Suddenly, the subtle, white noise of the hospital roared in my ears; the soft scuff of sneakers padding down the hall, and the ticking of the clock above the door of his office. My gaze touched on everything but him—the framed degrees and certificates on the walls, the filing cabinets, and the picture sitting on the desk of an older woman with two little boys. Obviously, he shared the space with a colleague. Somewhere in the back of my mind, I realized how these inane thoughts provided a distraction. A much needed one, because no way was I ready to hear whatever he was about to say. He had yet to utter a word, yet I already felt the impact of what remained unspoken in the pit of my stomach.

He got up and paced the floor, growing more agitated with each step. "I was young and stupid, and I've lived with the shame for over a decade now. I've spent every moment since trying to make up for it."

I cleared my throat. "Make up for what?"

"I was sixteen, popular and on top of the world, and my parents idolized me. All my dad cared about was my future in football. I was barely a junior, but I already had scouts looking at me. One night...it was just one night, but that night changed everything. It's the reason I became a doctor."

"What are you trying to tell me?"

"I'm saying that everything he's done to you is my fault." He fell into the chair beside me and dragged his hands through his hair. "I got drunk at a party...and was stupid enough to get behind the wheel."

A deep chill speared through me. "What happened?" I asked, my voice barely a whisper.

"I rolled the car." He buried his face in his hands for a moment, and when he looked up, his hazel eyes shone bright with the guilt he carried. "I had no business being with her in the first place, but she was older, and I fell hard."

I knew what was coming next. I knew, but I didn't want to hear it.

"Liz died. I killed her, and Gage has never forgiven me."

"How..." I cleared my throat. "How do you know him?"

He visibly gulped, as if he could swallow the words and keep them locked away forever. "He's my brother."

CHAPTER THIRTY-ONE

Did everyone lie and keep secrets? The question looped in my mind as I unstrapped Eve from her car seat and helped her to her feet. She took off running toward our doorstep, and I scrambled to catch up with her, despising my state of distraction.

"Eve, wait for mommy." I felt sick on the inside, disoriented, as if someone had turned me upside down and let all sense of reality tumble out. I couldn't form a coherent thought. It was all garbled words and phrases coming together in my head, and none of it made sense.

"Mommy, what's wrong?"

Even she could pick up on my chaotic state of mind. "Nothing, baby." I faked a smile for her sake and pushed the door open into our dark apartment. I flicked on the light, so distracted that I didn't realize anything was wrong until it was too late. The cold, hard barrel of a gun pressed into the back of my head, and though I couldn't see him, I immediately recognized the familiarity of his body pressing against my backside.

"Go to your room, Eve," he ordered. "I need to talk to mommy for a while."

Her wide eyes met mine, much too knowing for a three-year-old. A tear fell down my cheek as I forced another smile. "It's okay. Go. I bought you a doll. It's on your bed."

She hesitated, but the promise of a new toy lured her to safety.

Neither of us moved or said a word at first. The scent of his cologne, tarnished by the stench of whiskey, burned my nose. I swallowed the vomit rising in my throat. "What do you want?"

"What do you think I want?" he snapped.

"I don't know."

He snorted. "Don't play dumb. You know I can't stand it when you lie."

"I'm not lying. Please...don't hurt us." He nudged the barrel into my scalp, and I squeezed my eyes shut.

"I'd never hurt my daughter, but you're gonna pay." He pushed me further into the living room, but a knock on the front door halted him. "Fuck." Changing tactics, he tugged me in the direction of the door and folded his large body in the corner, keeping the gun trained on me. "Expecting someone?"

I shook my head.

"Good. Get rid of them." His gaze, colorless in a face that was too quick to deceive, leveled me. "Don't do anything stupid."

I turned the handle and peered out, and as I met Gage's stare, every part of me froze. I wanted to beg for his help, but Rick still had his gun pressed into my back.

"We're not done yet, Kayla," Gage leaned forward. "You're nuts if you think you can show up on my doorstep and pretend it didn't happen."

I raised my hand to ward him off. "I just got home with Eve. Can we talk about this another time?"

His eyes narrowed and then traveled the length of my body. "Are you okay?"

"Yeah, I'm fine."

His attention darted behind me, and he scanned the small space of my foyer.

"You need to leave." I slammed the door.

"Smooth move," Rick admonished. "You suck at acting normal." He pushed me into the living room and toward the couch. "You better hope he doesn't come back." Knocking me to my knees, he muttered, "Stubborn whore."

"Don't do this. Please."

"Shut up." He bent me over the cushion and jerked my hands behind my back.

"Please, Rick."

Blinding pain exploded at my temple. "I said shut up."

"Please," I begged again as he secured my wrists with rope.

He whacked me on the other side of the head and grabbed my hair, pulling tight. "Did you enjoy fucking him?"

"He forced me."

"But you liked it, didn't you? You keep going back."

I struggled to breathe, but my fear was too intense.

"Did your fucking vows mean nothing? You think you can forget about me so easily?"

"No," I choked. "I haven't forgotten you."

He laughed, a sound that struck more terror in me than any strike from Gage. "I'll make sure you don't forget me." He got up, and his shoes thudded across the carpet. He dragged a chair to Eve's door and wedged it underneath the handle. "You didn't think I'd miss my daughter's homecoming, did you?" The floor vibrated as he neared. "You and me are gonna celebrate all right. You owe me three years of fucking, Kayla."

He kneeled behind me and wrenched up my skirt, and I started sobbing, barely able to see through my tears. "Don't do this—"

"Did he fuck you in the ass? I hear he has a thing for that."

He shoved my face into the cushion, smothering my cries, and suddenly the memories flooded me. I'd almost forgotten how many times he'd choked me, how he'd smothered me with a pillow on a nightly basis. So many times I thought I was going to die, but then he'd allow me a gasp of air before continuing his suffocation methods.

"I bet he did do you up the ass." He pushed my legs together, tugged my panties down, and I heard the slide of a zipper.

I struggled, my lungs burning for life as the futility of my situation fisted my heart. He pulled my head up, allowed me a shallow breath, and then forced my face into the cushion again. I was going to die. The certainty of it gripped me, and I was no longer scared of being raped. Death was far worse. Death would take me away from Eve.

Eve.

Would he leave me like this? Lifeless for her to find?

Or would he disappear with her?

Head up...another gasp of air...then lightheaded darkness.

A loud, splintering crash tore through the apartment, and his hold on my head lifted. With a hoarse sob, I jerked my face up and sucked in air. Sucked it in until my lungs were full and near bursting. A grunt sounded, followed by a bang against the wall, and I rolled around to find Gage and my ex locked in a struggle. Eve screamed from her bedroom, tiny fists pounding on the door, and the chair shook under the force. I yanked at the rope binding my wrists, desperate to get to her, but the binding wouldn't budge.

"Stop it!" I yelled as the barrel inched toward Gage's head. They were engaged in a war, both exerting their strength to gain control of the gun. Gage was taller, but Rick had some bulk on him. He managed to kick free of Rick's hold for a moment, and Rick jumped to his feet and swung the gun in my direction. Time stopped as I stared past the barrel into his cold eyes. Nothing lurked in their depths; no regret, no anger. Just...nothing.

How had I missed this side of him all those years ago? The side of him that ignored his daughter's screams as he prepared to kill me once and for all?

"Please," I whispered, one last plea for mercy.

He cocked the gun.

Gage leaped into action, face distorted in the scariest mask of rage I'd ever seen. He charged Rick, a bull with red in his sights. They fell to the floor again, rolling, fists pounding, frantic fingers scrambling in a tug-of-war for the gun. The blast tore through the air just as the blaring sirens became noticeable.

Rick got to his feet and staggered back. He focused on the blood swallowing the front of his jacket, and for a moment he was entranced by it, the gun dangling from his fingers in distraction. And then he focused his attention on the broken door. The screeching sirens grew louder with every second.

He bolted, and I took in Gage's still form lying a few feet from me, watched the crimson spread across my carpet, and the sirens drowned out the hysterical cries of an innocent three-year-old.

And I welcomed blackness.

CHAPTER THIRTY-TWO

Snow trickled from the sky three days after Gage was shot. Not so much that driving in it was impossible, but enough to cause a stir of excitement. Normally, I would have been out in the wintery flakes like everyone else, throwing snowballs at Eve while we built a snowman. I watched the wintery weather through the window of the cheap motel we'd been hiding in. Eve was taking a late morning nap. Check out time was an hour away.

I couldn't bring myself to move. I was too busy torturing myself with what-ifs, too busy being a coward because I still didn't know if Gage had lived or died. Three days...and I didn't know if he'd died saving our lives. What kind of person did that make me? I'd left the emergency room three nights ago and hadn't looked back, and my phone had been powered off since. Ian was probably frantic by now trying to get ahold of me. But reality wouldn't step aside forever. I reached for my cell and switched it on, and I dialed Ian's number. He answered immediately.

"Where are you?"

"In a motel."

"I've been going out of my mind, Kayla. You freaking disappeared from the ER. Don't do that to me again."

"Is..." I swallowed and tried again. "Is he okay?"

"He's going to make it. They had to operate, but he's recovering." A train's horn blasted in the background, and I released a breath. "Where are you?" he asked.

I blinked a tear down my cheek. "Doesn't matter. I'm leaving today."

"Not without saying goodbye, you aren't."

I rattled off the name of the motel.

"Don't go anywhere. I'll be there in twenty."

By the time he pulled into the parking lot, Eve was already in her car seat munching on a graham cracker. I tossed our meager belongings into the trunk and slammed the lid.

"I can't talk you into staying, can I?"

"No. Eve's been having nightmares every night. I think a new environment would be good for her." I'd had nightmares too—paralyzing recollections of Rick trying to kill me. I leaned against the bumper. "Is he really okay?"

"That's what they tell me. He won't see me, but I hear he's been asking for you." He rubbed his chin. "I shouldn't have asked you to marry me. It was...selfish. I knew you were dealing with some stuff, but I was scared of losing you."

I dropped my gaze to the ground and kicked at the snow. "It was so long ago. Maybe what we feel for each other is an echo of what we could've been. Maybe we've been holding on when it's time to let go."

He tilted my chin up, and a snowflake danced on my nose. "I can't control how you feel, but I know what's in here," he said, placing his fist over his heart. "You've been here forever. It's always been you." He paused and gave a stubborn shake of his head. "I distracted myself with work, but I've never been able to get you out of my head."

His words squeezed the breath from me. "Don't do this to me now. I won't change my mind about leaving."

"I know, and that's why I'm not going to stop you. I know you need time. Maybe I do too." He stepped close and framed my face between his hands, and the warmth of his body penetrated mine. "I meant what I said, though. I love you, and no amount of time is going to change that." He wound his arms around me, and we held on to each other for a while, neither of us paying attention to the snow collecting in our hair. Another guest of the motel left his room and gave us a curious look as he headed to his car. Vehicles crept along the road, and one braked, going into a slide before stopping.

I wanted to hold on to him forever, frozen in this cold environment as the warmth of him surrounded me.

"Don't let him hurt you again."

"He can't hurt me if I'm not here."

"You don't know him very well."

"Turns out I didn't know you either." I backed out of his embrace. "Why didn't you tell me he was your brother? You watched"—I blinked the image from my mind's eye, but it refused to disappear—"you watched him with me. You screwed Katherine when all you had to do was be honest."

He kept his eyes downcast, and the guilt he wrestled with pricked at the part of me that still cared about him. Still loved him even. "I was stunned...when you came into that basement and got to your knees..." He shook his head, apparently at a loss for words. "And then I realized what was at stake...Jesus, Kayla. Your freedom, Eve's life. You begged me to go along with it, and I couldn't deny you."

"But you didn't tell me. You had every opportunity to, but you didn't."

"Chalk it up to cowardice. He'd ripped a hole in your life

and it was my fault." He pinched the bridge of his nose and closed his eyes. "I shouldn't have come back to town."

"Gage is a grown man. Don't beat yourself up over his actions. None of us are innocent, me included. I stole from him."

"To save your daughter. My crime killed someone. Yours saved the person you love most in this world."

"Doesn't make it right."

"No, but you shouldn't have a problem sleeping at night. At least, I hope you don't."

I refrained from answering—maybe someday I'd be able to let it all go. "Would you mind taking Eve to get something to eat? I could use an hour alone."

"You're going to see him, aren't you?"

I nodded. "I need to."

"There's something you should know. They found Rick, and when they arrested him, he turned everything he had on Gage over to the authorities. They've begun an investigation, and Gage is probably going to serve some time in jail."

"What about Jody?"

"They arrested her this morning."

I shook my head. "Typical. Of course Rick threw her under the rug. How did you find out about this?"

"They questioned me. The Feds didn't understand that Gage and I haven't talked in years. I expect they'll want to talk to you too." He grabbed Eve from the car before unbuckling her seat and pulling it out. "I'll meet up with you soon."

"Thanks, Ian."

I didn't budge for a full five minutes after he left. Finally sinking into the driver's seat, I pulled onto the road and took the long way to the hospital. I dreaded this visit. I had so much to say, so much to confront him about, and no words in mind. He didn't notice me at first, as he was too busy arguing with the nurse about taking his vitals, a deep scowl on his face. I stood in the doorway and stared at the flakes coming down outside his window.

"Get the doctor. I don't need my fucking vitals taken for the hundredth time—I need out of here *now*." And that's when he saw me. He froze, which gave the nurse the opportunity to complete her task. Noting the readings in his chart, she then frowned at him on her way out, making it clear he was not her favorite patient.

"Made anyone quit yet?" I forced a smile and took a step toward him, hoping to break the tense silence.

"I'm working on it." He leaned back against the pillows and winced.

"How are you doing?" I asked.

"Not too bad, all things considered." He frowned. "I wasn't sure if you were going to come."

"I wasn't sure either." I wandered around the room, finally stalling in front of the window, and became entranced by the falling snow. "I wanted to thank you for saving us, but Eve and I are leaving and we won't be back." I turned to face him. "I'll leave my resignation on your desk before I go."

"So that's it? You're just going to leave?"

I nodded. "I think the best thing for us is to move on from here."

He let out a bitter laugh. "You mean move on from me."

"You're part of it, yes. But I want her to have a happy life. She's been through so much."

"So have you."

"You're partly to blame for that."

He clenched his jaw. "I'm aware of that."

"Why didn't you tell me Ian was your brother?"

His eyes rounded, an unguarded second in which he couldn't hide his reaction, but then he smoothed his features. "*Half* brother. His dad's a bastard. Couldn't stand me." He studied me for a moment. "What else did he have the guts to tell you?"

"He told me about Liz."

"And now you're thinking I did this to you as a means of getting back at him."

"Didn't you?"

"It started out that way, Kayla. I won't lie. I wanted to make him pay. I still do." His attention veered past me, and he grew lost in memories of the past. "His old man got him off with a slap to the wrist. I wanted to hurt him all right."

"Maybe you should let it go."

"So that's what you think I should do? Let him get away with murder?"

"Like I've let you get away with beating and raping me?" My words brought his gaze back to mine. "You made me pay for his sins, Gage. Now let it go."

"Who's going to pay for mine?"

"I hear you are."

"Guess he's given you an earful. So you heard about the investigation?"

I folded my arms and nodded. "What I don't understand is why you did it. You're not hurting for money."

"Not now, but that wasn't the case during the recession. I did it to save the company." He paused. "I repaid every cent. That's when I realized Jody had been skimming too."

"Do I have to worry about going to jail, Gage?"

"No. I covered your tracks. If it comes up, I'll take the blame."

My mouth hung open. "Why would you do that?"

"You've paid enough. Go be with your daughter, Kayla."

That was one order from Gage Channing I could obey without hesitation. I stalled, my hand on the door handle as the heat of his gaze seared my back. "Goodbye, Gage."

CHAPTER THIRTY-THREE

One year later

"Kayla, he's staring at your butt again." My coworker's declaration made my eyes go wide.

"Stop it!" I hissed at Stacey. "He is not."

"Oh yes, honey," she drawled, her Texas accent pronounced, "he is."

I cranked my head to find that Stacey was right. Nate was a regular customer, and he focused on my ass now as if it looked tastier than the Gigi's breakfast special sitting in front of him.

"How are the eggs, Nate?"

He blinked and then lowered his head. "Great as always, Kayla."

Stacey snickered. "He'll ask you out eventually, mark my words."

I hoped not—it would save me the trouble of rejecting him. I'd waitressed at Gigi's for eight months now, and luckily most guys who pursued me quickly got the message. Stacey and I had gotten close, but she didn't know about my past. No one did, and that was part of the allure of starting over in a town where no one knew me.

Yet something was missing...or rather *someone.*

My demons had relocated with me. Both Gage and Ian stalked the shadows in my bedroom at night, and I spent too much time lying awake. Eve's nightmares lessened over time, but mine hadn't. It didn't matter if the days were getting easier to get through—it was during those few dark hours when echoes of the past haunted me that I realized how weak I still was.

How broken.

Thankfully, I couldn't say the same for Eve. She was doing well, physically and emotionally, and she continued to provide the brightest part of my day. She'd started preschool four months ago, and I'd watched her blossom since. Ian's phone calls also brightened my days, though lately the tone of them had changed. I knew he missed me, and I felt the same way, though I questioned what it was about him that I missed exactly. It was a myriad of things—the sense of security I always felt in his presence, the way his kiss set my head spinning, the fact that I trusted him with my daughter...I could fill pages upon pages.

I missed Gage for other reasons...reasons that reinforced how lonely I really was.

Once my shift ended, I said goodbye to Stacey and promised to meet her on Saturday for a movie. She also had a child—a boy a year older than Eve. They said they were getting married someday. We laughed about their innocent childhood dreams, but deep inside, the idea bothered me. Kids often said such things, but the thought of Eve ever getting married, of subjecting herself to the cruelty of a man, terrified me. I'd grown so distrustful and paranoid that it put the term "jaded" to shame.

On my way home, I picked Eve up from daycare. The last

thing I expected was to find an unfamiliar vehicle in my driveway. My world screeched to a halt at the sight of the man who unfolded from it. He leaned against his door and waited as I let Eve out of her booster seat. I hoisted her in my arms and carried her toward the door.

"Hello, Kayla."

"Hi..." My head spun with the reality of his presence. An entire year had passed since I'd walked away from my old life, and somewhere deep inside, I'd always known he'd come for me, but I hadn't allowed myself to dwell on that eventuality.

"Can I come in?"

"Sure." I pushed the door open. The duplex was small, but the place offered more room than our apartment had back in Oregon. "Just let me put on a cartoon for Eve." I got her settled in the living room with a snack, and then I ushered him into the kitchen. He leaned against the counter and silently watched as I turned on the oven and arranged chicken breasts in a baking dish. I kept myself busy with mindless tasks for several minutes, my heart tap dancing the whole time.

He was suddenly behind me, his hands on mine, pressing them to the counter and halting my movements. "Stop."

I went still. It'd been so long since a man had touched me. Months, though it seemed more like years.

He wrapped his arms around me and buried his face against my neck, inhaling as if he'd thirsted for the scent of me. "I've missed you." He tightened his hold. "So much."

I closed my eyes and focused on the weight of his arms across my chest, rising and falling with every breath. "Why are you here?"

"Isn't it obvious?"

Several moments passed, and I finally spoke the words I

wanted to say. "I've missed you too." I ran a finger along his forearm. "But—"

"Don't shut me out, Kayla."

Shutting him out was impossible. Always had been.

"Can you get a sitter for tonight?" he asked.

I nodded without thinking. Stacey would look after her, but why would I need a sitter? I voiced the question.

"Because I'm going to show you how much I've missed you." He reached into my purse and dug for a few moments until he produced my cell. He held it out. "Get a sitter."

My fingers curled around the phone, hesitating. I could send him away. He'd go—I knew he would. And I would go about my life in peace. In peace and alone, always keeping everyone outside the bubble I'd built, unable to let anyone in.

And I would never feel this way again.

Taking a deep breath, I opened the phone and dialed.

BOOK TWO

THE DEVIL'S CLAIM

"Lust is the devil's counterfeit for love. There is nothing more beautiful on earth than a pure love and there is nothing so blighting as lust."

—D.L. Moody.

CHAPTER ONE

He's waiting...and I could barely breathe in the small space of my bathroom. I gripped the sink, fingers curling around cold porcelain, and willed my galloping heartbeat to slow. He was going to hurt me. Physically, emotionally, psychologically. I knew this, yet it wouldn't change a thing. I would still unlock the door. Still pull it open and go to him...still give him my body.

"What the hell are you doing?" I asked my reflection. "Why are you letting him back into your life?"

The panicked woman in the mirror didn't have an answer.

I turned on the faucet in the tub and then removed my clothes, and for a few moments I concentrated on the roar of the water even though it did nothing to silence the alarm going off in my head. I hadn't been with a man in a year; a very long and lonely year, especially after experiencing how earth-shattering sex with him was. He'd given me a taste of something I hadn't realized I needed.

Like a dope dealer dangling a sample enough times until

he had me coming back for more, begging on my hands and knees and selling my self-worth *and* my soul.

A soft knock startled me. "Kayla? Is everything okay?"

I warily glanced at the door, as if he could bypass the lock and come inside. He was good at bypassing things—my protests, my will, even the damn law.

"I'm fine." My voice broke, giving away my shattered state of mind. "I'll be out in a few."

"I'll be in the bedroom. Don't make me wait long."

My body broke out in goose bumps, and I couldn't decide if they were the good or bad kind. I sank into the hot water, closed my eyes, and let myself remember. The first time he'd slid his fingers inside me, he'd had me strung up on my toes, gagged and thighs spread wide. I'd been helpless and terrified. That fear still lived in me, but so did the undeniable longing to be taken by him again. I throbbed all over just thinking about his hands on me.

Fear and arousal—why those two visceral reactions went hand in hand for me, I didn't know. I might never know.

I finished bathing, and twenty minutes later, I stood in front of the door, my hand trembling on the knob. The comforting scent of coconut wafted from my warm, naked skin. Skin he'd left bruises and welts on a year ago.

This was a bad idea. Seriously, in the history of bad ideas, I'd win the award.

Here goes nothing.

The darkness of the hallway swallowed me, and I blinked my vision into focus as I padded to the bedroom. He'd turned off all the lights; now only the soft glow of the nightlight I left on for Eve illuminated the way. Thinking about her twisted my insides. My daughter's presence was the only thing that would stop me now, but I'd sent her away with Stacey for the night.

I'd left myself with no way out.

The door to my bedroom stood wide open, like a gaping hole waiting to suck me inside. Or maybe it was the man waiting in there, reeling me in with his gravitational pull. My heart thudded with each step, and I couldn't deny the dampness collecting at the juncture of my sex. He hadn't even touched me yet, but just the knowledge of him waiting, of what he could do to me—what he *would* do to me—made me tense with equal amounts of dread and anticipation.

I stepped into the bedroom, and his body brushed mine. He stood behind me, radiating heat and arousal; the air was so thick with it, I smelled it, tasted it. His hands drifted down my arms, his fingers curling around my wrists like shackles. He pulled them behind my back and secured them with something soft and silky.

"Gage?" His name came out a shaky sigh, escaping my trembling lips and no doubt making him rock hard. I was scared. I couldn't help it, couldn't hide it, despite knowing how he thrived on my fear—how he'd *always* thrived on my fear. The pain he'd inflicted a year ago came rushing back, and I couldn't catch my breath. A year was a long time, but not long enough to make me forget. "I can't do this," I whispered, struggling to speak each word.

"Quiet." He spoke the command in a soft and gentle tone, yet the steel behind that single word ensured I pressed my lips together. "I'm going to make you come long and hard tonight, so long as you don't fight me."

"You know I can't," I choked, blinking back tears. "But I'm scared."

He fisted my hair, pulling until my neck became vulnerable to his mouth. His lips parted against my skin, and his tongue left a hot, wet trail down to my shoulder. The sensation was so arousing that my insides clenched from that single erotic kiss. I swayed into his body, feeling every hard plane of his nakedness, and shivered.

"I love your fear," he said, his confession rumbling along my shoulder. "But you don't have to be scared. Have you fucked anyone else?"

"No."

"Good."

His arms enfolded me and his palms shelved my breasts, thumbs and forefingers squeezing and twisting my nipples as he walked me further into the room. As soon as my thighs hit the mattress, he stepped away. I followed his progress around the bed, unashamed of blatantly ogling him. The soft light from the hall cast a glow on his skin, and I realized his body was just as firm as I remembered. If he hadn't tied my hands, I'd smooth them over his pecs, drifting lower until the muscles of his stomach quivered under my touch. Was he even capable of reacting like that? I couldn't recall; the past was a foggy recollection of pain intermingled with pleasure so hot it had branded me all those months ago.

He climbed onto the bed and stretched on his back. "Come straddle me."

Joining him became a challenge, considering he'd restrained my hands behind my back, but I managed to press one knee onto the mattress and hop up. His large hands reached for my hips, and my head spun as he settled me against the hard length of his cock. A simple adjustment, and he'd be inside me. A delicious shudder seized my body.

"Have you thought about me, Kayla? About this?"

Only every night. I blinked, refusing to give voice to the truth.

He dug his fingers into my hipbones. "Answer me."

My eyes drifted shut, and a small moan formed in my throat then broke free when he arched into me, just enough to tease. "Yes," I said with a groan. "I thought about you."

His hands glided up my sides and cupped my breasts. With a whimper, I leaned into his touch. "I thought of nothing else," he said. "A whole year thinking about you, of the way you smell..." He pulled my head down to his. "The way you taste." His mouth urged mine open, and his tongue swept inside for a mere second before he pushed me into a sitting position again. "It's not enough. I want to taste you all over."

I gasped when he hauled me up his body.

Oh God.

I lost my balance and almost hit the headboard, but his hands braced me as he settled me over his face. I remembered the measure of his strength when he'd whipped me a year ago, and now he held me upright with that strength. My thighs shook as he licked between my folds. He found my nub and added enough pressure until I was bucking my hips and moaning his name, but each time release threatened to take me, he went back to teasing with the tip of his tongue.

"Please," I begged, panting, "let me come. It's been so long."

He groaned. "You're so fucking perfect. So wet." In one swift motion, he moved me down his body and entered me.

"Oh!" This was what I'd been missing—feeling him pulsing and alive inside me.

"Ride me until you come."

My hair curtained my cheeks in red waves, falling into my eyes as I rocked my hips, and I moaned with every slow slide. The sensation was both ecstasy and excruciating. He held onto my hips, never allowing me to fully sheath him, but I needed him deep.

"Please..."

"Who am I, Kayla?"

I groaned. "My Master." A loud cry poured from me. "Gage...deeper..."

He pushed higher. So incredibly deep. Oh God, he felt amazing—one hundred percent man, hard and slick and rubbing all the right places. Our bodies slapped together, damp with sweat and pure madness, and my name rumbled from his lips as he thrust to the hilt.

But it still wasn't enough, and he must have realized it too. The room spun, and I was on my back with him hovering over me. His breaths came hard and fast as he pressed me into the mattress, settled my ankles high onto his shoulders, and made our bodies one with abandon.

"So fucking good," he growled, burying his cock so deep a pang resonated in my heart. "You're mine. I'm never letting you go." He expelled a long sigh, and I drank him in, growing dizzy from the poison that was Gage. His mouth crushed mine, opening and plundering, tongue thrusting in time with our bodies.

My hands bit into my lower back, and my shoulders burned from being restrained, but the pain didn't register. Exquisite tension started in the arch of my feet, in the muscles of my legs, and crawled up my thighs until it pulled so tight at my core I was about to burst at the seams.

His mouth ate up my cries as the intensity pulled me under before launching me free. I came and came and came in a shuddering ball of surrender, soaring to a realm so high I was sure the crash would kill me, but damn if it wasn't a place I wanted to visit every night of my life.

Nothing had ever felt so wrong but so right, so painful yet unbelievably good, and nothing and no one existed in that moment except Gage Channing.

CHAPTER TWO

"God, you're gorgeous." His whispered words woke me, though I didn't let him know I was awake. Early light crept beneath my lashes, and I listened to the morning song of birds, fearing he heard the drumming beat of my heart over the chirping melody.

His arms pulled me closer, flush against his chest, and he spooned me as if he didn't intend to let go. "I know you're awake."

"Pretend I'm not," I said, voice raspy from sleep. I wanted to pretend last night hadn't happened. Pretend I still had a modicum of sanity left. I'd built a life here for Eve and me, and I wasn't foolish enough to think that letting him back in wouldn't smash it to smithereens.

"I'm not good at pretending." His breath hitched, and for a few lengthy seconds, his silence pressed on me. "I need you. I need you so damn much it pisses me off. I'm crazy without you."

"You're just flat out crazy," I muttered.

His laughter vibrated against my shoulder. "I won't deny that statement."

The warmth and safety of his arms was an illusion, but I sank deeper into it anyway. "Where've you been for the past year, Gage?" Somewhere deep inside, I'd always known he'd come back for me...if he were capable.

He didn't answer right away. "Prison. I figured you knew."

"I...suspected." I'd seen the news reports about his arrest, but my own part in what went down haunted me, and I hadn't wanted to know what happened to him afterward. "What was it like in there?"

"It's not a place I'd ever send you." His arms tightened around me. "The worst part was being without you."

I stiffened. "What do you think is going to happen here?"

"You're coming home. That's what's going to happen."

"I am home. You can't just show up and start in on your demands. Things are a lot different from last year."

"Yes, they are. Fuck...I haven't felt like this since Liz."

His confession iced my veins. I untangled from his embrace and shot from bed. "No!" I cried, freaking out because he'd compared me to his dead girlfriend. The woman he'd loved—the woman he'd gone apeshit over. "Last night was—"

"Don't you dare say it was a mistake!"

I whirled at the sound of his rage, but it was too late. He pinned me against the wall, hips smashing mine as his fingers bit into my shoulders. I couldn't breathe, and I sure as hell couldn't speak.

"I know what I am." He swallowed hard as his attention fell to my mouth. "I accept that I'm a twisted bastard, but I don't think you realize who you are."

My lungs finally worked, and I sucked in a breath. "Who am I?"

"Mine."

"You're delusional. I'm better off without you."

"No." He gave a determined shake of his head. "You're alive when you're with me. I recognize it in you. You need what I give you. Even the discipline and pain. Deny it all you want, but I know what I'm talking about." He brought his face closer, almost nose-to-nose. "You *crave* it. Tell me you haven't thought of me and gotten yourself off every fucking night for the past year."

I blinked rapidly, but hot drops of shame still coursed down my cheeks. "Why can't you just leave me alone?"

A trace smile flitted across his mouth, as if he knew I was incapable of turning him away on my own. I'd only be rid of him if he decided it. "You know why."

I shook my head, because I really didn't. I had no clue what he found so appealing about me. Why me? It was a question I'd asked myself constantly since this messed up arrangement with him first began.

His eyes smoldered as he loosened his grip on my shoulders. Two warm palms rose to cradle my cheeks, and I was still incapable of moving. "I'm in love with you."

"No," I moaned as more tears spilled over. "You don't know what love is."

His fingers slid into my hair, tangling in the strands. He closed his eyes and brought his forehead to mine. "I'm selfish, controlling...cruel. Doesn't mean I don't know what love is." He brushed my lips with his. "I'm not in denial. What I did to you was fucked up. But Kayla?" His gaze found mine again, freezing me with the glint of resolve I saw there. "I'd do it again. I need you too much to let you go. I can be what you need, if you'll let me. I've had a year to find out what being without you is like, and I won't go another minute without you in my life, in my bed."

His mouth pressed against mine, and his kiss instantly possessed me.

Wrong. Bad. So bad. Tell him to leave and never come back.

"Gage?" I moaned into his mouth. I should have slept with someone else—maybe I wouldn't be so susceptible to his spell. "I hate you."

His mouth hovered, brushed mine again, and I felt the upward curve of his lips. The bastard was smiling. "Your head does." He settled a palm over my erratically beating heart. "But not here. And definitely"—he lowered his hand to the patch of hair between my legs—"not here. Here, you love me. You need me, so stop fighting it."

He forced my lips apart and dipped his tongue inside, but I wrenched my mouth from his. "It doesn't matter what I feel or don't feel. It's not important. I won't have you around Eve."

His eyes darkened to such a deep blue—the hue of the sky after sunset but without the beauty of reds, pinks, and oranges to soften the emerging twilight. Just the darkness. Just Gage.

"I told you I'd never hurt Eve." His lips thinned, and his fingers shot out and held my chin in place. "*Never*, Kayla."

"But you'll hurt me, won't you?"

"I'll also make you scream my fucking name every night. I could tell you that by the time I'm done, you'll beg me to take you again, but that's a lie. I'll never be done with you."

Shaking my head, I tried to push him away, suddenly self-conscious of my nakedness, but he wouldn't allow it. "I can't do this with you. I can't go through this again."

"Things will be different. We'll discuss boundaries." He dropped his hands to his sides. "You say you can't? Well I can't be without you. There's no one else but *you*." It was the closest he'd ever come to begging, and the honesty in his voice pulled at me.

Damn him.

"How about I make us breakfast?" I asked. He stepped back, and I took the opportunity to slip by him. His appreciation burned along my skin as I dressed, and I didn't have to look at him to know he was watching my every move. But I glanced at him anyway and caught him reaching for his pants on the floor.

My blood rushed hot through my veins as he pulled the slacks up his legs, past the powerful build of his thighs, and I was certain my cheeks warmed to an obvious pink. How could someone so dark and rotten to the soul be so beautiful? The heat in his expression rooted me to the spot, and I swallowed nervously as he buckled his belt. That belt...I remembered that strap of leather all too well, and from the upturn of his mouth, he did too.

I breezed past him and left the bedroom. The worst he'd done since showing up on my doorstep yesterday was tie my hands behind my back, and his actions and words were almost gentle in the way he treated me now, but I wasn't about to fall into his trap. He'd show his true colors again eventually.

But did I want to be around when he did?

The sight of the kitchen stopped me cold. The space was tiny, the linoleum cracked in some spots and the counters faded with age, but the sink was clear of the dinner dishes I'd left the night before and the counters were spotless.

He leaned into me from behind. "I cleaned up last night while you had your freak-out moment in the bathroom." His arms looped my waist.

"Thank you," I mumbled, unsure of how to handle the varying emotions boiling inside me. Was this a trick? Why was he being so...*decent*?

"It was nice having a home cooked meal with you and Eve. Prison food leaves much to be desired." He released me and took a seat at my small dinette. "So what are you making me?"

I blinked before moving into action. The contents of my

refrigerator made me cringe. I'd been so busy with work and Eve that I hadn't had time to go grocery shopping, but at least I had some eggs and cheese. "Omelets okay?"

"Yes."

I slammed the door shut, hating how off-balance his presence made me, and as I fixed our food, I allowed my mind to wander to a year ago. To the smack of his hand on my ass, to the force of his belt as it struck my skin.

The taste of his cock in my mouth as his hands held my head in place.

My breath grew shallow, from arousal, from fear. Gage was good at that—eliciting strong emotions that contrasted so sharply, they knocked a person on their ass in total confusion. I shouldn't want him. I should scream at him to get the hell out of my house and never come back. I should get a freaking restraining order.

As if the turmoil inside me didn't exist, I set our omelets on the table and calmly took a seat across from him. "What did you mean by boundaries?" I stabbed a bite and shoved it in my mouth. Raising my eyes to his turned out to be a mistake. His hypnotic stare paralyzed me; I couldn't look away if my life depended on it. I fell into the ocean of his gaze and almost missed the satisfied quirk of his lips. Almost.

"You know by now that a relationship with me won't be your standard variety. You'll have rules that govern your behavior."

"*My* behavior?"

"Yes. I expect you to obey me." He set his fork down and winced. "But last year I was cruel to you and that's not how I normally treat a woman. Not even when they beg me to hurt them beyond what I'm comfortable with."

"Then why?" I choked out. Everything he'd done hit me

square in the chest, and his admission that he'd been exceptionally cruel hurt more than it should.

"I wanted to destroy what was his." He lowered his head with a frown. At least he had the grace to look ashamed.

"Congratulations." I let my fork drop, satisfied with the clatter it made. "You succeeded."

"No, I didn't. Your strength is both my frustration and my undoing. There's nothing more irritating or sexier on a woman." He took a bite, and his gaze veered up to mine. "And to clarify on what I mean by boundaries, we'll set limits this time. You'll have a safe word."

"You're talking as if we're going to be together."

"I'm not leaving here without you, Kayla."

His words crawled up my spine, and every inch of my skin broke out in goose bumps. Definitely the bad kind. Before I could form a thought, let alone a reply to that loaded statement, a knock sounded on my door, loud and insistent enough to be heard from the kitchen.

Stacey had taken Eve to preschool for me, and I'd called in sick the previous evening so I'd have time to deal with Gage's unexpected appearance. I had no idea who knocked at the door.

Gage scooted back, and his eyes narrowed to dangerous slits as he rose to his feet. "Expecting someone?" he asked.

"No." Shaking my head, I left the kitchen, knowing he was on my heels as I headed to the front door. My lungs deflated when I pulled it open.

This wasn't happening.

"Hi, Kayla." Ian's gaze swerved over my shoulder, and I didn't have to feel the warmth of Gage to know he stood inches behind me, most likely giving off a nasty territorial vibe.

A dark shadow passed over Ian's face, extinguishing the

usual warmth of his expression. "I figured you'd be here," he told his brother.

CHAPTER THREE

Had anyone been around to witness the spectacle in my living room, the three of us would have dropped jaws. I stood between Gage and Ian, my arms spread wide, a palm flat on each of their chests.

If they wanted to kill each other, they'd have to get through me first.

"This isn't happening here," I warned.

Ian withdrew first, his shoulders dropping in concession, but then his gaze veered to my disheveled hair and bare feet before swinging to take in Gage's naked torso. He spun me around so he shielded me from Gage.

"How could you be such an idiot, Kayla?" His verbal attack astonished me; it was so unlike Ian to lose his temper, especially with me. "A whole year, and you're still falling for his bullshit?"

"Is it really that shocking?" Gage asked. "She's still falling for yours after eight." He ripped Ian away from me, and his jealousy crowded the atmosphere in the room. "I bet there's plenty you've kept from her. Does she know about your infamous reputation, or does she still think you walk on water?"

Ian balled his hands, and my own began to shake. This wasn't going to end well.

"Shut your damn mouth. That was a long time ago."

"Not long enough," Gage said. "I certainly won't forget."

Ian shook his head. "Doesn't matter what I do or say. You won't budge."

Gage lurched forward, his face twisted in hatred. "You have no idea what you did that night!" He pushed Ian against the wall. "No fucking idea."

I settled my hand on Gage's shoulder, but my touch only made him flinch. "Gage," I said, keeping my voice low, but steady, "calm down."

He flung my hand off and stepped away. "I'll calm the fuck down as soon as he leaves."

Ian laughed, a bitter, spiteful rumble that chilled me. "You're crazier than I thought if you think I'll let you hurt her again. If anyone's leaving, it's you. I'll drag you out myself if I have to."

I'd never before seen this side of him. Ian was synonymous with gentle, loving, kind. Not hateful, though obviously, his brother brought out his temper. My foolish actions did too. I was hurting him, and I hated myself for it.

Make a choice, Kayla, and stick to it this time.

Three choices. One stupid beyond recognition, one safe and comfortable, and one so lonely the thought made me ache.

"You don't deserve her," Ian said.

Gage went rigid, and I sensed things were about to get even uglier. I planted myself between them again. "This needs to stop. I'm not a possession you can fight over." I almost rolled my eyes at the thought. There were so many women worthier of this shit than I was.

"As soon as he's gone," Ian said, stepping closer, "I'll convince you there was never a fight to begin with."

Gage snickered. The bastard actually snickered.

I shot a finger toward the front door. "Get out. *Both* of you," I said through gritted teeth.

Ian took a step back, uncertainty on his face, while Gage crossed his arms. His mouth turned up in a self-satisfied smirk. I wanted to hit him.

"I'm not going anywhere," he said. "We have things to discuss, or did you forget? I suppose we can forgo the boundaries, though I doubt you'll like that arrangement since you didn't take to it the first time around."

His cocky tone unraveled the last thread of my patience, and I shoved him toward the door. "Get out of my house!"

He stumbled backward, his sapphire eyes narrowing, and yanked the door open. "You're making a mistake. Trust me—you're not going to like the outcome."

I slammed the door in his face and stood stock-still for a few moments, listening to the clock on the wall tick away the seconds, keenly aware of Ian behind me. A fist pounded, making me yelp.

"I need my damn clothes!"

I stalked to the bedroom and gathered the last of his things before throwing them onto the porch without a second glance. The door banged shut again, and I sensed Ian's gaze on me, though he didn't move. His presence only now caught up to me, and I fell into a state of shock, much like I had last night when Gage surprised me with his visit.

A whole year...

And I was still just as fucked up and confused as ever. A tear leaked down my face. I angrily brushed it away. "Why did you guys come here? I would have been okay."

Now he was moving, the softness of his flannel shirt rustling through the quiet as he neared me. I felt his heat, though he didn't touch me. "He got out of prison a few days ago, and I knew he'd come straight for you."

Which would explain why Ian had called more than usual this past week.

"I couldn't stand the thought of him hurting you again."

"He didn't." Not this time. This time, Gage had sent me soaring.

"I need to ask you something, and I want you to be honest with me."

I bit my lip.

"Are you in love with him?"

The space between us weighed heavily with silence, yet the roar in my head overshadowed it. In love with Gage Channing. Now wouldn't that be stupid? I gave him the only answer I could. "I don't know."

I was afraid to turn around and see how my words impacted him. Without warning, his arms came around me, and I tensed before sagging against him. His face nestled against my hair, nudging the strands aside and exposing my neck. His mouth caressed, open and hot and making me shiver until I melted. Ian still got me going and the realization came as such a relief.

"Did you sleep with him?"

A shameful sigh escaped my lips. "Don't make me answer that."

"You just did." The agony in his voice cut deep. He tightened his arms around me. "Give me one night, Kayla. If you can walk away from me afterward, then I'm gone for good."

"I don't deserve one night with you."

His protest vibrated against my collarbone. "Let *me* decide that. You need to stop blaming yourself."

He turned me around until we stood face to face, and his hands rose to frame my cheeks. "I want to show you what making love is really about because I think you've forgotten." His lips settled on mine and it was the briefest touch, the smallest of teases, yet achingly sweet all the same. "Let me love you."

"What if we do...and I still...let him come back?" I couldn't fathom it, had trouble saying the words even, but I didn't trust myself and I didn't want to hurt Ian anymore than I already had.

"Then I'll let you go."

"No," I said, shaking my head. "I can't do that to you."

"One night, Kayla. We'll go out and have a good time. No strings attached."

"There're always strings."

"You're right, but I'm cutting them now. Give me one chance to show you..."

My heart thumped at his words. "Show me what?"

"How much I still love you."

My mouth trembled, so I bit hard on my lower lip. Part of me wanted him.

Wanted to find out if I could still be normal.

But I feared the larger part of me that wanted Gage too much—the part that would hurt Ian because of the stronghold from which I couldn't break free.

"One night," he said again. "Besides, I think it's time we put all of our cards on the table. Gage is right—I have things I need to tell you, and I want you to hear it from me."

"Okay." The word was lost somewhere among the roaring in my head, and I knew I was making another mistake. Another wrong choice. Would I ever stop?

CHAPTER FOUR

"Good God girl, what happened?" Stacey exclaimed as I ushered her and the kids inside. Eve didn't give me a chance to respond. Not that I would've known what to say anyway. She demanded my attention with her excited chatter about how "Aunt Stacey" took her out for ice cream.

"And we had movie night last night!" Her eyes rounded with childhood innocence, and she failed to notice the strained curve of my smile. Thank God she didn't question why mommy had been crying as I pulled her into my arms and held on tight.

Stacey's assessing gaze followed me into my living room. I set Eve down, and she took off running toward her bedroom with Stacey's son Michael not far behind her. Turning to face Stacey, I fisted my hand and held it to my mouth.

Don't start crying again.

I was normal here, known only as the quiet woman with the adorable daughter. I wasn't the criminal who allowed abusive men to take advantage—the messed up woman who got off on being controlled and punished.

"Gotta let it out eventually, Kayla. It's been festering for months."

I raised my eyes and blinked. "Wh...what?"

She took me by the elbow and led me to the couch. We sat side by side, and she rubbed my back in the soothing way my mother used to, long before she'd died. Long before the world's darkness had seeped into my veins and turned me into a shadow of myself.

"I know you've been runnin' from something. I figured you'd tell me when you were ready. Seems like you're ready now. So, who was the hottie in the shiny Benz last night?"

I wasn't sure how long we sat in silence, me chewing the inside of my cheek while Eve and Michael played in the next room. Stacey didn't push, didn't say a word. She was older, in her early forties and divorced. Michael had been her miraculous surprise late in life because she hadn't thought she'd ever get pregnant. She'd been quick to take me under her wing months ago. And as usual, she was right. I did need to talk about it but finding the words was another matter.

"His name's Gage Channing." I closed my eyes, rubbed my hands down my face, and little by little, what I'd done last night seeped in. "Oh my God."

"Let it out. You'll feel better."

"Last year, Eve was sick. She had leukemia." I glanced up and took in Stacey's stricken face. "She's okay now," I assured her. "I have Gage to thank for her survival. I was working as his personal assistant and one day...well, I stumbled on a way to steal the money I needed for her treatment, but he found out."

More silence. Eve darted from her room long enough to show me she'd dressed her doll by herself. "Wow," I said. "You are such a big girl!"

"Michael says dolls are stupid." She pouted.

"He's a boy, baby. Most boys think dolls are yucky. I bet

he'll like your new puzzles though." She rewarded me with a toothy grin before returning to her bedroom.

"What'd he do when he realized you'd taken the money?" Stacey asked, bringing me back to our conversation.

A small laugh escaped, a bitter and crazy sound. "He blackmailed me into being his sex slave."

Stacey had no words, just wide and round eyes that assessed me in a different light. The whole story poured from me, and by the time I finished telling her everything, she'd gathered me into her arms. I muffled my cries so the kids wouldn't hear and gushed like a broken dam that wouldn't be stopped.

"I knew you carried a lot with you, but I had no idea, Kayla." She inched away to look at me. "Did he hurt you last night, or threaten you? Is that why you wanted me to take Eve out of here? We can call the police. He won't get away with this. Not while I'm around, honey."

I shook my head but couldn't meet her gaze. Shame warmed my cheeks, spreading until my body flushed. "He didn't hurt me. I...I..."

"You what?"

"I *wanted* him."

Her expression melted in pity, and I couldn't handle that look. I jumped to my feet, turned my back to her, and wrapped myself in my arms.

"It's classic, Kayla. He'll grovel and make you think he's sorry, promise not to hurt you again."

"Gage doesn't promise anything. That's what makes this so difficult. He is who he is and he doesn't hide or make excuses." Thanks to my ex-husband Rick, I'd become immune to those I'm-sorry-it'll-never-happen-again kind of tactics, but Gage was different. His hold on me was different, and I couldn't explain or categorize it.

Couldn't fight it.

"What does he want from you?" she asked.

"Me. He just wants me."

"What about Ian? Have you talked to him since all this happened last year?"

"He showed up this morning. He wants one night with me so he can...prove something, I guess." I rolled my eyes. "This is what most women fantasize about, right? Having two men fighting over them?" I collapsed onto the couch again. "I wish they'd never shown up. I was okay."

"No, you weren't."

My head snapped up at her matter-of-fact tone. "I was coping, Stace. I was *happy*."

"Coping? Maybe." She raised a perfectly shaped brow. "But you haven't been the picture of happiness, hon." She let out a heavy sigh. "So this is the reason you shoot down every man who shows any interest? This bizarre love triangle?"

"Trusting hasn't been easy. I don't have the best judgment when it comes to men."

"Your situation is far from normal, but for your own sanity you've gotta make a decision. Gage sounds like a monst—"

"He took a bullet for me." I paused, my throat constricting as tears threatened again. "He saved Eve. He's done *horrible* things, but..."

"Sounds like you've already made your decision."

I gave a rapid shake of my head. "No, Stace. No."

"If you didn't feel something for him, you wouldn't be sitting here so torn up. Some part of you must find him appealing, otherwise you wouldn't have called me last night to look after Eve." She grabbed my arm and my undivided attention. "You would've called the cops."

"I should've called the cops."

"But you didn't."

"It's just sex," I whispered.

She gave a sad smile. "It's never just sex, especially for someone like you."

I raised a brow. "Someone like me?"

"You believe in the fairytale—the happily ever after. I pegged you the minute you walked into Gigi's."

The corners of my mouth turned up. "Gage is *not* happily ever after. Ian is. He's what I need."

"But Gage is what you want."

"I don't know what I want. I thought I did, thought being away from both of them was the right thing to do."

"Maybe it is."

"I don't know anymore."

"Let me ask you this," Stacey began. "Which one would you trust with your daughter's life?"

When she put it like that...

"Both of them." But for entirely different reasons. One had used his money and power to save Eve, while the other would never hurt her, no matter what.

"Ian would make a great father," I said.

"Then maybe you should give him a chance. He isn't the one hurting you."

CHAPTER FIVE

Eve and I cuddled on the couch that night and watched *Beauty and the Beast* for what seemed like the hundredth time. It was her favorite Disney movie. It was also mine, which was why I'd introduced her to what I considered a classic. Now, having the perspective of a twenty-nine-year-old adult—and seeing the film through jaded eyes—I grudgingly realized why the movie had always appealed to me.

I was Beauty, and Gage was the Beast.

A submissive spirit had festered inside me for a long time; Gage had just brought it to the surface. But Stacey was right. I'd also dreamed of finding my Prince Charming since I was young, only I never imagined he'd come in the form of a true-life beast. Gage's ugliness stemmed from the core of his being, and unlike the beast of the fairytale, Gage was a master at disguise because you couldn't tell by looking at him.

Though once you glimpsed deeper, past the gorgeous face and sexy body, he was scary as shit.

"Why's he so mean to her? She's so pretty."

I swallowed hard, feeling as if Eve's question was

somehow significant. "I think he probably hides a lot of pain, baby, and he takes it out on people he shouldn't."

Too true.

If Gage was the beast, then I didn't know how Ian fit into this twisted real life fairytale. He was much too likable to be Gaston. I sighed. I *should* give him a chance.

After the movie ended, I gave Eve a bath amongst a mountain of bubbles and giggles, and afterward, I took my time tucking her in tight, wrapping her up like a burrito. Her Cupid mouth relaxed as sleep pulled at her. I tiptoed toward the door.

"Mommy?" Her groggy voice halted me. "Can Gage eat here again?"

My heart pounded upon hearing his name fall from her lips. "I don't think so. Now go to sleep. I love you." I crept down the hall, my pulse accelerating as I neared my bedroom. Eve's questions haunted me. *Gage* haunted me.

His memory lived inside that room.

So did his scent; it surrounded me as I settled in bed, but I couldn't bring myself to strip the sheets yet. Hesitantly, I reached for my cell and dialed Ian's number five times before allowing the call to go through.

"Why do you want me?" I asked as soon as he answered.

Silence.

"Ian?"

"Give me a minute. I'm thinking, because if you're asking me that question, then you must be considering what I said, and I don't want to blow it."

I sank into the pillows and nestled the phone against my ear. "Okay."

A minute passed before he finally spoke. "When we got close in college, you touched a part of me no one had before. You saw me for who I wanted to be. Someone worthy. I want you forever. I want everything with you, and I would be honored to be a dad to Eve. I want to take your pain when you hurt, and I want to be the reason you laugh, even if you're laughing at me because I've said or done something ridiculously stupid." The line grew thick with silence, and I held my breath. "I come alive when I'm around you, Kayla. That's why I couldn't let go, even after all these years. No one comes close to you."

I knew how he felt, except the person who made me come alive was my childhood fantasy—a beast for sure.

"You're leaving me hanging here, Kayla." His breath shuddered over the line and into my ear.

"I know," I said quietly. And I couldn't do it anymore. I either had to let him all the way in, or let him go. "How long are you going to be in town?"

"I have a lot of vacation time saved up. I'm here for a while."

"You mentioned going out. When?"

"Anytime. Name the day."

"Are you sure?" I asked. "What if one night is all I can give you?"

"Then I'll take it. I'd rather give us one last shot than go my whole life regretting I never even tried."

I closed my eyes and attempted to block out the bright depths of Gage's gaze, smoldering and lighting me on fire.

Get a grip, Kayla.

"How about tomorrow after my shift?" I knew Stacey would take Eve for me again, since she'd urged me to give Ian a chance.

"I'll be there."

The following evening came too soon. My room still haunted me, and I remembered Gage's hands on me in vivid detail. I got wet just remembering how his tongue lapped at me, how his body pressed me into the mattress and owned me. That night owned me. Gage had *always* owned me.

So why was I putting Ian through this? My heart refused to budge. It wanted what it wanted, and Ian wanted what he wanted; one more chance to make things right between us.

I finished dressing and quietly shut the bedroom door to the memories. He'd be here any minute and it wasn't fair to have Gage on my mind before our date even began. And wasn't that the only thing Ian had asked for? A final, fair chance? Letting him go would be the less selfish thing to do, but apparently, when it came to men, I wasn't the definition of selfless.

Ian made me hope. He made feel good about myself again. He wanted me so much he was willing to fight for me, even after a year. Even after the things I'd done.

His quiet knock unraveled me. I checked my hair in the hall mirror on my way to the living room, and my hands shook by the time I reached for the doorknob.

Dusk had fallen since I'd returned home from work, though the temperature was oddly warm. I was still accustomed to Oregon's cold and rainy weather in January. Ian stood on my doorstep, hands stuffed into the pockets of his blazer. His mouth curved into a brilliant smile, and God how that grin had the power to make me feel like the most important person on the planet.

I didn't deserve him. I knew this, yet I still allowed him to lead me to his rental car. It was nondescript, a white sedan to suit his needs while he was in town. Definitely not on the same playing field as the Mercedes Gage had shown up in a couple of days ago.

"You look...wow." He opened the door for me, and his eyes swept my body from head to toe. I wasn't wearing anything spectacular—just a lace cami and floral skirt that tickled my knees in the light breeze. A gauzy cover-up draped me, and my favorite part of the outfit was the white sandaled heels I wouldn't have gotten away with in Oregon this time of year.

"Thanks," I murmured with a smile. "You look good too, but you've gotta be hot in that." I gestured toward his jacket as I slid into the passenger seat.

"Not used to it being this warm." He removed his jacket, and the button down shirt he wore showed off his toned biceps. Instantly, a vision of him supporting his weight above me on those arms filled my head. I imagined his body sinking into mine, our foreheads coming together as our moans charged the air.

Maybe the problem wasn't the Texas temperature. Clearly, my hormones had taken me prisoner and had corrupted every facet of my being. Why else would I let Gage back in after all this time?

Oh God, don't go there. That's even worse.

"So where are we going?" I asked after he slid in behind the wheel.

His mouth quirked into a grin as he backed out of the driveway. "Into the city."

Butterflies took flight in my stomach. He was going all out.

What an understatement. We arrived at one of Dallas' more upscale restaurants. He ushered me inside, one hand resting at my lower back, and while he dealt with our reservation, I took a few moments to look around. Crisp, white linens covered strategically spaced tables small enough to offer the allure of intimacy, and a wall of trickling water sat tucked away in one corner. The hostess led us to a table near the waterfall, and the nervous flutters gained altitude once we were seated and left alone.

"So," he began, studying his hands. "I am curious about one thing."

I could only imagine. I braced myself, preparing for a difficult question I didn't want to answer. "And what is that?"

"How did you end up in Texas?"

I smiled, relieved. We'd had several conversations on the phone during the past year, mostly entailing of "how are you?" and "I miss you." He'd never asked how I managed to end up in such a small town so far from home.

"I got in the car and just started driving."

He raised a brow. "Seriously?"

"Seriously." I'd sold everything I owned to do it, though it hadn't been much. What hurt the most was letting go of my grandmother's locket my mom had passed down to me upon her death. "Never thought I'd make Texas my new home, but I stopped at Gigi's one morning for breakfast and that's when I met Stacey." She'd recognized a basket case when she saw one, and her kindness couldn't have come at a better time. I'd been on the brink of broke—in more ways than one—and tired of driving, but I'd been unwilling to return to Oregon.

"You continue to surprise me, Kayla." He dropped his gaze, and his expression melted in a frown.

"So," I said, my lips forming a smile despite the awkward silence. After a few moments, his did the same, though his grin came across as forced. Something told me he was thinking about his argument with Gage.

"I want you to know all of me," he said, "but once you hear the gory details of the person I used to be, I risk you walking away for good."

"It couldn't be any worse than what I've done." I lowered my head, and my hair obscured the shame flaming my cheeks.

"Kayla—" He began, but the waiter interrupted before he could continue.

With a formal smile that appeared plastered on the

man's face, he presented the bottle of wine Ian had ordered and filled our glasses. "Ready to order, sir?"

Ian asked me what I wanted, which was refreshing after all the times I'd gone to dinner with Gage and he hadn't cared what I wanted. He rattled off our dinner orders and as soon as we were alone again, he cleared his throat.

"I was a little prick as a teenager," he said. "I slept around...a lot."

I glanced up, wondering where he was going with this.

"Liz and I were screwing around for months before Gage found out." He dropped his head, letting out a breath. "I drank constantly, did drugs at parties. I was a mess, but my dad refused to see it. He treated Gage like shit, but me...he put me on a pedestal. I was gonna be the college football star, maybe even go all the way to the NFL. As long as I kept my grades up enough to play, kept showing up at practices and performing well, he turned a blind eye to the rest."

"Why are you telling me this? What does your past have to do with the three of us now?"

"I wanted you to hear about it from me, not him. I'm far from perfect, so the next time you say you don't deserve me, I'm gonna lose it, Kayla."

I fiddled with the deep blue linen housing my set of flatware and wondered why even a freaking napkin made me think of Gage's eyes. "Thanks for telling me, but the past is just that. It was a long time ago."

"To Gage, it's not." He leaned forward. "I won't sugarcoat this, Kayla. What happened that night was my fault, and he has every right to hate me. I'm the reason Liz is dead."

"Why do I feel a 'but' coming on?"

"But that doesn't give him the right to hurt you to get back at me." He reached across the table and enfolded my hand in his. "My dad abused him growing up." He swallowed hard. "I'm pretty sure he abused my mom too, but I was younger than Gage, and she protected me from it the best she could. Gage wasn't so lucky. When Liz died…I think it sent him over the edge. He's never been the same since, so don't kid yourself into believing you can change him."

"You changed," I pointed out.

He dragged a hand through his short brown hair. "How deep are you with him?" His question rattled me. Terrified me.

"I don't know what you mean."

"Bullshit. We're being honest here, remember? How deep?"

I locked my gaze on his. "When he comes around, I can't breathe, can't think, and for the life of me"—my voice splintered, and I looked away, unable to face him—"I can't say no to him. I don't *want* to say no to him."

"So it's sex then?"

"That's what I keep telling myself," I muttered.

"Jesus, Kayla. He's not gonna be your fairytale ending. He's gonna rip your heart out."

And I was going to rip out Ian's.

The certainty of it came on so suddenly that I grabbed my wine glass and downed the chardonnay in one gulp. Tense, inconsequential conversation filled the air during dinner—when we weren't immersed in uncomfortable silence. I emptied another glass of wine as Ian took care of the check.

Afterward, we ended up at a crowded dance club a few blocks from the restaurant where the music pulsed non-stop and the drinks flowed freely, though he cut me off after my third.

"Uh-uh, you're not getting drunk tonight. You're going to be in full control of yourself when I take you home." He palmed my ass and brought me tight against him as our bodies rocked to the rhythm. "And you're going to remember every second." His breath shuddered out against my neck, replaced an instant later by the pressure of his lips.

My blood pumped hard in my veins, and I held onto him to keep from melting to the dance floor. His erection pressed into my thigh as we moved together to the beat; he was more than ready to put action to words.

My head spun, from the alcohol, from the feel of his body against me. Heat and sexual tension smothered the air. "Can we get out of here?" Too many people closed in from all sides, and I wanted him alone. I wanted to lose myself, and I couldn't do that here.

"Hell, yes." He pulled me through the crowd, out the front entrance, and I sucked in fresh air until my lungs nearly burst with it. I was way too hot and it had everything to do with him.

He still got me going all right.

We covered the distance to his car in minutes, and soon we were speeding down the highway. He inched his hand up my leg, underneath my skirt, and slipped his fingers beyond the barrier of my panties. I parted my thighs and moaned as his touch sent tingles down my spine. He teased me the whole way home.

The car jerked into park in my driveway. He struck quickly, hauling me over the console and onto his lap. "Is this what you need? Someone burning up for you so much they can't make it to the door?" His mouth opened on my throat, hot and wet, and descended to my cleavage. "I want you so bad."

I leaned against the steering wheel, unmindful of the blast from the horn, and moaned as he yanked my top down over a breast. He sucked my aching nipple between his lips and grazed with his teeth.

I hissed in a breath. "We need to go inside."

He groaned. "I know, but I've waited so long to touch you

like this again, to taste you." He lifted his head and gazed at me. "I still dream of that night. Still hear the breathless way you cried my name. I want to hear it again."

I reached for the handle and pushed the door open. "Take me inside." I untangled from his arms and found solid ground. He immediately drew me into his embrace as soon as he got to his feet. One hand tangled in my hair as he coaxed my mouth open under his. We slowly backed toward my front porch, unaware of anything but each other.

"It's locked," I moaned against his lips once we reached my porch.

"Give me the key." He never let go of me as I blindly dug in my purse with one hand. His lips traced a winding path down my neck.

"If you keep doing that, I'll never find it." Even as the words left my mouth, I tilted my head so he'd continue.

He moved away with a sigh. "I'm not making love to you here on your doorstep, so find that key."

I finally pulled it from my purse and inserted the key, my fingers shaking. He picked me up, carried me inside, and the door slammed, echoing in my ears. He braced me against it and pressed his mouth against mine. His fingers inched under my camisole, sliding it above my breasts where his hands explored my tingling nipples.

"I love you so much," he said, inching back to look at me. "I'll never hurt you, never take you for granted or use you."

I couldn't say why, but his words brought tears to my eyes. "I'm wrong for you," I choked out.

He removed his hands from my breasts and framed my cheeks. "No, you're exactly right for me. You and I, we make sense. We always have."

Gage and I *didn't* make sense, so why was I suddenly consumed with thoughts of him? Ian's touch lit me on fire, but Gage's turned me into an inferno. His voice when he issued his commands, the way his eyes smoldered before he came—everything he did turned me to ash, and somehow he resurrected me every time.

The haze of passion I'd experienced at the club and in the car dissipated. "I can't do this," I whispered.

He leaned his forehead against mine. "Tell me why."

"You don't deserve this. I can't...I can't use you like this."

He sighed against my mouth. "Why do you think you're using me?"

The truth stuck in my throat, like a piece of something I hadn't chewed all the way before swallowing. I dislodged it anyway and spoke the words I knew he didn't want to hear. The words I didn't want to admit to myself.

"Being with you makes me normal, and I...I'm not... normal." I squeezed my eyes shut. "The things he does to me—"

"He's sick, Kayla," he interrupted, an edge to his tone. "He's made you question who you are, and I *hate* him for that. There's nothing wrong with you! He should rot in jail for what he did."

I opened my eyes and drew in a shaky breath. "I'm sorry. This was a bad idea. I think you should leave."

"How did we go from kissing and touching"—he whispered before his lips claimed mine for a brief moment—"to arguing about him? He doesn't matter."

I shook my head and gently pushed against him. "He matters."

His shoulders drooped. "You won't let me try, will you? You'll let him do unspeakable things to you, but you won't let me in, not even a little."

The defeat in his tone tore at me. "Ian, you mean *so* much to me."

"But I'm not him."

"You're better than him. Better than me. I can't give you

what you deserve. He...he wanted"—I gasped, trying to get the words out through the sobs rising in my throat—"to wreck you. Please," I begged, "don't let him." I wedged the door open. "Don't come back, don't call. Forget about me. I want you to move on and find someone who deserves you."

"Kayla"—his voice broke, and the sound alone bruised my heart—"*please...*"

"I won't sleep with you. That would be unforgivable of me. Go." I opened the door wider.

His hands fisted at his sides. "If I walk through that door, I'm not coming back."

"I...I know."

The next few moments were the longest of my life, but eventually he disappeared into the night, and I wasn't prepared for how his exit from my life broke my heart all over again.

CHAPTER SIX

I awoke to a crushing weight on my chest. Vise-like fingers encircled my wrists, rendering me incapable of moving, and a strangled cry tore from my throat. Instantly, I thought of Eve, but she wasn't here; she was with Stacey...

Oh God. No she wasn't. Stacey had dropped her off after Ian left. Someone had broken in, and she was asleep in the next room.

"Kayla!" A familiar voice said. "It's me. Calm down."

Gage.

I sucked in breaths of relief but then reality crept in again. What the hell was he doing in my bedroom in the middle of the night, pinning me to my mattress? He'd scared the life out of me until I'd realized he wasn't some random serial killer rapist. "What are you doing?" I squeaked. "If Eve wakes up, she'll be terrified. You can't pull shit like this!"

"Eve's safe."

I blinked, taking a moment to let his statement sink in. "Of course she's *safe*. She's in her bed, Gage." My words came out too calmly for the panic fisting my heart.

"She's on her way to my jet. She's safe, Kayla."

"What the fuck do you mean she's on her way to your jet?" I fought against his hold, kicking and screaming, though his strength made my efforts useless. Gage had always been and always would be too strong for me. Tears heated my cheeks, though these were born of rage just as much as fear. "Why are you doing this?"

He wrenched my arms to the mattress and held them down, and his strong thighs kept mine from lifting off the bed. "I told you I wasn't leaving here without you, and I meant it. Now we can do this the easy way or the hard way. It's up to you, but if you want to be reunited with your daughter, then *don't fight me.*" He loosened his grip slowly, as if testing to see if I'd attempt escape. "I'm going to let go, and you're going to get dressed, understand?"

With a gulp, I nodded. He let go and slid from the bed, and I got up on shaky legs, my breaths coming in choking gasps. I searched for the nearest pair of pants and pulled them on underneath my T-shirt.

"How can you do this to her? She must be terrified!" I wedged my feet into my sneakers and faced him, my body trembling. "I can't believe you kidnapped my daughter! Who has her? Please...you can't mess with Eve. She's innocent in all of this!" I fought the urge to get on my knees and beg, but doing so wouldn't help. He'd come this far and he wasn't about to change course now.

"She's fine. Katherine's with her."

Time did something funny. One instant I was standing a few feet from him, and the next I had my hands around his throat, squeezing as a red haze clouded my vision, fingernails digging in and scraping away skin until he yanked me out of reach from causing real harm. He twisted me, bent me over the bed, and used his thighs to trap me against the mattress. All the fight went out of me for a few seconds—

seconds I couldn't afford because he used them to secure my hands behind my back.

"You're only making this harder on yourself."

"You fucking bastard!" How could he let that bitch anywhere near my daughter? I wanted to kill him; the urge to crush his throat with my bare hands overwhelmed me.

"Eve's fine, so knock it off. Katherine won't hurt her. She's a mother too."

And that was supposed to make it all better? I gritted my teeth as he pushed me into the hall where the narrow space seemed more suffocating than usual. Helplessness stole over me as we approached the front door. He was really doing this.

Why was I surprised?

Deep down, I never thought he'd involve Eve like this. He'd used her against me a year ago, but she'd been safe from the fallout. Safe as expected, considering she'd been fighting her own battle. But now...

He'd gone too far, even for Gage.

"I'll send movers for your things, but everything you need is already waiting." He grabbed my purse and keys before opening the door. "Let's go," he said, gesturing for me to go first.

How fucking gallant of him.

He didn't even bother to keep a physical hold on me; he knew he had me where it counted. He had Eve and that was enough to make me comply without hesitation. I slid into the passenger seat of his car and ignored the burn radiating down my arms from being restrained. He rounded the hood and settled into the driver's seat.

"Where are you taking me?"

"The airport, and if you promise to behave, I'll free your hands."

"Fuck you."

With a sigh, he started the ignition and pulled onto the street. "Have it your way."

"My way? How about you bring my daughter back and leave us the hell alone?"

He clenched his jaw. Keeping one hand on the steering wheel, he unzipped his pants with the other. "Get your head in my lap."

My eyes widened. I couldn't fight him, and he knew it all too well. He'd make me suck his cock all the way to the airport if he wanted, and there wasn't a damn thing I could do to stop him.

"I'll shut up now, I promise."

"Yes," he said, grasping my hair and jerking me sideways into his lap, "you will. Open that sweet mouth, Kayla." He wound my hair tight around his fist so I couldn't move and forced his erection between my lips. His taste flooded my senses and an unwanted response traveled through my body, like sparks misfiring.

My body had to be misfiring. No way was I getting off on this. He bobbed my head up and down, painfully yanking my hair as he neared release.

"Deeper." His command floated above me, a breathless whisper as the road sped underneath us. To his credit, I didn't sense the car swerving at all, but that was Gage—always in control.

He pushed into my throat and came in a gush. "Swallow," he said, holding my head down to the point of smothering me. I couldn't *not* swallow.

Neither of us spoke afterward. I was too busy gulping in air as he dabbed at my mouth and chin with a napkin. I tried lifting my head, but he refused to let me up. His penis went flaccid against my cheek, and my tears drenched his lap as I cried myself into a doze.

The soothing hum of the highway was absent when he

woke me. I struggled into a sitting position and noticed his jet through eyes bleary from sleep. No one witnessed him escorting me onto that monstrous machine with my hands tied behind my back.

Even the pilot turned a blind eye once we boarded.

Katherine didn't. I expected her usual smugness, but something close to uncertainty pinched her face as she took in my restrained hands. She sat next to Eve, who lay sprawled on the couch at the front of the jet, fast asleep.

"Gage, I can't go to jail over this!" Katherine cried. "You didn't tell me you were kidnapping her."

"Lower your voice." He was so calm it was irritating. "Let's not wake Eve." He gave Katherine a pointed glare and then turned to me, as if her presence was of little importance to him. "If I untie you, will you behave? I'd rather not have a scene in front of your daughter."

Caging my anger, I nodded. He released my hands, and I rubbed my wrists until I got some circulation back. The severity of what he'd done hit me, and I was an instant away from panicking again. He pushed me onto the couch and took the cushion beside me. I wanted to go to Eve, but Katherine sat between my daughter and me, and Gage slid an arm around my shoulders anyway, keeping me at his side. His hold was just as possessive as always. I peeked up and got a spark of satisfaction upon seeing the nasty red scratches I'd left on his neck and throat.

As the jet sped down the runway and took to the air, I thought of only one thing.

He's gone too far this time.

CHAPTER SEVEN

The flight was shorter than expected. We beat the sunrise as we landed in Portland, not that we would have seen much of it anyway with the way the sky was crying. Now the four of us entered Gage's house. He shut and locked the door before turning to Katherine. "Take Eve to her room and sit with her. It's the last door on the right."

She gritted her teeth but went to do as ordered. Eve opened her eyes and looked over Katherine's shoulder, calling to me.

"It's okay." My voice cracked. "Go back to sleep, baby. She'll tuck you in." Comforted by my voice and words, she laid her cheek down, and I watched them disappear down the hall.

Gage clutched my arm. "Come on."

"Please stop," I begged, fighting our progress toward that door—the door leading to the one place I never wanted to see again. "Gage, don't do this to me."

Ignoring me, he inserted a key and the door creaked open, revealing the darkness beyond. I remembered how it infiltrated every corner, every implement of torture. Gage was at his darkest when in that space.

"You said you loved me," I cried. He pushed me in front of him, and through my panic I heard the door slam and the lock click into place.

"I do, Kayla. So fucking much."

He switched on a light and herded me down the steps. "Strip."

"No," I said, folding my arms.

He took a deep breath and seemed to deliberate for a moment. "You have no options. The only way through that door is by key. Now strip. I want you bare in front of me."

"Why?"

"Just do it." His tone was free of anger, free of anything other than resignation, and I wasn't sure what it meant.

I slipped off my shoes and brought my trembling fingers to the hem of my shirt. I wasn't wearing a bra, and his eyes glazed over at the sight of my breasts, nipples puckering in the chill of the room. I pushed my pants down my legs, followed by my underwear, and stepped outside the puddle of clothing to stand before him, reduced to a shivering mass of vulnerability.

This was about more than stripping me of my clothes.

"What do you want, Gage?"

"Every damn piece of you."

"Even my daughter?"

"Even your daughter."

I dropped to my knees from the force of his words. "Let us go!"

His tall frame became a blur through my tears, and I was unprepared for the ball gag he shoved deep into my mouth. He wrenched my hands up and secured them. His movements were measured but quick, and I had no time to adjust to what he was doing. He hauled me to my feet and kicked my legs apart, and I never thought I'd end up back here again—in Gage's basement of hell, strung up on my toes, hands secured above me and feet spread wide.

I'd come full circle, and I didn't like it one bit. Unlike last time, when fear and uncertainty had taken center stage, now an all-consuming rage filled my soul. I *hated* being helpless and at his mercy, rendered incapable of expressing the fury boiling in the vat of my being.

He had Eve, and no one messed with my daughter. Not even Gage Fucking Channing.

He sank into a seat, lowered his head into his hands, and didn't speak at first—just gripped his hair with those slender fingers that still managed to deliver lethal masculinity, as if he could hold himself together. Minutes passed. He didn't move, and I *couldn't* move.

What did he want?

"I have something to say, and you're going to listen," he said, rising from the couch and pacing in front of me. "I didn't want to do this. I tried doing the right thing, tried giving you time to come to me on your own, but then you fucked him." He stopped, and his face twisted, reminding me of how furious he'd been a year ago after catching me in Ian's arms the first time.

I jerked my head back and forth, trying to convey his mistake, but he didn't take out the gag and listen. His actions made sense now, knowing Gage the way I did. He thought I'd slept with Ian and now his jealousy had sent him off the deep end. I had to get through to him. Had to tell him he was wrong.

Some of my anger seeped from my limbs, leaving me shaking with weakness, and for the first time since he'd kidnapped me, I truly feared him. He had everything wrong, but he'd left me incapable of correcting his assumption. God. What would he do to me now?

He wouldn't hurt Eve...

I thought the words, turned them over in my mind, but a spark of doubt remained. He was too unpredictable in his jealousy. Especially when he appeared calm.

And he was calm. This was bad. I screamed around the gag.

"Damn it, Kayla! Don't look at me like that." I broke out in a cold sweat when he unbuckled his belt. "I'm going to prove I can get angry—fucking furious even—and still punish you without losing control." Brandishing that painful strap of leather, he disappeared behind me.

How did I get back here?

A year without physical pain had weakened me. His first strike purged more tears from my eyes, and the second lash crashed on top of the first, back to back, leaving me no time to acclimate to the overwhelming sting. I cried out in muffled abandon with each strike, and by the time he ceased hitting me, my legs were gelatinous, and I was sinking...

He released my hands, and I collapsed to my knees. I peered up through my messy hair, plastered to my face from sweat and tears, and met his guarded expression. Something lingered in his eyes. Hurt?

Was it even possible to hurt him?

"I'm no good for you," he said. "He's fucking perfect for you. He'll give you the idyllic life, white picket fence and all with two-point-five kids. I can give you anything and everything, but I can't give you that. I don't do *normal*!" His hands bunched as he came toward me. "But I can't let you go either. You're under my skin, in my head. I dream of you when I sleep and it's making me crazy." His eyes narrowed, alight with the emotion he didn't want to spill. "I want to kill him for touching what's mine, and whether you like it or not, you are mine. Your body knows it, and I think your heart does too."

I brought my hands up and pulled out the gag. "I didn't sleep with him!"

He dropped to his knees in front of me, and his hands came up to frame my cheeks. At first, his touch was gentle, but as he brought his face closer, he dug his fingers into my skin. "You better consider your next words carefully, because if you lie to me about this—"

"It's the truth," I interrupted. "I didn't sleep with him."

"I saw you guys. You were all over each other and barely made it through the fucking door."

"Obviously, you didn't stick around." I jerked back until his hands dropped. "I made him leave."

His mouth claimed mine, hard and insistent. I whimpered, but he ate it up, leaving me to question if I'd made any sound at all. He pulled away and searched my face. "You promise you didn't sleep with him?"

"Yes," I said, tears still streaming down my face. "I couldn't. It didn't feel right."

"But when we're together…it feels right, doesn't it?"

I choked on my answer.

"Do you love me, Kayla?"

"It doesn't matter what I feel. I can't live like this! You can't just do whatever you want because you're jealous."

He shook his head. "I won't live without you, so I guess that leaves you with two options. One, you can fight me every step of the way, but you're still not leaving. Or there's option two."

"What's option two?"

"You can accept we're meant to be together and compromise with me."

I arched a brow. "You, compromise?"

"Yes. Compromising isn't something I do easily, but I love you enough that I'd do it for you."

I scoffed. "How nice. You'll be a decent human being

because you love me. Are you listening to yourself? Does any of this really penetrate your thick skull? This"—I gestured between him and me—"isn't normal! You don't treat someone you love like this. This here...this is a watered down version of what Rick put me through. Why would I go back to that?"

"Don't you *ever* compare me to that piece of shit again. I might hurt you, but I'll never harm you."

"But you do harm me. Every time you take the choice from me, and I'll be damned if I let your methods corrupt my daughter. I want her to know what love is. If I stay with you, she'll grow up believing this is how relationships are supposed to be."

"No," he said in a level tone. "We'll contain the more unconventional aspects of our relationship to our bedroom and down here. She'll never be exposed to anything inappropriate. I'll protect her. I'll protect you too. No one will ever hurt you again, including me."

My gaze dropped to the front of his pants where his belt had been moments ago. "What do you call beating me?"

"Punishment." He slipped his fingers between my legs. "Your wet cunt suggests my belt isn't such a punishment after all. I'll have to come up with more interesting methods."

Every part of me tingled at his touch. I didn't have the energy to deny it. Everything this man did turned me on, and I'd long ago forgotten whether he'd conditioned the response from me, or if it had been there all along.

There were no more lines; they'd blurred until nothing but pixilated confusion remained.

He rose, picked up his belt from the floor, and wound it through his pant loops. I silently watched as he crossed the room where he pulled out a silky robe from a closet. Sticking out a hand, he helped me to my feet and held the garment open for me to slide my arms into. His fingers tangled with mine as he led me to the couch.

"Now, let's talk boundaries," he said after we were sitting side by side.

"I'm listening." I'd hear him out, and then I'd get the hell out of there with Eve the first chance I got.

"I need to know your hard limits."

I reached into the vault of my memory and tried to recall the research I'd done into BDSM last year. "Hard limits... those are things that won't be done under any circumstances, right?"

"Yes."

My gaze swerved to the wall where he kept his paddles and whips. The sight of the long and thin one, coiled against the wall like a lethal snake, sent terror into me despite his efforts to use it without anger. That night replayed in my mind, and I grew even wetter between my thighs. He'd done something to me that night.

The night I'd gone to him on my own.

But that whip...

"I don't want whips or paddles. Your belt"—I swallowed hard—"is my limit, as long as you don't use it when you're mad."

His attention landed on the whip too, and he frowned. "You're scared of the bullwhip." With a sigh, he dragged his fingers through his hair. "That's my fault. I wish I could take back what I did, but I can't." He paused, seeming to consider. "Okay. No bullwhip. We'll revisit this conversation in a few months. Maybe you'll change your mind by then."

I doubted it, but I remained silent.

"What else, Kayla?"

"Nipple clamps."

"Absolutely not. Those aren't going anywhere."

"Why?" I cocked my head and studied him. I was genuinely curious.

"They look sexy as fuck on you."

They also hurt like hell. "I don't like them."

He lowered his hands to my chest, parted the robe, and his eyes wandered over my breasts. I stopped breathing when he bent and sucked a nipple into his mouth.

"Gage..." Just like that, he stole my breath and the last bit of composure I had left. I fisted my hands until my nails bit into my palms. "No clamps," I mumbled, though my demand would have carried more weight if I hadn't said it with a moan.

He pulled back, and his eyes rose to meet mine. "This is called compromising. Bullwhip or clamps—you only get one as a hard limit."

I bit my lip. The clamps hurt, but the whip terrified me. "This isn't compromising. You're using my fear against me to get your way."

"Okay, the clamps will only be used as punishment."

"You're an asshole."

His mouth quirked into a grin. "Calling me names might constitute a punishment."

"I stand by my previous observation. I don't even know why we're having this conversation. You'll always get what you want."

He tilted his head. "True. But I do care what you want too. So no bullwhips, and clamps used sparingly. Now what else?"

"I want to see my daughter."

"Soon. What else?"

I opened my mouth, prepared to mention all kinds of horrible things I didn't want, but when I thought back to every moment I'd spent with him, nothing formed. My mind was a blank canvas, unnerving me so deeply that I shuddered. Why couldn't I remember the bad?

Why was the good—the *unbelievably* good—running through my mind like a hot porno? And then it hit me.

"No anal sex."

He laughed. "No deal."

I sprang to my feet and glared at him. "Then rape me again, Gage, because that's what you'll have to do. I'm done with this conversation. I've told you my limits, but you've shot down almost every one of them." I crossed my arms. "What's the point?"

He rose to his full height and stood close enough so his breath warmed my face, and his eyes smoldered in that familiar way—the way that made me fear and want him all at once. I tensed, waiting for him to grab me and force me to the bed. I was in for it now, since the subject of anal had precipitated this particular standoff.

He leaned down, and I thought he was going to kiss me, but he spoke instead. "No anal," he said, inches from my mouth. "No anal until you beg me for it."

"That will never happen."

"We'll see." He snaked an arm around my waist and pulled me against him. "I think we've covered hard limits. Now let's talk about what you *do* like."

Oh God.

I gulped. So not going there now. "I want to see Eve."

"Okay, we'll continue this conversation later. Maybe you can *show* me what you like, though I already have a few ideas." His mouth brushed mine, barely a touch but enough to make my pulse thready. "You're anxious to see your daughter, and I can understand that." He inched back, and his expression grew severe. New flutters of dread winged in my stomach. "But I need you to say yes to something before I let you through that door, Kayla."

"Wh...what is it?"

He reached into his pocket and withdrew a velvet box, and when he flipped the lid open, I thought I'd pass out. "I want you to marry me."

"No!" I shoved away from him, stumbling as my grip on sanity teetered. "You're insane. I'm not marrying you!"

He avoided eye contact as he shut the ring box. I couldn't even recall what the stone had looked like—my mind was too hazed with shock.

"I'm not letting you out of here until you say yes."

"You wouldn't." He'd never terrified me so much. "What would you do with Eve?"

"Let's hope you never find out." He strode toward the staircase, and I hurried after him, desperation fueling every step.

"Don't do this! She needs me." Tears threatened again, but I held them back. He didn't respond to them anyway. Not in a way that was favorable to me.

He whirled to face me. "If you come anywhere near these stairs, I'll tie you to the bed before I leave."

My body froze. "Please, I'm begging you, Gage."

"It's Master. When we're down here or in our bedroom, you'll address me as Master."

Like hell I would.

"Get some sleep," he barked. "I'll bring in lunch later, and hopefully by then you'll have changed your mind."

CHAPTER EIGHT

The day commenced with the biggest standoff of my life. He brought in lunch, opened that little dreaded box, and then promptly shut it and left without a word after I said no. The same thing happened at dinnertime. He wouldn't budge, and he refused to engage in conversation despite my pleading, so negotiating was out of the question.

Most disturbing of all? He didn't touch me, even though the heat in his eyes told me how badly he wanted to. His restraint said it all. I was screwed. He was being stubbornly serious about this, and I'd lost our battle of wills before it had begun. When it came to Eve, I'd already proven I'd do anything for her.

The sound of his entrance the next morning made my heart speed up.

"You can eat breakfast down here by yourself, or you can join Eve and me. It's your choice," he said as he pulled the ring box from his pocket. "Are you ready to say yes?"

No, not even close, but being away from Eve was killing me, and I couldn't stand the thought of how scared she must be wondering where I was. I'd do anything to get to her, even let Gage put a ring on my finger if it meant he'd let me out of this damn room.

"I'll marry you."

I was unprepared for the grin that widened his mouth; it wasn't smug, triumphant, or even cocky. I felt that unrestrained smile in the pit of my stomach. My answer made him *happy*.

Genuinely so, and I wasn't sure how I felt about that.

His hand slid along mine as he pushed the ring onto my finger, and God, it was gigantic. The diamond, a princess cut, sparkled in a beautiful antique setting. He gathered me into his arms and buried his nose in my hair.

"I can't wait to get you in bed underneath me. I've missed you so damn much."

I sucked in a breath and held it. He finally released me, took my hand, and pulled me toward the stairs.

Eve's eyes lit up the instant she saw me. She hopped into my arms with her usual exuberance. "I missed you. Are you all better now?"

I sent Gage a confused look.

"I explained to her how you weren't feeling well."

"Yeah, baby. I'm better now." My eyes stung as I held her tight. I was so much better now that I had her in my arms.

"Come see my room!" She slid down my body, and her feet pitter-pattered across the sheen of hardwood. I sensed Gage's presence behind me as I followed her down a hallway, past the master bedroom I couldn't bring myself to look into, and when I rounded the door frame to the next room, I stood motionless, my mouth hanging open.

The room was a four-year-old's dream come true. A canopy bed enclosed in filmy tulle sat along one wall, and shelves upon shelves of toys and books took up another. Every nook and cranny overflowed with the princess theme.

The bastard had bought my daughter, but what really

unsettled me was the evidence in front of me; he'd planned this.

I clenched my hands and tried to contain my anger. I couldn't compete, and she'd be so disappointed to go back to our life, assuming I could find a way out of there in the first place.

"Do you like it, Mommy?"

"It's very...nice."

"Look at the pretty tea cups!" She shot across the room to a table in the corner and lifted a dainty cup from its saucer. "Will you play tea party with me?"

"I will in a few minutes. I have to talk to Gage first." I backed into the hall and moved out of earshot of Eve. His presence filled the narrow space, and the shadows the early morning sun hadn't yet chased away only added to the threatening undertone of this situation, this moment. I made myself stand tall as I faced him.

"How dare you!"

He moved toward me, and instinctively, I backed away until my spine hit wall. "How dare I what? Make her happy? Give her things? She's had a blast since she's been here, despite missing you."

"You know I can't give her all of that." My voice shook, so I took a deep breath. "How will I explain all of this after we..."

"After you what?" He aligned his body with mine. "Leave? Entertaining thoughts of skipping out on me, are you? Even though you're wearing my mother's ring."

His words carried special weight, as if they meant something...something I was supposed to understand? But I didn't. I was floundering in a sea of turbulence, the waters deep and murky so the unknown remained just that.

He brought my left hand to his mouth and kissed the ring. "You're not going anywhere," he murmured. He pulled away but flattened his palms against the wall on either side of me.

He was right. I wasn't going anywhere, not even from this hallway.

"How long do you plan to keep us prisoner?"

"As long as it takes."

"You can't keep us locked away forever. Eve needs to be in preschool, and she's in remission. She has appointments—"

"You think I don't realize that? I'm aware you have obligations as a mother, but if I have to, I can hire someone to transport her." He leaned closer. "But I don't think it'll take long. I think you're exactly where you want to be."

"You're overly confident," I snapped, focusing on his chest even though I felt his gaze burning into me.

"And you're in denial." His hands smoothed over my cheeks before slipping into my hair. He tilted my head up. "You wouldn't have sent him away if you didn't feel this too."

My lids closed to the softness of his tone because the sight of him amplified everything. His lips pressed against mine, and our mouths opened, tongues sliding together slowly. He took his time kissing me, as if making up for the last twenty-four hours he'd gone without touching me.

I came back to myself sometime later, my hands fisted in his hair as his pelvis rocked with mine, and I thought of Eve's proximity. We needed to be more responsible; in fact, we needed to be more responsible in general. "If you intend to keep me here—"

"I *am* keeping you here." He lifted me and urged my legs around his waist. "And I'm going to sink into your body every night."

"Then we need to talk about birth control."

"What about it?"

"We didn't use any in Texas."

He paused. "I guess we didn't."

I moaned as he ground his erection into me. "We can't be so reckless."

"I'll get you a prescription today," he said, hips still rocking. At this point, our clothing was the only thing stopping us.

Eve.

I didn't want her witnessing something so inappropriate. I pushed against him until he let me down. "Not here. Eve's—"

"I know," he interrupted, his chest heaving. "Later. Go spend some time with your daughter. I'll make breakfast."

He stepped away, but I grasped his hand. "Wait...is Katherine still here?" The thought of facing her again was more than I could stand.

"No. She left yesterday."

"What is she to you?" Why had I asked that? I didn't want to know, didn't want to hear about her at all, but the question had nagged me since I'd seen her on the plane.

"She's nothing. She doesn't matter."

"She matters, Gage. You entrusted my daughter to her. Damn right she matters."

Gage's mouth flattened into a hard line. "We have an... understanding."

I narrowed my eyes. "What kind of understanding?"

"She helps me, and I help her fight her ex in court for custody of their son. Everyone wins."

Except for Eve and me. We didn't win.

I watched him disappear down the hall, and I waited a few moments before creeping after him. If I remembered correctly, I couldn't get to the front door without walking in direct sight of the kitchen. I peeked around the corner, and he stared right at me.

"Need something?"

I shook my head. The quirk of his mouth told me he knew what I was up to, and I said the first thing that came to mind. "Can you make pancakes? She loves them." I turned to join Eve, but his voice stopped me.

"You won't get around me, Kayla. I won't let my guard down."

Neither will I.

But I was lying to myself. The minute he got me in bed, he'd have me.

CHAPTER NINE

The three of us spent the day together watching movies and playing games. It was the oddest sight ever, seeing Gage crouched on the floor playing something as elementary as Candy Land. Witnessing how Eve responded to him disturbed me on all kinds of levels. He kept up a constant stream of chatter with her that night during dinner, as if he talked to kids on a daily basis. He asked about her favorite shows, if she knew how to sing her ABC's; he even asked what she wanted for her birthday, though that was still a couple months away.

He was using her innocence to worm his way into her heart, and I could do nothing to stop it. Not unless I wanted to cause a scene in front of Eve, which I didn't. He cleaned up after dinner while I gave her a bath, and afterward, as I tucked her into bed, he lingered in the doorway watching us. I wasn't ready to leave her alone yet, but even more so, I wasn't ready to be alone with *him*.

"Do we live here now? I like my room." Her question was so guileless, it broke my heart.

I forced a smile. "We'll see. Goodnight, baby." My gaze darted to Gage. "I'll be in the next room, okay?"

She nodded as she sank into her blankets, and her eyes fluttered closed. I turned on the nightlight before shutting off the overhead light. Gage led me down the hall, and we stopped in front his bedroom—the room he expected me to share with him. I couldn't fathom calling that space *ours*.

"What if she wakes up?" I asked.

"I installed monitors in our room and down in the basement. We'll hear her." His gaze wandered down my body. "I have to take care of a few things in my office first," he said, pointing to another door at the mouth of the hallway. "I'll leave the door open."

I didn't miss the warning in his tone. He'd always be watching me; that much was clear.

"There's a private bath off the master suite. Prepare for me. When you're done, I expect you on your knees waiting."

"And if I don't?"

"I'll punish you." He smiled as his attention dropped to my chest. "I wouldn't mind seeing your nipples clamped and aching. You think the ones I used last year were bad? I have worse sets."

Just like that, he'd transitioned me back into the role of submissive. I shrank into myself, keeping my eyes downcast as the sheer presence of his body closed in.

"Wait for me on your knees, thighs spread and hands behind your back." His breath heated my forehead. "I want you naked. Understand?"

I nodded.

"How do you address me, Kayla?"

"Master is my safe word."

"Like hell it is."

I raised my eyes to his. "You got what you want. You have me here following your orders, but I won't call you Master.

So beat me, rape me, show me how ugly you can get. I'll never call you that again."

His eyes narrowed. "You did the other night."

"What are you talking about?"

"In Texas, when we were fucking, you called me Master."

I reached into my memories and recalled the word slipping from my traitorous lips. "I was caught up in the moment."

His grin was positively evil. "So if we're 'in the moment,' and you utter that word because you want to come so badly, should that be my cue to stop since that's your safe word?"

I bit down on my tongue to keep from coming unglued. He was the most infuriating man I'd ever known. "You mentioned compromising."

He gave a slight nod. "I did."

"Can we at least compromise on this?"

He leaned into me. "What do you have in mind?"

"I'll call you Master when we're..."

"Say it. Fucking."

"I'll call you Master when we're *fucking*." That word struck me as all kinds of wrong. What we did transcended a casual coupling, despite my protests to the contrary. "But you have a name, and I'll use it."

"I *am* your Master. You don't have to say the word—we both know it's true." He smirked. "Wait for me on your knees. I don't care how long it takes. Don't move from that position until I say otherwise." He backed away a couple of steps. "I bet you're getting wet just thinking about it."

"You're an asshole." But he was right. I *was* getting achingly warm between my legs.

"And you need to be punished. I'll be in shortly." He turned and strode down the hall.

I stumbled into the room on jittery limbs and entered the private bath. He'd be a while. I was almost sure of it, so

I took my time in grooming for him. Like a good little slave.

God, what the hell am I doing here?

He hadn't left me with any other choice, but at the same time...I wasn't fighting him as hard as I could be. I shaved every inch of my legs and worked on my bikini area. Afterward, I pulled a brush through my thick locks.

And then I surrendered to his demands.

I kept my hands clasped behind me and thighs spread, and the floor became uncomfortable beneath my knees. Cool air drifted between them, igniting more heat in the place he owned. My nipples pebbled in the chilly room.

He was going to clamp them. I'd mouthed off to him one too many times, and now I'd pay the price. I almost groaned at the thought. Why couldn't he fuck me like a normal man?

Normal doesn't get you off so good.

So it was true; I was a masochist after all.

Even though I was waiting for him, I jumped when he pushed the door open. "Close your eyes," he demanded.

My lids fluttered closed, and I strained to hear him, picking up his quiet steps as he neared me. He covered my eyes with a satiny piece of cloth.

"Part your lips."

My mouth opened, breath escalating at the sound of his tone, which sparked through me like fireworks.

He pressed on my lower lip before slipping a finger inside to stroke my tongue. "Don't speak, and I won't gag you. I know you don't like when I do that, so I won't as long as you behave. But you will get the clamps. I won't stand for you disrespecting me."

His finger left my mouth, and he gently rolled a nipple between thumb and forefinger. His caress made me ache so intensely that I almost begged him to take me. His touch was a tease at first until he pinched hard. He applied the most excruciating clamp imaginable, and I managed to remain silent until he did the same to the other side.

I cried out and jerked away. "I'm sorry! I didn't mean—"

He pressed a finger against my mouth. "Don't move. Don't make a sound. When I'm ready to remove them, I'll remove them, but not a second sooner. Endure it, Kayla, and the next time you have the urge to call me 'asshole,' you'll remember this pain."

Asshole.

If I didn't rebel vocally, at least I could silently. I remained still as the dead and sensed him standing before me the entire time, his eyes on the vises that caused me so much pain but turned him on all the more. My eyes stung and watered, and after a while my nipples went numb.

It was going to hurt like hell when he removed them.

He did so without warning, and I bit my lip hard to keep quiet as pain flooded my sensitive peaks. He slipped a hand between my legs. "See? Not nearly as wet as you were after I used my belt on you. This is definitely a more effective punishment."

"Gage?"

"Yes?"

"We never established a safe word."

"Pick one now."

"Um...I can't think of one."

"Then we'll use yellow and red. Yellow means you're uncomfortable with what I'm doing and you want me to slow down. Red means stop so we can assess."

"Okay."

"Doesn't apply to punishments though. You don't get a safe word during those."

Of course I didn't. Had I expected otherwise? The sound of his clothing whispered to the floor, and I wished I could see him. His finger wedged between my lips and pushed down until my jaw went slack.

"Keep your mouth parted just like that." The wet tip of his cock tickled my tongue, and his taste brought back all kinds of memories; mostly of fear and hatred, overshadowed by intense desire. He bathed my lips with his moisture, and I didn't know if he was going to fuck my mouth like he had so many times in the past, or if he only intended to tease.

"We never discussed introducing new things. We'll try them, and if you're uncomfortable, you can tell me later, but you can't deny me something until we've tried it."

Nervous tension spread through me. What was he proposing now? And I was getting sick of him making up the rules as he went along.

"What do you—"

He shoved his cock all the way in. "I'm going to come on your face." He slipped in and out of my mouth, quick and rough, and his ragged breathing roared in my ears. I didn't have time to process what he intended—didn't have time to agree or disagree. I gagged as he pushed deep, and he came in a rapid burst. Some of his cum hit the back of my throat before he yanked out of my mouth. He pulled the blindfold from my eyes, and his thick and warm liquid flowed over my forehead, down my nose and cheeks, and lingered on my lips. I darted my tongue out to clean them.

"Fuck, that's a sight. My cum all over that gorgeous face of yours." He gazed at me, entranced for several moments before helping me to my feet. "Go clean up, then crawl to me on your hands and knees."

I scurried into the bathroom, my pulse thrumming at my collarbone. I didn't recognize the woman in the mirror. She looked insanely aroused with her face and lips damp from the essence of him, her eyes mud brown with want.

I wasn't me anymore. I hadn't been me for a very long

time. He'd taken what was left and had locked it away somewhere in the vault of his possession. I lifted my left hand, wiggled my fingers, and stared at the rock. He was steamrolling me again. Compromise didn't exist between us; he was getting exactly what he wanted.

"Kayla, hurry up!"

I splashed cool water on my face, dried off with a towel, and then got to my hands and knees. Cold tile smoothed into hardwood as I left the bathroom. Maybe I could talk him into putting carpet in; these floors were killing me. I glanced up as I crawled to him.

"Eyes on the floor."

Lowering my head, I watched my hands take me closer to him, ring sparkling from the light overhead. His bare feet came into view, and I stalled in that spot, staring at his beautiful feet. Everything about him appealed to me, and I hated it.

"Kiss my feet, Kayla."

The fucked up part about this? I leaned down and did so without a second thought.

"You are mine. You follow my commands so well. I bet if I brought out the bullwhip, you'd take it right now."

He was probably right. I was lost in my desire for him, but I still managed to utter two words. "You promised."

"And I keep my promises. No bullwhip. But I am your Master. Just because you refuse to say the word doesn't mean you don't think it, don't act on it." He stepped back a few feet. "Put your nose to the floor and spread your arms out in front of you."

I stretched my body, nose to the floor, in the ultimate pose of submission.

"You're so fucking gorgeous. God, Kayla, get up. I need you so bad right now I'm about to explode."

I got to my feet, and he swept me into his arms. The light

went out an instant before he crawled over me on the bed. I sank into the soft mattress, and we meshed together, naked body against naked body as he cradled my face in his hands. I breathed in his breath and tasted my own need.

"Kayla," he said before dropping his forehead to mine. "I've fucked you all kinds of ways, but tonight...I just want to love you."

"Then love me," I choked. A tear trickled down my cheek. His words filled me up so much. I gasped for air, overcome by it all, by the sensation of his body against mine, our hearts beating in sync. He was like several people rolled into one, but right at this moment, this version of him had me.

I was his forever.

"Do you forgive me?" he asked.

"I...I'm trying."

"Do you love me?"

"I'm trying not to."

"You're good at obeying me, so try less hard on that second point."

He raised my arms over my head, and his fingers trailed down the sides of my breasts as he kissed a wet path to my navel, over the scars of my past. "I could murder him for doing this to you." His fingers brushed over my stab wounds. "You're still perfection though." He swirled his tongue there, but I felt his kiss everywhere.

Another tear leaked out; he was cleansing me of the pain I'd carried with me for so long. "Don't break my heart, Gage."

"I'll protect your heart." He kissed his way south, down my thighs until he reached my knees. He placed a kiss on each one before pushing them apart, and I shivered as his breath fanned over me. "Come as many times as you need to. Don't wait, don't ask for permission. You have it." His fingers entered me first, followed by the intense heat of his mouth claiming me. I wrapped my fingers around the bars of the headboard and moaned.

He'd never made me come this way before, and I wanted it so badly—wanted my taste flooding *his* senses. His tongue circled, once, twice, three times, and I cried his name. He spiraled a finger inside me, plunging deeper. The headboard shook as I held on, my body arching...arching until I thought I'd break. Still, he didn't stop.

My legs trembled, cramped, and I bucked my hips in desperation, wanting more his mouth, more of his fingers. More of *him*. I couldn't stop. I didn't want to stop. The slide of his tongue felt incredibly good, so hot and wet and making me throb from the heels of my feet to the top of my head. I was about to fly apart underneath him.

And then he did the unthinkable. He stopped.

"Oh God! Don't stop!" I was a mess, tears drenching my face, body shaking, heart racing way ahead of me, and he was fucking *stopping*? "Please, I'm begging you. Love me."

"I do," he said, his voice floating to me on a hoarse whisper. "Say it."

"Say what? Damn it, Gage!" I raised my hips toward him, but he didn't put his mouth on me again.

"Who am I?"

I lifted my head and saw the shadow of him crouched between my knees, like a predator about to feast. "You're my damn Master! You own me, body, mind, soul. Please...God... don't stop." Out of breath, I collapsed against the mattress again, and when his tongue burrowed into my sex, I screamed and shattered. My hands left the headboard and fisted his hair, holding him to me like a greedy whore.

But I was his whore. Just his. Only his.

He crawled up my body, and his arms enfolded me as he slipped inside, agonizingly slow. He wasn't in a hurry this time, wasn't a beast driven by his wants and needs. The connection between us terrified and confused me, left me in awe of this brutal yet passionate man who turned me to liquid with his touch. He gripped my face, and his kiss reached the center of my being as our bodies moved together. God, he owned me in that kiss.

"Come for me again," he whispered, breaking our lip-lock and settling his head on my chest. "It's the sexiest sound ever, baby."

Another orgasm was already building, rushing through the dam he'd broken, and I cried out in short, breathless whimpers with each unhurried thrust. Warmth flooded where our bodies connected, and the heat seemed to span from here until never.

Oh God...Oh God...

"You feel so amazing," he said, burying his face in my breasts. "I'll never get enough." With one final plunge, he tensed and groaned my name.

And the truth hit me with the force of a hurricane. He was making love to me. This wasn't about fucking, wasn't about claiming or possessing me.

This was about loving me.

CHAPTER TEN

We lay together afterward, a twisted bundle of limbs. His hands never stopped touching or stroking, and I realized once you got beyond the darkness in him, the whips and pain, he was the most sensual man alive.

"Still awake?" he asked.

"Yeah." I let out a huge yawn.

His chest rumbled underneath my cheek in laughter. "Barely."

"You worked me over good."

"The working over was mutual, Kayla."

A question rose but caught in my throat. I swallowed and forced it from my lips. "Why me?"

He fell silent for so long, I was certain he had no intention of answering. "I didn't want to want you."

I could relate.

He drew lazy circles up and down my spine. "You got to me. I noticed how much you loved your daughter..." He heaved in a breath. "I don't want to talk about this right now."

"Gage, I just want—"

"Not now," he barked.

I flinched, and he let out a sigh. "I'm always going to fuck up. I've got a horrible temper." He paused. "But you already know that. You know that better than anyone." He hauled me on top of his lap and brought my left leg over his right thigh so I straddled him.

My head fell back, mouth open though no sound escaped, as I pushed down onto his cock. He rocked into me, slow and steady.

"How could you hurt me like that?" I gasped as he pushed higher.

The glow from the clock on the nightstand illuminated his expression. He closed his eyes, and his face tensed, as if he were in pain. "I looked at you and all I saw was him."

"What do you see now, Gage?" I lifted and slid down his smooth shaft, inch by inch.

He groaned, and his eyes opened but remained hooded. "I see this incredible, sexy woman who belongs to me." He plastered his hands on my breasts. "Only me."

His possessiveness shouldn't have sent me over the edge, but it did. I collapsed onto his heaving chest afterward, slick with sweat and spent, but still yearning for answers.

"You said it's your mother's ring. Are the two of you close?"

"We were, before she died."

Something clicked, and I recalled Ian mentioning her death years ago. "Cancer, right?" I said, my chest squeezing the breath from me.

"She passed a few months after Liz." He paused, his Adam's apple moving as he swallowed hard, and I sensed him shutting down. "People die, Kayla."

"Tell me about Liz," I pressed.

"I don't talk about her."

Each time we were together, he stole another piece of

me. I wanted the same from him. Answers. An idea of what made him tick. Was that too much to ask?

"You want this to work between us. You want me to stay and marry you, but you give me nothing in return. That's hardly fair."

"I gave you three orgasms tonight. That's hardly nothing."

Even though I heard the amusement in his tone, his words still irritated.

"You've taken everything from me," I said. "You literally turned my world on its head."

"I haven't taken everything. Not yet."

"What are you talking about?"

"Your heart. You still hold it close, still guard it."

"Can you blame me?"

He didn't answer right away. "No."

I lifted my head. "Gage? I...you..."

"Tell me."

"You have my heart."

He drew my face to his, and our lips met. "You still haven't said what I want to hear."

"You still haven't told me about Liz."

"You don't quit, do you?"

"Do you?" I countered. "You push and push until you get what you want. I've learned from the best."

His hands fell from my body. "She was my first. First everything. I was so fucking angry all the time, and she taught me how to let it out, introduced me to the deviant side of sex. We connected, understood each other."

"How did you find out about her and..."

"Say his name." The steel in his voice made me cringe. "If you can't even say his name, then we have a problem. I'll go mad knowing you still love him."

"I care about him, but I was so young when we were together, and we were barely together, Gage."

"In Texas," he said, his eyes narrowing. "Why didn't you sleep with him?"

I dropped my face to his chest with a groan. "Why are we talking about this? We were talking about you."

"This *is* about me. Now answer the damn question."

"Your anger is ruining this!" I was appalled at how close I'd come to admitting I loved him, but then he had to go and remind me why I shouldn't love him at all.

"And you're inability to answer a simple question is making me jealous as fuck. I can't stand the thought of you feeling *anything* for him. Now tell me! Why did you send him away?" He paused. "Or maybe you didn't." The timbre of his words grew deadly.

"Gage," I said, grabbing his face, "I *didn't* sleep with him."

"But you wanted to. You've always wanted him, so why didn't you fuck him?"

"Because he deserved better!"

"*He* deserved better?" He shoved me off and jumped from bed. "Better than you? Is that what you think? Perfect Ian Kaplan, golden boy of the century, can do no wrong, right?" The tall, rigid outline of his body towered over me, and I shrank away. "I've got news for you. He doesn't deserve to breathe your name. He knocked up Liz. She was six weeks pregnant when he killed her. I can't even think about it because it makes me so fucking mad I want to tear something apart!"

I blinked, only now aware of the tears streaming down my face. "Gage..."

"I saw you years ago, you know," he said, his tone eerily calm. "During a rare visit when he and I pretended to *fix* things. You were so entranced by him that I wasn't even a blip on your radar." He paused, and the disquiet rang through the room so loudly, I was tempted to cover my ears. "He never got over you, and me destroying you would've destroyed him, but you fucking destroyed me instead. You gave me a glimpse of something I thought I wasn't allowed to have. Fuck, Kayla, neither one of us deserves you." He pulled on a pair of pants and then stomped toward the door.

"Where are you going?"

"Away, before I do something else unforgivable." The door slammed in his wake, and his steps thundered down the hall. I was amazed the disturbance didn't wake Eve.

I sat in bed for a few moments, too stunned to comprehend what had just happened. Before I thought twice about it, I scrambled to my feet, wrapped myself in his satin sheet, and went after him.

It was probably a dumbass move, but I wasn't known for my rational decisions lately. I found him in the hall, his face against the wall, hands fisted at his ears. I tiptoed to his side. Complete darkness blanketed us, and the house was so still it unsettled me. *Gage* was too still.

"How did you know the baby was his?" I was poking an angry tiger with that question, but I didn't care—not if making him mad would get him to open up.

"You really want to do this?" He kept his voice low, probably so he didn't wake Eve.

I let out a breath. "Yes. You can punish me all you want, hurt me if you need to, but I'm not dropping this. You demand all of me? Well I'm demanding all of you. Tell me everything."

He didn't move, didn't look at me, and at first I thought he was going to flat out ignore me. "I can still smell her blood, and maybe it's on my hands as much as his because I went after them that night. I knew she'd been with someone else, but when I found them together...I just lost it." He tightened his fists further, as if he could squeeze the memory into nothing. "She died in my fucking arms, took everything good about me with her, and he never even knew about the baby."

I needed to touch him, possibly more than I'd ever needed to touch another man before. Tentatively, I smoothed my hand over his back, but he sprang out of reach.

"You want to know why I hurt you? I did it because I couldn't let go. It was all I saw at first. Him with his hands on her, and her blood all over mine."

"Gage...I'm..." I gulped, my eyes stinging.

"Go back to bed, Kayla."

"No."

He pounded a fist on the wall. "I could lock you in the basement for the night."

"Do it." God, why couldn't he open up to me? Why was getting him to tell me *anything* like prying a bone from a rabid pit bull?

He moved fast, like a snake striking unsuspecting prey, and hauled me into his arms. The sheet slid from my body, forgotten on the floor as his mouth crushed mine. His kiss silenced my protests as he carried me down the hall, thankfully in the opposite direction of the basement. He kicked the bedroom door shut behind us and threw me onto the bed, and his body followed. I became prisoner to his arms and legs as he slammed into me, his thrusts brutal while his mouth kept mine busy.

Unlike earlier, this was fucking in its basest form.

I couldn't ask questions if he was screwing me like an animal. Logical thought fragmented, leaving me with scattered pieces of the things I needed him to tell me. Ian, Liz, baby, death...Gage's brokenness. I'd never noticed that about him before. Thought I was the only broken one, and he was just the fucked up one.

Focus. What were we talking...no, arguing about?

My body betrayed me, and I stopped caring about anything other than the feel of him moving inside me. I came with a breathless cry, my hands fisting the pillows as I arched into him. This had to be a record. I'd never had so many orgasms in one night.

And I never wanted it to end.

His groan of release rumbled onto my lips, and in the afterglow of the explosion, he tucked me against him before sleep claimed us.

CHAPTER ELEVEN

Neither of us mentioned our argument, but it colored every word we spoke, every movement we made within that house. Gage worked from home in order to keep an eye on me, but also because his business wasn't the same since he'd gone to prison. Most of his clients had taken their accounts elsewhere, and he'd worked his ass off to regain the trust of the loyal few who stayed with him. I found it surprising he had any clients left after the scandal, but that was Gage; he inspired loyalty even when he didn't deserve it.

And that was the cause of my hesitation now. I gripped Eve's tiny hand in mine and pressed a finger to my mouth.

"Are we playing a game?" she whispered.

"Shh." I nodded and pulled her toward the front door. Gage's muffled voice drifted from behind the ajar door of his office. Agitation tinted his tone, and I imagined him pacing in front of his desk as he spoke into his cell. His distraction was my chance. A few more steps, a quiet turn of the knob, and Eve and I would be free. I'd find the nearest house and use the phone to call the police.

So why was I hesitating?

The past week replayed in my mind. Despite the tension between us, I'd seen yet a different side of him. Just yesterday, he'd taught Eve how to tie her shoes, which was amazing considering she was only four. He'd already won her over, and I knew she'd miss him when we left.

I couldn't stay though, no matter how much part of me wanted to—how much I was tempted to risk everything to be with him. My biggest mistake was allowing him in, because what he'd done was unforgivable. Normal, sane people didn't kidnap the ones they claimed to love. I firmed my resolve and gripped the cold doorknob.

"Don't go," he said softly behind me.

I whirled and found him standing a few feet away. Eve ran to him without hesitation.

"You found us!"

"I did." He grinned as he picked her up. "It's getting late. I'll tuck you in, princess."

She giggled at the nickname and wound her toddler arms around his neck, holding on tight.

I slumped against the door as his gaze pinned me. I couldn't read his expression, which was scarier than shit as it left me not knowing what to expect.

He closed the distance between us and dug a key out of his pocket. "Wait for me in the basement," he said, dropping the key into my hand.

"Is Mommy in trouble?" Eve asked.

"Everything's fine," he assured her, yet I detected something in his tone. Everything was *not* fine, and I was about to learn about it the hard way.

My body went cold. I hadn't been down there since the day he'd put his ring on my finger. "Gage..."

"Wait for me," he repeated.

Helplessly, I watched him disappear down the hall with Eve, leaving me a shaking mess in his wake. I wanted to run after him and snatch Eve away, but my feet wouldn't work. And who was I kidding anyway? Getting into a physical tug-of-war with him, my daughter the prize, wouldn't end well.

I forced my feet in the direction he'd ordered me, stumbling twice on the way to that closed off dark space. After turning the key in the lock, I swung the door wide and reached for the light switch. Not knowing what he was about to do to me, I undressed and waited for him on my knees, hands behind my back, like I had every night since he'd let me out of the basement. His voice drifted through the monitor as he wished Eve sweet dreams, and a few minutes later, the creak of the door echoed through the space, followed by the click of the lock. His quiet steps brought him downstairs.

"Please don't hurt me."

He strode to where I knelt and glared at me. "I'm not going to hurt you. I thought..." He took a breath and ran a hand down his face. "I thought we'd gotten somewhere this past week, but the second I'm not looking, you try to leave."

"I'm sorry," I said.

"Are you?" He threw a key onto the floor and stepped back. "Go. If you want to leave me so badly, then take Eve and go. I won't stop you."

Why wasn't I moving? I imagined my fingers clasping the key, saw myself dress and climb the stairs. Even heard the door opening. Felt Eve in my arms as we escaped into the cold. We'd go back to Texas and life would go back to the way it'd been before he showed up in my driveway. I'd work, Eve would go to daycare after preschool let out, and we'd spend our Saturdays with Stacey and her son. It was a good life.

"Why aren't you going?"

"I don't know."

"Yes you do. Stop lying to me, but more importantly, stop lying to yourself."

"I...I want you."

"You've always wanted me, Kayla. That's not why you aren't running right now." He unbuckled his belt, and I stiffened as he pulled it from his pant loops. "If you stay, I'm going to punish you, but you're not staying unless you tell me why."

"You'll make me leave?"

"Yes."

I squeezed my eyes shut and forced the words from my lips. "I love you."

His breath hitched. "Was that so hard to admit?"

More than he'd ever know. "I shouldn't love you."

"We all do things we shouldn't." He pulled me to my feet. "Get on the bench."

My body betrayed me again. Even though I shook with fear, desire bloomed low in my belly. I crawled onto the spanking bench and draped it like a rag doll as he strapped me down. He raised my ass, but instead of striking me, he palmed my bottom, both hands kneading flesh. His fingers teased the hole I knew he wanted to penetrate again.

"We only said anal sex was off the table. We didn't talk about anal play."

I moaned. The thought did funny things to me.

"Is that a yes?"

"Mmm-hmm." I swallowed hard as tingles shot down my thighs.

The chilly air stirred as he moved away. He returned moments later, and his fingers drew lazy circles around the opening of that forbidden place. I hissed in a breath when he inserted a finger.

"Do you like that?"

Unable to form words, I mumbled a yes.

"I'm going to make your ass red. Do you want my hand or my belt?"

"Your hand."

"Count them out loud. I won't stop until you tell me to."

What was he doing? Why was he giving me control of my punishment? I didn't have time to question him. His palm came down hard.

"One," I moaned, and he struck again. I gasped at the force and squeaked out, "Two."

Each strike grew in power, yet I kept counting. It didn't occur to me to say stop. Not when I was liquefying between my thighs despite the tears sliding down my cheeks, dripping off my chin to the floor.

With every strike of his palm, he brought out guttural cries, similar to the sounds I'd made during labor, but he didn't ease up, and he didn't order me into silence either.

"Fifty," I sobbed.

"Tell me to stop."

The word stuck in my throat, refused to form on my tongue. Instead, I kept counting.

And he kept spanking. Harder—so hard I was certain my ass would be one huge bruise after this.

"Fifty-eight!" I yelled, hands clenched in the restraints.

"Damn it, Kayla! Say stop!"

"Stop!"

He dropped his head onto my back, and his five o'clock shadow chafed my skin like sandpaper. I felt his heavy breaths puff across my burning ass. "Why didn't you tell me to stop?"

"I don't know." My body shut down, and I had nothing left in me, no more fighting power. I couldn't even gather my thoughts. Nothing made sense. I closed my eyes and wished for sleep.

"Yes, you do. Tell me why."

"Because I shouldn't want you. I shouldn't want this."

"But you do."

"Yes." I let out a cry, a cross between a sob and a hiccup. "What kind of person does that make me? What kind of mother?"

"What we do in the privacy of our bedroom or down here has nothing to do with your parenting. You're an incredible mother. Eve will grow up strong. Don't ever doubt that." He smoothed a palm over my bottom, and I gasped as pain radiated from where he touched. "You are the most sexy woman alive, especially when I mark you like this. God, baby. You have no idea what you do to me." He spread my wetness to my ass before slowly inserting a finger.

I groaned. "Are you trying to make me beg for it?"

"I don't need to try. I have no doubt you'll beg me to take you anally." He removed his finger and nudged me with the cool tip of a butt plug. I held my breath, enduring first the pressure then the burn as he shoved it all the way in. "But not tonight. Tonight you're being punished."

"Thought you already punished me."

"That wasn't punishment."

"It wasn't?"

He laughed. "Hardly. You wanted it too much."

"What are you gonna do then?" Fear snuck into my tone. Damn. Fear always got him going.

"How turned on are you?" He slid his other hand between my thighs.

"Oh..." Moaning, I rubbed myself against his fingers. "Very." I wanted him so badly, I could crawl inside him and it still wouldn't be enough.

"Good. That's your punishment. I'll keep you aroused to the breaking point all night, but you won't get off. It'll serve as a reminder that leaving me will leave you sexually frustrated for the rest of your life."

"You're evil."

He released my ankles and wrists. "But you love me, so I couldn't be that bad." His words reeked of satisfaction. "Come on," he said, helping me to my feet. "Let's move this to our bedroom. We might as well get comfortable, since you have a long night of punishment ahead of you."

CHAPTER TWELVE

This was the most wicked form of punishment ever. He'd restrained me to the bed, and I couldn't move.

At all.

Rope bound my skin in a soft texture, and my knees were bent and spread wide. He'd tied my ankles to my thighs and had extended the rope to the bed posts to keep me that way. My arms were stretched above and fastened to the headboard. He had me exactly where he wanted me—helpless and at his mercy, which was nonexistent.

He licked a slow path down my center, dipped into my entrance, and then glided his tongue to the aching bud of nerves he knew would break me if he put the right amount of pressure there. He'd been at this for the last forty-five minutes, according to the clock on the nightstand.

"You're so fucking wet. I bet you want to come so bad right now."

My only answer was a whimper. I'd clamped my lips closed since he'd started his torture methods. Why add to his pleasure with verbal confirmation his punishment was working?

"You're much too quiet." He turned around and eased his cock between my lips, and his tongue went back to work between my thighs.

I whimpered again as he pushed deeper into my mouth. The taste of him speared through me, and I felt warmth flood under his lips and tongue. An unrestrained moan vibrated around his cock. I was so close.

"Too close, baby," he said, ceasing his erotic kiss. "You're not coming tonight." He blew a cool breath over inflamed, heated flesh, making my insides clench. I squirmed in desperation. His hips bucked, and he deepened his possession of my mouth, hitting the back of my throat. My heart raced in fear.

Don't gag, don't gag, I told myself.

He came with a hoarse cry, and I was so hot with need I would have begged without shame, but I was too busy swallowing. He pulled from my mouth and knelt between my legs again, where he rubbed me to insanity.

I squeezed my eyes shut as involuntary sounds rumbled from my lips. "Please let me come," I said sometime later, for the fifth...no, sixth or seventh time. My hips rocked constantly, though I couldn't seem to bring myself closer to the hand causing so much pleasure and frustration simultaneously. "Please. I can't take it. Fuck me anally if you want... please..."

"No."

Why was I being punished again?

I must have asked the question out loud, because he answered, "You tried leaving without permission."

I drew in a shuddering breath as more pressure built. "You'll let me out of the house with permission?"

"Eventually, yes, when I can trust you not to bolt." His lips curved into a smile. "After tonight, the way you stayed, even admitted you loved me so you *could* stay, I think we're reaching that point."

Conversation distracted me from the ache he refused to relieve, so I kept talking. "If I asked to go to the mall for lunch or a coffee, you'd let me?"

"It would depend." He leaned down and added his tongue for a few strokes.

"God! Gage..." *Focus*. "Depend on what?"

He looked up from between my thighs, a sheen of my desire on his lips. "On whether you'd earn that privilege. I told you there'd be rules that govern your behavior, and I meant it. You'll be allowed friends—*female* friends—but only if I approve of them first."

"You're planning to control every aspect of my life?" Was he serious?

"Yes," he said simply. "I control your orgasms"—he pressed hard on my clit, making me shake—"your schedule, your relationships with others." He paused, growing even more serious. "I'm a jealous man, Kayla. That hasn't changed. You'll never be allowed to talk to other men in a casual or social setting. Your words are for me only, your ideas and dreams are mine. This body is mine."

"Am I supposed to ignore every man on the planet? Even to the point of rudeness?"

"No. You speak to other men only when necessary, and you excuse yourself when it isn't." He gave me a stern look. "And it is *never* necessary for you to see or talk to my brother. I want him out of your life for good."

I was pretty sure that wouldn't be a problem after our last encounter. Gage had allowed me to return Stacey's frantic calls, and I'd discreetly checked my call log. Ian hadn't tried to contact me once.

"This sounds like a lot," he said, "but you'll adjust. I do

want you to have friends and interests outside of me, but that doesn't happen until they go by me first, understand?"

Oh, I understood all right, and his tone was pissing me off.

"What if I decide to leave? Will you let me?"

He crawled up my body until we were face to face, and his intoxicating breath mingled with mine. "You can leave, but you'll never be allowed back. Ever. Leave me, and it'll be for good."

He'd given me my freedom, so why wasn't I jumping for it?

Because you love him, you dumbass, and he knows it. He knows you're not going anywhere.

"The good news about these rules," he continued, "is that Eve will follow them too when she's older. No boyfriends until she's sixteen, and they'll have to pass our inspection, as will her friends. I'm sure you can agree with me on this point."

He was right. I did agree, but I still didn't appreciate being treated the same way.

"I'm an adult, Gage. These 'rules' of yours leave no foundation for trust. You don't trust me, and you never will. You take and take and take, but you give nothing in return."

He was too quiet, and I wasn't sure if he was going to blow a fuse or ignore the issue entirely. "You're right," he said.

That was the last thing I expected him to say. "I am?"

"I have a hard time trusting. I'm working on it."

"Well...you've been working on compromising too, so why don't we go back to that?"

"Such as?" he asked.

"I won't flirt with men. I have no interest to anyway since I'm so hung up on you." I rolled my eyes. "God help me. I don't know why, but I am." A huge grin spread across his face. "But you need to trust me," I continued. "Just because I talk to some random guy at the coffee shop about the latest song or movie doesn't mean anything. It's called polite chatter, and people do it all the time."

He shook his head. "No. *You* don't. *You* belong to me and only me. If you have something to say about music or movies, you come to me. You don't seem to get it, Kayla. I want every part of you, and your behavior will honor that. If this hypothetical coffee shop guy asks you what you think of the new Britney Spears song, you say, 'thanks for the coffee, but I have to go,' and you fucking walk away." He gripped my chin so I had no choice but to look at him. "Do you understand me?"

"I understand," I mumbled.

"You're *mine*, and I won't compromise on this. If you want to leave the house, you ask for permission first. I'll expect a rundown on where you're going, who with, what you're doing, and when you'll be back—and you'd better be back in time or face punishment."

It was all I could do not to sneer at him. "So basically I *am* a child then."

He smirked. "Your tone right now suggests it, but no. You're simply mine, and you'll do as I say."

He reached behind him and produced a gag. "Now enough of this. If you're still able to form coherent sentences, then I haven't been doing my job." He glanced at the clock. "You have at least three more hours of writhing on this bed before I let you sleep."

He pushed the gag into my mouth before continuing with his torture methods. My eyes rolled back after he started in with a vibrator. Guantanamo Bay had nothing on Gage Channing.

CHAPTER THIRTEEN

"Mommy, are you awake?"

The whisper awoke me. I rubbed sleep from my eyes and found my daughter standing next to the bed. The wafting smell of something delicious drifted into the bedroom, and I sat up, realizing that Gage had freed my hands. He'd worked me into a frenzied state last night, and no amount of my muffled begging had changed his mind. He'd punished me all right. I still ached, still wanted him badly, but he'd made sure my hands were tied out of reach for the rest of the night. The binding had been loose enough to sleep comfortably but had left me incapable of reaching the aching spot between my thighs.

"I'm not 'spose to wake you up," Eve said, breaking through my thoughts. "How come you didn't sleep enough? Gage says you need sleep."

I ruffled her hair. "What's he doing?"

"Cooking French toast." She furrowed her brows. "How does the toast get Frenched?"

My mouth quirked as I peeked underneath the comforter to find my body nestled in one of his shirts. I must have been out cold if he'd dressed me without rousing me from sleep. "Come here," I said with a smile. "You silly girl." I opened my arms so she could pounce into them.

"I like our new house," she said as her arms tightened around me. "He's nice."

Her blind trust seared my heart. I glanced at the ring on my finger and gulped. Could I really go through with the wedding? He'd given us our freedom. I could leave anytime with Eve, and he said he wouldn't stop me.

But could I walk away from him? Each day we spent together, each small change I saw in him, slowly erased what he'd put me through last year. Something about him was different. The sadism was still there, the need for power and control still an innate part of him, but I'd also witnessed slivers of compassion and humanity.

Which one was the real Gage Channing? The cold, out-of-control sadistic man who'd whipped me until welts covered my body? The man who'd fucked me in front of his own brother for revenge? Or the man who'd won over my daughter? The man who was trying to take into consideration my needs and wants.

The man who said he loved me.

I closed my eyes, and my lungs expanded as I breathed deep. I felt so much with him—too much—and I couldn't imagine never feeling this way again.

"What's the matter?" Eve asked, her palms holding my cheeks. "Are you sick?"

"No, I'm fine." I flung the covers back. "Come on, let's go check on breakfast." We padded into the hall, and I was glad his shirt fell past my thighs since I wasn't wearing any panties.

The sweet aroma of breakfast wreaked havoc with my senses and my stomach. God, it smelled good. My belly rumbled, and I couldn't recall being so hungry in a long time.

"Good morning." He smiled at Eve as she hopped to his side. "Why don't you get to work on that picture you wanted to color for your mom? I got the art supplies down for you, princess."

"Okay!" She didn't walk—she ran down the hall toward her bedroom.

I narrowed my eyes. "You're trusting a four-year-old with crayons, unsupervised?"

"You worry too much. Let her have fun. They're washable anyway." He gestured for me to join him. The instant I got within reach, he turned me so my back faced him and pushed me against the counter. The plate of French toast teased my nose, sitting only a few inches away, and my stomach rumbled again.

His hands slipped underneath my shirt—his shirt—and he palmed my breasts. "You look so fucking sexy in my shirt. If Eve weren't in the other room, I'd fuck you right here on the counter." He nudged my bottom with his hard-on. "I like you bare-assed. From now on, you're not allowed to wear underwear. I want access at all times."

I groaned.

"Last night, you begged. I've been very patient, Kayla, but no more. This ass is mine."

Nearly breathless, I let my head fall back on his shoulder. "What you did last night was not fair."

"It was more than fair. You'll never escape punishment. Some will be easier to take than others, but I'll always punish you when you disobey me." He flicked my nipples, making me flinch.

"Does it hurt?" he asked, his voice husky at my ear.

"Mmm-hmm." My nipples were incredibly sensitive, and my breasts seemed heavier than usual in his hands.

"Good. That means you're still aroused."

Footsteps sounded in the hall, and Gage stepped away from me. "You have an appointment after breakfast, by the way."

"What?" I asked, freezing to the spot as Eve bounded to me, picture in hand. Numbly, I took the drawing and stared at the colors. A rainbow. A ray of hope in a grey sky. How symbolic. But rainbows were rare, and I'd yet to find a pot of gold at the end of one.

"What appointment?"

"The seamstress. She needs to measure you for your gown. She'll have designs for you to go through too. Pick any one you want. Don't worry about the cost." He picked up the plate of French toast and moved toward the table as if he hadn't just dropped a bomb on me. Eve followed on his heels. She liked to shadow him whenever possible.

I'm not ready for this, I thought as the two of them moved around the table, arranging plates and flatware. Eve beamed as she helped. I stood in a daze, my pulse pounding in my ears, and he had to ask me twice to join them.

"Gage..." I swallowed hard and pushed the food around my plate. A few minutes ago I'd been starving; now the thought of food made me want to retch. Would he go ballistic if I said I didn't want to rush this? My eyes fell on Eve, who remained unaware of the tension spiraling out of control in my stomach.

"What is it, Kayla?"

I glanced up and met his indigo eyes. They always deepened to that color when he was angry. Obviously, I was transparent to him. "Nothing." I pushed my toast to one side of the plate, then flipped the pieces over to the other.

"Say what's on your mind." He measured his tone, no doubt because a four-year-old witnessed our conversation, but I didn't miss the edge to his words.

"It's happening so fast."

"As it should. I know what I want, Kayla, and it's going to happen."

"What's gonna happen?" Eve asked.

I sighed, and Gage shook his head. "You and your mom are going out today. Maybe she'll take you for ice cream after lunch."

Eve grinned. "Can we have the rainbow kind?"

"Sure, baby," I said.

We finished breakfast in silence. Afterward, I retreated to the bathroom to shower. Gage checked on me several times to make sure I wasn't finishing what he'd started the night before. He'd made the rules perfectly clear, just as they'd been a year ago.

No masturbating.

He sat on the bed as I dressed, and his gaze never strayed. "Your purse is in the closet by the door. I'll have to unlock it for you. The keys to the Lexus are in there. I also gave you a credit card—use it for whatever you want. It's yours."

I dropped the ankle-length skirt I'd just pulled from the closet—the one he'd stocked with an unimaginable amount of clothing in my size four. It chilled me to realize the extent he'd gone to in order to get me here under his control.

"I'm not taking your money. I'm capable of making my own."

"Bullshit. Eve needs you home more than you need to work. That's a discussion that won't happen until she's in school full days."

I took a deep breath to sooth the anger roiling through me. "Gage, I'm not taking—"

"My money *is* your money. You're going to be my wife soon."

I set my hands on my hips. "How soon?"

"Three weeks."

My knees grew weak. "It's...that's too soon!"

"No, it's not."

How could he remain so calm? I was about to fall apart, and he just sat there, the perfect picture of relaxed. It was disturbing...and infuriating! I clenched my hands. "What if I say no?"

He rose from the bed. Eve's voice blasted through the monitor, and I jumped before realizing she was only playing. Gage moved toward me, a predatory glint in his eyes.

"You won't."

"You seem sure of yourself."

"I am." He grasped my head in both hands, not quite forcefully but not gently either. "I'm one hundred percent certain you'll meet me at the altar in three weeks, as I'm positive you'll be back tonight in time for dinner."

"How can you be so sure?" I whispered, my throat thickening because I sure as hell wasn't sure.

His lips quirked into a satisfied smile. "You're addicted to me. You were a year ago, and you're more so now. I'll never get the image of you last night out of my head. You were the definition of a wild animal, Kayla, reduced to your most basic desires and needs. You will always come back to me."

His mouth lowered to mine, demanded I let him in, and I did. I always did. He kissed me until I was breathless, until I couldn't remember what we'd been talking about, and I kissed him back just as greedily. I was lucky I still remembered my own name.

His hands slid from my cheeks, and I watched, in a trance, as he disappeared into the hall.

CHAPTER FOURTEEN

I had a major problem, thanks to Gage's new rule that I wasn't allowed to wear panties. I had to face the seamstress without any. She was gracious enough not to say anything, but it was just one more bit of humiliation at the hands of my future husband.

Husband.

That word stirred all kinds of feelings in me—all of them contradictory in nature. So I went through the motions, picked out a gorgeous dress that dipped low at the bust and sparkled with intricate artistry, and I smiled like a woman facing the best day of her life. The gown was designed to hug a woman's curves before flowing to the floor in satin and lace. If I was going to walk down the aisle, at least Gage would drool like a dog as I put one foot in front of the other. I even pretended the price tag didn't matter.

Though it did. Everything mattered, but what mattered to me didn't matter to him. I drove his car, spent his money, and took Eve out for lunch and ice cream. I even bought her a new princess Barbie because that was her new obsession since he'd handed her everything she'd ever want on a silver platter.

Time didn't understand my trepidation; it moved too swiftly and now the big day was only a week away. My stomach was in constant knots from the stress, and I could barely eat, despite Gage demanding I do so. Apparently, he liked my curves and expected me to eat enough so I wouldn't turn into a skeleton of myself. He'd already taken his belt to me twice over the issue, and God, those lashes had left their mark.

But the thought of food sickened me. Marrying him...I didn't know how to feel about it. I couldn't bring myself to leave him, but I didn't know if I could say "I do" either. Marriage was a big step—a bigger step than any conventional couple faced. Saying "I do" to Gage meant I would wait for him on my knees every night. I'd have no independence, no freedom. He would always hold my free will in his fist, and the difference between sleeping at his side or being locked in the basement lay in my ability to bend to his rules and demands.

He wielded his authority over me more powerfully than a parent did a child, yet he also loved me—loved me with single-minded focus and an intense need to own every part of me. His love was selfish and obsessive but also unconditional in a most conditional way. I couldn't even explain what that meant, but my heart understood. His love was sick and tainted and all wrong, but it was mine. He stood at the epicenter of my world, cast it in crimson, and I was ashamed to admit I rather liked living in red.

I *was* addicted to him.

"Mommy?"

I snapped to attention and found Eve's inquisitive eyes on me. We sat in the middle of the busy food court at the mall. Gage and I had met with the wedding planner earlier for a cake tasting appointment, and he'd gone to Channing Enterprises afterward to attend to some business. He was starting to trust me on my own, which said a lot. I'd promised to eat something, but I was beginning to think Chinese was a poor choice. The little I'd eaten sat lodged in my throat, holding the panic down so it couldn't bubble over.

I'm marrying Gage Channing in a week.

Only a week.

Seven days.

Am I crazy?

Stupid question.

Eve called to me again from across the tiny table. She'd refused to sit at my side in a booster seat. She was a *big girl* now. I shook my head and focused my attention on her. "Yeah, baby?"

"Can we come here for one hundred days?" She wrinkled her nose. "But not for Chinese!"

I forced a smile because I doubted Gage would let me bring her to the mall on a regular basis. "Maybe we can do this once a week. I'll have to ask..." I cut off, horrified by what I'd almost said. I did not want my daughter growing up thinking it was normal to ask a man for permission to do something as simple as leave the house. Relationships were supposed to be give-and-take—a partnership. Just because I'd become entrapped didn't mean she had to.

"You ready to go, princess?" I stalled, the nickname hanging in the air. When had I started using his nickname for my daughter? Acid burned my throat, and I swallowed hard. Suddenly, the urge to go home and fall into bed overwhelmed me.

When had I started thinking of his place as home?

Too many questions, and I had no answers. I was too drained to hunt for them. I disposed of our trash from lunch, and Eve and I window-shopped on the way to the mall's exit. She was a typical four-year-old who wanted everything her gaze touched.

"*Please*?" she whined.

"Not today," I said. She was about to argue, but the blonde entering the mall caught her attention.

"Mommy, look!"

I followed the direction Eve pointed, and my heart dropped. Katherine. Please, anyone but her.

Fate wasn't listening. She faltered at the site of us, and Eve squealed an excited greeting. I clenched my teeth, hating that my daughter liked the woman. Katherine's lips curved into a wicked smile as she sauntered toward us.

"Well isn't this a coincidence? How's Gage?" she asked, though her tone hinted at hostility.

"He's fine," I snapped. "How's your son? Everything work out for you in court?"

It was official; Gage Channing had turned me into a territorial bitch.

Her nasty grin vanished. "That's none of your business."

I brushed my bangs back with my left hand, purposefully flaunting the large diamond. "Well, we need to get home. Nice chatting with you."

She pursed her lips, her eyes narrowing as she stared at the ring. "Drive safe. The weather's horrid." She smiled at Eve, and as she brushed by, she leaned toward me, her mouth inches from my ear. "Just so you know," she said, lowering her voice, "Gage fucked me while you were down in the basement. He's better at it than his brother, isn't he?"

A deep chill traveled the length of my body, and I absently heard Eve call out "bye" to Katherine. My mind went numb, and the cold barely penetrated as we left the mall and found Gage's Lexus. Eve talked the whole way home, but my head was somewhere else.

I was still standing in the middle of the busy mall, hearing those words that knifed through my heart.

When we arrived back at the house, Eve barreled through the door in search of Gage. I figured he'd still be at work, so I was surprised when he appeared from his office. He picked her up, and as she chattered about our day, about the movie we saw and how she tried "yucky noodles" at the food court, his gaze roamed over me.

He let her slide to her feet. "I need a moment with your mom. You left the puzzles out from this morning. Go put them away, please."

At least he was polite when he demanded things of my daughter. She looked less than thrilled, but she wandered down the hall, swinging her arms and taking her time.

Gage crossed the space between us. "What's wrong?"

I opened my mouth but nothing came out.

"Kayla," he warned. "Answer me."

I wasn't sure what came over me, but my palm shot out and connected with his cheek. My eyes burned with unshed tears, and I moved to strike him again. He grabbed my wrist and squeezed.

"What the hell do you think you're doing?"

I blinked, and the tears spilled. "I ran into Katherine. She said you slept with her."

His eyes narrowed. "You already know about my past with her. I've never kept that a secret."

"I'm not talking about the past. You had me locked in the basement, keeping me from my own child, and you couldn't keep it in your pants for a day?"

"Is that what she told you?" He let go of my wrist.

"Yes."

"She lied. She wanted to, even embarrassed herself trying, but I didn't touch her." He grabbed my hands and held them at my back, and his arms imprisoned my body. "I'm not a cheating bastard, Kayla."

"You let her suck your cock in your office a year ago." Hearing their moans through the door hadn't bothered me at the time, but the memory of that trashy encounter now took my breath. My chest ached from holding back the hurt.

"A year ago, we weren't engaged." He let go of my hands and framed my cheeks, his thumbs wiping away tears. "A year ago, I wasn't in love with you." His voice grew stern. "Your jealousy is a major turn-on, but don't you *ever* hit me again." He glanced at his watch and then folded my fingers around a key. "Go to the basement and pick a corner. Face it, on your knees. I'll punish you once Eve goes down for her nap."

I nodded, my throat too constricted to speak. He took off down the hall toward Eve's room, and I headed for the basement. I removed my clothing and dropped to my knees in the far corner of the rectangular room. The flood of tears wouldn't stop, and as time passed, I wondered why I was still crying. I believed him. I wasn't sure how or why, but Katherine's claim rang false in my heart. So why was I such a mess over this? The thought of him with anyone else brought out my claws, and suddenly, I understood Gage a little better.

My knees were on fire when the door to the basement opened.

"Get up, Kayla."

I rose, rubbing my aching knees as I stood, and turned to face him. He grabbed a paddle from his collection, pulled a chair into the middle of the room, and sat down. "Come here."

I shook my head. "No paddles."

"I said no bullwhip. My belt and hand turn you on too much, and you need to be punished. This is going to hurt. Now get over here."

Wiping my eyes, I walked to him and forced down the pain that consumed me from the inside. He draped me over his lap, his thighs heating my abs as I tipped forward. I braced myself with both palms on the floor and teetered, feet in the air. He curled his fingers around my side and brought me against his waist.

"You understand why you're being punished so severely, right?"

"Because I hit you."

"That's part of it, yes, but you failed to trust me. You let someone else's lies cloud your judgment. I own you, Kayla. Don't you understand that you own me as well?" Goose bumps broke out on my skin, and the delicious chill spread when he squeezed my ass. "You're mine, and I'm yours, and no one is coming between that." He settled his hand at my side again. "If you get wet, I won't let you come."

Shit. I was already turned on. When had this happened? When had being spanked and humiliated gone from scary to arousing? His return to my life had done something to me, as if he'd come back and flipped the switch he'd installed a year ago but hadn't tripped. Until now.

The paddle came down in quick succession, and I lost count as I howled. He put a lot of strength into those strikes, probably more than he ever had. I squirmed with each one, but still, moisture collected between my thighs. He'd discovered a new form of punishment—one that gave him exactly what he wanted. I couldn't help my body's response, and he knew it. Just like a couple of weeks ago, he'd deny me again.

"No one is coming between us. Do you understand me, Kayla? Not Ian, not Katherine, *no one*."

"But Katherine wants to. Why?" I asked. "What's your history with her?"

"You want to ask questions?" The paddle hit my ass with two loud smacks. "One for every question."

I hissed in a breath. "I don't care. I want to know."

"We had a casual arrangement for a few months. We fucked a few times a week, and she let me do whatever I wanted. I ended it when she said she loved me."

I squeezed my eyes shut, trying to block out the image of them together, but it refused to vanish from my mind. "Did you bring her down here?"

Another painful smack rent the air.

"Yes."

"Was she better than me?"

The question seemed to catch him off guard for a few moments, and his next strike was especially hard. "That's a stupid question. No one compares to you. Come on, get up." He dropped the paddle and helped me to my feet. "Spread your legs." I did as told, and he slid his fingers into my drenched opening. "You are so busted," he said with a smirk. He unzipped his pants and freed his erection.

Our eyes met and held, and I knew he'd make me pay. He reached out, spun me around, and pulled me onto his lap so I sat astride but facing away. Grabbing my hips, he forced my body up and down his shaft, and I couldn't control my moans.

"I own you," he said as he pushed deeper. "Say it."

"You own me."

His fingers dug into my hipbones. "I want to hear you say it, Kayla."

"You own me, Master." I groaned as he hit my spot—*the* spot.

I was going to come.

He pulled me flush against him, cock buried deep, and went still. "You don't have permission."

"I can't help it, Gage. You feel so good."

"So do you," he murmured. "But you're not coming. If you can't control yourself, then suck me off."

Resignation, I got to my knees and obeyed.

CHAPTER FIFTEEN

I dreaded this day, possibly more than my approaching wedding day, because Eve was going back to preschool.

"Are you excited, baby?" I asked her.

With a nod, she picked at her breakfast.

"Nervous?" Gage used his fork to spear an untouched piece of sausage from her plate and brought it to her mouth. "Try it." She took the bite and chewed slowly. "So what do you think?" he asked.

"Good."

"So is preschool. You'll make friends and learn things. Before long, you'll be the smartest one in this house."

She giggled. "Will not! I'm only four." Her face grew serious. "I don't wanna leave."

"Why not?" I asked.

"What if the teacher isn't as nice as Ms. Barns? What if I miss you?"

Her words impacted me like a punch to the gut. I hated the thought of her going back to school, but I had to put my selfish feelings aside. "Everyone will love you, and you'll have so much fun you won't have time to miss me. I promise."

After breakfast, I got Eve ready, and we waited by the front door for the bus to pull up. Gage watched as he loaded the dishwasher. He demonstrated an oddly domestic affinity in the kitchen. Rain fell outside, hitting the roof in a calming staccato beat, and drops of water squiggled down the window.

"Bus is here," I said.

Eve gripped my hand. "Do I have to go?"

I crouched in front of her. "Remember how much fun you had in Texas?"

She nodded.

"See? You'll do great, and I'll be here waiting when you get back." I settled her Dora backpack onto her shoulders, adjusted her coat, and pulled the door open. We jogged through the downpour. Eve forced a smile, the picture of brave as she climbed those steps. The bus driver greeted her as I stood back, my eyes stinging as I folded my arms to ward off the chill. I watched the bus disappear around the corner before returning indoors, and without warning, tears erupted.

Gage gathered me in his arms and just held me. The gesture was so sweet, so unlike him, that I clung to his body and soaked up every second. His embraced tightened, eliciting a sigh from my lips. If he'd hold me like this forever, maybe I'd be okay.

He inched away with a frown. "You don't look good."

"I don't feel good."

He laced his fingers with mine and tugged me toward the hall. "Take a nap. I haven't been letting you get enough sleep."

No, he'd been worshipping my body every night, when he wasn't punishing me.

He stalled at the door to our room and held it open for me. I'd just taken a step toward the bed when nausea rose so swiftly, I knew I wouldn't make it to the bathroom in time. I sprinted anyway, determined not to make a mess, and slammed to the tile in front of the toilet. Chunks of sausage and eggs flew everywhere, mostly on the floor because I missed.

"I'm sorry," I mumbled after I'd purged the last bit of substance from my stomach.

"What the fuck for? Jeez, Kayla. Get up." He pulled me to my feet and shoved a cool washcloth into my hands. "I'll take care of the mess. Get in bed."

I climbed between the sheets, and a buzzing began in my ears, low at first until the sound grew so loud it made me dizzy. It wasn't actual buzzing—not like what people sometimes experience when they suffer from vertigo. No, this buzzing was a disturbing realization that didn't want to form in my mind.

But it did, and it took me right back to the morning, so many years ago, when I awoke in Ian's arms. I'd spewed chunks all over his floor then too, and later that day I'd stared at two lines while my mouth hung open, as if to catch flies.

No. Impossible. I was on birth control.

Except for Texas.

Oh God.

And we hadn't exactly taken precautions during the seven day waiting period when I first began the birth control pills.

Oh. My. God.

"Gage?" My voice wasn't my own. The high-pitched squeak belonged to some crazed woman who was a thread away from falling into the abyss.

"Just a second. Be right there."

I heard water running and the opening and closing of cupboards before he entered the bedroom. The mattress pressed low where he sat behind me, but I couldn't bring myself to turn and look at him. We'd never talked about kids. More kids, that was. He was patient and kind with Eve, more so than I ever imagined, but to add more children to this insane situation...well, *that* would be insane.

But I was getting ahead of myself. I was sick from a bug or bad food or side effects from being on the pill.

He settled his palm on my arm. "What can I do?"

Why did he keep showing parts of himself that made me love him more? I couldn't keep up with his personality shifts. "I think...I mean..."

"Just spit it out, Kayla."

"I'm worried I'm...pregnant." I peeked at him but saw no reaction on his face.

"You're not pregnant. It's likely a bug, or you're upset because today is Eve's first day back to school."

I pushed into a sitting position. "Regardless, I'll feel better knowing I'm not." I raised my gaze to his, not certain what I'd find, but his expression remained unreadable. "Will you get me a test?"

He opened his mouth, as if to say something, but shook his head instead.

"Gage?"

"You're worrying for nothing, but I'll get you a test."

He left the room, and I heard the jingle of keys followed by the slam of the front door. An hour went by, followed by another. I stalked the front entrance, arms wrapped around me as I waited for Eve. Waited for him. Eve's bus beat him back, and I did my best to push my worries to the back of my mind as she jumped down the steps with a huge grin.

"Have a good day?"

She nodded, going on about her new teacher and friends

and the new shapes she'd learned. I opened the door, and we escaped into the house, removing our jackets and wiping rain from our faces. Still preoccupied, I settled her at the kitchen table with a snack and returned to my post by the front door.

What was taking him so long?

Twenty minutes later, his car pulled into the driveway, and something was off about him when he stepped into the foyer. His eyes had darkened to indigo again, and I didn't understand what it meant. It was just a test, and he was probably right.

I wasn't pregnant. I *wasn't*.

He pushed the bag into my hands without looking at me.

"You don't want kids, do you?" I whispered. The idea of never having another child—I wasn't prepared for the pang of regret the thought produced. Part of me wanted another baby someday. *His* baby, as nuts as it was.

"Go take the test. We'll talk about kids another time."

"Why?"

"Just drop it."

That was his go-to phrase when he refused to talk about something. I clutched the bag, my fingers turning white at the knuckles. So that was it. He was against having kids. We were about to get married in less than a week, and he didn't find it necessary to discuss this with me?

I had nothing else to say, so I made my way to our bedroom. He followed, Eve on his heels, and lingered by the door.

"Come on, Eve. Let's give your mom some space," he said before taking her hand and disappearing from sight.

I eyed the bathroom long after they'd left me alone, and eventually, I forced my feet in that direction. What if I *was* pregnant? Would it change how he felt about me? Did the idea of me pregnant with a huge belly repulse him?

I enclosed myself in the luxurious bath, unsure of why I locked the door. I doubted he'd come in. He appeared to want *his* space. My hands trembled as I read the instructions, and finally, I sat on the toilet and took care of business.

Now just the wait.

Time ticked away in my head, a silent countdown that only spanned one hundred and eighty seconds yet seemed like hours. I sucked in a breath; I hadn't realized I'd been holding it for the last minute.

That little stick taunted me from the counter. Just two small steps, a tilt of my head, and I'd have my answer.

Two lines.

The floor dipped. No, that was me dipping to the cold tile, following the motion of my stomach.

But I'm on birth control...

Texas. Fucking Texas. One time and that was about... three weeks ago.

Holy shit. We were having a baby. My gaze veered to the door, and I never wanted to leave through it. Obviously, he didn't want a baby.

Suck it up, Kayla. The sooner you tell him, the sooner we can deal with it.

He was about to be a father because abortion was out of the question.

I got to my feet, turned the knob, and pushed the door open. He sat on the bed, apparently waiting. I expected to find a hint of worry tightening his lips, stiffening his posture, but he appeared unnervingly calm.

"Where's Eve?"

"I put a movie on for her." He rose and took a step toward me. "Feel better now? I told you not to worry about..." Something in my expression must have penetrated his nonchalant veneer.

"I'm pregnant."

"The hell you are!" His voice thundered through the room. "Where's the test?" He stormed into the bathroom, and I whirled, hot on his heels. I stood by helplessly as he gaped at the evidence.

Crazy, how two pink lines could change so much.

His gaze swerved to me, dark with something resembling hatred, as if this was my fault...as if he hadn't been there too.

"You lied to me," he growled.

What? Shaking my head, I tried to grasp the meaning of his words. When had I ever lied to him? He coaxed the truth from me effortlessly. Lying to him was about as easy as denying him. Impossible.

"I've never lied to you," I said, digging my hands into my hips. "I have no idea what you're getting at. I understand you're shocked, but we're having a baby, and we need to deal with this."

"No!" He lurched forward and slammed me against the wall. His hands pushed on my shoulders, fingers curling, squeezing, until I was shaking all over. "*You* are having a baby, and I have an idea who the father is." He dropped his arms and slumped as the fight left him. "Because it isn't me."

"How can you..." I swallowed, as if I could force down the hurt. Grasping my chest with both hands, I wished I could keep my heart from fracturing, but I couldn't. "How can you say that?"

"Because I can't have children!" He shouted, his hands balling at his sides. I flattened further against the wall; prayed I could sink right through it. He took one last look at me in disgust and tore out of the bathroom.

CHAPTER SIXTEEN

How had I ended up on the floor? I couldn't remember anything after he'd stormed out. Except for pain. It began in my heart, squeezing so tightly I couldn't breathe, couldn't think. I doubled over as his words took over my thoughts, torturing me with the echo of his contempt, and somehow I slid to the floor. Seemed like hours ago, though it was probably only minutes.

"Mommy?"

I glanced up from the ball I'd created. Eve stood in the doorway, her eyes bright with unshed tears and her lips quivering. I was trembling too. I pushed myself up, wiped my eyes, and reached for her.

"Where's Gage, baby?"

"He left. Why did he slam the door?" She pulled away, and her innocent eyes found mine. "I don't like him anymore. He yelled at you."

"He was mad. He'll get over it and say he's sorry." At least, I hoped he would. The idea of raising another kid on my own made my stomach clench, but maybe that was exactly what I should do. He was too volatile to be reliable. I swallowed a sob. How could he think I'd lie to him?

How could I have let myself fall for him?

I replayed what had just happened; searched for a clue as to what the hell he'd been thinking. His rage had taken over, but I'd never seen him so...unglued. He'd looked at me as if I'd torn him in two. I was pregnant, and he was the father, but he didn't believe me.

Why?

I hadn't been with anyone else, so unless this was a miraculous conception, his little swimmers worked just fine.

Eve's voice pierced the chaos in my head, trying to get my attention. I pulled her tighter against me and buried my nose in the hollow of her shoulder, inhaling the sweet and familiar scent of my daughter. I was supposed to comfort *her*, but she did the comforting.

"Everything's okay," I mumbled. "Sometimes people get mad and they need to leave for a while so they can calm down enough to talk."

"Like when you send me to my room for time-outs?" Eve asked.

"Yeah, like that." For a four-year-old, her wisdom astounded me. And she was much too observant. I couldn't fall apart with her here, and Gage and I couldn't go to bat here either, even though I feared we were about to.

Whatever he thought I'd done...I had to make him see he was wrong.

I picked myself off the floor, literally, and pulled myself together. Hours passed, but Gage still didn't return. I completed chores, cooked dinner, and played with Eve before tucking her in with a bedtime story. Another hour crept by, but still...no Gage.

He didn't allow me a cell phone. I only had access to one when he allowed it or I left the house. The phone, along with my purse and keys were locked in the closet by the door. I couldn't call him, and I couldn't leave unless I took Eve out of there on foot.

As I paced the living room, growing angrier by the second, I seriously considered it. I could wake her, pack a small bag of essentials, and just disappear. Never look back. But I'd tried that last year and look where it had gotten me. He would always find me...as long as he wanted me, and I wasn't so sure he did anymore.

A key turned in the lock, and I froze, eyes on the front door as it swung open. He stumbled in, swayed, and leaned against the wall as he kicked the door shut. He lifted his head and stared at me.

Stared through me.

"Gage, I—"

"Don't say a fucking word." He kept his tone quiet, though his words still produced a nocuous edge. He pushed away from the wall and came at me, his tall body stumbling closer. I backed away, alarmed by the hatred in his eyes and his obvious drunken state.

The back of my thighs hit the arm of the couch and I toppled over. He followed, trapping me with his body and his seething gaze. The scent of rum wafted between us. I clamped my lips shut and waited.

"You swore up and down you didn't fuck him."

Realization enclosed my heart with an icy grip. He was talking about Ian. "I haven't been with anyone but you. *No one*," I said slowly, enunciating each word in hope the truth would penetrate.

His hands shot out fast, fingers curling around my wrists, tightening to the point of pain. He held them prisoner above my head as his face lowered, his sneering lips an inch from mine. "Do *not* lie to me again."

"I'm not lying." My mouth trembled, and the words barely formed between us, despite the narrow space.

He yanked me to my feet, rough enough to make my head swing back, and I was already pleading as he dragged me toward the basement. "Stop! You're drunk. Don't do this now—"

He clamped a hand over my mouth and nose, muffling not only my words, but my air. Panic rushed up, bringing with it nausea and a flood of memories. I was suffocating...

I blinked and hot tears rolled down my face to pool on his hand. I couldn't breathe! I struggled as he unlocked the door; struggled for air, for escape. He switched on the light as I broke free, and I teetered on the top step as the bottom swayed closer, rushing to meet me though my feet still hadn't left solid ground. My hands flailed but found nothing to save me.

With a cry, I envisioned my body twisted and ruined on the floor—the baby and me dead—as gravity pulled at me with her powerful claws.

Gage grabbed me from behind. Not even gravity could match his strength. He fisted the back of my shirt and propelled me down the stairs before pushing me face first onto the bed.

"Don't fight me, Kayla. Cooperate, and it won't hurt as much."

A sob bubbled up. "What are you gonna do?"

"Punish you," he said as he yanked my shirt over my head. He unclasped my bra and pulled it from underneath me, followed by the rest of my clothing.

"For what? I haven't done anything wrong."

"You fucking lied to me!"

"Don't hurt us," I whimpered.

"Us?" He spat the word. "You think I care about you or

that…that…*fucking* mistake?" His voice fractured, and so did my composure. I bawled as he stretched out my arms and legs. He tied me to the bed with forceful efficiency, pulling the bindings so tightly they gouged my skin. I didn't even fight him—I didn't have it in me. His words had delivered the final, fatal blow.

I was dead on the inside. I was nothing. He could beat me until I gushed blood and it couldn't possibly hurt this much.

"I loved you!" he roared. "I told you shit I've never told…" His steps faded away. I twisted my head and watched through my tangled hair as he approach his collection of whips and paddles. He pulled that terrifying coil from the wall and unwound it.

"You promised," I whispered.

"If you can lie, so can I."

"I didn't lie to you! I never slept with your brother."

"Don't call him that." He stormed to the bed and made a cracking sound with his weapon of choice.

My muscles tensed. "Please," I begged. "Don't do it. You said you wouldn't. I trusted you!"

"And I trusted you!"

"The baby's yours, Gage. That's the truth. If you do this—"

Fire streaked across my ass, stealing the breath from me. I fisted my hands and tried to crawl out of reach, but he'd made sure I couldn't. Another strike landed, this time on the back of my thighs, eliciting a grunt. I sobbed his name. "I love you!"

That only seemed to anger him more. He swung that whip across my body again, and I screamed. My fingernails bit into my palms, and I concentrated on that pain, focused on the fire dancing up and down my skin—anything to drown out the unbearable ache within me.

I'd given him all of me, but it wasn't enough. He couldn't see beyond his past, couldn't see beyond his own pain.

"The baby's yours," I whispered with each strike, no longer screaming. No longer able. My voice faded as the count rose, but I grasped one tiny word and let it bleed from my lips. "Red."

His fist loosened and the whip slid to the floor. He followed soundlessly, his knees buckling, and burrowed his head into his hands. His body shook as he mumbled words I couldn't decipher. I swam in and out of consciousness for a while, but he didn't move, didn't stop shaking. Eventually, he got to his feet and headed for the stairs.

"You did it," I said. "You destroyed me. But I'm not his anymore, so I guess that means you destroyed what was yours instead."

His steps faltered, and I thought he was going to say something, but moments later the light went out and the door slammed.

CHAPTER SEVENTEEN

The darkness nearly suffocated me. I lay restrained to the bed, overcome by claustrophobia even though I had plenty of space around me. My bottom and thighs burned, and I focused on the pain so nothing else would touch me.

He'd gone back on his promise.

That still touched me. His words and actions hurt far worse than the whip he'd just unleashed on my body. Even drunk and enraged, he'd held back.

I wished he hadn't.

I wished he'd broken my body instead of my spirit. Hot tears soaked the sheet under my cheek, and I didn't recall the exact moment I dozed off, but I had to pee something fierce when I awoke. The blackness closed in more with each passing minute, and I had no idea what time it was or how long I'd slept. I was worried for Eve, especially since the monitor had offered nothing but silence. He must have shut it off. I didn't think he'd hurt her, but he wasn't operating on all cylinders either.

The door creaked open and a sliver of light beamed down the staircase. He switched on the overhead light, and I blinked several times until the sudden brightness no longer blinded me. I watched him stomp down the stairs and come toward me. His eyes were bloodshot, more so than last night, as if he hadn't slept at all. He held a bag and my purse in one hand, and he dropped them both before untying me.

"Don't move yet. I need to check your backside."

"It's fine," I muttered. I got to my hands and knees, turned to face him, but the room spun. Nausea hit me from nowhere. I shoved past him, sprinting to the bathroom, and my fingers gripped cool porcelain as I retched into the toilet. After the last dry heave, I flushed away the ugly brown and then relieved my screaming bladder before rinsing the vomit from my mouth.

He hadn't moved at all when I returned to the room. "Get on the bed. I need to take care of you."

"What do you mean?" I aimed my gaze at his shoes.

"Don't ask questions or argue. Just do it."

I stepped toward him, but apparently I wasn't moving fast enough. He took my arm and jerked me to the bed where he bent me over the end.

"Stay still," he snapped.

I squeezed my eyes shut and shivered as his hands slid over my sore bottom. He rubbed in some sort of cream.

"I'm sorry," he said, his voice gruff. "I shouldn't have punished you while I was drunk, but I didn't leave any welts."

This time.

He finished and stepped back, and a set of clothing landed by my head on the mattress. "Get dressed."

"We need to talk," I said, my voice cracking as I reached for the clothes. I was too close to splitting in two, and I didn't know if I could handle talking to him right now, but I had to try. I had to do something to relieve this ache in my heart, to make him understand he was wrong.

"We have nothing to talk about. You need to get dressed and leave."

My eyes widened as I pulled on a pair of jeans. "What?"

"You can take the car, the credit card—take what you want. I don't care about any of it. Use it as long as you need to, but don't come back here or call." He moved to the other side of the bed, as if he couldn't tolerate our proximity.

"So that's it?" I said, my voice wavering as I slipped into a T-shirt. "You're just going to send me away?"

"You're carrying that bastard's kid!" Seizing the lamp on the nightstand, he hurtled it across the room. The ceramic busted, echoing its haunting death through the basement. "I hate it, and I hate you. Now get the fuck out of my house and take Eve"—his voice cracked on her name—"with you."

Numbness stole over me. I couldn't process. He'd revealed so many sides of himself, so many personalities that all meshed to make up this complex, passionate, cruel, beautiful man in front of me. But this side of him...I hated this side of him as intensely as he now hated me.

"Go!" he screamed. "I can't stand the sight of you!"

I'd never seen him so livid, so destroyed by what he thought I'd done. I could have fallen to pieces at his feet, could have begged him to put me back together again. To make me whole. But I wouldn't. This was my chance to wash him from my life. Truly start over. Eve would be fine without him. I would be fine without him. The baby we'd created together, the one he hated, would be fine without him.

"Okay," I whispered, forcing my shaky limbs to move. I picked up the bag he'd tossed on the floor, pulled my purse strap high onto my shoulder, and headed toward the stairs. I said nothing; he wouldn't listen anyway. The man I knew was gone. I didn't know this stranger who had just cast me aside like I was nothing. Gage Channing had made me feel a lot of things in the time I'd known him, but never this—like I meant nothing to him.

I clutched the bag, knuckles turning to ash as the pain threatened to choke me. My whole body was ash. He'd incinerated me. A month ago, I wouldn't have thought it possible, but I loved him, and his hate almost brought me to my knees. Devastation welled in my throat, and I grabbed hold of my last thread of strength. I would not break down in front of him. I wouldn't.

"Wait," he said.

My lifeless feet halted on the first step. Slowly, I turned, a pang of hope fisting my heart.

His mouth never strayed from the mean line it formed. "My mother's ring." He marched to where I stood and held out his hand. "I want it back."

I blinked several times as I slid the ring down my finger, and I made the mistake of meeting his eyes as I dropped it into his waiting palm. That seething hatred wrecked what was left of me.

"You're the last woman on Earth who deserves to wear her ring." And with a wave of his hand, he dismissed me.

Just like that.

And I didn't know how I kept from breaking on the spot.

CHAPTER EIGHTEEN

We left before sunrise, and my tears fell in an endless stream once Eve and I sped down the road. I had a full tank of gas, a credit card with unlimited capabilities, and nowhere to go. No one to turn to. So I just drove, practically on autopilot because I was aware of nothing.

Only the hum of the road underneath me and the trickle of rain splashing the windshield.

Eventually, the flow of heartbreak slowed, and I realized I'd looped downtown Portland on the freeways twice when the first hint of pain began in my lower back. I straightened in the driver's seat and tried to get comfortable, but my head swam.

God, pull it together, Kayla.

Eve slept in the backseat. I glanced into the rearview, noticing how uncomfortable she looked with her head hanging over the edge of the car seat. I couldn't be a wreck when she awoke. Wiping my eyes, I looped the city again and gave myself time to calm down, but it didn't help much, especially when the traffic on the 405 came to a standstill.

Wonderful.

My stomach grumbled, and I was sure Eve must have been hungry too since we'd left *his* house without eating. Traffic inched forward at an agonizing pace—morning rush hour traffic at its finest for sure. My stomach grumbled again, this time accompanied by cramping that gripped my right side with the strength of pliers. I squeezed the steering wheel and told myself everything was okay.

It'd been a couple of stressful days, and I remembered cramping during my pregnancy with Eve. My stomach was too empty; I'd thrown up again before leaving his driveway and had gotten a bit of satisfaction at leaving my nasty bile on his pavement.

Pain spread through my abdomen, and my pulse sped up, thundering in my ears as I drew air into my lungs. This was more than hunger pains. The black interior of the car wavered, as if I saw it through warped glass, and a dull ache started in my shoulder. Suddenly weak, I let my head fall back against the headrest and closed my eyes.

Someone honked. Behind me?

I didn't know. Was traffic moving? I couldn't concentrate beyond the pain. Something was wrong, and I thought back to my first pregnancy; the one Rick caused me to miscarry.

Not again.

Last night, Gage had slammed me into the bathroom wall before he'd stalked out, and when he'd returned...

But he hadn't hurt me. Not really. He may have marked my ass and thighs, but the real damage had been psychological. Someone honked again just as my vision started to fade. Blindly, I reached for my purse, tried to get my hands on my cell as my foot let up on the brake. The car lurched forward and hit something...

I was on my back when I gasped to awareness. My arms

and legs thrashed, and someone held them down. Panic cut off my air, and I couldn't make a sound, so where was that screaming coming from? That gut-wrenching crying? Sounded much too young to be me.

Eve.

Eve was crying. Where was she? I needed her by me, needed her hand in mine so she wouldn't be alone and scared. I found my voice but no more than a whimper escaped as my right side lit on fire.

"...into shock! Let's move it!"

Voices, commotion, bodies crowding me, hands reaching, yet I could grab onto nothing. I sucked in each breath, as if through a straw, and a drop of sweat trickled down my face. My whole body heated—too hot, too drenched. I was burning alive where my baby nestled; my tiny baby who had yet to form arms and legs, fingers and toes. Who barely had a heartbeat.

I was losing him, and Eve had asked for a brother last Christmas.

My stomach dropped at the sensation of being lifted, and when I opened my eyes for a second, squinting against the colorful lights that strobed atop the ambulance, I saw the ominous clouds overhead. Thick and grey, they extinguished the brilliance of the rising sun and set the scene perfectly for this day.

"Wh...what's happening?" I managed to say.

"We're taking you to the ER. We're doing everything we can to help you," a deep voice assured.

But the crying hadn't stopped. My poor baby. Why was she crying? "My daughter..."

"She's okay. An officer is taking her to the hospital. Is there someone we can call to meet her?"

"Gage"—I felt myself sinking, much too fast—"Channing." Why had I given his name? He hated me, hated the baby.

The baby...

"I'm pregnant." I moaned as another wave of pain hit. I must be dying, I thought before there was simply...nothing.

CHAPTER NINETEEN

A low moan roused me, followed by a familiar voice saying my name with a hint of hope. Someone moaned again, and I realized it was me. I forced my lids open, squinting against the soft light that seared my eyes.

"Ian?" I had to be dreaming. Why would he be here? I hadn't heard from him in weeks. In fact, I wasn't even sure where *here* was.

"Hey." His gentle voice came from my left.

I swerved my head and blinked the room into focus. A small and windowless area, partitioned by curtains, enclosed us. Ian sat at my bedside, and I noticed a monitor behind him. "Why..." God, why did talking grate my throat like sandpaper? And why was I in the hospital? At least, I assumed it was a hospital. Sure smelled like one. "Why am I here?"

"How much do you remember?"

"Um..." Driving. Crying. Pain. "I was driving. We were stopped in traffic..." I drew a blank after that, though the feeling I should recall something—a voice assuring me everything would be okay—remained.

And crying. I remembered Eve crying.

"You were on the 405 when you passed out," he said, fingers folding around mine. "Another motorist called 9-1-1."

I squeezed his hand, mainly because I needed to hold onto something, and he just happened to be there. "What happened? Where's Eve?"

His gaze fell. "Did you know you were pregnant?"

Were.

I sucked in a quick breath. "The baby?"

"I'm sorry. Your pregnancy was ectopic." He pulled his hand from mine and wiped both palms down his face, and I realized how exhausted he seemed. "Your tube ruptured. I was the attending when they brought you in. I've never been so scared in my life. They had to rush you into surgery."

I comprehended his words, but mostly I felt numb. "Am I gonna be okay?"

He slumped into the chair. "The internal bleeding wasn't as bad as they feared. You lost some blood, and they couldn't save the tube, but you should recover fine."

"Where's Eve?"

He clenched his jaw. "She's in the waiting room with Gage."

He came.

A nurse appeared from behind the curtain. "Good, you're awake," she said. "They're about to move you to a more comfortable room. Are you in any pain?"

"Um, I don't think so," I said, though I hadn't tried to move yet either.

She fastened a blood pressure cuff around my arm, and a machine buzzed. "You'll probably feel woozy from the pain meds." She took more vitals and then made notes in a chart. "I'll leave you in Dr. Kaplan's hands." With a smile, she disappeared through the gap in the curtains.

Ian fell eerily silent, and I was too drowsy to ask what

was on his mind. I must have dozed off, because they startled me awake when they moved me into a private room. Ian never left my side.

"Aren't you supposed to be working?" I mumbled, rubbing sleep from my eyes.

"My shift was almost over when the ambulance brought you in. You're stuck with me." He settled into a chair and leaned forward. "Kayla," he began hesitantly, resting both elbows on his knees, "we need to talk about the bruises."

"What?"

"On your backside. You're black and"—he cut off and swallowed—"You're black and blue, and I'm pretty sure I know why."

I closed my eyes. "I don't want to talk about it."

"I'm not the only one concerned. The staff here mentioned abuse."

"And you helped them with their assumptions, didn't you?"

"I can't keep quiet about this anymore. He's hurting you. What are you gonna do when he starts in on Eve?"

I jerked into a sitting position, grimacing as pain seared my abdomen. "Gage would never hurt her."

"He's got you brainwashed—"

"You need to stop *right now*." The warning in my voice must have registered because he gaped at me. "I'm not blind to his ways, and I'm not a pushover either. What's important is how he's treated my daughter, and he's been nothing but good to her."

"And what about you? How does he treat you?"

The echo of Gage's mistrust pained my heart, and I pushed the memory into a hidden compartment of my mind. "What we do in the privacy of our bedroom is none of your business."

"You're in denial."

"No," I choked. "I just lost my baby and the last thing I need is another lecture from you."

"I know you're hurting, but I can't ignore this. Seeing you hurt like that..." He shook his head. "A social worker is waiting to speak with you. You need to talk to her."

"What good is talking to some stranger about my sex life going to do?" I didn't care if my words got under his skin; his burrowed into mine like a chigger.

He winced. "Talk to her. That's all I'm asking."

"I can't believe you got a social worker involved."

"Don't blame me. I didn't leave those bruises on your body."

Regardless of how much Gage had hurt me, he'd stopped when I said the safe word. That had to mean something, right? Or was I so far gone from logic and reason that I didn't recognize good from bad anymore? "I told you I was wrong for you, but you wouldn't listen."

"I did listen!" He sprang to his feet. "I've done my best to move on," he continued, lowering his voice, "but when you're brought into my ER, nearly dead and covered in bruises...I can't handle that. I'm not sorry for loving you, and I won't apologize for saying what you don't want to hear. You *need* help."

"You need to stay out of this."

His body tensed. "You're a smart, courageous woman, and you've always put Eve first. If I know nothing else about the person you've become, I know that's still true. You can't go back to him. If not for yourself, do it for her."

The sting of fresh tears threatened, but I refused to let them spill. "He doesn't want me anymore."

"What?" He sounded incredulous.

I let out a bitter laugh. "He thinks the baby is...was... yours. He says he can't have kids." I glanced up at him. "Did you know Liz was pregnant?"

The question hit him like a punch to the gut. He stumbled back. "No, she wasn't."

"Gage says she was. He also says the baby was yours."

"That's...nuts. Why wouldn't he tell me?"

"I don't know." I absently played with the edge of the blanket wrapped around my body. "Did he ask to see me?"

"I suspect you know as well as I do that Gage doesn't ask—he demands."

"I want to see him."

"I can't change your mind, can I?"

"We already went over this in Texas. I made my choice." Well, it'd been made for me, but I wouldn't tell him that. "I care about you, but you need to let me go." I narrowed my eyes. "And you never should have gotten a social worker involved."

"I didn't. Gage's abuse did."

I gritted my teeth. "It's unnecessary. If anyone asks, tell them the truth. I like kinky sex."

"Jesus, Kayla..."

"Can you please send him in? I need to see Eve."

"Fine," he said in a clipped tone. "I'll send the bastard in." He stormed from the room, and not two minutes later, Gage stood in the doorway.

I looked behind him, hoping to spot my daughter's short auburn curls, but she was nowhere in sight. "Where's Eve?"

"Ian took her to the cafeteria," he said as he closed the door. He stepped to my bedside and sank into a chair. "She'll be back in a while. I wanted to speak with you alone first."

"Why? You hate me, remember?"

I jumped when his hand settled over mine. "You need me."

"I needed you yesterday."

He dropped his head onto the thin mattress, next to my hip, and kissed the palm he held. "I don't hate you."

"But you don't trust me."

"We're not doing this now. You just got out of surgery."

"Why not? Ian didn't hold back."

"What are you talking about?"

I snorted. "Apparently, the hospital staff thinks you're abusing me. He wants me to talk to a social worker."

"Maybe you should. Maybe you should tell them everything. You could easily send me back to jail."

"I was willing, Gage."

"That's not entirely true. I kidnapped you, and last night..."

My breath hitched, then shuddered out. "What you did and said hurt, but I knew what I was getting into when I stayed. You gave me the option of leaving, but I stayed." I caught his gaze. "I was willing. You made me admit it, remember?"

"Yes," he murmured. "I remember. I molded you into what I wanted, and then I threw you out at the first sign of trouble."

"Why'd you do it?"

He fell quiet for a few long moments. "It was deja vu, Kayla. I should have punished you for lying to me, but demanding marriage and then making you leave was wrong." He held his mother's ring between two fingers. "This belongs on your finger. No matter what, you are and always will be *mine*." My mouth gaped as he slid the diamond onto my finger—as if he'd never demanded it back to begin with. "I was scared of hurting you," he said. "*Really* hurting you." He paused, avoiding my eyes. "Did I cause your miscarriage? I don't care that it was his, if I made you lose your baby—"

"The baby *wasn't* his!" I yanked my hand from his grasp. "You refuse to believe me, but it's the truth." Sorrow welled in my throat. "The baby was *ours*." Turning away, I buried my face in the pillow and muffled my sobs. I formed a ball, bringing about pain from the incision but instead of recoiling from it, I held on to it, breathed through it until I could think of nothing else.

His voice called to me through my despair, and I tensed when his arms came around me. Gage wasn't the comforting kind.

"I didn't mean to do this..." he cut off, strangled.

"You didn't. It was a tubal pregnancy. A miscarriage was inevitable." His embrace comforted me more than I wanted to admit, especially after what he'd said and done, but I needed his arms to live through the next second, the next minute, the next hour. "Why can't you trust me? You swore nothing happened with Katherine, and I took your word for it. Why can't you do the same?"

"It's not that simple." He withdrew his arms, sat up, and scooted to the edge of the bed, as if he needed distance.

"Then make it simple. God, you made me love you!"

"What else do you want me to say, Kayla?"

"Everything! I want answers. I want to understand why you're so adamant the baby wasn't yours."

He hung his head. "They told me back in high school I can't have kids. I sustained a lot of damage from...it doesn't matter."

"Damage from what?"

"A nasty brawl with the bastard my mother married."

A beat of heavy silence weighed on us, and I hurt for him as much as I did for myself in that moment. "Why didn't you tell me?"

"Because telling you would have led to this! You and your questions. I try not to think about the past, and I sure as hell don't talk about it."

"But you put me on birth control..." I shook my head as nothing about this made sense. "Why would you do that if you thought you couldn't father children?"

"I gave you a placebo, Kayla. I *can't* father children."

"Obviously, you can," I snapped. "Whoever diagnosed you made a mistake, or something changed—"

"I'm not discussing this with you," he interrupted. "You need to focus on recovering."

"I didn't sleep with him! It's only been you—in four fucking years, Gage, it's been you!"

The door opened, and Ian appeared in the entrance with Eve. Gage stood, his gaze dark and dangerous. He was still full of rage—toward me, toward his brother. "They tell me you're being released tomorrow," he said. "Call me. I'll come get you." He stepped around Ian, glaring at him the whole time, and closed the door upon his exit.

"You okay?" Ian asked.

"Yeah," I lied. I held my breath as Eve dawdled to my bedside, her head down, and told myself to get a grip. I wasn't about to fall apart in front of my daughter. "I'm sorry I scared you, baby." I scooted over and patted the space next to me, and she hopped up. "Mommy's okay." I tilted her chin up. "Okay?"

She nodded. "Are we going home with Gage?"

I blinked, my lids becoming heavy from the pain meds they'd given me. Instead of answering her, I glanced at Ian. "Thanks for watching her."

"No problem."

Eve cuddled into my side, and almost instantly, she fell asleep. "She must have been so scared," I said.

"She's a trooper like her mom." He wandered around the small room, and silence fell on us for a while. "I don't understand why you put yourself through this."

"It's...complicated."

"Don't give me that," he said quietly, though the vehemence in his tone hinted at frustration.

"You won't like the truth."

He let out a bitter laugh. "I'm sure I won't, but I think I deserve it."

"I love him."

"You loved Rick at one time too."

"It's different. Gage and I have our issues, but he's not Rick."

"No, he is exactly like Rick. Abuse is abuse. You're smart enough to know this, but you're letting sex get in the way of your thinking."

"I'm not talking about this with you. It's not fair to you, and I just don't have the energy." I brushed my hair from my eyes, and his gaze lingered on my hand.

Shit. I'd forgotten about the ring.

He strode to my side, snatched my hand between his, and glared at the diamond, as if he could make it disappear. "I should have been the one to put this on your finger. I can't believe you're actually going to marry him. Are you insane?"

"Please, don't do this."

"He has no remorse, Kayla, and he knows nothing about loving someone."

I pulled my hand from his. "That's not true. I've seen sides of him I would have sworn didn't exist a year ago. I can't help the way I feel, Ian."

"Me neither, so where does that leave us?"

"Nowhere."

He nodded, his mouth forming a tight line. "Okay. I get it." He opened the door, and his face and movements spoke of resignation as he exited the room. I'd gotten my wish—he'd given up. I'd just destroyed my first love, a decade long friendship, and I couldn't even muster a tear. I didn't have any left.

CHAPTER TWENTY

Two weeks. That was how long Gage shut me out after he brought me home.

That word bothered me.

This was no longer home, and Gage was no longer the man who lit my world on fire. I didn't know who this stranger was—this cold and detached man who couldn't bring himself to touch me.

At least where Eve was concerned, he hadn't changed. Clearly, he'd won her over again in the hospital, because she'd resumed shadowing him. They got closer every day, while he and I grew further apart.

He was in the wrong, and I should be furious at the things he'd said and done, at his refusal to believe the baby was his, but I experienced nothing but despair. I preferred him yelling or screaming; wished he'd bend me over his knee and beat me if it meant he'd feel *something*. As the days wore on and I slowly recovered, his indifference squeezed the last bit of warmth from my soul. I might as well have been back in that basement, my heart bleeding as his hatred lanced me.

The nights were the worst—the darkest hours being the darkest in my mind. He slept beside me, but we never touched. Never kissed. Never talked. I lay next to him for hours, inches from his heat but unable to take comfort in it, and I tortured myself with memories of the night he'd beat me with the bullwhip...and the fact that I'd lost another baby.

Being shut out like this...it sucked the life from me, and I'd done nothing to deserve it.

I couldn't take it anymore. The first time I waited on my knees for him, I'd hoped for even a marginal reaction; a stiffening of his muscles, a clenched jaw—anything—but he barely gave me a second glance as he ordered me into bed. Ignoring his command, I waited on the hardwood long after he shut off the light and slid between the sheets, and eventually I crawled in beside him, holding my breath to stanch the flow of sorrow. My tears drenched my pillow that night.

The following evening I did the same—waited on my knees and prepared to go to battle. I'd rather him furious than indifferent. He made me wait a long time, which I guessed was his way of avoiding my display of submission.

"What are you doing?" he demanded as he came into our bedroom and closed the door. "I thought I made myself clear last night." Like he did every night, he shed his clothes and headed for the bathroom. The door slammed shut behind him. I glanced at my ring, wondering why it still decorated my finger, wondering why I was still here if he no longer wanted me.

He opened the door a few minutes later, and I still hadn't moved. "Get up, Kayla." He strode to where I knelt, his cock standing proud, though apparently he had no intention of using it. I fisted his shaft, earning a low growl from him.

"Please," I said, raising my eyes to his, "Master." I paused, waiting for a reaction to that word. He gave none. "Let me suck you off." I closed my mouth around him, and he immediately shoved me back. I lost my balance and fell on my butt.

"Get up," he said through clenched teeth. Our breaths came fast and heavy, and I thought he was about to say something more, but he stepped away and headed for the bed, leaving me on my ass in the middle of the room. I wiped my eyes and got to my feet.

"Maybe I *should* fuck him, since you believe I did. I might as well do the deed and deserve the bastard way you've been treating me."

He whirled, grabbed me, and slammed me to the mattress. "You don't see him, you don't talk to him"—his fingers clamped around my wrists, and he wrenched them above my head—"you don't fucking *think* about him."

"I don't, Gage. I don't think about him at all. All I can think about is you and the way you've shut me out. It's killing me. Please. I'll call you Master again, I'll let you beat me with the bullwhip. I'll do whatever you want, just stop hurting me like this."

He blinked several times. "I...can't."

"Why can't you trust me?"

Loosening his grip, he turned his back and mumbled, "Go to sleep."

Tears silently streamed down my face, and I held my breath to keep quiet as we settled under the covers. I didn't know what to do, didn't know how to get beyond the wall he'd constructed. How could we work through this if he wouldn't talk to me?

Desperation took over, and I spread my thighs, slid my fingers between them, and rubbed my clit. I almost came on the spot—that's how sexually frustrated he'd left me. A cry escaped, but I focused on drawing out the pleasure. He'd taught me a lot about control. I opened wider and hooked a foot over his calf, and I blatantly worked myself toward orgasm.

Blatantly disobeyed him.

He kicked my foot off and turned to face me. His eyes darkened, narrowed.

I didn't stop. Let him be pissed. Let him punish me for masturbating. I didn't care. My eyes fluttered shut, and I moaned again.

"Look at me while you disobey me. I want to see your shame when you come."

Cheeks flooding with embarrassment, I arched my spine as my climax pulsed around my fingers. The blanket fell below my breasts, and my nipples puckered in the chilly room, begging for his hot mouth. I crashed from the high, my gaze connected to his, and the awkwardness of the moment wasn't lost on me. I withdrew my hand, but he pushed my fingers back into silky, wet heat.

"Come for me again, until it's painful, until you think you can't stand it anymore. Work your wet cunt, Kayla. Dip your fingers in and see what you've done to yourself."

"I...I don't think I can..."

"Oh yes, you can."

"Please, Gage..."

"Do it now."

I worked myself toward another orgasm and held my breath as the pressure built. My whole body shuddered and pulsed, and his groan only added to the intensity. Finally, a reaction.

"Again," he said, his voice hoarse.

He made me rub myself into multiple orgasms, and I didn't think I had it in me to come again until he sucked a nipple into his mouth. He covered my fingers with his, pressing hard on my clit, and literally forced my hand. An overpowering wave of pain seized my body.

"Stop, it hurts!" I cried.

"Keep going."

He pressed harder, keeping my hand in place. I writhed, squirmed...pleaded as moisture trickled down my cheeks. "I...I...please...can't."

"You can and you will."

I vocalized the pain in strangled grunts, openly sobbing as I came again. "Stop hating me."

"I don't hate you." He scooted away so we didn't touch at all. "Now stop pushing me and go to sleep."

"I didn't sleep with him," I choked. "It was your baby. Stop hating me for losing it."

"God, Kayla," he said, abruptly crushing me in his arms. "I don't hate you—I fucking hate myself!" He buried his face in my shoulder, and his body trembled as he held me. We stayed like that for a long time, his body wrapped around mine, shuddering with the emotion he'd bottled up since I'd come home from the hospital.

"I can't face what I said to you. I told you I hated it, told you I hated you."

"Gage..."

"I'm so fucked up." Something wet trickled down the side of my neck, and I was stunned to realize it was his tears. "I know it was mine. I didn't want to admit it, didn't want to face the monster I'd become. I'm sorry, baby. I don't deserve you."

"Deserve me then," I whispered. "Love me again. I'm dying without you."

His lips found mine, and he rolled me to my back, wedged my legs apart, and slipped inside where he belonged.

And it was like coming home.

He trapped my hands above my head and nipped at my neck, brushed his lips across my breasts, opened his mouth over first one nipple then the other, and like always, his body owned me. His thighs nestled between mine, rubbing my skin as he pushed into me with patience, though I knew he needed to come. It had been long for him too, these past two weeks.

"Fuck, Kayla," he said, voice ragged as he spilled into me with a violent thrust. His deep groan filled the air, and afterward, for the first time in what seemed like forever, he cocooned me in his embrace.

Definitely like coming home.

We lay in quiet harmony for a while, though neither of us slept. I played with the diamond on my finger, sliding it to the knuckle then down again. "You put your ring back on my finger, so I'm assuming you still expect me to marry you?"

"Damn right, I do. I made a mistake, and now it's rectified."

"This is what you call fixing things? Keeping your distance for two weeks, refusing to talk to me, and then pretending nothing's wrong?"

"I didn't trust myself with you."

"How will you ever trust me if you can't trust yourself?"

"Good question." He sighed. "Tell me what to do, Kayla, and I'll do it. I don't want to hurt you anymore."

"Go to counseling."

"So you think a shrink is the answer?"

I practically heard the scowl in his tone. "I don't know what the answer is, but I can't do this anymore. I can handle...tolerate...your rules and your need to hurt me physically, but I can't handle you not trusting me. I can't handle you shutting me out—not when I've given you everything." I grasped his arms and forced my next words out. "Either get help, or let me go for good."

Please, don't let me go.

"Okay."

"Okay?" I raised a brow.

"I'll get...help." He tightened his hold on me. "As soon as you marry me."

"I'll marry you as soon as you trust me."

"I do trust you."

"No, you don't."

"I'm working on it."

"Then prove it."

"And how do you suggest I do that?"

He had a point. Trust was something not only earned but shown through action, and he had a long way to go. What was the one thing he trusted no one with? My heart skipped a beat.

Control.

That was his Achilles heel—the single thing he never gave up because it left him too vulnerable. If he had to choose between his millions and control, I suspected he'd choose the latter.

"Submit to me for one night."

He laughed. "That will never happen, Kayla. I submit to no one."

"Then I can't marry you."

"Of course you can."

"Do you love me, Gage?"

"That's a stupid question."

I shook my head. "No, it's not. Ian wanted one night, and I tried, but in the end I didn't love him enough. Do you love me enough? You're asking for everything. You expect me to hand over my entire life to you—my free will, my decisions, my body. Give me yours for one night," I said, my voice going soft. "All I'm asking for is one night. Prove you can give me your trust, and I'll marry you."

"One night?"

I nodded.

"And what do you plan to do on this *one* night?"

My pulse sped up as all kinds of wicked things went through my head, though there was only one thing I really wanted from him, and if I could pull this off, he'd give it to me. He'd hate me for it, probably make my ass black and blue afterward, but it would be worth it.

"Guess you'll have to wait and see."

CHAPTER TWENTY-ONE

This felt wrong, but God if I wasn't tingling at the thought of making him submit. The idea was exhilarating, arousing... absolutely terrifying. We stood in the middle of the basement, three feet apart from each other, yet the aura of his presence wrapped around me as tangibly as his arms. I was a moment away from sinking to my knees and saying I'd changed my mind.

His lips quirked. "You can't do it, can you?"

I balled my hands. "Strip."

His smile never wavered from amused as he unbuttoned his shirt. "You're nervous. I can read you well. Having second thoughts?"

"I always have second thoughts when it comes to you, so obviously you don't read me well enough."

He let his shirt fall to the floor and then reached for his belt. "What are you going to do with me, now that you have me here under your control?"

We both knew it was a lie. I didn't have control. Not yet. "Give me your belt."

He pulled it from his pant loops and tossed it to me. My

mouth parted, breath moistening my lips as he lowered his slacks. Did anything fail to turn him on? His cock stood tall and proud. Suddenly, I lost my inhibitions.

Payback was a bitch.

"Lie on the bed."

"There are many ways to lie on a bed, Kayla."

Didn't I know it. "On your back."

He did so without a word, without shame, and his gaze followed me across the room. I found his leather cuffs and returned to him. I wasn't nearly as capable as he in restraining someone, but I managed to bind his hands to the headboard. I stood back and eyed him.

"Is this all you got?" he asked.

Dropping the belt, I laughed to cover my nervousness and retreated another step, far enough so he could see me from head to toe. I unzipped my dress and let it pool around my feet, revealing nothing underneath except for a pair of thigh highs and a garter belt. No panties. I still obeyed that rule, mainly because it would drive him wild.

His gaze lowered to the lace tops of my stockings, and his appreciation heated my skin. "God, you're sexy."

Fingers trembling, I lightly pinched my nipples, watching him the whole time. Truth was, I had no idea what to do, and I was scared of going to him. He still owned me, even though he was the one cuffed to the damn headboard this time.

Stop being a coward.

I sauntered to the bed and climbed up, my thighs sliding along his as I straddled him. "I'm going to tease you until you beg." I brought my hands to my breasts again, thumbs brushing the peaks until they pebbled into aching buds. His lips parted, as if he were about to speak, but he mashed them together instead. I stared at him, amazed at the sight of him restrained and helpless underneath me.

I dipped my fingers between folds already slick with need and stroked myself while he watched. His chest rose and fell more rapidly as my breathing escalated, and when I came, throwing my head back and arching my spine, I heard him groan.

"You want to come, don't you?" I said, moving down his body and lowering my head, my lips an inch from his wet tip. I raised my eyes to his.

"What do you think, Kayla?"

"I think you're about to beg." I darted my tongue out and lapped up his moisture.

He sucked in a breath. "You know what your mouth does to me."

"You're not coming tonight."

He flexed his hands in the restraints, his eyes deepening to indigo, and my heart pounded. I was going to pay for this, had known it all along, but that hadn't stopped me from strong-arming him into those leather cuffs. The fact that he was playing along with my pathetic attempt at making him submit said a lot.

But he'd still make me pay, especially after what I was about to do. I didn't have the sadist gene, and he had it in spades. I would hurt him though—I'd force his secrets from him and deal with the consequences later.

"You're not coming," I repeated, "unless you give me what I want."

"What do you want?"

"Everything." I licked down his shaft, tongue caressing silky skin, and kissed my way back to the tip. He groaned, his cock twitching under my tongue.

"I'm going to make your ass so red for this," he said through clenched teeth. He looked ready to either devour me, or make me hurt. He'd probably do both simultaneously if I freed him.

"I'm sure you will, but I want answers, Gage, so it's worth it to me."

"What are you talking about?"

Instead of answering, I took him deep, and he raised his hips, his hands bunching into fists as I worked him the way he liked. His body language spoke to me. He was close, his desire trickling out with each slide of my mouth. I curled my fingers around the base of his shaft and squeezed, grazing my teeth just under the head.

A warning.

He closed his eyes, his muscles strung tight as a guitar string. I held still, refusing to give him release, my teeth hinting at pain if he moved an inch. His eyes popped open when I got to my knees. I had all kinds of questions I wanted to ask—things he'd never tell me normally. I had him by the balls, literally, and I wasn't going to waste this opportunity.

"How long did you plan this, before I stole from you?"

"Fuck, Kayla. You're really going there?"

"I'm going there." I fisted his erection and worked him with my hand. "Answer me. How long?"

His hips rose and fell. "Years. Long before I hired you. He wanted you, so I did too."

"You hiring me...that wasn't a coincidence, was it?"

"No."

"Why'd you wait so long to make your move?"

"No opportunity," he gasped. "Put your mouth on me again."

"No. You're not the one in control this time."

"Shit," he said, strangled, "when it comes to you, I'm never in control. Haven't you figured that out yet?"

I paused. "That makes two of us."

"Don't stop, baby. I need your mouth."

I withdrew my hand, ignoring his protests, and circled my clit, though finding release a second time would take longer. "Doing what you did to me...did it help? Do you hate them less now?"

"Them?"

"Ian and his father."

"I can't believe you just said his name while you're straddling me, flicking your damn clit."

I imagined Gage's hands and mouth on my breasts and moaned.

"If you're thinking of him—"

"I'm thinking of you," I interrupted, glancing at his stiff cock. Not even our conversation turned him off. "Answer my question. Do you hate them less?"

"No."

"So it was for nothing, then?"

"I got you, didn't I?"

I sighed as the pressure at my core built. "You got me, so let it go. Hating him does nothing." I squeezed my eyes shut and focused because my next question wasn't going to be easy for either of us. "How bad did his father hurt you?"

"We're not going there. *Ever.*"

"Yes, we are. I want your trust, Gage. Trust me enough to talk about it."

"Not while your cunt is leaking all over my thighs."

I laughed. "After the messed up shit you've put me through, I think you can handle it."

He exhaled. "He beat me. Belts, paddles, sticks—anything he could get his hands on. But my mom...for years I was too young to stop it. So you see, I know exactly how much it hurts."

"Why do you do it, then?"

"Before Liz, I didn't. I hurt myself instead."

His confession broke my composure. My hand fell away, and my eyes burned as I looked down at him.

"Don't feel sorry for me," he snapped. "I've never

touched a woman who didn't want it—until you. I knew exactly what I was doing when I forced you into that contract. I'm beyond salvation, so don't think you can fix me."

"You don't need to be fixed. You just need to be loved."

"Kayla, I need to be fucked. Stop toying with me."

"You don't give the orders tonight." I reclaimed the wet, throbbing place between my legs. Later, I'd torture myself with what he'd revealed, but for now I concentrated on the touch of my hand, the heat of his thighs, and remembered the exquisite sensation of his mouth on me. My hoarse cries worked him into a crazed beast. He yanked on the cuffs and drew his knees up before I could stop him. His powerful thighs wrapped around me, and he locked his ankles, holding me prisoner while I worked myself toward another orgasm. His cock nestled against his abdomen, solid and dripping his need all over his skin in wax-like art.

My climax washed over me, a shuddering wave of intensity that gave him the upper hand. He tightened his legs and lifted, and I'd barely caught my breath when he pushed into me. I kicked from his grasp and crawled up his chest. "You're horrible at obeying. I didn't say you could fuck me."

"Free my hands," he said with a growl. "I need to touch you."

I smiled. "Don't like submitting? You make me do it all the time."

He smirked. "Enjoy this while you can. I assure you—you'll never get me here again."

I didn't doubt it for a second. I lowered my lips to his, and he forced them apart and sucked my tongue into his mouth. He might be helpless beneath me, but he made me submit in that kiss.

"You want me to beg?" he said, breathless as he wrenched his mouth from mine. "Fine. I'll beg. Please, let me go so I can punish your fine little ass and fuck you until you scream."

"Hmm, that does sound tempting," I said, "especially when you talk dirty." I brought my lips to his ear. "But I'm not about to waste this night. Now shush—you're balls aren't blue enough yet."

CHAPTER TWENTY-TWO

I kept him awake most of the night, his hands fisted and body rigid in a constant state of arousal. Considering what he'd done to me a few weeks ago, I couldn't say I felt bad about it. But the instant I released him, he pinned me to the mattress, and a slew of filth left his mouth as he fucked me like a hungry, uncaged tiger. He was saving the red ass for later, he'd promised.

Now we sat at the breakfast table with Eve, and I didn't miss the curve of his mouth every time he looked at me. Obviously, he had diabolical ideas running through his head, though if his preoccupation with punishing me kept him from pressing for a wedding date, I'd let him have his fun.

He'd done what I asked. He'd given me his body for one night, but I still wasn't ready to marry him. A large part of me was getting there, but he failed to understand the small part that still bled from his actions and words. I couldn't just turn those feelings off, no matter how far he went to prove himself.

I waved to Eve as the bus pulled away, and for the longest time I stood in the driveway, oblivious to the rain.

"Come inside," Gage said. "You're going to get sick."

"That's a myth, you know. Rain doesn't make you sick. Viruses and bacteria do."

"Okay smart ass, inside now. We have three hours before she returns, and I'm not going to waste them. Go to the basement and prepare for me."

"Gage, I—"

"Don't argue with me," he interrupted. "I've gone soft on you, but no more. You need to be reminded of who's submitting here, Kayla."

I gazed up at him, taking in the water dripping from his hair and into the collar of his jacket. He'd never looked sexier. I stepped passed him and headed toward the house. "Yes, Master."

"What did you say?"

"You heard me." I hurried through the door and left a trail of water and clothing in my wake. I didn't waste time in the bathroom, and when his feet thumped down the staircase, I not only knelt on the floor, but I had my nose to the hardwood. He was going to hurt me—I knew it with certainty—yet I couldn't contain the flutter of excitement in my stomach. It had been so long since he'd truly wielded his authority over me. His dominance and sadism had taken a backseat to my recovery.

But I knew he was hungry for it, and I was ashamed to admit I was too. I wanted him to take me.

He didn't speak as he neared me, though I sensed him removing his shirt. The heat of his body warmed my skin as he pulled my arms behind my back. He'd never tied them this way before—at the elbows and wrists. His fingers curled around my shoulders.

"Get up." He helped me to my feet. "Spread your legs."

I did as told. He knelt down and fastened a spreader bar between my ankles, and then he disappeared from sight. He wrenched my arms straight out behind me, raising them painfully high and attaching the binding to a hook in the ceiling. The position forced me down, bent at the waist. I dropped my head, and my hair nearly brushed the floor.

"How does that feel?" he asked.

"It hurts." Blood rushed to my brain, making me dizzy, so I lifted my head.

"Good. It's supposed to." He pulled out a set of nipple clamps.

"Please, no."

"No safe words during punishment."

"What am I being punished for?"

"I'm punishing you," he said as he clamped one nipple before moving to the other, "for getting yourself off so many times last night while leaving me in agony. For making me talk about things I had no plans of ever discussing with you."

I winced. These clamps were the worst yet; they had weights dangling from them. I sucked in a breath. "You're a hypocrite."

"No, I simply know my place. You do too, or you wouldn't have had your nose to the floor. You knew this was coming."

"What are you going to do to me?"

"Whatever I please."

I closed my eyes long enough to catch my breath, which was a mistake because I never saw the gag coming. This one was different; it forced my mouth open in a perfect "O" big enough for his cock to fit through. He stepped back, and I peeked up through my hair, my legs shaking under the pressure of keeping balance.

"I do love the sight of you like this. You're so vulnerable right now."

Reaching for his belt, he unbuckled it and lowered the

zipper of his pants. He fisted my hair, urging my head up, and slipped his cock through the opening in the gag.

"You have the sweetest mouth," he said, breathless. His hips rocked slowly at first before he jackhammered in and out of my mouth.

The taste of him turned me on, and if not for the gag, I would have closed my lips around him and worked him hard. Would have made *his* knees tremble the way mine did. His release hit me in a gush, but I had trouble swallowing with my jaw locked wide open. He let go of my hair, and I dropped my head, watching as his cum dribbled from my mouth onto the floor. He wiped my chin with a washcloth, and then he stepped back and pulled the belt from his pants.

I suddenly feared that belt. I couldn't say why, as I'd grown used to it during the few weeks we'd had together before I'd found out I was pregnant, but now, the thought of him using it made me cry. I squeezed my eyes shut, and my tears were lost in my hair. The first strike was soft, a warm up. As the second one landed, harder, on the back of my thighs, I realized why this lashing reduced me to a blubbering mess.

All I could think about was the baby I'd lost, and how he'd said he hated it. I trembled from the force of my sobs as drool dripped down my chin. The sounds coming from me were gut wrenching and deep, and I couldn't hide them.

He removed the clamps and gag, pushed the hair from my eyes, and cradled my face, his thumbs brushing away the tears. "Tell me what's wrong."

"I...I can't...can't do this now. All I can think about is..."

"The baby," he said, regret strangling his tone, "and the way I treated you that night."

Another sob hitched, and as he moved behind me and freed my arms, a wave of guilt overcame me, swift and dark and suffocating. I hadn't cried enough over the loss; I'd locked the grief away instead. Now it choked me. He removed the spreader bar and then carried me to bed. His body spooned mine, both arms wrapping me in his embrace, and I thought about how he'd stopped. He could have ignored my tears and kept going—it's what he would have done in the past.

But this wasn't the Gage I'd known back then.

"Do you think about the baby?"

"All the time," he said, voice rough and deep. "But I try not to. That night...it was one of the darkest moments of my life, and I hate to think I contributed to what you went through."

"You've changed."

"Or maybe you didn't know me before."

I shook my head. "No, something's changed."

"I had too much time to think in prison."

"About?" I laced my fingers with his.

"Eleven months, twenty-five days, four hours, and thirty-nine minutes—that's how long it took to realize what you mean to me. You make me want to be a better person, Kayla. No one's done that in a very long time."

"Did you consider that while you were kidnapping me?"

"I wasn't considering much of anything. I couldn't get the image of you and *him* out of my fucking head. So yes, I went crazy. Haven't you figured out by now that crazy is what I do best?"

I let out a breath. "You could say that."

"I won't apologize for who I am, for loving you this way."

I found his words eerily similar to Ian's in the hospital. "I don't expect an apology from you, Gage. I know better."

"But I *am* sorry."

I stiffened. "But you just said..."

"I know what I said, and I meant it. But I'm sorry I said those things to you, sorry I took back the ring. It belongs on your finger, and you belong to me, so let's set a date already."

"I'm not ready."

"Kayla..." He paused, taking a deep breath. "Pick a date, or I'll pick one for us, but this isn't negotiable. We're getting married."

"You're not being fair!" I pushed against his arms, but he only held on tighter.

"I'm rarely fair, but I am your Master and you will obey me. Now pick a damn date—any date in the next few weeks."

"You pick it, since you're in such a hurry."

"Baby, I submitted to you last night. That was the deal. Now pick a date, or I *will* take my belt to your ass, and I won't stop this time, no matter how much you cry."

"Why do have to be such a bastard?"

"It's in my nature." He fell silent for a beat. "Do you still love me?"

"Define *love*."

He rolled us over and pinned me, but his deep blue eyes did the job just as effectively. "It's all-consuming, leaves me unable to breath when I look at you, and when you submit, truly submit your very being to me, there's no better feeling in the world. That's when I know you love me—when you lie in wait of my every whim and desire. I don't give a fuck what the world thinks of us, Kayla, but we need each other. Tell me when you'll marry me."

"As soon as you want," I whispered.

His lips claimed mine, and we became a tangle of tongues and limbs as our bodies came together.

"You overwhelm me," I gasped. "Gage...I'm gonna come."

"Not yet," he moaned. "Not until I give you permission." He held my wrists in one hand above my head as he sank into me, again and again with slow madness.

"Oh God…you're killing me."

"That's the idea." His mouth curved into his devil's grin before he sucked a nipple between his teeth.

"What will you do…if I come anyway?" I was about to, if he didn't stop teasing my breasts with his mouth and fingers.

"I'll deny you for a week."

"I hate you."

"You love me."

"I do," I said, arching as my toes curled.

"Then come for me."

Thank God he gave me permission because I was a goner anyway.

A long while later, he still lingered inside me, and his lips and hands never stopped exploring my body. He left a wet path down my neck.

"Eve will be back soon," I said with a sigh.

"I know." He placed one last kiss on my lips before sliding from bed. We showered and dressed in under ten minutes, and I was just about to climb the stairs when he stopped me.

"Wait. I have something for you." He opened a drawer, pulled out a box, and came toward me. Removing a necklace from the black velvet encasing, he said, "It's an infinity collar." The choker appeared to be made of stainless steel and minimalist in design, save for the diamonds sparkling in the symbol at the front.

"Do you like it?"

"It's beautiful."

He inserted a key into the discreet lock on the backside and opened the collar. "Get on your knees."

I dropped to my knees and clasped my hands at the small of my back.

He swept my hair aside and fastened the choker around my throat. "You make the collar beautiful, Kayla. You'll always be mine, and this piece of jewelry, to which only I hold the key, signifies that. We'll exchange rings during the ceremony, but this is the true token of our relationship. Our love never ends, and neither does my possession of you." He tilted my chin up. "So if you want to back out, do it now."

"Leaving would be the sane thing to do, but you're under my skin, Gage Channing. You've shown me there's a good man hiding somewhere inside your rotten soul."

He grinned. "Don't tell anyone."

CHAPTER TWENTY-THREE

"Are you sure about this?" Stacey asked as she adjusted my veil.

"I'm sure," I reassured her for the fifth time. She'd flown in yesterday, and besides Gage and Eve, she was the only person I knew at my own wedding. The rest of the guests, acquaintances and business associates of Gage's, were only there to witness the wedding of the year.

That's what the local media called it, anyway.

"Okay, then," she said. "Let's get this show on the road." She knelt and straightened the hem of Eve's dress that matched my own. "You know what to do, right, hon?

My daughter nodded, a wide grin on her face.

The music filtered into the back where Stacey had fawned over me as I'd gotten ready. She left the room and walked down the aisle, followed by Eve. I waited, wringing my fingers and shuffling my feet. The first strains of Pachelbel's "Canon in D" began, and I stepped outside the sanctuary of my hiding place.

Everyone stood and faced me, their eyes widening as I came into view. Amongst a chorus of "oohhs and aahhs," I scanned the audience and gave a sigh of relief that Ian was nowhere to be found. Deep down, I feared he'd make an appearance and try to stop the wedding, but he really had given up. The realization caused a pang of sadness in me; I hated how things had ended between us. Mostly, I hated the way I'd hurt him.

I walked over the rose petals Eve sprinkled in her wake, bringing me one, two, three steps closer to *him*. I sensed the heat of his gaze and finally lifted my eyes to his. Oh God…I'd forgotten how well Gage Channing wore a tux. A shiver ran through me at his expression; it encompassed so many things—smoldering desire, lethal resolve, but above all else, ownership. I was his, and this ceremony was only a technicality to make sure the world realized it too.

That walk was the longest of my life, but when I joined him and we laced our fingers together, the significance of the moment left me in awe. I was being reborn from the ashes he'd created.

The wedding officiator recited his introduction and then the vows began.

"Gage Channing, do you take Kayla Sutton to be your wife, to love, honor, and cherish now and forever more?"

"I do," he said, his gaze never leaving mine.

He would push me beyond my limits, always demand more than I wanted to give, but damn if he didn't make me feel alive. I needed him to breathe, and my humiliation and submission were small prices to pay. My body would endure him, because without him it would petrify.

"Kayla Sutton, do you take Gage Channing to be your husband, to love, honor, and obey…"

Obey.

Gage's mouth curved into a satisfied smile. The man performing the ceremony had no idea the weight that word carried in our relationship. Above all else, I would obey him.

"...now and forever more?"

My heart thumped—a drumming beat that grew louder with every second *obey* flitted through my mind. Obey and owned. Two little words, both beginning with the same letter but holding so much meaning in the complexity of our union.

Gage waited for my answer, his sapphire eyes alight with absolute confidence. I was his.

His to command. His to set on fire. His to punish.

His.

I cleared my throat, parted my lips, and confirmed in front of God and the world what Gage and I already knew.

"I do."

His.

Now and forever more.

BOOK THREE

THE DEVIL'S WIFE

"Lead me not into temptation; I can find the way myself."
—Rita Mae Brown

CHAPTER ONE

Snip. The first lock of hair drifted to the tile. I brought the scissors to the left side of my head. Tears rimmed my eyes, threatening to spill over.

Snip. Snip. Snip.

My bare breasts heaved, nipples puckered. I didn't want to be warm. Warmth let feeling in, and I was suddenly and amazingly numb. Besides, warmth deceived with its inherent comfort, and comfort didn't exist in my world—not when he wanted me on my knees. Not when he wanted a meek and pliable and *obedient* robot for a wife.

Snip. Snip. Snip.

The severed strands circled my feet, freeing my shoulders from the weight of the red hair he loved so much. I couldn't help but recognize the significance in this moment, the symbolism, and it terrified me. It was only hair, but this rebellious act would change the tenuous dynamic we'd settled into for the past year. This very moment was about to fracture our world and expose the guts of our lies.

Narrowing my brows in determination, I faced the reflection of the woman whose eyes lit up with something foreign. Something challenging.

Something he wouldn't like.

This strange woman from another time—before rules and rituals and Gage Fucking Channing—was reborn as she lifted the shears and cut off the last section of hair.

Movement in the mirror drew my attention. He stood in the open doorway behind me, his posture inflexible as always. My eyes swerved to his before dropping to the belt clasped in his determined fist.

I whirled, crossed my arms, and silently threw down a challenge. A belt wouldn't cut it this time. I knew it, and now he did too. No, on the eve of our first anniversary, Gage would have to do better than that.

CHAPTER TWO

One week earlier

I was late. Not in the oh-my-God-I'm-pregnant kind of way, but in the I'm-going-to-get-my-ass-punished-for-this kind of way. As I inserted the key with an unsteady hand, Eve squirmed at my side on the stoop.

"Mommy," she whined. "I gotta pee."

"Okay, just a sec."

Gage's car isn't in the driveway.

I kept repeating that phrase in my head, trying to calm my nerves, but that wouldn't happen until this stubborn door opened. As I cursed under my breath and jiggled the key, my heart thundered at the thought that he could pull into the driveway any second and realize I was fifteen minutes late. The lock clicked over, and I shoved the door so hard it banged against the wall.

"Hurry up and use the potty, baby. I need to start dinner."

Fifteen damn minutes.

If I didn't act fast, Gage would learn of my tardiness, and

then he might take away the key to my car. Heck, that wasn't even my biggest problem at the moment. As I set my purse on the entryway table, a text notification sounded from my cell.

Almost like an omen reflecting my thoughts.

I pulled the phone out of my purse and read the message.

I just want to talk. Think about it, ok?

That was the problem. I *was* thinking about it. I'd thought of nothing else since I'd run into him at the hospital.

It's not a good idea, I replied.

Neither was marrying him.

Ouch. He sure wasn't holding back the punches. Gnawing on my lip, I fired off another text, doing my best to ignore the time as it ticked away.

That's exactly why it's not a good idea. I don't want to fight.

A car approached, the whine of the engine muffled through the door. I peeked through the small window in the foyer and slumped in relief. Just a neighbor. Another text sounded, making me jump.

I don't want to fight either, Kayla. I just want to talk.

My thumbs hovered over the screen, ready to type *no*. But somewhere between thought and action, the no became a yes.

Ok, tomorrow.

I took a deep breath. Oh my God. What was I doing? I honestly didn't know, yet my fingers tapped the screen, telling him when and where to meet me. Telling him not to text again. Because him texting was dangerous. No, it was just plain reckless. Gage searched my phone at random.

I deleted the messages, shrugged out of my coat, and hung it in the closet. As I headed into the kitchen, I told myself to calm down. Otherwise, Gage would take one look at me and know something was up.

My hands were still trembling as I turned on the oven and slid the casserole I'd prepared that morning onto the rack. Next, I worked to set the stage with a wine glass sitting on the breakfast bar, half full as if it had been there a while. Hopefully, Gage wouldn't take a sip because the Pinot Gris was too cold to have been poured fifteen minutes ago when I *should* have been home.

"I'm hungry," Eve said, appearing at my side as I fretted over the preheat beep going off.

Please go off before he gets home.

"Dinner will be ready soon. Did you put your things away?"

Eve nodded, pride in her eyes because she was a big girl now. "Can I watch TV?"

"Sure, but just until dinner."

Five minutes later, the oven sounded its preheated status, and Gage walked in. Sipping my wine, I relaxed my face into an expression of serenity, but my foot itched to tap against the leg of the bar stool.

"Sorry I'm late," he said, embracing me from behind. He looped an arm across my abdomen, turned my face toward his, and planted his mouth on mine. We might have kissed for an hour because I lost track of time as our tongues mated.

Sighing into his kiss, I brought my fingers to the spot below his ear and ran the length of his jaw, loving the prickle of his five o'clock shadow.

He drew back, leaving my head spinning from the intoxication that was purely him. "How was yoga today?" he asked.

"It was..." I blinked, recovering from his heated greeting. "Relaxing."

He nudged my neck with his nose. “Did you talk to any men today?”

“Of course not.” Right then, I’d never been more grateful that he couldn’t see my eyes and the lie in them.

“Good girl.” He gingerly nibbled the side of my throat, right where my pulse throbbed.

“Hungry?” I asked, breathless.

“Mmm-hmm. Depends on what we’re talking about.”

Despite my frazzled nerves, I laughed. “Food, you pervert. Dinner will be ready soon.”

Eve bounded into the kitchen, and Gage let me go so he could greet her. He swung her into his arms and asked her about her day.

“Ms. Sherman teached us the letter *M*,” she said.

Gage glanced my way, debauchery in his eyes, and that intense stare stripped me of my defenses from across the kitchen. M for Master. We were both thinking it.

“It makes a sound like *moo*,” she said with a giggle.

Gage set her back on her feet, laughing as he mussed her hair. “You’re getting too smart for your britches, princess.”

“Am I as smart as you now?”

“Way smarter than me.”

She giggled again before racing out of the kitchen, her little feet pounding the hardwood.

He returned to me at the breakfast bar, and his hands landed on my shoulders, massaging some of the tension away, making me relax into him. Until he spoke. “I’m taking away your yoga privileges next week.”

My eyes widened. “Why?”

“I have other plans for you.”

Heartbeat rising to a furious staccato, I slid off the bar stool, needing distance. Some space to decipher what he was up to. “What kind of plans?”

“Guess you’ll have to wait and see.” His tone gave

nothing away, and I had no idea if these *plans* were good or bad.

Having this discussion with him would be easier if I had a reason to keep my hands busy, my attention focused on something other than him. I crossed the kitchen and pulled salad makings from the fridge.

"Simone will be disappointed," I said, rinsing a tomato.

"Your friends have no bearing on my decisions, Kayla."

I bit my tongue. Last thing I wanted was to give him another reason to harp on my choice of friends. He didn't like her, and it had taken a lot of effort on my part to get him to allow our friendship. His high-handed attitude was starting to burrow into my skin a little more each day. I sliced into the tomato with extra oomph, slamming the knife onto the cutting board with a loud *chop*.

"I agreed to your yoga classes as long as you didn't forget your place." He leaned toward me, his long and slender fingers curling around the edge of the granite counter. Granite just like his expression. "Do you need a harsher reminder tonight?"

I dropped the knife and tried not to glower at him. "That isn't necessary."

"Glad to hear it." He picked up the discarded knife and took over, moving on to peel and chop a cucumber. "After next week, we'll revisit your yoga classes with Simone."

And right then I knew this wasn't about yoga at all. He didn't like Simone. Clearly, he was trying to put a wedge between our friendship.

"Gage, please. It's only twice a week."

"I don't care. I want you here and available. Can I trust you to obey me, or do I need to work from home next week to make sure you stay put?" His sideway glance tingled down my spine. I studied the profile of his gorgeous face, searching for signs that he *knew*.

"That was a question, Kayla."

I tamped down rising panic. "There's no need for you to do that. I'll talk to Simone and let her know I'm not free."

Damn it.

"Good, then it's settled."

Neither of us spoke until we sat down with Eve at the dinner table. Gage and Eve chatted easily like they always did, but my mind wandered to next week and my new dilemma.

"Are you excited about the slumber party next weekend?" Gage asked Eve.

I picked at the chicken broccoli casserole on my plate, my stomach twisting into knots over my half-discussion half-argument with him. Even worse, my lie ate away at me more than ever.

"Leah said it's a *pajama* party, Daddy."

Gage's sapphire eyes sparkled with meaning, not only because she'd called him Daddy—something she didn't do very often—but the slumber party was a reminder of our anniversary next weekend. Knowing Gage the way I did, I figured his plans included something equally diabolical and romantic.

After dinner, I cleared the table and gave Eve a bath. Our nightly routine of chores, bedtime stories, and at least five kisses and tuck-ins before she settled underneath her princess comforter passed quietly.

This was our life. We sat down for dinner every evening, and on Mondays we played board games as a family. Wednesdays were movie and popcorn night. Fridays... Fridays ended late, long after we said goodnight to Eve since Gage had decided a month ago that I needed a weekly session with his belt to remind me that I belonged to him. That Friday ritual had started after he'd given me access to my purse, keys, and phone. It had started after I'd begun using yoga classes as a cover.

Each week since, when the sharp bite of his belt flamed my ass, I fretted over the idea that he knew. Considering the tension between us tonight...I hated that today was Friday.

I switched off the lights in the kitchen, grabbed a raunchy romance from the bookshelf in the living room, and headed toward the hall. Gage had retreated to his office and would probably be in there for a while dealing with the pile of paperwork on his desk. I expected him to be at least an hour, giving me a short reprieve from his Friday ritual, so I was surprised to find him blocking my way to our bedroom. The novel slipped from my fingers.

We didn't need words as he took my hand and ushered me into our bedroom. The door shut with a soft click, followed by the turn of a lock. As he unbuckled his belt, I crossed to the bed and bent over the mattress.

I widened my stance, willing my four-inch stilettos to support me. Willing my legs to stop quivering. Silence blared through the room, a disquiet that brought the *thump-thump-thump* of blood rushing through my veins to the forefront, amplifying everything.

The chill in the room, drifting over my skin and causing gooseflesh. The slow and deliberate way he slid the belt from his pant loops. The soft but insistent pad of his shoes on the floor as he neared me.

Despite the phantom echo of pain roaring along my nerve endings, I'd never felt so sexy, bent over the way I was with my hair splayed on the mattress, one cheek pressed to the comforter. Vulnerable to his every whim.

I gripped the hem of my skirt and waited for his command. Seconds ticked by until a full minute passed. I bit my lip to keep from squirming, to remain quiet as he expected. I knew he waited behind me with that strap of leather looped in his fist. This preamble was part of the thrill for him, part of the ritual. He enjoyed making me wait with my breath suspended. Fear crept in during this time like it had last week and the week before. Fear that he knew, and this was his way of punishing me for it.

"Lift your skirt."

Pound. Pound. Pound.

How could he not hear my heartbeat? It throbbed in my ears as I pulled up my skirt, sliding the silky material over an ass left bare for his pleasure.

Always bare. Always ready for him.

I sucked in a breath, let it shudder out, and gripped my skirt so tightly my fingers ached. We entered another unbearable period of waiting, and I shook with knowing that when his belt did strike my ass for the first time, it would come as a surprise.

Like the week before, and the week before that.

That first lash would steal my breath and make my eyes burn, would cramp my legs and—

Thwack!

I opened my mouth, but no sound came out.

"One," he said because I wasn't allowed to speak during these weekly *reminders*.

I blinked several times to hold back tears, and my deception wrapped around my throat, cinching until it nearly choked me. Another lick of fire streaked across my ass, followed by his hoarse voice.

"Two."

Eighteen more to go.

The strikes were few compared to his usual allotment, but they were three times the strength. On number eleven, I almost pleaded for him to stop. But like the week before, and the week before that, I pressed my lips together and endured the next one in quiet anguish.

It wasn't so much that it hurt. Wasn't that it was degrading. This new ritual of his was...

Confusing.

And if I spoke and fractured our unspoken code of silence, I was scared of what would come out. Would I show my weakness by begging and crying? Would I confess? Would he utter the words I dreaded most?

I know your secret.

I didn't want to find out, so I took the beating. Week after week, our ritual settled into something that just *was*, something that transpired between Master and slave in unnerving silence.

"Twenty."

Finality rang in my ears, bounced around my mind. His belt clattered to the floor, and the sound of his zipper stabbed at my control, primed me to tremble under the firm pressure of his palms on my stinging ass.

I wanted to moan.

I wanted to push my ass toward him in invitation.

God, I *wanted*.

And he knew it, tortured me with it, had me wrapped long before his cock nudged the center of my depravity. My breath hitched, stalling in my lungs until the edges of my vision grew fuzzy.

Until my world narrowed only to him.

To him dangling me over the precipice with his strong hands gripping my hips, holding me in place as he rocked into me. To the stillness of our interlocked bodies and the rush of adrenaline begging me to move against him. Begging me to beg him.

But I understood without him saying a word. I was to have no control. He didn't permit me to take pleasure, nor to voice my distress in having to hold back. And God, it was torture not to grind against him, to moan and plead for more as he began to thrust.

Finally, he slammed into me the way I needed him to.

Then he did it again.

Deeper.

So rough and brutal and animalistic that the power of his cock drove me to my toes, pushing me higher onto the mattress until my back arched under the onslaught. He grunted while I sucked in quick, shallow breaths as our bodies slapped together.

I balled my hands around my skirt, squeezed my eyes shut, and tried to block my impending orgasm. And I would. I'd do whatever it took to hold back. I gnawed on my lip, bit down on the comforter, ground my fists into my sides. Desperation threatened to swallow me whole. Desperation appealed to the pressure building, whispering to *just let go*.

But I couldn't. I'd broken my oath to obey enough already, and I'd atone for it. If—*when*—he learned of my deceit, I'd pay dearly. But stopping the eruption seemed damn near impossible.

Don't come.

In my mind, I visualized a cage where I locked away my free-fall into ecstasy, but my pussy tightened around him anyway, becoming slicker. Needier. Greedy.

Shit, he felt good. Not even my burning ass overshadowed the way in which he claimed me.

With a strangled groan, he lifted me onto the mattress, spread my knees, and shoved me to my elbows before plunging deep—so deep that the base of his cock stretched me wide. He tugged on my hair, yanking my head back, and the smack of his balls on my clit almost sent me over the edge.

I will not come.

Not until he uttered the word. And he would, soon. Because he was close.

Just a little bit long—

"Come."

A muted scream tore from my gaping mouth, and I did the only thing I could. I obeyed.

CHAPTER THREE

I often asked myself why I'd married Gage. He wasn't the easiest to love, and he wasn't the easiest man to live with. But on those dark days when his intensity became too much to bear, all I had to do was watch him with my daughter.

The following morning, I stood to the side of the dining room entrance and did just that. Pushing my bangs from my eyes, I saw him turn her pancake into a smiley face. He loved her, but more importantly, she loved him.

He'd not only kept my baby girl alive by bringing her back from the brink of death, but he'd given her something I feared she'd never have. He'd given her a father. So during those times when I hung from the ceiling, my toes barely touching the ground, and endured the bite of his belt, I remembered.

I remembered on days when the belt wasn't enough, and he moved on to harsher toys. The paddle riddled with holes. The riding crop that induced a mystical sensation between my thighs—a feeling I couldn't discern from sexual hunger. And the deceptive flogger with its soft strips of leather. That thing inflicted more pain than his belt if he put enough strength behind the lashes.

But paddles and floggers were child's play to Gage. He reserved the truly horrific implements for severe infractions despite them being hard limits. Every time my gaze crossed paths with the bullwhip in the basement, a knife ripped through my chest. That symbol of agony bled memories from its coiled place on the wall. I couldn't help but cower at the sight because I knew I wouldn't escape it forever.

He'd promised a caning if I left the house without permission.

He'd promised to gag me if I lied to him.

He'd promised a date with the bullwhip if I spoke to his brother again.

I was three for three.

"Mommy!" Eve's smile, along with the sweet scent of pancakes, pulled me into the dining room. As I greeted her, I spied the upward curve of Gage's lips. He loved making her happy. I was certain the few times he'd scolded her for stepping out of line had upset him more than it had her.

I would have never guessed a man as complex, sadistic, and controlling as Gage could harbor such a soft spot for a child. Perhaps that hint of vulnerability in him, that glimpse of kindness he rarely displayed, was the reason he'd captured my heart a year ago when I agreed to marry him. If I were truthful though, I'd hurtled headfirst into loving him before then, and it hadn't mattered if my sanity shattered upon the fall.

"Gage made me the smiley face again. Do you want one too?"

"I'd love one," I said with a shaky smile as I slid into a seat. I wanted to share her enthusiasm, her perspective on life, seen through the veil of innocence. But for me, enthusiasm was only found in the bedroom, and I'd lost my innocence long before Gage had gotten his hands on me.

Somehow, that quiet acknowledgment made what I planned to do today a little easier, made the guilt a little more bearable. I liked to think I was an honest person, someone with a healthy moral compass, but I was far from a saint. I'd crossed that line the day I'd stolen ten grand from Gage to save Eve.

And I'd do it again without hesitation or remorse.

Eve shoved a huge bite of pancake into her mouth and dripped syrup onto her nightgown. She didn't seem to care, and neither did Gage, even though some of the sticky goo dropped onto the dining table, which would surprise most people if they didn't look beyond the carefully groomed man in the expensive suits. Something could be said about a man who didn't mind the sticky fingers of a six-year-old.

Gage set a plate in front of me, squirted a smiley face made of whipped cream onto the perfectly golden pancake, and then he bent and pressed his mouth to mine. It wasn't a passionate kiss. We didn't even part our lips. But the way he brought his hand to my cheek and feathered his fingers over my suddenly flushed skin melted my heart.

Eve giggled and said something about kissing and a tree, but I was too breathless and flustered to hear if she'd recited the ageless rhyme correctly.

He drifted to my ear and imparted a whispered, "Good morning, beautiful."

He made me *feel* beautiful, and that only added to my treachery because I'd dressed with someone else in mind.

"Morning," I said, sidestepping my guilt as I cut my pancake into neat little sections. "I forgot to pick up the dry cleaning yesterday. They close early today, so I thought I'd take care of that after breakfast." Willing my face to give nothing away, I met his eyes and silently asked for his permission.

We had a system in place to protect Eve from our alternative lifestyle, an unspoken code of rules and protocols. If the answer was yes, he'd give the go-ahead, but if I wasn't allowed to leave the house, he'd tell me not to worry about it today.

I held my breath and waited. Not only would I get a spanking for my failure to do the chore, but I'd "forgotten" on purpose so I'd have an excuse to leave the house. Deep down, I'd known I'd go, regardless of what I said in my texts yesterday. Even so, I'd deliberated too long over stopping by the cleaners, and the consequence had been coming home late.

A close call, and all because I couldn't help but flirt with disaster. Flirt with the forbidden.

I continued to hold his gaze, praying he wouldn't read the subterfuge in my expression, the stress threatening to pull at the corners of my mouth.

Finally, he gave a slight nod. "I need to speak to you before you go."

"Okay," I said, hoping my relief wasn't too apparent. Showing signs of relief upon confirmation of an impending punishment wasn't a typical reaction. He made it hurt when he spanked me for an infraction, and if I got wet, he used the nipple clamps and started over.

After breakfast, Gage loaded the dishwasher while I settled Eve in her bedroom with her collection of Barbies. While she quietly played, lost in her own realm of pretend, I waited with my stomach in knots.

Gage stepped into view, and one glance at his firm mouth commanded me to my feet. I bent and placed a kiss on the crown of Eve's head. "Be good, baby. I need to run an errand. I won't be long, okay?"

"'Kay." She was too wrapped up in her dolls to notice me leaving. I quietly shut the door before following Gage down the hall to our bedroom. He'd had the room soundproofed after we'd married. Neither of us wanted Eve to hear our loud cries of ecstasy. Or my howls of pain.

He didn't punish me often in this room—usually only when Eve was home, and we needed an accessible space where we could still be close in case she needed us.

Gage turned down the child monitor, and Eve's soft voice faded to a static whisper. He sank into the designated spanking chair, but I stalled in the middle of the room.

I fucking hated this.

I loved the kinky play between the sheets, even the more brutal sessions with his various toys in the basement because he usually mixed pain with pleasure. But the punishments...they were bullshit. I thought I could tolerate his never-ending need to control me, but I had to admit, if only to myself, that these past few weeks of stolen freedom had opened my eyes to how he'd isolated me inside his vortex of sex, dominance, and sadism.

Why couldn't I have the good without the bad? Did I not deserve that? More importantly, *why* did he need to hurt me? To punish me. I'd turned this puzzle over in my head too many times to count. I figured it stemmed from losing Liz. His world had cracked and fissured under him, and that single, irrevocable moment had forever changed him.

Part of me wondered if this was his way of punishing her for her affair with Ian. Was he unconsciously using me as a proxy?

"Look at me."

My gaze snapped to his, and only then did I realize I'd been staring at his feet. I loved him in pajama pants, his feet bare, hair mussed. God, he was sexy as hell, more sinful than the devil himself because he appeared more human that way. Less intimidating.

"You know the rules, so quit stalling."

I wanted to argue with him, but that never ended well. In fact, it ended with an extended date with his firm hand, and I didn't have time for that today. The sooner I gave him what he wanted, the sooner he'd give me what I wanted.

The freedom to walk out the front door.

I trudged across the room and let him pull me over his knee. He lifted my skirt, using his usual method of slow torture. It shouldn't take thirty seconds to bare my ass, but he managed to draw it out that long.

"Do you have anything you'd like to tell me, Kayla?"

"I forgot to pick up the dry cleaning yesterday. I need to be punished."

He gripped my hair and tugged. "Who am I?"

"My Master."

"I will always be your Master, but apparently you've forgotten lately."

The title had never settled on my tongue with ease, but in certain situations, he wouldn't let me get away with calling him anything else. I'd learned when to choose my battles, and calling him Master wasn't one I intended to fight.

He settled me against his abs, tucking me in with a strong arm and leaving his right hand free to deliver the punishing strikes. "Your disobedience needs to stop."

"I'm sorry, Master."

"Apology isn't enough. You're going to beg me for each swat."

I gritted my teeth. He was infuriating! His rituals and rules and consequences for the slightest offenses...they were too much. They were downright absurd. But I had no one to blame but myself. He'd shown his true colors from day one

—that day in his office when he'd used Eve's cancer to blackmail me into sexual submission.

Shameless and without remorse, he'd forced my legs apart and fingered me while my coworkers went about their business like any other day. But my entire life had changed in that fifteen minutes. I'd signed the contract on his terms and promptly fell down the rabbit hole.

Fell into an addiction named Gage Channing, and not even putting a year between us and running half way across the country had stopped him in the end.

"Beg," he said.

"Please spank me."

"I'm not convinced. Convince me, Kayla. Tell your Master how badly you deserve to be punished."

"I need to be punished. Please, Master. Spank me."

"No." He pulled me flush against his hard body. "Explain to me why I should give you my hand."

"Because I forgot to pick up the dry cleaning?" A note of question entered my tone.

"That's part of it, but I think you know the real reason."

He knows! Shit, he knows.

Icy dread sludged through me. I hoped he didn't notice the shudder in my bones. How I managed to keep my voice steady remained a mystery.

"I don't know what you're talking about. If you tell me, then I can beg you for what I deserve."

"You've been absent from this relationship lately. I don't know where your mind is, but it's not on how to serve and please me. Remind me again what your job is."

"To serve, please, and obey my Master." I recited the oath with such precision it fell flat to my ears.

He didn't seem to hear the lack of truth in those words. "And what is my responsibility to you, baby?"

"To love and care for me."

"Have I not done those things?"

"You have."

"Then I won't ask again. Beg me to make your ass red, and mean it."

I closed my eyes and uttered the words, swallowed the self-disgust in my throat. His hand came down with too little force but with obvious intent. The easier he went on me, the faster I'd get wet.

And he never passed up an opportunity to clamp my nipples.

I willed my body to behave and waited for the next swat, but it never came. Silence ticked by, ringing in my ears, increasing the speed of my pulse. What was he waiting for…?

Oh.

"Please, Master. Again."

"Should I go easy on you?"

"No, Master."

"Why not?"

"It pleases you to hurt me." It was true enough, and if he stopped playing with me and just fucking struck me with a punishing hand, maybe I could control myself. "Please, Master. Spank me hard."

He complied, and I asked for another. I asked for so many that I lost count. When would it be enough for him?

"Please…" My voice trailed off, and I resisted squirming on his lap as my ass blazed. I didn't want to push him and prolong the punishment. I'd learned to accept his sadism, his need to mark me as his for the smallest of reasons. Life was easier when I gave in.

"Please, what?"

Please stop.

"Please spank me again, Master."

His hand came down with a loud smack.

Harder.

Faster.

He was escalating from punishing to vicious. I couldn't contain my strangled cries after a while. I'd never been more appreciative of the soundproofed room. Last thing I wanted was for Eve to hear me.

"Please!" I yelped, then forced a plea for more between tight lips.

"More, you'll get. My hand loves your ass. I have all day." Each time he hit me, I jerked atop his lap, blinked through the burning tears pooling in my eyes. But on some masochistic level, I knew I deserved every strike of his hand.

A desolate tear fell to the floor, and I fell silent for too long.

"Do you think you've been punished enough?"

I thought long and hard about my answer, but there was no right one because either option could potentially land me in his lap for another twenty minutes...or longer. "Yes, Master. I won't forget the dry cleaning again."

"Are you wet?"

"No, Master."

But it wouldn't take much to get me there. I stood, facing away, and bent so he could complete the punishment by *checking* me. It was a degrading thing to do—bending over, fingers grasping my ankles so he could probe my sex for signs of forbidden arousal. At the first touch of his fingers spreading me open, seeking my hot center, I bit my lip hard.

"Spread your legs."

I did so, and he pushed his fingers so deep, I was sure the full length of them laid claim to my treacherous cunt. The needy thing *was* a cunt. It didn't know when to fucking behave, and I was a stroke away from creaming all over his hand. I counted the various lines in the hardwood, watched the way my hair gently swished the floor. And I thought of the front door and how I needed to be going through it *now*.

That wouldn't happen if I let my body betray me. Again. I should have more self-restraint by now. How many times had he tormented me with denial? With orgasm control? He'd trained me so well that I rarely came unless he commanded me to. But controlling my body on the cusp of a punishment, no matter how degrading or hurtful, was torturous, and he knew it.

"Good girl," he murmured, slowly withdrawing his fingers from me. I rose to an upright position. But he wasn't through with me; he spun me around and pulled me onto his lap.

"You did well, baby." He caught my mouth, drawing me into a kiss that made my muscles tense and freeze. A kiss that torpedoed through me and did what his punishment hadn't; turned me to liquid fire. Unfurled me into abandon. Obliterated my mind because I couldn't think beyond his tongue sliding against mine.

His cock grew heavy between my legs, and I fell victim to need. I was free of thought, doubt, or regret as I pushed against his hard shaft, tainting his pajama bottoms with my arousal and wishing like hell the flannel wasn't between us.

He broke our fevered connection and inched back, pinning me with hooded indigo eyes. "Do you deserve to be fucked?"

I almost said yes, but the gleam in his gaze bespoke of sadistic fuckery. It was a trick question. "No, Master."

"Good answer." Gently, he untangled my quaking body from his and pushed me to the floor between his spread knees. I must have fallen under some devious spell because I couldn't tear my eyes away as he tugged his pants down and freed his erection.

Adrenaline rushed my veins, heat erupted at my core,

and I licked my lips, already tasting him on my tongue. Already hearing the way he groaned low in his throat whenever I teased the head of his gorgeous cock.

Imagined him surrendering to me, if only for a few minutes.

"You want me in your mouth?"

"Yes, Master."

"That's too bad." He folded his fingers around his shaft and stroked the length. Up. Down. Slower than slow. "You don't deserve to suck my cock."

My breath hitched, but I bit my tongue to keep from arguing with him.

"Open your mouth." He began pumping his smooth shaft. "Now, Kayla. *Open* your mouth."

I did as told and waited with parted lips. A few more strokes of his hand was all it took. Striking my ass had been all the foreplay he needed. Letting out a deep cry, he jumped to his feet, height towering over me, and squirted his release onto my face. I wiped his cum from my eyes and swallowed what had landed on my tongue.

A few heavy seconds passed. For some reason, he avoided my gaze. And that's when I realized it. When *he* realized it. Mutual understanding flowed between us. I needed freedom, and he needed absolute control. But which one of us would fold first? The foundation of our marriage had shifted, had been shifting for a while, and I suspected neither of us had acknowledged it until now.

He broke the silence. "Freshen up and take care of your errand." He offered his hand—an act of kindness, or a trap? Cautiously, I fit my hand into his and allowed him to haul me to my feet. But when I tried to move past him toward the bathroom, he halted me with a harsh grip on my chin, his thumb and forefinger pressing into his cum on my face.

"I want you back here by noon and not a minute later. Do you understand me?"

"Yes, Master."

He dropped his fingers to my collarbone, caressing the infinity collar that trapped my neck—the symbol that enslaved me under his ownership until the day I died...and maybe not even then.

"I don't enjoy being harsh with you. You probably don't believe that, but it's true."

He was right. I didn't believe him. His sadism often did the driving. Gage was just a passenger to its depraved needs.

"But I know something is going on with you," he said. "Don't keep shit from me. Dishonesty will get you nowhere." He let me go, but his warning had the desired effect because I was shaking by the time I found sanctuary in the bathroom.

CHAPTER FOUR

A constant mist dampened my hair and coat. I preferred rain, as it dropped from the sky without giving the hope of leaving you dry. Mist was a creeper—you didn't realize you were soaked until it was too late. I feared that was how this meeting with Ian would go.

I can't believe I'm doing this.

But in the most secretive corners of my being, I'd known an eventual confrontation of some sort was on the horizon. It was only logical since he was Gage's brother. And I knew Ian well enough to know that he wouldn't settle for the way things had ended. The day we parted ways had haunted me for a while, as if we'd left something important unsaid, left a window open that needed closing.

Maybe that's what drew me to volunteer at the hospital in the first place. The idea that I'd bump into him...eventually. That I'd get the chance to do what I'd failed to do that day in the hospital after losing my baby. Make things right.

Was that even possible?

I was about to find out. As I entered the coffee shop next to the cleaners, flutters of anticipation took flight in my stomach. The door swished closed behind me. Wiping the moisture from my temples, I scanned the space for him, my gaze falling on several men with dark hair before I found Ian.

He sat by himself at a small table at the far end of the shop, and something about his demeanor bothered me. Made me consider him in a different light. He wore his hair in a buzz cut, much shorter than I ever remembered, and his clothes were unusually rumpled. He seemed distracted as I approached—preoccupied as he stirred a spoon in his coffee. One brown loafer tapped the floor, and he gazed out the window, failing to notice my presence.

I almost turned and fled. Meeting him was wrong, unfair to both him and Gage. But...I had to see him. My selfishness disgusted me, and suddenly I was grateful Gage had wailed on my ass that morning.

Drawing a fortifying breath, I gathered the last threads of my resolve and slid into the seat across from him. His attention broke away from the fascinating show of birds flocking through the trees lining the street.

"I wasn't sure you'd come." His gaze dropped to my modest cleavage for a moment, then his eyes settled on my face again.

"I wasn't sure I'd come either." A lie. The instant the elevator at the hospital yesterday had confined us for the duration of seven floors, I'd known this was the moment I'd been waiting for. The moment I'd been dreading.

My opportunity to play with fire.

He leaned forward, and his hazel eyes imparted an intensity that almost matched Gage's. I could detect the relation so easily now. I wasn't sure how I'd missed it before. They both commanded with their presence, though Ian did it in a quiet, unthreatening way compared to his brother. Suddenly, I wondered if that made him more dangerous.

A creeper mist waiting to drench me.

"You look good, Kayla."

The way he said my name sent a sharp ping through my heart—not big enough to be a knife, but not small enough to be a harmless pinprick either. I'd missed him this past year, but I couldn't voice it. I could barely admit it to myself.

"I probably shouldn't have come."

"Does Gage know you're here?"

My first instinct was to lie. Ian wouldn't like the answer, and I didn't have the energy to defend my marriage to him. Before I could answer, he scowled, indicating I was as translucent as sheer silk.

"Is he going to beat you for seeing me?"

"No." Even as I spoke, I knew there was more deceit than truth in the denial. When it came to Ian, Gage would blow a gasket in a heartbeat. "He's been seeing a counselor."

"Still making excuses."

"I'm not making excuses." No. I was flat-out lying to myself. Now it was my turn to watch the birds zipping through the mist outside, their wings fluttering.

"So this won't bother him? You and me," he said, gesturing to the space between us, "sitting in a crowded coffee shop, simply *talking*?"

It would definitely bother him. More than bother him. Even worse, it bothered me because I had no business being here. But a force I couldn't fight had propelled me to volunteer at his place of employment—essentially putting myself in his path. Now I sat across from him, an arm's length away from the one man on this planet I was forbidden to think about, let alone talk to.

My web of lies had me teetering on a slippery slope.

"I'll take your silence as a yes," he mumbled.

"You're right. He wouldn't like it." No doubt about it. Gage would feel betrayed, flayed to the bone. For someone as strong and dominant as Gage, he wounded easier than most people.

Ian raised a brow. "Why did you agree to meet me then?"

I stared down at my hands. "I'm not sure."

"Maybe your subconscious is trying to tell you something."

I risked a peek at him. "What do you think it's trying to tell me?"

"That you married the wrong man."

That was bold, even for Ian. "I don't regret marrying him."

He grabbed my hand. "Then *why* are you here, Kayla?" He thumbed the ring on my finger, but his quizzical gaze remained fixed on me.

I pulled my hand back and stood, and the chair scraped across the floor with an earsplitting screech. "Why are you here?" I tossed his words back into his face with a glare. "It's been a whole fucking year, Ian. Why now?"

"Sit down."

His tone was too similar to Gage's. Too commanding. That was the only reason I sank into my seat again. Habit. Gage had trained me well, though bending to another man's commands wasn't the result he'd aimed for. I tried not to fidget in my seat, especially when Ian leaned toward me again.

"Do you believe in fate?" he asked.

That was a difficult question. If I said yes, then did that mean Gage blackmailing me had been fate's doing? "I don't know."

"Well I believe in fate. Running into you yesterday was a sign." He took my hand again, refusing to let go this time. "I hear you've been volunteering in the children's wing. Is that true?"

I nodded as acid rose in my throat.

"What prompted you to do that?"

"I don't know," I whispered.

"You don't know much of anything, do you? Do you even know why you married him?"

"I'm not talking to you about this. I shouldn't have come." I tried removing myself from his grasp, but he held steady.

"He's got that much power over you?" he asked, incredulous. "He fucks you a few times and you're hooked. Unbelievable."

My heart sank. Apparently not even a year of distance had lessened his bitterness. "My marriage is none of your business. You have no idea what you're talking about." What he didn't understand was that Gage had power because I gave it to him. I gave him control. I willingly called him Master, gave him my body freely. I allowed him to hurt me when and how he liked. I followed his strict rules, wore toe crushing stilettos daily because he wanted me to. I bent, and bent, and bent some more because I got off on the obsession. No man would ever love me as fiercely and possessively as Gage Channing.

Yet I missed being *me*, the old me...the me who didn't have to ask for permission to do something as simple as pick up the fucking dry cleaning. The me who, despite a year of not seeing Ian, refused to stop caring about him in some small corner of my heart.

This day—the day I'd irrevocably stepped out of line—could be the day that brought everything crashing to the ground.

"Fine, Kayla. Your marriage to him is none of my business. But the fact that you're sitting across from me now, barely able to look me in the eye, is my business."

"This was a mistake," I said, finally extricating myself from his hold. Ian and I had too much history for this to feel so awkward. Yet it did, and it was my fault because I had no valid reason for meeting him. A year ago, I'd chosen his brother over him. Nothing had changed since then. Gage was still my husband. Still the man who owned me, whether I wanted him to or not. The man I loved, whether I wanted to or not.

"You've made plenty of mistakes," he said. "What's one more?"

My breath caught in my throat, and I couldn't hide the surprise in my expression. "What do you want from me?"

"I want to see you again. Meet me in my office on Monday? I've got a short shift, so I'm free around noon."

"I can't do that."

"Yes, you can. I talked to your boss. She already told me you volunteer on Mondays."

"What do you think is going to happen between us?" I held my breath, afraid of his answer.

"Nothing, unless you want something to happen."

I jumped to my feet. "I need to get home." My voice came out a strangled mess, revealing too much. The pain that fisted my heart. Would I ever be able to look at him and not want to crack in two?

He rose, slowly rounded the table, and before I could process what was about to happen, it happened. He pulled me into his arms, held on tight, and buried his face in my hair. I went stiff in his embrace, knowing that I was on shaky ground. Knowing that letting him touch me was the worst idea ever. But as the seconds ticked by, I couldn't help but relax into him. I was weak. Needy. I needed this.

Because Gage never *just* held me. He made me feel a spectrum of emotions, from fiery passion to lust to rage to suffocating possession, but he refused to show vulnerability. The part of him I loved the most—the man with a heart made of more than just ice—was barely around anymore.

And I missed that man so fucking much.

"I took so much for granted," Ian said, his tone thick with regret. His fingers tangled in my hair, and he tilted my head back. "I'll never make that mistake with you again."

I freed myself from his tempting arms and put some much-needed space between us. I'd made a massive mistake by meeting him today. The realization clenched my insides, and I felt on the verge of throwing up.

If Gage ever found out, not only would he be livid, but this would hurt him.

"I have to go." I pivoted and strode toward the front of the cafe without looking back, and I prayed to whoever was listening that I'd have enough time to pick up the dry cleaning and make it home by noon.

CHAPTER FIVE

I arrived home with two minutes to spare. The house was too silent, giving off a vibe of abandonment. Too quiet because my daughter and Gage were nowhere to be found. The living room and kitchen were empty. I checked Gage's office before peeking inside Eve's room, but they were vacant as well.

Trepidation clutched my gut as I halted outside our bedroom. I knew he was home—I'd spied his car in the driveway. I could practically feel him beyond our bedroom door. Pushing it open, I wasn't surprised to find him waiting in the spanking chair. His guarded expression made me nervous. I couldn't read him, and I hated his cool and collected mask more than anything.

"Where's Eve?" I asked, clutching the dry cleaning in my hands.

"Leah's mother picked her up. She's spending the day with them."

Alarm bells rang in my head. "You didn't discuss it with me first?" I tried to keep my voice level, but in the back of my mind, I worried that he'd had me followed, was terrified he'd seen me in Ian's arms. This morning had convinced me that he knew *something* was up, but if he figured out I'd met with his brother...

I tried not to shrink at the thought.

"Who's in charge in this marriage, Kayla?" He rose, took the dry cleaning from me, and placed it on the bed. His expectant gaze settled on my face, and I realized it wasn't a rhetorical question.

"You are."

He nodded. "I'm not just your husband. I'm your Master. I don't discuss things with you."

"When it comes to me, maybe, but she's my daughter. You can't—"

He pressed a finger to my lips. "You should quit while you're ahead." I ceased arguing, and he dropped his hand. "Prepare for me in the basement."

"Am I in trouble?" I asked, anxiety thundering in my chest.

He knows. God, he knows.

The severity of his expression softened. "No, baby." He stroked my cheek with the back of his hand. "You're not in trouble."

I let out a small breath of relief, hopefully inconsequential enough that he wouldn't notice. But if he didn't intend to punish me, then that could only mean one thing.

"So today is about play?"

He gripped my jaw between his forefinger and thumb. "I know it's been a few days since I've had you on your knees properly, but that doesn't excuse you." His firm hold wasn't designed to inflict pain—he only did it to emphasize that he held all the power. "How do you address me?"

"I'm sorry, Master."

"No need for an apology. Just be a good little slave for

your Master and do as you're told." One corner of his mouth quirked up. "You might like what I have in store for you. Or not, depending on how you look at it."

My heartbeat took off without me. God, how could he still make me this nervous? I'd lived with him for a year—a whole damn year—but the problem wasn't familiarity. The problem was the exact opposite; I knew him *too* well…which meant I knew better than to guess at what was coming next because Gage was as volatile as he was sexy.

"Don't take too long. I'll be down shortly." He brushed his lips over mine before disappearing through the doorway.

I made my way to the basement's entrance, found the key in its hiding place above the door—out of Eve's reach—and ventured inside. The temperature dropped, and the air grew chillier as I descended the stairs. He liked the way the cold hardened my nipples, so I didn't dare turn up the thermostat.

I eyed the floor where he expected to find me, naked and kneeling. Waiting. Even though I didn't have much time, I wandered into the bathroom and finger-combed my deep red locks. The distressed expression of the woman in the mirror gave me pause. Uncertainty strained her features, but her cheeks were also flushed from the exhilaration of the unknown.

My fingers caught in a stubborn tangle, and I nearly growled because I didn't have a say in how I wore my hair. It had grown too long, too heavy, and I was tempted to cut it despite Gage's orders that I leave it be. He liked to yanked on it during sex, so I wasn't allowed to come near it with scissors. But it was *my* hair, and I was the one who had to comb through the knots every day.

Expelling a weary sigh, I removed my blouse and exposed my breasts, shoved my skirt down my legs until it bunched around my feet. Save for the infinity collar that never left my neck, I stood in the bathroom, unclothed and shivering. Unless I wanted play to turn into punishment, I'd better quit stalling and get into position.

He entered a few minutes later, his shirt and shoes gone. The tailor made slacks he favored hugged him in all the right places, showcasing the huge erection straining beneath his zipper. I knelt on the hard floor with my thighs spread just how he liked, hands clasped at the small of my back, eyes downcast. I thrust my breasts upward to offer him the best view of my nipples.

"Good girl."

Why his approval traveled through my system, heating the core of what made me a woman, I'd never understand. I'd stopped agonizing over the whys of our relationship dynamics a long time ago. We were what we were. I was who I was. No point in fighting it just because what we had wasn't conventional. It just *was*.

He neared me with purpose, unbuttoning his pants, pulling his zipper down. With confident hands, he took his cock out and folded his fingers around the base. He didn't have to command me—simply standing before me with his erection aimed at my mouth was enough. I knew my place, anticipated his needs so well that pleasing him became the fuel for my hunger. It was second nature.

Keeping my hands clasped at my back, I leaned forward and ran my tongue along the underside of his cock. The tiny breath he took, sucked in between clenched teeth, was my reward. I softened my lips and pressed a kiss on his tip. His arousal moistened my lips, teased my tongue with the salty taste of him.

He groaned, his fingers sifting through my hair, holding me to him with a tender, hypnotic caress as he pushed into my mouth, shoving deep so I had no choice but to take his entire length.

He moaned as he plundered, his hips swiveling with each thrust, his cock as forceful as it was merciful. The need in him took over, and his pace increased. Breathing escalated —his and mine.

Shit, he was in a weird mood. Gage either fucked me hard, regardless of what hole he was using, or he just...loved me. Something about this felt in-between, on the edge of a brutal mouth fuck. Yet I sensed his restraint, and it confused the heck out of me.

"Kayla—" He halted with a gasp, his cock throbbing on my tongue, the head finding respite between my tonsils. My gag reflex kicked in, spasmed around his shaft.

He breathed in ragged bursts. "You know what gagging does to me."

I did, and I was bewildered because he held back instead of shoving deeper. I lifted my eyes, and I would have gladly knelt at his feet all day, his cock taking residence between my lips, if he'd look at me like that forever. With heated, indigo eyes that imparted his obsession in waves of longing, lust, and possessive madness.

I yearned for all of those things—yearned for our bodies twisted in the sheets, slick with the kind of sweat only mind-blowing sex could inspire. And I ached. Hell, how I ached and craved and thirsted for his weight on me, for his fists pinning my wrists to the bed. Taking what was his.

Leaving me helpless to stop it.

A shiver traveled through me. I whimpered, resisting the urge to touch myself, and silently begged him with my gaze.

He gritted his teeth. "You're not coming."

My heart sank, and I slammed back to reality with a harsh jolt. What if he'd found out about my clandestine meeting with Ian? What if this was all a sick and twisted game, and I'd be better off coming clean? With my mouth full of cock, I couldn't even do that.

"Don't give me that look. You always think the worst of me. Stop thinking you're being punished because you're not. *I'm* not coming either." He closed his eyes for a few moments and just breathed, as if he couldn't fathom not climaxing down my throat.

I couldn't fathom it either.

"Baby..." His eyes popped open, and he inhaled, exhaled. "We're not coming until we celebrate the day I got your stubborn, sexy ass down the aisle." Letting out a furious groan of frustration, he pulled out then helped me to my feet.

"I don't understand," I said. "What are we doing down here then?"

Hauling me into his arms, he attacked my mouth as he carried me across the room. We all but fell into the St. Andrew's cross, his hands supporting my ass as my legs wrapped around his waist, our tongues clashing in battle. In the space of a few minutes, the basement had gone from freezing to an inferno. Perspiration crawled between my cleavage, bathing my skin in a sheen of pure lust.

We broke apart, and our eyes met and held.

"What we're doing down here," he began, nipping my bottom lip, "is beginning a torturous week of teasing." Another nibble, and then he whispered, "Practicing restraint through denial." He tempted the seam of my mouth with his tongue, and I parted my lips, inviting him inside again. "Practicing the art of edging."

Inch by agonizing inch, he pushed his cock into me, right to the hilt, and pinned my back to the wall with nothing more than his strong body.

"Arms up," he said.

I lifted my hands, already reaching for the chains meant to shackle me.

"You feel so damn good." His groan of self-control vibrated against my lips. He fumbled with the chains for a few moments, too caught up in the blaze roaring between us. Finally, he locked the cuff around my left wrist. "Too fucking good."

"So do you," I whispered, trembling as he pulsed inside me. "I need more."

"Who am I?"

"My Master." I gave him the title without hesitation. Would have given anything to feel him move.

He worked on securing my right wrist, and soon I hung from the cross, held up by nothing more than my wrists and the power in his thighs, the force of his cock.

"Tell your Master what you want."

"I want you to fuck me." Except I didn't. I wanted more. I wanted his body wrapped around mine, his arms caging me within his warmth and protection.

I wanted his love.

I hungered for the last decaying brick of his fortress to crumble, because even after being his wife for a year, he still hid parts of himself from me. Parts of himself I feared he'd never uncloak. It was easier to command me, to have me on my knees with his cock in my mouth, or bent over our mattress while he beat and fucked me than to expose the tatters of his soul.

"I'll fuck you," he said, thrusting in a slow, sadistic way designed to make me his. To keep me at his feet, underneath him, against the wall. "But sliding in and out of your sweet cunt won't end in orgasm for either of us. Think beyond sex. If you could have anything, what would it be?"

"To not be helpless." Once the words were out, settling between us, there was no taking them back.

He glanced at my outstretched arms. "Yet here you are, your cunt begging to cream on my cock." He withdrew then dived in with a brutal thrust. A cry tore from my lips, part pain, part ecstasy.

"What do you want, Kayla?"

"Your submission." I felt my eyes go wide. Where had that come from? Someplace deep inside that craved him at my mercy, where he could deny me nothing. Demand nothing. "You submitted once. I want that again."

He stilled inside me. "That's what you really want?"

I remembered him beneath me, his hands tied to the headboard, muscles straining with unchecked power. Remembered how teasing him to insanity had been the most intoxicating night of my life. His desperation and frustration. The way he'd watched me as I brought myself to orgasm again and again. How he'd given me a piece of himself he'd never planned to give.

Yeah. I wanted that again.

My silence must have been answer enough. He pulled out, lowered me to my feet, and stepped back, appreciation blanketing his face as he studied his helpless slave whose body begged for whatever he was willing to give.

He rubbed his jaw, considering. "If you can go the whole week without coming, I'll think about it."

My jaw about dropped to my breasts.

"But don't think I'll make it easy," he warned. "I'll have you out of your mind with needing to come before the week's over."

My need for him shuddered in my core, and I moaned, a moment away from pleading with him. "A whole week?"

He couldn't be serious. Neither one of us would make it.

But he nodded, fell to his knees, and brought his fingers to my mound, spreading my wet lips. "This will be the ultimate test of control, don't you think, Kayla?" He raised a brow. A challenge. "Can you handle it?"

My nipples peaked, and my chest rose and fell too fast. With a sigh, I let the back of my head thump against the wall. "Can you, Master?"

"I won't deny that it'll be a challenge." He ran a finger up my slit, drawing a tremor from my bones. "But you know I can never resist a challenge." His lips curved into his devil's grin, then he leaned forward and sucked my clit into his wicked mouth.

CHAPTER SIX

Monday morning arrived with rain. The deluge gushed from the sky, leaving pools of water that tempted little feet to splash through them. Eve thought about it, but a stern look from me changed her mind.

I blew kisses to her as she climbed the stairs of the school bus, her sneakers lighting up with each step. After the bus disappeared down the road, I returned to the house. No matter how hard I tried, I couldn't displace the feeling of dread settling in my gut.

Gage still hadn't left for work.

Ian still wanted to meet today in his office.

I wanted to crawl back into bed and sleep the dilemma away.

No such luck. I found Gage in his pajamas. He sat on a bar stool in the kitchen, reading the newspaper and sipping coffee.

"Running late this morning?" I asked, rinsing the few dishes left over from breakfast.

"I'm the boss. I'm never late." I heard the bar stool scrape across the floor, followed by his quiet steps bringing him closer. "It's a hard decision, choosing between work and chaining you up in the basement."

A plate slipped from my sudsy hands and clanked into the sink. Luckily, it didn't break.

He pressed his lips to the side of my neck, his warm breath inducing a delicious shiver. "I want to spend some time with you, just the two of us. In fact, I plan on spending a lot of time with you this week." He leaned into me the slightest bit, his cock nudging my ass. "I've been hard all morning, Kayla. Do you know how difficult it is not to bend you over and fuck you right now?"

I clutched the edge of the sink, biting back a groan. He ran his fingers through my hair, taunting with what I would miss this week.

"I need a cold shower," he muttered, backing away. "When you're done in here, I want you on your knees in our bedroom."

"O-okay." My heart battered my ribcage long after he left the kitchen. I finished loading the dishwasher, then for a few moments, I gripped the counter. Let it prop me up. Once again, I couldn't ignore the hunch that he was punishing me. Was he playing a cruel game? A game designed to mess with my head?

Psychological instead of physical.

Or was he simply amping up his need to conquer and control, and my guilt was wreaking havoc by making me read more into his behavior? Either way, I was frozen. Under his thumb, life had become restrictive and suffocating.

But it's never dull.

Sometimes, that voice in my head was too fucking right. I tuned into the sound of the dishwasher and let the steady *swoosh swoosh* calm my nerves, let it wash away the annoying voices in my head. I was supposed to be somewhere today, but that wasn't going to happen since he'd forbidden me to leave the house this week.

Taking a detour to the foyer, I grabbed my phone from the table and crept down the hall toward our bedroom. As I peered through the door, my cell pressed to one ear while I listened for the sound of the shower, Simone answered with her usual to-the-point greeting.

"Hey," I said, keeping my voice low. "I can't come in this week."

A pause came over the line, and even though Simone wasn't standing in front of me, I imagined her dark blond brows furrowing. "Why?"

Her suspicious tone pricked at my defenses, and I let out a sigh, growing tired of arguing with her about my marriage. But she was the only person who knew of the type of relationship Gage and I had...besides Ian, but I didn't want to think about him or how I'd done the unthinkable by seeing him over the weekend. Or how I was tempted to do something even more stupid, like see him again.

"Something came up. I'm sorry."

"You mean Gage came up. Is his dick more important that those kids?"

"That is—" *Not fair.* Shit. His cock wasn't even an issue right now since he had no intention of fucking me until our anniversary. And those kids...they *were* important. So important that I'd gone to great lengths to hide my volunteer work from my husband because no amount of logic would penetrate his thick skull when it came to my being in the same building as his brother twice a week.

Sick children or not.

"I'll be back next week." I owed Simone more than I could ever repay. She'd been Eve's favorite nurse in the hospital. And she'd become a true friend since I'd married Gage. The kind of friend I talked to, which didn't always work in my favor at times like these. I'd shared too much of my life with her, and she didn't always "get it."

She didn't understand that I owed Gage even more. He would own every part of me until the day I died.

"Damn it, Kayla. I promised Emma you were coming in this morning. Your visits are the highlight of her week."

Simone's words fisted my heart. I remembered Eve in that hospital, alone and scared because I hadn't been there when she needed me. I'd been too busy selling my soul to the devil to save her. Emma spent a lot of time alone in that place too, since her mother was a single parent who couldn't afford to miss work. Nurses and volunteers helped fill that gap, just like they had for Eve.

Emma was only six, the same age as Eve. And she could die...like Eve almost had.

"I'll try to stop in today for a little while. I want to be there."

"Then be here. This is ridiculous. You're a grown woman. When the hell are you gonna stand up to him?"

"It's not that simple."

"Yes, it is. He either respects you, or you walk. You can't get much simpler than that."

She'd never felt the need to hold back. Simone told it like she saw it, right or wrong.

"Gage is complex."

"I don't care if he's Jesus. How can you justify his behavior?"

I ground my teeth and counted to ten. "I knew what to expect the day I married him. Nothing about him has changed." I was beginning to sound like a fucking broken record.

"But *you've* changed. I see how unhappy you are. You might have agreed to this insane arrangement the day you married the bastard, but you're not happy about it now."

"You don't need to resort to name calling."

"Look," she said in a clipped tone. "You're my friend, so that means I'm going to have your back no matter what. But—"

"There's always a 'but,'" I interrupted.

"*But*," she began, "you deserve more than this. After everything you went through with Eve, you deserve to be happy. You deserve to be safe."

So did Eve, and that's what Simone and Ian didn't understand. Gage made *her* happy. So how could I justify walking away when things got bumpy, knowing that it would devastate her?

I couldn't.

"I'm sorry." I peeked through the ajar door and saw steam rolling from the bathroom. So much for the cold shower. "Tell Emma I'll try to visit today. If I can't, I'll make it up to her. I won't let her down."

"You just did."

I couldn't argue with her because she was right. Not only was I disappointing a little girl fighting to live, but I was disappointing myself. Disappointed *in* myself. Disgusted, even. What happened to the ballsy woman who'd stood up to him that first night in the basement? The first night he'd fucked me.

Raped you, the voice of reason whispered in my ear.

That night felt like a lifetime ago.

The spray of the shower shut off, and a few seconds later he entered the bedroom wearing a towel around his waist. I relaxed my face, willing my mask of *everything's a-okay* to fall into place, and pushed the door open.

"I've gotta go," I told Simone.

"He's there, isn't he?"

"I'll call you later," I said, skirting her question.

"See?" Her tone came out testy. "You're lying to him

about something you shouldn't have to hide in the first place, but mostly, you're lying to yourself."

I had no argument left, so I ended the call and calmly set the phone on the dresser.

"Was that Simone?" Gage asked, brows furrowing in a way that hinted at his irritation.

"Yeah." I swallowed hard.

"Did you tell her you're not available this week?"

I sat down on the bed and eyed his hard body as he let the towel drop to the floor. "I let her know, but I don't understand why this is an issue." I'd only been a volunteer for a few weeks, but I was growing attached to those kids, and I hated the idea of not being there for them this week, especially Emma.

"Don't argue with me, Kayla," he said, the tick in his jaw speaking volumes. "This week, you're mine and mine alone." He pushed me back onto the mattress and shoved my legs apart. Dropping to his knees, he pulled me toward his face with a rough, demanding grip.

My lips parted, and I closed my eyes as a sigh escaped. His hot breath teased between my thighs, hovering. Barely there, but potent enough to scatter my thoughts.

"I'll forgive you for not greeting me on your knees, seeing as how you were distracted by your *friend*." He shot a hand out and pinched my nipple. Squeezed. Twisted.

I cried out and instinctively tried moving out of reach, but he intensified the pressure between his thumb and forefinger.

"You will not move unless I tell you to. You're going to lie here, spread wide, your cunt aching for my mouth." He nudged my thigh with his nose, drawing a whining plea from my throat. He took my other nipple between two sadistic fingers and pinched.

The pressure was never ending—between my legs and in

my nipples. They both ached in two entirely different and unbearable ways. My whole body trembled as I willed it to remain unmoving, even as the vise of his fingers tortured me.

Another small cry tumbled from my disobedient lips. "Please, Master."

"You desperate little thing," he whispered, his words a heated caress on my pussy. "Fucking turns me on so much." Abruptly, he let me go.

I sat up, placing my weight on my elbows, and watched him through my confusion. He turned his back on me and began dressing. "What are you doing?" I asked.

"Going to work."

Of course he was. I flopped back on the bed and squeezed my eyes shut.

"I'm not touching your sweet cunt, Kayla. And neither are you."

I must have groaned out loud because he laughed. Even when he laughed at me, I found him sexy—that deep and rich sound that shivered along my skin. "You're the devil."

The mattress depressed on either side of my head, and when I opened my eyes, I found his face inches away. Tempting me. Drawing my head up until our lips met.

He moaned into my mouth, and strength seemed to drain from his bones. He blanketed my body, his weight growing heavier by the second. "But I'm your devil. Always, Kayla. I love you so fucking much." Inching back, he gave me a severe look that stole my breath. "You know that, don't you, baby?"

I nodded, barely able to breathe, and somehow managed to tell him that I loved him too. And right then I knew I wouldn't see Ian again. I couldn't do that to Gage, no matter how much his behavior infuriated me.

"Good," he said. "Because I do. There is no one more important to me on this planet than you and Eve."

My body felt like a limp noodle. I remained speechless as he finished dressing. He kissed me one last time before heading toward the bedroom door, adjusting his cufflinks as he strode with purpose.

"I want you to come to the office today. I'll text you." The door shut quietly upon his exit, and I hated myself because I knew what I'd be doing all morning.

Anxiously waiting for the devil to summon me.

CHAPTER SEVEN

"Go into the women's restroom on the second floor and touch yourself."

I stopped dead in my tracks in the lobby of Channing Enterprises, and a man in a charcoal power suit almost ran into me from behind. As my cheeks flushed, he strode by me, casting a glare my way. Since standing in the middle of the lobby, unmoving with the phone pressed to my ear, was probably more attention-grabbing than Gage's words, I wandered to the edge and stood in the middle of two towering tree-like plants. Rubbing a leaf between two fingers confirmed they were real.

"Why the second floor?" What a crazy question. My first question should have been *why* at all.

"The PR department takes their lunch about now. I imagine the ladies room will have plenty of activity in it."

"I can't do that in there!" I said in a fierce whisper.

"You can and you will. Tell me when you're in the stall."

Panic ate at my composure. I remained motionless, eyes unseeing as people bustled around me, their bodies little more than moving blurs.

"Are you moving, Kayla?"

"Yeah." Instead of taking the elevator, I used the stairs, figuring I could at least delay this uncomfortable task for a minute or two longer.

"Taking the stairs won't save you from this." The bastard said it with barely contained amusement.

"I'm in the elevator."

"Do you remember what the punishment is for lying?"

Dread snaked down my spine. "Yes, Master. I'm sorry." I was grateful to be in the stairwell then, where no one else was around to hear me. And I was even more grateful that Gage didn't know the *real* lie. The one I'd perpetrated every day for the past few weeks.

I hefted the door to the second floor open and stepped into the hall. The women's restroom was up ahead to my left, and Gage was right about the busy time of day. Three women entered as I approached. I shouldn't have been surprised though. He knew what went on in this building at all times.

One of the women held the door for me, and as I stepped inside, snippets of conversations filled the space. A toilet flushed and water ran. The hand dryer blew. Maybe I could do what he demanded without being detected since the noise level in here was close to ear-splitting. I entered the last stall and firmly shut the door, double checking the latch.

"I'm here," I whispered.

"Good. Hold the phone with your left hand."

"What if I already am?"

"You aren't."

I swear the man had eyes in the walls of every room. I switched the phone to my left ear. "What now?" I asked in a hushed voice.

"Tease your clit with one finger."

This was beyond humiliating. I shifted inside the stall,

standing in the center of the door with my back to it, thankful the stalls were made with privacy in mind; they didn't have gaps between the door and the frame.

My reluctant hand dragged my skirt up my thigh, and I slipped a finger between the lips of my pussy. Heat instantly flared. My head fell back against the door, and I let out a breath.

Two days of being teased and denied. God, this was torture.

"Are you touching yourself?"

"Mmm-hmmm..." Chatter continued on the other side of the door. Gossip about coworkers, stories about the men they were dating, the assholes they'd dumped and the assholes who'd dumped them. I closed my eyes and blocked it all out. Everything but my finger caressing, slipping through the moisture growing between my legs.

"Cup yourself, Kayla." Blocked out everything but Gage's seductive voice in my ear. "Fingers in your cunt, thumb on your clit."

Swallowing a moan, I widened my stance and forced my fingers inside. "Gage..." His name was a breath on my lips. An oath. Bringing my thumb to my clit almost destroyed me, but I did it.

The hand dryer blared on again, and I used it as a cover. "I'm so close."

"I know, baby. That's where I want you. On the edge..." He groaned, and I knew then that he had his cock in his devious hand. His breathing escalated. "Rub yourself and mean it. I want to hear you moan."

I *didn't* want to make a sound. Not with a bunch of gossip mongers who wouldn't hesitate to spread this humiliating task around the office. The flesh under my circling thumb throbbed, skyrocketing my pulse. Biting back a moan, I willed my hips to stay still.

"You're holding back. If you don't moan for me right now, I'll gag you when I get my hands on you."

He knew me too well. The strangled sound escaped my throat just as someone entered the next stall.

"You're very naughty, Kayla." He tsk-tasked. "Touching yourself in the middle of the day and turning me on. Do you know how hard my cock is right now?"

I grunted, unable to do more beyond my constricted throat.

"Do I need to call you into my office for a spanking?"

"Please, Master." The words tore from my tightened lips, breathless enough to count as a whisper. I'd rather he bend me over his desk and whale on me than lose control in this bathroom.

"Fuck, you're sexy. Come to me. Don't wash your hands. I want the smell of your beautiful cunt on your fingers. I want you wet. Do you understand me?"

Several women had exited the bathroom, and the sudden quiet seemed to echo. I mumbled a yes and ended the call before he could issue another command. Thirty long seconds ticked by as my heartbeat slowed. I straightened my skirt and was about to slide open the lock and push the door open when a single name froze the blood pumping through my veins.

"Did you hear about Katherine Mitchell?"

"Crazy, right?" a woman with a pitchy voice said. "I heard she's coming back."

The sound of rushing water interrupted for a moment. "I'd bet a month's pay the boss is fucking her again."

"Well that's obvious. You don't spend over an hour in his office without him taking out his dick." Laughter echoed. "Rachel told me Mr. Channing's wife disappears in there for *hours* sometimes."

Fire erupted in my stomach, and something dangerous

and venomous collided inside me. Possessive jealousy. If I was his and only his, then he was fucking mine and only mine.

"What a pig," one of the women said.

"A hot, rich pig." More giggles. "Think he'll give Katherine the PA position?"

"Ugh. No doubt. That bitch has always had a hold on him."

"It's bullshit. At least four girls have been waiting for a shot at that job."

A door squeaked open then banged shut, muffling the words coming from their running mouths. My cheeks flushing with rage, I tiptoed from the stall I'd been hiding in and faced an empty bathroom.

Listened to the pulse throbbing in my ears.

He was waiting for me, but I didn't want to move. I didn't feel capable of doing anything besides gripping the counter until my knuckles turned white. Their words raped my mind, making me want to claw and scratch and *scream*. They believed he was screwing Katherine. The whole damn building probably thought my husband was fucking another woman.

At some point, I left the bathroom and moved down the hall at a pace that defied the stilettos on my feet. As I waited for the elevator, I practically ripped the shoes off and held them in my shaking fist. No one paid me any attention. I was invisible—just another employee among many. After all, why would the wife of the CEO be on the second floor using the ladies room?

As I rode the elevator to the fourth floor, I couldn't stop the speculation, the mistrust and hurt and jealousy from taking hold of me. After our wedding, I'd insisted he transfer Katherine to another office. He'd owed me that much, considering all he'd put me through. Considering all he expected of me. If he wanted control of every aspect of my life, then he could at least give me this.

He'd shocked me by agreeing, by putting *me* first. But he'd brought her back. Why?

Was I not good enough?

The elevator dinged. I despised how my eyes burned with unshed turmoil as I stepped onto the floor where I used to work. The place transported me to the past—to a time I'd been but couldn't quite remember. As if someone else had worked here. Someone who'd been strong and independent.

"Hello, Mrs. Channing. He's waiting for you."

"Thank you," I mumbled to his secretary—a woman who was thankfully married and much older than Gage. I thought I trusted him…I *wanted* to trust him, but my reaction to overhearing the gossip of those women told me otherwise. We were both jealous people. Possessive. Obsessed. Maybe that's why he'd ultimately won my heart, because it recognized its own kind.

Clutching my shoes in one hand, I turned the handle with the other, pushed the door open, and stepped inside.

He sat at his desk—the same one he'd bent me over countless times to ravish or punish. He glanced up as the door clicked shut behind me.

"Took you long enough. Come to me on your hands and knees."

Instead of dropping to the floor, I stood motionless.

He leaned back in his chair and folded his arms. "Kayla, don't make me tell you again."

"Why is Katherine back?"

The question seemed to startle him. "Who told you?"

"It doesn't matter who told me!" My knuckles whitened around the straps of my stilettos. "You promised me she was gone."

He sighed, and the way he did it—as if he were dealing

with a recalcitrant child—enraged me. I dropped my shoes so I wouldn't throw them at his smug, I'm-in-charge face.

Bastard.

My vision blurred, narrowed to where he sat as if the walls were closing in on me. Or maybe the memories were coming to claim me. This office held too many of them, most of which were still raw and bleeding. They flooded my mind, flaying me with their brutality. With their sensuality. Me, bent over the desk as his belt punished my ass. On the floor between his knees, eating cock while he ate his turkey on rye.

And the walls...we'd broken in each one. He'd taken me many times in this space, in many ways, from slow and loving to fast and harsh. Time hadn't wiped the slate clean, despite marriage. Despite the fact that I loved this insane man more than he deserved.

Because in that moment, I wanted to kill him.

He studied me for a few seconds—seconds that felt like minutes. Finally, he stood, and rather than beam me with anger and the promise of degradation, his eyes widened in a way that was foreign to me. As if he'd been caught red-handed.

My stomach lurched. Vomit rose. When it came to him, my instincts were usually on the money, and they were screaming bloody murder. I failed to breathe as I brought my hand to my throat, brushing trembling fingers over the collar he'd locked around my neck before we'd married. I had no key to it. He kept it on him at all times.

Because he owned me. Because I was his plaything he kept locked away, ready and available to use and fuck when it suited him. I didn't want to ask, let alone hear the answer, but I had to know.

"Did you sleep with her?"

"God, no, Kayla." He rounded the desk, creeping toward me like one would sneak upon a skittish animal.

I held a hand up. "Don't you dare come near me."

He halted at my venomous tone. "Don't do this, baby. You're overreacting."

His cautious demeanor, and the fact that he didn't have me over his desk, ass reddened from his belt, spoke louder than the thunder in my ears. A tear finally slipped free. Glaring at him, I swiped it away. Pretended it wasn't there.

I wasn't crying. Crying meant he was hurting me, and I'd let him hurt me enough. Day after day, I let him wreck me. Crying meant those women were speaking the truth.

"Why aren't you punishing me, Gage?"

"Seriously? You're picking a fight with me because you want to be punished?" Ignoring my protesting hand, he took a step toward me. Helplessly, I watched him take another, and another until my back hit the door.

Trapped. Nowhere to go. Right back at square one... where I always ended up with him.

He wrenched my arms above my head and shackled my wrists in his strong fist. "Is there a reason you need to be punished?"

"N-no." I hated how shaky my voice was, how the lie seemed to dance off my lips too easily. My face heated, flushing my cheeks with deception.

"You're looking guilty as fuck, Kayla. Are you sure you don't need to be punished?" The uncertainty in his eyes had disappeared. Now that he had me subdued and back under his control, those few moments of unsteady ground he'd stood on were no more. His world was solid again.

Mine was crumbling beneath my feet.

"The thought of you with her kills me." Another tear dripped down my cheek. "Why is she back?"

He brushed the sorrow from my face, and the gesture

was so gentle and caring, I wanted to sob. His mouth settled on mine, coaxed my lips apart, plundered away my insecurities. Tightening his hold on my wrists, he shoved his free hand under my shirt and cupped me, thumb whisking the hardened nipple poking through thin silk.

"Gage..." I sighed against his lips, disarmed by his touch. Pliable submissive waiting to bend upon his command. That was me.

"There is no one but you. *No one.*" His gaze sparked with meaning. "Can you say the same?"

"Yes." Though not in the way he meant. Not in the way he was hoping for. No matter how much I loved him, needed him, was bound to him...Ian would always have a tiny piece of my heart. Deep down, he knew that, or he wouldn't have asked.

"You're it for me, baby." His gorgeous blue eyes, fringed by thick lashes that normally shadowed his secrets, held steady. He didn't avoid my gaze, didn't look away in shame or regret. They bespoke truth.

I'd misunderstood. He would build me a new foundation, assure me that I had nothing to fear. Those women were wrong. Katherine wasn't—

"But there is something I need to tell you." He swallowed hard, and my legs almost gave out. If he hadn't pinned me to the door, I would have leaned against it to prop me up.

"Tell me what?" I wanted to take the question back. Wanted to cover my ears and sink through the door to the other side, where I wouldn't hear the words he so clearly didn't want to say. Gage didn't do nervous.

"Katherine's son is mine. That's why she was here the other day. We were arguing over visitation."

A blade sliced through my heart, freshly sharpened. She'd given him the one thing I hadn't been able to. We'd tried. Jesus, we'd tried. Day after day, week after week. We'd fucked more times than most people fucked in a lifetime, yet my curse still showed up like clockwork every month.

"How long have you known?"

"A couple of months." He paused, hesitating. "But I suspected last year after..."

After we lost the baby.

The truth crashed over me. He hadn't believed he could have kids, so finding out the doctors had been wrong—that he was capable of knocking up a woman—had changed everything. Why hadn't I given thought to Katherine's son? I remembered seeing him once, long before Gage had blackmailed me into sexual slavery. Now that I considered it, there had definitely been a resemblance.

How could he have kept something this huge from me? We'd turned a new page the day we married, left the lies and blackmail in the past.

Except you've been lying for weeks.

That annoying voice in my head was right. How hypocritical to feel betrayed when I'd kept something from him as well. Only my lie was small in comparison. I'd only wanted a little freedom. A few stolen hours each week to give something back for the gift I'd been given.

The gift of Eve.

I yanked my hands free and pushed against his chest. "Let me go."

"We need to talk about this."

"No, we don't." Putting all my strength into freeing myself, I shoved him back, inch by hard-won inch, and managed to jerk the door open before he could grab me again. He glanced at the busy room full of his employees, and the boss mask fell into place.

"Don't you dare walk out that door." Though he wore a neutral expression for show, his tone dropped to a range that never failed to ring my warning bells. “We aren’t done here, Kayla.”

How could he wipe all signs of feeling from his face? Was part of him always pretending? Always keeping an iron grip on control?

“I can’t even look at you,” I said, not giving a shit if the entire floor heard me.

All sign of pretenses vanished. He tugged me into his office and slammed the door. “How do you address me?”

“You don’t get to be my Master today. Today you’re just my husband who had a kid with another woman and failed to mention it.”

He hauled me to the desk, his fingers grasping my bicep with enough strength to bruise. “You *will* call me Master, even if I have to beat it out of you.” He reached for his belt. “Bend the fuck over and lift your skirt.”

“No.”

His mouth formed a severe line. He wasn’t used to being defied. And he hadn’t punished me out of anger in so long that the determination in his hands as he unbuckled his belt tore through me. I hadn’t stepped out of line since we’d married. Not that he knew of, anyway.

“You don’t tell me no.” He lunged for me, grabbed a fist full of my hair, and forced me over his desk. My palms slapped the smooth surface. “Fuck, Kayla. Your defiance is only turning me on.” He kicked my legs apart and thrust his fingers into me.

I pushed to my toes with a startled cry.

“Who am I?” His grip on my hair tightened.

“A liar.”

“Wrong.” Slowly, he inched his thumb into my ass, igniting a ring of fire I couldn’t escape. My stomach roiled from the intrusion.

“Gage, stop.”

"You don't issue the orders. I'm your Master, and if I want to finger your tight little asshole, I will."

I struggled for about two seconds before flopping onto the desk, my body a boneless mess of defeat. Fighting him only prolonged the pain. My breaths blasted the mahogany surface of his workspace. I relaxed my muscles and accepted his probing thumb.

Accepted that I was helpless.

The hardest part of accepting that I was helpless was accepting that I'd put myself in this position. I'd married him when I should have walked. Loved him when I should have hated him. Bent when I should have stood on my own two feet and not only said no, but meant it.

Instead, I found myself bent over with my ass bared. Again. And the truly fucked up part was my body's reaction to everything this man did to me.

"Your cunt is so damn wet, Kayla. It doesn't lie. And that low groaning in the back of your throat? That's you begging me to take you, whether you want to admit it or not."

"Fuck you, Gage."

"You'd like that, wouldn't you? I'm sorry to break it to you, but two of your holes are occupied at the moment, and the only one left is spewing some dirty shit right now."

"Oh my God, you're insufferable."

"Say it, Kayla."

"I'm not calling you Master."

The bastard laughed, and I wondered why until he curled his fingers inside me. His thumb added pressure in my ass that stopped hurting and started feeling *good*.

Damn it.

He was relentless in holding me prisoner on the desk, my hair in his fist and my cheek to the wood. Legs spread wide for his plundering fingers.

I couldn't stop from pushing my ass into him, couldn't

hold back a plea for more. Couldn't deny that I wanted him. I *needed* him.

What the fuck was wrong with me?

I had no backbone. That was my problem. Because he had me anytime he wanted, and he knew it. I let out a breath that ruffled my bangs.

"You win, Master. Fuck me. Please, for God's sake, fuck me."

He leaned into my back, his cock pushing against my tender ass where his thumb had been two seconds ago. "Do you remember what I said I'd consider if you made it the whole week without coming?"

My heart skipped a beat. Him, at my mercy. How could I forget? "I remember."

He brought his lips to my ear. "If I fuck you right now, I won't stop until you come. Are you sure you want that?"

Yes, I wanted it. Wanted *him*. But the chance to have the upper hand tempted. Taunted.

"Let me go," I whispered.

He released his grip on my hair and stepped back.

As my blood pumped steady in my veins, I regained my bearings. Regained my damn mind and recalled the reason he'd had me bent over and taking his thumb up my ass.

The words of the grapevine duo tumbled through my head, end over end, an incessant provocation. I rounded on him, anger rushing through me like a flash flood in the bereft of deserts. But the burn in my ass served as an annoying reminder. Screaming at him would accomplish nothing, except for a return to his desk. So I tried leaving, my mouth a straight line to keep my tongue in check.

He blocked my attempts, first stepping to the left then the right.

"Move," I said through gritted teeth. "I'm done here."

His answering smirk grated. "How can you be done? I haven't even started yet."

"You can use sex all you want, but this isn't going away. You have a kid with Katherine. She gave you what I couldn't." What I might never be able to give.

Pain flickered in his eyes, matching the ping in my heart, and I took the opportunity to force my way past, scooping up my shoes on the way to the door. As I reached for the handle, I glanced over my shoulder.

He leaned against the desk's edge, in the place where he'd had me sprawled and vulnerable. "If you walk out, prepare for the consequences when I get home."

I paused, surprised by the way he held on to his executive desk with whitened knuckles. He thrived on control, and right now, he straddled the ledge.

We'd battled, and though he'd won, I wasn't down yet. I threw one last glare in his direction. "Don't hold your breath, Gage. I might not even come home tonight."

CHAPTER EIGHT

Insufferable didn't come close. Insufferable was the pebble digging into your heel, the itch you couldn't reach to scratch. Insufferable was getting stuck in rush hour traffic with a full bladder and no exit in sight.

Gage's behavior transcended insufferable.

Entering the hospital's lobby, I willed my anger to subside, my pulse to slow. If one good thing had come from our argument, it happened to be that I wasn't sitting at home waiting for him to snap his fingers so I could drop to my knees.

I'd walked out of his office of my own free will, and though part of me dreaded the eventual price I'd pay—taken from my flesh with each agonizing strike of whatever implement he chose—mouthing off to him had been...liberating.

I punched the button for the tenth floor and waited for the arrival of the elevator. Standing up to him had sparked something alive inside me. The woman I used to be, if only for a blip in the grand scheme of things. Being bad hadn't felt this good in such a long time.

I stepped into the elevator and found myself alone until

the seventh floor. As the doors slid open, a chill traveled down my spine. I almost expected to find Ian waiting on the other side, just like the other day.

But Ian wasn't there. Two doctors entered, mid-conversation. I tuned out their talk of cancer stages and grades, research, and cutting-edge treatments. Each time I entered this wing, the past threatened to punch through the walls I'd built to protect myself. The memories were never far, and sometimes they crept up on me to bind around my chest until I could hardly breathe.

And that's why coming back to this place was good for me, no matter how difficult. No matter how the antiseptic smell took me back each and every time to the utter despair of Eve's illness. To the hopelessness of watching her become sicker and sicker. To the desperation that had spurred me on to embezzle thousands of dollars from Gage.

If I hadn't stolen the money, he would have never caught me in the act, would have never blackmailed me into loving his sadistic ass. But the most important takeaway from that tumultuous decision was Eve; without my thievery, he would have never moved obstacles to get the care she needed.

The elevator arrived on the children's floor. I stepped out and made my way toward the circular nurse station that served as a hub for activity. A rainbow mural decorated the walls, and the counters of the center island were a mix of complimentary sky blue and shades of gold. The nurses had proudly displayed artwork from some of the children above and below the rainbow. Compared to the rest of the hospital, this floor had the vibe of warmth and innocence.

I spotted Simone immediately. She glanced up from a chart, her reading glasses perched on her dainty nose.

"Emma's been asking for you," she said, tucking a stray blond hair behind her ear.

"Is she awake?"

"Yeah, but she started another round of chemo yesterday, so her spirits are a little low. I'm sure a visit from you will cheer her up."

As I wrung my hands, Simone marked something on a chart, shelved it, then studied me with an assessing eye. "Is everything okay? You seem upset."

"It's nothing. I don't want to get into it right now."

She crossed her arms. "What'd he do this time?"

I blinked, despising the sting in my eyes. My problems were a speck compared the issues these kids faced every day on this floor.

"Hey," Simone said, her voice softening. "I'm sorry. I didn't mean to upset you."

"It's not you." I avoided her gaze and forced myself to pull it together. "Gage and I had an argument. I don't have the energy to talk about it right now, so I'm gonna see if Emma's up for a story."

"That girl is always up for your stories." She squeezed my shoulder. "Let's meet for lunch sometime this week, okay?"

I nodded then headed down the hall, making a stop at the hand-washing station before stepping into Emma's room. Flowers and stuffed animals covered most of the surfaces, and her mother had brought photos of her siblings from home. I tiptoed to the side of her bed and sank into a chair.

Her lashes fluttered and opened, revealing two brown eyes. A weak smile painted her lips—the only feature brightening her face because she was pale otherwise. But nowhere near lifeless. Not yet. This little girl was a fighter, and she reminded me so much of Eve that coming here was more difficult each time I walked through the door.

Yet I also found it therapeutic in some ways. Bringing a smile to her precious face was my biggest reward.

I picked up the *Cat in the Hat* from her bedside table. "You wanted me to read this one to you next, right?"

She nodded and settled against her pillow. I turned the first page and started reading the story of odd cats and rhymes. After a while, my voice blended with the din of the hospital; the continuous beeping, intercoms, and feet padding down the halls. It was all so achingly familiar.

After a while, Emma's eyelids drooped, but I sensed she was still listening. I read page after page, each word an octave above a whisper. I wasn't sure how long I sat there, content to give her comfort through mere words. Probably no more than twenty minutes, but it felt like an hour. I closed the book and carefully placed it back on the table. Emma's chest rose and fell in steady cycles, her breathing deep and even, indicating she'd succumbed to sleep.

A tingle traveled through my extremities, and that's when I noticed Ian standing in the doorway. My heart skipped, jumpstarted by the sensation of deja vu.

"You're a natural," he said.

"I wish I could do more for her."

"You're here. That's all you can do, Kayla, and it's enough. More than enough."

I rose and tiptoed across the room, careful not to rouse Emma from her slumber. "What are you doing here?"

"Can we talk for a second?" He nodded toward the hall, and I vacillated between returning to Emma's side, and allowing him to usher me from the room.

The latter prevailed.

I followed him down the hall a few feet, out of earshot of little ears.

"You didn't meet me for lunch," he said.

"I wasn't planning to meet you. I'm just as married today as I was Saturday."

"Normally, that would matter to me."

A doctor approached, and I stepped toward Ian, lowering my voice. "Well, it matters to me."

He brushed his fingers against my cheek. "Do you really want to do this here?"

His touch careened through my system, forbidden and unwanted, but I couldn't displace the familiar longing he'd sparked in me for years. That ember was a shameful entity flaring inside me.

"Why are you doing this?" As I stumbled back, my sneakers squeaked on the linoleum.

He folded my hand in his and refused to let go. "Come with me?" he asked, though he didn't leave me much choice unless I wanted to risk causing a scene, which I didn't. He pulled me down the hall toward the elevator. I swallowed with a hard gulp, my protests catching in the vise of my constricting throat.

The silence between us grew heavy as we traveled the distance of ten floors. The elevator halted at the bottom, and the doors slid open to reveal the busy lobby. Ian led me past the receptionist and through a double door. We journeyed through a maze of corridors before coming to a halt. He'd switched offices since the last time we'd spoken within the privacy of his workspace.

As he shuffled through his keys, I questioned how I'd ended up *here*. Entering that room was a bad idea, yet my feet had no intention of doing the sensible thing by turning around and navigating the labyrinth of the hospital. My stubborn feet suddenly had a mind of their own, planting me in a precarious situation I didn't want to be in.

He reached for the knob, key shaking in his hand, and missed the keyhole three times before managing to unlock the door. He motioned for me to enter. A small window allowed dreary light in, obscured by the shitty weather. A mixture of paperwork, folders, cups, and office supplies cluttered his desk, which was at odds with his tidy personality.

Ian not only closed the door, but he locked it, and he didn't bother turning on a light. I backed up a step, hating how he stood between me and the exit.

"What do you want?" I asked, folding my arms. Maybe it was true—curiosity did kill the cat.

I was fucking roadkill then.

"What do you think I want?"

I had no answer. None that I liked, anyway.

"Sit down. I just want to talk." He took me by the elbow and ushered me to the small sofa tucked against one wall. Taken completely off guard, I plopped onto it as he claimed the cushion next to me.

"How is Eve?"

"She's great."

"How are you?" He devoured me with eager, hungry eyes. Despite the low light casting us in shadow, I still clearly saw that he didn't *just* want to talk. He wanted something he couldn't have.

"I'm great. Everything's *great*."

"One big happy family, huh? He hasn't started abusing Eve yet?"

Blistering anger roared through my veins. I moved to stand, but his forearm blocked me.

"It's a valid question, Kayla."

I slapped his arm away. "No, it's not. Do you think I'd allow anyone to hurt my daughter?"

"No, but I never saw you for a doormat either. I never thought you'd go through with the wedding."

I gritted my teeth. "You're about a year too late to question my decisions."

"Better late than never." He leaned in, caging me between his body and the sofa. "You fucked up, Kayla. You let that fucking bastard abuse you. But the real kicker is how you let him near Eve. What the hell is wrong with you?"

I wanted to throw the question back at him, but I couldn't find my voice. His confrontational tone stunned me.

"You sold yourself to save her, but when it comes to him, you put her last." His upper lip curled in a sneer that was foreign to his features. "Fantastic parenting skills there."

My palm sent a sound slap across his cheek. "You don't know shit about my life."

He rubbed his cheek, though he appeared unfazed by my loss of control. "Explain it to me then." He brought his face forward until we were nose to nose.

I placed a hand on his chest, my fingers brushing his stethoscope. I despised the way he had me trapped. Gage had me in this position often—cornered and helpless—but I was used to his overbearing nature, was drawn to his dominance in a way that sickened me if I let myself dwell on it too long.

Ian's behavior unsettled me beyond words, and it wasn't because I didn't like the feel of him being close. With much shame, I realized that I did. No, what sent off my internal alarm was the feeling that something was *wrong*.

I inched back and met his hazel gaze. "Why are you mad at me?"

The festering anger seemed to flee from his bones. He let out a breath. "I'm not mad at you. I'm mad at myself. I should have stopped your wedding, even if it meant crashing it."

"Thank you for not doing that," I said quietly. "I've built a good life with Gage, and Eve is happier than I've ever seen her. She has a father. A *real* father this time. She loves him."

"Do you?" His heartbeat thumped under my palm.

"What type of question is that?"

"One you obviously don't want to answer."

"Because it's none of your damn business." When I got down to the grit of what Gage and I were, love just didn't cover it. What we had was unhealthy and wrong, yet we both thrived on it, craved it, needed it.

"Let me go," I told him. "Being here with you is just... torture. It accomplishes nothing. All we're doing is dredging up the past and hurting each other."

"We don't have to dredge up anything. I'm content to sit here and *not* talk."

I pushed him back an inch. "Ian, stop."

He nuzzled my neck. "Am I making you nervous? Are you feeling things you're not supposed to feel?"

I bit my lip, denying with a quick shake of my head.

"What if you could go back and do it differently?" he asked. "Would you?"

I flipped through the days and weeks and months of the past year, the scenes going off in my mind like flashcards.

My wedding night, when Gage had taken me with the tender patience he rarely allowed me to see.

Our first argument as a married couple. I'd made the mistake of saying hello to the neighbor while checking the mail—the very attractive and very *male* neighbor. Gage and I had gotten into a shouting match over his ridiculous control issues, and that had resulted in him gagging me until Eve came home hours later. Needless to say, I now steered clear of the neighbor, and I'd been careful to obey since that day.

Until recently, when I'd risked it all to volunteer, knowing full well that Ian worked here. What did that mean? Not for the first time, I wondered what my actions were trying to tell me.

That I missed him?

Definitely.

That I still cared about him?

"I regret many things," I said. "But changing the past isn't possible, and even if it were, I'm not sure I'd want to."

"I think you would." He leaned forward and pressed his lips on mine. The kiss barely lasted a second, but it was enough to knock the air from my lungs.

"Don't," I said through thinly veiled anger.

"You're not the same woman you were a year ago. You're stronger, more determined." He narrowed his eyes. "You're staying for her, aren't you?"

I shook my head, mouth gaping. Was it true? Did I endure Gage's rigid rules and brutal hand for Eve? Or was I staying because no one worked my body the way he did? The heat flaring between my legs—heat that had nothing to do with Ian's brief kiss—gave me my answer. I loved Gage for the way he made me feel; wild and out of control. But I also hated him for the way he made me feel.

Like a caged animal.

Just as Ian was doing now. "I love him."

"I don't believe you."

"You can choose to believe what you want." I shoved him back, surprised by how easily he relented. Compared to Gage, Ian was weak...or less determined to make me bend.

He fell back against the couch, his hand grasping his head. "I'm sorry, Kayla." Wincing, he cursed under his breath. "This is harder than I thought." He was about to say more, but my cell went off.

Gage.

"You going to get that?" Ian asked.

"No," I whispered. "If you need to get something off your chest, do it now." I pointed at the door. "Because once I walk out of here, I'm not coming back." My cell blared again.

Ian rose to his feet. "I can't do this with him calling every fucking thirty seconds."

His constant mood shifts made the hair on the back of

my neck stand on end. "Do what?" I stood and faced him, clutching my obnoxious phone like a lifeline. "You're worrying me."

He wasn't acting like himself, and it scared me.

"You know what?" He paused, his attention veering to the ceiling for a moment. "You're right. It's too little, too late. If you're truly happy, then I can accept that. I can leave you be." He exhaled. "I just...I had to know."

I moved to place a hand on his arm but thought better of it. Hell, his cryptic-speak was messing with my head. My phone went off again, and I answered on the second ring with a clipped, "Hello?"

"Where are you?" Gage's question dripped with fury.

"On my way to pick up Eve."

"Don't bother. I picked her up early."

My fingers tightened around the phone. I cast a furtive glance at Ian and noticed the tightness of his features. Afraid he'd see the alarm in my eyes and do something about it—like alert Gage to his presence—I turned my back on him.

"Why did you take her out of school early?"

But I knew the answer before I'd tossed the question out there. He'd done it because maneuvering me was what he did best, and if he wanted me home, getting the upper hand by using Eve would ensure I walked into his trap.

"We need to talk, so get your ass home and maybe I'll go easy on you."

CHAPTER NINE

The front door stood between me and my surrender, silently mocking with its facade of normalcy. Beyond that door waited a prison. Waited passion. Waited punishment. Waited *him*.

Most people would stay on the side where I stood. The safe side. The *sane* side. Too bad I needed the insanity to feel sane anymore. Needed his soul-crushing possession to feel free. Because it was freeing…until the last wave of rapture crested and the bars of my world clanked into place again.

Folding my reluctant fingers around the handle, I wedged the door open inch by inch. He had my daughter in there, so entering Gage's domain of fucked-up was a sure thing.

I dawdled in the foyer and hung up my coat, set my purse on the table, fiddled with my wedding ring. The quiet unsettled and that alone sent my feet moving in the direction of the living room, in search of my daughter. Instead, I found Gage on one end of the white sectional, still as stone.

"Where's Eve?"

"In the dining room coloring. She's got a snack, one of

those juice pouch thingamabobs you buy her, and enough crayons to draw a rainbow masterpiece." He patted the cushion next to him. "Sit down."

I took a step forward, my gaze on the kitchen. The dining room lay just beyond, irritatingly out of sight.

"For fuck's sake, Kayla." He reached out and planted me on his lap in a way that left no question about his state of mind. I straddled him, and his firm hand on my back brought me closer until my breasts smashed against his chest. His cock throbbed between us, refusing to be ignored.

"Where did you go?"

"The mall." The lie left my lips in a near mechanical way. "Then I went for a drive. I needed some time to think."

With a sigh, he dropped his head against the back of the couch. "I was going to tell you."

"Why didn't you?"

He slid his palms up my thighs and squeezed. "I knew it would hurt like hell. We've been trying for months—"

"Gage...please." Closing my eyes, I pinched the bridge of my nose, sensing the onset of a headache. I didn't want to go down this road. Not today—not when my emotions were a mutilated, bloody mess. Dealing with Ian's cryptic presence and then facing the fact I might never have another child was too much to handle in one day.

"This is why I didn't tell you," he said. "I didn't want to rip that wound open."

"The truth had to come out eventually."

Just as all secrets do.

"I know, Kayla. Fuck. Don't you think I know that? I wanted to give us time...I was hoping...never mind."

What he didn't say busted through with clarity. He'd banked on the appearance of two lines to soften the blow when he told me about his child with *Katherine*.

Katherine, of all people.

My stomach lurched. God, how I hated that woman. I could already imagine the smug curve of her lips. She'd hold this over my head, milk it for all it was worth. She was the mother of his child…and I wasn't.

But I *was* his wife. He'd put his ring on my finger. He shared a bed with me every night. He got what he needed every time he took his belt to my ass. Every time he pushed me to my knees, past my limits. Every time he fucked me. Suddenly, I wanted to curl up at his feet and beg him to do as he wished.

I had power.

My mind turned itself inside out mulling over the realization. She had his son, but I had him where it counted—I had him by his obsession, by his heart, *and* by his balls.

And now I had his mouth opening under mine, allowing me two seconds to claim until he rose up from rock-bottom and remembered who he was. He held me by the nape and took control, plundering my mouth in a way that only Gage could. The taste of him on my tongue pounded the memory of Ian's chaste kiss to dust.

I completely lost my shit, grinding my slick pussy against the bulge in his pants. He swallowed my moans, let loose one of his own, then abruptly broke free. He glanced down at our bodies, practically interlocked despite our clothing.

"Don't think this changes anything." He brought his lips to my ear. "Your hot little cunt won't tempt me," he whispered. "No orgasms."

My head was still spinning from dry-humping him like a horny teen, but at least I was lucid enough to catch what he'd said. To grasp the meaning of it.

"No?" I challenged, moving my hips.

He shook his head. "It's going to be torture, Kayla."

My eyes drifted shut. "Why's that?"

"You're in big trouble," he said, palming my breasts, "and your punishment is going to make my cock throb like hell."

I groaned, knowing that I couldn't throw his deceit in his face without my conscience lambasting me.

"But we're getting sidetracked here, aren't we?" He let his hands drop. "You might not believe it, but I *am* sorry. You deserved the truth."

I'd never felt shittier than I did in that moment. This was a rare occasion for Gage. What had gone down in his office earlier today had knocked him off his game, and he was still reeling.

"So she's not coming back to work for you?"

"No, baby."

A lengthy pause fell upon us, and I sensed the wheels in his head turning.

"We'll tell Eve together. But I think it would be better for her to get to know him first. He's about her age, and for all intent and purposes, he's her brother."

"That bitch's spawn is *not* Eve's brother."

Gage narrowed his eyes. "He's part of me too. I realize we have a lot to deal with, but don't take your hatred for Katherine out on my son."

I pushed off his lap and wandered around the living room, since in a way, it beat pacing. This would change everything. Later it would really hit me. I felt the weight of his keen gaze on me, so I gave him my back and folded myself in the protection of my arms.

But then he had to go and melt my heart by embracing me from behind. By showing me we were in this together. "Baby, you're strong and compassionate and caring. I know you'll accept him as your own."

The way he'd accepted Eve as his own. He didn't have to voice it. I heard the truth.

"Are you going for custody?"

"I won't take him from his mother, but I do want to be part of his life." His arms tightened around me. "I want the three of us to be part of his life."

"Like one happy family, in between the whips and chains."

His low laugh vibrated against my neck. "Whips, chains, and nipple clamps. Don't think I've forgotten how you stormed from my office earlier."

The doorbell rang, fracturing our private bubble.

Eve raced from the kitchen. "Is that Leah?" she asked as Gage let me go. I cast a confused glance in his direction, one bordering on suspicious.

He eyed me in a way that set my teeth on edge. "No, princess. There's someone I want you to meet."

The world seemed to freeze as he disappeared into the foyer. When he returned, ushering Katherine and her son into our house, the earth lurched forward again with too much force.

Oh hell no.

I would not let that woman get under my skin in my own home. Rather than avoid her gaze, I met it head-on, refusing to let her haughty expression draw a response from me. I'd expected her nasty disposition, had prepared for it from the moment I learned Gage was her son's father. All I had to do was remind myself that his pants were still damp from my arousal. I hoped the bitch smelled it, tasted it on her vapid tongue.

Folding my arms, I clenched my teeth as I watched them interact. Eve warmed to her son immediately, which wasn't surprising because she welcomed everyone. Katherine took a step closer to Gage and opened her mouth, about to spew her venom, but he halted her with a raised hand.

"This isn't the time or place."

Just like that, she clamped her lips shut and fumed in silence.

He returned his attention to the kids and spoke to Eve. "You're going to spend the day with Katherine and Conner."

His words were a jolt to my system. I lurched forward, hands fisted at my sides, about to shout my disapproval, but Eve's expectant face cooled my wrath. "She's not going anywhere with that woman."

Gage threw me a dark glance. A warning to behave. "We aren't discussing this right now."

"But—"

"Not now," he said in a tone that proved more effective than him raising a hand.

Now I was the one fuming in silence.

"Mommy, can I go?"

Biting my tongue, I nodded.

"But what about game night? Today is Monday," she said with pride.

Gage bent so he could meet her eyes. "You're going to have game night with them."

"Are you and Mommy coming?"

"Not this time, princess. Your mom and I have a date." He tilted his head. "Do you know what a date is?"

She shook her head, curiosity and dejection coloring her features.

"A date is when two people go out and do something special."

"Like what?"

Gage glanced at me, his grin hinting at a devious plan brewing in his mind. "I can't say. We wouldn't want to ruin the surprise for your mom, would we?"

Katherine glowered at me. If looks could maim, I'd be a pile of shredded skin and bones. Gage's words cooled my ire some because he'd not only put her in her place with a lift of his authoritative hand, but he'd shown her beyond doubt that she had no place between us.

She left with her son, taking Eve with them, and my spirits plummeted. Gnashing teeth seemed to take over my gut, cutting me to pieces. Knowing that she was walking out the door with my baby girl and watching her do it were two different things.

The resulting disquiet scraped my mind like claws on a chalkboard. I crossed my arms. "You should have asked me before you let that bitch take my daughter." I didn't want Eve around her. Hell, I didn't want *him* around the bitch.

"I thought she was *our* daughter."

"She is." I dipped my head. "You know you're the only father she has."

"And I'll make decisions for her, same as you." He lifted my chin. "If I thought Katherine posed a risk to Eve, I'd be the first in line to do something about it." The firm set of his mouth softened. "This is more about jealousy than anything. I know you well."

I couldn't deny it, as she'd been nothing but kind to Eve in the past.

"Don't think I've forgotten about your tantrum in my office." His fingers tightened around my chin. "On your knees, now."

Strength trickled from my body, escaping through the holes he'd poked in my armor. I dropped and assumed the position. He stood before me, his feet planted with grating confidence shoulder-width apart on the floor.

"Kayla."

I peered up through the strands falling over my right eye. The ones he brushed away with a touch so soft and gentle, it stole my breath. "Yes, Master?"

The corner of his mouth quirked up, and I knew I'd hit the right button. He was helpless against that title when I gave it to him of my own free will. It was one of the few ways I had of manipulating him.

Tucking my hair behind my ear, he moved even closer. Caging me in. Making my world narrow to the hard floor under my knees, the blazing warmth in my extremities, and the larger-than-life posture of the man who owned me.

"I'm in a merciful mood, so you're spared from taking a lashing." He reached into his pocket and dangled a set of nipple clamps at eye level. Upon further inspection, I realized they were the kind he reserved for going out. The kind that made me feel beautiful, despite the agonizing pain they caused.

"However, I think you deserve these. What do you think, Kayla?"

If I disagreed with him, he'd only lash me for it, and my nipples would still end up between his sadistic vises. "Yes, Master. I deserve them."

"Go into our bedroom and prepare for me. I left the coconut bath products out for you." He fisted the clamping set. "I expect you on your knees, naked, no later than thirty minutes from now. Do not move from that position." He pivoted and headed into the kitchen.

As I dragged my feet toward the hall, I spied him opening a bottle of his favorite red. He perched on a bar stool and made himself comfortable as if he intended to stay put for a while. He'd probably sit there for at least an hour, his cock growing thicker, straining against his pants, forming a hard ridge behind his zipper at the thought of me on my knees in the next room.

On my knees waiting for him. Hurting for him. Powerless to do anything other than pass the time in supplication.

I entered the bedroom and quietly shut the door. Thirty minutes didn't give me much time to bathe, shave my legs, do something with my hair.

But he'd expect me to look like a damn model anyway. I shook my head, kicking myself for feeling a modicum of surprise. Gage had never made my life easy, and he never would. His talents lay in other areas, like making me insane with want and need when he got me under his powerful body in bed, up against the wall, bent over a table...chained to the St. Andrew's cross.

Humiliated on my knees with his cock on my tongue.

I sighed as I switched on the faucet to the tub. Despite all that, he made me feel loved. Cherished. Possessed. There wasn't anything he wouldn't do to have me, to fight for me, to protect me. He would crash into hell and charm the devil out of his throne if it meant giving me the world. Of course, he'd chain me to it. The world and I...we were both treasured possessions in Gage's fist.

I shut the faucet off, twisted my hair into a messy up-do, and sank into the blessed hot water. I wanted to lean my head back and close my eyes for a few minutes—just long enough to prepare myself for whatever he had planned. But I couldn't. Every minute counted. Two minutes to shave the barely-there stubble on my legs. Another minute lathering my steaming skin with the coconut body wash he'd left on the edge of the tub.

Ten more minutes to dry off and spread lotion on every inch of my skin. What little time I had left, I used for hair and makeup, and at the thirty-minute mark, I dropped to my knees in the middle of the bedroom and watched the clock to pass the time. No matter how much I pleaded with him to lay a rug down, he refused. The sadist in him gleefully smiled at my pain.

He appeared in the doorway forty-five minutes later, and my knees ached something fierce as he laid the clamps, along with a butt plug, onto the bed. He disappeared into the walk-in closet and emerged a few minutes later wearing tan slacks paired with a soft navy knit shirt. He'd left three buttons at the neckline open. Damn, I wanted to kiss down his throat and make him moan. Gage's idea of casual was no less arresting than the business suits he wore to the office.

"What have you learned from this?" he asked as he wandered to where I kneeled.

"To obey you." The strong, more recent voice in my head rebelled, threatening to throw a verbal punch at his beautiful face.

He reached out and pulled me to my feet, and his eyes sizzled as he scoured my body with a single glance. "God, I'll never get over how gorgeous you are."

His words cast a sheen of desire down my spine. "Same here," I whispered.

Reaching for the clamps, he smiled. "Is your cunt wet, Kayla?"

"Yes."

"Yes what?"

"Yes, Master."

He gestured to my chest. "Present your breasts."

Pulling my shoulders back, I thrust them forward, peaks hard and tingling at just the thought of him clamping them. The fierce pinch would hurt like hell and cool the fire between my legs.

He held up the jeweled chain, and I lifted my chin to allow him access to the discreet built-in ring in my infinity collar. He attached the top of the contraption to the collar, and dainty layers of chains draped my chest. At first glance, people would think it was an elaborate necklace. But if they looked closer, they'd noticed two single chains lowering between the valley of cleavage.

He took a nipple between two fingers and rolled with a light caress. He did the same to the other side, making them extra sensitive, causing an ache that would intensify the sting once he tightened the clamps. Gage often found reasons to punish me so he could play with my nipples in his most favorite and sadistic way.

"These belong to me. Your cunt belongs to me. Don't ever forget that." He pressed one vise against a tingling bud and closed the prongs. A sharp twinge shot through me, coalescing at the tip of my breast.

"I'm the Master of your pain, the Master of your pleasure." He clamped the other side, eliciting a whimper.

"Loosen them, Master. Please," I whispered, barely able to catch my breath. Stones the color of his sapphire eyes dangled, and the added weight heightened my agony.

"Sorry, baby. You're going to suffer tonight." He held my chin in his hand—his modus operandi when it came to putting me in my place. "Don't you ever walk out on me like that again."

What he wanted was an apology, but he wouldn't get one. My nipples throbbed, leaving me with nothing nice to say, so I said nothing at all.

Pulling another clamp from his pocket, he bent and gathered the two sapphire stones together. He attached the additional chain to the tiny hooks at the ends, and the chain tickled my belly.

I watched him in fear and a little wonder as he spread the lips of my sex and placed the third clamp. I gave out a stunned cry, but instead of the familiar sharp ache I expected, that contraption between my legs felt so damn good. Too good. One glance into his eyes told me that was his intention.

To keep me on edge, aroused with no end in sight, my nipples connected to my clit. Pain connected to pleasure. All of his toys chained together for his gratification.

The next five days until our anniversary seemed to span for decades.

Sliding his palms up my thighs, Gage remained kneeling on the floor. I lost my breath because it wasn't often that I had my husband on his knees at my feet. An expression of awe blanketed his face. His eyes heated, darkened to indigo, and the need for control arose in me once again.

I wanted to dominate him.

Wanted to make him writhe.

Make him howl and beg.

Make him submit to *me*.

Warmth crept up my neck and flushed my cheeks as he stood and reached for the butt plug.

"Bend over," he said, his voice thick with seduction.

I planted my hands on the mattress and gave him my ass. Holy hell, this man was my Master all right. And he was absolutely shameless. I told him as much, to which he laughed as he worked the plug in, using enough lubricant that it wasn't too uncomfortable. But then the thing went off, sending vibrations through every nerve in my lower extremities, and I arched my back, expelling a deep moan.

He whirled me around and pushed me onto the bed, then he pulled a pair of lacy thigh-highs from his pocket. Taking my foot in his hand, he began rolling one up my calf, past my shaking knee until the lace top banded around my thigh. He grazed my pussy with his knuckles for a few laborious seconds before giving my other leg the same treatment.

"You're fucking exquisite." He rose to his full height, rubbing the front of his pants. "A test of control indeed. Finish dressing. Something light with a short skirt that flares. I want easy access to that sweet ass."

Oh my God. My nipples were pinched to the point of numbness, and I couldn't move without my clit aching, but he somehow ignited me with mere words.

Dressing was a no-brainer. A flirty black dress with a draped top to hide the clamps, and a strappy pair of the standard four-inch heels he required I wear most of the time. The simmering lust in his eyes told me I'd chosen the right outfit.

"Ready?" he asked.

Was I? I honestly didn't know, but I took his hand, anxious to find out.

CHAPTER TEN

The restaurant gave off a vibe of sin. Low lighting invited couples to sit close and whisper dirty things to each other. Red walls and sleek black tables made me think of passion and sex. Bypassing the section of tables in the middle of the room, the petite hostess halted at a private dining booth and pulled back a gauzy gold drape.

Dining booth didn't come close. The alcove had all the makings of a place to share a meal, but the horseshoe shape of the black cushions, along with red and gold accent pillows, spoke of something else. Something sinful, dark, and forbidden.

Gage had more than dinner on his mind.

"Mr. Channing, your private dining booth is ready."

Gage gestured for me to slide in before him, all the way to the back wall. As he settled next to me, he ordered a bottle of wine.

"Excellent choice, sir."

The way she said "sir" made me bristle, and I couldn't explain why. I didn't like the flirty smile she aimed at Gage or the way her cleavage threatened to spill over the white top of her uniform.

"Have you been here before," I asked after the hostess left to fetch our wine.

"A few times, yes."

"With Katherine?"

He frowned. "Do you intend to waste the whole night talking about her?"

I dipped my head, letting my hair hide the flush in my cheeks. "No."

He swept my hair back. "The past doesn't matter, Kayla. There's only now." He turned my face toward him, refusing to let me hide. "No one has ever captivated me the way you do." He leaned forward and brushed his mouth over mine, barely touching, merely hovering with the promise of more.

"The thought of your pretty nipples pinched between my clamps is enough to make me hard. Only you can do that."

Keeping my lips parted, I closed my eyes and breathed him in. Allowed myself to fall into his snare. He lowered a spaghetti strap, his warm fingers trailing over my goose-bumped skin. His touch skimmed over a clamped nipple through my dress.

I sensed the slow unraveling of his control, felt his lips teasing mine, his tongue aching to mate. To own.

The hostess fractured the moment with her presence. "Your wine, sir."

Gage and I broke apart, and I was glad I wasn't the one on the other end of his dark glare. "We require privacy. Announce your presence before entering next time."

"Of course. I'm sorry." But she didn't seem sorry at all as she set two menus onto the glossy table, followed by wine glasses and a bottle of red. I didn't bother reaching for the menu since Gage always ordered for me anyway.

She filled our glasses half full. "Your server will be here

momentarily to take your orders." Her red lips curved into a suggestive smile. "Is there anything else I can do for you, sir?"

I swallowed a growl as Gage dismissed her. Silence fell upon us, giving me time to stew over how gorgeous my husband was. He turned heads, commanded respect without earning it. His entire being harvested power and sexual prowess.

Had his jealous streak rubbed off on me?

Our server arrived, and this woman was no less attractive than the hostess, but she showed respect by not openly flirting with a married man. Gage rattled off our orders before she exited through the curtains, leaving us alone again, stowed away in our intimate booth.

"Your jealousy is a major turn-on." He downed his glass of wine in two drinks, which was so unlike him. Then he set the glass down with a heavy hand, leaned back, and lowered his zipper with a taunting smile.

"Come over here and grind on me."

"What?"

He raised a brow. "Did I stutter?"

"N-no." But I couldn't help but observe the people on the other side of the gossamer drapes, their movements resembling shadowed ghosts in the dim restaurant. This place had been designed for public displays of indecency.

Gage took my chin in his firm hand. "The only thing that matters right now is your Master's cock."

I opened and shut my mouth at least three times. I'd married this sex-crazed, brazen man a year ago, yet he still managed to knock me off my axis way too often.

"Kayla, my cock isn't going to fuck itself."

He had no shame. None. Zilch.

"Here?" My eyes shifted around the private space, and I almost expected the waitress to appear.

He thrust his hips the slightest bit, flaunting his hard-on with too much pride. “Yes, *here*.” He aimed his patented devil’s grin my way. “Now hop on before I bend your sexy ass over the table and take my belt to it.” He tilted his head. “Somehow, I think that might gain more attention than you quietly riding my cock.”

Swallowing nervously, I stood and was about to lift a leg over his lap to straddle him when he whirled me around and fit my body between his knees. He lifted the back of my dress then pulled me down in one swift motion until his erection nestled against my bare ass. He spread my thighs wide, making me shoot a hand out to grip the table for balance.

“I want deep inside you.” His low tone whispered down the side of my neck. “Lift up,” he said, hands on my hips. I raised my bottom, and he pulled me down until I sheathed him. And we both moaned, on the brink of madness.

I arched my spine and sank against him, back to chest. He ran his fingers down my thighs, teasing with each inch of material he touched before he reached underneath my skirt and carefully removed the clit clamp.

“Ow!”

“Shh,” he said. “Unless you want to be heard.” His tone was much too satisfied.

I breathed noisily, trying to survive the sudden rush of blood to my pussy, and trying not to cry out again.

“This isn’t so bad, is it? I might just eat my dinner like this, with my cock buried inside you.” The plug in my ass started vibrating.

“Oh God...”

He wrapped his arms around my waist, remote to the plug clutched in his hand, and rested his chin on my shoulder. “Can you stand it, Kayla? Me inside you like this? Can you stand the thought that when the server brings our dinner, she'll see you spread and sitting on my cock with nothing but your skirt hiding your beautiful cunt?" He stroked my throbbing clit. "Hiding the way our bodies are joined."

"You wouldn't!"

"You said I'm shameless. I'm about to prove you right."

"Why are you doing this?"

"I take great pleasure in making you squirm." He tilted my head back, and his mouth opened over my throat, left a wet trail to my ear.

"Mmmmm..." I lifted my hips the slightest bit, aching to feel him pushing in and out, rubbing that mystical spot that sent me out of my mind every time.

"Damn, Kayla." His breath blasted my neck, and his hands returned to my hips. "Fuck me to the edge."

I lifted then sank back onto his cock, the table shaking under my grip. "What if I can't stop? It's been days. I don't know—"

He bounced my body up and down, cutting off whatever I'd been about to say.

"More," he groaned, yanking me down to glove him again. "Give it all to me. Everything but your orgasm, baby. Save that for our anniversary."

I melted into him, not only molten lava between my legs but deeply touched by his words. This meant something to him. Beyond the sexual games, the teasing and denial, lived a man who wanted to make a single night special. Memorable.

I gently rode him, my hips swiveling at a steady pace that brought him deep inside me on each rotation. The point of no return neared for us both. But I wouldn't stop until he told me to. My job was to take his cock for as long as he wished, as deep as he wanted, and hold back my orgasm.

And holding back would give me the ultimate prize—his

submission for a night. He hadn't been kidding though when he said he wouldn't make it easy. He slipped his fingers under my dress, up my sides, and unclamped my nipples. Blood rushed my sensitized peaks, and a hoarse cry escaped my throat.

"Keep fucking me, baby."

I hadn't realized I'd stopped. I pushed upward then impaled myself on him again, making him moan. God, how I wanted to send him hurtling over the edge, take control from his iron-willed fist.

"Harder," he growled, taking my nipples between his fingers.

A desperate plea fell from my lips. Desperate and treacherous. I couldn't let him win this cruel game. The stakes were too high, meant too much.

"I mean it. Fuck me until you're there. I can wait on the edge for hours. Can you?"

Frustrated tears slipped from my eyes. Gage had practiced the art of control for years, and I was weak in comparison. He'd won this battle before it had begun.

"Take my cock like you mean it." He tweaked my nipples with teasing fingers, keeping time to my undulating hips.

"Please, don't make me come."

"That's a first. You usually beg for the opposite." He grabbed my earlobe with his teeth, pulled, then let go. "But you want something, don't you?"

"Yes!"

"Yes, what?"

"Yes, Master."

"Tell me what you want again. This time in detail."

Drawing an unsteady breath, I visualized it, held onto it, and willed my body to stay strong.

Don't give in.

"I want you tied to the bed, naked. Unable to move."

"What else?"

"I want to suck your cock for hours, but I won't let you come."

I'd make him *hurt*. He'd regret every wretched thing he'd ever done to me.

"I believe you have a little sadist in you, Kayla. What else?"

"I want you gagged, blindfolded."

Helpless.

He grabbed my hips and yanked my body down with a vicious thrust. "I should make you come right now just to end this madness."

The idea of a role reversal unhinged him, made him grasp for the upper hand. A year ago, he'd promised his submission was a one-time deal, and he intended to hold to that promise, even if it meant fighting dirty. A blizzard would grace hell before he'd willingly give me control again.

He not only meant to push me to the edge, but he meant to throw me off without a parachute. Thank God our dinner beckoned because I was ready to leap, to hell with the consequences.

CHAPTER ELEVEN

Beyond frustrated from Gage's week of sexual games, I gave caution the finger and took a logic-defying risk on Friday morning.

I went in for my shift at the hospital.

If Gage found out, it would ruin our first anniversary. But I was going stir crazy in that house, cooped up like Rapunzel. Only I wasn't a girl held captive by an evil sorceress that thirsted for power. I was a sex slave held prisoner by my husband's deviant desires.

He'd given me explicit instructions with no room for bending the rules, yet here I was, not only at the hospital to see Emma, but I was sticking around afterward to have lunch with Simone. I entered the cafeteria, attention on my cell as I read the text Simone had sent, telling me she'd snagged us a table. Two steps into the busy hub of the hospital at lunchtime, and I collided with a warm body.

I lifted my head and took in Ian's masculine jawline, shadowed with stubble. Forgoing his normal white doctor's coat, today he wore teal scrubs.

"Excuse me," I muttered, veering to the right and attempting to go around him.

He followed my movement. "Do you have a minute?"

I'd managed to avoid him for weeks, but now everywhere I turned, he was in my way. Literally. "There's nothing left to say."

"I know where I stand, Kayla. Is it too much to ask that you have lunch with me?" His mouth quirked in an endearing way. A sexy way.

I couldn't do this. He was trying so hard to squirm back into my life, but he was wasting his time. Folding my arms, I focused on his chest. "We can't be friends."

"Because of Gage?"

"Yes, because of Gage. He's not okay with this."

"I don't give a fuck what he's okay with." He tilted my chin. "You shouldn't care either. Are you not your own person anymore?"

I frowned, once again thrown off by his odd mood swings. "I'm not doing this with you."

"Doing what? Getting a harsh dose of truth? Or sharing a meal?"

"Take your pick. Besides, I'm meeting someone, so if you'll excuse me...?" I stared him down.

"Your wish is my command." His barbed tone pricked at my roller-coaster emotions. God, the way he spoke to me hurt. He stepped to the side and swung an arm out in a display of grand gesture, his body language screaming at me.

Go on, he silently taunted. *Pretend I don't exist.*

His presence shook me up, made me want to bolt, but I wouldn't give him the satisfaction of knowing his words chewed my heart up and spit it out. I went through the lunch line in a blur, my spine tingling with the notion that he was watching me. I turned around and scanned the raucous room, but he'd disappeared. Instead, I spotted Simone, who raised a questioning brow.

Carrying my food, I squeezed between tables, went around a small group of nurses chatting, and settled into the seat across from her.

"How do you know Dr. Kaplan?" she asked as she dipped a chicken strip into a ranch cup. She could put the king of junk food junkies to shame, yet she never gained a pound.

"I met him in college." Stirring my soup with a spoon, I wished like hell she wouldn't press for more info.

She narrowed her brown eyes. "Now that I think of it, I do recall him hanging around Eve's room. He sat with her a lot while you were gone."

That reminder only made me feel like shit. Ian was kind and caring and fucking sane. Gage was the opposite of all those things.

"So what's the story there?" she asked.

"There's not much to tell."

"Uh-uh. You're not playing the vague card on this one."

Spooning up a bite of chicken noodle soup, I blew on it. "He's Gage's brother."

"Get the hell out. No way."

"Yes way." I sipped on my hot soup for a couple of minutes, Simone giving me the stare-down the whole time.

"C'mon, gimme the 4-11. Did you and Dr. Kaplan have a *thing*?"

"Why would you think that?"

She raised a brow. "You wear everything on your face, Kayla."

Funny. Gage told me the same thing once.

"I guess you could call it a thing." I nibbled my lip, debating on how much to tell her. "I was in love with him."

"This is getting juicier by the second. Dr. Kaplan is a sweetheart. So what happened?"

"My ex-husband happened."

Simone was aware of my history with Eve's biological father...Eve's sperm donor. DNA didn't make a father. Being there did. Loving and caring and giving *time* to a child made a father.

Gage was that to Eve.

"When did you meet Brother Number Two?"

"A few years ago. He hired me on as his personal assistant." I pushed a bite of salad into my mouth and chewed. Simone didn't know about the blackmail or the kidnapping, and she didn't know that Gage had paid for Eve's care. Very few people did, as he'd gone to great lengths to remain an anonymous benefactor.

"So you ended up falling for both of them." She mulled over that piece of information for a bit. "Looks like Dr. Kaplan still has a thing for you." She pointed to my left hand. "Regardless of that shackle on your finger. That's why you're hiding your shifts here from Gage, isn't it? There's still something between you and that fine specimen of a doctor."

"Not on my end," I said, my cheeks flushing, contradicting the denial. "Things are complicated." What a clichéd cop-out.

Simone shook her head. "Your life is like a soap opera, only more entertaining." She glanced toward the entrance of the cafeteria, where I'd run into Ian. "Do you ever wonder if you made a mistake?" She shrugged her shoulders. "Maybe you're with the wrong brother."

"Jesus, Simone. Gage is my *husband*. Not some guy I've been dating for a few weeks."

"He's cold and distant. Does his heart even beat?"

Letting out a frustrated breath, I swept my bangs to the side. "You met him once. I don't think you can judge the character of someone during a single dinner."

"It's called intuition. I don't know what happened to yours, but when it comes to him, you can't see shit."

I wouldn't bother telling her that Gage didn't care for her either. She was too crass for his taste, too immodest. Mostly, she was too independent—a trait Gage did *not* find attractive in a woman.

He wouldn't like the rebellious streak of independence sparking to life inside of me either. These last few weeks reminded me of how amazing it felt to go places, talk to people, order my own food, and wear whatever the hell I wanted before I'd said "I do" and gave those things to my husband. I just didn't know how to voice what was in my heart because anytime I came close, he turned me to mush with the way he adored me, lusted after me, and made me feel like I was the only woman in his world.

Except I wasn't the only woman in his world. Katherine was the mother of his child. What little soup and salad I'd eaten threatened to come back up.

Simone frowned as if she saw the turmoil darkening my face. I didn't like the pity straining her features.

"You've got serious baggage, girl." She picked up a French fry and chewed, her forehead creased in contemplation. "If you want your marriage to work, you need to tell him. Sneaking around like this isn't good for the soul." Simone had stood by her opinion since the day I'd decided to volunteer at the hospital.

Since the day I confided the nature of my relationship with Gage, because I'd needed to use her as a cover. She genuinely cared about people, which made her a damn good nurse. She'd cared enough about me to lie on my behalf, to play the part of yoga companion.

"I know I need to tell him."

"So bite the bullet and tell him, and don't back down."

"He won't give permission for this. Not as long as Ian works here."

"Uh-uh." A low growl escaped her mouth. "I'm not talking about getting his fucking permission. Don't let him railroad you. If he really loves you, as you say he does, then he'll want to see you happy."

The subject of Gage never failed to rile her up. She was headstrong, self-sufficient, and no man would ever make her kneel at his feet.

Of this, I was sure.

I picked at my salad, and for a few minutes, the din of the cafeteria lulled me into a state of calm. I loved being in the thick of people. Loved the dichotomy of voices that filled the space, making my chaotic thought processes fall silent.

"What if he can't accept it?"

"Then you and Eve are always welcome at my house."

A tumultuous story tainted her past. I was sure of it. A story that had left her battered. But she didn't talk about her life much, or the scars I sensed she carried around with her. Maybe I recognized myself in her, except she was strong where I was weak. She stood on her own two feet while I dropped to my knees on a daily basis.

I envied her, yet I wouldn't change who Gage was for anything. I wanted him to give me some slack—not become someone else. Embracing my submissive nature was liberating.

I just needed…more.

I needed to tell him everything, then maybe I could breathe again. The idea of this hanging over my head the whole weekend while we celebrated our first anniversary suffocated me.

"You're right. Lying to him is eating me alive." I took a long swig of my water to quench my suddenly parched throat. "I think I'll drop by his office. It's going to be hard as hell, but getting this off my chest before we go away for the weekend is the right thing to do." I scooted back and rose to my feet.

Maybe he wouldn't come undone with his employees on the other side of the door. Right. And maybe I'd hallucinated him bending me over his desk and forcing his thumb up my ass. It wouldn't matter where we were when I spilled my guts.

"Don't back down. Make him respect you." She pounded a fist against her palm. "If you need me to beat him up, I'm more than willing."

The idea of a woman beating Gage was laughable. "Thanks for the pep talk."

"Anytime. Let me know how it goes."

I emptied my trash and placed my dishes in the respective bins before leaving the way I'd come. As I made my way through the hospital toward the main entrance, I expected to find Ian waiting around every corner.

As if he were stalking me and waiting to pounce.

I was losing my damn mind. When I'd first started at the hospital, I'd known running into him was a possibility. So why had I done it? Gage would want an answer to that same question, but I didn't have one.

CHAPTER TWELVE

Maybe the real question I should have asked was why the hell Katherine had her slutty ass planted on my husband's desk. She sat to the side, her perfectly tanned legs crossed toward him, hiking her red skirt up her thigh.

Gage was busy scanning the paperwork in his hands, and Katherine had her back to me, so neither of them noticed my presence.

I stepped inside his office and let the slam of the door announce my arrival. Gage lifted his gaze. Katherine startled, her ass sliding off his desk. She whirled, but when she saw me, her surprised expression turned into one of calculation. A slow smile widened her red lips. She held my gaze as she buttoned the top four buttons of her blouse.

"Get out," I said between clenched teeth, venom dripping from my tone.

Gage stood with a sigh. "Kayla, calm down. It's not—"

"Don't you dare tell me it's not what I think. Get this bitch out of your office now."

A brewing storm darkened his expression, but I didn't care. I couldn't explain the fury roiling through me.

Katherine had a way of getting under my skin. My jealousy manifested like a malignant tumor, reproducing bad cells faster than I could handle.

Katherine strutted toward me, hips swaying. "Piece of advice, Kayla. Men find jealous women unattractive."

She didn't know Gage at all, had no clue what made him tick. I did though, and I knew my jealousy fueled his desire for me. Maybe that's why I embraced the nasty emotion, rather than shove it below the surface. We fed off each other like wild animals. We fucked like wild animals too.

I wrenched the door open. "Don't presume to think you know shit about my husband or our relationship." I gestured to the doorway, ignoring the watchful eyes of the people on the fourth floor. "Get out."

She looked at Gage expectantly. "Are you going to let her treat the mother of your child like this?"

Gage parted his lips to speak, but I snapped my fingers in her face, bringing her attention to me again. "You might have popped his kid out, but I'm his wife. Conner is always welcome. You, on the other hand, are not."

She left in a huff, her overbearing perfume poisoning the air in her wake. I slammed the door and rounded on Gage.

"What the hell has gotten into you?" he shouted.

"Why was she here?"

"Shouldn't I be asking you that question? You think it's okay to barge into my office when you don't have permission to leave the damn house?"

"Fuck your permission, Gage." I jabbed a finger at his workspace. "What was she doing in your office, sitting on your *desk*? If you caught me in the same position, you'd go ballistic."

"Well that's the difference between you and me. I have reason to be jealous, don't I?"

Forget the elephant in the room; Ian stood like a brontosaurus.

"No more reason than I do," I said, willing my voice to remain steady. "The fact that you're refusing to answer is reason enough. You're fucking her, aren't you?"

He gritted his teeth. "We were talking about Conner. We'd almost reached an agreement on visitation when you stormed in and threw your tantrum."

"She needed to unbutton her shirt for that?"

He slammed his fist onto the desk. "Enough. I'm not doing this here. Go home and cool down." He rose, meaning to intimidate me with his full height.

Was he really not going to explain? The bastard expected me to return home to my prison, tail between my legs, and ignore how I'd found him in a compromising situation with another woman.

I folded my arms. "Her buttons, Gage." No way was I letting this go.

"You'd have to ask her," he said, rubbing his jaw, "seeing as how I paid her little attention. I was too busy going over the parenting plan." He came out from behind his desk. "Do you honestly think I notice anyone else? You're all I see, Kayla. How can you not know that?"

Because he wasn't all I saw. The truth washed over me like sour milk. The truth fucking reeked. I'd flirted with disaster, so maybe on a subconscious level, I expected him to as well. My gaze fell to the floor, and for the first time since finding her on his desk, I doubted my too-quick reaction.

"You have history with her." He had a *child* with her—a DNA connection he and I might never share.

"Are you kidding me?" He covered the distance between us. "My history with her means nothing. Not when I'm obsessed with fucking you into next week!" He clenched his hands, careful not to touch me. "You're behaving like a jealous adolescent. I mean it, Kayla. Go home."

I jutted my chin. "I'm tired of taking orders from you. This is bullshit," I said, swinging my hand in the air. "Have you ever heard of a courthouse? She has no business being in your office behind closed doors."

He grabbed my chin, applying enough pressure to make me back down. "I didn't want to punish you on the eve of our anniversary, but you're making that next to impossible."

"Don't kid yourself, Gage. Punishing me is the same as breathing for you."

"You want it? *Fine.*" He brought his face close to mine. "You've got it, baby. Go home and wait for me. If you're not on your knees in our bedroom, I'll give you more than my belt."

We faced off in a hushed battle for a few moments until Gage broke the standoff. He opened the door and waited for me to walk through it.

To submit to his orders.

My gaze lingered on his desk, remembering how her legs tempted just inches from his arm, how she'd unfastened her buttons to seduce him.

She was after my husband.

And I was a hypocrite because Ian was after me. I'd behaved no better than Gage. Worse, actually, because he wasn't attempting to hide her presence. He met with all sorts of people in this space—clients, PR people, financial advisors, employees of all levels. She was only one of many.

Afraid I was wearing my guilt on my face, I turned and fled.

CHAPTER THIRTEEN

I returned home a half hour later, no calmer than when I'd left Channing Enterprises. His voice flitted through my mind, on constant loop. But instead of repeating what he'd said, my chaotic mind put words in his mouth, filling the holes of my insecurities with lies my heart believed were true—with things I was sure he hadn't had the guts to say.

If you hadn't interrupted, I would have fucked her on my desk.

You're just a slave, a toy I use for pleasure. She's the mother of my child. You can't compete with that.

I'll always be right, and you'll always be wrong.

Entering the bedroom, I let the door bang against the wall, and the nasty voice in my head changed his tune.

Do as you're told.

Don't argue.

Get on your knees.

On your knees, Kayla.

On your fucking knees now.

The sight of the floor set my teeth on edge. Hardwood, a means of torture for my joints, and he expected me to drop and wait until he decided to show his face. I tore across the room toward the bathroom, wondering if I were finally cracking. These past few weeks of sneaking around and stealing moments of freedom had finally caught up with me. This week alone had broken my spirit. Ian's reemergence into my life, the revelation of Conner's paternity, and the sexually frustrated nature Gage had left me in.

Going on autopilot in the bathroom, I stripped the clothes from my adrenaline-flushed body, dragged a brush through my wild hair. Prepared to become the slave he craved.

Always a slave.

Not a woman with feelings and wants and needs. My vision blurred with the hot sting of tears. The brush snagged on a tangle, and the dam finally broke.

Always crying, always bending, always taking the blame. He was right, and I was *always* wrong.

I glared at my reflection, hating the shell of a woman staring back. If he wanted to punish me, I'd give him a reason. Because blowing a gasket over finding another woman practically in his lap was a bullshit reason—an excuse to revel in his sadism at my expense. I'd done *nothing* wrong, unless I counted visiting sick children, eating lunch with a friend, and finding my husband with that...that *bitch*.

I yanked drawer after drawer open, contents rattling under my fury. My pulse skyrocketed, then dived toward the ground at the sight of the red-handled shears. I reached a hand out but faltered.

He would be livid.

So what? Gage Channing would be mad. Big fucking deal. I grabbed the scissors and straightened my spine with purpose. Parting a thick section of hair, I counted to ten before raising the shears.

Snip.

The first lock of hair drifted to the tile. I brought the scissors to the left side of my head. Tears rimmed my eyes, threatening to spill over.

Snip. Snip. Snip.

My bare breasts heaved, nipples puckered. I didn't want to be warm. Warmth let feeling in, and I was suddenly and amazingly numb. Besides, warmth deceived with its inherent comfort, and comfort didn't exist in my world—not when he wanted me on my knees. Not when he wanted a meek and pliable and *obedient* robot for a wife.

Snip. Snip. Snip.

The severed strands circled my feet, freeing my shoulders from the weight of the red hair he loved so much. I couldn't help but recognize the significance in this moment, the symbolism, and it terrified me. It was only hair, but this rebellious act would change the tenuous dynamic we'd settled into for the past year. This very moment was about to fracture our world and expose the guts of our lies.

Narrowing my brows in determination, I faced the reflection of the woman whose eyes lit up with something foreign. Something challenging.

Something he wouldn't like.

This strange woman from another time—before rules and rituals and Gage Fucking Channing—was reborn as she lifted the shears and cut off the last section of hair.

Movement in the mirror drew my attention. He stood in the open doorway behind me, his posture inflexible as always. My eyes swerved to his before dropping to the belt clasped in his determined fist.

I whirled, crossed my arms, and silently threw down a challenge. A belt wouldn't cut it this time. I knew it, and now he did too. No, on the eve of our first anniversary, Gage would have to do better than that.

"Do you mean to goad me?" he asked, flexing his hand around that strap of leather.

"What are you going to do about it? Lash me with your belt?" I grabbed the brush and yanked it through my newly cut hair. "Or maybe you'll have me sit on your desk next time, half dressed since you seem to enjoy that sort of thing." I raised a brow. "Huh, Gage? What are gonna do?"

He opened his mouth, shut it. Opened it again.

I blinked, feigning apathy, but I was shaking on the inside. He'd never looked so...at a loss. Unsure. After a year of submitting to his every order and whim, a single act of rebellion had knocked him on his sanctimonious ass. What a powerful, addicting feeling this was.

The belt slipped from his hand. "What do you want from me?" He spread his arms. "I've given you everything—"

"No! I've given *you* everything." My voice rose. "I've spent more time on my knees than at your side. Have spent more time with your cock in my mouth than actually talking to you. You've forced your damn rules and jealous tirades on me, but I'm not allowed to feel anything when I see that bitch sitting on your desk like she fucking owns it?" I threw the hairbrush at him, but instead of hitting his face, it thumped against his broad chest. He caught it, folded his fingers around the handle, and I realized too late that I'd just given him a weapon.

He stalked into the bathroom, his body moving in a way that warned. I had no room to retreat, no way to defend myself as he grabbed my arm.

"Don't you dare judge me when you've been sneaking around for weeks working at *his* hospital."

I gasped, and the sails of my anger dropped, leaving me bobbing in a sea of blatant deception. Leaving me stagnant with guilt.

"That's right, Kayla." His gaze wandered my face,

assessing the flush of guilt spreading across my cheeks. "I've known since you started." Letting go of my arm, he grabbed my chin, holding me prisoner in his furious indigo eyes. "Did you see him?"

"Yes." My admission crashed a wrecking ball through his heart, and my own fractured at the flicker of betrayal in his eyes. "Nothing happened. I ran into him a few days ago, and I told him to leave me alone."

"You really don't want to lie to me right now."

"Please, Gage. Don't do this."

His fingers slid from my jaw, and he fiddled with my short hair. "You started it, baby."

"I'm sorry." And I was. Not because I'd defied him. Not because I'd blown my top over Katherine. I was sorry because this was the worst time to poke at the frayed past named Ian Kaplan.

He lowered his eyes. "I've tried so hard not to come down on you about this. I've waited and waited and fucking waited for you to tell me."

The Friday ritual...I was right. He'd done it to punish me, maybe even to coax a confession out of me.

"I only wanted to do something meaningful with my spare time."

"You should have asked for permission."

"You would have said no."

He cocked his head. "You sound so sure of that."

"Are you saying you would have given your blessing?"

"That depends."

"On what?"

"On whether or not you're still in love with him."

For a few seconds, my lungs ceased working. The room and everything in it, including Gage, blurred, shifted. My eyes stung with the truth. I wasn't supposed to care about another man, especially when that man was his brother. I was certain my silence gave him all the answer he needed.

"Kayla..." he said, voice thick with pain. "What do you want from me? I've gone to counseling. I've been the best father I can be to Eve. I've worshipped the fucking ground you walk on, yet you go behind my—"

"You're slowly killing me!" I barreled past him and paced the bedroom, tired of being cornered, especially since he still held that brush with purpose. "Your love is toxic. I can't fucking breathe anymore."

Spanning the distance, he held my left hand and ran his thumb over my wedding ring. The one that meant so much to him because it had belonged to his mother. "I've given you everything I can. Everything that I am."

"You don't get it!" I yanked my hand from his. "I need more than this. I need to be able to walk out the door when I want. See who I want. Wear what I want. Get a damn job if I want."

"Then explain it to me. Why do you need those things?"

I blinked several times. That was not the reaction I'd expected. "Because...because I just do." I brought my fist to my chest. "I need a piece of *me* back."

In the space of two seconds, he had my chin in his strong grip. "But you gave every piece of yourself to me the day we married. I need you to submit, always."

Like a flash going off behind my eyes, it all became devastatingly clear. Control. It would always whittle down to his thirst for complete control over every aspect of his life, and now mine. He'd had none growing up. I'd known this, and maybe I'd understood it on a subconscious level. I'd bent for him for a year because I'd wanted to make him happy—because giving him everything meant giving him the security he needed.

"The question goes both ways, Gage. Why do you need

it?" I wondered if he'd figured out what I had, or if it was still a need that chewed inside him, mostly uncategorized.

His forehead creased. His eyes narrowed. He struggled to speak.

"You don't know why you need it, do you?"

"You're asking me to change who I am. I can't, Kayla. I've already bended the most I can bend."

"No, I've bended. Every damn day, I've given up myself for your needs."

"You're more limber than I am, baby."

"Don't joke about this."

"It's not a joke. You're the strongest woman I know. Nothing can break you, not even me. You're my miracle."

"I shouldn't have to be so strong."

"But you are." He held my gaze with meaning. Paused a beat. "Only you can handle what I need." He tapped the hairbrush against his palm. "And what I need right now is to blister your ass."

"Just when I think we're getting somewhere." I yanked at my infinity collar, brimming with restless energy—a tonic of anger, desperation, and even regret. "Take it off, Gage. I'm done handling your shit."

He struck so fast, I didn't have time to gasp. I dangled over his shoulder, the hardwood floor of our bedroom my only view as he stalked toward the bed.

"Let me go!"

He dropped me to my feet and forced me over the end. "Ass up, Kayla."

I kicked and yelled and slung obscenities at him.

"Knock it off. Take your punishment like a fucking adult."

"Why should I, when you treat me like a child?"

"If you don't behave, I'll make you wish you had."

"Let. Me. Go."

"Do you remember your wedding vows, or do you need a reminder?"

"Do you?" I fired back.

He smacked my ass with such strength, the world seemed to halt. I cried out, my eyes stinging, muscles rigid from the fiery imprint of his hand. That hairbrush was going to be torture in comparison. I held to no delusions; he had every intention of beating me with it. The thought stole my breath, and I fought for air until my lungs filled. The world jerked forward, returning to its laborious orbit around the sun.

Just like I would. I'd orbit Gage because he was that powerful. He was the center of my solar system, the God of my gravity, the devil of my desire. The Master of my mind.

He was the dean of my discipline.

"Let's try this again," he said, squeezing where his palm had just put me in line. "Do you remember your vows?"

"Yes! Of course I do."

"I want to hear them. One at a time." He shifted and stood to the side. With ceremonial significance, he placed the brush on the mattress in front of me. Fisting a hand in my shortened locks, he forced my gaze on his chosen implement of punishment.

Wooden, square, made durable for long hair...which I no longer had.

Warm fingers skimmed the back of my thighs, inching my skirt up to expose his naked canvas. "You're getting five strikes for each vow, but for each one you've broken, you're getting twenty-five." He released his grip on my hair and picked up the brush again. "Don't plan to sit anytime soon."

I wanted to scream at him. Wanted to tell him to go screw himself. But he had me right where he wanted me, and I knew from experience that the only way out was to follow his orders.

"Okay, Gage. You win."

Whack.

"Ahhh!"

"Address me properly."

"I'm sorry, Master."

"Start reciting."

"I promised to love."

"Love me, you have. I know I'm difficult to love, but I feel the way you love me every time you drop to your knees."

Whack.

"Every time you make yourself gag so I'll come that much harder."

Whack.

"Every time you take my belt."

Whack.

"Every time you've let me kiss your tears away."

Whack.

"Every time you come with my name on your lips."

Whack.

"Every time you watch me with Eve." Dead silence followed his words. He cleared his throat. "You don't realize that I'm paying attention, but I am, Kayla. I see the amazing smile that lights up your face. Your joy is a fucking weapon." He drew in a shaky breath. "Next vow."

I couldn't breathe, couldn't see through my tears, so I wasn't sure how he expected me to speak. But that didn't matter. I'd better find a way to utter what he wanted to hear, or face even harsher consequences.

"To honor."

"Have you, Kayla? Have you honored me?"

If I were being truthful... "No, Master. But you haven't honored me either."

"How do you figure? You've been sneaking behind my back for weeks. How have I dishonored you?"

I figured now wasn't the time to bring up the double standard—the fact that he'd hid something from me as well. But there were no double standards with Gage. Only my obedience.

"You don't respect me," I said. "You don't care how I feel. You'll always do what you want, and what I want doesn't matter."

"You're right. I will do what I want, but that doesn't mean you don't matter. You matter more than you realize. I've made concessions I didn't think I was capable of making. I stood by knowing you were seeing him, and I said *nothing*."

God, he was right. I had no argument to stand on.

"We'll call this one a draw," he said. "Next vow." The tone of his voice dipped to a dangerous level.

We both knew what was coming. His triumph over punishing me, and my struggle to endure it because I had broken the last vow. I'd stood on that altar and promised to obey him. It didn't matter that his expectations and demands were beyond fucked up—I'd married him with both eyes open.

He hadn't changed. He'd remained his usual volatile yet ironically dependable self. If I could count on anything, it was that Gage Channing would *always* punish me.

"Obey," I whispered.

"Did you break that vow?"

The words wouldn't come at first. A lifetime seemed to go by in the time it took to force out the answer he thirsted for. "Yes, Master."

"Yes, you did. Even worse, you broke my cold as fuck heart." He brought the brush down with maximum strength, stealing the essence of my life-force. My lungs refused to work. My muscles refused to relax and take the strike. My brain's synapses were stuck firing down a one-way street.

The boulevard of broken man. Gage had a heart—fragile and infested with love for me.

I'd stomped on it by not giving him all of mine.

"You could have volunteered anywhere. Any goddamn fucking place, Kayla. But you chose *that* hospital. Why?"

"I don't know," I cried, not even flinching when he hit me again.

"Yes, you do. You just don't want to admit it."

Whack.

"Fuck, Kayla, out of every man on this planet for you to be in love with, why'd it have to be him?"

My body quaked from the force of his words.

"I love you more." I shuttered my eyes, too ashamed to look at him because my non-denial spoke volumes. I was in love with two men. To finally admit and accept it shredded my soul. "Forgive me, Master."

I glanced over my shoulder, and for the second time ever, I watched him struggle to hold it together. Tears hinged on dark, thick lashes. He blinked rapidly, each drop purging him of turmoil and grief and heartbreak.

"I'll die trying, Kayla." He lifted the brush, and my ass became the devil's playground.

CHAPTER FOURTEEN

This was the worst way to start off our anniversary trip. We'd pulled ourselves together long enough to welcome Eve off the bus and get her ready for when Leah's mother picked her up for the sleepover.

But we'd barely said two words to each other since we'd loaded our bags into the trunk over an hour ago. I shifted in my seat, hissing between my teeth because no matter how I moved, I couldn't escape the pain from the force of that brush.

He'd walloped my ass good.

I shot him a sideways glance. A shadow darkened his jawline. I imagined a dark cloud obscured his eyes as well.

"How many times did you see him?" His question filled up the festering space, piercing my ears louder than the highway rushing beneath us.

"I met with him once," I said then lowered my voice. "Ran into him twice after that."

He gripped the steering wheel as if the thing threatened to break off and roll away. "Did you *run* into him on purpose?"

"No, Gage. It wasn't on my end."

"Address me properly."

I sighed. This was getting us nowhere.

"I mean it, Kayla. Address me properly, or I'll pull the car over." He threw me a look full of devious meaning. "After what I put your ass through earlier, trust me—you don't want more."

"Yes, Master."

"Did he touch you?"

Shit. He wasn't about to let this go any more than I'd been willing to let him off the hook about Katherine and her undone buttons. I recalled how Ian had grabbed my hand, how he'd trapped me between him and the couch. How he'd kissed me for the merest of seconds.

All of those things would jab at Gage's anger.

"Just tell me the truth, Kayla. Don't overthink it."

"He touched me," I admitted quietly.

"How?"

"Grabbed my hand, mostly."

His Adam's apple bobbed in this throat. "Did you touch him?"

"Only to push him away."

His jaw was so rigid, I wondered if it would split in two.

The remainder of the drive went by in utter disquiet. Gage focused his attention on getting us safely over the worst part of the snowy pass. By the time we pulled into the driveway of a secluded cabin, nightfall had descended hours ago. Fluffy, white snow weighed down the surrounding pine trees, and the inches on the rooftop must have reached a foot or more.

I opened my door, grateful that someone had plowed the driveway and cleared a path to the front door. My boots crunched on packed-down snow, fracturing the cold serenity of winter. Gage popped the trunk, hefted a suitcase and a duffle out, and gestured for me to precede him to the stoop.

"It's beautiful out here," I said.

"It's secluded. I had to pay a premium to get someone out here to ready the place for us. No one's around for miles." We reached the front door, and the way his gaze lingered on me sent nervous flutters into my belly.

"For two days, it's just you and me, Kayla."

Just the two of us...and me at his mercy. Eve wouldn't provide a buffer between us. His work wouldn't save me with a well-timed distraction. Being in the middle of nowhere with him was nerve-wracking enough on its own, but considering how hurt and furious he was...

He set the luggage down long enough to unlock the door. I entered first, and a blast of warmth hit me. A fire raged in the insert. The plush throw rug in front of the flames would be the perfect spot to make love all night.

The thought squeezed my heart. I missed making love with him. These past few weeks, he'd been more dominant than loving.

He dropped our luggage by the front entrance. "No TV, no distractions. I'd planned to make you come all weekend until you begged me to stop."

Past tense.

Forget making love by the fireplace. I'd ruined this weekend and any chance of that happening.

No, a logical voice in my head piped in. We'd ruined the weekend. I'd been in the wrong, but he wasn't innocent either. He should have never allowed Katherine inside his office, let alone plant her ass on his desk.

He dragged a hand through his hair. "I want you naked, now."

Blinking several times, I held it all in, refused to fall apart. But the way he was acting stabbed at my hurt, opening old wounds. I couldn't take it when he grew cold and distant. I could take just about anything but that.

"Yes, Master," I choked out, shrugging out of my coat. I reached for the hem of my sweater, but his warm palm on my cheek stopped me. He leaned down and took my mouth. The slow slide of his tongue against mine melted all my doubts, all my fears.

The tears finally broke free, streaming down my cheeks, dampening the stubble on his face. Cleansing us. I clutched his jacket, needing his reassurance more than ever.

"I'm sorry, Master," I said with a gasp.

"Shhh." His command feathered across my well-kissed lips. "I know, baby." The low, sexy tenor of his voice hit me in places where I was most vulnerable. Right at the center of my heart and between my thighs.

"Get naked for me, then go lie down on your stomach on the rug." He pointed toward the fireplace. "I'll put our bags in the bedroom."

Less than five minutes later, he had me sprawled by the fire. The rhythmic movement of his hands as he rubbed lotion into my skin cast me under a curious spell—one where the pain from the hairbrush ceased. But his gentleness also widened the crack in my spirit, until every last bit of sorrow and regret gushed from me in a torrential downpour. As I replayed my punishment, in which he'd extracted each vow, I wasn't sure if I hurt for him or for me.

He said I'd broken his heart.

"I'm in love with *you*." My voice hitched on a sob.

"I know." He hovered over my back and pressed his lips to my shoulder. "I never doubted that, Kayla."

"I never meant to hurt you." My diaphragm spasmed with a hiccup.

"I know that as well." He scooted down my body, placing kisses along my spine, and his breath heated the small of my back. Gentle fingers kneaded my stinging flesh. Then he ran a finger between my ass cheeks and stalled at my puckered hole.

"Are you done punishing me?" I tensed, waiting for his next move. The simple act of him teasing my asshole made me nervous.

"I'll never tire of punishing you." He rolled me to my back and gently wedged my thighs apart. "Every Friday night until the day I die."

So the ritual was permanent. For the rest of my life, I'd endure his belt. Just because.

Because that's who he was.

"What if I don't want that?"

He crawled up my body and grasped my hair. "As long as you're my wife, you'll get my belt." He nipped at my neck, right above the collar. "But you'll also get me, Kayla. Every part of me. You have my fucking soul."

"Not every part of you," I pointed out.

"What do you mean?"

"I want your control."

"So we're back to that, are we?"

Wood crackled in the fireplace, drawing my attention. The clock above the mantel ticked.

Tick, tick, tick.

Each second brought us closer to our anniversary when the shackles on my orgasms would unlock and fall to the ground.

"That was the agreement. I make it to our anniversary, you give me what I want." I gestured toward the clock. "Our anniversary begins in fifteen minutes."

I expected worry to darken his features. Maybe even resignation. Anything but the devilish grin that widened his mouth.

"Guess that means I've got fifteen minutes to make you come."

As he lowered his head between my thighs, I became dizzy with delirium. It seemed like weeks instead of days since he'd gone down on me. His warm breath hit my aching core an instant before his mouth did. And he didn't start off slow. Instead of teasing, like he'd been doing for days, he flattened his tongue on my clit and added the perfect amount of pressure.

My spine arched, and I moaned deep in my throat, seconds away from coming undone. My fingers found their way into his hair and clutched him to me. Begged me to push him away. What a dilemma.

I dug my heels into the rug, pushed up on my elbows, and tried to scoot out of reach. His hold on me tightened. Upon my frustrated cry, he raised his head and ensnared me inside blue eyes full of cunning design.

"Don't move." His do-as-I-say-or-else tone put an end to the fight in my bones. I froze, my gaze prisoner to his.

"That's better." Letting go of one hip, he slowly dipped a finger into my pussy, watching me the whole time. Studying my reaction. Calculating how far he'd have to go to push me over the edge before midnight. "You're going to come on my tongue, whether you want to or not."

"If I don't, will you honor our agreement?"

Rubbing his rough cheek against my inner thigh, he smiled—just a tiny curve of his lips, but I saw it.

"You'll come." He sounded way too confident as he thrust another finger inside me, and I wondered if he wasn't right. "Don't move," he warned again before returning his mouth to my clit and moving his tongue in a steady back and forth rhythm. My head plopped to the floor, and a soundless breath escaped.

Back and forth, up and down.

Flick, flick, flick.

Pressure...God, the pressure. I was nothing but a throbbing bundle of nerves between my legs.

I clenched my fists at my sides and willed myself not to move. Not to push my mound more firmly into his mouth. Not to let the upsurge of release burst through my faulty barricade.

Because I wanted him underneath me, tied to the bed, his mouth gagged. I wanted him at my mercy, only this time, I wanted to have none.

I wanted to unleash my demons and watch them rain down on him.

But hell, if he kept this up, I had no doubt he'd make me come before midnight. I cast a glance at the clock. Eight more minutes. Seemed like forever. I fastened my attention on that slow moving hand as it taunted with its lazy jaunt through each number. Zeroed in on the constant *tick, tick, tick* that kept perfect timing with his expertly timed tongue.

"Eyes on me."

He would allow me no distractions. No way out. But he couldn't command my thoughts. He couldn't read my mind, so I mentally counted the ticks.

One...two...three...four...

His finger brought me back with a devious crook, pressing *that spot* just right. I launched his name from my lips with a painful groan.

"Who am I, Kayla?"

"Master," I choked.

Counting...

God, where was I?

Eight...nine...ten...eleven...

Another come-hither crook. Another concentration break. I whimpered for more, even as I relaxed my muscles and hurtled every thought and feeling away from the rush of heat building in me.

Away from his vicious tongue.

"That's right, baby. Come for me. You know you want to."

I squeezed my eyes shut. "No...please. Stop!"

Another flick of his tongue, followed by a snicker. "You're drenched. There's no stopping this, so let go. Come on my tongue."

He went in for the kill, intending to rocket me into deep space. I shook my head, chanted *no, no, no* in time with the incessant ticking that brought me one second closer to freedom.

The freedom to jump off the ledge. God knew I clung to it until the last possible second. Cried in disappointed anguish as his lips and tongue and devious fingers sent me plummeting head first.

Spiraling.

Screaming.

Shattering.

"Gage..." I held on to his head for the ride, squirming underneath him, back arching. Mouth gaping.

His triumphant moan vibrated to my core, making me claw at his shoulders.

"Oh God!" A week of denial had primed me for the ultimate surrender, and another body spasm bent me to his will. I succumbed to his tongue with everything I had, turned to lava, flooded his greedy mouth.

More.

There was only more.

By the time I slammed back to Earth, my body drenched in sweat and utterly spent, I was malleable flesh in his hands. Easy prey. Too susceptible to his guile.

He almost had me—had almost obliterated me beyond thought or reason. But I remembered to glance at the clock, and a slow grin stretched across my face. "It's four minutes past midnight."

His gaze swerved to the instrument that would ultimately be his downfall, because I had no intention of letting him get out of this.

"So it seems," he said with a frown.

"I want your control."

He shot a hand out and squeezed my nipple. "I'm still your Master. Don't forget that."

"Please, Master?" I fluttered my lashes at him.

He shook his head with a sigh, but something about the way his mouth twitched gave me hope. He almost seemed... amused. Last year, he hadn't believed I had it in me, and he'd been right. I'd tested the waters of making him submit, but I hadn't gone after it with purpose. With absolute bravery.

With the obsession that ran through my veins now.

A year had twisted my psyche into something beyond innocent. Not only did I want to watch him writhe, but I wanted payback.

"A deal's a deal," he said.

My pulse thrummed in anticipation.

"Under one condition."

Of course there was a condition. Gage specialized in the language of contingencies.

"What do you want, Master?"

"I want you to remove anal as a hard limit. Give me your tight little ass whenever I please, and I'll give you what you want for *one* night."

"That doesn't sound fair. How about a night of anal for a night of your submission?" I countered.

"You're lucky I'm negotiating at all. I can do what I want, whenever I want. That's what owning you means, Kayla. That's what it means to be a slave. You yield to me—not the other way around."

"Why are we having this discussion then? Take what you want. Force me. Hold me down and show me what it means to be a man." My voice rattled with scorn. "Hurt me. Make me cry. Is that what you want?" I was on the verge of tears again.

Something in my tone must have gotten through to him. The severity of his expression softened. "I want you to give it to me." He slid a hand under my ass and teased the spot he was dying to penetrate. "Don't make me force you."

"Don't make me beg you not to."

He dropped his head between my thighs, his sigh of concession a feather on my skin. "Remove the hard limit. In return I'll give you what you want every year on our anniversary."

It was more than I could have hoped for. More than I thought he'd ever give.

"Promise?"

"I swear on my love for you."

"Will you be gentle?" He'd been gentle in Vegas, but I sensed a restless energy in him that scared me.

"Always."

I chewed on it for a few moments, bottom lip pulled between my teeth, and nodded.

"Since we're laying our cards on the table," he said, bracing himself above me on his forearms, "your volunteer work at his hospital is ceasing *yesterday*. Do you understand me?"

"Gage—"

"Don't even think about arguing with me."

I clamped my mouth shut.

"You may volunteer at any damn place you want, but if you ever set foot in that hospital again, or talk to him, or touch him, you will *not* like the consequences." He grabbed my chin with the harshness of the pre-marriage Gage, who was not only a controlling and sadistic bastard, but a psychotic, controlling, and sadistic bastard.

There was definitely a difference.

"I don't share, least of all with him," he said. "Are we clear?"

I nodded, my throat too constricted to speak.

"Good. Now enough of this bullshit. My cock is in desperate need of your mouth." He climbed to his knees, unbuttoned and lowered his zipper, then moved to perch on my chest. Prepared to *take*.

I shot a hand out and placed it against his abs. "You said a deal's a deal. It's our anniversary, so I believe it's my turn to call the shots."

He dropped his head with a laugh. "You wicked, wicked woman. You might have the world fooled with those I'm-innocent eyes, but I'm on to you."

I veered upright and shoved him back. He dropped to his haunches, his dark hair a sexy, disheveled masterpiece. I rose to my feet and crossed to where he'd set a single duffle bag next to the couch.

Gage's bag of tricks.

For the next 24 hours, it would be *my* bag of tricks. I felt his attention on my back as I unzipped it. Glancing over my shoulder, I found him in the position I'd left him.

"I'm going to miss that hair," he said. "But I've got to admit the short length is not without merit. You're gorgeous no matter what you do."

My fingers caressed a buckle. "Are you trying to sweet talk me, Mr. Channing?"

"Maybe just a little, Mrs. Channing."

Spending time with him like this—with the air full of laughter and love and happiness—was amazing. As I pulled the cuffs from the bag, I realized how harrowing our lives had become. But maybe that was the cost of harboring such intense passion. We felt things deeply. Loved with depth, lusted with insanity, angered with the burn of an inferno, hurt with the force of a blast.

We were both a little insane.

I carried the cuffs to him, but instead of restraining his wrists, I dropped to my knees and let them crash to the floor. I launched myself at him, much like I had the first time I'd gone to him of my own accord, free of coercion. My hands ended up in his hair, our mouths melded together, and his arms circled my waist, pulling me closer. I wasn't sure who was submitting—seemed like we both were.

We were submitting to something bigger than the two of us.

"Do I have to call you Mistress?" He was nowhere near taking this seriously.

"I don't care what you call me, as long as you get naked and let me cuff you to the bed." I rose, picked up the restraints, and sauntered toward the bedroom, not bothering to see if he would follow.

I knew he would.

CHAPTER FIFTEEN

Gage lay spread-eagled on the bed, his wrists and ankles trapped inside his own cuffs. I'd buckled those fuckers tight. He wasn't getting free. The way he followed my movements with his nervous gaze told me that he knew it too.

Digging through our suitcase, I selected one of his silk ties—a deep blue color that brought out the brightness of his eyes—and climbed over his powerful abs to straddle him.

"Lift your head," I told him.

"You're having too much fun with this."

"You have no idea."

"Did you forget who you're talking to?" He raised his head off the mattress by a couple of inches. "I know you better than you know yourself. You've hungered for this."

"You're right, I have. Now shut up." I fastened the tie around his eyes. "No talking unless you're begging."

He pressed his lips together, but a devious curve hinted at a smile. I scraped my fingernails down his chest, enjoying how his muscles jumped under my touch, and hunched between his muscular thighs.

His cock was huge, harder than the man himself. I wet my lips, my pulse racing in my ears as I hovered. Waited. Drew out the torture. I lowered my mouth over the tip, and he balled his hands, rattling the chains tethering him to the four poster bed. I'd barely touched him, but he was already squirming.

God, I loved this power.

He could hold off for hours when he was in control, but take control away from the sadist, and he came undone at the slightest provocation.

I fondled his tight balls as I swirled my tongue. He raised his hips, bringing his cock deeper into my mouth. I squeezed his sack and clamped down with my teeth, not enough to hurt, but enough to tame him.

"Fuck, Kayla."

"I don't hear you begging yet. Are you allowed to speak unless you're begging?" He didn't answer, so I increased the pressure on his testicles. "Answer me. Are you allowed to speak?"

"No!"

"That's right, my sexy husband. I don't want to hear it unless you're ready to admit defeat. I want your surrender." I ran my tongue along the length of his shaft, from base to head.

"Baby, take me in." He raised his hips again, seeking entrance into my mouth. I flicked the slit at the end, and he sucked a painful breath between clenched teeth.

"I'm in charge," I reminded him. "You don't get to shove your cock into my mouth. You'll get what I give you when I give it to you."

"You've learned too fucking much from me."

"You're the best teacher, Gage. Just think of all the things I'll pick up before our next anniversary."

He groaned. "Giving in to you was a bad idea."

"I disagree," I whispered, licking and tasting. "I love this idea." I softened my lips and sucked on his tip, flicking my tongue back and forth. Keeping my eyes on him, I glorified in the sweat that broke out on his temples as I bobbed my mouth on and off his shaft.

Just the head of it.

Just enough to get his blood pumping.

Gage would hold onto his last thread of control until I wrenched it from his being. And I wasn't fooled—taking him there would require some work.

Steady, patient work. My mouth had a long road ahead of it. I let my eyes drift shut and gave myself over to the heady taste of him on my tongue, to the sensation of his silky soft tip sliding between my lips.

Tonight, I owned his cock, and I could kiss it for as long as I wanted. Tease it for as long as I wanted. Torture it for as long as I wanted.

I *wanted.*

"Good God, you're killing me." He lifted his hips again, and I gave his sack another squeeze.

"You're not behaving. Don't make me punish you."

That drew a laugh from him. "I'd like to see you try."

Letting go of his balls, I sucked on my finger before inching it up his ass.

He howled, a cross between pain and intense arousal. Taking advantage of his helplessness, I pulled his entire length into my mouth and gagged.

"Shit," he groaned. "Take my cock down your throat." He pulled at the restraints, his spine arching, his lips imparting groan after groan. Every muscle in his body had turned on him, holding him captive to my torture.

I had him.

For the first time ever, I had him.

"Dammit, Kayla. Give me your mouth. Stop fucking around."

"Is your cock throbbing for me?"

He growled. "You know it is."

Grinning like a true sadist, I took him in my mouth and drew his shaft down my throat like I meant it. He veered upward like a man possessed. I circled the base with one hand and kept time with my busy mouth as my finger played with his ass.

And I took him there—that tricky place where one more slide of my lips would send him spinning out of control.

"God, yes...oh fuck...don't you dare stop."

Abruptly, I pulled away.

"Kayla, for God's sake, make me come."

"Maybe in a few hours."

"Baby, I need you. It's been too fucking long."

"What you need doesn't matter tonight. You're not coming until I say so." A wicked grin captured my lips. "I can make you edge all night long."

He groaned, thrashing his head back and forth, and wrenched at the restraints with real effort, as if determined to break free from the metal chains keeping him at my mercy.

"You'd better make me come long and hard before you unlock me."

"You think you deserve to come?"

"I think you're going to *want* me to come."

"Why would I want that?"

"I promised I'd be gentle with your ass." He licked his lips. "If you don't fuck me like you mean it, I won't be held responsible for my actions."

Oh, boy.

If he kept talking like that, I might lose my nerve. I scrambled from the bed and returned to the bag of tricks I'd dropped on the floor inside the door of the bedroom. Digging through the various implements of torture and pleasure, I settled on a solid rubber ball gag. I also grabbed a flogger. For some reason, approaching him with these foreign items in my hands made me question my ability to go through with this.

Don't back down now. Do it right or don't do it at all.

Sitting astride his chest, I pushed the rubber ball to his lips. "Open your mouth."

"Jeez, Kayla."

Shifting positions, so I was able to reach his cock, I gripped the handle of the flogger and brought it down on his throbbing, wet tip. He cried out in shock, every muscle in his body spasming.

"Take the gag, or I'll keep striking your prized possession."

"You're my prized possession."

"Open your mouth," I demanded, pressing the gag to his lips once more.

He fought me for a while until the fifth strike landed with the kind of force that drew a high-pitched cry from him. Breathing hard, he gave in and parted his lips. I wound the strap around his head and fastened the buckle, my pulse skittering at my throat.

He was mine.

Unable to move.

Unable to break free.

His eyesight taken.

His voice silenced.

With a sigh of satisfaction, I mounted him and positioned myself over his erection, holding shy of his tip for thirty seconds before taking him deep inside, inch by slow inch.

He moaned, writhed underneath me, his body a

powerful machine disarmed by my longing to conquer. His hips took over, held hostage by his current state of mind. They wouldn't stop thrusting. Right when I sensed him teetering on the edge of orgasm, I jerked up and let his cock slip free. The gag made anything he said unintelligible, but I was positive he slung muffled obscenities at me.

This was going to be hell for him and heaven for me. I counted to sixty, one palm pressed against his chest where his heartbeat thundered, then I sank onto his cock again and rode him to the next edge.

And the next.

There were an infinite amount of edges on this night when time ceased to exist. I let my head tilt back, my short hair brushing the back of my shoulders, and rolled my nipples between two fingers.

"Do you want to know what I'm doing right now?"

I took his stifled moan as a yes.

"I'm playing with my nipples. Pinching them hard, Gage." Taking control from him was empowering. Exhilarating. I could do this until the sun rose.

But two hours later, my resolve wavered. Sweat drenched us both. I'd ridden him slow and steady the whole time, pulling off whenever he came close to blowing his load. But I was getting antsy. I wanted to feel his lips under mine, our tongues clashing together in mutual madness, and when I came again, I wanted him to take the plunge with me.

If that made me weak, then so be it. I found more satisfaction in pleasuring him than hurting him. Leaning forward, I unbuckled the gag and tossed it on the floor.

"You're in deep shit, Kayla."

"Shh," I said, placing a finger against his mouth. His ragged breaths puffed against my skin. "Don't make me put the gag back in."

"I hope you enjoy a red ass."

"I'm only doing what you gave me permission to do." I removed the tie and watched him blink me into focus. His deep blue eyes trapped me, dragged me under. I was sitting astride him while he couldn't move, but I was the one submitting now.

With a quick thrust of my hips, I impaled myself.

"Fuuuuck..." He bucked, angling up to meet me. "You're so fucking beautiful."

I whimpered, my mouth colliding with his, and our tongues tangled as we joined in a new tempo.

The dance of languid fluidity.

"So fucking good," he rasped. "You want control? Take it. I'm all yours."

"What will you do if I untie you?"

"Do it and find out."

Deliberating between having him exactly where I wanted him, and being exactly where I wanted to be, I ran my fingers along his bicep. "If I release you, no anal."

"I can't promise that."

"I don't mean *ever*, I just mean tonight." I bit my lip. "I want something else, Gage."

"You're a demanding little thing tonight, aren't you?"

Bringing my lips to his, barely touching, breathing him in, I worked on unbuckling his left wrist. "I don't want chains, cuffs, whips, or clamps. I just want you."

"You have me," he said, threading his fingers through my hair. "I'm at your fucking mercy."

"Then love me."

"I do love you. So damn much."

"That's not what I meant. You used to make love to me, but lately, all you do is fuck me."

Licking his lips, he pulled on the restraint trapping his right hand. "Let me go."

I studied him, uncertainty straining my mouth.

"Baby, trust me."

"I do trust you," I whispered as I released his right wrist, followed by his ankles. He hauled me into his arms and flipped us.

Hands in my hair.

Mouth coaxing mine open so his could plunder.

He slipped inside me with the sort of patience I didn't expect. The weight of his body grew heavy. Each thrust wrenched synchronized howls from us, his a heated blast on my neck, and mine unleashed into the air as I arched underneath him, head thrown back. He laced our fingers together and shoved my hands to the mattress.

It had been so long since he'd done more than take; tonight, he gave something priceless in return. Gave a little piece of himself in the way he held me, the way he kissed me, the way he surrendered even though I was on my back again with my hands pressed to the bed.

Mostly, the unhindered loss of control strangling his vocal cords was the real gift. "You feel so fucking good. I can't stand it." He jerked to a halt. "So good. Come with me."

With a breathless cry, I followed him over the edge.

CHAPTER SIXTEEN

I lived off the high of that night and Gage's submission for three weeks straight. That weekend had been a tipping point for us, and we fell into a new routine of sorts. Friday night still came around like clockwork, but something had finally settled, finding its rightful place in the midst of our marriage.

Our anniversary and the unveiling of my deception had helped us build a new foundation.

But with new beginnings came new endings. I hadn't been allowed to visit Emma at all, despite begging him for the privilege. I had many freedoms I hadn't had before our anniversary meltdown and reconstruction, but he wouldn't budge on the subject of Ian or anything about Ian.

Sadly, that included what he referred to as *his hospital.*

A rare occurrence of blue skies and sunshine made the day perfect for running errands. A nippy breeze rustled my hair as I unlocked the front door. I hefted a bag of groceries in one arm and pushed my way inside. My phone went off in my pocket on the way to the kitchen. I set the bag on the counter and dug out my cell, finding Simone's smiling face flashing on the screen.

"Hey, what's up?" I held the phone between my shoulder and ear so I could unload the bag of groceries.

"Kayla," she said, her tone immediately putting me on alert.

I halted, and a jar of spaghetti sauce thudded on the counter. "What's wrong? Is Emma okay?"

"Emma's fine. Great actually. She's going home in about another week."

I let out a relieved breath. "That's great to hear."

"It is." She paused. "I didn't call about Emma though. Can we meet somewhere to talk?"

I glanced at the time on the microwave. Gage had given me four hours to do my errands. I still had an hour left. "Of course. Where should I meet you?"

"Can you come to the hospital?"

I hesitated. "I haven't eaten lunch yet. That pizza place a few blocks away sounds good. You up for that?"

She sighed. "Don't bullshit me, Kayla."

"I can't meet you at the hospital. I'm sorry."

"The pizza place it is then. See you in twenty." She hung up, and I stared at my cell for a few moments, bewildered. Something was wrong. She was never that curt, even for Simone.

I rushed to put the groceries away, checked for any new messages from Gage, then hurried out the door. Traffic was heavier than usual, causing me to walk into the pizza place ten minutes late.

Simone sat in a booth by herself. "I ordered pepperoni," she said.

"Okay." I slid in across from her, studying her distraught face. Fear tightened my gut. "You're worrying me. What's going on?"

She wouldn't quite look at me, and when she wiped a tear away, I reached out and grabbed her hand.

"He needs you right now," she said, holding onto my fingers like a lifeline.

"Who?" I squeezed her hand back, wishing my ears would rebel and not listen. There was only one *he* she could be referring to.

"He came looking for you a couple of weeks ago. I told him you'd quit your job, and things just...happened. We started having lunch together every day."

"Okay..." I eyed her cautiously, wondering where she was going with this. As much as it hurt to think of Ian with anyone, I wanted him to be happy. I also wanted Simone to be happy, so if they were hitting it off... "If you guys are dating, I think that's...it's great, Simone."

"We're not dating. I've grown attached, but we're not dating." She chewed on her bottom lip. "He didn't want me to tell you, but I can't keep my mouth shut on this. Kayla, he's sick."

"Sick?" Like with the flu or bronchitis or pneumonia. As I swept my bangs to the side, the tremor in my fingers said otherwise. That tremor knew the truth before she said it.

"He's got cancer."

I shook my head, denying. "But I just saw him three weeks ago. He was fine."

"He's far from fine," she snapped. "He hasn't been to work in days. He's stopped treatment. I think he's given up." Another tear slipped down her cheek. "You need to talk to him. He's still in love with you. Maybe he'll listen to you because I can't get through his thick skull."

"What are his chances?" I blinked, willing my eyes to stay dry. If I started crying, I wouldn't stop, and that wouldn't help anyone.

"Without treatment?" She dropped her head. "Not good."

Our order arrived then. The waitress set the steaming pizza between us, but neither of us had an appetite.

I didn't want to believe her, and I knew part of me would refuse to accept it until I heard it from him. I stood, glanced around the restaurant at the half-filled booths, the people from the nearby hospital and other businesses gathering to share lunch. The setting appeared too normal. Just another day. I wanted to scream at everyone and ask how they could go about their day as the earth shook under my feet. It all seemed so unfair.

"Do you have his address?"

She pulled a pen from her purse and wrote on a napkin before pushing it into my hands. "You'll talk to him?" Hope held her vocal cords captive.

I clutched his address to my chest. "I'll try."

"Get him to start the chemo again. We both know how fast things can turn around. He's throwing away any chance he has of living."

It was true. Volunteering in the oncology wing had taught me a lot, and Simone had more firsthand experience with this frail thing called life than I did. Fear seized my gut. Eve had come close to dying, and she would have if Gage hadn't intervened. People could definitely take a turn for the better with the right treatment...but it didn't always play out like that.

"I'll talk to him." Vomit had found a new home in my throat. Simone and I exchanged one last glance before I exited the restaurant in a fog and slid behind the wheel of the shiny Lexus Gage had bought for me. I wasn't sure how I'd gotten to the car, or how I made it to the other side of the Willamette River.

I pulled into his driveway, or at least, what I believed to be his driveway. The parking spots were empty, so unless he'd parked his SUV in the garage, he either wasn't home, or

I'd found the wrong place. I exited the car, cringing when the slam of the driver's side door ricocheted in the quiet, and headed toward the front door.

Stepping onto his stoop, I raised my hand, readying myself to knock, and almost turned around. Simone had to be wrong. Ian was fine. He'd seemed perfectly healthy three weeks ago, if not a little...off. Swallowing my fear, I pounded on the door. Footsteps sounded from the other side. Something crashed, a curse whispered through the door, then the lock clicked over before he yanked open the barrier standing between us.

My knees nearly gave out at the first sight of him. The pallor of his skin was too familiar, and the sweatpants and T-shirt he wore were too big on him. He'd lost weight. Dread coiled my heart, constricting with lethal power. I denied the truth staring me in the face, even though Simone had laid it out straight.

"What are you doing here?" he asked, gazing past where I stood as if he expected someone else behind me.

"Simone gave me your address. Can I come in?"

"Why? You made it clear you want nothing to do with me. I'm done, Kayla."

"You can't give up."

He scowled. "She told you, didn't she?"

The air knocked from my lungs. "So it's true?"

He ushered me inside and shut the door. When we reached the living room, he sank onto the sofa and let his head fall back against the cushion.

"What kind of cancer is it?"

"A brain tumor. Inoperable."

I shook my head. "No...no. You're gonna be fine. You just need to start the chemo again. Simone said you'd stopped." Desperation clouded my tone, strained my expression.

"Kayla...no. Don't do this now. I can't handle any more pressure. I've made my peace with it."

"Well I haven't! They made a mistake. You need a second opinion."

"I got a second opinion, and a third and a fourth."

"I don't care!" I spun around, my hands clutching my hair because if I let them loose, I'd put a hole in the wall. He was going to beat this. There was no other alternative. "Gage can help. Like he helped Eve." I didn't recognize my voice, could barely see through my tears. Barely heard him through the shrill ringing in my ears.

"Our situations are completely different. Besides, we both know he won't lift a finer to help me."

"You're his brother! This goes beyond grudges." I blinked hot tears down my cheeks, hating the turbulent cyclone of terror that had taken over my stomach. "You can't die on me. You just...you can't."

"Come here." His voice held a quiet note of resignation, and I didn't like it.

Crossing the few feet between us was a no-brainer. "What do you need from me?" I whispered, drained to my soul. "What can I do?"

He opened his mouth, seemingly at a loss. "Just let me hold you."

I placed a knee onto the cushion and straddled him, squeezing his frail body with enough force to steal his breath. As I laid my head on his shoulder, he buried his face in my hair. My heart cracked in two at how much weight he'd lost.

"I dig the new haircut," he said.

"I was pissed at Gage."

His chest rumbled underneath me. "You've still got it in you."

"Instances of temporary insanity? Yeah."

He pressed his lips to my neck. "Do you remember our first kiss?"

"Of course I do."

"That kiss knocked me on my ass."

"Me too."

"That night was the most intense bout of temporary insanity ever. We were so young, so fucking clueless." He inched back and caught my gaze. "But I wouldn't change it for anything."

I leaned my forehead against his and closed my eyes, remembering the intoxicating taste of first love on my lips, the exhilarating way his fingers had slipped beneath my panties. The first time he'd pushed inside me. Like he belonged there.

Like I was home.

"I loved you so much," I said, my voice cracking.

"Past tense, Kayla?"

I only hesitated a moment. "No."

"Jesus. This isn't easy for me. I planned to go quietly."

"You would have done that to me?"

"I didn't want to put you through this." His sigh fanned across my mouth. "You chose him—"

"Ian, please..." A sob hitched in my throat. One more ding to my composure.

"Let me finish, sweetheart." He nudged the bangs from my eyes with his nose. "I don't like that you chose him, but it was your decision to make. I just...I needed to know you and Eve were okay." Tears rimmed his hazel eyes. "I can accept the cancer taking me. But leaving you...that's really killing me."

"Don't talk like that."

"I have to be realistic." He paused. "Is he still hurting you?"

I lowered my gaze.

"Tell me the truth, Kayla. No matter how ugly or hard to hear. Give it to me straight."

"He's sadistic, controlling, domineering, possessive, jealous—"

"Sounds like a great guy," he interrupted, his mouth twisting in disdain.

"But he's also passionate…" I softened my tone. "Caring, protective. He's a disaster, but he's my disaster. And he's incredible to Eve."

"You're head over heels."

"He loves me more than I deserve."

"That's bullshit."

"It's true."

"That could never be true."

"I can't give him my whole heart."

Ian closed his eyes. "If there's anything I regret, it's not being with you in Texas. Texas could have changed everything." His chest shook with holding back what he didn't want to express in words.

I didn't think, didn't analyze the right or wrong in my actions. I only knew that he needed me. As I brought my mouth to his, I forced Gage from my mind. Shattered the images of him as I brought my fingers to the first button of my blouse.

I'd hate myself later.

Ian deserved this. *I* deserved this, because in spite of everything, Gage had taken this from us. And God, I loved that cruel and fragile man, no matter what he put me through. I forgave him for every lash, every bruise, every time he forced his will on me.

I prayed he'd find the same capacity to forgive.

"What are you doing?" Ian gazed at me with bewildered eyes.

"Giving us Texas." My fingers quaked as I unfastened a button, then another.

"Don't do this for me." He moved to push me away, but his arm was weak, ineffective in fighting me off...in fighting off his own desires. He placed his right hand on my chest, and the instant his palm conformed to the softness of my breast, he lingered until the tips of his fingers brushed my aching nipple through the thin silk of my bra.

Thrusting my breast more firmly into his hand, I let my shirt slide off my shoulders, and the garment fluttered to the floor. Desperation possessed me. Fear. The idea that the earth and everyone on it would lose him. That *I* would lose him. I pressed my mouth to his, lips parting. Tongue questing for acceptance.

He opened to me, groaning deep in his throat, and sucked my tongue into his mouth. We kissed until neither of us could breathe. I reached between us and slid my hand down the elastic band of his sweatpants, and closed my fingers around his erection.

"Jesus..." He jutted his hips, bringing him deeper into my hand. "Jesus...fuck, Kayla. Stop."

"Let me give you this."

He swallowed hard. "I want this. Jesus, I want this. But only if you're doing it for you, because I know it'll rip into your conscience."

"I don't care." I swirled my thumb through the moisture collecting at his tip. "You can't give up yet."

A hoarse groan rumbled from his throat. "This isn't going to change anything. I'm still going to have cancer—"

"Shh. Come for me." I wanted him to purge the sickness from his body, free his mind of death and doom. "Let it out."

Live for me.

Sex was living. Loving was living. Giving in and letting go, embracing the free-fall...that was living.

Ian needed to fucking live.

I pushed to my knees, giving myself more room to work at coaxing him over the edge. As I pumped his cock with frantic strokes, illogical thoughts assaulted my sanity with trickery disguised as truth. As if I could keep him alive by making him fly.

The way Gage had made my fly while in the depths of despair over Eve's illness. My heart blanched, and another sob squeezed from my throat, except I didn't know who I was crying for now—Ian or Gage.

I was hurting both of them.

Giving one a taste of ecstasy as a bon voyage, and breaking into shards the iced-over heart of the man I'd married. The man I loved with such intensity and possessiveness and all-consuming passion that I couldn't wrap my head around what my hand was doing.

It didn't have permission, just as Ian didn't have my fucking permission to die.

Every breath he drew was a laborious, wordless plea. A plea for more. A plea for me to stop and let him go. But there was no stopping this. The orgasm came over him in a violent assault, seizing his muscles, cutting off his vocal cords. He came in a muted full-body spasm, his release spurting over my pumping fist in an unstoppable eruption. As soon as he caught his breath, my name fell from his twisted mouth, almost as if it killed him to say it.

"Why did you do that?" His eyes shuttered as he rested his head against the back of the couch.

"I…needed to."

His arms flopped like lifeless noodles at his sides. "I want to touch you. Taste you on my tongue." A tear streaked down his cheek, and there was something especially heart-wrenching about a man crying. "I'm sorry, Kayla. I never wanted to hurt you like this."

The disease had weakened him, stealing his energy reserves, the ravages of cancerous cells holding a strong man prisoner.

I folded my arms around him and sobbed, leaving tear stains on his T-shirt, and my guilt sucked the strength from me. I'd done the unforgivable. I'd betrayed Gage, and in doing so…it would change nothing. Ian would still have cancer when I walked out the door. Now that the frenzy had abated, and rational thought took hold again, I felt close to vomiting.

"I can't…" he began, his voice a mere whisper, "keep my eyes open."

"Shh, just let me hold you."

A sigh escaped him. "So tired."

"Sleep. I'm here."

"Don't want you to see me this way."

As he let sleep take him, I held on to him so tightly I thought I might never let go.

CHAPTER SEVENTEEN

Late afternoon shadowed Ian's living room. He was warm and breathing steadily in my arms. The clock on his end table pushed time forward, minute by minute. I was frozen, wrapped around him, holding him with everything I had.

He mumbled something in his sleep, but when I pushed back and studied him, he appeared peaceful in slumber. Healthy. Alive.

Being careful not to wake him, I slid from his lap, pushed my arms into the sleeves of my blouse and buttoned it, then went in search of a towel. I found one tucked away in a cupboard in the hallway. As I headed to the door I assumed opened into the bathroom, I pulled my cell out and dialed Simone.

She answered before the first ring completed. "Did you talk to him?"

"Yeah." Swallowing hard, I blinked back tears. "He's made up his mind."

"You gotta keep trying."

"I will," I said as I entered the bathroom. "But I need you to do something for me." I held the phone between my shoulder and ear as I turned on the faucet in the bathroom and dampened a blue cotton towel.

"What do you need?"

"Can you pick up Eve from school and keep her for the night?"

"Sure thing. I'll get someone to cover the last couple hours of my shift."

"Thank you." I squeezed the excess water from the towel before exiting the bathroom. "You're already on the list for picking her up." Pausing halfway to the living room, I lowered my voice. "If Gage calls you, tell him you haven't heard from me."

"What's going on?" The alarm in her tone unnerved me. She had reason to be concerned. *I* had reason to be terrified because there was no way of knowing how he'd react when I returned home.

"Nothing to worry about," I told her. What a blatant lie. "We're going to need some time to talk, and it's best if Eve isn't around for that."

"Kayla," she warned.

"It's okay. I can handle it."

"Call me *immediately* if you need me."

"I will." I halted at the entrance to the living room, where Ian lay sprawled on the couch where I'd left him. His sweatpants were a mess from his cum, and I realized I probably had it on my skirt as well.

I told Simone I'd talk to her later before hanging up and making my way into Ian's bedroom to hunt for a clean pair of pants. When I returned to him, he was mumbling in his sleep again. I placed the clothing onto the cushion next to him and worked the soiled sweats down his thighs.

His lashes fluttered open. "Hey, beautiful."

"Hey." Bringing the towel to his lap, I cleaned him up as quickly as I could, trying to avoid embarrassing him.

"You don't have to do that. I'm not an invalid."

I glanced into his stormy eyes. "I know you're not. I just want to help. Let me help." I had to do something, even if it was something as simple as cleaning up the mess we'd made and helping him into a fucking pair of clean pants.

He let me do so grudgingly, and then he patted his lap.

I wanted so badly to go to him, but if I put myself in that position again, I wasn't sure I'd be able to stop at touching him.

"It's okay. I understand," he said, reading the indecision spreading across my face. He leaned forward and rubbed his head.

"Is it a headache?"

"Yeah." He rose to his feet, taking a few seconds to gain solid footing. As he moved toward the kitchen, his left arm hanging limply at his side, I realized he was having trouble using it.

My lips trembled. Grief stung my eyes and nose. But I refused to give in to my weakness. He needed me to be strong right now, and I needed him to keep fighting.

I followed him into the kitchen. "I need you to do something for me."

"Anything."

"Go back on the chemo."

He frowned. "Anything but that."

"Please, Ian. Don't give up."

"I fought for six months." He grabbed a pill box and single-handedly flipped the lid on one of the sections. "I don't have anything left."

"You have *me*," I said, my voice and soul splintering in two.

He dropped the pills into his mouth and washed them down with a swig of water. "We both know that's not true."

Unable to argue with him, I found myself speechless.

He set the glass of water on the counter with a loud thud before spanning the few feet between us.

"Ian," I said, my heart pounding something fierce as he backed me against the refrigerator. The stainless steel chilled me to my bones.

He fingered a strand of my hair before lowering his right hand to my collared neck. "Does he make you happy?"

"Most of the time." My guilt leaked through the fissure in my soul. I tried ignoring the lingering scent of Ian's cum on my body, but I couldn't, just as I couldn't ignore what I'd done.

"Don't tell him about this, Kayla. He doesn't need to know."

I nodded, even though I knew I would tell Gage. Not only tell him, but beg for forgiveness. Keeping this bottled inside would end me. And Gage would know anyway. He'd spot the treachery in my eyes as soon as he walked into the house.

"Thank you for loving me too," he said.

I clung to his T-shirt, burying my face in the soft fabric, and cried. "You're saying goodbye."

"Yes."

"Why are you giving up?"

"I refuse to spend the last few weeks I have left on chemo."

"But it could save your life!" I fisted my hands and pounded against his chest, hoping to beat some sense into him. "Please, Ian. *Please*. It could work. Look at Eve! She—"

"It's different!" He halted my furious fists with his working arm. "My fucking brain is quitting on me. I can't do this anymore. The chemo wasn't working. The tumor isn't going away. It's only getting worse." His chest stilled as if he were holding his breath. "I'd rather go with dignity. On *my* terms. You need to accept that."

"Why do you have to be so damn stubborn?"

"It's in my blood."

That was true. Gage shared that same blood. But could he find it in his heart to forgive Ian before it was too late? I honestly didn't know, especially after what we'd done on the couch less than two hours ago. I never believed myself capable of betraying Gage, but I had. I'd done the unthinkable. The unforgivable.

And I couldn't find the strength to regret it, other than for the pain it would cause him. I gulped just thinking of how he'd react—how I was about to tear his heart out.

"You should go home."

"Who's going to take care of you?"

"I'll be okay. Stop worrying about me."

"That's impossible."

"This is why I didn't want you to know."

"Then why did you meet me in that coffee shop?"

"*Not* seeing you was impossible. I've thought of nothing else since I walked out of your hospital room a year ago."

"But why now?" I already knew, heard the words before he spoke them.

"In some irrational part of my brain, I thought if I could win you back, maybe I'd have more reason to fight." He frowned. "But I realized it wasn't fair to you. It's not your job to give me a fucking reason to live."

"If you need a reason, I'll give you one."

He lifted a brow. "Are you willing to divorce him?"

I gaped at him, unable to find words because I didn't like the answer. Even now, faced with his illness, I'd still choose Gage.

"I knew the answer before I asked, Kayla. And I'd never ask that of you anyway. I'm just making a point. You can't give me a reason. I have to *want* to fight, and I did fight. I tried all kinds of treatments. But some things can't be fixed."

"Don't say that."

"It is what it is!" He stepped back, no longer touching me. "You need to accept it."

"Please. I'm begging you."

"And I'm begging you to go home. I can't argue with you about this anymore."

I leaned against the refrigerator, frozen in that position for what seemed like forever with my hands balled at my sides.

"Jesus, Kayla. You told me in my office that being near me was torture. Well this is worse. I need you to go. Please, just go."

"Okay," I choked out. As I left his house with tears dripping down my cheeks, splattering the ground with despair, the ache in my gut shoved the truth into my head. Into my heart.

This was goodbye.

CHAPTER EIGHTEEN

Gage found me naked and kneeling in the basement, the bullwhip coiled in front of me, waiting to strike me like a snake. The thing *ticked, ticked, ticked* like a rattler in my mind. Or maybe that was time ticking by, bringing me a second closer to the annihilation of my marriage.

To the sharp sting of leather that, for the first time, I'd gladly welcome. I wanted the strikes to take away my pain—pound to dust Ian's illness and my shame over what I'd done.

He halted in front of me, his shiny black shoes coming into view. I tilted my head and wanted to sink through the floor as his suspicious gaze flickered between the bullwhip and my face.

"Where's Eve?" he asked.

"Gone for the night."

He knelt before me and held my chin between two harsh fingers. "I called you hours ago. Where were you?"

No words or explanation could express the chaos inside me. I thought I was void of tears, but I was wrong. I'd been so, so wrong for betraying him like this.

"I'm sorry," I said, a sob squeezing from my throat. This

was going to hurt him so much, and the knowledge rose like acid.

"Baby..." He broke me to pieces by brushing the tears from my cheeks. Doubt colored his features, and in that moment, I read him so easily, had an idea of what he was thinking.

Maybe he was wrong. Maybe the dread in his gut was lying to him.

"What's wrong? Is Eve okay?"

"S-she's fine." I swallowed hard. "I did something you're going to hate me for." I lifted the whip and pressed it against his thighs. "I didn't mean to hurt you. I...*God*..." Shaking my head, I let the tears drop.

"Just tell me." A familiar tick went off in his jaw.

"I saw Ian."

"What do you mean you saw him?" He furrowed his brows. "Because I know my wife, the woman I love more than anything in this world, would never *see* my brother."

"More than saw him," I said, my voice a croak that echoed my shame. He pushed away, and the whip crashed to the floor.

I grasped it by the handle, scrambled to my feet, and offered him the implement I feared the most. The one I deserved the most.

"Please, Gage—" Everything inside me fractured. "Strike me with it. I deserve nothing less." I couldn't bear the devastation my words drilled into his eyes. Every emotion he rotated through came off him in a tangible blast.

I hadn't voiced my sin, but he heard it anyway. He stumbled back, hands clenched at his sides, shaking with the need to punish. To maim the way I'd maimed him.

"Gage, please."

"What did you do?" he asked between tight lips.

"I..." I'd never felt so broken, so helpless. He'd taken me

to hell and back, but it turned out my actions were the final accomplice in my destruction. "It just...happened."

"You fucked him." No question, only harsh certainty.

"No." The denial felt like a lie. "Let me explain."

"God, Kayla—" His voice broke, and that anguished sound alone brought tears to my eyes. He buried both hands in his hair and paced the room like a lost man. "I don't want to hear it. The reasons don't fucking matter."

"Please—"

"Nothing you say will justify you cheating on me with *him*!" He propped his back against the wall and slid to his haunches.

I couldn't fix this. I'd done the unforgivable, and I absolutely could *not* fix this. After everything we'd been through, I'd hit him in the one place capable of destroying him.

"I'll do anything," I said, forcing the words out beyond my constricted throat. "It was a mistake."

"A *mistake*? We're fucking married. This isn't like Texas when you had a choice to make."

"You didn't give me a choice!" Probably the wrong time to point that out, but I couldn't help it.

"I gave you a choice!" his voice bellowed through the basement, making my muscles lock and tense. My legs threatened to go out on me. He jumped to his feet and stormed to where I stood with the bullwhip gripped in my nervous hands.

"On your fucking knees. *Now*."

And just like that, I dropped. Groveled at his feet. Let my tears bathe the floor.

"I gave you a choice," he repeated, calmer this time. "I dragged your stubborn ass back home, but right here in this spot, I gave you the option to walk."

"I couldn't."

"Why?"

"You know why."

He let out a cruel, bitter laugh. "You claim you love me but—"

"I do love you."

"Then why? Make me understand how you could *almost* fuck my brother after I gave you what you wanted on our anniversary? I gave you everything, Kayla. *Everything!*"

My mouth trembled as the truth stalled, frozen on my tongue. I didn't want to say it, but not voicing Ian's illness wouldn't make it go away. "He has a brain tumor."

He blinked. "A...what?" That hadn't been the answer he was expecting.

"When I found out..." I hiccuped, holding back another sob. "I was blindsided. Simone called me, otherwise, I wouldn't have known. I wouldn't have gone to see him."

He shook his head, disbelieving, and I rushed to explain.

"He's refusing treatment." My limbs quaked in defeat, and only my willpower to obey him kept me on my knees instead of sprawled on the floor. "He's got a few weeks left."

His jaw worked in a frightful way, and his eyes brightened with the threat of tears. No matter the decrepit bridge between him and his brother, this news affected him.

But my betrayal was the real clincher.

I slumped, and as I dragged the memory of what I'd done to the forefront of my mind, my ashamed gaze fell to the floor. I didn't understand how I'd ended up on that couch with Ian, my hand in his pants, my lips pressed to his.

"Get into position and look at me." His tone left no room for argument.

Letting the bullwhip slip from my grasp, I forced my body to fucking work. I dredged the last of my strength and straightened my spine. Hands behind my back, breasts thrust out. Eyes on him.

"How far did it go?" he asked...no, *demanded.*

"Please don't make me tell you." My cheeks flamed under his scrutiny.

"How far, Kayla?"

"We kissed."

"What else? You're going to tell me every detail."

He was going to make me drown in my guilt. "I took my shirt off, and I…I…"

"You *what*?"

"I touched him. I made him—" The word hitched in my throat. I couldn't do it. I couldn't describe Ian coming. And no matter how long I analyzed my behavior, I couldn't explain what had been going through my mind while I'd had my cheating hand around his brother's cock.

"Spell it out for me, and address me properly when you do."

"I jerked him off, Master."

"Look at me."

I lifted my gaze, realizing after the fact that I'd been staring at his shoes. "I'm sorry, Master."

"Do not lower your eyes again." He took a step closer. "Did his cock fill your hand the way mine does? Did you want to take him in your mouth?"

His caustic tone made me nauseous—so fucking sick to my stomach that I couldn't speak.

"Answer me!"

"I don't know! I don't know what I was thinking." I held my chest, as if to keep my heart from spilling to the ground. "Whip me, Master. I'm begging you."

He kicked the bullwhip out of reach. "I'm not taking this away for you. You did it, now you get to deal with the consequences."

I bent at the waist, nearly falling sideways. I'd never regretted something so much in my life. If I could take it back…

But would I? Knowing that I might never see Ian again? Never touch him or hear his voice?

He was *dying*.

But the reasons didn't matter to Gage. There were no ands, ifs, or buts with him. Only obedience and my unconditional loyalty.

"Please, Gage. I need you so much right now." I was a selfish bitch for needing him to comfort me in my time of grief when I'd broken his heart.

"Don't move," he said through clenched teeth. "When I get back, your knees better be redder than your damn cheeks."

"Where are you going?" I crawled after him, reaching with desperate fingers, hysteria rising and careening through me, pushing me to the edge of deranged.

"I said don't move!" His contempt rained down on me as I kneeled at his feet.

"Yes, Master," I choked out, closing my eyes and letting my tears burn my face.

I listened to his unsteady breathing, his fight to hold it together. "I love you so damn much, Kayla." A pause…a beat of irreparable damage passing us by. "But right now I need to clear my fucking head."

My eyes flew open, and through my misery, I watched him climb the stairs. His feet raged war with each stomp. He wrenched the door open, and an instant later the light went out. A ricocheting bang signaled his exit. My stomach heaved and erupted, and I spewed my fear all over the floor.

The interesting thing about darkness was how it amplified everything—silence, the pungent smell of puke, even the unfaithful heart beating a furious tempo behind my breastbone. I pushed to my knees and clasped my hands at my back.

And I waited.

CHAPTER NINETEEN

Gage returned some time later. The light switched on before his heavy feet brought him down the stairs. He stopped in front of me, where I'd kneeled like a statue for the past... three hours, maybe? The only thing I knew for certain was how badly my knees ached. How my whole body ached.

"Can I please stand, Master?"

He grasped me by the shoulders and helped me hobble to the bed. My legs were numb, full of tingles, and I could hardly walk without his support. I sat at the end and waited for him to speak. The way the corners of his mouth twitched told me he had much to say.

He sat next to me and entwined his hands as if to keep them busy, so he didn't lose control and use them on me. "I went to see Ian," he said.

I held my breath, my heart pounding too loudly in my ears.

He lowered his head. "He's my fucking brother, Kayla, but all I could think about as I looked at him was you." Pushing to his feet, he paced the area in front of me. "You touching him, kissing him, fucking jerking him off."

"Gage, I'm sorr—"

"Let me finish." He pushed a hand through his hair in agitation. "I'm rotten to the soul because all I could think about was how his death would affect you. Call me a selfish bastard, but I don't want you grieving him. He doesn't deserve it."

I held my breath, deliberating between anticipation and dread.

"So I convinced him to check into a special treatment center out of state." He held up a hand, silencing anything I might say. "I love you enough to give you the world, and that includes doing everything in my power to save his life."

To say I was shocked was an understatement. "Master—"

"Can you *shut up* and listen?"

I nodded, clamping my lips.

"But that doesn't mean my motives are selfless. He's leaving in two days, and you won't ever see him again." He paused, and the hard line of his mouth put me on alert. "It doesn't matter if he lives or dies, Kayla, because he agreed not to come back. I made it clear that if he comes near Oregon, or contacts you in any way, I will punish you for it."

Gage knew how to play people to perfection. Ian loved me enough to stay away. I hoped to God he loved me enough to live.

"I own you." Gage bent and twisted his fingers in my hair, jerking my head back. "With the exception of Eve, there is no one else in your world but me. Do you understand?"

"Yes, Master," I said, my words drifting across his lips in a breathless whisper.

"You had better, because I'm demanding every last molecule of your heart."

"I understand, Master. I never meant for any of this to happen. If I could take it back, I would."

"Well, when you fuck around with temptation, you get

burned." He let me go, rose to his full height, and crossed his arms.

"I hate myself for ruining your trust in me."

"You think I forbade you to see him because I didn't trust you? Fuck, trust has nothing to do with it. It's just cold, harsh reality. You're weak when it comes to your greedy cunt, and even weaker when it comes to your heart. I exploited that, baby." He paused long enough to let out a cruel laugh. "I can't even blame you for it because I *knew* you loved him. Hell, Kayla, I wrecked any fucking chance you had with him from the moment I forced your legs apart."

Matching action to words, he bent and slipped a hand between my thighs. "Spread them, now."

"Yes, Master." I opened wide for him, and he feathered his fingers so lightly over my pussy that I wasn't sure if he meant to touch me at all.

"I stole you from him," he said, voice ragged. "And I'd do it again. I have no remorse or shame in making you mine. My only regret is allowing you to stumble."

"I did that on my own."

"No, you didn't. I own you, which means I own your mistakes. And you can be sure this one won't happen again. That taste of freedom you got? Savor it. This is the last time I leave you to your own devices."

Unable to speak, I simply nodded. My heart beat in a frenzied tune of fear. I'd backtracked us by months...years possibly.

"I confiscated your cell and the key to your car. It'll be a frozen day in hell before you get them back." He gave my inner thigh a sound slap. "Thank me for disciplining you."

"Thank you, Master."

His fingers pinched my thigh. "Beg me to punish you."

"Punish me, Master. Please." I gazed at him through my tears, meaning every word, despite the terror of the unknown rising in the form of vomit. "I deserve whatever you decide."

He palmed my cheek. "This decision wasn't easy for me. I want you to know that. But I feel this is the only way to ensure you never stumble again."

I swallowed hard, barely getting past the huge lump of terror in my throat. "What are you planning to do to me?"

He dipped a finger between my legs, crooking it in just the right way. "No orgasms for the duration of your punishment. That's a start." He stood and gestured to the bed on which I sat. "You'll sleep here tonight."

I blinked a tear down my cheek. God, this hurt. The distance growing between us, the way he couldn't quite look me in the eye. I already missed him.

But he'd gotten Ian help. If anything good came from this, it was the chance Ian now had at living.

CHAPTER TWENTY

He made me sleep in the basement for a week. I did my best to act normally when Eve was home, which was the only time he let me out, but it was harder than I thought. I missed my daughter. I missed my freedom.

I missed him.

One mistake had destroyed our happiness, and I wasn't sure how long it would take to get that back. But I had to try. No matter what he had in store for me, I had to do everything in my power to earn his forgiveness.

On the eighth morning, the door creaked open, just like it had during the previous week. Like clockwork, he brought my meals down to the basement. As he descended the stairs, I wiped my cheeks, certain I had tear stains on them from crying so much.

Every night as I fell asleep, first thing in the morning, and every time he left me alone in his dungeon. The separation was killing me. I wished he would punish me and get it over with, even if it meant taking strikes from every implement of pain he owned.

His heavy feet landed on the bottom step, and I realized

something was different about today. He wasn't dressed for work, and he wasn't carrying a plate of food.

"Strip," he ordered.

I peeled the long T-shirt I'd been sleeping in from my body.

"Put on a pair of heels." He gestured toward the collection of stilettos against the wall, right under his paddles and floggers.

I crossed the room, selected a red pair because I knew he liked the color, then slid my feet into them, one by one. As I bent over, I missed the way my hair used to curtain my face, trailing toward the ground. Straightening my spine, I faced him. And I waited.

He held out a hand.

"Come here."

I went to the hand beckoning me, as eager as a well-trained dog. Knowing this didn't change a thing. I gladly slipped my palm into his.

"Today you begin the first day of your punishment."

Something ominous tingled down my spine. We climbed the stairs in silence—the kind of quiet that was the polar opposite of comfortable. As he led me through the house, I wanted to ask questions.

What are you going to do to me?

Will it hurt?

Will you ever forgive me?

He pulled a keyring from his pocket and unlocked his office. This was a new development, as he'd never felt the need to lock his office before now, and that made me question what waited on the other side of that door.

Fitting his hand to the small of my back, he ushered me inside, and that's when I spied the cage standing upright in a corner, barely big enough to fit one person.

I gulped.

"For every day that Ian is in treatment, you will spend your time in that cage while Eve is in school. I've arranged to work from home for a few weeks."

Paying attention to the intricate details, I inspected the cage and guessed he planned to put me in there facing the corner. There was an open area about the right height for my ass.

I cast a pleading glance his way. "Please don't do this, Master."

"I didn't do this. You did."

"I don't blame you for being angry."

"Kayla, I'm not angry. I'm fucking destroyed."

"I'm sorry," I said, falling to my knees and kissing his bare feet. I was that desperate.

"I know you are, and that's why I know you'll take your sentence with gratitude. I expect you to thank me every goddam day for it." He grasped my hair with his unyielding fingers. "Get up."

I was certain my heart was about to claw its way out of my chest and die a slow, torturous death on the floor. I hadn't been this scared in a long time. That cage seemed larger than life with its door wide open and waiting for me to cross the threshold.

I cast a nervous glance at Gage. "I'll do anything else. Anything."

"Begging won't save you from this."

My voice rose to an unnatural level. "Please—"

"What I did for *him*," he interrupted, "I did for you." He gestured to the small prison. "Now you're going to do this for me."

He was punishing me for wanting Ian to live, and in a way, he was also punishing his brother. The longer Ian fought the cancer, the longer Gage would imprison me. He was possibly the most sadistic man on the planet.

"When it's over, will you forgive me, Master?"

For the first time in days, he touched me. Raising his palms, he framed my cheeks. "Pay your penance, baby, then we'll talk forgiveness." He swept away my tears with his thumbs, and it was those sparks of gentleness, of compassion, that kept me forever under his spell.

But with that spark of empathy also burned an ember of a wound that wouldn't heal anytime soon. My week spent in the basement hadn't softened him a bit. I deserved the consequences, but knowing what I was in for and getting it were two different things. I eyed the cage with its cold bars, various hooks and stockades, and shivered.

"Don't move." He crossed to his desk and pulled a ball gag out of a drawer, along with a set of nipple clamps and leather cuffs. I stood like an inanimate object—save for the shivers of my naked body—as he revealed the biggest, most gag-worthy contraption of rubber he owned.

"Gage—"

"I'm your Master right now. Not your lover, not your husband. I'm your fucking Master, and you *will* obey me." He held the rubber ball in front of my trembling lips. "Open your mouth."

"Can we talk about this?" I asked in a rush. "I know what I did hurt—"

"Kayla, open your mouth now."

Seconds passed—silent, agonizing seconds that weighed heavily on us. I realized that nothing I said would help my case or absolve me of my sin. My temporary moment of insanity didn't matter because, on the most fundamental level, I'd betrayed him.

My terror of enduring that cage didn't matter. He would impose his will on me until I relented, and he'd do it because that's what he needed to get past what I'd done.

I swallowed hard, utter dread coiling around my neck

like a boa constrictor. The collar I wore, the ring on my finger—both bound me to the spot with the inescapable strength of chains. Parting my lips, I let him inch the ball in, allowing the contraption to spread my mouth unbearably wide...wider still until the gag filled every crevice. He fastened the strap around my head, and I drew in slow breaths through my nose to calm my raging pulse.

To quiet the panic that flared inside me.

Saliva collected on my tongue and threatened to leak past my lips. The gag would have me drooling like a fool in no time. That was the thing I hated most about being gagged. The humiliation and the accompanying saliva that would drip down my chin before landing on my breasts.

"Give me your hands."

I met his eyes and pleaded for mercy. Mostly, I hated not having a voice, despised not being heard. Another tear fell as he buckled leather cuffs around my wrists.

"You lied to me when you promised to stay away from him," he said, moving on to my ankles. "Which is why you're going to endure that gag." He stood and gripped my chin. "Blink if you understand."

I blinked, and blinked some more. One, two, three times with deliberate meaning.

Forgive me, Master.

"Stop it." He took my nipples between two fingers and pinched. "Did he touch your nipples?" He tilted his head and studied me, almost as if my forced silence would answer. "He did, didn't he?" He gave them a hard twist. "Did he make them hurt like this? Or maybe he sucked on them. I know how much you like your nipples played with." He let go and lowered a hand between my legs. "Did he touch you here? Did he fuck you with his fingers? Maybe he even dipped his tongue into *my* cunt. Did you let him taste what's mine, Kayla?"

My body reacted to his touch, to the images they produced in my poisoned head, and I spread my legs a little wider.

"Did you spread your legs for him?" He thrust angry, punishing fingers inside me, bringing me to my toes, wrenching a pleading moan from my gagged mouth.

Sick. I was so sick. He was about to discipline me for the ultimate sin, and I couldn't stop from dripping onto his fingers, down his wrist.

Who knew self-loathing could be so toxic?

"I'm going to take your flushed cheeks as a yes." He stepped closer until we were nose to nose. "But *I'm* the one who owns you. I'm the one who decides when you come. The only one who decides if you ever come again." His claim to my pussy took on the tempo of a jackhammer, fingers plundering my slick heat. "I'm the one who decides if you ever talk again. If you ever exist outside of that cage again."

I wanted so badly to be strong, but my moans gurgled in my throat, barely held back, and my eyes begged him for more. I pushed my breasts out, hoping the tightness of my nipples would distract him. Tempt him.

But Gage was a man of his word. Stubborn, steadfast, and immovable. No amount of temptation would appeal to him because he was in his *zone*—that dangerous place where the only thing that tempted him was my pain and humiliation.

"We *will* get past this." He positioned himself in front of me, feet shoulder-width apart on the floor, his fist clenching a set of nipple clamps. "Because I love you."

I felt my eyes widen at the change in his tone. The hope it brought forth.

"I'll find a way to forgive you for this, because you've forgiven me for so much shit, Kayla." He clamped my nipples, and then I stood before him, his decorated slave. He gestured to the awaiting prison. "Inside, now."

Oh God.

That space seemed so tight. On shaking limbs, I obeyed and tried not to squirm as I faced the corner, but it was futile. Gooseflesh licked my ass, a precursor to what I instinctively knew. He was going to whip me through the opening of the cage. Maybe not now. Maybe not even today.

But eventually, he would take the bullwhip to my ass.

"Good girl." He spread my arms out, locking my wrists to the bars at my sides. Then he used a foot to nudge my feet apart so he could anchor them as well. After he finished securing me, I stood in four-inch heels, spread-eagled, and incapable of moving or even shifting my weight.

Panic took hold of me, increasing my heart rate, making me breathe heavily through my nose. How would I stand this, day in and day out?

I honestly didn't know.

CHAPTER TWENTY-ONE

I cracked after three days of imprisonment. Locked inside his cage of hell with my mouth gagged and nipples clamped, my wrists and ankles bound—I cried harder than I'd ever cried before. Sobs wrenched from my gut, and I worried I was close to hyperventilating.

Snot ran from my nose, mixing with the saliva escaping the gag. I was a hot mess. A blubbering mess. A mess he mostly ignored, other than to free me for ten minutes every two hours so I could move around and regain circulation. So I could eat and use the bathroom.

So I could feel like a fucking human being again for the small amount of time he allowed.

He had yet to strike me with anything, but just being inside this contraption was soul-sucking, and thinking of the endless weeks to come…

I was going insane, my mind shattering, my nerves teetering on the ledge. If Gage intended to make me forget about Ian, he'd done a bang up job because his idea of imprisonment tormented me to the point that I couldn't think of *anything* else.

The touch of his warm hands on my ass cheeks startled me. My chest heaved every couple of seconds, spasming with sobs.

"Baby, calm down. Getting so worked up isn't going to help."

Calm down? *Calm down?* My mind screamed at him because I sure as fuck couldn't do it vocally.

He slid his finger between my legs, and that had an immediate effect. Not necessarily a calming one, but it was something.

"I'm trying to work, but you're over here about to have a panic attack." He plunged a finger into my pussy. Instantly, arousal flared. It had been over two weeks since he'd let me come. But even worse, two weeks had gone by since I'd slept at his side.

"If you can calm down and behave, I'll think about making you come tonight."

I shook my head, protesting despite the gag. I only wanted him—like a druggie craving the next fix. Like a child craving candy. Like I craved Gage Channing.

"So you *don't* want to come?" He sounded surprised and amused. He smacked my ass hard. "You want me to punish you?"

I shook my head again.

Another smack brought me to my toes. The impact of his palm tingled over my skin, more arousing than painful. I heard him insert a key, and the door squeaked open. He unbuckled the gag then wiped my face with a napkin.

"What does my naughty prisoner want then?"

"Master, I want to sleep in our bed tonight."

"Why do you want that?"

Another sob hitched. "I miss you so much. Please, Master. I will stand here all day without making a sound if you'll just hold me tonight."

I heard him suck in a breath, which gave me hope because he didn't seem as collected as he would have me believe.

"Behave yourself, and we'll see."

He reinserted the gag, and for the next few hours, I stood silent and still, determined more than ever to do as I was told. When afternoon rolled around, and he freed me so I could tend to Eve, I'd allowed hope to settle in, and hope was a dangerous thing when it came to a man like Gage, especially considering how angry and hurt he was over my actions. Today he'd been gentle, even kind, but on other days, he'd had nothing but snide remarks and scornful planes on his gorgeous face.

My mistake had snowballed into something horrific and ugly, and I worried no time in the world could erase what I'd done, could patch his heart back together. Or mine, for that matter.

"What's wrong, Mommy?"

I picked at my salad that night at dinner. "Nothing baby. I'm just tired." I mustered a smile and met her inquisitive gaze. "How was school?"

"At lunch, I sat with Vanessa and Toby."

"What happened to Leah?"

Eve's face crumbled. "She said she's not my friend anymore."

Her sadness pricked at my heart. "Why did she say that?"

Rather than answer, Eve shrugged and spooned in a bite of mashed potatoes.

"Answer your mother, Eve."

She sat up straight upon hearing his no-bullshit tone. It was a tone I knew well, and though I appreciated him backing me up, it also bothered me that he often talked to us both in the same manner.

Like children, only Eve *was* my child.

"She said I was being mean, but I wasn't."

"Did she tell you why she thought that?"

Her lower lip poked out. "Some kids called her names. She said I wasn't her friend anymore because I laughed."

"Did you say you're sorry? That wasn't very nice."

"I wasn't laughing at her, Mommy! The names were funny."

"Princess, just tell her you're sorry, and you didn't mean it." Gage's attention landed on me. "People make mistakes. I'm sure she'll forgive you."

I held my breath for a full minute, unable to erase his words from my mind. I wanted to believe that forgiveness was possible, that we could find our way back to each other, but the road ahead seemed endless and full of rocky mountains I'd have to climb over first.

I came across the first rocky hill later that night after Eve went to bed. I'd been so out of my mind all week with being locked in that cage, that I failed to realize tonight was Friday.

Gage had no problem reminding me. A little after 11 p.m., I found myself bent over the end of our bed, my fingers gripping my skirt and exposing my ass to him. Only this time he wasn't using his belt.

He gripped the bullwhip.

"Master, I'm scared."

"You should be."

"Please don't hurt me."

"Did you stop to think how your cheating would hurt me?"

"Yes, Master."

"But you touched him anyway." The tail cracked an instant before the strike landed. My entire body tensed. I remained silent, but only because the pain knocked the air from my lungs. Before I was able to catch my breath, he struck again.

I tried managing my breathing, willed my muscles to relax and accept the brutality of his arm, but my screams fractured the air. After the twentieth lash, he dropped the whip, pulled the drawer to our nightstand open, and grabbed a tube of cream.

A groan almost escaped me as he applied the ointment to the reddening welts on my backside. I knew I wouldn't be able to sit for a while.

"Do you still want to sleep in our bed?"

My heart skipped. "Yes, Master."

He crossed the room and turned off the light. I didn't move from my bent over position at the end of the mattress. He scooped me into his arms, stunning me into a boneless mess, and tucked me against him under the sheets. His warm embrace surrounded me, and my heart wouldn't stop thumping a furious beat as I sank into him.

The intensity of the moment washed over me, and I drew on the vestiges of my strength to hold back my tears.

"I know I've been harsh with you."

I didn't know how to answer that. His punishment was more than I could bear, yet I understood him. No sane person would, but he was my crazy, and I understood him. I also knew how deep his hurt ran. His wounds would bleed for a long time, slow to scab over.

"I'm sorry I hurt you, Master."

"I know, baby." He nuzzled my neck. "Get some sleep."

For the first time in two weeks, I slept in complete harmony, wrapped in my husband's arms.

CHAPTER TWENTY-TWO

Eve didn't have school on Monday, so I got a break from the cage. While Gage worked in his office, I spent most of the day playing with her. We battled each other in the game of Life, made up our own rules for Monopoly, and played Go Fish for hours.

It was freeing to have so much time to myself. A whole day with my daughter. A whole day of not having to set foot inside that cage. Things were looking up. Gage hadn't sent me to the basement since he'd allowed me back into our bed, and he'd held me every single night, though he still refused to make love to me.

He wouldn't even fuck me, nor did he use my mouth for his pleasure. I'd heard him groaning his release in the shower over the weekend, more than once, finding satisfaction by his own hand. I wasn't worthy enough for him to fuck, and that stung. The spooning at night, however...that I couldn't complain about. It was all he could offer me now, and I'd eat it up like a starved animal.

But Tuesdays came around like they always did. I'd never

despised a Tuesday with such intensity, but with Eve back in school, Gage didn't hesitate in returning me to the cage. As he held the gag in front of my lips, I thanked him for his discipline and accepted the rubber ball. I behaved like a model prisoner for fear that he'd send me back to the basement if I lost my shit again.

The days came and went, most of them spent within the confines of those bars. My bars of shame. My bars of penance. In the back of my mind, I knew to be grateful for each day in that contraption because it meant Ian was still fighting. The day when the cage became no more...I couldn't allow my thoughts to go there.

But two months, three weeks, and five days later, that day crashed through my world like a wrecking ball.

"Why are you taking me down here?" I asked as Gage ushered me through the door of the basement.

"Your time in the cage is over."

I froze on the bottom step, my heart in my throat. Looking over my shoulder, I opened my mouth to ask the one thing he wouldn't want to hear.

"Don't even think about it, Kayla. It doesn't matter if he lived or died. All you need to know is that you're free of your prison now."

"Master, I'm beggin—"

"I suggest you don't, unless you'd like an additional two months in that prison."

I clamped my mouth shut, shaking my head, but in the back of my mind, resolve formed. Some way, some how, I'd learn of Ian's fate.

"Let's get on with this," Gage said, pulling me back to the current moment.

"Get on with what?"

"The last phase of your punishment." He grabbed my arm

and led me into the middle of the basement. I expected him to order me to strip. Instead, he pulled me into his arms. "We need to be able to trust each other. That's going to take some time."

"I know," I whispered, my face hidden in the fabric of his shirt. I squeezed my eyes shut, willing away the burn in them.

"I'm going to make love to you for hours."

I held onto him with more strength, unashamed of the moan that rumbled from my throat. His words hit me right between the thighs. His erection grew, pressing against my stomach, and his chest rose and fell too quickly.

"It's been too fucking long, baby. Punishing you was torture."

"I've missed you so much."

"Me too," he said, nuzzling the crown of my head. He held on for a few seconds longer before letting go. "Strip."

Anxiety stormed through my veins as I removed the T-shirt and sleep shorts I'd worn that morning while seeing Eve off to school. As I stood motionless, my skin erupting in goose bumps while my nipples puckered, he sorted through his toys.

"Get into position at the cross," he said, his back to me.

The air in the basement seemed chillier than usual. Or maybe the tremor in my limbs stemmed from fear because I had no idea what he had in store for me.

The last phase of my punishment...that could mean anything.

I moved the few feet to the St. Andrew's cross and aligned my body with it. He joined me, holding the cuffs that would hold me at his mercy, along with the gag that would silence my ability to beg for any.

But I was eager to end this torturous sentence. Frantic to have my husband back. My grief over Ian's illness had caused me to stumble, but Gage had scraped it out with his psychological confines. Now I brimmed with his will.

A small piece of my heart still hurt when I thought of Ian, but my husband, my Master had crashed through any remaining barriers by locking me inside that cage. He'd conditioned me back to a state of total obedience. I didn't put up a smidgen of fight when he anchored me to the cross. Didn't protest when he pushed the gag into my mouth.

He stepped back and perused his possession, and as his gaze wandered over my exposed and vulnerable body, something dark flashed in his eyes.

I didn't like that look. That indigo glint was an omen of bad things to come.

He reached into his pocket and drew out his cell, brought it to his ear with calculation. "You can come down now."

Silence screamed between us as the minutes ticked by. He said nothing, and I *couldn't* say anything. Then the door at the top of the stairs creaked open, and time seemed to screech to a violent halt as Katherine descended, tainting *our* space with her rancid presence.

Reality was a fragile thing, too easily shattered by the figments of our imaginations. Because what I was seeing couldn't be real. No way was Katherine standing beside Gage while I was naked and chained to the cross.

The old Gage would have done something this wicked—this fucked-up and *wrong*—but not the Gage I'd married. His brutal side had owned my punishment, but we'd moved past Katherine.

Hadn't we?

So why the hell was she standing there, her mouth curled in a triumphant smirk?

Memories of the last time the three of us had occupied this room blew through my head like a category five hurricane. Ian and Katherine on the couch. Gage forcing me over the bed and fucking me hard so he could torture his brother. So he could exact revenge.

Was this his grand finale of revenge on me? Was he going to make me watch him fuck Katherine, bent over the bed, slamming into her with the force of his anger? I almost retched at the thought, and only the knowledge that I'd choke on my vomit held it at bay.

The severity of his mouth scared the hell out of me. I could tolerate him fucking me in front of her, using my body for his sadistic pleasure. I could even tolerate him subjecting me to degradation.

I could *not* handle watching him touch that bitch.

God, had he experienced this same all-consuming jealousy at the thought of me with Ian? Roiling and ravishing the spirit like a monstrous storm? No wonder he'd locked me in a cage.

He pulled his shirt over his head, and my thought processes crashed into a cement wall. His shirt lay discarded on the floor at his feet.

Pound, pound, pound.

My heart became its own entity behind my ribcage, taking on a rhythm of unnatural origin. No one's heart should beat this hard and fast—not without sending them into cardiac arrest.

He turned to Katherine. "On your knees," he said, setting his hands on her shoulders and applying pressure until she kneeled before him.

"Unbutton my pants."

Undiluted rage coursed through me. I lurched forward, wrenching my wrists as far as the restraints allowed. She brought her fingers to his pants and followed his command.

"Unzip me."

Ziiiip.

She curled her fingers at the waistband of his boxer briefs, ready to expose his hard-on, but he batted her hands away. "I didn't say you could touch me. Hands at your back." He cast a meaningful look in my direction, one Katherine didn't miss, and it became clear that this had nothing to do with her.

This was all about me.

He pulled his cock out and aimed the tip at her willing mouth. "Do you want to suck me off?" he asked her.

"Yes."

"Yes *what*?"

"Yes, Mr. Channing."

"Do you want me to fuck you?"

"Please, Mr. Channing."

He leaned forward and almost brushed her lips with his cock, but his words were for me. "Capture this picture, Kayla. Keep it at the forefront of your mind. If you *ever* touch another man again, I'll not only fuck her, but I'll do it in front of you."

Katherine studied him, a brewing storm shadowing her features as realization dawned. But he was too busy watching for my reaction to notice. Too busy shooting a promise of dark truth from his eyes.

"I'll fuck her for hours. She'll take my cock in her cunt, in her ass, in her damn mouth. I'll make her scream my name for as long as it takes until the thought of *looking* at another man makes you sick."

I detected no bullshit in his tone. No bluffing. The warning was real. Set in stone. He'd laid down the law. For the rest of my life, if I stepped out of line again, he held the power to hit me where it would hurt the most...just like I'd hit his bullseye.

Silence descended upon the three of us. Gage drew in a breath as he zipped his pants.

"You're free to go," he told Katherine.

"But—"

"That will be all. You know where the door is."

Hell, if that bitch didn't look disappointed as she left us alone in the basement.

CHAPTER TWENTY-THREE

The two of us were like oil and water, fire and ice. Love and Hate. None of those things mixed, but Gage and I were drawn to each other, nevertheless. Apart, we straddled the border of sane, but together we were a nuclear meltdown waiting to happen. Toxic chemicals emitting fatal fumes.

None of that mattered when we were in bed because our compatibility in that single, intense place overrode the incompatibilities.

Katherine's presence in the midst of our chaos was but a faint memory as his arms sheltered me, enclosed me in his possessive embrace. We sat in the middle of the bed, naked, the sheets a puddle around our joined bodies. Moans rent the air between frantic kisses. I clung to his sweat-slicked chest, my cheek on his shoulder as I rode him.

"Baby, yes." His strong hands gripped my hips, jerking me onto his cock in forceful plunges. "Fuck yes." He groaned. "Take me deep."

We came together at regular intervals. Up. Down. Up. Down.

Steady.

Sensual.

Sex in its basest form, yet what we were doing eclipsed fucking. We were crashing into each other in a wave of forgiveness, of absolution.

I cried out, just a few strokes away from creaming all over him. "Gage, please...oh God, please. I need to come." I panted, teeth pulling on my lower lip.

"You don't have permission."

"Please...please...can't hold back. Begging you..." I clawed at his shoulders, about to climb out of my skin and burrow into his.

He brought me down on his cock hard and held me there. "Look at me, baby."

I veered back, my breath coming fast between parted lips, and met his gaze—his heated, seductive gaze that pulled me into the depths of intense blue. I could lose myself forever in those eyes. In his arms. In the joining of our bodies.

Forever didn't seem long enough.

"Do I have your whole heart?" he asked, watching me closely.

"It beats for only you."

"Do I own this body?"

"Always."

"Am I yours?"

"I hope so." I leaned forward and caught his mouth, taking what I needed. Hoping he'd give it to me.

And he did. He thrust his tongue into my mouth and moaned in a way that made me whimper. Low and deep in his throat. The taste of him sent me reeling.

"I need you," I whispered against his lips.

He expelled a shaky breath. "You have me. Nothing and no one is taking you from me, or I from you." He ran a thumb over my lower lip. "Do you have something you need to ask me?"

Only every day for the rest of my life. "Will you forgive me?"

He pushed my damp bangs back and kissed my forehead. "You taught me about forgiveness, Kayla. You showed me what it meant to be forgiven. Because of your grace and heart, I learned to love. Baby, you were forgiven before you ever committed the crime."

I kissed him again, tears flooding my eyes. Joy grabbing hold of my soul. "I love you, Gage."

"Who am I, Kayla?"

"My Master."

Always.

BOOK FOUR
THE DEVIL'S SPAWN

"Hell is empty and all the devils are here."
— William hakespeare

CHAPTER ONE

Present - 1 day before Thanksgiving

I will not fucking cry. "Damn it," I muttered as a tear escaped. Gritting my teeth, I blinked rapidly and stuffed more clothing into the overflowing suitcase. An absurd amount of dresses rose above the rim, and as I shoved the pile down, I wished like hell I had some pants. Or even a few pairs of sweats. Definitely some underwear. But those finer things in life weren't allowed—not when it meant blocking my husband's access to his favorite place between my thighs.

I wrestled with the zipper, adding my body weight to the top of the case, and finally zipped it shut. If I walked out that door, I'd have nothing but what lay in a tossed mess inside. The remainder of my clothing filled the shelves, drawers, and hangers inside the walk-in wardrobe I shared with Gage.

Oh, God...Eve.

How was I supposed to tell her? She'd miss her bedroom, her toys. She'd miss *him*.

The reality of what I was doing hit me, and in a fit of anger, I dragged the suitcase off the bed and kicked the damned thing until it fell over on its side. Okay, so I wasn't exactly thinking logically, but didn't a pregnant woman have the right to a meltdown after finding out her husband was nothing but a lying—

Don't go there.

But I went there anyway, torturing myself with every word the bitch had spoken. Nearly doubling over at the thought, I pressed a desperate fist to my lips and stifled a sob; sucked in quick breaths before letting them out in hot spurts that dampened my knuckles. Where had the tears come from? I'd promised myself I wouldn't cry anymore.

Pull it together, Kayla.

He was due to arrive in the driveway any minute now. Simone had begged me to leave before he got home, but if I were going to do this, I had to confront him first. Otherwise, he would never let me go.

A hand dropped onto my shoulder, warm with comforting support. Simone didn't say a word, but she didn't need to. I knew she wouldn't leave my side, and that's why I'd called her. She was my safety net, the one person who wouldn't hesitate to hand Gage his ass if he tried railroading me. She was here to make sure I got out.

"You don't owe him anything," she said.

Nodding, I wiped my eyes. "I know."

I didn't know shit. My husband was the fucking devil incarnate, but he loved me. Didn't he? Or had it all been a lie? That was the problem—I didn't know anymore. My emotions had me trapped in the eye of a typhoon named Gage Channing.

Simone's hand slid from my shoulder as I rebuilt my emotional fortress. I stood to the side in bitter numbness while she hauled my suitcase upright. She headed toward the bedroom door, rollers sounding on the hardwood behind her.

"It's okay to need some space, you know. If he loves you, he'll understand."

Folding my arms, I sank onto the end of the mattress. This particular spot bled with memories. He'd bend me over in a heartbeat and blast some sense into my ass if I let him. I couldn't let him get that close, or I'd crack wide open. Hell, I'd probably fracture regardless.

"I need to do this," I said, shaking my head just as his car sounded. "I need some space, but I also need..."

Answers.

Simone lingered by the bedroom door, chewing her bottom lip. Uncertainty was a strange feature on her face. She didn't do uncertain—she was a pick-a-path-and-follow-it kind of woman.

"I'll be okay, Simone. I promise."

She let out a sigh. "I'll be right out there," she said, jabbing a finger in the direction of the living room. She left the door cracked open upon her exit, and her absence echoed in my ears. The room hummed a solitary tune, and each lonesome note poked at my will. But a single question repeated on loop within the chaos of my foggy mind.

Could I really go through with this?

CHAPTER TWO

Past - 18 days before Halloween

I was going to be sick. The inevitability of it sat in the back of my throat, burning like acid. My stomach cramped, and a sweaty chill broke out on my skin. I wasn't immune to the irony in that, but it was true.

As I watched Katherine trail a manicured hand down Gage's arm, I seethed hot and cold, raged with clammy sickness. I lifted a hand, a millisecond away from shoving his office door all the way open, but his harsh voice made me freeze.

"Get your hands off of me."

Katherine jerked back as if he'd burned her, and only then did I realize that I'd seen her touching him for maybe two seconds.

But two seconds had been enough to make me sick. Literally sick. Before Gage or Katherine spotted me, and before anyone on this floor questioned why I was lingering outside my husband's office, I strode toward the women's restroom, my head held high with false confidence. Hopefully, anyone looking at me wouldn't see the truth on my face.

That I'd caught him with her *again*, and I was about to come undone over it.

A phone rang, fingers clicked over a keyboard, and I heard the distinct scratching of someone jabbing down quick and purposeful notes with a pencil. I held my shit together long enough to reach the safety of the ladies room. Thank God it was empty. I scurried to my knees in one of the stalls and lost my pride along with my breakfast.

He'd told me to meet him for lunch. Why would he do that if Katherine was going to be here? He knew how the sight of that bitch got under my skin. Gage had a sadistic streak as black as the desert at midnight, but when it came to Katherine Mitchell, he exercised care. In fact, he went out of his way to spare me her presence.

Because he was fucking her? Or because he loved me enough to shield me from her?

I hated how she was the weak spot in my armor, the single chink that made the rest of me fall apart. I didn't want to doubt him, but the image of her four months ago in the basement, eager and on her knees, was a searing brand on my memory. It didn't matter that he'd only threatened to follow through to make a point, to show me what *could* be if I dared to betray him again.

The mental damage had been done.

Tears stung my eyes. Damn, I had to get my shit together. I couldn't go back out there and face the employees of Channing Enterprises—face *him*—looking like I'd just had a breakdown in the women's restroom. Even if that was kind of true. Turning the faucet on, I shot my reflection a stern frown then splashed cold water onto my face.

Five minutes later, I left the restroom mostly composed. As always, the curious gazes of my former coworkers burned into my back. I didn't check to see if they were watching me, but I felt it. Maybe I was paranoid, though I didn't think so. My marriage to CEO Gage Channing was a cesspool for gossip mongers, especially since Katherine and her son had come into our lives. The selfish, jealous wife in me wanted to keep Conner at arm's length, but he was just a kid, and he had the best parts of Gage in him, so much so that I found it shocking his paternity hadn't come out sooner.

Not for the first time, I wondered why Katherine had waited so long to tell Gage about Conner. Maybe marrying me had been the final push that sent her over the edge. Maybe she'd always believed Gage to be hers, so coming clean about a secret like that hadn't seemed important. Maybe the idea of coming clean had even scared her—until another woman had taken him away and that had scared her more.

Well, the bitch couldn't have him. And speaking of Katherine, she was thankfully nowhere in sight when I entered his office.

"You're late," he said, dark head bowed toward the screen of his laptop.

I shut and locked the door. "I know. I'm sorry." I crossed to the front of his executive desk and bent over, lifting my skirt as I did so. I could explain how seeing Katherine had caught me off guard, but I didn't want to stir that pot right now, and I definitely didn't want to go into how I'd puked in the women's restroom, even if telling him might spare me a punishment.

He might think it meant something else, and with a stab to the heart, I acknowledged once again that it wasn't going to happen. Not after all of this time. We'd been married for over a year and a half now, screwing like rabbits the whole time without any form of protection, yet I continued to be... broken.

The painful reminder of that almost drowned me in despair until the texture of his suit against my outer thigh pulled me from my dark thoughts. I bit my lip as he grabbed my ass with a warm palm. He wasn't gentle, and the rough way he handled me made my insides clench in the best way imaginable. Anticipation zinged through me as I waited for his punishment. I had no doubt he was going to spank me for arriving late, but he knew what the heat of his palm on my bare ass did to me, so calling it a form of discipline was a stretch.

"I can practically hear the wheels turning in your head. What's on your mind?" he asked.

I gnawed on my bottom lip some more and considered what to tell him. What not to tell him. "I'm thinking of how turned on I am."

"Are you aching for my hand? Is that why you were late?"

I groaned. "No."

"I'm going to need a little clarification."

"I wasn't late on purpose." A dark note entered my tone, and I hoped he didn't pick up on it.

"But you'll take a spanking for it anyway?"

I nodded.

"Fuck," he groaned. "You've got me so damn hard." He smacked my ass to punctuate just how hard he was. "Spread your legs."

I gripped my skirt and did as told, exposing myself to the gentle caress of air on my pussy. The remnants of Katherine and her whorish fingers vanished from my mind. There was nothing but wet heat between my legs. I ached for him there. Tingled. Burned.

He'd been away at a conference for a few days and had gotten back late last night. I'd already gone to bed, and instead of waking me to claim what was his, he'd shown a rare bout of sweetness by letting me sleep. But going so long without his cock was beginning to drive me insane.

He trailed a finger between my butt cheeks, drawing a surprised gasp from me. "I need you," I moaned.

My words gave him pause, and his touch lingered but did little more. God, he could be such a tease.

"Please."

Finally, he touched me exactly how I wanted…no, *needed* with his thumb teasing my asshole while two fingers slipped inside me.

I moaned at the welcome intrusion. "Feels so good."

"I'm going to spank the fuck out of this ass."

And he did. He walloped me with more force than I expected, considering his playful mood. I gritted my teeth to keep quiet, dancing from foot to foot between each hit, but on his final, most brutal strike I failed to bite back a yelp.

He palmed my right ass cheek and squeezed. "Beautifully pink."

My legs were rigid pillars of steel, driven wide open by the strength of my need for his cock. "Please," I said, groaning the word. I fisted my skirt to keep from touching myself.

"Shhh," he said, shoving his fingers between my lips. "I have other uses for this mouth. Do you have any idea how badly I want you gagging on my cock? I've thought of nothing else but getting into your mouth and ass since I've been gone."

My heartbeat stuttered, and I would have begged for mercy if he'd given me a chance. Instead, I moaned my protest around his fingers. He understood exactly what I was objecting to.

"I've gone easy on you, but you've grown spoiled. Entitled even. I own your ass. We agreed on our anniversary that it's mine to take as I please." Leaning against my back, he pressed his erection into my ass cheek and brought his lips to my ear. "I *please*," he said.

I bit down on his fingers in response, instinctively clenching my ass at the thought of him shoving his cock inside. Abruptly, he sprang back. Turning to face him, I gripped his desk behind me.

"Not here, Gage. Please."

He gestured to his desk, eyes smoldering. "Bare your cunt."

Oh hell. I was a pile of goo at his feet, sculpting clay in his strong hands. I hopped up, bunched my skirt around my waist, and spread for him much too eagerly. Propping myself up on my elbows, I watched him as he inched closer with that burning indigo gaze zeroing in between my thighs.

Hot energy blazed between us, and exhilaration squeezed my heart, rushed through my veins.

Then he smiled and asked his favorite question. "Who am I?"

"My Master."

"Always, Kayla." He dropped to his knees and placed his hands on my thighs, his thumbs digging into my skin as he spread me even wider. He wet his lips with a furtive dart of his tongue. "Who decides when you come?"

"You do, Master."

Please, please, please, please. I need to come. So fucking ba—

"I've decided you're not coming." He shot me his devil's grin. "But I'm going to lick you right here on my desk until you beg me to."

I almost cried at his words. Defeated, I closed my eyes and let my head fall back, swallowed a frustrated growl. Fuuuck...his breath would be the end of me, drifting over my exposed pussy with enough heat to make my blood rush right *there*. And his tongue...damn, that tongue.

Wet and on fire, sliding between my lips with perfected

finesse. Easing through my slickness with lazy purpose, as if he had all day to eat me out. Which, of course, he did. He always had time to torture me.

"You're not leaving here satisfied." Slowly, he inched two expert fingers into my pussy. "You're going to leave my office with pink cheeks, a throbbing cunt, and beyond excited to get fucked in the ass tonight."

I groaned.

"Eyes on me, Kayla."

"Master, I'm begging you." With a roll of my shoulders, I dipped my head, chin to chest, and returned his gaze beneath hooded lids.

He had me gone already. Primed and ready. My nipples puckered to the point of pain, the very tips straining against my bra, begging for freedom from the sheer fabric so he'd fondle them. Lick them. Pinch them.

"There you are," he whispered, crooking his fingers inside me before sliding them in and out. Slooooow. So damn slow.

"Oh God, Gage. Please, please..."

"Will you do anything to come?"

The bastard was trying to trick me again. I bit my lip to keep from answering. If I said yes, he'd take advantage of any number of things. Nipple clamps. A cane or bullwhip. His favorite gag, nearly as big as my fist.

My husband was beyond sadistic. He had no qualms about pushing me past hard limits if I gave him the go ahead, and he'd hold me to my green light even if I gave it while under duress.

"That's not fair."

"The only rules I play by are my own," he said, then he lowered his mouth to me again.

Nothing could be as erotic as watching him go down on me. Nothing. I reached under my splayed thighs and gripped the edge of the desk with both hands. He'd given me plenty of lessons on the art of limber movement, and right now I used my body's capabilities to grind against his face.

There. God. So close. I was going to come, and I didn't give a fuck about the consequences. He'd find a reason to take his pound of flesh anyway because he was Gage. "Yeah, yeah," I panted, barely above a whisper. "So close."

He jackhammered his fingers a few more times until I writhed on his desk, and then he shot my hopes down the drain by pulling away. "Good. That's exactly where I want you." Wiping his mouth with the back of his hand, he pulled himself upright and towered over me. "I'll see you at home. I won't be late."

The fight went out of me, and I plopped onto his desk, trying to catch my breath. "Don't leave me like this."

"You know what I want, Kayla. Give it to me, and I'll take you there."

He wanted to fuck me in the ass—only he wanted me to give it to him willingly. More than willingly. He wanted me to beg him to take me in the one way he knew I despised. If that wasn't sadistic, then I didn't know what was.

CHAPTER THREE

Awareness could be a cruel thing, especially when it was of one's self. The whisper in my head, an irritating voice that sounded eerily close to my own, chanted vicious truth. I was a sex addict. No. I was a Gage Channing addict. I'd given up the idea of quitting him a long time ago, but tonight, as I set the table and prepared to greet him, I realized just how pathetic I was, how far I'd fallen through the fissures in my sanity.

He'd thrown down the anal gauntlet at the most opportune time—for *him* anyway—when he had me out of my mind and foaming at the mouth from withdrawal. I could think of nothing else since I'd left his office. My head was crammed full of Gage and sex and the pain he'd inevitably inflict. Poor Eve had been dealing with my dazed-like distraction all afternoon. I'd managed to get my head out of my ass long enough to help her with her homework. We spent thirty minutes gathering leaves from the ground, each one a bright shade of autumn splendor. Afterward, I patiently watched her glue them to an outline of a tree on a white piece of paper.

But the glue hadn't even dried before I'd gone back to obsessing over Gage's plans for my ass. Something rose in my throat. Fear? Maybe. I swallowed that bitter lump of emotion as I layered the ingredients for lasagna into a baking dish. It was Gage's favorite, but I guess tonight was all about Gage's favorites, especially anal.

That word had such intensity to it, such power and control. And fear it I did, because anal was so unpredictable. Sometimes it felt good. Unbelievably good. But other times…

Gage was careful, but his definition of careful and mine were two entirely different things. Sometimes his sadism took over and my ass became the casualty. We didn't do it often, and I suspected that was the reason why. Even he didn't quite trust himself. How could he, when he craved my pain on such a fundamental level?

Fifteen minutes before I expected him home, a text pinged my cell. He'd given back my phone a few weeks ago, with parental controls to restrict my access, of course. In addition to emergency contacts, and Eve's school and doctors, I could only call or text him, and vice versa.

Gage: *what's Eve doing?*

Me: *watching tv*

Gage: *did she finish her homework?*

Me: *yep, all done*

Gage: *good, go into the bedroom and touch yourself. I'm checking you when I get home. You'd better be wet.*

I bit back a groan as I tapped out a *yes, Master*.

Gage: *lock the door and get on all fours on the bed. First thing I want to see is your ass in the air. I'll be there in a few.*

Damn him.

Setting my cell on the counter, I eyed the oven and the minutes ticking by. Eve was engrossed in her "TV time," which gave me a chance to slip down the hall and quietly push the bedroom door open.

I couldn't help but love this game that Gage and I played. The rules always changed, and he always won, but the ride was the biggest thrill ever—like sitting white-knuckled at the top of a roller coaster, on the cusp of hurtling down into the unknown. I locked the door, well aware he had a key, and crossed to the bed and got into position. Head down, ass up. I slipped my fingers between my legs and started stroking, going easy because it would take so little to get me there, and that was, under no circumstances, allowed.

I heard his car through the cracked window in our bedroom, followed by footsteps that led him to the front door. Then silence stole over me, save for my rapid pulse. I listened for a hint of him in the hall but detected not a single footfall. Besides, I didn't need to hear or see him to know the exact moment he entered the bedroom.

His presence tingled on my skin, sparking my nerve endings until they sizzled with electricity. My body flushed, and the satin comforter seemed to grow hot under my skin.

He had me boiling already.

"Dinner smells wonderful," he murmured, taking my vulnerable ass in his hands. "According to the timer, we've got six minutes."

"Six minutes for what?" I gulped. He had to notice the shaky quality of my voice. Six minutes wasn't nearly enough time. Not for anal.

"Relax. I'd never rush this. You should know better by now." His clothing rustled, and I heard a cap open, followed by a squirt. "I'm only prepping you with a plug."

I let out a breath. Those weren't so bad. Sometimes, they were even...arousing. He pressed the cold, hard tip against my rectum, but he didn't shove it in right away. Instead, he swirled the plug around my reluctant hole, spreading the lubricant.

He really was taking care with this, but considering my meltdown the last time he fucked me in the backdoor, I shouldn't be surprised. Gage lived to make me submit, and though my pain never failed to harden his cock, he'd come a long way from the monster he'd once been. Either that or I'd trained myself to accept his will because it was easier than fighting him.

He nudged my ass with the plug, and I winced, my body automatically tensing.

"Just relax for me."

I blew out a breath. Easier said than done. He probed my ass more firmly, and this time he didn't hesitate. I didn't dare move away from him, no matter how much I wanted to. It didn't matter that this was the biggest fucking butt plug he'd ever used. It didn't matter that it hurt. If I didn't hold still and take that plug in silent submission, he would punish me into next Sunday. Finally, the horrendous ring of fire abated, leaving in its wake an anus brimming with his toy.

He dragged a finger through my slit. "You are so damn wet. Such a dirty, needy girl." He swatted my ass with enough force to extract a yelp from me. "Take a minute if you need to. I'll get dinner on the table." The soft pad of his feet carried him away from me, and his quiet exit echoed in my ears.

My heartbeat thundered as I made my way into the bathroom. Acclimating to the foreign object in my ass took a few moments, but by the time I'd wiped away the excess lube from between my cheeks, it felt mostly...comfortable.

Not really arousing though, considering the size. But Gage didn't have a small cock, so I understood why he'd chosen this one.

I turned toward the door, mentally preparing to endure

an evening of playing by Gage's ever-changing rules, but my toiletry bag caught my eye. Had I left it out this morning? I must have because I'd been the last one in here.

Stupid. So stupid.

Holding my breath, I listened for footsteps. There were none. I wandered closer to the bag and dug through it until I found what I was looking for. The makeup compact felt cool and solid in my hands—a sharp contrast to the dread that burned in my gut. Before I questioned the wisdom of my actions, I pulled out the tiny piece of paper and unfolded it.

I'd found the note taped to the front door one day, shortly after Gage had ended my sentence in his cage, and things between us had gone back to a weird sort of normal. But if he found this...

I shuddered to think of the consequences.

The paper was worn around the edges from taking it out often and reading the simple two-word message, jotted down in a familiar heart-wrenching scrawl.

I'm okay.

CHAPTER FOUR

"I thought you could help me with something next week," Gage said after dinner. As Eve splashed in the tub, I turned and found Gage's impressive form filling the open doorway. At first, I thought he was talking to her, as he often came up with things for her to do because she loved helping.

But he was talking to me. His blue eyes held that familiar sparkle that turned my insides to mush. Gage wore many faces—Master, sadist, disciplinarian, and right now, loving husband. He had something up his sleeve. Something I was going to be happy about. He stepped into the bathroom and sat at the edge of the tub.

"Channing Enterprises is sponsoring an event in a couple of weeks."

I raised a brow, wondering where he was going with this.

"Basically, it's an overpriced masquerade ball." He let a beat pass. "But a portion of the proceeds will go to The Eve Foundation."

Wow. Over the summer he'd formed The Eve Foundation to help fight childhood cancers, claiming it was something he'd been thinking about doing for months. But I suspected he'd done it because regardless of his questionable actions, he did have a conscience. Maybe he even felt a little guilty for demanding I stop volunteering at the hospital. I still had no life outside of motherhood or my marriage, but at least he was beginning to cut me some slack.

And I couldn't help but find a sliver of hope in the unexpected arrival of this conversation. Unable to stop myself, I leaned forward and pressed my lips to his.

He laughed. "Does that mean you'll help me with this?"

"I'd love to. What do you need me to do?"

"Each sponsor is helping with the organization of the event. I have a team working on theme and decor, but they might as well be color blind, so I fired them yesterday."

"Oh," I said, a touch of nervousness painting my utterance.

"I want elegant, classy, *and* seductive. What I don't want is a standard costume party." He lowered his voice, shifting his attention to Eve for a moment, but she was too busy building a humongous bubble castle in the tub to care about boring adult conversation. "You are the epitome of all three, and I know you can do this, even on such short notice."

His confidence in me heated my belly in a way that wasn't sexual for once. Sex drove our relationship to the extreme, which made these small moments of coexisting as husband and wife all the more special. "I'll do my best. I mean, I do know your tastes pretty well. I was your personal assistant once upon a time."

He raised a brow as if giving what I'd said consideration. "Good. Then it's settled. I'll clear my afternoon for you on Tuesday and Wednesday." With a smile, he leaned down and scooped up a bubble, then smeared it on Eve's nose. As she giggled and squealed, he took the opportunity to whisper in my ear. "But enough about work. After you tuck in Eve for the night, I want you downstairs on your knees. I laid something out for you."

My full ass was a reminder of what was to come, and the happy vibe of a moment ago dissipated. The fact that he was going to do this in the basement filled me with even more dread. I didn't know why the idea of anal terrified me so much. It wasn't like we hadn't done it before. In fact, he'd introduced anal sex within the first week of blackmailing me into being his.

But things had been different. Back then *everything* about him had terrified me, and I hadn't had a choice.

And you have a choice now?

In a way, I did. Or at least, I had. He'd given me a choice before I'd stupidly let go of my right to refuse on our anniversary. Now anal sex had become this huge *thing* between us—and an even bigger thing in my head—where I waited in dread for him to do it while he taunted me with the fact that he was going to fuck me that way.

And he always took his time, as if he lived to take me in such a demeaning way, drawing out my discomfort and fear along with the mind-blowing orgasm at the end.

I finished bathing Eve and tucked her in for the night, then immediately wished I'd come up with an excuse to stall. Hovering outside her bedroom, I did my best to come up with something that needed to be done *now*.

There was nothing. I'd finished the nightly chores, and Eve was already snoring softly in that precious way she had about her. The only thing left was my avowed duty to my husband.

It was time to be his obedient slave.

I padded down the hall and spied Gage in his office. He sat at his desk, one hand propping up his head while his sharp gaze roamed the screen of his laptop. I should just head down to the basement and prepare. It's what he expected. What he wanted. But I couldn't bring myself to do it. Pushing the door open further, I glanced at the cage in the corner, now hidden behind the facade of a cabinet that locked. The black metal panel stared me in the face whenever I set foot inside his home office, a constant threat. I was one serious misstep away from finding myself back in there.

"Eve in bed?" he asked.

"Yes."

"Do you know how hard I am for you right now?" He didn't lift his head, and I wanted to go to him just to run my fingers through his thick, dark strands.

"No, Master," I said with a nervous swallow. "How hard?"

"Hard enough to break you in two. Don't make me punish you for stalling."

Shit, shit, shit.

He had me wound so tightly I could hardly breathe. I hurried from his office and down the stairs of the basement. Something sat on the end of the bed, just like he'd promised, but it took me a full minute to find the courage to see what it was.

Thigh highs and a garter belt. No panties. That wasn't the distressing part. No, the O-Ring gag and nipple clamps had me pulling my hand back, as did the accompanying note.

Put them on, then wait for me on your knees.

Was I in trouble? But that didn't seem right. He was always the one to put the clamps on and shove the gags in. I couldn't imagine him giving the honor to me if I were about to receive a punishment.

But I hadn't misread the note. He wanted me to do it this time. God, Gage would not be happy until I surrendered every last piece of myself. He'd been slowly breaking me down from the moment he caught me stealing from him.

Even after we'd married, he'd continued to play me like a well-loved guitar.

The Friday Night Ritual, which still occurred without fail. The sly introduction of all the things I'd "negotiated" against before we got married.

No bullwhip? Now used once a month to remind me of how I'd failed him with Ian.

No nipple clamps? Now used whenever he fucking felt like it.

As far as gags went, he didn't wait to catch me in a lie anymore. He used them freely as well. Ever since I'd flirted with disaster all those months ago, he'd basically tossed my hard limits out the window, and he'd been pushing past them ever since.

Week after week with more severity. Pushing just a little...bit...*more.*

My guilt hadn't let me object at first. I'd felt he was justified in doing whatever he wanted, considering what I'd done. But then things had shifted, and we'd found our footing. He'd even returned my cell and the key to my car—albeit with restrictions.

But the hard limits...he kept bulldozing right over them as if they didn't exist.

And I kept surrendering, just as I was doing now, knowing that my ass was about to get fucked. I undressed, then rolled the stockings up my legs, stretched my lips around the gag that was big enough to accommodate his cock, and pinched my nipples tight between his clamps, making sure they hurt like hell because if I didn't, he'd make me regret it.

Unclipping my hair, I let the red locks fall to my shoulders as I dropped to my knees. Hands clasped at the small of my back, and breasts thrust out. I'd perfected this pose over the last year and a half, and he ate it up every time.

He made me wait longer than usual tonight—probably because he wanted me slightly unhinged. By the time his confident gait sounded on the stairs, my nipples were numb, my knees throbbed as much as my pussy did, and drool bathed my chin and chest. I didn't dare look at him. Suddenly, I was scared. This felt like...

Like a punishment.

He sauntered closer, bare feet coming into view, and pushed his eager hands into my hair—hair that had grown by a few inches since I'd whacked it off in anger. Gently, he tilted my chin up.

"I see the confusion in your eyes. You're wondering if you're in trouble." He knew me so well. As he ran his thumb over my lips, tracing the shape of my stretched mouth, I could do nothing but return his stare. "You're not in trouble *this time*, but I am disappointed in you."

I tried talking, despite the humongous gag making my jaw ache, but he pressed a finger to my tongue.

"I wanted you unable to speak for a reason. You're going to listen carefully, Kayla. There is *nothing* between Katherine and me, except for Conner."

He saw me earlier. Damn.

"I have never been unfaithful, baby. Not in the flesh, and certainly not in here," he said, pointing to where his heart beat. "I live and breathe to be your Master. To be your everything."

Couldn't he see that he was? I'd fought it like hell, but in the end, Gage was my everything. I'd given so much of myself to him.

"I only want to protect you. Things are about to get ugly between Katherine and me, and I don't want you caught in the crossfire. She can be downright vindictive when she doesn't get what she wants." He stepped back, lowering his fingers to the front of his unbuttoned slacks, and slowly pulled down the zipper. His cock sprang free, a hard piston already leaking at the tip. "She's not even close to getting me in her bed, and she knows it." He exhaled on a long sigh as he took his cock in his hand and slowly stroked the length from base to tip.

"This is all you, baby. The thought of your mouth on me, the way you submit even when you're scared, the fire you carry around inside of you. I've got a fucking cramp in my wrist from jacking off so much this week."

Crouching in front of me, he pinned me with an earnest gaze full of intensity. "She showed up at my hotel room. I won't lie to you and tell you she wasn't at the conference."

Of course she'd attended. He hadn't fired the bitch—he'd merely transferred her to another office after I'd thrown a fit about her working with him. My eyes must have grown huge with jealous rage. He sifted his fingers through my hair—a habit he'd picked up whenever he figured I needed calming.

"When are you going to learn that you have nothing to worry about?" he asked. "I slammed the door in her face, then I jacked off to thoughts of ramming my cock down your throat. I don't know how much more honest I can get than that."

Matching actions to words, he rose to his feet and shoved his cock through the opening in the gag. He was silky smooth on my tongue and big enough to fill the cavity of my mouth to the back of my throat.

"Ah, fuck, baby. You own me with that wicked mouth. You take my cock so well—better than any woman ever has." His gaze ignited a burn so deep that I felt it to my bones. Every atom in my body sizzled for him, existed solely for this man who had no qualms about turning me inside out.

"Why would I want anyone else when I've got you here on your knees, so fucking eager to please me?"

His words made me light-headed with a sense of power. I

grabbed his hips and brought his shaft deeper until I had him moaning and thrusting in abandon.

"Trust me, baby," he said with a grunt. "You take my cock like you were born for it. Give me your sweet ass too." He grabbed my head between two steady hands and held me in place while he plundered.

He wasn't gentle.

He wasn't merciful.

He had my number, read my body language as if it had been written for him, and he wasn't about to let me steal a shred of power. Self-preservation kicked in, and I pushed against his hips. Useless. He gripped me tighter and rammed his cock more roughly down my throat.

I gagged so hard that my stomach cramped, and my knuckles whitened as my hold on his hips turned to one of desperation. My throat burned, and tears of frustration leaked from the corners of my eyes. I tried relaxing my throat to accommodate his thrusts, but my gag reflex seemed to be on steroids. I glanced up at him, silently seeking mercy, and found his eyes hazed over with domination.

"I own you. Own you, *own* you," he chanted with each plunge. "Fuck, Kayla..." Letting out a ragged groan, he withdrew from my mouth with a quick jerk. "Almost ended me."

Reserved, control-freak Gage was nowhere in sight. In his place was this lust-filled man who was slowly letting his walls crash right before my eyes. I wasn't sure how it was possible for two people to live in the same house, month after month, and never really know each other.

But we'd managed it. I hid parts of myself from him—like that forbidden note at the bottom of my bag which had given me the answer to a question I wasn't supposed to know. Wasn't *allowed* to know. But in this moment, our truest selves shone through, and the protective veil between us lifted. He had me on my knees with my ass plugged and nipples clamped as he fucked my mouth, yet he was as vulnerable as me.

My reaction to seeing him with Katherine had pulled at something inside him. He didn't like that I doubted him. And he had every reason to be upset because he'd never given me a reason to suspect he'd cheat.

But I couldn't say the same for myself. I'd not only given him a reason, but I *had* touched another man, and not just any man, but the one he despised most in the world.

"As much as I adore your mouth," he said, rolling the tip of his shaft against my tongue, "my cock is going in your ass. You can love it, or you can tolerate it. Either way, you're taking it." He pulled out, removed the gag, and hoisted me to my feet. "Get on the bed. I want you on your stomach with your knees tucked under you."

I obeyed his commands, my breathing as erratic as my heart beat. "Like this?"

"Almost. Raise your ass." He climbed behind me. "That's better. Reach behind you and spread your cheeks."

Silence followed his words. This was it. The ultimate surrender.

"Do it now, Kayla."

"Master..." My voice faltered, but my body knew its place before my brain did. I submitted to his orders, even though I found it humiliating. Fingers shaking, I spread my cheeks in invitation, leaving myself open and vulnerable. This was about trust. If I could offer myself while remaining completely still...truly submitting the one hole I didn't want to give...then he'd win this game tonight.

But maybe I would too because meeting the challenge of pleasing him fulfilled me in a way that most would view as sick and wrong. And maybe it was.

But it *felt* right.

Whether or not his cock felt right inside my tight hole

was another story. He inched out the plug that had grown too dry, applied a liberal amount of lube, then held a palm in front of my mouth for good measure.

"Spit."

I spat saliva into his hand.

"Are you wet?" he asked.

"Yes, Master." Shamefully so.

"Good girl. Now beg your Master for a good ass-fucking."

The word *please* was on the tip of my tongue, just waiting to spill off my lips. That single word would give him exactly what he wanted, and in a roundabout way, it would give me what I wanted too.

But the journey was going to hurt like hell. No doubt about it.

"I'm waiting."

"Master...please." My voice sounded small and uncertain.

"Please, what? You're going to have to be more specific."

Gage was at the top of his game, and he wasn't about to back down. Splaying my ass cheeks wasn't enough—he intended to drag the words from my soul.

I cleared my throat and forced my pride down, but it sat in my gut like deadweight. "Please put your cock in my ass, Master."

"Sexiest fucking words I've ever heard." He eased inside me, just the tip at first, and stretched and pushed, gaining more of my ass with each inch forward. Fuck, it hurt. No denying that it did, and I could do nothing but lay there and try to relax, try to accept his girth because he was filling me no matter what.

And that was the most disturbing part of our relationship. Gage didn't need my consent because I'd given it the day I married him. He was in charge. *He* decided all things. Sure, I could change my mind. If I left him.

He knew I wouldn't. He made sure I wouldn't. Our marriage was unhealthy and distorted, but I didn't care anymore. Like a true addict, I kept coming back for more.

With a growl that bordered on possessive, he seated his full length inside my tight space, and somehow, despite the pain and the fear that had grown too big in my head, taking his cock in my ass felt a little like him coming home.

CHAPTER FIVE

Weekends were always busy, especially when Conner came to visit. The kids got along, for the most part, filling the house with their boisterous games and laughter.

Except for when they didn't.

I'd take rambunctious play any day over the bickering going on in the other room, escalating to a feverish pitch with each "stop it!" from Eve. This wasn't good, especially since Gage was trying to catch up on work so we'd have the day to spend with the kids.

Abandoning the pita pockets I was putting together for lunch, I hurried from the kitchen and spotted the two of them sitting side-by-side on the couch in the living room. Conner held a game controller in his hand, but he focused mostly on Eve. Every few seconds, he flicked the crayon she clutched in her fingers, making her draw a jagged line.

"Conner!" I said before Eve could screech in protest again. "Leave her alone. That isn't nice. I'm sure you wouldn't want her picking on you like that."

He sprang up from the couch, tossing the controller onto

a cushion, and faced me with his arms crossed. "You're not my mom. I don't have to listen to you. My mom said so!"

Oh boy. I gaped at Conner for a couple of seconds, trying to come up with an effective response to get through to him, but his angry expression settled into one of apprehension. Conner's blue-eyed gaze darted past me, and I sensed Gage's presence before he spoke.

"Go to your room. *Now.*"

"I hate it here!" Conner stomped toward the hallway in a grand ceremony of disapproval.

Gage sighed. "I'll talk to him." He squeezed my shoulder before following his son.

Helpless frustration burned my eyes. I should've handled the situation better. Unable to sit and do nothing, I told Eve to stay put before creeping down the hall toward Conner's bedroom. Gage had moved the gym equipment into the basement so Conner would have his own space when he visited...which wasn't as often as we'd like, considering Katherine fought Gage every step of the way. If she'd stop being a bitch for one second and do the right thing, maybe Conner wouldn't keep having these outbursts. The poor kid needed a little stability—not random weekend visits with a father he barely knew.

Gage's voice filtered through Conner's open doorway. I hesitated on the outskirts, not knowing if I should intrude or not. Better to stay put. Conner wouldn't likely open up with me there anyway.

"This is stupid. Why do I have to come here?"

"Because you're my son," Gage said, drawing in a deep breath. He softened his tone. "I know this is confusing for you. I know you miss your mom and Sean," he said, referring to Katherine's ex, who, for several years of Conner's life, had been the only father he'd known. But since Katherine's deceit had come to light, Sean had washed his hands of the boy who wasn't biologically his.

"I just wanna go home."

"This is also your home, and you have a family here that loves you too."

"They aren't my family."

"Yes, they are, and I won't put up with you disrespecting Kayla or Eve."

"My mom said they'd be gone soon." Conner's voice hitched. "It's supposed to be me, you, and my mom!"

Heavy silence followed his words, then Gage cleared his throat. "That isn't going to happen, Conner." Footsteps sounded, and Gage muttered for him to take a few moments to calm down before coming out to apologize for his behavior.

Gage halted in the hallway as soon as he caught me lingering outside of Conner's bedroom, his indigo gaze blazing with ire.

"You know how I feel about eavesdropping." Closing the distance between us with purposeful steps, he gently took me by the elbow and escorted me to our bedroom. The lock clicked into place, and he whirled to face me, arms crossed.

"I'd have you on your knees right now if we had time."

"I didn't do anything wrong." The instant the words left my lips, I wanted to yank them back. Okay, so eavesdropping wasn't exactly an innocent act to engage in, but it was a minor fuck-up. The problem with Gage was he punished all infractions, no matter how small.

"You know that's not true," he said, his tone calm and even. Moving around me, he sauntered to the chair he used to dole out spankings and settled into the soft leather. "Which is why you're going to come over here this instant and present your ass. I don't have time for you to stall." He patted his lap.

I blew out an exasperated breath, but I went to him without further prompting and draped over his thighs. He flipped my skirt up and exposed my bare bottom, and a hot tingle erupted between my legs as I waited for the first strike of his palm.

"You're getting wet, aren't you?"

I dropped my head with a groan. "I'm sorry, Master. I can't help it."

"I believe you. So here's what I'm going to do to help you refrain from becoming aroused. I'm going to use a different method of punishment."

Before I could ask about this "different method," he shoved his thumb into my tight hole. Abruptly, violently, and uncompromisingly.

"Ow! Master, please!" I hissed in a breath, clenching my ass around the dry intrusion of his thumb.

"Spanking is losing its effectiveness. Hell, even my belt turns you on, and a punishment should hurt. It should, at the very least, make you uncomfortable. Don't you agree?" Slowly, he withdrew his thumb and forced it back in again.

"Ow!" I shrieked.

"Answer me, Kayla."

"Yes, Master!" Ow, fuck *ow*! He wasn't using a drop of lube, and that made it hurt even more. "I'm sorry! Please, Master. I won't do it again."

"I don't imagine you will after this." The horrible burning eased up for a mere second as he removed his thumb, but relief was short-lived. He pushed it in once more, to the hilt, and stretched my burning anus in every direction.

"Please stop," I sobbed. He hadn't truly hurt me in months. He'd played with my backdoor, even fucked it a couple of times, and of course, he spanked me regularly. But he was correct in assuming spanking no longer worked as a punishment.

"I will not allow you to backtrack in your behavior," he said, keeping his thumb lodged in my ass. "The last time I gave you an inch, you took a hundred fucking miles and ended up in a compromising situation." He let a significant beat pass. "Or do you need to spend some time in the cage to remind you?"

"No! Please, no, Master."

"You know what is and isn't allowed. Eavesdropping has never been and will never be accepted. Do you understand me?"

"Yes, Master."

"I was in there scolding Conner for disrespecting you, only to find you doing the same to me. When I told you I'd speak to him, you knew I meant alone. Did you not?"

"I did. I'm sorry I overstepped." I hesitated, wanting to say more but not sure if I should. Eventually, the need to be heard won. "I hate being left out. I feel like I'm the last to know about everything."

"Baby, I have no intention of leaving you out. I was going to discuss Conner's behavior with you later after I'd talked to him alone." Even though he softened his tone, he did not cease his assault on my ass. "If you want to know something, you need only to ask. Eavesdropping will not be tolerated."

Some tiny part of me acknowledged he was right about the eavesdropping. But the headstrong part of myself—the facet of my being he was most challenged by—called bullshit. Considering his growing fascination with all things anal, I knew he'd find excuse after excuse to use my ass for his sadistic pleasure by putting the stamp of punishment on it.

A girl, no matter how obedient and submissive, could only stay silent for so long. "Is this really a punishment, or is this just another way for you to get your rocks off?"

He laughed, the sound so rich and unexpected that I

jumped. “Both, Kayla. You want to know if my cock is hard? Fuck yeah, it is, in case you hadn’t noticed. If we didn’t have two kids needing us in the other room right now, I’d fuck you senseless.” He dug his thumb in a little more deeply, and I cried out another plea for him to stop.

Useless pleas because Gage operated by his own rulebook, and the word “stop” wasn’t part of his repertoire.

“Hell, I’d fuck this ass senseless, and you’d let me, wouldn’t you, baby?”

The hardwood floor blurred through the tears collecting in my eyes. They weren’t tears of sorrow; they were pure drops of pain burning my eyeballs—a testament of my frustration.

“What if I said no?”

He laughed again. “You don’t know how to say no to me. Let’s talk about the fact that I have you willingly lying across my lap with my thumb up your ass. Does it hurt?”

“Yes!”

He added a sound wallop to my butt cheek in addition to his anal probing. “Address me properly.”

“Yes, Master! It hurts.”

“Does it turn you on?”

“No, Master.” Not unless he added some lube and played with my clit—behavior he wasn’t likely to engage in at the moment.

“Do you like it when I punish your little hole?”

“No, Master.” What type of questions were these?

“Then all things considered, I’d say this is a very effective form of discipline. And it pleases me how willingly you accept it.” With a final swat to my bottom, he removed his thumb and gently helped me off his lap.

Silently, I vowed to be on my best behavior because pleasing him not only made my life easier, but it caused my body to hum in a way I couldn’t help but crave. I dropped to my knees and let my lips linger on his left bare foot, followed by his right.

"Thank you for your discipline, Master."

His eyes widened the slightest bit. He hadn't expected such a display of voluntary acceptance on my part. Truth be told, I hadn't either. But sometimes accepting my place was far better than fighting it. My reward lay in his eyes; a warm hue of appreciation.

"You're welcome. You can always count on my discipline. As for this particular kind of anal punishment, I plan to use it often. So remember that the next time you think of stepping out of line. Not only will I spank your ass, but I will punish your hole as well."

"I understand, Master." I didn't, but I understood it was what he wanted to hear, and the submissive in me delighted at his surprised reaction. Sometimes, a girl just had to keep her Master on his sexy toes. "May I finish fixing lunch now, Master?"

"You may. I'll get the kids ready."

I rose fluidly, aiming for graceful yet sexy, and moved to leave. At the last second, he pulled me onto his lap again, this time to sit.

"I forgot something," he said, voice raspy with sudden desire. His attention fell to my mouth, and in response, I parted my lips. Tangling a fist in my hair, he angled my head and claimed my lips with a ravenous mouth. His tongue pushed inside, battling my own, and we both moaned into the kiss.

Then he let me go as suddenly as he'd grabbed me. "*Now* you may finish making lunch."

CHAPTER SIX

Conner was downright morose during lunch. But at least Eve had bounced back from our rocky morning.

"Then Leah said she liked Toby, but Toby and his stupid friends found out. The boys were so mean to her!" She glared at Conner. "I'll never like boys. Gross."

He glared right back, and that warning glint in his blue eyes sent a chill down my spine. He certainly had the best of Gage in him—his fierce loyalty, for one—but every now and again I glimpsed the same dominant curve to that boy's smile.

But Conner was far from smiling now. He hadn't said a word since we'd all sat down for lunch. To say he was unhappy at losing video game privileges was an understatement. Eve either didn't care, or she was oblivious. She continued her hundred-mile-per-hour chatter.

"I'm sooo glad Leah isn't a boy," she said. "Or we couldn't be friends." Eve scrunched her nose. "But she likes boys!" she said, rolling her eyes. "Why do girls like boys, Mom?" She'd stopped calling me "Mommy" at the start of first grade, because apparently, Leah said it was a baby thing to do.

"That's a good question." Why *did* we put up with men? We not only liked them, but we fucking loved them—even when they left our asses tender from obscene punishments. It was insanity.

"Is Simone still your best friend?" Eve asked me.

The girl had a sharp memory. Before I could answer, Gage interjected.

"Actually, your mom is spending the day with Simone on Monday."

I turned a stunned gaze on him. He shot me a grin, the tilt of his mouth hinting at how happy my submission earlier in the bedroom had made him.

"Your mom works hard around here to take care of us," he told Eve. "I think it's time she had a day to herself. What do you think, kids?"

"Can I go, too? Pleeease?" Eve whined.

"Sorry, princess. You've got school."

Conner shoved his plate away. "Can I be done? I wanna go to my room."

I thought Gage was going to object, but the dejected sigh he let out instead pricked at my heart. He was trying so hard to connect with Conner.

"Go ahead."

The legs of Conner's chair scraped the floor, and he left the room without ceremony. The boy spent most of the day in his room until Gage made him join us for a board game.

And that was how the weekend passed—uneventful and unbearably slow. Normally, it wouldn't bother me so much, but I had plans for the first time in months, set in stone later that night after Gage programmed Simone's number into my cell and gave me permission to call her. For whatever reason, he was giving me a reprieve from the monotony of my life for a day.

My fingers clutched my cell, but I didn't move to make the call. No, my first instinct was to question him on his unexpected generosity, but upon his eyebrow quirk, I shoved my reservations aside and dialed Simone.

Permission was permission. And hell, I was excited at the prospect of a girls' day out.

Regardless, I couldn't help but dissect the implications. Either aliens had taken over Gage's body, or punishing me in the ass had put him in a damn good mood. It was the only explanation I could come up with because Simone had been a sore spot in our recent history ever since she'd come to me about Ian's cancer. Not that Gage had cared for her to begin with, but this was the first time in...*ever* that he'd given me the go-ahead—on his prerogative, for that matter—without so much as a sideways glance.

And that made *me* the suspicious one. It made the stubborn part of my mind latch right onto Katherine again, agonizing over the what-ifs. By the time Monday arrived, I'd given in to the poisonous doubts plaguing me. I was in full-on paranoid mode.

Simone was unusually quiet from across the small table for two at our favorite bistro. Tilting my head, I tried catching her gaze. She'd barely said two words since we'd given the waitress our lunch orders. I knew she wasn't happy with the way I'd gone MIA for the last few months, but I'd naively thought we could pick up where we'd left off. I'd naively thought she'd understand. I should have known better.

"I'm kind of surprised you called," she said, breaking the silence.

"I'm sorry, Simone."

I didn't have a choice.

She'd disagree. Everyone had a choice, she'd say in that indignant tone of hers. The rational part of my brain—the part that wasn't led around by Gage's cock—would agree with her.

"That's all you're going to say after giving me radio silence for so long?"

The waitress arrived with our orders, which gave me a few moments to figure out how to go forward with this tricky conversation. Spilling my guts to her used to be easy, but now tension simmered between us, and I hated every second of it.

"You know I have certain...rules to follow. Things got complicated after..."

After Ian.

So much to discuss, but I couldn't even bring myself to say his name. She shifted, tilted her head, and I recognized the signs. Go on, she silently told me.

"After everything that happened, Gage and I had a lot of issues to work through." What a fucking understatement. She didn't know the half of it. She knew more than most people did about my fucked up arrangement with my husband, but I wasn't about to speak of those torturous months spent in his cage, bound and gagged for my sins. If I opened that can of *disturbingly wrong*, I'd have to justify his actions, and somehow, they only sounded justifiable in my poisoned mind. There was just no way of explaining that to her. "I didn't mean to shut you out, Simone."

She took in a breath, then blew it out, ruffling her blond hair. "I get it. You obviously have baggage you don't want to get into. I'm just glad you're finally back." Her brows furrowed over deep brown eyes. "You are back, right? No more disappearing on me for months at a time?"

A weak smile took hold of my lips. "I think things are starting to settle down again."

"So you worked shit out?"

I heard so much more in that question—all the ones she didn't ask. The ones she would probably never ask because she respected my boundaries too much to pry. Hell, she respected my boundaries better than my husband did.

"We're getting there," I hedged.

"I've got a nosy ear, you know." She fit her palm behind her right ear, and I had to laugh. But then the image of Gage and Katherine whirled through my head and blew that small amount of joy to the next county over.

"I'm scared he's fucking her." The words tore from my mouth before I could stop them. And damn, they weren't even true…entirely. I believed him when he said he wouldn't touch her…didn't I?

"Who?" Simone bit into her BLT sandwich.

"Katherine."

She halted her chewing long enough to raise a brow, then a few moments later, she wiped her mouth with a napkin. "She's still an issue?"

Hell, Katherine had been an issue since the day Gage had first hired me on as his personal assistant. She was the weed that refused to go away. Her presence just spread and spread until the bitch sprang up in the cracks of our marriage.

"I don't know. He swears nothing is going on with her."

"You think he's lying?"

"I…" I replayed his words in my mind, and deep down I knew he'd meant them. "No. Not really. But she just has a way of getting to me. She touches him every chance she gets, shows up at his hotel room—"

"She *what*?"

I nodded, feeling even more miserable. "He said he slammed the door in her face." I wondered what Simone's reaction would be if I told her the rest—how he'd jacked off while imagining his cock in my throat. I parted my lips and drew in a thready breath.

"It really boils down to one thing. Do you trust him?"

She made it sound so easy, but as I examined my feelings and tore apart his words, dissected his actions, I realized that I did. Mostly. There were plenty of things *not* to trust him about—anytime he came near me with his cock at the ready and a belt or whip in his fist, for instance—but on a fundamental level, I did trust him.

If I didn't, why would I keep putting myself through this? Why keep bending and bending and bending?

"I do trust him," I said, swiping my bangs to the side. "I love him. More than I could ever say. More than even makes sense."

"Then I'd put the baby mama out of your head. He married *you*, and though I won't begin to understand or approve of your...weird relationship, he has always come across as pretty fucking whipped."

I almost spluttered my tea all over the table at her words. Gage, whipped? But the more I thought about it, the more it clicked, because when you got down to the nitty-gritty, we had each other wrapped. "I guess you're right. I just wish I could get that woman out of my head. The way she touches him, and the way she glares at me...God, Simone, she makes me see red and green at the same time."

"You need a fucking hobby." Simone's mouth twisted into a scowl, but her gaze softened as she said it to take out some of the sting.

"A hobby?" I asked, absently picking at my half-eaten quiche. Apparently, the subject of Katherine made me lose my appetite. Or maybe it was the smell of overcooked cheese. I pushed the plate away, scrunching my nose. "Why do you say that?"

Simone made a scoffing sound, and I glanced up to find

her reclined in her seat, arms crossed. "To hear you talk, it sounds like your whole life revolves around Gage and what he may or may not be doing with Katherine."

A hobby might not be a bad idea. Maybe I could start collecting trinkets, like dolphins or dragons.

Or elephants.

Definitely elephants. Lord knew I had plenty of those in my life. Gigantic ones that ate up too much space and sucked up all the air. One stood between Gage and me in the form of Katherine. But the biggest one sat smack in the middle of Simone and me.

This elephant's name was Ian, and he'd grown too secure in his comfy spot since that damn note had magically appeared on my door. But it was easier, *safer*, to focus on my marriage and the interloper named Katherine. The subject of Ian was too dangerous. Too painful.

Simone must have agreed because she didn't bring him up once. Not to tell me he was okay—the note had already done that—and certainly not to tell me whether or not she'd spoken to him or seen him.

And maybe it was better this way.

"If you're really worried about Katherine," Simone said, "then talk to Gage. Just be honest with him. Tell him how you're feeling."

She made it sound simple. If only it were that easy.

CHAPTER SEVEN

The following day I met Gage in his office at Channing Enterprises to work on the charity ball project, but it wasn't until Wednesday when I finally found my lady balls to broach the subject of Katherine. Even then, it took me a good hour of perusing color schemes while situated firmly on his lap, distracted beyond belief by his depraved hands.

"So this is your final decision?" Gage asked, gesturing by way of a nod toward the various colors, fabric textures, and decorations splashed across the screen of his laptop. His fingers tapped a staccato beat on top of his desk.

"You said elegant and sexy."

He pressed a kiss to my neck, and I felt the curve of his smile. "Mmm, you most certainly are."

"Did you really need my help with this, or were you just looking for an excuse to have me on your lap for a few days?"

"I never need an excuse to have you on my lap, Kayla. For any reason."

Damn, he was turning me on.

"Truth is," he said, "I miss you here at the office. I

wouldn't mind you coming back as my assistant if that's something you'd like to do."

I angled my head and shot a wide-eyed gaze at him. "Are you serious?"

"Absolutely."

"I'd love to." More than love to. I ached to fill the void that leaving the workforce had caused.

"Then consider it a done deal." He pressed his mouth to mine before focusing on our project again. "Besides, where would I be without you? You pulled this together in two days flat, fixing the blunders of the idiots I hired to do this job in the first place."

Two days seemed too long for the amount of work I'd done, but at least I'd finally whittled the color scheme down to burgundy, mahogany, and the accent color of gold. "I'm thinking creme china trimmed in gold, red masks with gold feathers for centerpieces—like those," I said, pausing to point at a picture, "and sable linens for the tables."

The visual made me think of sex and sin—just like that restaurant had the night he'd taken me there before our anniversary. Riding his cock in that private dining booth had been terrifying and exhilarating. I wasn't comfortable with public displays of indecency, but apparently, Gage had an exhibitionist streak in his blood. God, the surprises kept coming when it came to my husband.

Thing was, I was tired of being the last to know about shit. Taking comfort in his assertion over the weekend that I need only to ask, I finally found the words and did just that. "Why was Katherine here last week?"

He stilled the casual tapping of his fingers. "Was that so hard?"

I narrowed my eyes. "What?"

"Asking about Katherine. Was it so difficult to come out and say what's on your mind?" His fingers resumed their tapping. "You've taken to eavesdropping lately, and I don't like it. You don't have to be afraid to come to me, baby. I'd rather know what's on your mind than assume and guess."

"I'm sorry."

"Don't be sorry. Just tell me what's on your mind."

"Why does she keep coming here?" My breath hitched. Lord knew I wanted an explanation, but now that one was forthcoming, I didn't know if I were ready.

"She's the mother of my child. I'm afraid we're not getting rid of her anytime soon."

"She's only using Conner as an excuse to see you, and you know it."

"I won't deny it."

His words tunneled deep, impacting the center of my being. "But you promised nothing is going—"

"Because nothing *is* going on." He took my right nipple between two punishing fingers. "Don't you trust me?"

"I...I want to," I whispered, barely able to form the words beyond my pounding heartbeat and the piercing ache in my nipple.

"Well that's great to hear, Kayla," he said, tone brimming with sarcasm, "because I've been trying so fucking hard to trust you again. I need you to do the same. Katherine is not a threat to you. I promise you that."

"But she wants you." The admission soured my tongue.

"Yes, she does, and being the bastard that I am, I can't help but throw my hot-as-fuck wife in her face every chance I get. Does that explanation make you happy?"

Oh, yeah. More than it should. But it did nothing to alleviate the doubt in my heart. Gage might not be fucking her now, but what if he changed his mind someday? What if, years later, he grew bored with me?

"You said I was playing with fire with—"

"Don't you dare say his name." He practically growled

the words, his voice beyond harsh, and his grip on me even harsher. "I will beat your ass red if you say his name."

"How is that fair? Katherine is like a fucking leech that won't let go, and you keep encouraging her. You're playing with fire, just like I was."

"I'm not interested in sleeping with Katherine, and I'm sure as fuck not in love with her. That's the difference."

I felt my face heat with humiliation and regret. How could I respond to that? I couldn't.

"I look at that cage every night," he said, "and I *yearn* to lock you in there forever. Then I'd know you're mine."

"But I am yours. Can't you see that?"

"Prove it to me."

"How?" I asked, voice rising in disbelief. What more could I possibly do to prove it to him?

"The night of the ball. It just happens to be a Friday, and I have special plans for you afterward."

"But..." I trailed off, confused. "I take your punishment every Friday without complaint. What more do you want from me?"

"Everything, Kayla. I want everything." He gestured to the color schemes on the screen, his index finger hovering over a photo of a jeweled mask in burgundy. "I told you about the charity ball, but I didn't tell you about our plans afterward." Grabbing my hair, he tilted my head back and placed his warm lips on my neck. "After the masqueraders leave and it's just a handful of Portland's most wealthiest deviants, I want you to submit *everything* to me. No ands, ifs, buts, or whys. I say spread your legs, and you ask, 'How wide, Master?'"

A lump formed in my throat—a mass of sickening fear. "You want to fuck me in front of other people?"

"I want you to submit in front of other people."

"I don't know if I—"

"I don't care about your feelings on this. You will do as I say." He pushed me from his lap. "Because you always do what I say." His gaze lowered to his hard-on. "Get on your knees and suck me off."

Yielding to his command, I knelt between his legs. His desk hid most of my body, but he pushed back a few inches to give me more room. Shoving the masquerade ball and what would come after from my mind, I had him unbuckled, unzipped, and his cock in my mouth in about five seconds flat.

He pushed his hands into my hair and gripped the strands, holding me to his lap with suffocating force.

"I guess now would be a good time to tell you that Katherine will be here any minute."

The movement of my eager tongue stalled around his shaft, and I tried pulling away, but he wouldn't let me. With a groan, he forced his cock deeper. "Take it all, baby. I want her to see how fucking unglued your mouth makes me. I want her to see this, Kayla. Let's give her a show she won't forget."

This plan of his excited me too much, and I gagged extra hard. He wound my hair around his fist and drew my lips up and down his velvety cock. As my lips closed around the tip, I raised my eyes to his, entranced by the startling blue depth of his need for me.

"God, you're sexy," he breathed.

A quick rap sounded an instant before a door creaked open then closed. Feminine footsteps crossed the room. Over the ruckus of heels, I detected the soft groan that escaped Gage's tight lips.

"I'm glad you called," Katherine's said in her grating voice, "though I would have met you someplace more private. Your office isn't my idea of—"

"As you can see," he said with a grunt, responding to the

way I worked the underside of his cock, "I don't care about privacy. I get what I want, where I want, and when I want. And right now I want my wife's very talented mouth wrapped around my cock while I give you these." The sound of rustling papers drifted to where I knelt on the floor, and as he slid them across the desk, he leaned forward, thrusting deeper.

Silence ensued for a few heavy seconds. "What is this?"

"A petition for parenting time."

I imagined Katherine's beet-red face and envisioned steam coming out of her ears.

"We were working out visitation just fine. You don't need to do this!"

"If you mean you used our son as a bargaining chip, then yes, I do imagine the status quo was working in your favor."

"Gage!"

"Do not fuck with me, Katherine. You won't like the outcome." Voice stringent with a warning, he fisted my hair even tighter, and I felt his thighs quake under my clenched hands. He was losing his shit, though it was a toss up if his crumbling composure was a result of his argument with Katherine, or from the way I swirled my tongue around the head of his cock. I studied his face and found a mixture of both.

"I'll see you in court." A telling tick hardened his jaw an instant before he showed his teeth. "Now get out of my office so I can properly fuck my wife."

An indignant huff sounded, followed by stomps and a slam of the door. Gage yanked me to my feet, lifted me with one arm as he shoved the laptop out of our way with the other, and we crashed onto his desk. I wrapped my legs around him, my skirt bunching around my waist.

"Wish you could have seen her face," he said as he thrust into me with unapologetic violence. My body slid across his desk from sheer force. He crushed his lips to mine and devoured, our tongues tangling as he slammed my hands to the surface of his workspace. Clamping a hand around my wrists, he pinned them above my head as he plundered me into oblivion.

Fucked me to Neverland.

Loved me with more passion and obsession and loyalty than I deserved.

This crazy, obscene, and powerful man loved me. He hungered for me so much that he was about to rattle the screws loose that held his desk in one piece. He was definitely rattling the screws loose that held my mind together. With each thrust of his cock, they shifted a little more, slowly working their way out of the holes in my head. This was how my will shattered, how my sanity and the very essence of who I was broke into pieces.

Then he'd take those pieces and play with them as if they belonged to his favorite puzzle—one custom made for him. Maybe I was. Maybe I was born to be broken down and put back together by him.

"Fuck, baby," he said, pulling his mouth from mine. "If you believe nothing else, believe how much I belong to you. Feel me, Kayla." He slowed to a crawl, his cock annihilating me with measured strokes meant to push me right to the edge.

"The energy between us doesn't lie. It's more than fucking. It's mutual ownership. You have my heart. You *are* my heart."

Tears flooded my eyes, and a sob strangled from my well-kissed lips. My pussy clenched once around him, begging to go over the edge. Begging, always begging.

"I love you, Master."

"Ah fuck." He let go of my hands and engulfed me in an embrace rife with possessive restraint. "I love you so damn much." He huffed ragged breaths against my ear. "Come for me. Come so fucking hard the entire building hears it. Do it, baby."

When he was this worked up, holding back was impossible. I clenched around the steel-like shaft of my husband and cried his name at a decibel I was sure even Katherine heard.

"God, you feel good. So fucking good, squeezing my cock like you own it." His fingers grasped my hair and pulled.

I let out a high-pitched mewl, instantly forgetting where I was. In fact, I was pretty sure I forgot my own name. "Master," I cried, tears wetting my cheeks. "I need you...need you so much—ahhh! Don't stop! Oh God! Not yet."

I thought I'd plummeted off the cliff already, but I'd merely been floating, weightless in my desire for him. That first orgasm had been extraordinary, but this...I had no words, and no mind left to keep my wits about me. My cries escalated to a pitch that was ear-splitting. He shoved a sweaty palm over my mouth.

"They've heard enough. This is only for me." He swiveled his hips, his shaft rubbing in a way that slowly marched me to my end. I was going to tear myself apart in his arms. We fucked all the time, so why this time was so different, I didn't know. More emotions were involved, more *feeling*, more...everything.

"There, baby. You're *right* there, aren't you?" His lips curved into a sly grin. "But you're not coming again."

"Why?" I whimpered into his palm, eyes wide with a plea for mercy. Why was he doing this to me now? There was no way I could hold back, and the way he moved inside me told me he knew it. No, that sparkle in his indigo eyes spelled it out.

"Because I said so. But what I say doesn't matter right

now, does it? You love my cock so much you're gonna cream all over it anyway."

I squirmed underneath his powerful body, spewing muffled protests into his sweaty palm.

"You don't have my permission." He closed his eyes for a moment and let out a harsh breath, then he removed his hand from my mouth.

Our bodies moved together like a well-oiled machine. We were meant to interlock in exquisite harmony, in rapturous agony. He was born to own, and I was designed to bend to his iron will.

"Please, Master," I whined. "Please let me come again."

"What will I get in return?"

"Anything you want."

"Be careful what you promise," he groaned. "I'll always hold you to your word."

Oh, he was sadistic as hell. I had no weapon to fight him, nor the strength. He plunged me to the heights of another orgasm—one that would cost me greatly—and as I contracted around his cock, I didn't miss that familiar devil's smile.

CHAPTER EIGHT

My time spent in Gage's office this afternoon had left me fucked on an emotional level. But it also shot me to a high from which I never wanted to come down. However, as soon as I pulled into my driveway and spotted Katherine's shiny red car sitting in Gage's parking spot, my mood plummeted so fast it could have caused whiplash.

She alighted from her vehicle with grating nonchalance as I shut off the ignition. Her arms, enhanced by subtle muscles that some men found sexy, crossed over the white bosom of her suit. I hated how she managed to embody the definition of *put-together*. Her red lips matched her nails to perfection, and hell...I wasn't blind. She'd look perfect and gorgeous on Gage's arm—another observation that gutted me.

Shoving aside my petty, envious thoughts, I headed to the front door, muttering a "what do you want?" on the way.

"Don't be nasty, Kayla. I'm only here to talk, woman to woman."

I unlocked the door before turning to confront her toxic presence. "We have nothing to talk about." Shooting her a fake smile, I added, "So why don't you take your jealous ass home and go cry into a pint of Ben & Jerry's?"

Much to my irritation, she didn't seem affected by the barb. Casually, she glanced at her diamond-studded watch. "In about an hour, the only thing I'll be gorging on is your husband's cock." Her icy blue eyes widened, feigning incredulity. "You didn't think you were the only one sampling that fine cock, did you?"

"Get the fuck off of my property," I seethed.

She tsked-tsked. "You're just the trophy wife, Kayla. So that makes this *his* property. I'll leave when I'm ready."

I folded my arms and prayed for composure because I was two seconds away from tearing into her flawlessly made-up mug. I thought of Eve, and how she needed her mother at home instead of in jail.

Katherine pursed her painted lips. "Don't get me wrong. I'm sure Gage enjoys having you cook and clean and cater to his cock at his beck and call, but I've got a child to think about too. So I'm here to give it to you straight. Gage is in love with me. He's been fucking *me* for months, ever since he found out about Conner." For a fraction of a second, she had the nerve to appear contrite. "It's really not fair to you, or to me, so I think it's past time you know."

Clinging to my outward front of stoicism, I remained silent. But a porno of epic proportions flashed through my mind, starring Katherine and my husband, and I found my pretense in jeopardy of crumbling at any second.

Don't lose your shit now.

"You don't believe me, do you?"

"I trust my husband." Even as I said the words, I couldn't ignore the ever-present niggle of doubt. Forget the hypothetical porno. The memory of Katherine on her knees crashed into me with the violence of a hurricane. I ached to wash the recollection in red, ached even more to tear into the bitch and scratch the smugness from her face, blast the haughtiness from the curve of her pouty mouth.

I wanted her blood on my hands. I'd spatter every last piece of clothing Gage owned with crimson if he were fucking her.

Combing a manicured hand through her blond curls, she sauntered toward her car. The click-clack of her heels was akin to nails on a chalkboard.

"We both know there's no love lost between us, but you need to know the truth. I'm the mother of his child, and I refuse to be the mistress. Since he doesn't have the balls to tell you, then you need to come see for yourself."

She was lying. She had to be. Gage wouldn't...he *wouldn't.* If there was one thing I knew about Gage Channing, it was that I was the center of his universe.

Then why did she look so...triumphant?

I shook my head, refusing to buy into her lies. But as she pulled her car door open, lifting a shoulder as if to say, "Fine, don't say I didn't warn you," my lips parted and betrayed me.

"Where?"

She walked to my car and set a keycard on the hood. "The Hilton," she said, then rattled off a room number.

I waited until she slid into her driver's seat and backed out of the driveway before snatching the keycard from my hood. And as her luxury sedan disappeared down the road, I chewed over the decision ahead. I had three options.

Option A: Call Gage.

Option B: Ignore what Katherine had said.

Option C: Walk into that hotel room in an hour and see for myself.

The first option was not only the smartest, but it was the only option that would keep me out of trouble. The second was the most maddening, and the third was the one my unwavering doubt would demand I go with, to hell with the consequences. If checking this out for myself and finding that she was lying—that my husband was *not* cheating—would land me in hot water with Gage, then I'd accept the consequences. At least then, I'd finally be able to put these doubts to rest.

An hour later, I found myself creeping toward the door of an upper-floor room of the Hilton. Whatever lay beyond, I would accept and deal with it. But if what Katherine claimed were true...

Could I find the strength to forgive him? I wasn't sure, and that drove home how difficult it must have been for him to forgive my betrayal. I loved him so much at that moment, needed him more than I ever had because we'd both made mistakes, yet somehow we still formed a united front.

At least, I fucking hoped we did.

Sucking in a fortifying breath, I swiped the card and slowly pushed the door open. Nervous energy tingled down my spine as I crossed the threshold. With each step forward, my heels moving silently over the light textured carpet, I felt as if I were stepping into a bear trap, metal claws just waiting to rip into flesh.

Because if Gage were having an affair in this suite, wouldn't I hear something? And this hotel...it wasn't his style. Clearly, the room was a corner suite, outfitted with plush furniture that complimented the neutral theme of the space. Straight ahead, I spied two sitting chairs, but both were empty.

The place was nice, though nowhere near Gage's high standards. If he were going to cheat, I'd expect him to fuck me over in the Presidential suite of a place like the Heathman, at the very least.

I cleared the wall partitioning the vanity and bath area from the rest of the suite and found the king bed empty as well. The white comforter hadn't been disturbed, and the drapes were wide open, affording a view of the neighboring skyscrapers of downtown Portland.

What kind of sick game was Katherine playing? I reached for my cell. Calling Gage would mean he'd find out how I'd doubted him, and that would mean a harsh punishment on top of his hurt and disappointment, but I needed answers—answers only he could provide at this point.

A beep sounded, and the quiet swish of the door reached my ears, followed by the soft pad of feet. I put my phone away and watched with a mixture of curiosity and apprehension. The last person I expected to see was Ian.

Apparently, he felt the same way. We both froze, eyes wide as we took each other in. I opened my mouth, trying to find a string of words that would make sense, but could find none. My mind raced ahead, mentally cataloging every detail of him—the healthy tint of his face and the subtle weight he'd put on since the last time I saw him.

Without thinking, I launched myself at him, overcome by too many emotions to name, and just held on to him. Tears dripped from my eyes, running in rivulets down my cheeks before soaking his black shirt.

"I'm sorry," I said with a sniffle. "I'm just so glad to see that you're okay."

He stepped back and tilted my head up with a gentle finger underneath my chin. "Hey, don't cry. I'm fine."

Nodding, I wiped my eyes, and the precarious predicament I now found myself in hit me hard. I stumbled toward the bed, only stopping when my legs gave out, and I sank onto the end in a stupor.

"But I am confused as to why you're here," he said as he claimed a spot on the other side of the mattress, being sure to keep plenty of distance between us.

"Umm," I blinked several times, running my fingers over

the down comforter. "Katherine told me she and Gage..." Humiliation burned my cheeks, and I felt utterly ridiculous for believing her, for falling for her lies. I let out a long sigh that blew my bangs out of my eyes. "God, I was so stupid to believe her."

"You're not the only gullible one," he said. "I got a message that Gage wanted to meet with me, accompanied by this." He held up an identical key card.

"Bitch set us up," I muttered.

"Why would she do that?"

"Because she wants Gage, and..."

"And?" Ian prompted.

Oh, God. Panic fisted my heart, and all I could see was my husband's cock just mere inches from her lips. And Gage's threat that if I touched another man again...I covered my mouth, suddenly feeling sick. Upchucking would accomplish nothing, besides more embarrassment. I pushed down the burn of vomit in my throat and dropped my hand.

"I can't talk about it, so please don't ask." How could I be so fucking stupid? But damn, I still couldn't bring myself to regret that hug. Not one bit. Because the last time I'd laid eyes on Ian Kaplan, I'd been certain his death was imminent. But here he was, alive and healthy and...ironically all because the brother who hated his guts had found a morsel of mercy in his sadistic blood.

"Last thing I want is to cause you trouble," Ian said. "After the way I behaved earlier this year...."

"This isn't your fault. This is Katherine's doing, and I'll explain that to Gage." Never mind that he would be furious. I eyed Ian. Now that he was here, I could finally get some answers. "He told me what he did for you."

"Did he tell you his terms as well?"

Averting my gaze, I nodded. "You're not supposed to be here."

His mouth flattened into a stubborn line. "I know that's what he wants, but I can't live my life with our history hanging over my head forever. Don't you think it's time we put this behind us?"

"Of course I do! But Gage would rather burn in hell first. He's not going to budge."

"Well, getting a second chance at life has made me see things in a new light, Kayla. I have no control over what he does, or how he treats you." His hazel eyes, overflowing with the familiar kind of warmth I ached to wrap myself in, held me captive. "You're a strong, capable woman, so when you say you love him, I'm going to take you at your word." A beat passed. "I'm going to believe that you know what you're doing and can protect yourself."

"What are you trying to say?"

"I'm not leaving Portland, and I'm sorry if that's going to cause you problems." He shuttered his eyes for a moment. "I'm sorry if my decision to come back gets you hurt. But I've gotta live my life. I've accepted a job here, and..."

I raised my brows. "And?"

"And I'm seeing someone."

"Simone?"

He cocked his head in surprise. "How did you know?"

"Just a hunch."

And it was at that precise moment, as we were finally on the cusp of putting all of our cards on the table, of burying past hurts and broken dreams, that another beep rang through the hotel room. A hint of footsteps kept me in suspense, breath stalling in my lungs. Terror tore through me, and my back stiffened, as my first thought was that Katherine had sent Gage.

But those footsteps weren't confident like my husband's. He had a unique way of walking, in which every step touched the ground with complete ownership of the path he chose to walk. These footfalls were dainty, completely feminine. When Katherine came into view, I shouldn't have been surprised. Of course she'd want to witness the coup she'd pulled off single-handedly.

However, I was even less prepared for the camera flash that went off in our faces.

CHAPTER NINE

For the next two days, I stewed over one question: when would Katherine drop her bomb? Confessing to Gage was inevitable, but anytime I came close to opening up to him about what I'd unwittingly stepped into, my throat closed up on me.

I couldn't eat, couldn't sleep. Hell, I was so twisted up over Katherine's trickery—and her ultimatum that I leave Gage or she'd show him the photo—that I'd puked twice in 24 hours. At first, I thought it was due to stress, but then Eve came down with a stomach bug, so I blamed my sickness on a virus. Katherine and her nasty ultimatum faded into the background, as taking care of Eve trumped everything.

The scent of vomit seemed to cling to my skin. My poor baby hadn't been able to keep anything down for the past two hours since I'd picked her up from school. At least the worst had passed. I smoothed a palm over her hair while she snuggled into her princess themed sheets, lashes lowering from exhaustion. Gage would be home soon, so that didn't give me much time to shower.

Ten minutes later, as I towel-dried my hair, I heard his

car pull into the driveway. I dropped the towel in the laundry hamper, ignoring how it hung over the side, and moved down the hall in time to greet him in the foyer.

"How's Eve doing?" Gage had barely stepped through the front entrance, smelling of autumn and pure sexy man, before he set his laptop case by the door, which was so unlike him. "I came as soon as I could. Where is she?"

"In bed." I hastened to keep up with his urgent stride as he headed down the hall toward Eve's bedroom. Finding her fast asleep, he stalled in the open doorway and let out a breath. I placed a hand on his back, touched by his concern.

"She's feeling much better. You didn't have to rush home from work."

He whirled, grabbed my arm, and pulled me a couple of feet down the hall. "Of course I did. You said she had a fever. She was puking..." Pacing a few steps, he pushed his hands into his hair.

"It's just a stomach bug. There's a lot of nasty stuff going around right now." I lowered my voice. "Really, Gage. I talked to her doctor. She doesn't think there's any reason to worry."

He turned to face me again, and something dark haunted his eyes. "How can you be so calm? So fucking sure? What if she's...?"

Sick again.

I swallowed hard to keep hysteria from choking me. The fear that she would get sick again bordered on paranoia, and it would pull me into weeks, or even months of despair if I let it. I crossed the few feet separating us and wound my arms around him.

"I spent a whole year in Texas, in and out of the hospital. Every cough, every fever...I was a basket case convinced she was going to come out of remission."

"I hate that you had to go through that alone." Gage

practically crushed me in his arms. "You're not alone now. Never again, baby."

Blinking back tears, I held on a little tighter. Eve coming down with any illness, no matter how common or normal, would always send me spiraling, and that was why I'd slowly learned to cope instead of freak out.

"She'll be fine," I said. "Remember the last time she got a cold? You went all protective daddy on her then too."

Which made me love him a million times more.

Exhaling on a sigh, he let me go. "Okay, I'll try to scale down the overprotective parent role. But Kayla...I can't help it. She's our girl."

I wanted to launch myself at him again, only this time with no clothing barring us from becoming a tangle of two bodies made for each other. I reached for his face, figuring I could settle for a kiss, but the hallway seemed to tilt. I shuffled backward until my spine hit the wall.

Gage frowned. "What's wrong?"

"I don't know. I'm a little dizzy."

"Did you eat lunch?"

"Umm...not that I can remember." I'd been too worried about Eve to eat, and too busy taking care of her to find time to have lunch anyway. At the thought of food, my stomach revolted. What little I had eaten earlier that day rose so unexpectedly that making it to the bathroom wasn't a possibility. I tipped forward and vomited in the hallway, narrowly missing Gage's shiny black dress shoes.

He helped me to the bathroom and held back my hair as I lost more of my stomach's meager contents. "I'm sorry," I gasped during a spell. "Guess Eve's not the only one—"

My whole body seized, muscles tensing as vomiting turned to dry-heaving. "Oh God," I moaned. The dry-heaves lasted for maybe a minute, but it felt like forever. I fell back into Gage's arms, utterly spent.

"I happen to know a bed with your name on it," he said, carrying me as if I weighed nothing. Though his tone was light, he couldn't hide the worry in his eyes as he tucked me between our silky sheets.

"Thank you, Master."

Brushing the damp hair back from my head, he frowned. "Don't 'Master' me now, Kayla. Just rest. I'll keep an eye on Eve."

My eyelids suddenly felt as if they weighed a ton, but the fact that I was sick too was a huge relief. "See," I mumbled, halfway to a much-needed slumber. "She's fine. It's just a bug."

"Hopefully a short-lived one."

"Tonight's Friday, after all," I said. Now would be the time to tell him about my accidental meeting with Ian. Then I could wash away my guilt over doubting Gage with the force of his punishing arm. But I didn't have any strength left, and I'd already spilled my guts enough for one day. I tried to muster a small smile, uneasy with the dark cloud hanging over my head. "Wouldn't want a pesky illness to get between your belt and my ass."

"You mean bullwhip," he said.

"It's been a month already?"

The sculpted shape of his jaw hardened. Hell, he was so damn beautiful. "It's been a month," he confirmed. "But I'm not about to use the bullwhip on you while you're sick, so we'll put an extension on it."

"An extension with interest?"

"We're discussing an ass-whipping, Kayla." He rolled his eyes. "Not negotiating a complex contract."

He was the king of complexity. Everything he did was calculated to break down another layer of my protective armor. A few hours later, after Eve and I sipped chicken broth and managed to keep it down, I sat in bed flipping through a fashion magazine.

Gage tucked Eve in for the night before returning to our bedroom. "You seem to be feeling better."

"I am," I said, putting aside the magazine as he settled onto the edge of the mattress.

His dark brows furrowed over indigo blue. "Could you possibly be…pregnant?" A note of hope colored his voice, ripping my heart to shreds.

"I don't think so." A small part of me wanted to hope too, but…

No.

Not worth the agony. Besides, I'd had a period a couple of weeks ago. "It was just the stomach flu." My shoulders slumped. "What if…?"

He took my hand and folded our fingers together. "What is it?"

"What if it's not in the cards for us?"

"I will not allow you to give up hope. Someday, I'm going to watch my child grow inside your gorgeous body. Have some faith, baby."

Faith didn't come easy. Deep down, I knew I'd disappoint him, and in more ways than one. Not only would I fail to conceive his child, but delaying my confession about Ian's return would crush him.

Crush him and make him irate enough to go off the rails.

CHAPTER TEN

By Saturday afternoon, Eve had fully recovered and was back to her rambunctious self, so we let her spend the night with Leah. Since we were kid-free for an evening, Gage took me out and wined and dined me.

"You're unusually quiet tonight," he said, taking a sip of his red wine. "Are you feeling under the weather again?"

"No, I'm fine." I gave him a small smile, but I felt sick as I forced a bite of steak down my throat. The need to spill my guts was eating me alive.

My reprieve from the Friday Night Ritual wouldn't last much longer. After we returned home from dinner, he would take the bullwhip to my ass. Time was running out. I had to find the courage to tell him about Katherine's trickery because I'd rather withstand a brutal punishment all at once and get it over with than suffer through his ritual, only to be punished again once he found out.

And he would find out. Katherine hadn't gone to all of that trouble for nothing. She would send that photo to Gage eventually. My only advantage was coming clean before she did.

"You don't look fine. You seem upset."

A nervous breath escaped my mouth. "I did something you're not going to like." What an understatement.

He paused, fork dangling halfway to his mouth, and darkness shadowed his features for a moment. But then he quickly washed his face of it. "Finish your dinner, Kayla. Whatever it is, you can tell me when we get home."

"Okay," I said, relief choking that single word. There was no going back. Now that he knew there was something to tell, he would pry it out of me. I no longer had to agonize over how and when—it was in his hands now.

The rest of our meal slid down my throat, mostly tasteless. As for the wine, I'd barely taken two sips, knowing I'd need a clear head to handle what was to come. We left the restaurant, and he escorted me to the car with one hand pressed gently to the small of my back.

Heavy silence overshadowed the drive home, and the quick twenty-minute jaunt from the restaurant seemed much longer. Halfway through, Gage took my hand in his and offered his support. It was a simple gesture meant to reassure me that I could come to him about anything. But even as his fingers entwined with mine, I couldn't help but notice the anxious downturn of his mouth, and the way he steered the car single-handedly, his knuckles turning whiter with every mile.

As soon as we pulled into the driveway, Gage let go of my hand, and I missed the warmth of his touch instantly. He rounded the hood and opened my door—ever the gentlemen despite the brutality of his dominance. The wind rushed through the trees, scattering autumn leaves in a whirl. As we approached the front door, a cold drop of rain fell onto my nose.

"Just tell me one thing," he said, ushering me into the foyer. "Were you unfaithful?" His voice shook with nervous anger. But his eyes...fear had taken over, leaving him open and defenseless. It was such a foreign look on Gage that I did a double-take to make sure I wasn't hallucinating.

I wasn't. My dominant husband was terrified of what I might say.

Unable to help myself, I fit my palm against his cheek. Not touching him was impossible. "I haven't been unfaithful. I promise."

"Address me properly, Kayla." Warning tinged his tone. Now was not the time to fuck up on protocol.

"I'm sorry, Master." I sank to my knees, then dipped even further to kiss his shoes. "I wasn't unfaithful," I repeated.

Never again would I cheat on him, but he obviously still had reservations, or he wouldn't have brought it up the instant we crossed the threshold. Lifting my chin, I saw some of the worry fade from his gorgeous eyes.

He held out a hand. "Come on," he said, hauling me to my feet. After he removed my cashmere sweater and shed his overcoat, he ordered me to prepare for him in the basement. I'd known that was where I'd end up tonight, but a chill still tingled down my spine.

"Yes, Master." As I moved in the direction of his dungeon, limbs weak, I spied him pulling at his tie from the corner of my eye. Because he was eager to dress down to punish me? Or because the tension spiraling between us was choking him? I unlocked the door to the basement, switched on the light, and descended the stairs, chewing over his reaction the whole way.

I was Gage's only real weakness—something I failed to remember between the rituals and rigid expectations. He'd imprinted his power and mastery onto my soul, and I often forgot that underneath the confident veneer of dominance and control lived a vulnerable man with family issues.

And ex-girlfriend issues.

How could I prove to him that I wasn't going anywhere?

As I unzipped my dress and let it slide to the floor, the answer to that question tormented me. The only way to prove my loyalty was on my knees, unwavering in my surrender to his disciplinary decisions, no matter how intense the degradation and pain. I unclasped my bra, stepped outside the puddle of Haute Couture at my feet, and kneeled, preparing to speak Gage's language in the form of "yes, Master."

About fifteen minutes later, the door creaked open, and his loud footfalls brought him down the stairs. He walked with heavy feet as if the next hour or two weighed on his shoulders as heavily as they did mine. A single glance at his expression—eyes narrowed, jaw tense, and a pasty hue to his skin—and I knew I was too late. Katherine had gotten to him. As if to confirm my suspicion, he tossed a photo onto the floor in front of me.

"That just hit my inbox." He gestured to the incriminating evidence. "Is this what you need to tell me about?"

A glossy photo stared me in the face. Though Ian and I sat with plenty of space between us, our identical caught-in-the-headlights expressions made us look guilty. So did the fact that we were sitting on a bed in a hotel room.

"I can explain, Master."

"Can you, now?" He arched a contemptuous brow. "You said you weren't unfaithful. But Kayla," he said, crouching to confront me at eye level. "As far as I'm concerned, you cheated the instant you had any form of contact with him."

"It wasn't intentional, Master." God, I despised how tiny my voice sounded. How wobbly and terrified. The disconcerting part was the *why* of my fear. I wasn't afraid of getting punished—that was inevitable, and I'd accept it. No, what had my gut turning was his reaction to that picture. He wasn't only angry, but his entire body exuded betrayal, from the strain of his voice to the devastation in his eyes whenever his attention fell on the image of me with his brother.

"Wasn't *intentional*?" he said, rising to his full height. "Let me guess—someone kidnapped you and dropped you on that fucking bed with him. How convenient."

"I went there looking for you!" I squeezed my eyes shut, horrified at losing my cool. Raising my voice to my Master was never tolerated, a fact that was abundantly clear when I lifted my lids and found Gage rifling through the drawer where he kept my least favorite things. He strode toward me with a ball gag clutched in his hand. His breaths heaved in and out, and his massive chest expanded with every draw of air.

"Explain yourself." He dangled the humongous gag in front of my trembling lips.

Suddenly, I didn't want to explain. Recounting Katherine's unwelcome visit and how I'd fallen for her bullshit…no, how I'd doubted *him*…was almost more than I could stand.

"You're only making this harder on yourself," he warned.

The need to stall rose inside me, and I did my best to squash it. Submit. *Submit, submit, submit.* I chanted the word but finding the right way to explain how I'd essentially let my doubt tear a gaping hole into the fabric of our trust…that was easier in theory.

He exhaled on an exasperated sigh. "You've got sixty seconds before you lose the privilege of speaking."

His threat busted through my resistance. "After I left your office on Wednesday, Katherine was waiting for me in the driveway." The lies the bitch had spewed seemed thin to me now. I should have seen right through them and had I not reacted with too-quick judgement born of emotional overload, I would have recognized the trap in her accusation.

I blinked, and a tear squiggled down my face. "She said you were going to meet her at the Hilton. She left a keycard."

Meeting his eyes, I silently pleaded for understanding. "But Ian showed up right after I did. He said he got a message from you. He thought he was meeting you at the hotel." Pissed at myself, I dashed away the moisture collecting on my cheeks. "She set us up, and I fell for it. I'm sorry, Master."

With a long sigh, Gage dropped the ball gag and paced a few feet away, turning his back on me for a few seconds that were long enough to ratchet up my anxiety. Eventually, he turned around, dragging both hands down his face. "Did you touch him?"

And that's when I wavered again. The truth clogged my throat, but if I didn't come clean, he'd think the worst. "I…I hugged him."

"Why?"

"I was shocked to see him, and…" My stomach turned, making me ill. My reasons were unimportant to Gage, as I had no business laying a finger on Ian Kaplan.

"And?" he prompted.

"Please don't make me say it."

"You were happy to see him alive." His tone was so matter-of-fact that I wondered if he had mind-reading capabilities.

"Yes, Master." God, how my cheeks burned with shame. I shouldn't feel guilty for finding joy in knowing that someone I cared about was alive and healthy, but I did. "I'm sorry, but it's the truth."

"I appreciate your honesty, baby."

"But?"

"But I'm hurt as fuck. When will you learn that you need to come to *me* about things? In fact," he said, walking in a slow circle around me, "I demand it. You come to me, or you get punished. This wouldn't have happened if you'd trusted me."

"I know, Master." I hung my head, misery fisting my gut.

"Please don't take away my phone and car. I'm begging you. I'll take any other punishment you wish to give."

"Yes, you will, because you don't have a choice. As for your privileges, we'll discuss that later."

His words crashed over me like a frigid wave, and they were a much-needed wake-up call because everything he gave me was a privilege and not a right. I had none in this marriage—in this fucked up union I agreed to every damn day by staying. There were no victims here—only obsessed people who knew the fucked-uppedness of their relationship and stuck through it anyway.

"Get up." He held out a hand and pulled me to my feet, and as he escorted me to the other end of the room, near his wall of pain-inducing implements, I experienced a new level of fear. A piece of equipment I hadn't seen before had been stowed away in the corner of the room, hidden underneath a black cloth.

He whipped the material off and revealed a wooden stockade. "I had this delivered earlier this week while you were out with Simone."

"What is it, Master?"

"A device designed to position you for anal discipline."

Holy shit, the thing looked medieval. It had an upright panel that tilted toward the surface at a slight angle. Holes for wrists and ankles sat top and bottom, and a cutout for where I assumed my bottom would fit took up the space front and center. He was going to lock me in that contraption and objectify my ass. Instinctively, I backed up a few feet.

"What are you going to do to me, Master?"

"To put it mildly, I'm going to make it *very* difficult for you to sit."

My body shook, and I tasted blood from gnawing my lower lip.

"Come here," he ordered.

My feet refused to move, and my heart refused to stop pounding in my ears.

"Baby, don't fight me on this. You won't win." Gage stormed the few feet between us and propelled me forward. His hold on me was harsh and absolute, but his voice had softened, sending a gentle breeze onto my fiery terror.

My submission was the key to everything—freedom, forgiveness, fortitude.

Of my own free will, I slipped my sweaty palm into his and let him help me climb onto his new torture device. "H-how do you want me, Master?"

The sexy timbre of his voice cast me under a spell as he explained how to position myself. I settled horizontally onto the bench, my cheek to the wood, and spread my knees before tucking them underneath my abdomen. The wood was surprisingly smooth against my skin.

"Higher," he murmured, fitting a palm under my bottom and pushing upward. Then he pulled his hand away and ordered me to scoot all the way back until my ass protruded through the cutout in the wood.

A mechanism sounded, and I gripped the edge of the table as Gage fastened my ankles below my exposed ass and pussy. With surprising gentleness, he pulled my arms behind my back and secured my wrists in the openings situated at the top.

It was a humiliating position, a variation of a kneeling hogtie—only more painful because a single panel of wood trapped my ankles, ass, and wrists behind me. I'd never felt so helpless, so immobile with my bottom exposed to the chilly air of the basement and cheeks spread in preparation for what I knew was going to be an excruciating punishment. My ass was well and truly stuck within the confines of his stockade.

And undoubtedly fucked.

"Before we begin, let's get something straight, Kayla. Forgiving you earlier this year wasn't easy, but it was necessary because I refuse to live without you. My brother, on the other hand, will never be forgiven. He knew better than to come back."

"Please, Master. He's not—"

"You are not to beg tonight," Gage interrupted. "You're going to accept this punishment without a single 'please' or 'stop.' Do you understand?"

"Yes, Master." I did understand. Begging for mercy was not only pointless, but it was humiliating.

"Ian knew the consequences of coming back. His decision to go against my wishes was not in the scope of your control—I understand that—but you will be punished for it regardless." He walked out of sight, and I felt the heat of his body at my backside.

He slipped two fingers inside me, then forced his thumb into my dry asshole. "This is going to hurt. But I think you need a painful reminder of who you belong to." He paused a beat. "Who owns you, Kayla?"

"You do, Master."

"We both know I don't need your permission to punish you, but I'm asking for it anyway. Do you give me permission to punish you as I wish?"

Oh, what a sadistic question. I considered saying no, mostly because I was curious if he'd honor my wishes for a change. I faltered for a mere second, and that was all it took to come to the conclusion that he would *not* bow to what I wanted. If I went against him, even verbally, he would still go through with the punishment, only he'd do his worst.

But what if I were wrong? What if accepting his firm hand and sadistic need for retribution was the only way past what I'd done today? I'd kneeled with the intention of asking for forgiveness in Gage's language.

So I answered in the most honest yet harrowing way I could. "You have my trust and permission, Master."

I heard him exhale—a telling sound indeed. And as he placed one palm on my left ass cheek, rubbing some warmth into my skin, I knew I'd given the right answer.

"Your submission is like a drug, baby. It's precious, and it means the world to me." He landed a smack that not only smarted, but it fucking turned me on. Then he repeated the stinging swat on my other cheek. Back and forth, he continued the spanking, escalating in velocity and strength until he had me tensing with each calculated swat.

Gage wasn't doing this to punish in the painful sense; he wanted me aroused before he went haywire on my backside.

God, why did I love this sadistic prick so much?

"I love how vulnerable you are right now. You are physically incapable of denying me anything. I can beat your ass for as long as I wish, fuck it for as long as I want. Or," he said, his tone dropping to a dangerous level, "punish it until you lose the ability to scream."

My blood turned to ice. "Master?" I said, a mere whimper.

"No begging. I won't warn you again. Next time you disobey me, I'll gag you." He commenced with the spanking for a while longer, working me into a quivering mass of arousal. "Your cunt is leaking all over the wood."

"I'm sorry, Master." Closing my eyes, I gnawed on my lip.

"Don't be. I want you on edge, your cunt dripping in shame even as you tense from not knowing what I'll do next." He rubbed his palms over my smarting backside, then he inserted a finger into my disloyal cunt. "Are you wondering how I'm going to hurt you?"

"Yes," I moaned, wishing I could squirm from his touch, or at the very least, block it out. I'd give anything to have control over my body, to be able to deny him in some small way.

"We're going to go slow and steady, working our way through each implement one by one." His hands disappeared from my backside, and he came into view, stopping in my line of sight to work the buttons of his white dress shirt free. The material slid over his shoulders and down his arms, and he laid it over the arm of a chair before unbuckling his belt.

Swish.

The belt slipped free of his pant loops. "After your ass is nice and red, and beautifully welted, we'll move on to the punishment of your hole. I made you wet first to ready you for punishment because I do intend to make you scream."

Tears threatened to flood my eyes. I blinked them back with sheer willpower. Crying would not endear me to him right now. He didn't want crying or begging—only my absolute acceptance of his discipline.

And right then I understood more than ever how his mind was wired. Accepting pain equaled disowning my past with his brother. I ached to wrap my arms around him and tell him how much I loved him. Tell him I'd never betray him again. But Gage didn't need that. A normal man might. For Gage, true apology lay in the steadfast way I took his strikes. My redemption lay in an ass left so red and beaten and welted that the mere act of sitting would be impossible.

So I apologized in the only way he understood—I gritted my teeth and silently accepted the first strike of his belt.

The smoldering ash of Gage's retribution encased my backside. He wasn't counting tonight, which made receiving the lashes of his belt even more challenging because I didn't know when they'd stop.

I thought they'd never stop.

Through the strikes, I refrained from sobbing, bit back every moan of pain, every whimper at the bone-chilling *crack* of leather against flesh. But then he moved on to a paddle riddled with holes, and I couldn't help but let loose a whimper. The real test came with the cane, never mind the bullwhip because I couldn't begin to comprehend making it through that, and I prayed to anyone listening that Gage would stop after the cane.

Crack!

"Ahhh! Plea—" I choked on the plea, horrified at the thought of starting from square one.

He walked to the front of the bench and stared down at me. I could only imagine what I must look like—blotchy skin from the tears that finally escaped, mouth open to pant through the pain, and strands of hair caught in my eyes, stuck to my cheek from sweat and saliva.

His soft, warm fingers brushed my hair back from my face. "What could you have done differently?"

"What do you mean, Master?"

"At the hotel when you first saw him. Tell me what you could have done differently that might have saved you this level of punishment."

"I could've called you."

"You *should* have called me, at the very least."

"I know, Master. I'm sorry I let you down."

"You disappointed me," he said, brushing a thumb over my lips, "but you didn't let me down. You weren't unfaithful, and this punishment will ensure you stay loyal to me until the day you die. I won't allow you to stumble again."

He disappeared once more, and the next blow to my ass stole my breath. I couldn't make a sound if I tried. His evil cane cut across my ass in sharp lines, one on top of the other, and I knew from experience that those wounds would stay with me for a while, above and below the surface.

Some time later, the cane clattered to the floor. He'd been dropping implements left and right, which was so unlike him. He reached for the bullwhip, and that's when I slipped up. That's when a sob escaped, and I cried out a plea in the form of his favorite title.

"*Master...*" God, how I choked on the word, but I almost threw up at the thought of his whip landing on top of the welts from the cane.

He came to stand in front of me again, bullwhip held in a white-knuckled grip. "Do we need to start over?"

"No! I want the bullwhip!" Desperation strung those words together, screeched in a high-pitched tone.

"Don't lie to me. We both know you hate the bullwhip."

"I'm sorry, Master. Don't make me start over again." My

voice was near to pleading, which terrified me even more. "I just want this to be over."

And that was the honest fucking truth.

He leaned down, and his lips claimed my mouth. The kiss was too brief; a fleeting moment of bliss that seemed more like a dream in my current mental state. He pulled away, and I ached to do something—anything—to bring his mouth back. As long as he kissed me, he wouldn't hurt me anymore.

"This will be over soon, baby. Then we can move on."

Soon was not the word I'd use. His inner sadist had taken control, and he wasn't likely to unhand the reins anytime soon. Gage lost himself a little more to that monster with each minute that passed. And there were a lot of them. Minute after minute after minute of his bullwhip cracking through the air before it thrashed my thoroughly abused ass.

Forget composure. Forget acceptance. I screamed and cried and even cursed.

"I hate you!" I sobbed.

"I don't blame you for saying that right now," he said, a note of hurt tainting his voice as he brought the whip onto my ass once again.

"Fuck you! How can you be so cruel?" Hell, I lashed out in any form he'd allow. As long as I wasn't begging for it to stop, he let me throw my agony-induced tantrums, similar to a woman in the throes of labor during the horrendous stage of transition. And that's where I was—out of my mind with pain and so high on adrenaline that reality was a nebulous concept viewed through warped glass.

"You don't love me," I whined.

"I love you too much."

Whack!

"This isn't love!" My words echoed off the walls, and only then did I realize I'd screamed them.

"You're probably right, but it's the only way I know how to love."

Whack!

"Oh God! Fuck! Fuck! It hurts, Gage. It hurts!"

"It's supposed to hurt."

"No," I moaned, unable to find the strength to keep screaming at him. "Love isn't supposed to hurt like this."

He dropped the whip, and as that fucker hit the ground, echoing with hope through my ears, I'd never experienced so much relief. I would never, ever cross this man again. Ever.

"Thank God," I mumbled.

"We're not done yet."

But I didn't care. He could stick his thumb up my ass all night long if he wanted, because that was a hundred times better than getting spanked, lashed with a belt, beat with a paddle, struck with a cane, and tormented with a bullwhip. I was in no hurry to examine my backside in a mirror.

Gage opened a drawer and pulled out a rod-like toy of some sort, and that's when it hit me that he wasn't planning to use his thumb. The instrument was long and fat, bigger than his cock, and one end had a rounded head designed for penetration.

Begging for mercy was on the tip of my tongue, so I bit it instead.

"I want anal sex to be amazing for you. To achieve that goal it's going to take time and patience, and harsh anal punishments to remind you of how pleasurable my cock can be in comparison. You're going to learn the differences between anal penetration for pleasure and punishment."

"It's too big, Master."

He pressed a finger to my lips. "I allowed you to cry and insult me during the first portion of your discipline. But now you will remain quiet and reflect on the behavior that got you here. Don't make me start over, Kayla."

I clenched my teeth, knowing that I'd summon the strength to get through this. I was stronger than he realized...or maybe he did realize the extent of my resilience. Maybe that's why he pushed so hard—because he knew I could bounce back from his shit. Maybe I was the one woman capable of surviving Gage Channing's all-consuming sadism.

But as he inched that steel shaft up my ass, using a minimal amount of lube, I wondered if maybe they should just toss me in a loony bin and throw away the key.

CHAPTER TWELVE

Warm water sluiced over my head, spraying from the multiple shower heads, and dripped off my nose, running over my breasts before sliding down my spread legs. Facing the shower wall, thighs open to my husband's questing hands, and arms over my head with my palms flat against the tile, I bit my lip as he washed me...and coaxed me to arousal.

But my mind replayed his vile use of that anal rod. He'd punished my ass slowly, first inching the thing in, allowing my anus to stretch and burn around the intrusion for a few minutes before he removed it.

Then he'd insert it again.

He must have penetrated me with that rod a dozen times —as many times as it took to lose a whole hour or more to his sick punishment of my hole.

"I'm proud of you," he said, his fingers moving between my thighs.

"I'm pissed at you," I bit back. Even as I sassed him, uncaring of the consequences at this point, my legs betrayed me and opened wider to accommodate his touch. I didn't know whether to lash out in anger, sob from the despair fisting my heart, or come all over his teasing fingers. Leaning my forehead against the wall, I pushed my ass toward him, an invitation to touch me deeper.

"How do you do this to me?"

"Do what, baby?"

"Make me want to come after everything you just did."

"It's a talent of mine," he said, finally slipping his fingers inside me.

"I'm still pissed at you, Master."

"That's okay. You're entitled to your emotions, Kayla. I put your ass through the wringer."

"I'm scared to look at it."

In response, he brushed his fingers over my stinging backside. "Your ass is gorgeous. I was careful not to draw too much blood, but you really won't be able to sit for a couple of days. I wasn't kidding about that."

"Can I speak freely, Master?" The last thing I wanted was to push too hard and earn an additional punishment.

"You may."

His gentle manner was my undoing. I plummeted in a brutal mood swing more powerful than his strikes, and a sob wrenched from my soul. "How can you love me and hurt me like this? How? I don't understand."

"I told you a long time ago that I'm a bastard. But I'm your bastard, Kayla. And I do love you. I love you more fiercely than the burn in your ass right now, with so much loyalty that I'd gladly kill anyone who hurt you."

"But *you* hurt me."

"And I'm the only one who ever will." He thrust his fingers in a steady rhythm, propelling me to that glorious edge I craved. Oh, how I needed to jump off right now.

I moaned and groaned, my hands balled into fists against the tile. "Master, please."

"Please, what?" He blew a warm breath over my bottom, and I liked that he was on his haunches behind me, practically worshipping the handiwork of his sadism while simultaneously gifting me pleasure.

"Can I come, Master?"

"You may not."

"Grrr!" Bumping my forehead on the tile, I gritted my teeth to keep from slinging hateful words at him.

"You're still being punished. You don't get to come during a punishment. You know that."

Still being punished...

A flash of Katherine on her knees, her slutty mouth inches from his cock, sprang to mind, causing my body to go rigid. But recalling his words truly iced my heart.

If you ever touch another man again, I'll not only fuck her, but I'll do it in front of you.

I hadn't betrayed him, but a hug could be construed as touching another man. "Are you going to...?" Suddenly, vomit burned my throat.

"Spit it out, Kayla. Whatever it is, don't hold back. That's what got you in trouble in the first place."

"Are you going to use Katherine against me?" Closing my eyes, I failed to breathe as I waited for his answer. But he was quiet, leaving me close to panicking. "Please, Master. I need to know."

"You don't have to worry about Katherine. When I made the threat, I was so angry that I thought I could do it. But fuck, Kayla, I don't think I could ever touch another woman. You're it for me."

The breath I'd been holding whooshed from me in a torrent of relief. "You're it for me too. I need you to know that."

His lack of response worried me. He stopped caressing between my legs, but still, he didn't say anything.

"Gage, I mean it. Please know that."

"You don't have any feelings for him?"

"Not like I used to." Gage had purged my love for Ian the instant he'd sentenced me to that cage. "Honestly, after I got over the shock of seeing him, I was more worried about how you'd react."

He rose behind me, pressing his erection against my sore ass, and gripped my hair in an uncompromising fist. "Swear to me that he means nothing."

"He means nothing."

Gage pulled on my hair, angling my head so he could claim my mouth. The spray from the shower misted over our faces, wetting our lips as we came together in an open-mouthed kiss that sucked the will right out of my bones.

I whimpered against his lips, needing more...so much more.

He inched back with a groan. "I want in your ass so badly right now."

My breath hitched, and I turned horrified eyes on him. I could not, for the fucking life of me, comprehend taking his cock right now. Not with the way my ass burned.

"Relax, baby," he whispered, brushing his mouth over mine again. "I know you're in pain, so I'll settle for your mouth instead." He let out a breath that shivered against my well-kissed lips. "On your knees."

His command, spoken soft and low yet full of authority, shot straight to my pussy. I turned around and kneeled before him, then eagerly accepted his cock into my mouth. He pushed his hands into my hair, brushing the wet strands from my eyes.

"Baby, look at me."

God, he was beautiful. Dark hair drenched, blue eyes more startling than usual—I was helpless against this man, especially when he gave in to the speck of tenderness hiding inside his sadistic soul. Instead of grabbing my hair and ramming his cock down my throat, like he normally would, he combed his fingers through my hair as he slipped in and out of my mouth.

Intense heat flared between my thighs, and I whimpered around his shaft, tongue massaging the softness of his head.

Propping an arm against the tile, he groaned deep in his throat as he gazed down at me in wonder. "Don't stop doing that with your tongue. It feels unbelievable." His mouth flattened into a determined line. "You're being such a good girl. Fuck, I want to make you come into next year."

But he wouldn't. Gage had many sides to him, but he rarely wavered on punishment, and holding my orgasm at bay was part of it.

I sucked him to release, accepting every last drop, and despite the desire blazing between my thighs, I felt mostly... content. We finished washing up, then he towel-dried my skin, paying careful attention to his favorite areas before instructing me to bend over the counter.

"I love marking you like this." He opened a tube of cream and squirted a dollop into his palm. "Your ass was made for me." As he gently rubbed the soothing balm into my skin, I wondered how he'd managed to coach me through fear, then anger before molding me into a content pile of skin and bones, subservient to his wants and needs, and pliant in his hands.

I had no answers and no chance to mull over his sorcery-like mojo any longer. He scooped me up in his arms and carried me upstairs to our bedroom, winding a path through the darkness to our bed. He set me on my feet before turning down the covers.

"Grab your ankles."

I did so without question. He probed my pussy, gliding his devious fingers through the evidence of just how fundamentally screwed my body was. And even in the darkness, his face cast in shadow from my bent over position, I knew he was pleased.

He'd punished my ass to his liking and had nearly brought me to orgasm enough times to leave me drenched around his fingers. Gage Channing's work for the day was done. His self-satisfied sigh confirmed it as he pulled me into bed beside him, yanking my stinging ass snug against his thighs. And though he didn't voice the words, his long sigh told me all I needed to know.

That night, I fell asleep wrapped in his forgiveness and love.

CHAPTER THIRTEEN

Gage was having my masquerade gown designed. He'd stuffed most of my closet with custom made clothing from some of the top designers in the world. Every button and bead had been added down to his specifications. If I were going to be his trophy wife, then he'd outfit me like one. Considering the charity ball was less than a week away, he'd put a rush on my dress, no doubt paying a ridiculously high premium.

"Not even a teensy little hint?" I needled him, lying on top of his body because I still couldn't sit without pain after the punishment he'd issued the previous night.

"You'll see it Friday night." His warm hands drifted over my naked backside, his caresses downright hypnotic. The same hands that delivered excruciating pain were also the same hands that moved over my skin in a way that made me feel treasured and loved. I buried my nose in the crook of his neck, suddenly overcome.

"What's wrong, baby?"

"I don't know. Nothing." Maybe I was having a woman moment. In fact, that particular curse was due any day.

"Are you worried you'll lose your privileges?"

The issue had crossed my mind a few times, but I couldn't say I'd thought about it tonight. Not with the way he'd...*God*...

He'd made love to me.

"You had honest intentions, Kayla, so I won't punish you further by taking your car or phone away."

"Thank you, Master."

His chest went still as if he were holding his breath. "Are you still angry with me?"

"No, Master. I just wish..." I swallowed hard before forging ahead, knowing he'd want me to share what troubled me. "I wish we had more moments like these."

Moments where we lost an endless amount of time, tangled as one in the darkness of our bedroom, bodies swallowed in the sheets. These kinds of nights were few and far between.

He grabbed my hips, pulled, and urged me to my knees. "I vow to you right now that we'll have more of these moments, Kayla." Nudging my opening with his cock, he shuddered a breath into my hair. "Ride me."

"Again?"

"Did I stutter?"

With a slow downward thrust, I sheathed his cock.

"Look at me," he said, fisting my hair with both hands. He pulled my head up by force, too impatient for me to unbury my face on my own. "Don't forget that I'm calling the shots here. You being on top means nothing."

I wouldn't dare to be so foolish. He'd allowed me the sacred privilege of control twice since I'd known him—only because I'd tied him to the bed in a role reversal he probably still regretted to this day. But truthfully, Gage had wielded power over me both times, because that's who he was. Even gagged and tied, he'd owned me.

And he always would.

"I don't want fast and hard," he said, fingers loosening in my hair. "Fuck me slowly."

Undulating my hips, I dropped my forehead against his, and our gazes locked together as surely as our bodies did. His breath became my own, and the adoration in his eyes hit me square in the chest, stealing my life-force.

"I have no fucking words for how good you feel right now," he said, sliding his hands along my cheeks. Gage could do tender when he wanted to—when he wasn't preoccupied with taking me by force or delivering a punishment.

Sometimes, he loved me like a normal man.

Fuck, I was going to cry and ruin this moment. I shuttered my eyes against the threat of tears, but it was too late. He swiped at the moisture creeping out from underneath my lashes.

"Baby, eyes on me."

Exhaling the sob I'd been holding back, I opened my eyes, and confusion overshadowed his blue gaze.

"Why are you crying?"

"I don't know." And I truly didn't. Maybe his tenderness on the tail of such brutality did me in. Or maybe I just needed him too much, and a tiny part of me wept over the hold he had on me.

Cradling my cheeks, he nipped at my lips before drawing me into a kiss that destroyed me. Our tongues came together in sync with our bodies. The salt of my tears infused our taste buds with a spectrum of emotions, cleansing us of past hurts. We kissed and fucked in perfect harmony, each note falling into place, every high and low executed with mastery.

He let go of my face with a groan, grabbed my hips, and yanked me down until I took his cock to the hilt. "I'll never get enough. Your body enchants me—"

Another upward thrust hit my G-spot, and I cried out with a delicious shudder.

"Your smile lights my world, baby. And your stubbornness...hell, you can't help but challenge the bastard in me." As if to punctuate his words, he dug his fingers into my tender ass. "I know loving me isn't easy, but you do it so damn well."

The tears would never stop at this rate. I clutched his hair and fucked the *fuck* out of him, mindless of the way his hands gouged my red and welted flesh. His touch guided me, punished me, but above all else, he held me to him with fierce possession.

He'd never let me go, and the certainty of that knowledge swaddled my heart in absolution.

"No more doubts," I cried, lips damp against his skin.

"No more doubts," he agreed, then he sucked in a sharp breath. "You're making me lose my shit. I'm gonna come, and if you don't come with me, I'll spank the fuck out of your ass."

That was all I needed—the mental picture of his authoritative hand on my bottom. I fell apart within the confines of his embrace...no, we fell apart in each other's arms, groaning and grunting and moaning incoherent nothings as we grasped for that wondrous high together.

CHAPTER FOURTEEN

The week began with torrential rain. I found the downpour symbolic as if Mother Nature was urging us to wash away the darker aspects of our histories and focus on the future instead. And the future held a bright new beginning, in more ways than one.

For the first time since we'd married, Gage allowed me to find purpose in something other than motherhood or being a wife and slave. He'd hired me on as his personal assistant again, this time on a part-time basis. For the first two days, I worked at his side until noon, at which point he sent me home to perform my wifely duties. Housekeeping, shopping, and meal preparation were still my responsibilities, though if I started working more hours at Channing Enterprises, he'd allow me to hire help at home.

But for now, my new job was on a conditional basis until I proved that I could keep up with my duties. Everything was going smoothly until Wednesday when life slapped me in the face with a huge wake-up call.

I'd just walked into the foyer when the lunch I'd had with Gage turned in my gut. I barely made it to the bathroom before losing the contents of my stomach. As I held onto the gleaming porcelain, heaving for all I was worth, I could no longer deny it. Getting sick all the time wasn't due to stress, and the stomach bug that had visited Eve was long gone.

This was something else. Something I couldn't bring myself to hope for just yet...until I ran the calculations in my head and realized I was late.

I should have called Gage, but when I picked up my cell, Simone's number was the one my fingers dialed. Late or not, I wasn't about to get Gage's hopes up for nothing. A piss stick would have to show me two lines first.

Then I'd tell him...if I had anything to tell at all.

Simone answered on the fifth ring. "What's up?"

"Are you working today? I was hoping we could get together."

A few seconds of quiet passed. "Ian told me he ran into you," she finally said, hesitancy lacing her tone. "I'm sorry I didn't tell you about us."

Her words caught me off-guard. "That's not why I'm calling." The incident with Ian seemed like weeks ago instead of days, considering everything that was going through my mind now.

"Oh," she said, sounding surprised. "You seem a little upset, so I thought..."

"I'm not upset about you and Ian." Sure, I shared enough history with Ian that the idea of him moving on wasn't the easiest thing to face, but the pain was but a phantom ping—an ache stamped on my heart like a fading tattoo. "I was actually hoping you'd want to help me shop for...Halloween costumes."

Not pregnancy tests. No siree.

Besides, I did need to find a costume for Eve. I was fairly certain Gage would give me permission to leave the house if

I told him I was shopping for Halloween costumes. "I need to find something for Eve."

"Okay." But doubt tinged her voice. "My shift ends in an hour."

I told her where to meet me, then she hung up without a goodbye, which was a very Simone-like thing to do. Two hours later, we were sorting through the racks at a costume shop in comfortable silence.

"Are you sure you're okay?" Simone asked, breaking the quiet between us. Okay, so comfortable wasn't the word I'd use, but I hadn't realized my distress was that noticeable, and she obviously mistook it for unhappiness over her new relationship status.

"I'm fine," I said, fingering the lace on an Elsa ensemble —which was *so* two years ago according to Eve. "Why?"

Simone gave a sarcastic quirk of her brow. "You've been touching that hideous costume for the last three minutes while staring into space."

Expelling a sigh, I let Elsa's cheap and scratchy blue skirt slip from my fingers. It was now or never. "I need to buy a pregnancy test." My emotions were all over the fucking place. The threat of tears burned my eyes, but on the opposite end of the spectrum, my belly fluttered with the possibility of a positive sign.

A literal fucking positive sign.

Cool it, Kayla. It's probably nothing.

"Hey, this is great news...isn't it?" She frowned. "You've been trying to get knocked up with that devil's spawn for... well, for what seems like forever."

"Gage doesn't know I'm buying a test."

"*Oooh*," she said, drawing out the word. "You're worried he's going to turn you over his knee for going *mum's-the-word*?"

"Something like that." A spanking over his knee was

foreplay. More than anything, I hated the thought of him finding out about the test if it ended up being negative. I wasn't sure I could handle the disappointment in his eyes. He tried to hide it, but after living most of his adult life believing he was unable to have children, only to find out the diagnosis had been incorrect, I knew how much he wanted this.

A baby of his own.

Katherine had robbed him of Conner's early childhood years, and Eve had been three-years-old when he'd forced his way into our lives. He wanted this badly...possibly more than I did.

"You know how I feel about that man," Simone said, "but I think he'd want to go through this with you, no matter the results."

"I know you're right."

"What's the problem then?"

"I need to be sure before I tell him."

She grabbed my arm and escorted me to a bench designated for shoppers to try on shoes. "And you'll have an answer soon, but first you need to take a few deep breaths and calm down." She settled beside me, and I buried my face in my hands, drawing shallow, hot breaths from between my palms.

"We'll go to the pharmacy together, okay?"

"What if I'm not?"

"But what if you are?" she said. "Only one way to find out."

And that's when I realized that both outcomes equally terrified me—a reaction I hadn't expected. I figured I'd be overjoyed at the possibility of being pregnant, but now that I had a real chance I considered things I hadn't thought of until now.

Like the fact that I was prone to miscarriages and tubal pregnancies.

Or how my slave duties would make carrying a baby difficult. How would I handle Gage's rituals and punishments on top of pregnancy? And then, after the baby arrived...would I be too exhausted to want sex, let alone kneel on command, ready to please?

Simone pulled me to my feet. "Okay, no more freaking out about this. Let's buy a test and get an answer." She ushered me through the mall and to the parking lot with a purposeful stride.

Simone was a life savor that afternoon. She ran into the pharmacy and came out fifteen minutes later with half a dozen tests, each one advertised at being the best, most accurate on the market. Somehow, she knew I wasn't ready to go home yet, so she drove straight to her house.

Now I found myself pacing in front of her bathroom door, the bag of tests in my hands, terrified to hope. My heartbeat was a wild beast behind my breastbone. I should have called Gage. Deep down, I knew I was going about this the wrong way, but the idea of taking a test while he eagerly waited was too upsetting. Once again, vomit pushed its way into my throat, and I bolted into the bathroom and threw up for the second time that day. The situation felt too reminiscent of another day.

The vomiting. The test. The reminder of Gage's reaction afterward.

I curled into a ball next to the porcelain God and sobbed. Taking the test wasn't even important—it would only confirm what I already knew in my heart. The impossible had happened. My remaining ovary had produced an egg, and Gage...

His reaction would be so different from last time, but in that moment, all I could hear were the echoes of his rage.

The accusations and hatred. Forgiving was easy. Forgetting was harder.

"What can I do?" Simone set a hand on my shoulder, her touch light and gentle as if I might jump out of my skin. I pulled myself upright.

"I'm pregnant. I know I am."

"You won't know for sure until you take a test."

"I'm scared to."

"I thought you wanted to have a baby?"

"I do!"

"Then why are you falling apart before you've even pissed on a stick?"

"I don't know! I guess it's...Gage didn't handle it so well last time."

"But he's onboard now, right?" She gentled her tone, infusing her words with the power to coax.

"Yeah."

Simone grabbed my hand and dragged me to my feet. "No point in having a breakdown until you at least confirm it." She picked up the bag I'd dropped and pushed it into my shaking hands. "I'll be right outside the door."

I gave a solemn nod as if headed to a firing squad instead of taking a test that was bound to give me news I'd been hoping to receive for months. The next three minutes were the longest of my life—at least that's what it felt like when I finally picked up the stick and read the results.

Two lines.

CHAPTER FIFTEEN

Gage slid the razor over his jaw and down the side of his neck in hypnotic strokes, erasing his five o'clock shadow. I sat on the edge of the tub and rubbed jasmine scented lotion into my smooth legs. I liked watching him do mundane things. Standing barefoot with nothing but a towel wrapped around his waist, he didn't come across nearly as intimidating as he normally did.

Until he turned that steel blue gaze on me in the mirror.

I didn't know what propelled me to kneel behind him, my hands tugging at the terrycloth around his waist. The towel floated to the floor, and I wrapped my fingers around his cock. It only took a few strokes to get him hard. He dropped the razor onto the counter.

"What are you doing?"

I didn't often take the initiative. He'd conditioned me to follow his lead, and that was a hard lesson to break.

"Serving you, Master." Swiping my thumb over the head of his cock, I bit my lower lip, hiding a smile at the bead of moisture on my fingers.

"Did I give you permission to grope me?"

"No, Master."

He chuckled, but as soon as I stroked the length of him, his laughter turned to a deep-throated groan. "You're being very bad. You interrupted my shaving, Kayla," he said, but his tone teased rather than admonished. "Now I have no choice but to punish your mouth." He whirled and had my head between his hands before I had a chance to move out of reach. As he pushed between my lips, his gaze roamed my face, as if he were searching for the answer to my out-of-character behavior.

"You've been quiet tonight, and now you're on your knees playing with my cock of your own accord. Something is obviously going on here." He thrust deeper, ensuring I couldn't answer him.

And that's when things took a turn for the worst. My gag reflex kicked in, stronger than ever, and I jerked my head back. But he moved with me, wordlessly forbidding me to pull away. Gagging was a huge turn-on for him, and he wasn't about to give me any slack.

"While I fuck your mouth, why don't you consider telling me what's on your mind?" He paused for a moment, a dark brow arched. "Something *is* on your mind, right?" Ceasing his thrusts, he allowed me a quick nod of my head.

Would my entire pregnancy be like this? Struggling with the side-effects of growing a baby inside my body while he took his pleasure from me? All evening I'd worried over how to tell him, but suddenly, I wanted answers first.

He moved his hips in a lazy circle, keeping his cock buried deep in my mouth, and hitting the back of my throat with each rotation. His eyes deepened to my favorite shade of indigo. Sometimes, that hue was a warning, but more often than not, it was a sign of his raging arousal.

Gage was possibly the most passionate man I'd ever met.

With a grunt, he pushed further into my throat, and I

gagged so hard my eyes burned from unshed tears. My belly roiled—a sure sign I was in trouble if I didn't get him off pronto. Renewing my efforts, I worked his shaft with my tongue and lips, hoping against hope that it would be enough to make him come. I wasn't sure how much longer I could stand his cock trapped in my throat, no matter how much I loved making him go wild with my mouth.

And this was why I needed to tell him, or at the very least, open a conversation about the what-ifs of pregnancy.

He withdrew without warning, causing my lips to make a popping sound. Then he bent over and hefted me to my feet with two hands under my shoulders. He spun us around, lifted me onto the counter, and buried his half-shaven face between my legs, smearing shaving cream on my skin in the process. My elbows hit the counter hard, but I didn't give a fuck. Not as long as he kept flicking his tongue over my clit like that.

"Master...feels so good."

He lifted his head. "I lick, you talk."

My head fell back against the mirror. "About what?" His wondrous tongue derailed my train of thought.

"Tell me what's bothering you, or I'll stop." Again, he lifted his head and stared at me, brows narrowed over eyes that saw too much. "You haven't been yourself all afternoon. I know when something is off."

"I've been thinking about..." He darted his tongue into my opening, and I gripped the edge of the counter with white-knuckled fingers. "Oh, God. Don't stop."

"Then finish what you were going to say. You've been thinking about what?"

"What if...what if I do get pregnant?"

As soon as I said those words, he backed away completely, and I lamented the loss of the heights he would have surely sent me to. But the way he watched me, with a mixture of suspicion and hope, told me that our oral session was over. Reluctantly, I slid to my feet.

"What do you mean *what if*?" He folded his arms, and somehow he didn't look ridiculous standing buck naked like that. If anything, he seemed more formidable. "As far as I knew there was only *when*. Are you trying to tell me something, Kayla?"

"No! I just never gave it much thought until now, but..."

"But what?" His voice rose, on the edge of anger. He was taking this all wrong. Or I wasn't explaining myself in the right way.

"How will you treat me during the pregnancy, or after the baby is born?" Considering the what-ifs—the ones I'd never given much thought to because getting pregnant seemed like a pipe dream—were making me nauseous.

Either that or it was morning sickness.

"I've done research, Kayla. You need to trust me to know what is safe and what isn't."

"I'm not just talking about safety. I'm talking about... about what I want." I wrung my hands before forging ahead. "If I were to get pregnant, I'd want more freedom. And once the baby arrives..." I gulped, kicking myself for the slip-up. "I mean I can't comprehend taking care of a newborn and kneeling at your feet daily, or taking your belt or...or your anal punishments. Gage, I'd need you to tone it down."

A tick went off in his jaw, and for a second I thought he'd figured me out. "You sound like you don't want a baby. First your talk the other night about how it might not be in the cards for us, and now this?" He took a step toward me, but my back hit the edge of the counter, leaving me no room to escape.

"Have you been taking birth control pills behind my back? Is that why you're not getting pregnant?"

"What?" My eyes widened. "No! These are just things...

I've just been giving this stuff some thought lately."

"Well here's all you need to know. I'm your Master, and I *will* take care of you. You might not always like my methods, but I won't hurt you beyond what you can handle."

"What if I don't want to 'handle' it while pregnant or taking care of a newborn?" My voice climbed higher with every word, and I regretted it immediately because I knew what he was after before he disappeared from the bathroom. A few moments later, he returned with the ever-dreaded ball gag clutched in his fist.

Shaking my head, I flattened my lips together in pure defiance. "I'm sorry I lost my cool, but this is serious, Gage. We need to talk about this."

"I'll talk. You're going to listen." He pressed the gag to my lips, but I batted his hand—and the gag—away. Even as I did so, I was horrified by my actions. Not because they were out of line, but because they were out of line according to *his* standards.

"Kayla," he warned, once again coming at me with that horrid gag.

"Please, Master. Can't we just talk about—"

"We will talk. We'll talk about anything you want, but *after* you've accepted your punishment."

"What am I being punished for? Will you at least give me a damn reason?"

His mouth formed an indomitable line. "The way you just spoke to me is a fine example of why your disobedient mouth is getting punished."

Why bother protesting? Even if I were ready to tell him about the baby, he wasn't willing to hear me until I took my discipline like the dutiful slave I was. I parted my lips and stretched them around the gag. After he'd tightened the buckle with extra oomph, he ordered me to my knees in the middle of our bedroom.

I did as told, and Gage surprised me by producing a set of leather cuffs. He secured my wrists behind me, and I had to wonder why. He rarely restrained me anymore—he didn't have to. A slight chill stirred by body as he walked in a slow circle around me.

"I may be your husband, but this is not a normal marriage. You knew going in that I would have absolute authority over your life, your body, and your decisions." Completing another circle, he came to a stop in front of me. "You have no control here, Kayla. And though I love your feisty spirit—God, I truly do—I won't hesitate to put you in your place, pregnant or not."

He cocked his head to the side. "And this is your place—on your knees, naked, bound, and gagged. Your place is on all fours, offering your cunt and asshole whenever I wish. Your *place*," he said, raising his voice, "is in any damn position I see fit with your mouth wide open and eager to please me."

Sliding his fingers under my chin, he forced my head up, eyes on him. "There is only one path to freedom, and it's one I know you'll never take. I've made sure of it."

Everything he said was true, and it rose inside me, an insidious truth I couldn't deny. He'd manipulated and molded me, trained and conditioned me. My will was strong and always present, but he'd somehow rewired it to exist for him.

"I'm not just your husband. I'm your *owner*." Crouching until we were at eye level, he caressed my cheek. "And that takes a lot of trust on your part, but I do realize it's something we're still working on. Your first instinct is to withhold and deceive, and I will not stop until I've eradicated that behavior. You will not doubt me, nor question me, nor fear me. You will learn to submit and serve with total trust."

Something dark and dangerous crossed over his features.

"But we aren't there yet, are we? Even after the harsh punishment I put you through last week, you still feel the need to hide things from me."

I shook my head with vehemence.

"The sudden onset of these questions about pregnancy are more than a little suspicious." He pointed to where I kneeled. "Do *not* move from that spot." He hurried back into the bathroom, his stride full of purpose, and my stomach dropped. This couldn't be good. If he planned to search my things for birth control pills that didn't exist…I began to shake. He was going to find the note.

The fucking note I'd forgotten about until now.

To top it off, I was going to choke on my own vomit because I hadn't told him about the baby. That should have been the first thing I'd done this afternoon, as soon as he came through the door.

Instead, I'd stewed and overthought it too much. I'd worried myself into this position. If I'd only been honest, we'd be celebrating right now. But there would be no celebration tonight. How could I expect him to wield his power over me with caution and safety if he didn't have all the facts? No matter the sadistic bastard that lived inside him, I knew he would have never left me gagged, unattended for even a minute if he'd known I was suffering from morning sickness.

Calm down. Deep breaths through the nose.

Breathing deeply and purposefully staved off the nausea. I focused on drawing air in and out of my lungs in a slow and steady rhythm as I waited for him to return. Drawers opened and closed, cupboards squeaked then slammed shut. The unmistakable sound of him rifling through my things filtered to where I kneeled. Finally, he appeared in the open doorway of the bathroom, long after my knees had begun to ache from the hard floor, and my burning shoulders slumped.

Entering the bedroom again, Gage came to a stop in front of me. Dread chewed my gut as I saw what he held in his hands. Struggling to dislodge the gag—which was impossible—I whined and shimmied, begging him with my eyes to let me speak.

He took mercy on me. Leaning down, he loosened the strap and pulled the rubber ball from my mouth. But he didn't free my wrists from the cuffs, and that bespoke of the degree of trouble I was in.

"It's not what you think," I hurried to explain, then winced at that particular cliched tripe.

"You're right. It's definitely not what I thought." He began pacing. "I thought maybe you didn't want another child, but you didn't know how to tell me." He clutched my makeup compact in a fist. "I was looking for contraceptives. Instead, I found this."

"Gage—"

He cut me off by swiping a hand through the air. "How long have you been keeping this from me?"

"It doesn't mean anything."

"*How* long?" he demanded, opening the compact before tossing it onto the floor. He balled his fingers around the note, crushing it.

"A few weeks. I would have gotten rid of it last week, but I forgot about it."

Shit. That was *not* the right thing to say. His face darkened, a storm brewing on the horizon.

"Wait, that came out wrong, Master. I meant that the note didn't mean anything to me anymore. I saw that he was okay. In fact, I found out he's dating Simone, and I'm okay with it!" I struggled to my feet, pleading with my eyes for him to understand. "I would have mentioned it, or thrown it away, but I *forgot*."

"How can you just forget something like this?"

"I don't know! I'm sorry, but I did. A lot has happened since that day. You punishing me, starting work with you this week, and then today..."

Oh God. I'd ruined this moment for us. We'd waited so long, and I'd stupidly withheld the news from him, if only for a few hours. But it was long enough for that damn note to spring up and wreak destruction.

"What else, Kayla? What else are you hiding from me?" He towered over me, and I dropped to my knees. Kissed his feet.

"Stop groveling and just tell me."

Lifting my head, I gazed into his eyes—blue orbs filled with anger and hurt and suspicion. "I'm scared to tell you."

For so many reasons, the biggest of which lay wrapped in superstition and the echoes of a painful history. We'd gone down this road before, and it hadn't ended well.

"Jesus, baby. Whatever it is, we'll deal with it together."

"I'm..." I swallowed hard, and maybe it was the speck of tenderness in his expression—the softening of his mouth, and the way he unclenched his hands. The crinkled piece of paper, a souvenir from a painful time that seemed eons ago, floated to the floor, forgotten.

Gage saw my fear, and instead of feeding off it in his usual sadistic way, he empathized. He showed patience and love and even anxiety for what I was about to throw his way. Again.

I'd proven that I was more than capable of letting him down, of wavering when I should stay the course. I kissed his feet once more then smiled up at him through the tears forming in my eyes.

"I'm pregnant."

CHAPTER SIXTEEN

The following morning, Gage got me in to see the best obstetrician that money could buy. We sat side-by-side in the waiting room, hands clasped together. He seemed as nervous as I was. The wait to see the doctor wasn't long, but it seemed to span forever. By the time they called me back, I was sure my blood pressure would rocket through the roof. After the nurse took my vitals and asked a dozen or so questions, she left Gage and me alone with the assurance the doctor would be in shortly.

I hopped onto the table, my ass sliding over the paper, and eyed Gage. He'd unfolded into a chair near the door of the exam room. Between the glaring lights overhead and my lack of sleep the previous night, this whole situation seemed...surreal.

What bothered me most was all the things we hadn't said. After I'd finally gotten the words out about the pregnancy, Gage had flipped through a plethora of reactions, from shocked to elated to disbelieving to...worried.

And that last one set me on edge the most, possibly because it reflected my own fears. Everything was changing so quickly—within my body and in my marriage. I needed his rock solid presence right now. Hell, I even needed his stringent disciplinary measures. They kept me grounded, and I needed that more than ever.

I'd grown accustomed to bowing to his decisions, to depending on him to keep me in line. But a pregnancy... maybe we'd both underestimated the realities that would come with such a life-changing event.

Deep down, I hadn't worried about it much because after those first few months, when it became obvious I wasn't getting pregnant, I hadn't thought it would be an issue we'd have to face.

Turned out I was wrong.

I glanced up and found him staring at me. "What do you need from me, Kayla?"

That was the last thing I'd expected him to say. "I...I'm not sure what you mean."

"You tried talking to me last night about what you'd need, should you become pregnant. I could have handled that conversation a lot better. Instead, I jumped to conclusions, and for that I'm truly sorry. So now I'm asking. Tell me what you need."

I parted my lips, but nothing came out. The best I could do was shrug my shoulders. Problem was, I had no idea what I wanted or needed. My head was still spinning from seeing those two lines yesterday, and the fact that Gage was sitting in that chair, looking so damn lost, just about unhinged me.

"I need you to be *you*," I whispered, my throat constricting. Why was I so upset? Having a baby was a dream come true for us. But neither of us could deny the risks—not with the type of lifestyle we lived and my previous track record with pregnancies.

He rose and crossed to where I sat, legs dangling over the

edge of the table. As I drew in a lungful of air, he slid his palms along my cheeks, and it amazed me how gentle he managed to be at times. The tender way he cradled my face was incongruent with his basest self.

"Baby, I'm still the same bastard I was yesterday before you told me. Trust me, there will be times when you wish for more leniency. But damn," he said, caressing my temples with his thumbs. "This is fucking real. It's happening, and I want to do right by you, so tell me what you need."

A breath shuddered from my lips. "I don't know. I thought I'd want things to change between us, but I...I just want you the way you are." A large part of me *needed* to kneel at his feet to feel loved. He cherished me best while on my knees, and I craved that connection with him.

Out of nowhere, tears erupted, and I swiped them away, angry at myself for crying. "I need you to take care of me like you always do. I need the security of being yours."

"That's a given, so why am I sensing a 'but' in there somewhere?"

Was I clinging to a caveat? I searched within myself and found the perpetual need to be owned by him, but also to have a piece of me that I could call my own. The strikes of his implements wouldn't quiet it, nor the penetration of my ass—it would fester until I took my last breath because as surely as Gage was a sadist, I was a reluctant slave with a nagging need to be my own damn person at least part of the time.

"I want to go back to the negotiation table."

"We're talking about your needs, not your wants."

I met his gaze with the glare of firm resolve. "I *need* to go back to the negotiation table."

His fingers slid into my hair, and he tugged my lips to his. "You had it right the first time, but for the duration of your pregnancy, we'll compromise. I don't expect things to stay the same while we navigate this."

"Thank you."

"But this habit you have of withholding shit? It ends now. Do you understand me?"

I nodded, blinking in quick succession to fight back the tears. "Yes, Master."

"My job is to help you carry these burdens, but I can't do that if you don't tell me what's bothering you."

I reached for his cheeks, and as we stood there, face-to-face, holding on to each other while we waited for the doctor to tell us everything would be okay, I finally found the words I needed to relay what my heart had been telling me for a year and a half.

"I need your permission to be imperfect. What if I'm too sick to take your cock in my mouth? What if I'm not in the mood for sex? And anal," I said with a gulp. "I don't want you to be disappointed if I...if I say no."

Dropping his hand to my chin, he ran his fingers along my jawline. "You're not allowed to say no to me, which makes your job simple. Trust me. I'll be careful with you, baby. Why can't you see that?"

"Because you hurt me."

"I've always hurt you, long before we married. Part of you even gets off on it, so this preoccupation of yours lately leaves me with one conclusion. You don't trust me enough to submit fully. You've given so much of yourself, but you're still holding on to the doubt in the back of your mind. It's an ugly voice in your head, and it'll do nothing but pick apart our relationship."

"I'll try harder, Master," I said, lowering my eyes.

A knock sounded, shattering our moment.

"We'll talk about this more later," Gage said as he moved away from me. The door opened slowly, revealing a petite woman in scrubs. The doctor introduced herself as Dr. Keenan, and her warm smile put me at ease instantly.

The appointment went as expected; first we went over our concerns about another tubal pregnancy, talked about our alternative lifestyle—Gage had found Dr. Keenan for a reason, as she wasn't quick to judge when it came to kink. Then came the degrading part. After changing into a gown, the doctor helped me fit my feet into stirrups and performed the exam. I kept my eyes on Gage the whole time, counting the seconds until she finished.

"I'd like to do an ultrasound," she said. "I believe you're further along than you thought."

"By how long? A few days?"

"More like a few weeks."

I pushed myself up on my elbows, and she held out a hand to help me into a sitting position. "But I had a period about...five weeks ago, I think."

She asked me a few more questions and mentioned something about implantation bleeding before readying the ultrasound machine. I reclined once more, and as Dr. Keenan squirted a jelly-like substance onto my flat belly, Gage moved to my side and took my hand, squeezing my fingers.

I kept my gaze glued to the monitor, but terror fisted my throat. What would we do if that machine trampled our dreams?

"Everything's going to be okay, baby," he said, his voice low yet full of certainty.

I grabbed onto his words and wrapped myself in them. I had to trust that he was right. Besides, if I were further along than I thought, then didn't that mean the truly nail-biting stage of my pregnancy had passed?

The doctor pressed the hand-held device to my belly and moved it around until she found the right spot. "There's your baby," she said with a smile. "My, hear that strong heartbeat."

Thump-thump, thump-thump, thump-thump...

"You're about ten weeks."

"Oh my God." Through my tears, I stared at the image of our tiny baby in awe. Tearing my gaze away long enough to meet Gage's eyes was so damn hard, but I wanted to see his reaction as much as I wanted to take in the black and white picture of the child growing inside me.

Gage brought the back of my hand to his lips, his blue eyes bright with wonder, and that small gesture was nearly my undoing.

CHAPTER SEVENTEEN

"Eve!" I called out, thrusting my arms into the sleeves of a knee-length sweater. "Where's your jacket?"

"Um...I think I left it in the bathroom."

As I tied the sash around my waist, she ran down the hall, and I called after her to hurry up. "The bus is going to be here any second!"

She returned thirty seconds later, trying to shove her right arm through a sleeve that was partially inside out.

"Here, baby. Let me." Pulling the garment from her body, I tugged on the sleeves then helped her push her arms through. We rushed out the front door, and a misty rain fell, leaving tiny pin-sized drops of water in our hair and on our clothes.

"Did you get my Halloween costume yet?"

Shit.

"I'll get it tomorrow."

"Mom," she whined.

I sighed, ill-equipped to handle her mood swings this morning. I was barely able to keep up with my own, and it didn't help that what little breakfast I'd eaten sat lodged in my throat, just waiting to make an appearance.

"You'll love it, I promise." As soon as the bus pulled up, I bent and gave her a hug. "Have a great day at school."

"Bye, Mom!" She stomped up the stairs, and as the yellow bus started to wheel away, she waved at me from her seat at the front. I waved back, then I stood for a few minutes, eyes closed, face upturned toward the falling mist, and just breathed. The cool air soothed the nausea, and the serene chirping of birds, combined with the gentle rustle of leaves, eased the tension from my muscles.

I sensed Gage's presence before he touched me.

"What are you doing out here?" he asked, resting his hands on my shoulders.

"Fresh air helps the nausea."

Wrapping his arms around me, he rested his chin on my shoulder. "Then we'll stand out here as long as you need, though I'd hate for you to come down with a cold."

"Cold weather doesn't cause—"

"Illnesses, I know." He let out a soft laugh into my hair. "Viruses do."

"And bacteria."

"That too."

Standing in the rain with him like this gave me a sense of deja vu. He let me have my meditative moment for a couple minutes longer, then he tugged on my arm, and I followed him back into the house. The day held a weird sort of energy I couldn't put my finger on. The air was rife with it as we settled in at the dining table again, where we'd gathered for breakfast before Eve had to leave for school.

Gage folded his newspaper and set it aside, and the way he scrutinized me made me edgy. I crossed my arms, suddenly chilled despite my sweater. The ball was tonight, and he'd taken the day off from work so we could...talk.

"You should try finishing your breakfast," he said, nudging my partially eaten plate of pancakes toward me.

"I'm sorry. I'm just not hungry right now."

"Do you want me to fix you something else?"

"I don't know. Maybe in a while."

With a sigh, he grabbed my hand. "Are you nervous about tonight?"

Avoiding his gaze, I darted my tongue out and wet my lips. "Which part?"

"The latter half of the evening."

"Yes."

He leaned forward and brushed the hair from my eyes. "You have nothing to be scared of, baby. Just let go and trust me."

"I'm trying, but I still think we should go over a few things."

He settled back into his seat. "I was up most of the night considering everything you said yesterday at Dr. Keenan's office, and I came to a decision, Kayla." The tone of his voice put me on alert, and I sat up straighter.

"You said you needed security, so I'm going to give it to you in the only way I know how. There will be no negotiations. The only thing I want from you is trust. In return, I will give you a safe word after tonight."

"A safe word?"

"Yes."

Technically, I had a safe word, but I never used it, and he didn't allow me to use it during punishments. "In what way will this be different from what we do now?"

He cleared his throat. "You know how I dislike giving you control, but in this situation, a certain amount of it is necessary, so long as you don't abuse the privilege. Because that's what it is. A privilege. You're my slave, but you're also carrying my child, so I want you to feel...safe." Lowering his head, he ran his fingers through his hair, and I realized how difficult that concession had been for him to make.

"I do feel safe, Gage."

"Do you?" he asked, lifting his head.

"Yes."

"Even when I'm punishing your ass?"

I gulped. "Yes, Master." Didn't mean I liked or even handled his punishments well, but I hadn't truly feared him since...

Since the day I cheated on him with his brother.

"Then why are you having trouble submitting?"

That was a good question. Fear of the unknown, perhaps, or that voice inside me that constantly shouted how love shouldn't be like this. "I guess it's in my nature to dig my heels in."

"Baby, I love that part of you more than anything. But rules are rules, and you'll never be allowed to deny me." He paused, letting his statement sink in. "That being said, if something I'm doing is too difficult to handle, no matter how well-deserved, you have my permission to speak up about it."

"Kinda hard to speak up when you gag me half the time," I grumbled.

"I don't gag you to quiet your opinions. I do it when I need you to hear what I'm saying, without interruptions or distractions. And Kayla," he said, a gruff note entering his tone. "I do it because it turns me the fuck on."

God, how I loved turning him on.

"Are you still feeling ill?"

"No, Master." Why was my voice suddenly raspy? Tight with need and want? Had he conditioned my body's response to fall in tune with the way he spoke to me?

"Don't move," he said, scooting his chair across the hardwood. "I'll be right back." He gathered our dishes before disappearing into the kitchen. Running water sounded from the other room for a few seconds before he returned.

"Hop up here," he said, patting the middle of the dining table.

"Master?" My attention swerved between his face and his hand, which still rested on the table.

"I'm fairly certain you understood me. I want you up here now, legs spread. I intend to make you edge all day."

Just in time for tonight, so I'd be so out of my mind with wanting him that I wouldn't question the things he planned to do to me. Even as I slid onto the table in front of him, opening my legs and exposing myself to his darkening gaze, I knew his end game, and it would be one hell of a ride that would soar me to the highest of highs before dropping me into the bowels of agony.

He buried his face between my thighs, and that's how much of the day passed. Between bouts of morning sickness, Gage pushed me to within inches of tumbling over the forbidden ledge of ecstasy.

On the table, bent over his desk, in the shower, even against the window with the curtains drawn. That had been particularly fucked up, as he'd positioned me facing our street while he crouched between my legs, out of view. He'd licked me to madness underneath my skirt, and the only way to save my dignity had been to keep my face blank as the cars rolled past.

In the end, I'd failed. With my hands balled against the glass, I'd begged him to let me come, heedless of who might be watching my grand moment of weakness as my husband pushed his tongue into my pussy again and again.

Of course, he'd ignored my pleas. But at least there was one positive side effect to having been pushed to the edge all day; I throbbed for release so much that the nausea subsided, and I I figured I'd have no problem digging into dinner like a starving, ravenous pig.

After Leah's mom picked up Eve, and the evening fell into darkness, I entered the bedroom to prepare for the charity ball. That's when I noticed a box sitting on the end of the bed.

Gage hovered behind me, his body heat warming my back as excitement zinged through my veins. Damn, this man...his biggest achievement in life was turning me inside out and upside down. Tonight would challenge me, scare me, but knowing Gage, it would also make me stronger in my submission. Tonight would be the first true test of our roles since finding out about the baby.

"Are you curious what's inside?" he asked.

"Of course I am."

"Address me properly."

"I'm sorry, Master."

"Your pregnancy doesn't give you license to act like a brat, and it won't prevent me from punishing your hole." To drive home his point, he drew a finger between my butt cheeks, bottom to top. "Anal penetration won't harm the baby if done with care."

I wanted to argue, mostly because I hated when he punished my asshole, but the doctor had given us the rundown on what was safe and what wasn't. As long as my pregnancy continued on a normal, healthy path, Gage still had plenty of room to make me bend.

"May I open the box now, Master?"

"You may," he said with a playful swat to my bottom.

It was enough to send me into motion. I sensed him lingering a couple of feet behind me as I crossed to the bed. That box drew my attention like a beacon, with its gorgeous burgundy color, accented with black lace and trimmed in gold. I pried the top off and pushed the tissue paper aside to reveal black rope and a jeweled butt plug. Dread and longing collided inside me until I couldn't decide whether to run from what he had planned, or beg for it. I lifted the rope and turned to face him.

"I thought you could use a couple of accessories to match your dress." His mouth curled into a smug smile.

"My dress?" I rubbed the silky rope between my fingers.

"Come," he said, holding out a hand.

Sliding my palm into his felt as natural as breathing. He led me to our wardrobe and unzipped a garment bag that hadn't been in there that morning when I'd dressed.

"Wow," I breathed, more than taken with the gown that spilled from the bag. The dress was the same deep burgundy as the butt plug, and the skirt was as full as a ballroom gown. I ran my fingers over the black and gold beadwork that adorned the front of the strapless corset-styled bodice.

"What a divine creation," he said, fingering the satin material, but his gaze never left me. "Wearing clothing should be illegal. If I could escort your naked body to this ball and get away with it, I would." A corner of his mouth tilted up. "I guess this dress will have to do, at least until we get to the better portion of the night."

The *after* party.

He freed the dress from the bag before escorting me back into the bedroom. I clutched the rope, which was long enough that the end trailed behind me on the hardwood floor. He carefully arranged the dress on the bed before moving toward me with purpose, one hand outstretched, palm up.

"Hand me the rope, please."

It slipped from my fingers, like silk pouring from my hand to his, and a chill broke out on my skin as I watched him fold it in half. I had no clue what he was about to do.

The upcoming night held many intrigues—beginning right here in our bedroom.

"Extend your arms."

As I stood with my arms spread and feet shoulder-width apart on the floor, he wound the rope above and below my breasts, his fingers grazing my skin in a way that caused gooseflesh. Then he drew the rope over my nipples—fuck, they were sensitive—and weaved it into neat little knots as he worked, before making a loop around my neck. Finally, he finished by running the rope between my legs. All of my most sensitive parts came alive under the restraining friction of the silky twine. I couldn't move without arousal flaring to life.

He halted in front of me, his eyes bright with mischief and lips curved in a knowing smirk as if to say how he'd be the one stroking me by proxy all night long.

"Bend over the bed," he said, grabbing the butt plug.

I found freedom in yielding to his commands, despite fighting myself daily on giving him my unconditional trust. The more I resisted, the more firm his resolve to exorcize my last thread of independence tonight. As he slipped the plug in, making my pussy shamefully wet from that single action alone, I thought he might just achieve his goal. I was tired of battling an internal war I'd never win.

"The plug is synced to my cell. For the duration of the night, when it vibrates, I expect you to touch yourself."

My breath caught in my throat. "Where? The women's restroom?" Damn it. He knew how I hated submitting in public places.

"No, that's too easy. An empty hallway or room will suffice. I want you in fear of getting caught."

I turned wide, frightened eyes on him. "Master, please!"

"Shh," he whispered, pressing a finger to my lips. "The ball is being held at the Davenport Estate. There are plenty of semi-private places to masturbate. I expect you to find one upon command, but you're not to bring yourself to orgasm." Running a palm down my ass, he pressed his lips to my neck. "This will help you get into the right mindset for our plans after the ball."

Plans that included other people. Oh, how I despised these plans, probably more than he'd ever know.

"It's getting late. Time to dress," he said, slapping my ass. He crossed to the bureau and produced two masks—one for him and one for me.

"What's a masquerade ball without a mask?"

CHAPTER EIGHTEEN

Gage pulled through the iron gates of the Davenport Estate, and as we approached the front of the traditional brick mansion, I marveled at the lush, sprawling lawns that seemed to reach the horizon. Rolling to a stop at the main entrance, he alighted and rounded the hood, warding off a well-meaning valet who moved to open my door. As Gage assisted me from the car, helping me maneuver the full skirt of my ballgown, I took in our surroundings. By no means did we live in anything other than the lap of luxury, but this place was on a whole other level of opulence.

Fitting my hand in the crook of his arm, Gage escorted me onto the stone walkway that led to the front door. A light breeze blew through my hair, and I brushed the strands from my face, my wide-eyed gaze riveted to the nearby pond. The night was mild, absent of even a drop of rain. Fluffy clouds parted, allowing the silver light of the crescent moon to ripple onto the pond. The moon seemed to hover—just a tiny dip and the bottom would touch the pond, breaking the glass-like surface.

A man in a tux greeted us at the door. He took our jackets before pointing us in the direction of the mansion's host. And speaking of tuxedos...good God, how I ached to rip off my husband's and have my way with him. I peeked at him from the corner of my eye, appreciating how his chest filled out the vest and overcoat. But he caught me ogling, and his eyes sparkled behind the black mask he wore.

"Mr. and Mrs. Channing. Welcome to our home," said a man who also knew how to wear a tux, though he lacked Gage's commanding presence, not to mention a pair of sexy indigo eyes and a cock I wanted to kneel for at this very moment.

Gage shook hands with the man as he introduced us.

"Nice to meet you," I said, failing to offer my hand because I knew the rules. No other man was to touch me, no matter the social etiquette. In the beginning, Gage had allowed that tiny concession, but not since I'd betrayed him with...

Better to not go there.

Mr. Davenport seemed unsurprised by my lack of manners, and something niggled in the back of my mind. Suddenly, I felt on display, naked despite wearing a gown heavier than seven layers of clothing.

"Pleased to meet you," our host said, and even though he didn't possess Gage's innate dominant manner, he had a head full of thick, blond hair and a broad smile that revealed the kind of perfect white teeth I'd seen in toothpaste commercials. "This is my wife, Virginia." He indicated the brunette holding onto his arm. Her hair was sleek and straight, and she had the kind of curvy waist I envied.

But her smile was as genuine as her husband's, and that was all that mattered. She stepped forward and gently took my arm. "How about we allow these men to do what men do at these shindigs? There are several ladies just dying to meet the woman who snatched the one and only Gage Channing."

Something about the way she spoke of Gage made me curious, and a little cautious. I shot him a quick glance, relaying so much with a furtive dart of my gaze.

May I go, Master?

With a slight nod, he bent and kissed my cheek. "Have fun, baby," he said, voice too intimate to be overheard. "Don't forget your task for the night."

I'd grown used to the butt plug. It wasn't overly big, so I didn't find it uncomfortable, and I certainly didn't miss the rectal burn the larger ones caused. Even so, now that Gage had reminded me of what I was to do, my ass suddenly felt too full—brimming with the promise of humiliation.

I swallowed hard as Virginia led me through the throng of people. Ballgowns of all colors brushed the parquet flooring, and men wore a variety of tuxedoes, from traditional black with long-tailed jackets to contemporary attire, embellished with colors from tasteful to...less tasteful.

She ushered me into another room where tables were grouped in strategic patterns around the dance floor. I instantly recognized the decor because I'd helped pick out the colors. Ironically, the ballroom matched my dress, and I wondered if that had been Gage's intention all along.

Probably so. Gage did everything by design.

"Over here," Virginia said, yanking on my hand and leading me to a table where four other women, also decked out in extravagant ballgowns, sat.

"Kayla," my hostess said, "I'd like you to meet..."

Too busy taking in the features of each woman, I tuned out their names, as I likely wouldn't remember them anyway. Not in this setting, with my heart pounding an irregular rhythm behind my breastbone.

The blonde with enviable curls and dark brown eyes

nibbled on a crab-stuffed mushroom, her gaze shyly taking me in. The other three were all various shades of browns, but their hairstyles couldn't have been more different. One sported a cute pixie while the other two had longer lengths. The girl wearing a dress that could pass as a wedding gown wore her hair past her ass. The last of this brunette trio ran her fingers through layers that feathered around her flawless complexion.

These women were, in a word, gorgeous. And something about the way they interacted with each other—with ease and familiarity—told me their friendships had withstood the test of time. I sat with them for about forty-five minutes, nibbling on hors d'oeuvre and listening to their casual chatter.

But I felt disconnected, unable to relate to Blondie's endeavor to find the perfect piece of jewelry for her upcoming trip to Paris. Nor could I empathize with Pixie Girl's indecision on which boarding school to send her daughter to next year.

Over my dead body would I send my children away.

Despite the world of differences between this group and myself, I still found their company pleasant, and I could see meeting up with them for lunch, or even a day of shopping if Gage allowed it.

Something told me he would. My gut chewed over this whole night in a way that frightened and excited me, and I sensed these women and their as yet named husbands were going to play a big part in our lives. Maybe Gage wanted us to have friends. The concept sounded kind of...nice.

I was lost in Virginia's talk about the next fundraiser she was in the process of organizing when the plug in my ass vibrated me out of my stupor. The telltale mechanical sound blazed my cheeks red, but no one seemed to hear it over the excited discussion of venues and caterers.

Rising from my chair, I excused myself to use the ladies room and headed in the direction that Virginia pointed out. But that wouldn't do. Gage had given me specific instructions, and they didn't involve hiding in a bathroom, safe behind a closed door.

Damn him.

A wall of French doors caught my eye to the right, and before I could give it more thought, I slipped outside and immediately wished I had my jacket. But the weather wasn't too bad, and doing Gage's bidding would be easier out here, where I had plenty of space to explore, between the stone walkways, spotted with benches and lanterns that invited people to meander through the gardens surrounding the gazebo.

Only a few stragglers braved the chilly night, but most of them kept close to the estate. Gage hadn't said a word about *not* going outside to touch myself, so I took off down the path, eyeing the shelter of trees that provided a backdrop for the gazebo. Ash trees were prominent throughout the grounds, and their autumn leaves—the color of burnt sienna and gold—quietly drifted to the grass like confetti at a party.

I found an unusually large tree a few feet from the gazebo, its trunk wide enough to conceal most of my body. And that's where I settled in for the duration of my first task, my back against the smooth bark as I gathered my gown up in the front and wedged my hand between my thighs, pushing Gage's rope to the side.

Oh God. The friction of that rope in the valley of my ass cheeks, and the way it pressed tight against my nipples amped me even hotter. Between the vibrations from the plug and the slickness of my needy pussy, left aching all day from Gage's denial games, I wasn't sure how I'd survive this.

But I had to, even if that meant visualizing spiders

crawling all over me to keep from coming. Because I knew my husband well enough to know that he expected me to touch myself until the vibrations stopped.

It was all about control, and I'd better find some, or else.

But damn...

With a groan, I let my head fall back against the tree and increased the circling motion of my fingers. And they were playing a dangerous game—touching in the perfect way with enough pressure to bring a massive rush of blood to my core.

So damn good. Could I get off and lie about it?

Not even an option. Not only would he know I was lying, but I'd break under my own guilt in two seconds flat. But shit...I was going to come. So close.

Too fucking close.

Growling, and more than a little angry, I banged my head against the trunk as I wrenched my fingers away from temptation. Just a few seconds, I promised myself, concentrating on breathing until my heartbeat slowed. But my ass still vibrated Gage's command, and I imagined his words as surely as if he'd spoken them into my ear.

Fingers in your drenched cunt, Kayla. Don't stop now.

Why did he have to torture me so damn much? I was never free of him—if his control didn't wrap me in metaphorical cellophane, then his voice echoed in my head, uttering filthy words that never failed to make me do his bidding.

Pushing my wet fingers back into the center of slick heat, I worked myself into a frenzy. My pussy throbbed with each stroke, and I climbed higher—so high I worried I'd float away, regardless of the consequences. Squeezing my eyes shut, I pleaded with a higher power to help me resist.

"Please, *please*..." My frantic whispers got lost in the

breeze, drifting on the leaves, finding the kind of freedom I wasn't allowed. "Oh please...I *can't...*"

And that's when the vibrations stopped.

I wasn't sure how long I leaned against the tree, eyes closed, chest expanding and collapsing with each hard-won breath. Coming down took time—more time than I thought it would, considering I hadn't reached nirvana.

After a while, I started shivering, and I had just taken a step away from my hiding place when I heard voices. Pressing as flat as I could against the trunk, I prayed the cloak of darkness would conceal me to whoever had decided to encroach upon my private moment.

Two people stalled in front of the gazebo, and I recognized Gage immediately. The build of his shoulders, the way he walked, and the authority inherent in his tone—if nothing else gave him away behind his mask, those traits certainly did.

But he wasn't alone, and it took me an extra five seconds to realize the woman with him was Katherine. I pressed a fist to my mouth to cover a gasp.

"You've got five minutes before I have you thrown off the grounds," he said, and the undeniable anger in his voice leeched some of the tension from my body. This was not a rendezvous between two lovers on the down-low.

This was...I had no idea what this was, but forget the rules against eavesdropping; I wasn't about to blow my chance to find out more.

"Don't be so mean. No one's around, Gage. It's just us."

He closed the distance between them and grabbed her chin. "How pathetic are you? In what world would I want you here? You *weren't* invited."

A nearby lantern cast their faces in dim light, and I saw her full mouth curve into a sultry grin. "I can have anyone I want, Gage. It was child's play getting a date to this thing."

"Like I said," he growled, letting go of her chin in a move that bespoke of frustration. "Five minutes, Katherine. If you used our son to lure me out here—"

"You can't take her into the circle," she said, her voice rising in desperation. "It was supposed to be me!" She dropped to her knees and kissed his black dress shoes.

I chewed on my fist, swallowing vile hatred because the bitch was laying her nasty lips on what was mine. Those were my feet to kneel at. *My* shoes to kiss. I clenched my hands so tightly they cramped, but my gaze...I was transfixed, lost in the scene unfolding, like one would watch a horror film.

He stepped back, arms crossed, mouth in a scowl. "Get up. You're only embarrassing yourself."

"Please, Mr. Channing."

"Don't you dare 'Mr. Channing' me! She is my *wife*. When will you get that through your thick skull?"

Katherine lifted her head, but instead of the submissive pose I'd expected her to take—the one I adopted every fucking day—she sneered at him, her hands forming tight balls at her sides.

"Fine," she snapped. "She can be your wife all she wants. Little Miss Perfect with the adorable daughter and a penchant for scrubbing your house and serving your meals, but we both know you need more than that. I can give you what you need, baby."

"You never gave me what I needed. Why do you think I broke it off after a few months?"

His words blasted a hole in my heart, and I almost threw up on the spot. Rage simmered in my gut, heading for a full-on boil, and only closing my eyes and counting to ten kept the vomit at bay. He'd been fucking her.

For *months*.

I stepped forward, my thirst for a confrontation blazing

an inferno in my veins, but he spoke before I exited the cover of shadows.

"Katherine, seriously, get up. What we had meant nothing. Hell, it was years ago. You need to move the fuck on."

"Like you were able to move on from her?"

"That's different."

"No, it's not, and I know you want me. Deep down, you know it's true. Why else would you have called me down to your basement?"

"That was about her. It had nothing to do with you." Leaning down, he grabbed a chunk of her hair. "I will not repeat myself. Get the *fuck* up."

She struggled to her feet, and he instantly let go of her. "After the shit you pulled last week, you're lucky I don't go after full custody. Your behavior makes me question how fit you are to be a mother to Conner."

She smirked at him. "You're just pissed because I forced your wife to face her past in that hotel room." Planting her hands on her hips, she cocked her head. "The photo I sent you was nothing. They were all over each other."

That was it. I stormed from my hiding spot, and her face stopped my out-of-control fist. She covered her cheek, eyes wide. In my periphery, I registered Gage's equally stunned silence, stowing that rare expression away in the dregs of my mind to process later.

"Thank you for that," I told Katherine, forcing my voice on an even keel. "With these damn pregnancy hormones, I never know when my fist might go flying." I held my right hand up and contracted my fingers. "The thing has a mind of its own sometimes."

Slowly, she dropped her hand, and I was way too fucking pleased to see red smarting across her skin. Her face wasn't so perfect anymore.

"Wh...what?" Her eyes grew wider if that were possible.

Two blue pools of utter disbelief—though whether from the punch I'd landed or from my pregnancy announcement, I didn't know. And I didn't care.

Planting my fist in Katherine Mitchell's face had felt... way too satisfying.

She turned incredulous eyes on Gage. "Are you seriously going to let her assault the mother of your child?"

I stepped forward before he could answer, invading her space. "You're nothing but a lying bitch, jealous over what you can't have," I said, meeting her glare head-on. "You think you're a special snowflake because you gave birth to his child?"

Something ugly took over me—maybe my own version of jealous and possessive woman—but I felt my lips curl into a nasty smile. "You keep forgetting one vital fact. You're just the baby mama. But me?" I lifted an elated brow. "I'm his wife *and* the mother of his unborn child, so I guess that makes me the winner here, sweetie."

She stumbled back, and only then did I realize that I'd inched forward with each verbal strike to the bullseye of her venomous core. I would have kept on pushing, refusing to back down until the bitch fell flat on her ass, but Gage grabbed my shoulders.

"Come on, Kayla. She's not worth it, and this stress isn't good for the baby."

I knew he was right, but hell, I wanted to keep going at her until not a trace of her claim on my husband remained.

"If you're not gone in five minutes," Gage told her, "I'll send security after you." He veered me in the direction of the estate, and I caught a glimpse of something dark passing over her face, settling into the depths of her eyes.

The promise of payback.

She might be down this round, but she fully intended to

dig her claws into what was mine....one way or another. Beneath the mask of momentary defeat lived an irate woman who issued a silent challenge.

Game on.

CHAPTER NINETEEN

"Why were you out here?" he had the audacity to ask as he ushered me toward the party.

"Why were you?" I shot back. Once again, I tried to pull from his grasp, but he wouldn't allow it. He had my hand in the crook of his arm, the picture of a perfect gentlemen, but as he placed his palm over the back of my hand, I knew the true reason he held onto me.

Power and control. It was such a Gage type of move that I shouldn't have been surprised.

The lights from the mansion lit up the patio several feet in front of us, but Gage steered us toward a bench. As I settled into the seat, he removed his jacket and draped it over my shoulders before taking the spot next to me.

"Do not disrespect me, Kayla. Answer the question."

"I'm sorry, Master," I said, lowering my gaze to my twiddling thumbs. But I wasn't really sorry—a large part of me still seethed from my confrontation with that bitch. Adrenaline pumped through my veins too fast, and I took a deep breath to get a grip on my emotions.

"I came out here to touch myself." From the corner of my

eye, I noted how his shoulders seemed to release some of his tension.

He let out a breath. "Of course you did." He shot me a sideways glance. "Did you come?"

"No, Master."

"But you got close?"

His line of questioning more than frustrated me. "Shouldn't we talk about Katherine?"

"You still don't trust me," he said, matter-of-factly. "But to answer your question, Kayla, I went for a walk with Katherine because she said she needed to talk about Conner."

I turned to face him and laced our fingers together. "I do trust you. That's not what this is about. I feel like..."

He squeezed my fingers, and that small gesture of encouragement gave me the strength to forge ahead.

"I guess I feel like there's something I'm missing, or not understanding. We've been married for over a year, but she just won't let go. You were with her for *months*, but that was years ago."

The instant the words left my mouth, I realized how ridiculous I sounded, considering my brief time with Ian years ago. Cheeks flaming, I lowered my gaze, ashamed that I'd let my jealousy and doubt cloud what was right in front of me.

It was like a bulb flashing behind my eyes.

"I feel so stupid," I whispered.

He tilted my chin, refusing to let me hide. "You're not stupid, baby. You're mine, which makes me yours, and you have every right to get angry. She's overstepping, but it won't last forever. Eventually, she'll move on." His hold on me tightened. "She'll move on because she has *no choice*."

His assertion was layered in meaning. People always had a choice, but in Gage Channing's world, his decree was law, and he always got what he wanted. I wasn't sure he was right —not after I'd punched the bitch before throwing my pregnancy in her face.

"I'm only going to say one more thing about what went down back there," he said, nodding in the direction of the gazebo, where thankfully I found no sign of Katherine. "Because I won't allow her to ruin this night for us."

My breath stalled in my lungs as I waited for him to continue. Whatever he wanted to say, I sensed the importance.

"You were fucking amazing," he said, voice hoarse as he palmed my cheek. "If you're wondering why I didn't stand up for you, it's because I didn't have to. Watching you in action, with your claws bared and fighting for what's yours, was the best foreplay imaginable. I can *not* wait to get my hands on you tonight."

His words arrowed straight between my legs. "Master?" I breathed, fighting the urge to cover my suddenly aching nipples as visions of the two of us tore through my mind.

"What is it, baby?"

"I'm so wet." A whimper drifted from my lips, and I pressed my thighs together.

"Spread them," he ordered, a seductive timbre holding his voice captive.

"But what if someone—"

"I don't care who's watching. Spread your legs." And he truly didn't give a fuck. His gaze remained on me, and he brought his hand to my cheek again, preventing me from searching our surroundings for bystanders.

Wetting my lips, I inched my thighs apart, horribly self-conscious as a hint of air drifted up my legs.

"If you don't spread your legs like you mean it, I will bend you over my lap and expose your ass."

Oh, fuck. That shouldn't make me so hot, but it did.

I spread wide open, and he slipped a warm hand underneath my full dress. He didn't bother easing into it—his fingers filled my pussy in a forceful thrust.

"Master," I groaned, arching my back.

"So fucking wet." He licked his lips. "Who owns this sexy-as-fuck cunt?"

"You do, Master." And he was driving me crazy because he refused to move his fingers. They'd laid claim to my drenched opening, and they seemed content to stay seated there as if my body was but a glove for those digits.

"Please," I practically sighed, falling into the deep sea of his eyes. No one else existed—it was just the two of us, nose-to-nose, his left palm on my cheek while his right hand drove me insane.

"You can beg all you want, but you're not coming."

"Why are you doing this to me?"

One corner of his mouth lifted. "Because I can." Leaning forward, he dipped his tongue between my parted lips. "Because I love to watch you come undone, nothing holding you back." He crooked his fingers inside me, and I moaned against his lips. "If I told you someone was watching us this very minute, would you still beg me to fuck you with my fingers?"

"Yes, Master." I kissed him, eyes fluttering shut, and spread my legs as wide as my tired muscles would allow. He tangled his tongue with mine for a few lust-filled seconds then pulled away.

"What if I wanted to lick your beautiful cunt while strangers watched? Would you beg me to do it?"

"*God*," I choked past the desire strangling my throat.

"I'm not your God, but I am your Master. Beg me, Kayla."

"I need you," I said with a whimper. "Fuck me, Master. I'm begging."

"Mmm," he murmured, scraping his teeth over the sensitive part of my neck, "your cunt is begging. Know the difference, baby."

"It needs you. Bad."

"Yes, it does. But your belly is growling, so your cunt will have to wait." He rose to his feet, and it was a good thing he pulled me to mine because I knew my legs would have folded without his support.

He led me back inside in time for the first course of an elaborate meal, and I wondered if everyone could guess at the mess between my legs with one glance at my flushed face. My lust for Gage consumed me, and I was certain I gave off whore-like pheromones that no mask in the world could disguise.

CHAPTER TWENTY

I made it through dinner and dessert in a daze, politely nodding upon what I hoped were the right cues, and speaking only when directly spoken to. But my mind had zeroed in on the hot need between my thighs. Gage had mastered the art of controlling me through denial, and when he played with my head like this, I might as well be a puppet dangling on the other end of his strings.

Sometime later, long after we'd eaten our last course, he dragged my reluctant feet to the middle of the dance floor. Couples crowded around us from all sides—at least that's what it felt like despite the cathedral ceiling over the spacious ballroom. My husband's unyielding finger titled my chin in his direction, demanding my undivided attention. He pressed a hand to the small of my back and brought me into his arms. We swayed to the music, lost in our own world, mindless of the time passing. I could dance like this with him forever, one cheek nestled against his chest, moving more to the sound of his heartbeat than to the music.

"It's time," Gage whispered into my ear.

He might as well have poured ice water over my head. I withdrew from the circle of his arms, and only then did I notice how the guests had mostly disappeared. Hired help in crisp black and white uniforms began clearing tables.

Wordlessly, Gage ushered me from the ballroom. We headed toward a grand staircase with ornately carved wooden banisters, but instead of climbing to the second or even third floor of the estate, he steered me to the left of the stairs where we disappeared through an archway.

"Where are we going?"

Instead of answering, he laced our fingers together and escorted me halfway down a long corridor before opening another door and urging me into what appeared to be the library, going by the floor-to-ceiling shelves housing books. Some of them were old and worn, possibly antiques. The room offered privacy in a claustrophobic nature, as not a single window allowed a beam of light from the moon or a ray of warmth from the sun during the day.

Even though he'd removed his mask, I recognized Mr. Davenport instantly. He sat in a chair in front of the fireplace, his lean body nestled in dark brown leather. "It's an honor to have the two of you join us tonight," he said, his smile reaching his eyes.

I turned to Gage for instruction because I was way out of my element here. I didn't know what to expect or what was expected of me.

"My wife is in the dark about all of this, so please forgive her lack of protocol. She'll know better after tonight."

Our host narrowed his thick brows. "Do you need a few minutes to discuss it with her before we get to the nondisclosure?"

"Thank you, but that won't be necessary. This is a lesson of trust for her."

"I see," the other man said, nodding. "Please, make yourself comfortable, Channing." He gestured to another chair to the right of him. A crystal decanter sat on a table alongside two tumblers.

Gage led me to where the other man sat and pointed at the floor in front of the table. "You may kneel here."

"Yes, Master." Regardless of our audience, the title slipped off my lips, as natural as breathing, and I sank to my knees, arranging my dress over a plush Persian rug as I did so.

Gage poured two fingers then settled into the high back armchair.

Mr. Davenport laid a document and pen down on the table. "It's standard, but feel free to read through it."

Burning with curiosity, I watched Gage go over the paper, certain his astute gaze left not a single word unread. With no hesitation, he signed his name at the bottom before passing the pen to me.

"You need to sign as well. It's just a standard nondisclosure agreement. You're not allowed to speak to anyone about what goes on during these sessions."

Sessions...as in plural. I tried not to gulp as I pushed upward, standing on my knees so I could reach the paper.

"Welcome to our circle," Mr. Davenport said. "I must admit to being pleasantly surprised you finally took me up on my invitation," he told Gage.

My husband merely shrugged. "I guess I was waiting for Kayla." He leaned forward and brushed his fingers under my chin. "And she wasn't quite ready until now."

The other man rose. "Wonderful. You'll find a robe for your slave at the top of the stairs. We require that new slaves disrobe in front of everyone their first time in the circle."

I felt my jaw slacken, but I didn't dare look at Gage. If I did, I might beg for him to take me home.

"If that's all then," Mr. Davenport stated rather than

asked, "we'll see you down there in a few minutes." He gathered the document and crossed to the wall of shelves before pulling out a book. Much to my astonishment, two bookcases wheeled outward and to the sides, revealing a secret staircase.

"Is this some sort of secret society?" I asked after those stairs seemed to swallow our host.

"In a way, yes." Gage stood and held out a palm, assisting me to my feet. "Let's get this dress off."

I shrank back, fists crossing over my breasts. "I want to go home."

Gage frowned. "Now is not the time for you to rebel, baby. I've waited years for this. You're the only woman I've ever wanted to take into the circle."

"Why me?" It was a stupid question, and a desperate one I'd thrown out to stall him.

"Address me properly."

"I'm sorry, Master." Sorry wasn't even close—my mind spun in all directions, trying to latch on to something that made sense. How had we gone from Master and slave in the privacy of our home to this?

"When spoken to by the men in the circle, you'll address them as *Sir*, myself excluded. I'm your Master, and you'll address me as such." He straightened his spine, rising high over my quivering form. I stood on my feet in front of him, but my will was but a tiny ball of nothing, cowering on the floor.

"As for the other slaves," he continued, "you won't speak to them unless directed to." Carefully, he removed my mask and set it on the table before taking his off as well. But as he reached for me, I stepped out of line again.

"Please don't make me do this, Master."

"Do you trust me?"

"Yes, Master." But wanting to trust someone and doing so were two different things.

"Then prove it," he said. "Obey me. I promise you won't be touched by anyone but me."

No, I'd just be used and humiliated in front of his societal bigwig friends. Allowing him to unzip my dress took more self-control than I thought I possessed. As that zipper slid down my back, I clenched my fists and mashed my lips together. Why did the idea of submitting to him in front of others seem so daunting? Compared to what he put me through daily, having an audience shouldn't bother me so much.

My dress fell in a heavy pile on the floor, surrounding my shaking limbs with the finest fabric money could buy. Gripping his offered hand, I worked my heels off before stepping outside the circle of discarded formalwear, and goose pimples erupted on my skin as he slowly freed my body from his rope binding.

"Are you ready?" he asked, folding the silky twine before pocketing it.

Not even close, but I'd be damned if I allowed this night to be the catalyst for a breakdown.

"As ready as I'll ever be, Master."

Gage herded me to the top of the stairs, where the "robe" hung on a hook. Robe, my ass. The garment was nothing more than a sheer peignoir.

"Whether you receive pain or pleasure tonight is up to you," he said, holding the lingerie open so I could push my arms through the long, flowing sleeves. Impossibly, I felt more exposed with it on.

"How so, Master?"

"If you behave, you won't be punished."

"That doesn't reassure me, Master."

"Why not?"

"Because you love my pain." Promises or not, he'd find creative ways to make me stumble.

Taking my chin between two commanding fingers, he pressed his lips to mine for a fleeting moment. "You know me so well."

The winding staircase took us to a room hidden below where the ball had been held. My skin chilled from the cold, or maybe from nerves. A door came into view, and Gage halted.

"You will follow my directions and only mine. Do you understand?"

"Y-yes, Master." I swallowed hard, but nausea busted through my resolve. "Can I have a safe word?"

"You don't need a safe word. You asked why you? This is why. You give me what I crave most. You give me the honor of truly owning you. Trust that I know what you can and can't handle."

Oh God. I was close to panicking.

"No gags," I begged.

He ran a thumb across my lips. "Considering your condition, I wouldn't have gagged you anyway. This is what I'm talking about, Kayla. You don't trust me to take care of you." Sharp disappointment drew his face taunt, deepening his indigo eyes.

"I'm sorry, Master." My failure at pleasing him sucked the strength from me, and my knees gave out. Wrapping my arms around his legs, I nestled my cheek against the smooth fabric of his pants. "I want to make you proud."

"You're making me hard."

Those words had the power to flip that mysterious switch inside me. From despair to arousal in less time than it took to inhale. Gazing up at him, I exhaled my reservations and grabbed his offered hand.

He propelled me to my feet, and though my body still shook from fear of the unknown, I felt stronger at my core as he wedged open that door and ushered me toward the next test of my submission.

CHAPTER TWENTY-ONE

The sweet aroma of cigars drifted through the space that could only be described as elaborate…or decadently sensual from the candlelight that washed the room in a soft glow. This was not a basement, but a huge circle of a room, and Gage and I stood at the edge. Directly in the center sat a group of people, unsurprisingly in a circle. The men relaxed in chairs, their formal attire in various stages of undress as they talked, drank, and smoked. The five women I'd met earlier in the evening kneeled at their feet, sans their masks.

Blondie was completely naked, and her husband had gagged her mouth. Tears lingered on her long lashes, and I wondered what she'd done to earn the punishment of silence. To their left, Mr. Davenport puffed on a cigar, his legs spread to accommodate his wife's bobbing head. He helped her along, his fingers sifting through her sleek hair. He downright petted her as she sucked him with lazy strokes of her slurping mouth.

The other three women kneeled like Blondie, only none of them were entirely naked. The girl who'd worn a white gown earlier now sported thigh-highs and nothing else.

Pixie Girl was trussed up in shibari that concealed her private areas in the intricate design. The rope wound around her breasts, torso, and limbs in gorgeous weaving. She was bound to the spot, unable to rise to her feet with the way her arms and had been tied behind her, wrists connected to ankles.

The fifth woman wore only nipple clamps, and I resisted the urge to cover my breasts at the sight. Clenching the chain between her teeth, she tensed her jaw as she struggled to pull on the clamps. I watched her in morbid curiosity, wondering if she wanted the extra pain that pulling on that chain caused, or if she was yanking on it because the alternative would be worse. What would happen if she let it slip from her mouth?

I wasn't sure I wanted to know.

This place set me on edge, and not because it was home to displays of painful implements or torture stockades. Rather, the understated deviance in the room unsettled me to the bone.

Gage tugged on my hand, and as I followed him to the circle, I couldn't take my eyes off the two beds situated opposite each other across the room, with their canopies draped in gossamer gold. Those beds weren't made for privacy; they'd been set up as a stage for fucking, sitting high atop platforms that necessitated a five stair climb just to reach them. Love seats and chairs surrounded each platform, inviting the remaining couples to watch...or join in on the fun.

My stomach wanted to take a dive at that disturbing realization, but all I had to do was remind myself of Gage's possessiveness, and the fact that he'd promised no one but him would touch me.

"Welcome to the circle," the men chorused in sync as if they'd rehearsed that greeting.

Mr. Davenport, regardless of having his wife's mouth wrapped around his cock, leaned forward slightly. "The floor is yours," he told Gage.

"Thank you." Gage came to a stop and gently pushed on my shoulders, telling me without words to kneel.

My body obeyed, practically on auto-pilot, and the position put me at eye level with his hard-on. God, how I wanted to unzip him and take a page from Virginia Davenport's book. The woman's escalating moans as she feasted on her husband's cock did funny things to my insides.

"I need to go over one important ground rule," Gage said, his voice echoing through the room for all to hear. He grabbed my hair as if to ready me for a good mouth-fucking. "No one touches what's mine."

"Understood," someone said.

With a nod, Gage let me go. "It's time to disrobe," he said as my hair slid through his fingers.

I trudged to the center, watching as Gage settled into the only available seat in the circle, and slowly brought my hands to the front of the peignoir. The sheer fabric grazed my nipples, making my cheeks flush with awareness, and as I opened the material I imagined his mouth nipping at my breasts. I nearly moaned at the thought as the garment slipped from my shoulders and drifted to the hardwood under my bare feet.

"Good girl. Now turn around so everyone can see what's mine."

I made a slow circle, taking in the features of the men more closely than before. And while their eyes were on my erect nipples, I cataloged each couple. Blondie's husband was on the husky side, his shirt unbuttoned and pants undone. Pixie's man was as tall as Gage. His red hair was his most arresting feature; it was on the longer side, unruly and entirely sexy. The remaining men had classic dark good looks, but I found nothing interesting or special about them.

"Kayla?"

"Yes, Master?" I said, whirling back to Gage.

"Crawl to me."

And here came the real test. As soon as I got down on all fours, everyone would see how wet I was between my thighs. I wasn't sure why, but I found revealing my arousal more distressing than stripping in front of these people. I had no authority over the nakedness of my body, but my drenched pussy...I wished to be able to control that more than anything.

As I made my way across the floor to where Gage waited, I sensed five pairs of eyes on my ass—possibly even more if the women watched as well. He pulled the rope from his pocket and looped it through the discreet ring in my infinity collar, effectively leashing me with the rope I'd worn on my body all evening.

"Unzip me," he commanded.

That's when I hesitated, and not because I fretted over what he planned to do with me, but hell...I didn't want those women ogling my husband's cock. Fierce possessiveness rose in me, pumping blood through my system in pulsing bursts.

How could he stand those men's eyes on me? Especially with how jealous and possessive he was?

"Do I need to spank you?"

"No, Master," I said, reaching for his pants and freeing the button. As I pulled down his zipper, it dawned on me why Gage wasn't bothered by the prying eyes of other men. He was in control here, and they could look until their eyes fell out of their heads, but they couldn't touch.

The same could be said for the women. Mine, I mentally chanted as I parted his pants and revealed his cock, beaming with pride that I could call it mine. No other woman would come near it again. They'd have to get past my flying fist first. I balled my hands, darting my tongue over my lips to wet them as I gawked at my husband's impressive erection.

"Do you want me in your mouth?" He lifted his head, a sparkle in his gaze. "Davenport's slave seems to be enjoying the task."

I couldn't see the other couple, but I heard him chuckle over his wife's moaning.

"Yes, Master." The need to please him clawed at my composure. He had me too worked up, too wet at the epicenter of my depraved core. He'd managed to break me down like this in a mere day—to this desperate *thing* that would strip in front of strangers and beg to suck his cock.

Gage was a fucking sorcerer. I could come up with no other explanation.

"Baby, what if I don't want my cock in your mouth right now?" He withdrew a travel-sized packet of lube. "What if I want it someplace else?"

Cringing, I grabbed his knees for support. "As you w-wish, Master."

"Kayla," he murmured, tilting my chin up, "stand up and grab your ankles."

I pushed off his knees and stood on gelatinous limbs, and as I turned around to do his bidding, I found the others watching with appreciation and desire in their eyes. They were getting off on this voyeuristic showcase. Would watching these men dominate their wives get Gage hot and bothered as well? Would witnessing such sinful behavior get *me* off?

Listening to Virginia's moans had hit my bullseye, but only because I'd envied her at that moment. Fuck, I still did, considering that packet of lube and what it was obviously intended for.

I bent and grasped my ankles, and blood rushed to my

head as Gage inched out the dry plug. He took extra time with the removal, being careful not to hurt me upon the toy's exit. Then I heard him tear into that packet, and between my spread thighs, I watched him lube his cock.

"You're going to sit your pretty ass onto my cock while we watch the show." He grabbed my hips and yanked me toward his lap, and I planted my hands on my knees to steady me. I tensed, body already fighting the intrusion of his shaft inside my tight hole, but he didn't bring me down onto him like I thought he would.

Quick and brutal, and powerless to stop him.

"Take me in as slow as you need to," he instructed, shocking me with his unexpected gift of control.

Holding onto the arms of the chair, I pressed onto his cock and willed my body to stretch around the intrusion. Minutes passed as I carefully worked him inside my ass, my knuckles going white even as I relaxed the muscles below my waist. Accepting his length and girth into my backdoor was a tall order, but I wasn't there yet, so I thrust downward and impaled myself fully. A gasp stalled in my lungs, and I held my breath for a few moments until I grew accustomed to the fullness in my ass.

"So good," he groaned into my ear. "Just sit like this for a while and watch."

His tone had a drugging effect on me. Or maybe it was his cock laying claim to my ass, but my belly heated, and my head spun with disorienting wooziness. Lifting heavy lids, I watched the going-ons happening inside the circle of this lair in a fog-like state.

Pixie had been released from her restraints, and now she sat on her husband's lap and rode him, her hips lowering her onto his cock over and over again.

Mr. Davenport yanked his wife's head up with an uncompromising fist in her hair.

"You haven't earned the privilege of getting me off yet."

She whimpered her disappointment.

"You're out of line, slave." His harsh voice stunned me, as did the way he addressed her. "You don't decide when I come down your throat. I do." Without further discussion, he pulled her head back into his lap and returned to sipping his drink.

The man to his left laughed, and they resumed their quiet conversation about stocks or some other crap I had no interest in listening to.

My attention veered to Blondie again, who'd switched positions with her husband. She reclined in the seat with her legs bent and feet on the chair's arms, knees spread wide. Her man stood before her, rubbing his chin as he watched her touch herself. His right arm dangled at his side, hand clenching a belt.

And now I understood why he'd gagged her. Even with her mouth full of rubber, her shrieks bounced off the walls. How the fuck did she manage to make so much noise behind that gag?

He brought his belt down on the rapid movement of her fingers. "No orgasms!" he hollered. "You took it without asking, and now you need to pay. Isn't that right?"

She nodded, but her whine indicated she felt differently about her husband's methods of punishing her. Just as Blondie's Master ordered her to touch herself again, Gage yanked on the rope attached to my collar. "Close your eyes," he said. "I want you to feel only me right now. They can watch all they want, but you'll feel and listen to only me."

"Yes, Master." My words were but a whisper, my body but a vessel for Gage to own. He pulled my head back until I reclined against his chest.

"Touch yourself," he said, placing his hands on my hips and lifting. As I buried my fingers between my thighs, he moved me up and down the entire length of his cock, sliding in and out of my ass with surprising ease.

And he was launching me to new heights, to the realm of ecstasy he'd teased me with all day.

My fingers practically spasmed over my clit. "Can I come, Master?"

"I haven't decided yet. Tell me how good my cock feels in your ass." He pushed in again, drawing a long shuddering moan from between tight lips.

"So fucking good, Master. Please let me come."

"Does it bother you that everyone here knows what a dirty girl you are?"

"No," I breathed, ten seconds away from exploding. Nothing mattered except the friction between our bodies and the trust flowing between our hearts.

Gage nipped at my earlobe, and his voice dipped low so only I could hear him. "You've made me so damn proud. Baby, come for me."

I'd never heard sweeter words.

CHAPTER TWENTY-TWO

The circle changed us, or maybe it only changed me. I'd found the experience empowering. Accepting Gage's dominion in the trenches of the Davenport Estate, while ten other people watched, had not only been kinky as hell but liberating. That night bound us together more tightly than the day we'd said "I do" in front of hundreds of people. It was magical how my doubts faded to nothing, almost as if they hadn't existed in the first place.

But insecurities have a way of camouflaging themselves in the absence of trials, and life threw me a mean curveball the day before Thanksgiving. As I pulled out a pumpkin pie from the oven, I heard the front door burst open before banging against the wall. Tossing the pot holders onto the counter, I wondered if Gage had come home early. Eve had gone to Seattle to visit her paternal grandparents for the holiday, so I knew she hadn't made the ruckus, though she'd normally get off the bus at this time.

I rushed from the kitchen and slid to a quick stop upon the sight of Katherine seething in the foyer. "What the hell do you think you're doing?" I shouted, planting my hands on my hips. "Get out of my house."

"This is *your* fault," she said, taking a menacing step toward me. "You've done nothing but ruin my life since the day Gage set eyes on you."

I held my ground, refusing to give her an inch, especially in my own home. "Are you on drugs or something?" She didn't appear to be under the influence of anything other than pure hatred, but the unmistakable odor of whiskey assaulted my nose, and I gave that assessment a second glance.

She backed me into a wall before I saw it coming, and that's when I got scared. For all the things Gage had done to me, this was the first time in over a year that someone managed to transport me back to the days of my first marriage, when Rick had lost his temper while drunk off whatever bottle he'd gotten his hands onto for the day.

"Katherine, what are you doing?" My voice shook with the fear I couldn't hide, and I despised myself for the weakness.

"If he thinks he can fuck with my child, he's wrong."

"I-I don't know what you're—"

"Of course you don't," she spat. "Anything to protect the little wife. He wouldn't dare subject you to an unpleasant court battle."

Oh. The court date had arrived. Maybe it was due to pregnancy brain or preoccupation with the upcoming holiday, but I'd forgotten today was the day Gage had court over Conner's parenting plan.

"If you cared about your son at all, you wouldn't try to interfere with visitation."

"Visitation?" she shouted, pounding the wall to the left of my head. I closed my eyes, body tensing as my heart thundered in my chest. "He's going for full custody," she said, breath hot on my face. "Look at me, you bitch!"

Jumping, I opened my eyes, but I was frozen to the spot. I'd never seen her so unhinged. She'd always had a nasty, catty way about her when it came to me, but this was the woman who'd had my daughter over for play dates because Gage had demanded it.

This was the psycho he'd entrusted Eve with when he'd kidnapped me from my own bed in Texas. Letting my mind go back there for even a moment made me question my mental health because I'd married him.

And right then I wanted to strangle him for allowing Eve anywhere near this woman, not to mention for putting me in the position of needing to defend myself against her now.

"Get the fuck away from me." I shoved her, and she stumbled back a couple of steps. "I have no idea what you're talking about. Full custody?" Last I'd heard, he'd only wanted visitation.

Katherine gave a snide arch of her brow. "Didn't he tell you? Obviously, you convinced him I'm not fit to be a parent."

"You're giving me too much credit. You did that all on your own."

Her laughter grated, like a screeching cat at midnight, or the squeal of a braking train. "Wow, you really are dense. Things were fine before you came along. But he traded his old obsession for a new one, so I guess that leaves me in the dust."

"What are you babbling about now?"

"I'm talking about Liz and Ian."

My eyes widened, and she laughed again.

"You know exactly what I'm talking about, don't you? But I'd bet money he didn't give you the really juicy details." She folded her arms. "Well, he wants to play hardball? He's got it.

I bet he didn't tell you how Liz and I were besties in high school, or how he turned to me for comfort after she died."

"You're lying."

I knew she wasn't. Her words impacted me in the gut, stinking to fucking high heaven of truth—the sort I didn't want to face. I tried clinging to a mask of *I don't believe you, bitch*...but tears of betrayal dripped down my cheeks, giving me away. I swiped at them, angry at myself for letting her witness yet another episode of me falling short when it came to trusting Gage.

"He told me everything I need to know about you," I insisted, my words little more than a script my heart wished were true. "He was only involved with you for a few months."

"Oh my God—" She cut off and doubled over, laughing and laughing and laughing some more. "You're so fucking naive. Is that what he told you? A few months? We've been wrapped around each other for over a decade." Her expression sobered, and she straightened until she stood taller than my average height. "But then you came along, and suddenly I couldn't even get him to fuck me anymore. It's like he let go of a decade-long grudge to marry Susie-Fucking-Homemaker. How the fuck did you get him to do that?"

Maybe I *was* naive because I should tell her to leave, and threaten to call the police if she refused. But she'd obviously been drinking, and in my experience, people had loose lips when inebriated. They also tended to be dangerous, but I squashed the warning that buzzed through my head before it had a chance to take flight.

"Enlighten me then. Since I'm so naive as to believe what my husband tells me," I said, experiencing a small thrill at how her lips flattened upon my use of the word *husband*, "then why don't you set me straight?"

"You have no idea how happy I am to knock you off your

high horse finally." She pushed past me and headed toward the kitchen. "Pour me a fucking drink, and I'll talk about Gage's sordid past all you want."

This was a bad idea. She'd barged into my home and put her hands on me, and I wasn't stupid enough to believe for a moment that she was trustworthy.

But I was powerless to turn back now. Unlike the first time she'd duped me—when my instincts had screamed that she was lying—this time they hummed. Something was different about Katherine. She was a woman at the end of her rope, all hope lost with nothing to lose, and a woman like Katherine...she didn't go down without dragging someone else with her.

She knew things about Gage. Things I wished more than anything he'd tell me, but I knew he never would. Despite his grandstanding about coming to him with my concerns or questions, he remained closed-off to discussions of the past.

For someone who lived to inflict pain, he sure avoided the emotional kind at all cost.

I pulled down a bottle of rum and poured a small amount into a glass before adding cola. She'd taken a seat at the bar, so I leaned against the opposite side, feeling safer with the counter between us. But the position also put me at an advantage. While she cast her attention on the drink between her manicured hands, I carefully slid my cell off the countertop and hit the record button. After what happened the last time we'd spoken alone, I wasn't taking any chances. If the bitch said or did anything wrong, I'd have it on audio.

"Start talking."

CHAPTER TWENTY-THREE

I will not fucking cry. "Damn it," I muttered as a tear escaped. Gritting my teeth, I blinked rapidly and stuffed more clothing into the overflowing suitcase. An absurd amount of dresses rose above the rim, and as I shoved the pile down, I wished like hell I had some pants. Or even a few pairs of sweats. Definitely some underwear. But those finer things in life weren't allowed—not when it meant blocking my husband's access to his favorite place between my thighs.

I wrestled with the zipper, adding my body weight to the top of the case, and finally zipped it shut. If I walked out that door, I'd have nothing but what lay in a tossed mess inside. The remainder of my clothing filled the shelves, drawers, and hangers inside the walk-in wardrobe I shared with Gage.

Oh, God...Eve.

How was I supposed to tell her? She'd miss her bedroom, her toys. She'd miss *him*.

The reality of what I was doing hit me, and in a fit of anger, I dragged the suitcase off the bed and kicked the damned thing until it fell over on its side. Okay, so I wasn't exactly thinking logically, but didn't a pregnant woman have the right to a meltdown after finding out her husband was nothing but a lying—

Don't go there.

But I went there anyway, torturing myself with every word the bitch had spoken. Nearly doubling over at the thought, I pressed a desperate fist to my lips and stifled a sob; sucked in quick breaths before letting them out in hot spurts that dampened my knuckles. Where had the tears come from? I'd promised myself I wouldn't cry anymore.

Pull it together, Kayla.

He was due to arrive in the driveway any minute now. Simone had begged me to leave before he got home, but if I were going to do this, I had to confront him first. Otherwise, he would never let me go.

A hand dropped onto my shoulder, warm with comforting support. Simone didn't say a word, but she didn't need to. I knew she wouldn't leave my side, and that's why I'd called her. She was my safety net, the one person who wouldn't hesitate to hand Gage his ass if he tried railroading me. She was here to make sure I got out.

"You don't owe him anything," she said.

Nodding, I wiped my eyes. "I know."

I didn't know shit. My husband was the fucking devil incarnate, but he loved me. Didn't he? Or had it all been a lie? That was the problem—I didn't know anymore. My emotions had me trapped in the eye of a typhoon named Gage Channing.

Simone's hand slid from my shoulder as I rebuilt my emotional fortress. I stood to the side in bitter numbness while she hauled my suitcase upright. She headed toward the bedroom door, rollers sounding on the hardwood behind her.

"It's okay to need some space, you know. If he loves you, he'll understand."

Folding my arms, I sank onto the end of the mattress. This particular spot bled with memories. He'd bend me over in a heartbeat and blast some sense into my ass if I let him. I couldn't let him get that close, or I'd crack wide open. Hell, I'd probably fracture regardless.

"I need to do this," I said, shaking my head just as his car sounded. "I need some space, but I also need..."

Answers.

Simone lingered by the bedroom door, chewing her bottom lip. Uncertainty was a strange feature on her face. She didn't do uncertain—she was a pick-a-path-and-follow-it kind of woman.

"I'll be okay, Simone. I promise."

She let out a sigh. "I'll be right out there," she said, jabbing a finger in the direction of the living room. She left the door cracked open upon her exit, and her absence echoed in my ears. The room hummed a solitary tune, and each lonesome note poked at my will. But a single question repeated on loop within the chaos of my foggy mind.

Could I really go through with this?

I had no time to mull over the question, or to second-guess my knee-jerk reaction to what Katherine had told me. The front door opened and closed, and I heard murmuring in the living room, then footsteps. Firm, urgent steps that brought him down the hall. I withdrew my cell from my coat pocket and gripped it in a sweaty hand. He shoved the door open, and my pulse skyrocketed.

Gage took one look at my red eyes and splotchy face, and his complexion blanched.

"Are you okay?" He covered the distance in a few long strides, but I held up a hand.

"Please don't touch me."

He halted a couple of feet in front of me. "What's going on? Tell me you're okay."

"Physically, I'm fine." I rose, tilting my chin up, and met his eyes. "Katherine pushed me against the wall, but that was the extent of it."

A vengeful storm brewed in his gaze, and he clenched his hands at his sides. I wondered what his reaction would be after he heard every detail of his sordid history from Katherine's own mouth, courtesy of the recording the bitch knew nothing about.

"What did she do?" he asked, his voice ominous enough that I shivered.

"She told me all the things you wouldn't." I handed him my cell, screen displaying the play button.

He glanced at the phone, brows furrowing in confusion. "Kayla, you'd better start explaining right now."

"Press play. I'd rather let Katherine explain since she's so good at it." I edged around his body and stood a few feet away.

His thumb moved over the screen, and as Katherine's voice infiltrated our private space, some of her words slurring a bit, Gage captured me in his gaze. For twenty minutes we listened to the foundation of our marriage fissure at our feet, all the while looking at each other as if the other could save us from the wreckage.

He shut the recording off. "I've heard enough."

"No," I said, gesturing to the phone. "You haven't gotten to the best part. She threatened our baby." I settled a hand over my belly, seething at her parting shot. "The bitch actually looked at my stomach and threatened to hurt me if you take Conner from her."

His face twisted into something ugly, and he launched the phone through the open door where it thumped against a family portrait in the hall before dropping to the hardwood. I probably had a cracked screen now, if the cell still worked at all. A few seconds later, Simone appeared in the doorway.

"Kayla?"

"I'm okay. I'll be out in a minute."

Gage thrust an irate finger in her direction. "She's not going anywhere with you."

Simone wasn't someone Gage could command, and she made that clear by the way she planted a hand on her hip. "Good thing she has a brain of her own and two feet to carry her out of this house."

"Simone, please. I'm okay."

"And there's this little thing called the Portland PD," she added. "So if you think of laying a hand—"

"What I do with my hands is none of your business, and neither is this conversation." He stalked toward her, and his expression must have been fierce because Simone backed into the hall. "Get the fuck out of my house before *I* call the police to have you removed for trespassing." Indignation arched her brows as Gage slammed the door in her face. He turned the lock then crossed to me, and he wasn't stopping this time.

"Gage, no—"

"It's Master."

"Fuck you!" I spat as he lifted me and tossed me over his shoulder. "A real Master wouldn't hide an engagement. You lied to me!"

"I didn't lie to you." He set me on my feet in front of the spanking chair.

"What do you call it then?"

"I call it fucking history." Settling into the seat, he pulled me over his knees.

"You said you fucked her for a few months. Ha! You've known her since high school. She was Liz's best friend, for fuck's sake."

"It's in the past, Kayla. It was history the instant I—"

"Had me in your sights as the ultimate plan for revenge?" I scowled at him. "I can see why you fucked her now—anything to further your quest against the bitch that betrayed you!"

He yanked up my skirt. "Have you told me every little detail about your past with my brother?" He ended the question with a smarting strike to my ass.

"No!" I anticipated the painful intrusion of his thumb, but a yelp still escaped.

"Honest to fuck, baby, I don't want all the details. Do you think I want to know how he fucked you? I know you loved him, and that's hard enough to swallow." Another slap landed on my ass. "The details would drive me insane."

"Get your thumb out of my ass."

He fisted a hand in my hair. "Would you rather I give you my cock instead?"

"You can take your cock and your lies and shove them up your ass, Gage."

"I'll forgive your verbal rampage. I know how pregnancy hormones can make a woman crazy."

"I'll show you crazy!" I struggled atop his lap, kicking my feet and tipping precariously head-first toward the floor. He tugged me back into position by the hair, and it became clear that no matter what I did or said, he wouldn't dislodge that thumb until he was ready. "Let me go."

"No," he said. "We're going to sit here like this until you calm down and find a little rationality. I understand you're angry, but you're reacting like this because of hormones."

"Stop pretending you know me better than I know myself! Katherine busted your lies wide open, Gage. You can't just wash it away like it never happened. You didn't fuck her for months—you fucked her for years! You put a goddamn ring on it."

"We were engaged for a few months, and those months were a mistake."

"Why were they a mistake?"

"Because I didn't love her."

"You used her."

"I'm a bastard, so yes. I admit it."

"Just like you used me." The fight seeped from my tired bones, leaving me limp on his lap. "Am I just a conquest to you? Do you love me at all?"

He withdrew his thumb and pushed me to my feet. "I'm going to pretend you didn't just ask me that."

I stumbled back, heeding the reminder of my sore ass as cause to keep my distance. "Don't you think it's time we stopped pretending? How can I trust you after you kept something so momentous from me? Did you put my ring on her finger?" I thrust my left hand toward him, displaying the large diamond that had once belonged to his mother.

He dropped his head and dragged both hands through his thick hair. "Of course not."

"I don't understand," I said. "Why ask her to marry you?"

"Fuck, Kayla. I don't know, okay? I have no answers for you. You think I'm a mess now? You should have seen me back then. She was the closest thing I had to Liz."

A sob caught in my throat. "She still is." I whirled and headed for the door, but everything blurred through my tears. As I reached for the knob, he shot out a hand to stop me.

His powerful form brushed my back, and I sensed the rapid rise and fall of his chest. "Don't go. She doesn't matter."

"If she didn't matter she wouldn't be standing between us."

"The only thing standing between us is your doubt."

Closing my eyes for a few moments, I sucked in a calming breath. "You kept her around, Gage. All of these years, she's been working for you. Even after we married, you kept her on your payroll."

"After today, she's gone."

"It's too little, too late."

"Don't say that, baby." He nuzzled my neck, breath hot on my skin. "I only kept her on because she threatened to tell you shit I'd rather forget about."

That somehow made it even worse. She'd blackmailed him to keep her job. "Why were you so afraid to tell me?"

"I knew you'd take it wrong."

I turned the knob and pulled. He pushed.

"I'm taking it the way any *rational* woman would." Gritting my teeth, I yanked hard and got the door open by an inch. "Let me go, or I'll scream for Simone."

He backed away immediately, allowing me to slip into the hall. I rushed toward Simone, who would undoubtedly strengthen my resolve to put some distance between Gage and me. But with every stride of my trembling legs, I sensed him on my heels. The hold he had on me was undeniable, and it threatened to pull me back into that room and over his lap.

Hell, I'd probably spread my cheeks for him.

Simone rose from her perch near the edge of the living room, suitcase in hand. "Ready?"

To throw up? Maybe.

Unable to form words, I nodded.

Gage tangled our fingers together, holding me back while Simone escaped through the front door. "Watching you walk out that door is going to wreck me. You know that, right?"

I couldn't look at him—if I did, I'd crumble. "I need some space. Please, just let me go."

And I wondered how much it had cost him to let my fingers slip through his.

CHAPTER TWENTY-FOUR

"Hey, baby. Happy Thanksgiving! Are you having fun with gramps and gran?" Eve hadn't seen them in a year or so, other than the time they'd come down for her sixth birthday, so even though I hated sharing her with them on a holiday, they were her grandparents—the only ones she had left.

"We had lots of fun. They took me to the Space Needle yesterday! Did you know it's like the highest place *ever*?"

I closed my eyes, simultaneously cringing and celebrating how grown up she'd become. She was still my little girl, but she'd matured, possibly beyond her years, and she had opinions and ideas and dreams.

Thank God she hadn't developed an interest in boys yet.

"Have you ever been there, Mom?"

"Nope. We'll have to go sometime. I'm sure Gage—"

I shot a stricken look at Simone, who returned my stare with a sympathetic tilt of her mouth.

"Listen, I'm so happy you're having fun, but I'm gonna let you go so you can spend some time with your grandparents. Tell them I said Happy Thanksgiving."

"Okay! I love you," she said.

"Love you too. See you on Sunday."

With a sigh, I handed Simone her phone. "She's going to be devastated, unless..."

Simone shook her head. "Give yourself a day or two, then figure out what you're going to do. Maybe you'll be back in the devil's lair by then..." She halted upon my scowl. "Or maybe not. Either way, teleport across that bridge when you get to it."

How she managed to turn my scowl into laughter was beyond me. "What do you need help with?"

She quirked a brow. "Only everything. I kinda suck at cooking. I managed to get the turkey stuffed and in the oven."

"Good thing I'm here then." We got to work, and as I peeled potatoes, she chattered about some relationship drama at the hospital between a doctor and a head nurse. But she was also trying to follow the directions on putting together a green bean casserole. Watching her multitask was entertaining, and a little scary when she almost dumped in too much cream of mushroom soup.

"Jeez, Simone. I think you need to take a breather."

She plopped onto a barstool. "I'm sorry. I'm just really fucking nervous right now."

"How come?"

"Because I invited Ian."

The peeler stalled in my hand. "Oh, well...that makes sense. You guys are dating now, so why shouldn't you spend the holiday together?" As I resumed peeling the last potato, I didn't have to peek at her from the corner of my eye to know she was studying me.

Rising from the stool, she crossed to the oven and checked on the turkey. "Are you sure about this? I was your friend long before his..."

"You can say it, Simone. I'm not going to burst into pregnant tears, I swear."

Closing the oven, she afforded me a sheepish smile. "Just checking. You're already in enough turmoil. I don't want to make it worse."

"You're my friend. My *best* friend, in fact. And he's Gage's brother, *soo*..." I said, moving the pot of peeled spuds onto the stovetop. "This is something I'm just going to have to get used to." Needing to keep busy, I rinsed the few dishes that had collected in the sink before stashing them away in the dishwasher.

"You think you'll be able to work shit out with Gage?"

"I hope so." I propped against the counter and let my hands dangle over the sink. "Maybe I made a huge mistake by leaving." If he knew I was about to spend the holiday with not only Simone but Ian too, he'd blow a gasket. But after the dirt Katherine had spilled, I couldn't bring myself to care.

"I don't think you made a mistake at all. He kept a huge part of his life from you while demanding you give him everything. That's pretty fucked up."

"That's Gage," I said, a note of tender sadness strangling my words.

Simone sighed. "I'm not blind. You'll go back, probably before the turkey's done. But Sometimes, a girl's gotta breathe. Especially with you being pregnant. A little time to deal and process won't hurt anyone."

She made perfect sense. It was a talent of hers. But usually, her logic defied my heart's, because my bleeding organ beat for Gage.

Except it skipped a treacherous beat upon the knock that sounded. Simone rushed through her moderate-sized apartment and flung the door open. I remained motionless in the background, unnoticed as Ian drew her into his arms and planted one on her lips.

I wouldn't lie, least of all to myself. Seeing him with someone else wasn't the easiest thing in the world, but I couldn't stop the curve of my lips at witnessing how happy he seemed.

Or how head-over-heels Simone was for the man who'd at one time held my heart in his gentle hands. I'd returned his kindness and devotion by ripping him to shreds. But she'd weaved him back together, and I refused to let my drama get in the way of that, or ruin this holiday.

Simone broke away as Ian shut the door, but his hazel eyes widened upon the sight of me standing just outside the kitchen, wringing my hands because I didn't know what else to do with them.

"Hi..." His surprise registered in his deep voice.

"Hi," I said, my cheeks heating from the sudden awkwardness in the room. I looked to Simone for help.

"Kayla's spending Thanksgiving with us," she rushed to explain.

Ian took a step toward me. "Are you okay? Where's Gage?"

"He and I are...taking a break."

The astonishment that washed his face attested to the momentous nature of my news, and it told me how bad of an idea being the third wheel was. I moved to grab my coat. "I shouldn't be here. This is just..."

Way beyond awkward.

I had one arm in my jacket sleeve before Ian placed his hand on my shoulder. "Don't go. You're always welcome." He glanced at Simone, including her in the conversation. "Right, babe?"

So they were at the "babe" stage. I wondered how much time they'd spent together. Had Simone visited him at the treatment center, wherever that had been? Just how long had he been back?

And that's when I realized there were things I'd probably never know, and for a good reason too, because our histories were cocooned in hurt, and crisscrossed in a web of wrong. We only had two options at this point; remain hung up on the past, or salvage what little friendship we had left.

The third choice—walk away for good—was unfathomable.

Simone gave me a reassuring smile, so I assumed she voted for the second option. "Of course she's welcome. We're all adults, but more importantly, we're friends."

My husband excluded, for obvious reasons.

Ian removed his jacket, and we settled in to watch parts of the *Macy's Thanksgiving Day Parade* while the food cooked and boiled. When it came time to carve the turkey, Ian took on that task as I set the table for three. With each minute that passed, the nagging awkwardness subsided. We settled around a table crammed full of turkey and all the trimmings. I loaded up my plate, overjoyed that my morning sickness was mostly a thing of the past since I'd entered the second trimester.

"How about we say what we're thankful for?" Simone arched a brow at me. "Would you like to go first?"

I set down my eggnog with a slight gulp. "Um, sure. I'm grateful for..."

The baby.

But thinking about my unborn child brought tears to my eyes, and I didn't know if Ian was aware of my pregnancy. The last thing I wanted was to rub it in his face.

"I'm grateful for your unconditional friendship." My gaze swerved between the two of them. "Both of you. You've been there for me, each in different ways, for such a long time. So that's what I'm thankful for."

Simone took Ian's hand. "You're next."

"I'm gonna have to cheat and mention two things. I'm

grateful to be alive." He brought her hand to his lips. "And I'm grateful for you."

Silence fell over the table, neither comfortable nor uncomfortable. It just was.

Simone cleared her throat. "I'm grateful for the three kids whose cancer went into remission this week. By the grace of God, they got to go home and spend the holiday with their families."

I raised my glass. "That takes the cake, Simone. It deserves a toast." Our glasses clinked together—three glasses representing three lives that had come together through trial and tribulation, yet here we were, sitting around the same table and thankful to do so.

But God, how I missed Gage just then. And Eve. Frigid air whistled through the holes in my heart where they should have been. With a little distance, I saw things more clearly, and Gage's past with Katherine didn't lance my heart as badly as it had yesterday. But not being with him did.

A bang on the door went off like an omen as if the universe heard my pain and wanted to reply. Even so, dread formed in my gut. I didn't know how I knew, but that angry fist pounding on Simone's door belonged to Gage.

She scooted back, the legs of her chair scraping loudly across her floor. "I'll deal with it, Kayla."

Except that I beat her to the door. She tried stopping me from opening it, but nothing and no one would keep me from seeing him. The instant I laid eyes on his disheveled appearance—his uncombed hair and the redness that rimmed his eyes—I fought against myself to fall at his feet.

He barreled into Simone's apartment, letting the door slam behind him. Everyone seemed to hold their breath for a few heavy seconds as Gage and Ian exchanged a look. But it wasn't a look I could put a name to.

"What are you doing here?" I asked.

"It's Thanksgiving, and my wife isn't at home. What do you think I'm doing here?"

Simone tried wedging between us—always the protector—but Ian gently held her back. He pulled her to his side, one hand curving around her shoulder, and Gage didn't miss the obvious bond they'd come to know in such a short time.

"I think you should leave," she said, though her tone was far from harsh. She might not like Gage, but she managed to rein in her temper for my sake because that's the type of friend she was—the type of friend who invited the ex-girlfriend of her new boyfriend to Thanksgiving.

"I'm not leaving without my wife."

"Gage, please don't do—"

"I mean it," he interrupted. "What do I need to do to get you to come home?" To my utter astonishment, he dropped to his knees and nuzzled my belly. "You want me to beg? Well here I am, baby. For you and our children, I'll do anything, even if it means getting on my knees, and I don't give a fuck who's around to see it."

God, I was going to cry.

"Gage, please get up." As much as I loved him kneeling at my feet, we both knew he didn't belong there. "I'll go home with you."

"You don't have to do that," Simone said.

Gage shot her a glare. "This is between my wife and me."

"Then why did she come to my house with a packed suitcase? You need to give her some time."

"She's had time. Slumber party is over."

My friend was about to explode, so I interjected before she did. "Thanks for everything, Simone," I said, silently pleading with her to understand. "I think I should go home."

"But you were a mess yest—"

"Babe," Ian said, massaging her shoulders as if that would be enough to calm her. Who knew? Maybe it would.

He probably knew her buttons and how to set off each one better than anyone. “Let them go. Kayla’s a big girl. She can take care of herself.”

His new attitude astounded me, and I couldn’t help but wonder if a second chance at life was the only reason behind the change. I knew Gage had spoken to him the night he sent him away, but I’d never had the guts to ask what they’d talked about.

And I probably never would. That was a conversation Gage would likely never tell me about. We both had our flaws; I relapsed into the land of trust issues every time new doubts arose, and he refused to open up emotionally. We could fight each other on those two things until we destroyed our marriage and each other, or we could accept them.

Everyone had flaws. Some more than others.

“Thank you for having me,” I said. Not everyone was lucky enough to be blessed with a friend like Simone. She’d always have my back, and I prayed that when the time came, if it ever did, I’d get a chance to have hers as well.

Gage laced our fingers together. “Where’s your suitcase?”

“By the couch.” I pointed to the sofa where I’d slept last night, tossing and turning and agonizing over my impetuous decision to leave. There was a saying I’d once read in some pregnancy book, or maybe I’d seen it on a forum, but I’d found the advice sound.

Never make big decisions while pregnant.

Gage fetched my suitcase as I put on my coat. Before we reached the door, I stopped to give Simone a hug. But I didn’t dare touch Ian, and the glance he exchanged with Gage spoke volumes. Just because they’d managed to occupy the same room for ten minutes without tearing each other’s heads off didn’t mean they were on the way to becoming best buds.

But I was optimistic. People changed. Gage had, in spite of his habit of hiding painful things from his past. I had too, in spite of my penchant for doubting first and asking questions later. Even Ian had gone through a metamorphosis. Maybe, by some miracle, these two would someday bury the past and find some common ground.

We left without another word, having already said our goodbyes—for now anyway—and Gage pulled my luggage behind him as he led me to the car. After stowing the suitcase in the trunk, he opened the passenger door and helped me into the seat.

Gage settled in beside me and amped up the heater before digging my cell out of his pocket. "It still works," he said, handing it to me as if it were a token of apology. "But I'm afraid the screen is cracked. We'll get you a new one."

I merely nodded, my thoughts still lingering on what had happened in Simone's apartment. Gage steered the car onto the road. Fog hung over the city, obscuring skeleton trees and roadway signs, and though the heater blasted warm air toward me, I shivered in my cold leather seat. Neither of us spoke until we were on the freeway.

"Did you know he was going to be there?" he asked.

"No."

A few nail-biting beats passed. "They seem happy together," he said.

I could not have given him a more stunned expression. "I think they are."

Letting out a breath, he ran irritated fingers through his messy hair. "I didn't sleep at all last night."

"Neither did I."

"Baby...I was wrong."

I had no words. My mouth was too busy gaping.

"I should have told you."

"I'm glad you can see that now," I said.

"But if you ever leave me like that again…" He shook his head, jaw rigid.

"So I'm to be punished then?"

"What do you think, Kayla?"

"Am I not allowed to have feelings?" I angled to face him head-on. "What about space? Is that out of the question too?"

"You're allowed to have feelings. But space? Fuck no. Not only are we married, but you belong to me. If you need space, I'm happy to put you in the cage for a while. You can have all the time in the world to think things through in there."

I gulped. "Gage, please."

"Please, what?"

"Please don't hate me for what I did."

He glanced at me, raising incredulous brows. "That's not even possible. Jesus, Kayla. I'm upset that you bolted like that, but I don't hate you. I could never *hate* you. I'm so fucking in love with you that I can't see straight."

"You might want to tone down the love a little, so you don't wreck the car."

He laughed. "Fuck, you're crazy, and I love you for it."

"When she told me those things, I *went* crazy, and I doubted you. *Again*. This nasty voice in my head told me you only wanted me to get at him, that I'm only a possession to you. A thing you use."

"You're everything to me."

On that note, with those words echoing in my mind in the soft way he'd spoken them, we rode the rest of the way home in silence. By the time we reached the driveway and rushed to the front steps, the sky had opened, but we beat the worst of it by seconds. Rain pounded the windows and danced on the rooftop.

And something smelled delicious. My stomach growled, reminding me that Gage's arrival had interrupted dinner.

"Come," he said, reaching for my hand. He escorted me into the dining room where a man I'd never seen before readied the table for us. A full Thanksgiving dinner had been set out.

"Dinner is served, Mr. Channing. Do you require anything else?"

"No, thank you."

The man made himself scarce, and a couple of moments later, I detected the front door open and close.

"You knew I'd come back."

"I was hoping." His mouth tilted up in a halfway grin. Bringing a hand to his tie, he loosened the knot before reaching into his pocket. "First things first though." He fisted a set of clover clamps—the worst kind I'd ever been punished with.

"If you weren't pregnant, you'd have a date with my bull-whip in the anal stocks right now. Lucky for you," he said, coming closer, "your womb is growing my baby and making your belly sexy as fuck." Stopping in front of me, he cocked his head to the side. "Just how sensitive are your nipples these days?"

I covered my breasts on instinct until he flattened his mouth into a firm line. Slowly, I let my hands drop and dangle at my sides.

"Good girl," he said, beginning with my left nipple.

"Ow!"

"It hurts, does it?"

"What do you think?" I said, scowling.

"Good. Now address me properly before I change my mind about the stocks." He raised a thoughtful brow. "Or you could spend some time in the cage after dinner."

"No, Master. Please. I'll be good."

"It is Thanksgiving, and I'm feeling grateful and a bit lenient, so assuming you get rid of that bratty attitude and let me feed you," he said, pinching my other nipple between his horrible clamp, "I'll offer you some mercy. No cage."

I was relieved to hear the words *no cage* fall from his lips, but my mind had latched onto the first part of what he'd said. "Feed me, Master?"

"Mmm, yes." He whirled me around, causing my head to spin, and used his tie to bind my hands at the small of my back. "I imagine you'll have a difficult time eating without the use of your hands." Happy with his handiwork, he pushed me into a chair and ordered me to spread my legs before taking a seat a mere arm's length away.

And in between bites of turkey, mashed potatoes and gravy, and the best damn cranberry sauce I'd ever had, he fingered my pussy until I teetered on the edge of orgasm, then he yanked on the chain connecting the clamps every time I uttered a plea to come, no matter how small. Even a whimper for more got my nipples punished. My face had become a tear-stained mess from the vises trapping my overly sensitive buds in never ending torture. And yet the pain faded the instant he pushed his fingers into me again.

Arching my spine, I curled my toes. "Please let me come!"

He brought those same digits, slick with my arousal, to my chin. "You will not come tonight."

I groaned.

"But you'll be happy about something else." Turning intense blue eyes on me, he slowly dipped his fingers between my lips. "The next time you do come, it'll be at the expense of the bitch who made you leave me in the first place."

CHAPTER TWENTY-FIVE

I stood inside the bathroom in the basement and listened to the thump of footsteps on the stairs. A few seconds later, Gage's voice filled the space, his tone arrogant and authoritative. I hated that tone of his, but I hated that he was using it with *her* even more.

Katherine. The bitch who'd nearly torn my marriage apart by preying on my insecurities. That whole *fool me once* phrase echoed through my mind, and I chewed over how it fit me perfectly.

"You'll park your ass against that cross because I said so. Don't make me change my mind about this," he said.

"Where's your wife?" The racket of her heels faded away from where I hid. "Is she out shopping for groceries?" Her laughter got under my skin. "Or maybe she's at a bake sale."

"That is why I'm going to gag your irritating mouth."

"But I want to suck your—" A muffled whine cut her off, mid-sentence.

"See?" he said. "That's one thing you never understood about me." Chains clinked, and I could almost hear the cuffs locking her wrists and ankles in place. "I don't care about your wants."

Creeping closer to the entrance, I waited for my cue.

"Kayla understands though. She knows and accepts that her wants come second to mine."

A few seconds later, Gage called for me to come out of hiding. I stepped into the main part of the basement, my own four-inch heels noisy on the floor, and the look on Katherine's face was one I wanted to catalog and pull out to gawk at for years to come. Six months ago, I'd been in her place, chained to the St. Andrew's cross and silenced with a gag, while Gage taunted me with his hard cock and her eager mouth.

Turnabout was fair play, and it tasted sweeter than ever.

Straining against her bindings, she attempted to shout epithets around the ball of rubber stretching her lips.

"I said I wanted to fuck, and you couldn't wait to get over here, could you?" he said to her, tilting his head as he held an arm out toward me. I fit at his side like I belonged, and I couldn't imagine ever leaving my place again. "I never said who I was going to fuck."

Katherine shook her head, a desperate whine emanating from her throat, but her eyes spit venom. Gage crossed to her fully-clothed body and grabbed her chin. "If you ever come near my wife again, a little bondage and humiliation will be the least of your worries."

Gage turned his back on her, but when I met his eyes, longing sparked between us. And Katherine? For a few intense moments, she failed to exist. I parted my lips, standing like a pillar to keep from pressing my thighs together. Only a couple of days had passed since we'd torn up the sheets.

But I was ravenous, hungry to feel him inside me, and

the bed a few feet away called like a siren at sea. I couldn't wait to rock it.

"Take your dress off," he said, his feet slowly bringing him toward me.

Katherine's angry protests grew louder. As I reached behind my back and pulled the zipper down, I threw her a triumphant look.

"Eyes on me," he ordered.

The dress slid down my body, pooling around my feet. "Yes, Master."

"She doesn't matter." There was a double meaning in his statement. "Say it, Kayla."

"She doesn't matter."

He lifted a hand and drew a line between my breasts. "Right now, the only one who matters is me." Leaning forward, he teased my mouth with his lips. "Only me, baby."

I ached to kiss him, to undress him, to do *something*. But I did nothing. He gave me one night a year to take the lead, and tonight wasn't it.

He led me to the bed and pushed on my shoulders until I sat on the edge, then he brought my hands to his buttons. I undid each one in haste, my fingers jittery yet eager to remove the barrier of his clothing. His shirt parted, and I couldn't help but smooth my palms over his warm skin. His stomach muscles quivered under my touch, making him hiss in a breath.

"I love your hands on me."

Katherine's muffled words drew my attention to the cross, but Gage palmed my cheek and brought my gaze back to him. "If you look at her again, I won't let you come."

The idea just about destroyed me. "I'll be good, Master," I whispered.

"That's my girl." He shrugged out of his shirt and let it drift to the floor. "Lay back and spread your legs."

As I reclined on the mattress, heels pressing into the comforter, he reached for the button of his pants. But watching him shed the rest of his clothing put me in too precarious of a position, as Katherine struggled to get free just to the left of Gage, and she was doing her best to grab my attention.

Even rendered powerless, she still believed she could drive a wedge between Gage and me.

Letting my legs drape to the sides, I focused on the ceiling and tuned her out. The mattress dipped, and he grasped my inner thighs, gently pushing, opening me wider to the heat of his gaze. A hot tingle rippled through me. God, his touch alone was enough to flood my pussy with want.

"Master," I moaned, shuddering. I was about two days past due for my next fix.

"So wet," he murmured, his breath making me even wetter. "Are you going to be a good girl?"

I wanted to behave more than anything, but my grasp on control slipped by the second. "Master, please. I want to be good."

"You want to come."

"I want you inside me."

"Trust me, baby. My cock wants inside you too. But first I'm going to lick you for a very long time, and you will *not* come. Do you understand me?"

I rolled my head back and forth on the mattress. "Don't do this to me. I can't take it."

"Yes, you can."

And then he lowered his mouth to my clit, teasing with gentle closed-mouthed kisses at first. I grabbed the bedding in both hands, thighs trembling from the overload of sensation. I was pathetic. He'd barely touched me, but I was ready to fly apart under his cruel mouth.

That cruel, sadistic, sexy mouth that went to work in driving me higher. He whirled his tongue, teased with his teeth, and when he lodged his thumb into my ass, I knew the gesture was far from a punishment. He had me squirming, moaning, begging, and crying tears of frustration for having to hold back for what seemed like an endless session of oral pleasure-turned-torture.

I lost track of time and space and reality. He'd dropped me in a realm where my pussy and his mouth were the only two things in existence. Eventually, I fell through the cracks and throbbed in suspension, my entire being aching for him to fill me.

"Master, please!"

He slid his palms over the gentle swell of my belly before settling on my breasts, and the friction of his hands pebbled my nipples. He climbed onto the mattress and entered me with a forceful thrust that declared his ownership.

And I came.

"Oh God!" Clawing at his shoulders, I held on and rode the wave. "Please don't punish me."

"Shh," he said, nipping my lips. "You're beautiful when you shatter. I want to watch you come again."

As our bodies locked together, he dragged me to that otherworldly high again, cock plundering me to orgasm after orgasm. His thrusts were manic, partly driven by the need to show Katherine that we were made for each other.

But his ultimate end game was to make me cry, "No more, Master!"

This level of exquisite torture wouldn't be complete without first driving me to beg for it, then making me plead for it to stop. Even then, he launched me deeper into madness. This crazed man wouldn't stop fucking me until he was good and ready.

Exhausted, I lay beneath his thrusting body, limp with weakness and powerless to do anything but let him extract painful orgasms from me.

CHAPTER TWENTY-SIX

As I came down gradually, silence descended over the basement like a protective fog that shielded us from the outside world. Every few seconds, a long, satisfied exhale would dent it.

But not break it.

We lay wrapped up in sweat and each other, loathe to fracture this moment, until Katherine let out a muffled screech, and the real world came pounding on our fortress.

Gage pressed his lips to mine for one last stolen kiss, then he slipped from the bed and reached for his pants. I sat up, hair falling into my eyes as he buttoned his slacks. He fetched my dress, and I didn't dare look at Katherine until I stood on solid ground again, fully clothed, even if my husband's cum dripped down my thighs underneath my skirt.

A sheen of hostility cast her face in red, and she'd balled her hands into fists so tight that they were nearly colorless. Doubt sank into my gut. Fucking my husband in front of her had been the best payback ever, but I worried we'd achieved little more than the sharpening of her claws.

Gage removed the gag from her drooling mouth.

"I'll have you arrested for this!" she shrieked.

"No, you won't." He freed her ankles and wrists before crossing to the nightstand next to the bed, where he kept smaller items like lube and nipple clamps inside the drawer. He withdrew a set of documents and thrust them into her shaking hands.

"What's this?"

"You've been served."

"What?" Pursing her lips, she shuffled through the papers. "What the hell is this?"

"Can't you read? It's a restraining order. You're not allowed within 500 feet of Kayla or our children. And since she's an employee of Channing Enterprises, with duties that may take her to any of the company's offices, you no longer work for me."

"On what grounds?"

He advanced on her until her back hit the wall. The papers fluttered to the floor around them in a disarrayed mess. I didn't like him anywhere near her, but I found a small amount of justice in the maneuver because she'd done the same thing to me a couple of days ago.

Only she'd put her hands on me. Gage didn't need to touch her to intimidate—not when the tense set of his jaw and the broadness of his shoulders did the job for him.

"You threatened my wife and unborn child," he said, placing his left palm flat on the wall next to Katherine's head. "You barged into my home while drunk and put your fucking hands on my wife."

"I wasn't drunk, and I didn't touch her."

"Don't bother trying to lie about this. Kayla recorded your conversation, including your threats." He leaned forward, invading her space to the max, but he still refrained from touching her. "You can bet your ass I'll use it in court. If

I had any reservations about going for full custody before, I don't now."

She shook her head, eyes glistening with tears. "You can't take my son from me."

"I didn't want to go this route, but you've caused nothing but trouble."

She dropped to her knees and grasped his pant legs. "I'll leave your wife alone. I promise. Please don't take my son from me!"

He moved out of reach, and she tipped forward, palms flat on the floor in the midst of strewn papers.

"Nothing you say will change my mind," he said. "Now get the fuck up and get out of my house." He bent and gathered the documents.

As Katherine rose to her feet, her expression hardened, and I expected her to go off on a tirade. Instead, she started laughing—a deep and smug sound that emanated from her belly. It was manic and disturbing on so many levels.

"You're as gullible as your wife." She yanked the documents from his hands. "I honestly don't know why I wasted so many years on you."

"The feeling's mutual. Now get the fuck out and don't come back. I won't allow you to fuck up my marriage anymore, and as for Conner, I'll do what I have to do to protect him from you."

Her lips curved in pure viscousness. "He's not your son."

"Excuse me?"

She shrugged. "You're not the father."

"Of course I am!" Gage roared. "I have the paternity test to prove it."

She let out another laugh. "I wanted it to be you, but it's not, and you've made it clear tonight that it won't ever be."

"Why are you pulling this shit now?" His voice bellowed through the basement.

"Because you left me no choice! I wanted you to be the father, but I'll be damned if I let you take my son from me."

Gage clenched his teeth, but before he could unleash his anger, I entwined my fingers with his. Katherine had blindsided him with this, possibly to provoke him into doing something he'd regret.

He inhaled then let the breath out five seconds later. "We did a paternity test," he reminded her, his tone calmer than she deserved.

She shrugged. "You share DNA with the father, so that test gave a false positive. But Conner's not yours. It's impossible, based on the date of conception."

"Who *is* Conner's father then?" The question echoed off the walls, but he already knew the answer, same as I.

"Ian." She lowered her head, fingers thumbing the restraining order. "I slept with him a few weeks after you broke up with me."

"Why didn't you tell me? Or hell! Why didn't you tell Ian? You fucked with Conner's head for years."

"Because I wanted you back!" she shouted. "If you'd known I'd gotten knocked up by your brother...? C'mon, Gage. We both know you would have never spoken to me again."

"Ain't that the truth."

"Ain't that poetic justice." She folded the papers and gripped them in both hands. "I have more in common with Liz that you ever knew. Your brother knocked us both up." She headed for the stairs, and Gage worked his jaw, watching in a state of anger and shock and disbelief as she climbed to the top.

"I guess that makes you his problem then!"

The door slammed shut, leaving us in the wreckage of a plan that had backfired horribly. Gage pushed his hands through his hair, breathing hard, but when his eyes met mine, that was my undoing. I crossed to him, but he slid to the floor before I could touch him.

"He's not my son."

Falling to my knees in front of him, I wedged between his legs and grabbed his face. His eyes glassed over with tears, and one slipped free, hanging on his lashes before dripping down his cheek. I brushed it away, wishing I could wipe away the devastation I saw in the slump of his shoulders and the sheen of his eyes.

"He's not my son," he repeated as if saying it again would make it sink in. "But I love him like my own."

"I know." I had no words to take away his pain, so I wound my arms around him and held on. Getting through this seemed impossible just then, but we were stronger together, and I knew we'd find a way to overcome Katherine's final curveball.

EPILOGUE

Five and a half months later

"I fucking hate you!" Holding Gage's hand with enough force to crush bones, I screamed through another contraction. I was certain his fingertips had gone white, cut off from blood flow by my unnatural grip, but he didn't seem to care. Using his free hand, he wiped the sweat from my brow.

"You're almost there, baby."

"I'm hurting you," I groaned, squeezing tears from my eyes. They dripped down my flushed face. "Your fingers..."

"It's okay. I'm not going anywhere. I'm right here." As if to get his point across, he rubbed a thumb over the back of my hand.

The horrid peak of the contraction subsided, and I collapsed against the pillows, trying to catch my breath. How was I supposed to push a baby out when I had no strength left? I hadn't given birth in over six years. Funny how time had a way of erasing just how fucking insane women were for going through this again and again and again.

Fucking loons.

Forty seconds later, another contraction began the climb to agony, and I looked at Gage, tightening my jaw in panic.

"Oh no…another one…"

Through the pain and delirium, some part of my mind acknowledged they were coming faster and harder…that was a good thing, right?

No! Fucking make it stop. Make. It. Stop.

The pain was…I had no words for this level of torture. Nothing Gage had subjected me to had ever hurt this badly. Each contraction brought me closer to meeting our baby for the first time, but it was hell—an endless sentence to purgatory where a vise stronger than anything known to man clamped and squeezed and pulverized from the inside. I grabbed hold of the bedside rail, certain the power of my grip would shake that fucker to pieces.

"I can't do this!" I said in a high-pitched shriek. "Oh God, Gage. I'm scared!" Wrenching my hand from his, I scooted to my side and clutched the railing with both fists. Pressure built between my thighs, rushing faster until it settled low in my womb. Instinctively, I lifted a leg, and Gage wound a strong arm under my thigh to prop me up.

Because I couldn't do it on my own.

He pushed strangled locks of hair from my cheeks. "You're doing amazing."

"I think she's coming."

"She, huh?"

We'd decided to keep the sex of our baby a surprise, but I'd had dreams, and as crazy as it might sound, I was positive the universe had given me signs. Like the time we'd gone shopping for Eve's Christmas presents and a pink sippy cup had somehow ended up in the cart. Deep down, I knew the baby was a girl. I didn't need an ultrasound to confirm what my heart already knew.

"Yeah, she. And she's coming…fuck…oh *fuck*…" The bed

rail became my birthing partner, and I gave it another shuddering assault before collapsing again. "Where's the doctor? I think I need...I need to push!"

Gage cursed under his breath. "The nurse was here a few minutes ago. As for the doctor..." He searched the room. "Baby, you can't push yet."

"Don't you think I'd stop if I could?" I shouted, glowering at him, wishing *he* was the one going through this.

He jabbed the call button a dozen or so times, but it didn't matter. She was coming, and she wasn't waiting.

"Gage..."

"Hold on, baby. I'm trying to get—"

"Gage!" Something unnatural hurtled from my lungs—a cross between a howl and a grunt. It was purely animalistic. In that moment, as my baby moved down the birth canal, I felt like an animal.

Wild, uninhibited, and human in the basest form.

A flurry of motion erupted in the room. Dr. Keenan rushed in, pulling gloves on in a hasty manner as a nurse readied the bed for delivery. Gage took my hand again, murmuring encouraging nothings.

I was in my own dimension, already pushing, despite the world not being ready for this child to be born. She was coming. *She* was ready, zooming to her first breath of air on her own terms.

"Doctor, she's crowning."

I glanced up at Gage and watched in complete awe as a tear slid down his cheek. During a break between pushes, I brought his hand to my mouth. "I'm sorry. I didn't mean it."

"Didn't mean what?"

"When I said I hated you."

"It's okay. You're allowed to say whatever you want right now."

More pressure built, stronger than ever, and as I grunted,

powerless to do anything except let my body do its job, I managed to groan a question.

"What should we"—another long howl burst from my throat—"name her?"

And he chuckled through his tears, a sound as pleasant as wind chimes, or as comforting as rain on the rooftop. His laughter soothed my soul.

"She *or* he...you pick the name. You should definitely have the honor."

Bearing down again, I knew this was it. I'd never forget the way our child's tiny body slid from mine, or how the sound of that first cry was the sweetest thing I'd heard since Eve was born.

Our baby arrived on the eighth of May at 11:28 a.m.

Squalling the music of life.

Warming my belly and my heart.

Perfectly healthy with ten fingers and just as many toes. I knew because Gage counted.

Oh, and I was right. We were the proud and exhausted and overjoyed parents of a little girl.

When Gage held her for the first time—swaddled in a customary striped hospital blanket—and cooed about how special she was, and how he couldn't wait for her to meet her big sister, Eve and cousin Conner, that's when her name came to me.

"Grace," I said, barely above a whisper.

"Grace?"

"Her name. It's Grace."

He treated me to a devastating smile, accompanied by a flash of his indigo eyes. "Fits her perfectly."

ABOUT THE AUTHOR

Gemma James is a *USA Today* bestselling author of sexy contemporary and dark romance. She loves to explore the darker side of human nature in her fiction, and she's morbidly curious about anything dark and edgy, from deviant seduction to fascinating villains. Readers have described her stories as being "not for the faint of heart."

She warns you to heed their words! Her playground isn't full of rainbows and kittens, though she loves both. She lives in Florida with her husband, children, and a gaggle of animals.

Visit Gemma's website for more info on her books:
www.authorgemmajames.com

Made in the USA
Columbia, SC
28 May 2025

58539212R00450